BLIGHTED WARRIOR

A WARRIOR'S PRELUDE

BLUE TEARS OF SOLARIA
BOOK 1

JONATHAN J MICHAEL

CONTENTS

1 MACHINA JUNK
AND KELPMALLOWS

Slice! Hack. Tuck and roll. Slice! Kick. Tuck and roll. Slice! Flip. Tuck and roll. Gallagher pauses, his hands on his hips, panting, and looking over his shoulder to see the damage done. Several bull kelps as thick as his waste lie scattered on the ground, harvested to perfection.

"Gallagher!" Bannik, his superior, leans against his cart whittling a small piece of driftwood.9

He's an elf who's taken pride in kelp picking. He stands tall with a mid-section the shape of a plump, perfectly ripe kelpmallow. His hair is loose and disheveled as all kelp pickers wear it. But not Gallagher. Gallagher has two braids framing his carved jawline and the rest of his hair is pulled tight into a tail. He has the hair of a warrior.

"What are you doing?" he questions Gallagher.

"My job, sir. Did I not fell the kelp properly?" Gallagher grins with pride, his fists on his hips with his sickle in hand, and his chest puffed.

"Bale 'em and load 'em. And stop wasting energy with that ridiculous dance you're doing. It does you no good, Gallagher."

"I can never stop training, sir. One day, you'll thank me for protecting the harvest, and the product of my training will be in full light."

"The harvest!" Bannik stops whittling as a chortle escapes him. "You mean the Solari Harvest?" More bellows of laughter pump from his gut. "How many times are we going to have this conversation? You're lying to yourself. Look at that fin of yours. You'll never be a warrior. And you don't need to be training while you're laboring for me. Now, get back to it."

Gallagher looks down at his fins. He presses his toes into the soft, damp sand and lifts it to reveal the finprint left behind. Two of the five digits are absent with the webbing between the others torn beyond repair. "Yes, sir." He trudges toward the fallen kelp, eyes focused on his damaged fin. It doesn't alter his step or his ability to fight on land, but he'll never be able to swim as fast as the warriors, in the sky or the sea. And because of that, he'll never have the opportunity to join the Warrior's Guild.

Even to be a harvester would be a great honor, but they're expected to swim faster than the warriors. So, he's stuck with the other landlubbers as a kelp picker. It's not an ideal role for an elf. His mother and father have made peace with it, but not Gallagher.

The Elders have earned their place on land after a life of honoring the Warrior's Guild. The harvesters risk their lives to nurture the clan with Blue Tears. The mothers give birth to new warriors, which is more honorable than any of the other roles. Even the smiths, carpenters, and textile artists all have their fulfilling duties. And then there are the blighted—the damaged elves who will never make the cut to take part in any of the honorable roles. This is what Gallagher has become, no thanks to his overconfident ego when he was a child.

Gallagher heaves a bull kelp over his shoulder and, dragging the whip-like plant, he carries it toward the picker's cart where Bannik dawdles next to the carabao. One by one, he pulls all the kelp he slayed and tosses them onto the cart. When it's loaded to the brim, Bannik climbs into the saddle and pats the bovid animal on the rump. It shakes its robust horns and lunges forward, off to the mill where they'll pluck all the kelpmallows from the end of the stalk and bag them for a savory treat to be roasted over a flame. Then, process the trunk into a less-than-desirable, but edible meal.

Standing just outside the kelp forest, he stares into the everlasting overcast above the mountainous ridges surrounding their small bay. The eye in the everlasting cloud cover is visible over the swaying bull kelp. The sun's rays will light the way for the Solari Harvest soon.

Silhouettes of the warriors in training can be seen swimming overhead, far above the forest to the east. An outpost resides just on the other side, planted atop the stone bulwark. It's another role Gallagher could have aspired to—a point-elf standing watch over the clan as they scan the skies for truce-breaking Indra—which has been in place for millennia, long before Gallagher's time. More importantly, they spy swarms of venomous wraiths drifting by and watch the depths of the ocean to alert the clan of any leviathans lurking too close to the shallows within their bay.

The leviathans are the real threat within the Knuckles of Morshine. Gallagher would know. He looks down at his damaged fin, then back to the kelp forest as he trudges forward to continue the day's work.

Hours later, after he's met his daily quota for Bannik, he finds himself swimming through the skies. His steel sickle at his hip, and a hunting spear in his grip, he breaks from his daily routine to calm his mind.

His stout frame weighs heavier in the dense air with less buoyancy than the majority of his clanmates, making it that much more important to have two whole fins to propel through the air. But it doesn't prevent him from hunting.

Water pours from the clouds in a steady stream, a waterfall flowing from the Caelum Ream above. Flying fish dance around it in a thrum of idiocy, searching for food.

Gallagher's spear flies, piercing two or three. He bursts forward to retrieve his catch, and a looming shadow appears overhead. He halts with a heavy backstroke, wary of its existence.

The border that the Elders have defined is the clouds themselves, but consequences come to the elves who linger too close. They'll chastise him for it, should they find out. He should swim away, but curiosity binds him where he treads.

Could it be the dreaded Indra the Elders warn them about? He has his speculations, but they're *only* speculations because he's never been above the clouds. He learned his lesson about trespassing beyond their boundaries many years ago.

The gloom hovers just above the waterfall, like a murderous thundercloud waiting to strike its next victim. Gallagher treads the air just beneath it.

Watching. Waiting. A thin line drops from the fluffy ceiling, something glowing on the end of it. Something aromatically sweet.

Blue Tears!

It's a trap.

Gallagher's desire overpowers his intuition.

He watches his fishing spear drift away with his meal pierced through the belly. It's no longer relevant.

His gaze quickly fixates on the glowing iridescence before him. He places a hand on the sickle at his hip. The sweet aroma draws him in, irresistible. A small pinch of the magical spice can change a kelp picker's story. It's worth the risk.

The school of fish continues to circle around themselves, and only scatter when he gets within an arm's reach. With a swift jab, he snags the wad of Tears with a hasty backstroke to follow. Cloudy bubbles fill the dense air around him as high velocity projectiles shoot downward. A dark net encapsulates him, sending him skyward.

The dense air grows heavier as Gallagher traverses into the clouds. He touched the ceiling once when he was a conniving child testing his limits, but since his incident—beyond the opposite boundary within the depths of the ocean—he doesn't test the boundaries anymore. Never has he swam into the clouds. The infamous Indra live up there.

The clouds are thick, a heavy weight on his lungs. Then, suddenly all is clear. The pressing weight lifts and shocks his system as the air above the clouds is quite the opposite. Too thin to breathe. He gasps, and his lungs burn.

The serenity of the space surrounding him holds him captive, temporarily dissolving the pain in his lungs, and putting a halt to his struggle against the net.

A blue ceiling spans across the sky. Not the marbling greys and whites he's accustomed to. The mountainous bulwarks and sandy shoreline have disappeared, replaced with a sea of clouds.

The sun shines brightly. Too bright for his eyes. He squints. It hits his skin like a heated kelp blanket. He only witnesses the sun once a year on the day of the Solari, and not to this degree. Its warmth and energy saturate him. He tries to sprawl out to take it in, to melt in its glory, but the netting doesn't allow it, and it pulls him back into the severity of the moment.

The line hoists him toward an enormous dark silhouette above. It blots out the sun and most of the blue sky as he's reeled in. His lungs burn in the thin air.

Gallagher has trained for this moment. Not officially. The Warrior's Guild has shunned him since his accident. He's unfit. A blight on the colony as his tormentors have labeled him. But he's been training alone, without the means of the guild, to withstand the depths of the ocean where he plans to collect his first stone and prove himself as a warrior.

The thin air up here is no different than submerging himself beneath the ocean currents. He can breathe it all the same. Thinner or denser, he merely needs to collect himself and gain control of his lungs. He flattens his lips, allowing a slow stream of air to seep in. His chest balloons as far as it will go, then slowly exhales. A few more repetitions and it calms his nerves.

It's a new world above the clouds. Mira will be thrilled to hear about this.

If he returns, that is. If the Elders don't punish him for breaking through the boundaries and making contact with the Indra.

He continues his methodic breathing exercises. The fresh air replaces the dense air hunkered deep within him. Several more repetitions and his breathing comes easier, but not without a dry burn like pouring sand into his lungs.

By the time he collects himself, the parapet of the sky vessel sinks beneath him, and the blue sky and sun become visible once again, but not without the silhouette of a grand cityscape. Gallagher shields his eyes to get a better view.

The ship is massive. Ship isn't even the right description. It's a floating island with rails. A civilization above the clouds. A landship. How it floats in such thin air, he isn't sure.

The net raises him above a pier where several squatty elf-like individuals stare up at him with their mouths agape.

Indra!

This is the first he's witnessed them in the flesh. He freezes, unsure what they're capable of. He only knows what he's been told: the De'wi avoid the Indra because their magical machina will decide the fate of all species if they so choose. They're a hostile race.

The pulley system used to hoist him up looks primitive compared to everything around it. A wide, green meadow lies beyond the pier, covered in short grasses and bright-colored plants. Clusters of larger plants with leafy appendages tower around it. Trees, perhaps. He's heard stories and seen them from a distance, but never has Gallagher been this close to them. As far as he's aware, the only trees within the Terra Realm grow high in the Morshine Peaks beyond their borders.

Further off, behind the trees, castles and towers aplenty mark the horizon. They could house ten thousand of his clans. Yet they're not made of stone or wood as they do within the Knuckles of Morshine, but rather a shiny material like the steel of his sickle. Could their entire civilization be built on steel? How could they possibly acquire so much of it? It's a rare mineral, only used by his clan for the worthiest of tools.

A steel, mechanical gauntlet picks at the net, pulling his attention from the stunning floating civilization back to a crowd amassing before him. He jerks backward. "Ma-machina!" he stutters. The gauntlet is attached to a long shaft, which is attached to one of the Indra's shoulders. A machina appendage? The sight of it paralyzes him, eyes wide and mouth agape, not so different from the dreaded Indra on the pier.

Wild, short breaths consume Gallagher. He gasps for air, unable to control his breathing any longer. Tugging on the net does nothing but further tangle him. He finds the sickle at his hip and slices at the netting. Pain stings his forearm, and a hole opens.

He hasn't trained for *this*. An experience he's never encountered Before. *Falling.*

His fins paddle against the thin air without effect. His arms flail with no grasp on the air around him. He's too heavy above the clouds, like a leviathan out of water. Then, a puff of clouds catches him, and it quickly turns back into his ceiling—a dull, grey, comfortable ceiling. The view of the Knuckles of Morshine calms him. His velocity slows. He's safe.

Later that afternoon, Gallagher putters through the village where deep ruts from the kelp-filled carts mark the roads. The hardened sand on the thoroughfares makes it easier for him to trudge through. His fellow clanmates prepare for the Morshine Clan's big day in a couple days—the day of the Solari Harvest. Finely crafted sunbursts made from dried kelp, leathers, and a splash of crumbled coral for color decorate every building. Colorful windsocks with long streamers emulating the rays of the sun line the roads. The air is buzzing with smiles and excitement.

For Gallagher, this day is a reminder of his blight.

He armors himself with a jovial façade around his companions, but until he can join the harvest team, this day won't fill him with the same delight as it does for the others.

The smith's daughter and another maiden elf Gallagher isn't acquainted with stand on the upper deck of the parlor. They serenade the street with a spirited hum while they dance and hang more decorations for the big event.

"Hey, Gally!" The smith's daughter waves down to him with a smile.

Gallagher tries his hardest to curve his lips in the same manner with a lame attempt at a wave.

Gallagher passes by Crumbaker's, a bakery full of the finest pastries. Not that Gallagher would know any better, but when you find something good, you hold onto it. And Crumbaker's pastries are worth holding onto.

The sweet aroma of sugar and dough wafts through the air. Samara's crumble cake is the most sought after. Only made for those with special orders. Her patrons supply the Blue Tears, measured by her, and she bakes its sweet goodness into the bread. Gallagher has only been allowed to take in a whiff of its splendid aroma. Never has he had a taste. With the Solari Harvest coming, that same smell infiltrates the streets, as each member of the harvest team will be gifted one.

"Oh, Gallagher, do you have a spare hand?" Samara calls from an open window in her kitchen.

Gallagher cringes. Of course, he does. But he doesn't want the temptation of the Blue Tears or the sweet dough. He'd rather continue his pouting as he trudges through the streets glowering at all his clanmates going about their merry days.

"Err… Miss Crumbaker, I know nothing about baking. Are you sure? I'd only be a bitter spice in your sweet kitchen."

She flashes a dish with a cerulean glow emanating from it. The Blue Tears wadded on the plate leave him speechless. Samara says something to him, but he doesn't hear her. She shoves the plate out the window, nearly spilling it in his face, and he doesn't even flinch. He welcomes the proximity to the Tears, and their sweet aroma.

"Meh, don't give me your excuses. I've got plenty of spice in this kitchen," she says. "You won't cause me any trouble. Here, take it!"

"Gallagher, there you are." His mother approaches with his father in tow.

Gallagher's head snaps in their direction.

Little do they know they saved their son from more heartache—helping Samara Crumbaker make her famous crumble cake for the guild of warriors of which he'll never be a member. The only thing worse would be handfeeding it to them.

"Sorry, Miss Crumbaker. Maybe next time." He gestures to his parents as his scapegoat.

"Of course, of course. Maybe next time." She waves him off.

Both his parents don generous smiles with grey streaks highlighting their mud-brown hair. Solid lines of hard-earned wisdom stretch above their foreheads and beneath their eyes, and reaching from the corners, too. Their labor-filled lives are on display with their callused hands and toned physiques. A healthy couple, considering they're more than two hundred years old.

"Lady Lightcloud." He addresses her formally with a dull delivery.

She glares at him in return, saying nothing to acknowledge her disapproval of his acrid greeting.

"That's Mister Lightcloud to you, son." His father chuckles, implying his son was addressing him, and not his mother. He looks around for more smiles but gets none.

Gallagher dismisses his father's lame attempt at humor. He's trying to lighten the mood, but Gallagher's trudge is holding him together right now. There's nothing that puts him into a tarter mood than the celebration of the Solari Harvest. The only thing he can think about during this time of the year is how he'll never surmount to what he aspires to be. He expects his parents to either join his trudge or leave, but not to prevent him from sulking.

"Hold on, Gally." His father grabs his arm causing him to wince.

"Branford!" His mother scolds his father.

He lets go. "Daya, I was just…" Her glare keeps him from saying more, but his eyes gesture toward Gallagher's injury.

"What have we here?" his mother asks. "What happened?" This time, *she* grabs his arm and pulls him closer to inspect the wound.

"It's nothing. An accident with my sickle is all." He wouldn't dare tell them he was above the clouds earlier that day. Word would spread and there would be severe consequences to follow. To think if he could sink any lower than a blighted kelp picker. He shakes his head in silence.

"It's not nothing. That's a deep cut, son." His father insists, but he won't do anything about it. He's never been one to stand up for what he believes. He accepts the world as it's given to him.

"And what can we do with it? No need to fret over what's out of my control."

Gallagher pulls his arm back. His mother reaches for the small amulet hanging around her neck. It's a silver conch shell, something she's always worn. She twists it open, and he rolls his eyes at her.

"What?" She dabs her finger inside the trinket, then rubs the iridescent paste across Gallagher's wound. He winces again, then experiences a subtle coolness where she touched him. "I can't leave your wounds unattended. I'm your mother."

"I'm sixty-four years old, mother. I don't need you taking care of me. Besides, it'll hardly make a difference. It's diluted with kelp paste. There's only a dash of spice in that salve."

"It's induced with Ceto's will. It's better than nothing," she says.

"As kelp pickers," his father speaks up, "we must cherish what Ceto offers us and make our rations last." He waves a finger in the air. "That ration of Tears has lasted all year because of that kelp paste."

"And what good has it done you? Don't you ever aspire to more than kelp picking?" Gallagher cringes after speaking to his father in such an insolent tone. It's not his way.

His father is speechless, not with anger but confusion. His lips part to say something, though only silence can be heard.

"I'm sorry, father," Gallagher quickly adds. "The Solari Harvest flares my ambitions... *and* my blight." He looks down at his damaged fin. His anchor to the reality of his future.

His father wraps a warm arm around him, but Gallagher nudges him away.

"I'd rather be alone at the moment," he admits. "Plus, Mira and I—"

"I insist." He wraps Gallagher tighter. "It'll be quick. I promise." He looks to Gallagher for permission to continue. A subtle nod is given, and his father continues. "Ceto..."

At that one word, Gallagher rolls his eyes. He knows it'll be a short lecture on gratitude and patience. One he's heard a thousand times.

"Pride is the worst of all flaws, Gallagher. Community and family must always come first. Ceto has blessed us all with the life he's given us. And we cannot take that for granted. Where do you think the Tears come from? These are his offerings—health and prolonged life—from creator to creation. And as lowly elves, we are not entitled to his offerings. We must earn them. We must prove ourselves to Ceto, consume his Tears, then return ourselves to him upon our demise. Only then will our blessings come."

"And hard work," Gallagher adds. "And determination. And wishful thinking that our traditions will be muddled by a blight becoming a warrior. Only then will I have the opportunity for this blessing."

Now it is his father's turn to roll his eyes. He lets go of his son and looks him up and down. "A blight you may be, but you're a Lightcloud. And you're full of excellence."

Gallagher nods to show respect for his father, but with an unconvinced quirk fully displayed in his grin. He offers them a traditional parting of heart, strength, mind, and soul before he turns his back to trudge alone.

"You have your mother twisting on the inside, you know," his mother chimes in before he goes. "Will you be joining us later? There remains much to prepare for the festivities tomorrow. We have ganderberry juice to make... coral wreathes... and we must tune our pipes for the melodies to come... There's much to do."

He looks over his shoulder at her. "Of course, mother. I would never skip on tradition."

"Heart, strength, mind, and soul." His father thumps the left side of his chest, then the right, followed by a tap to his forehead and carries it down to his abdomen. "Don't be tardy. I know how you and Mira love to get lost in your adventures." His father leaves him with empty words. As if there would be any consequences if he were to be tardy. And as if his self-discipline would even allow such a thing as tardiness to take advantage of his day.

Gallagher finds the edge of the colony along the shoreline and dangles his fins in the shallows. He finds himself here often, staring into the depths, wondering what adventures the warriors get to partake in. The leviathans are the triumph of a warrior, but other dangers and escapades lurk down there too. Run-ins with octopuses, wolf eels, and occasionally wraiths—though they tend to drift the skies. He's heard stories of the treacherous dragon's tongue too, a paralyzing plant that grows within the canyon. But it's always just stories.

He looks up toward the ceiling of clouds pondering his brief act of betrayal within the Caelum Realm, and to see if any wraiths are on the horizon. The jelly-like creatures aren't aggressive, but they come in swarms and are mindless about what victims they engage with. Mira despises them. Where is she?

"Hey, Gally!" A voice is heard from behind, right on cue.

Only a few call him by that name. Only a few are allowed to. "Hey there, Mira."

"Dreaming about seadragons and puffers again?" Rivee swims up next to Mira.

Rivee is blighted like Gallagher. She lost a leg just above the knee in an accident about fifteen years ago and may not even be able to surmount to as much as a kelp picker. She helps gather driftwood for the carpenters and assists

Bailey in the infirmary, but her options are limited. As is her growth. For whatever reason, she's a short elf. She's just a youngkin at twenty years, but she ought to be nearing her adult height. Some murmurs blame it on the accident. Other murmurs, which only come in the form of whispers, say an Indra was involved. Rivee doesn't seem to be concerned, though, and that's all that matters.

"Wraiths, actually," he replies. It's a better answer than telling the two about his incident above the clouds. He rarely keeps secrets from Mira and Rivee, but he's hesitant to let anyone know.

"Why would you dream about wraiths?" Rivee cringes with a scowl on her face. "Nasty things. Not fun at all."

"Agreed," Mira chimes in. "It's because his dreams are filled with blades and blood and danger." She smirks at him.

Gallagher stares at her, admiring her beautiful smile. Her dark braids hang to one side of her face, and the rest of her hair is wadded into a chaotic bun. She just finished training, wearing her worn, molded leathers that protect her chest and upper thighs, along with bracers on her forearms. She dons a silver circlet with her stone mounted in the center—a testament to her strength and rank within the clan. It's mostly transparent with a subtle green hue to it, coordinating with her eyes.

"Would you like to add some fun to your brooding, today?" she asks with a devious grin. "We're about to head out on an adventure."

The word perks his interest. "Adventure?"

"Yeah!" Rivee blurts out with the excitement of a child. "We're going to the Crisper Coral to explore."

As a youngkin, it makes sense that she's excited about this, but when you've reached young adulthood and should already have your first stone, climbing your ranks through the Warrior's Guild, you've been to that place a thousand times. He has a longing to tell them about his adventure above the clouds, but too many reasons force him to keep quiet. The foremost, if he tells Mira about it, she will find reason to go. And if the Elders find out about it, he could be banished from the colony. But he doesn't keep secrets from these two.

He feigns a smile, looking at Rivee. He can sulk about what he'll never have—he stares at the stone upon Mira's forehead—or he can join two of his favorite elves on an adventure. "Let's do it."

"Yay!" Rivee chirps. Her shoulder-length curls bounce with her joyful movements.

Mira rests her fists on her hips, leaning slightly to one side as she dons that striking smile again. Gallagher cannot resist ogling. He'll never have her hand, however. It would be selfish of him to court her as a lowly kelp picker. She's a warrior from a prestigious family. She's better off as one of his favorite elves and no more.

"C'mon," Mira says, watching him stare at her. "I can see your excitement. Your ears are getting erect." She glances down at the malo covering his groin and snickers, obviously not referring to his ears or the exploration of the Crisper Coral.

Gallagher's face flushes. "What..." He brushes at his loin cloth several times, smoothing it out. "No you can't. I'm not... What?"

"Yeah, c'mon, dreamy," Rivee fires at him, unaware of Mira's immature and inappropriate comment.

Gallagher pops to his fins and ruffles her short hair, then flicks the point of her left ear. "Beat you there!" He speeds off without them, mostly trying to flee the awkward situation Mira has put him in.

The coral reef is on the opposite side of the bay, still within the protection of the knuckles—natural stone bulwarks that reach from the Morshine Peaks into the shallows.

Rivee, quick with one leg and one fin, is thrilled when she outpaces Gallagher with his damaged fin. The two young adults let her win, of course, but it's a believable win. Mira could have easily dominated the race to get there. She's the fastest elf in the clan. So fast, it's a surprise she's a warrior and not one of the harvesters. Family obligations.

"I know you could've won, Mira. Don't play the sea slug for my sake. As long as I can outswim this sucker, I'm good." Rivee jabs at Gallagher with a playful scowl, then does a cartwheel through the air.

Mira snickers.

"Why aren't you a harvester, Mira?" Rivee asks bluntly.

Mira's smile fades. "Oh... Well... It's complicated, Rivee." Mira leaves it at that.

"You could be the best harvester there ever was," Rivee boasts. It's not a preposterous boast, either.

"Yeah, well..." Mira hikes an eyebrow. "I'm not all that interested in gathering. It might come as a shocker, but I'd rather discover new species of plants. I'd rather go on expeditions to explore the vast ocean outside our borders." She waves her arm across the horizon. "Maybe an excursion into the Caelum Realm..." She looks up. "Wouldn't you?"

"Yes!" Rivee shouts with much emotion.

"And you, Gally?" Chin up, she gives him a pointed look. "What would you like to do?"

Gallagher freezes. Could she possibly know he was in the Caelum Realm earlier? Why would she say that if she didn't? He must tell them.

"What is it that you desire, Gally?" she asks again as she leans in closer.

The rephrasing of the question combined with the warm feeling she imbues distracts him from his anxiety about the incident above the clouds. Embracing her is the first thing that comes to mind. Slaying a leviathan to claim his first stone is the second. Earning himself the right to cerulean steel is among his desires, but that is long-term for it would require five stones. It's out of reach at the moment, but someday... It may be what it takes to have Mira's hand.

"Me?" An earnestness overcomes him. He bats his heart with a fist and stares deep into Mira's green eyes. "All my desires will come to me if I follow my heart..." Then he smacks the right side of his chest. "...and allow my strength to carry me there. I must only be in the moment and one stroke ahead at the same time."

The two girls stare at him for an eternity before they erupt with laughter.

"And what of your mind and your soul?" Mira leans in to tap his forehead and playfully slap his gut. "Shouldn't they be a part of your decisions and desires?" She lingers close, casually pressing her body into his, but not overdoing it. She looks up into his eyes.

As much as Gallagher wants to hold onto this moment, he mustn't. She is not within his reach. Not yet.

"I would rather be the first to discover something new in the Crisper Coral," he blurts out, then points his arms overhead and dives through the air into the ocean waves where most of the coral life flourishes. Some coral, urchins, and other sea life live within the Terra Realm, but the trio are not likely to discover anything new above the waves. Thankfully, the shallows aren't off limits like the clouds of the Caelum Realm. The border lies at the canyon's edge beneath the waves where the knuckles fade into the ocean bed.

Rivee and Mira follow his lead.

In the shallows, they swim and explore. Seahorses bob this way and that, skittles follow along with them, only seen as a colorful flash ducking behind the sea plants—skittish creatures. And sea anemone, urchins, and shellfish are everywhere. Schools of fish curl in and out of the coral and scatter when Rivee flirts with them. Mira smiles.

Strength culminates within that smile. She's a warrior who protects her clan; a shining star to a youngkin elf; a loyal daughter; a blessing to her kin. Gallagher finds himself ogling not the coral life he should be, but Mira.

Hovering just above the coral bed, she looks over at him. Her smile turns into something of genuine passion. He only ever sees her in this state when she's on an adventure with Rivee. She's happy here.

Rivee points to the surface, asking for them to follow. They all pop their heads above water, bobbing in the gentle swells.

"How big do seadragons get?" Rivee asks. "I've only ever seen these tiny ones." She shoves her head underwater and points to a cluster of them dancing amidst the swaying sea grass. They're as large as her forearm and blend well with the swaying foliage, but apparently that's tiny in her eyes. Her hair sprays water on their faces when she pops back out.

Gallagher wipes droplets from his face. "They're dragons, no?" Gallagher replies in an enigmatic fashion to exude wonder.

"Yes…" She eyes him carefully.

"And dragons are monstrous beasts who feed on youngkins. So…"

Rivee darts toward him, and playfully swings at his shoulder, but he twirls out of the way and catches her instead, wrapping her up tightly.

"You don't know anything," she protests.

"You're right. I have no idea," he says with a chuckle. He looks back to Mira whose breezy expressions never fade out here. Someday he'll count how many variations of grins she has. They're all contagious.

"And what about *blue* dragons? How big do they get?" A sparkle of marvel shines in Rivee's eyes.

"Ah, the blue dragon…" Gallagher looks at Rivee with a mixture of mystery and wisdom, as if this is a topic that shouldn't be discussed. He looks back at Mira. "I don't know. Mira is the one who dreams of them day and night. Large enough to ride, I'd say. How big are they in your dreams?" He smiles at her.

"Hmph…" Mira swims toward him and gives him a playful nudge. "Legend says they read your soul, and only reveal themselves to those with the heart of a warrior with the purest of intentions."

Gallagher frowns. "Are you saying I'll never get the opportunity to find out how big they are?" He tries to turn his frown into a smile, but she's touched on a delicate topic. He knows it wasn't intentional.

"I'm saying your intentions aren't always pure, Gally." She pokes at his bare chest and swims past him with a burst, brushing close enough to taunt desire. She flicks at his braids as she speeds away.

His head swiftly turns to follow her. As he's admiring Mira once more, a peculiar something catches his eye on the shore, stealing his attention away from her. Nestled into a bushel of bright-orange coral, its dark color is stark against the noisy colors of the coral bed.

He casually releases Rivee, who's been struggling in his grasp, and wanders toward the oddity. Rivee and Mira watch him in suspense due to the odd change of attitude from casual glee to intense focus.

"Come!" he suggests. "Look at this?"

"What is it? Is it something new? Is it something wonderous?" Rivee speeds toward him.

Mira follows in silent curiosity.

"Better," he replies. He struggles to break it free without damaging the coral, then holds it up for them to see.

"It's a piece of junk!" Rivee spits. "What world do you live in where garbage is better than something wonderous?"

Mira, standing in the shallows behind them, closes her eyes and withholds a laugh while grabbing onto Rivee's shoulders.

"This is...*machina*..." Gallagher holds it higher, admiring its novelty.

"*Was* machina," she corrects him.

"Looks like it fell from above the ceiling." Mira looks up.

"Exactly!" Gallagher inspects the chunk of metal. "Indra machina. It's heavier than my sickle, but—"

"Of course it is. It's as long as your arm and three times as thick."

Gallagher glares at her before continuing. "For its size, it's much lighter." He lifts it up and down.

"May I ask..." Mira starts, but waits for acknowledgement from Gallagher before proceeding, "...what is it about this... *junk*... that interests you so much?"

He knows exactly why he's fascinated with the Indra's machina, but he's hesitant to tell them. He looks down at his damaged fin and wonders what could become of it with Indra technology.

Mira watches him intently. A screwy grin forms on her face. "You know... a kelp picker is an honorable role. Think of all the smiles you're putting on youngkin's faces with the kelpmallows you're gathering. It's a part of our culture. A joyous part."

"Easy for a warrior to say who's already earned her first stone. You have so much more to be proud of. So much, nobody needs to remind you of your great accomplishments. My life is all machina junk and kelpmallows."

Gallagher leaves it at that. He splashes the machina into the shallows where it drifts to the sandy floor beneath them. He continues wandering the Crisper Coral, aimlessly, and in much thought about one bad choice that side-tracked his entire life.

"Gally, wait!" Mira rushes to catch up to him. She curls her arm around his. The simple act adds so much warmth to his brooding, it nearly dissolves all his woes. "What's wrong?"

Gallagher is hesitant to unfold his problems. Mira doesn't need to deal with them. She would probably think them childish, anyways. If he keeps to his ways as a lowly kelp picker, he'll always be a part of her life. "Do you ever desire more, Mira? Do you ever wonder where life will take you?"

"You should know better than to ask such a silly question. My curiosity pulls my mind across all three realms: sky, land, and sea. To float above the clouds with the Indra, or to race an Ebisu through the darkest parts of the ocean. Even to escape the confines of our bay and explore the vastness of the Terra Realm would excite my heart. To explore all the places…" Her voice trails as her gaze drifts into the depths of her mind.

"There's always something more to aspire to, isn't there?" Gallagher's message is positive, but his tone suggests he doesn't believe it.

She tugs on his arm, bringing him to a halt. "Heart, strength, mind, and soul." She presses a hand into his chest. "These are what carry us forward."

"Sounds like something your father would say," he replies.

"Or you!" She smiles and a brief silence follows before she points to the eye in the sky. "Look, Gally."

"It's the eye. What of it?"

"It's the Eye of Solari. The eye that brings fortune to our clan. It's the eye that allows the sun's rays to shine down on us once a year to bring warmth and kindred feelings to all the De'wi elves. And wherever life takes me, as long as I look up and see that eye, I'll know you're close by. Wherever my wonder takes me, I won't let it take me far from you."

The eye in the sky also brings a raging storm and chaos every year. But he doesn't say that out loud. Gallagher pulls her in closer, enjoying the moment, for it will never turn into more. Not until he can prove to her he is an elf worthy of her hand. And to do that, he must overcome an entire clan who has labeled him blighted.

2 WRAITH DECOY

T he morning light touches the top of the knuckles, revealing dark rugged silhouettes spearing toward the forever-grey heavens. The Solari Harvest is almost upon them. One more day for Mira's stomach to churn with anxiety before it comes and passes. She treads in the air, remaining in place just above their home as her wandering mind pulls her into the vast wild beyond their outposts. She longs to explore Solaria. She'd much rather be there than at the training grounds preparing for the harvest.

"Mira!" her mother calls to her from below. "Shouldn't you be training right now?"

She swims lower to address her mother properly. She's a strong elf and has earned the respect of not being hollered at from a distance—unlike Mira, it would seem.

"Rivee Rayfin!" She smiles at her adopted sister who's standing next to her mother. "Lady Rayfin…" Mira nods politely. Her mother stands rigid, slightly taller than Mira, with auburn braids draped over her shoulders blended with flowing tresses. Her face is stern. She expects the best from Mira, and Mira has no intention of disappointing her. "I respect your concern, but I have my priorities in alignment with the time. A gaze upon the morning light wakes my mind." She taps her forehead. "My mind wakes my body. You could say, my daily training has already begun."

"You know I don't appreciate being addressed as such. Not by you." Lady Nessa crosses her arms. "If *mother* is beyond you, you can at least tone your conceit down to Lady Nessa." She flattens her lips and shakes her head at her daughter.

"Rivee doesn't address you as mother." Mira cocks her head with a know-ing smirk, intentionally being brazen.

"Please." Her mother rolls her eyes. "I would never force Rivee to address me as such." Rivee remains silent, distracted by the elves getting an early start to hang sunbursts and tear drop decorations for the Solari Harvest. Lady Nessa looks down at her. When she decides Rivee is not paying attention, she quietly continues. "She may have taken our name, but it would be narcissistic to force her to call me mother." Lady Nessa looks down at her again, this time with a deep adoration that cannot be missed.

"Of course, mother. My snideness was intended as a jest. My apologies." Mira looks down at Rivee as well. She's like a sister to Mira.

The story behind Rivee's parents has been kept quiet. Nobody from their clan knew them, and the Elders have requested the clan to refrain from discuss-ing the matter for Rivee's sake. The only thing that is known is that they were De'wi drifters traveling from a distant island in search of a new home, and Rivee is the sole survivor found by the point-elf working the outpost that day. Whispers point her origins as far as the Caelum Realm. Others point toward the lost Isle of Imperius. Nobody knows for sure. Not even Rivee. But she seems comforta-ble with it.

Lady Nessa took Rivee in when she was an infant. Since then, Mira has helped raise her… And destroy her future.

A frown sets into Mira's face.

Rivee begins singing a common melody as her attention lies elsewhere.

"Kings, kings, kings of the isle
Giants of old, no need for guile
Head in the clouds
Feeding on wraith stings
Kings, kings, kings of the isle
Giants of old, bringing a smile
Stepping over mountains
Bedding in stone rings
Kings, kings, kings of the isle
Giants of old—

She abruptly stops singing and looks at Lady Nessa with large, desperate eyes. "I'd like to help with the decorations, Lady Nessa. May I be excused?"

"Of course. Swim along." Lady Nessa shoos Rivee with a waving hand. Mira and her mother both watch as she swims away, unable to walk with only one leg. "You have a wandering mind, dear," she says to Mira.

Mira looks up at her mother to see her amber eyes staring at her. Her worry is obvious in those eyes, like looking through the transparent flesh of a wraith and witnessing its inner workings.

"You may call it many things, but training is not one of them." She steps closer to her daughter and places her hands on her shoulders. "Are you ready?"

She refers to the Solari Harvest. It's an annual excursion followed by a festival of triumph. Rays of the sun will penetrate the clouds, bless their colony, and shine into the depths of the canyon where the Blue Tears bloom. It's their one opportunity to restock their provisions for the year. The bioluminescent spice offers strength and healing and plays a dominant role in their culture. It prolongs the lives of those who have earned the right to consume its sweet bliss-fulness. It's a miracle from the depths of the ocean, given to them by Ceto. But it comes with its sacrifices.

"I'm ready, mother. How many harvests have I taken part in now? I'm one of the fastest elves out there. I must only swim faster than the next elf, right?" She smiles.

"This is no joking matter, Mira. You are out there to protect your clan. Think of the wolf eels. Think of the dragon's tongue. Too many dangers prowl within the depths. You are there to protect the harvesters."

"I know, mother. My apologies. I understand the severity and importance of the harvest. I am ready, and I *will* protect every De'wi out there. I promise."

"I know you will." Nessa brushes rogue tresses of hair out of her face, then rubs a thumb across the stone embedded in her circlet. "You're strong, Mira. You always have been." A moment of silence passes as the trepidation of the harvest hangs over them. It hangs over the entire clan because not all the elves return home every year. Mira knows this all too well. "A leader you may be, but you're young, yet. You haven't even made it to your century mark. Be-havior is contagious, dear. Act immature, and your team is likely to emulate that behavior. Be a respectable leader and you'll all come home safe."

"I'm hardly a leader, mother." She slides her circlet from her brow to gaze upon it. "This stone might offer me rank within the Warrior's Guild, but you said it—I'm young. At a notch above the half-century mark, nobody looks to me for guidance. Plus, we know this stone represents death. For every stone that is earned, a life reacquaints itself with Ceto in the depths of the ocean. And my stone is extra special. Two lives went to the afterlife. Alariya…" Mira taps her

heart with her right fist, her right breast with her left fist, then touches her forehead and carries it down to her abdomen. "It should have been buried with her."

"What are you saying?" Nessa recoils and continues in a near whisper
even though nobody is around to hear her. "You landed the first blow and the
final blow. That stone belongs to nobody but you." Her tone sharpens. "Act the
warrior you are!"

"If death gives me stones, and stones make me a leader, is this what my
companions should strive to accomplish? Death? Is this the behavior they should
emulate?" She holds it up like a trophy to be admired.

"I don't know what to do with you, Mira." Her mother turns her cheek to
her. "That stone is a symbol of strength and triumph. Your mind sees the world
in a different light, and I'm not sure how to offer you guidance." Nessa stares at
her daughter for a quiet moment. "Go. Get to your training. Maybe your father
will have better luck with you. Show him your priorities are in alignment with
the time."

"Yes, mother." Mira leaps into the air with a blend of finesse and power,
eager to be free of the lecture.

Mira treads air at the designated training grounds waiting for the rest of her
harvest team and other members of the Warrior's Guild to arrive. She could
blame her mother for arriving so early, but if she's honest with herself, it's her
own bad habit. Whether it's to get it over with or to prove to her family there's
no lack of interest, she isn't sure.

Their training grounds rest high above the kelp forest where Gallagher
works almost daily. She's further to the east, closer to the mountainous bulwarks
protecting their colony, which is a good thing, otherwise she'd be distracted by
him.

"Early again, I see." The Elder swims up beside her. His square jawline
and defined build make him look younger than he is. The grey hair and lines of
wisdom on his face portray his true age. From a distance, however, he could be
mistaken for a warrior of the guild. "Dedication will take you far, young lady.
And you are stout with it."

She offers him a half smile, unsure how to take the compliment, or
whether she's even due. "Thank you, Elder Rayfin."

His warrior days are long past him by a few hundred years. Now, he trains others to achieve the same. Thus far, he's a better warrior than trainer, but worthy candidates to replace him are slim.

"The horizon is beautiful, isn't it?" He stares toward the ocean, the only true horizon visible to them with the knuckles towering over them on all other sides.

Mira looks at him with concern. It's not a typical comment that would come from this elf. "It is," she replies dutifully.

"Our borders are locked down, but there will be a day our eyes get to witness up close the secrets the horizon holds." He places a hand in the center of his chest. "Well... Maybe not in my time, but it will come."

A gleeful warmth briefly subdues the anxiety growing within her gut. "Beyond the borders of the Morshine Isle?" she exclaims. "To the Luna Isle in the east or the Rhizo Isle in the west? Meandering upriver, past the rice crops and the Morshine Peaks to the north? Or south even? Does the ocean go on forever? How many isles are there?"

The Elder chuckles. "Everything you said and more."

Mira's lips curl into her cheeks, the idea of seeing the horizon, *actually* seeing it up close and not from a distance, tempers all the fear she has going into tomorrow's harvest. "How do you know these things, Elder? And when? What can I do to open the borders?"

His smile fades. "My apologies, I'm getting ahead of myself. It's a mere dream, Mira. Nothing more. We must remain in isolation. You know this."

Mira's apprehension returns. "Yes, but it's nice to dream. It's where the best ambitions derive." Silence fills the air between them until Mira overcomes her hesitation to explore his knowledge on the matter. "How do we know the Indra and the Ebisu are so horrible, Elder? If we haven't made contact in thousands of years, I mean. Cultures change. *They* could change."

The Elder grunts. "Our races have drifted apart, Mira. The Indra have melted into something docile beneath the heat of the sun. Though, it is not their physical threat, or lack of, that we shy away from. We fear their narcissistic culture. They abuse machina for the worse. They are above anyone but themselves. They look outwardly for honor and virtue, not inwardly. And we cannot have that ideology creep into our realm. The Ebisu... They are somewhat the opposite. Aggression formulates many of their decisions. Both cultures rely heavily on the machina that dilutes their societies into something less than respectable. So, we create borders to distance ourselves from toxicity, Mira, and Ceto forbid it, violence."

"And nothing will change your mind? No worthy emissary to make amends that would at minimum open our borders to trade or... holiday?" Her brow lifts, hopeful lines stretching across it.

A subtle shake of his head, hardly perceivable. Mira knows it's wishful thinking, but the thought of exploring the vastness of Solaria electrifies every nerve in her body.

The Elder's eyes become distant and dark as he stares at the horizon. Something about her inquiries trouble him. She lets go of their more formal interactions between Elder and warrior to probe deeper. "What is it, father?"

"If only history could be rewritten... it is nothing, dear. Please understand, these borders we create, they are for your own safety."

"Yes, Elder."

"The Solari Harvest is tomorrow," he says, clearly in need of a change of subject.

"It is." She's not ready for it. Not as ready as she would have her mother believe. She never is. This is her fifteenth Solari Harvest, and she has the jitters just as she did on the first one. The Elder's and other warriors alike have high expectations for her, except those who realize the luck involved. She's fast, but she's not as talented or skilled as some believe.

"Do you get nervous?" he asks.

"A little." It's not exactly a lie. She would never lie to one of the Elder's. Especially Elder Rayfin. He has earned her respect for many reasons.

"I still get nervous, too. I didn't achieve any of these without fear in my gut." He holds up the silver torque he wears around his neck. It has five stones embedded into it. An ornament of the highest status. An ornament displaying the renown he deserves. If you care about defeating the leviathans and protecting the clan, that is. "I learned early it's not the fear that kills you, it's the hesitancy. Don't hesitate. Trust in your stones."

"But a bad decision can kill you just the same as hesitancy." She speaks before she thinks. She shouldn't question the Elder's advice.

Elder Rayfin smiles before replying. "Allow me to amend my words. When facing a leviathan your odds of success are not great, and that disturbance in your gut will usher you to make good decisions. Trust your stones, Mira. Don't ever let it flee you when in the face of danger. Follow that instinct."

"Understood, Elder Rayfin." She offers him a curt bow as she treads air before him. Not another warrior has arrived yet, so she dares to ask him a question. "Why do instincts flounder within our soul, or... err... guts? Wouldn't it be better if they were directly linked with our thoughts?" She points to her head.

"Checks and balances, I suppose." He proceeds to rubbing his abdomen. "Your instincts are good in some situations… Your thoughts in others…"

"And your heart is there to keep them both in line. Your strength to fortify your decision and carry you forward. Heart… strength… mind and soul."

"Sound words from a true warrior, I would say."

"They're hardly my words, Elder. They are the words of a thousand years of tradition." Mira goes quiet and stares pensively into the distance. Little does he know those words are at the forefront of her mind because of her most recent conversation with Gallagher—an elf deemed blighted and incapable of being a warrior in his eyes. Her heart is aimed at him—an elf forsaken by her own father. She knows this. Her head is aimed at wonder—despised by her own mother. She knows this. But what does her soul tell her? She doesn't understand how to translate that unsettled feeling deriving from her gut and creeping through her skin. It could be faith in Ceto's will, an emotion only meant for the deity to interpret. It could be fear. Fear of owning more death.

The other warriors begin arriving, and Mira shakes away her heavy thoughts and straightens her posture in the air. Hands crossed behind her back, fins shoulder-width apart and gently swaying to keep her afloat.

"In line, warriors," Elder Rayfin commands once they all arrive.

Several lines, ten warriors each, tread before him. Mira is in the front line. Andolas, the chief of her squad is lined up next to her—the only elf in the guild who leaves her feeling exposed. This isn't the entire Warrior's Guild, but just one squad. And only a portion will take part in the harvest tomorrow.

"The Solari is on the horizon," he continues his morning address, "but today's training is no different than any other. You will work hard to perfect your skill. You will work as a team. You will work to defend one another. You will compete. The only difference in today's training will be when it's over. Your self-discipline will be in full effect as all your kin enjoy the festivities partaking around you. Your role as a warrior or harvester is to smother temptation this evening. Save your merrymaking for tomorrow when triumph saturates our clan. Now… begin with your sparring routine."

The warriors pair up. Tanniv Windstalker and Veras Elreid, two of her regular sparring partners, line up across from one another. "Mira!" Haltuk calls to her. She finds him in the line, but a hand firmly grips her upper arm.

She turns to find Andolas pulling her in his direction. She retracts from his grip but follows. "Sorry," she mouths to Haltuk. He offers a sympathetic cringe in return. Andolas is not anyone's preferred partner. She'd much rather spar with Veras, Tanniv, or Haltuk, but she won't deny her chief.

Each is armed with a yari, a long-shafted, piercing, melee weapon, with a long, curved blade-and-hook on one end and a traditional spearhead on the other. It's the weapon of choice when dancing with a leviathan. The long shaft offers reach, and the various blades allow for a variety of attacks, which is needed with an unpredictable sea demon. With a flattened shaft they cut through the water with ease, unlike morning stars or the typical variety of spears.

Mira's yari is fashioned with steel blades, but not all are so blessed. Like the stones the warriors don, the type of blade the warriors wield is earned. Steel isn't readily available within their borders. The only steel they have drops from the Indra above. Most tools are made of shale or stone. Shale the preferred of the two as it's sharper, but also extremely brittle. A warrior needs to carry at least one stone to earn the steel. Three stones will earn a warrior cerulean steel—a blade augmented with Blue Tears. It can cut through virtually anything.

The warriors line up across from each other, ensuring they're a safe distance away from all other sparring pairs around them. They each casually swing their yari full circle to ensure none will reach another, creating their imaginary blood-circle before they begin.

"Ready?" Mira calls to her partner, Andolas. He's many years older than her—they all are—with at least twenty more years of experience, but that doesn't matter much when sparring. The movements are choreographed, intended to warm up the body and generate muscle memory.

"Ready," he replies.

They torpedo toward each other, spinning with yaris outstretched, clashing shafts. The dense air is more challenging to gain traction than they would experience in the ocean, but it's close enough to improve their skillset. Andolas' first blow is powerful and sends her backward. She scrambles back into their blood-circle. They clash shafts, alternating sides, two-handed, single-handed, spinning, and repeating. The longer they spar, the more forceful Andolas' attacks get. He repeatedly knocks her out of the sparring ring and into the neighboring pair, who glare each time it happens.

"What's wrong?" She questions his integrity. He holds onto a grudge from the past she cannot do anything to correct. But she questions him as if she doesn't understand.

"I don't know what you mean?" Andolas pauses, treading out of reach of her yari. He's a tall elf with lighter hair braided into a tail. His physique is well defined, firm, and masculine, as are all the elves of warrior age, but Andolas is noticeably more toned than the others. He works for his place in the guild, and his attitude isn't afraid to announce his achievements.

"We only spar. Do I look like a leviathan?" she spits back with stabbing eyes and an even sharper jab with her yari.

Andolas squints and looks her up and down. "No. Not a leviathan, but—"

Mira goes off the choreographed moves with a spin and strike. Andolas raises his shaft and blocks the attack with a delighted grin.

"Very well." He strikes back, sending his hooked blade a fingers-width from ripping her nose off.

"Jelly spittle!" she curses at him, followed by her own aggressive attack.

Andolas hooks her shaft and yanks, pulling her yari from her grip. He could have grabbed it and handed it back to her, which would have been the respectable thing to do for a warrior who's on your team, but instead he watches it drift away, gliding down to the kelp forest below.

"What's your problem, Andolas?" She shoves his shoulder as she swims by.

He snatches the circlet from her forehead, drawing blood as he does. "*This* is my problem. You don't deserve this stone." He feigns ripping the stone from the circlet. Mira flinches. "It should've been you in the grave. Not her."

"That was two Solaris ago!" She keeps her voice low, glancing at the others. "What do you expect me to do?" She feels the same as he does, but she doesn't dare tell the truth with the damage it would do to her own pride, and the pain it would cause so many others. "An elf died, and so did the leviathan that killed her. She was brave. End of story."

"Alariya is still in the grave," he growls.

Mira wants to put her fist between his eyes, but she wouldn't be able to participate in the Solari Harvest tomorrow if she did. She inhales, biting her tongue, and snags her circlet from his grip. She slides it back on, tucking it beneath her hair as she swims away to gather her wandering yari.

A conch shell bellows from the outpost atop the knuckles—an alarm to warn them of an invading threat.

Mira beats her fins with intensity and snags her yari before it gets lost within the swaying kelp below. If that alarm hadn't sounded, her yari would still be drifting toward the forest below, and she'd be seeking a glance at Gallagher instead.

"Mira! In line!" Elder Rayfin calls to her before addressing the entire squad. "A swarm of wraiths curls over the knuckles. Hundreds! Stick to your training. Partner up with whoever your sparring partner was and protect one another. Don't engage with those above you. Stay on the perimeter. Should you find yourself surrounded, pray to Ceto you come out alive. Now, go! Protect your clan. More squads will be on their way." He waves a hand for them to charge.

Mira makes eye contact with Andolas and gives him a nod—an unspoken truce until they're through this. He's the ranking warrior with two stones and is the most experienced in the squad. Despite her differences with the elf, she trusts him as a leader. They'll find victory under his command.

His eyes narrow, but he nods in return before speeding ahead. Mira mentally prepares herself for the massacre they're about to unleash on the foul creatures.

This far out, the swarm could easily shift direction and not come any closer. They're a wandering, nomadic species, following the winds and the food, harmless unless they actively engage the clan. She despises the creatures, but she doesn't fully approve of slaughtering them.

"We're almost there. Flank out!" Andolas calls to the rest of the squad.

"Yes, chief!" several call out in return.

The elves spread out wide enough and high enough to frame one side of the wraith swarm. It's more massive than it appeared from a distance. Hundreds was an understatement. These wraiths would devour her entire clan if left unattended. Her gut doesn't feel so bad about that massacre, now.

The wraiths come in many sizes from as small as a palm to larger than an elf. They have a pink, purple, or blue translucence to them when pinned against the marbled-grey cloud cover. However, when staring at certain angles, all that can be seen is a glimmer in the air. And when above them, they're nearly transparent aside from their innards, which are camouflaged with the kelp forest below. Deceptive creatures.

They bob casually through the air, occasionally rippling their hoods to propel themselves. Overall, their movement is slow and imminent, like a rising tide.

"Defend your clan!" Andolas calls out with the first strike of his yari. Using the spearhead it pierces the hood with ease, but the wraith continues to bob through the air. He strikes again, keeping his distance, and hits in the center of its innards.

Mira jabs with quick consecutive strikes of her spear. She gores the first wraith and attacks all that are within reach, then twirls the shaft and switches to the blade. Slice, hack, slice. Tentacles and pieces of gelatinous flesh float all around her. She stays clear of the tentacles as they're still venomous.

Mira backstrokes as the swarm surges forward, and she moves onto the next cluster. Slice, hack, slice.

Minced jelly spittle surrounds her, and suddenly she feels a sting on her ankle. A petite wraith about the size of her forearm has broken through their wall of defense. It bobs away without a care for her presence.

As she curses, movement in the kelp forest below steals her attention. More movement than ought to be made by the kelp pickers themselves, and too aggressive and isolated for wind to be the cause. The plumes atop the long stalks disperse as if several waterspouts push through. She lowers herself beneath the swarm to tend to her ankle. But that's just her excuse. She swims lower to investigate the anomaly in the forest.

"Seadragons!" The word comes out with a gasp. Seadragons parade through the kelp forest. If only Rivee were here to witness them. These aren't the small variety they see dancing through the Crisper Coral, however. These seadragons are the size of a large manatee. And mounted atop them are elves, dark in nature.

Ebisu! Mira has only heard the Elders speak their name with minimal description, but she has no doubt these are the aquatic elves from the Ocean Realm. Their flesh is several shades darker, and their hair as black as the canyon's depths. Even the armor strapped to their chests, legs, and forearms is dark. They're armed with two-pronged tridents. From this distance she cannot get a clear visual, but it appears as though they carry a bluish-green glow—the same glow that radiates from the Tears. The kelp around them illuminates as they trample through it. They are headed toward the colony.

Why was there not an alarm from the outposts?

Mira gasps. The squad assumed the wraiths were the concern when it was an invasion from beyond the border.

She must warn Elder Rayfin and the rest of the clan, but her duty is with her squad to fend off the wraith swarm.

Torn between racing back to the colony or fulfilling her duty to battle the wraiths, she hesitates, but others will die if she wavers any longer. She swims toward the cloud cover where the pink and purple mass of wraiths press closer.

"Andolas!"

The chief lances a wraith. "What?" he shouts between pants and sends her a quick glare.

"The wraiths are a decoy!"

"Hardly." He flinches as a tentacle brushes across his forearm. "Their venom is real. And they press into the knuckles, headed straight for our colony. I'd say that's a true threat. Why are you not striking?"

"Ebisu are attacking the colony. I need to hurry back. I'm sorry. I would suggest you lead our squad home, too."

"You what?" His head snaps in her direction with a mixture of confusion and anger, but he doesn't cease his attacks, nor does he command any of the others to.

Mira grins internally. Not for abandoning her companions, but because of the emotions she's drawing out of Andolas. She zips away without waiting for approval in pursuit of the Ebisu.

3 ALLY IN THE SKY

"Leviathan!" A shout is heard in the distance. But how could it be? In the kelp forest? It must be a mistake. The leviathans are monsters of the deep. The air won't hold their mass the same as it does the De'wi elves. It can't be possible.

The long tentacle-like stalks push out of the way and Gallagher witnesses the commotion. The face of a dragon stares him down, not slowing as it charges. Nostrils puff and its leafy ornaments whip about as it comes at him faster than the speed of a harvester. Faster than the winds of a waterspout.

Gallagher, fearless of a harmless seadragon, despite this one being larger than he is, stands his ground and waves his arms in the air to try and stop the panicked creature. Or so he thinks. When the seadragon refuses to slow, Gallagher leaps out of the way just before being run through. Only then does he realize these seadragons are mounted.

More follow right behind the first. This time Gallagher shouts. "Hey!" He waves his hands again. "What's with all the unnecessary stampeding? You're destroying our kelp."

They don't listen. Several more race through, trampling the kelp. One of the riders stares him down on his way through. His features are dark and malicious aside from the glowing breastplate. He's never seen elves so dark before. Although, he's never seen elves other than the De'wi and Indra races. And these are neither. Could they be the Ebisu?

The seadragon slows and swings around to face him. The Ebisu atop it grimaces. A challenge? The dark elf charges. Gallagher leaps to the side and grips his adversary's leg as he does, pulling him from his mount. The dark elf grunts and hits the ground in a tangle with Gallagher.

"Get off me, little elf!" he carps.

Gallagher pins him to the ground, face down, with his hands wrenched behind his back and all his body weight on top of him. He's right, this dark elf is much larger than he is, but he doesn't let that stop him from interrogating him. "You belong in the depths, no? Why are you here?"

The dark elf remains silent and struggles to free himself.

"Answer me!" Gallagher shouts.

More mounted seadragons tear through the forest. Gallagher is forced to lay flat against the dark elf as they pass overhead. The Ebisu, hands now free, presses into the ground. An immediate surge of light follows, and Gallagher launches into the air.

Gallagher's arms flail. His fins kick unexpectedly as he tries to gain control of his angle of departure. Something blunt smashes into the back of his head and a wash of colors fills his vision as he rolls in agony on the ground.

When he gathers himself, the dark elf and company are out of sight and headed in the direction of the colony. A fellow clanmate swims above the forest in the same direction. Gallagher's vision remains fuzzy, but he recognizes her slender figure and curves.

"Mira!" he yells. She doesn't hear him. She's fast enough, she'll catch up to them, but then what? If chasing them would make a difference, he would follow her. He looks down at his damaged fin. He doesn't have the means to catch them. He clenches his jaw, frustrated with his blight. There must be some way he can be useful. He looks around, all he has is his sickle and fallen kelp. It'll do him no good. If only he had a yari like the warriors, and a pinch of the Blue Tears to give him the strength he needs to swim as fast as Mira.

He considers the wraith swarm above. The fight rages on. *Why aren't they following Mira?*, he wonders. The wraiths can be dealt with later. He swims toward the cloud cover.

"Tanniv! Veras!" He calls to the closest two elves he recognizes.

Veras Elreid is a slender elf with a pointed beak for a nose. Easy to spot in a crowd of warriors as he's the only one with ribs telegraphing through his flesh.

Tanniv Windstalker is handsome warrior who comes from a long line of champions. Broad shoulders, toned physique, and sturdy build overall. He looks more like the type who should be battling a legendary grendelin than these pathetic wraiths that attack in droves.

"A tad busy at the moment, Gally." Veras pants, not looking to see who's calling his name, as he repeatedly thrusts at the enemy.

"Gallywog, is that you?" another elf taunts. "Are you here to join us? Because I'm afraid you might get eaten alive by one of these extraordinarily slow-moving predators. Doubt you could outmaneuver them if you put all your might into it. Go home, Gallywog."

"Shut it, Andolas!" Gallagher swims closer but keeps a good distance from the wraiths. He's not prepared to defend himself with just a small sickle at his hip. "The colony is under attack."

"And we're dealing with it, you fool," Andolas growls as he pierces the wraiths in rapid succession. "Trust in your stones, Gallywog." He pauses a moment, likely to let the satisfaction of his words soak into his ego. "Oh wait, you don't have any. And you never will! Go home." A spin of his yari, and one massive slice takes out three wraiths at once.

"The colony is under attack by invading elves."

"The Indra haven't been at odds with us for centuries. Millennia, in fact. And the conches would bellow if they did. We'd know if they were coming."

"And if the outposts were distracted by a swarm of wraiths? Would you know, then?" Gallagher rebuts. "Besides, they're not the Indra. They arrived on seadragons. I presume from the ocean depths. Their chests were glowing with the color of the spice. They're Ebisu."

"Now you're blowing waterspouts out your ass. Get out of here, you blustering fool." Andolas strikes several more wraiths, shredding their gelatinous hoods.

"I'm not lying, Andolas. They were dark of nature. Their flesh, their hair, their attire, it was all dark. And they were larger than the average De'wi. Nothing like the squatty Indra. I'm not mistaken because I just wrestled one to the ground."

"Or maybe it's that you're a petite De'wi, who's blighted, and everyone appears large in your eyes."

"Why are you such a schmuck?"

Andolas retreats from the wraiths to a safe distance. "Why are you a persistent, finless guppy?" Andolas slaps Gallagher on the side of his head with the flat of his yari.

It's a challenge. Gallagher has every right to defend himself, now. Chief or not, warrior or kelp picker, he has been assaulted and he will take this opportunity to save his pride.

With no intention to draw blood, Gallagher twirls in the air with his sickle, slicing past Andolas' leather bracer, leaving a large gash and no blood. Andolas retaliates with his yari, but they're in close combat, now, and Gallagher has the advantage. The finless guppy swats away the schmuck's weapon with ease, and takes another jab, and another slice. This time he leaves a mark on Andolas' leather breastplate.

"That's a kill." Gallagher retracts from the semi-playful fight to point at the situation where their attention should be. "Please, Andolas, your squad is needed back at the village. Look for yourself!" Gallagher thrusts his pointed finger, urging for him to look. The edge of the kelp forest can be seen, and so can the dark elves riding atop their seadragons. Miniature from this distance, but visible all the same.

Andolas twirls his yari in the air and strikes Gallagher with the spear end. It slices past Gallagher's arm with a bite and a dark red line forms where it struck. Then another twirl, and another strike, which lands directly across his face with the flat of the blade. Gallagher's wits are shocked momentarily.

"What in Ceto's name…" Andolas circles in place to get a better view. "Warriors! Retreat. And ready yourselves for battle! Immediately. Go! Go! Go!"

The warriors look at him questioningly, still battling the wraiths. The first warrior retreats with enough force to send him spiraling through the air toward the colony. Then another. And finally, all of them follow in unison, including Andolas.

"C'mon, Gally!" Veras shouts back to Gallagher as he spirals away from the swarm and toward the colony.

Gallagher watches with envy. They easily speed through the air—the only thing holding him back from becoming a warrior.

"Argh!" A severe pain shoots through his leg.

Gallagher unsheathes his sickle and carves the venomous creature in half that stung him. Another wraith bounces overhead, its tentacles too close for comfort. He cuts and dodges the ends as they drift away.

More wraiths surround him. He slashes, dismembering their tentacles as well. More wraiths, more slicing. He is surrounded on all sides. A tentacle grazes against his shoulder and pain explodes through his arm and into his chest. He hacks frantically. Wraith bits float all around him, as do hoods and tentacles. He bludgeons the hoods of those lower than him to push them away. It's hardly effective.

Another tentacle contacts him, and this one seems to grip his chest like an orca's tongue, slightly adhesive and scratchy. More tentacles slap against him.

The pain is unbearable. His entire body aches, but he's a warrior at heart. He will not fall to wraiths. His sickle splits the air with ease dicing through several wraiths at a time.

Dozens of lifeless bodies float around him, but the tentacles remain venomous, and more wraiths press in to fill their place. Dozens more are cut down, and dozens more sting him. His vision is blurry, his arms grow weak, and his articulated swings turn into hashing cleaves. His vision fades and his mental capacity no longer outperforms the pain.

𝒜 warmth touches Gallagher's flesh. He has felt this once before. It is pure energy. The same energy that brings the Blue Tears to bloom. Gallagher opens his eyes and immediately shuts them due to the overwhelming brightness from above. Just as he suspected, the sun shines brightly. He's above the ceiling of clouds. He's ventured into the Caelum Realm.

"Dubious and blasphemous, this is. We cannot eat you, and I do believe we're breaking the truce, somehow."

Gallagher squints to see who's speaking to him. He can only see the silhouette, but it is certainly an Indra with their short stature, elongated ears like the fins of a ray, and a plump midsection. He's shaped like a kelpmallow. Maybe they eat too many of them.

"Jelly spittle!" Gallagher blurts. The reality of being in the Caelum Realm lying before an Indra hits him like an unexpected geyser. He feels at his hip. No sickle. It's likely at the bottom of the kelp forest by now. He has no other weapon aside from his fists and mass. He pops to his fins without a scoop of grace. The air within this realm is scentless and…sterile. Thin too. His body doesn't move with finesse as it would in the Terra Realm. He hits the ground and falls over, his breathing short and strenuous.

"Lie back down, you pollywog. Your lungs don't work the same up here."

"Wh…" Gallagher tries to speak. "What did you ca…" He gasps for air. He can't get it out. This squatty little elf called *him* a pollywog. A pollywog!

He sits upright and presses against the furniture he was just lying on. He employs his breathing techniques, the same techniques he'd have to use in the deep. It takes a long time, the Indra staring down on him all the while, but he finds his breath. "Kelpmallow," he mutters.

"Excuse me?" the Indra replies. His hands are crossed in front of a belly protruding from an open jacket, and his head tilts at the comment. He wears attire unlike anything Gallagher has ever seen from the De'wi. It's a heavy fabric, likely durable, and restricting, too. Pale grey with several layers and folds, and metallic fasteners.

Gallagher glares at him. Should he overexert himself by trying to get out of here, he'll certainly overwork his lungs. So, he stays put. This Indra, whoever he is, doesn't seem threatening, anyhow.

"Why do you swim so close to the border? This is the second time I've witnessed your face above the clouds. You were pulled aboard down by the Godmadina's piers. Are you trying to find your way into our realm?"

"No." Gallagher's response is sharp. "I was—" He erupts into a coughing fit.

"Here, try this?" The Indra adjusts a single lens in his left eye, then holds out a strange mechanism.

Gallagher has to shade the sun from his eyes, and he continuously blinks and squints as his eyes adjust to the intensity of the rays above the clouds.

He holds a tube the length of the Indra's forearm—which isn't long—with an oddly shaped opening on either side. "It's a breathing apparatus," he continues. "They're not used often by the Indra anymore, but I always have some lying around. I have my reasons. I can get you a pair of shades, too."

Gallagher jerks back and dismisses him with a wave of his hand and chooses wheezing instead. It looks like machina, and he's not about to betray his clan by falling to the first of the Indra's persuasive tactics to get him to do so.

He explores the area with his eyes as he takes in his predicament. He's outside, but he's not. Dark metallic walls surround him. A door too, but no ceiling. It's open air above him with the sun shining brightly, blue skies, and several trees as he remembers seeing upon his first visit. He closes his eyes as the intense light strains them.

"Those are trees?" He gestures to the large plants. Speaking a few words leaves him short of breath. He focuses on his breathing technique. Mira would do anything to explore this place. He needs to learn what he can, so he can at least describe it to her when he returns. *If* he returns. No. He *will* return. He's a warrior at heart, and no Indra will prevent him from getting back to her.

"Trees," the Indra responds. "Trees with bees and leaves galore. The scent from the white blossoms is one to admire. Smell it." He sticks his nose to the air. "You don't see too many of them beneath the clouds, do you?"

Gallagher sucks in the aroma, careful not to overdo it and mess with his controlled breathing technique. He hadn't noticed it, but the Indra is right. The sweetness is more intoxicating than anything he has smelled beneath the clouds. "Only from a distance," he replies cordially, and sucks in a gasp of air. "They grow mostly…" He gasps. "…in the Morshine Peaks…" More air. "…beyond our borders. The Elders have stories, but I've never see—" A cough chokes his words.

"Magnolias to be specific. The large leaves and voluminous flowers require too much moisture, however. They do much better in the Morshine Peaks," he nods to Gallagher, "where the land is fertile. Takes machina to keep them flourishing within the city." He points to large cylindrical structures towering above the walls and all the trees in the distance. "Our irrigation system. Hydrates the plants and all other life above the clouds. Occasionally we get the stratus clouds passing overhead, but they don't offer much for precipitation. Oh, but the noctilucent clouds are quite marvelous. Do you have those within the Terra Realm?"

"Nocti…"

"I suppose you don't. It requires a bit of a sunset to witness. Beautiful things they are. They glow brightest when the stars decide to wake up."

"Stars! I've heard of those." Even Gallagher, who's not as much of a dreamer or wanderer as Mira, has many thoughts of what it would be like to see the stars. All De'wi do.

"Heard of them?" the Indra questions. "Heard of them?" His voice grows higher. "Oh, dear Ceto, you must stay. You must witness the stars. Please do. It would be a blessing in itself just to see your expression while seeing them for the first time. Any elf can lose themselves in the depth and grandeur, and it puts all our tiny squabbles in perspective."

"Ceto?" He sucks in another gasp of air. "You know Ceto?" Gallagher had thought this was the De'wi's deity. But perhaps all the races worship Ceto.

The Indra scrunches his already scrunched face. "No. He's a god, for goodness' sake. Whoever claims they know a god is a lying skimplefruit. He, however, is more of a wishful hope amongst the Indra. Machina have taken over our belief system."

Machina! He glances down at his damaged fin, undesirable thoughts creeping in about how machina could help his situation. "I'm Gallagher," he introduces himself with an outstretched hand.

The Indra straightens his posture and shakes Gallagher's hand. "And I'm Brunswick. A pleasure to meet such a fine De'wi."

"Likewise." Gallagher politely gives him a half smile in return, but he remains skeptical of this strange place.

4 ELDER FAE

The Sky Plaza is in abundance today. Elves of lesser houses scurry about, making decisions toward a promising future that will never fulfill. Elves of greater houses observe and plot, always three steps ahead in maintaining their power. And the elves of the working class... The backbone of any society who thrive on giving back to the community, never taking more than they need, cherishing the moments they live in, and thus obtaining no true ambition. Their bliss in the present is both their freedom and their manacles.

Lady Fae cruises past her inferiors on her ferry, following the lane of wheeled traffic, surrounded by her armed guard. It's delightful to have all the citizens hustle out of her way, but she doesn't ask for it. It is a mere benefit of her elevated status as the Elder of the Caelum Realm. And it allows for a much more efficient day in their overpopulated sky-metropolis.

They come to a halt on the edge of the plaza at the Aricafé, one of many throughout the city. An Arilight investment to give back to the citizens and maintain her civility with the elves she rules over. All meals and beverages are free for the working class.

She parks her ferry in the stalls designated for the greater houses, which are never taken, and her guard crowd in around her. They disperse amongst the patrons as she steps off her ferry and ventures over to her son, Jarnes Arilight.

"Look at all the beauties livening the café today..." She stares down on him in his seated position, legs crossed, where his face is buried in a book.

He glances up at her from beneath his blond brows, then quickly resumes his consumption of whatever piece of literature he's discovered today. She wouldn't be surprised if it were his fifth or sixth time diving into this particular book, as he has likely read every book the Caelum Realm has to offer.

Lady Fae waits for a chair to be pulled out by one of her guards. She smooths the folds of her white gown as she sits. The chair is pushed in for her, and the guard doing so blends in with the surrounding crowd when done attending to her. Her son, sitting across from her at a petite metal table, doesn't pull his eyes from his book.

"How was the delegation?" she asks.

"Hardly productive," he admits.

"The limelighters and the provocateurs are a part of the political game. They waste all of society's time, but you must navigate around them and take care of your business, nonetheless."

"It has yet to be determined which crop the Tear shortage is coming from. We may have to send scouting ships with observers across the globe to discover where the issue lies."

Lady Fae grunts. "Hardly. Look only where the Ebisu colonize in proximity to our crops. You'll find your shortage. No doubt, they have destroyed one of our combines and laid claim to the crop themselves. Those greedy, salt-sucking elves scarcely have any civility in them at all."

Jarnes finally marks his page, closes his book, and lays it on the table. He straightens his white collar and smooths out his grey vest before leaning in to properly take part in the conversation with his mother. "I will make your suggestion to the other great houses next time we collaborate."

"Your suggestion, not mine." She stares at him as a mother does when laying out a lesson before her child.

"Yes. Of course, mother." He reaches for his book and thumbs the pages, already bored with his mother and her politicking. "Is the shortage of Tears as bad as some claim? House Godmadina would love to blame this on us and are making quite the stir over it."

"It would take much more than the loss of a crop of Tears to defile our state." She shakes her head at the absurd notion. "The Tears are in abundance. Ceto has seen to it that Solaria will never fall short. If you ever get the chance to see the ocean at night with your own eyes…" Her gaze grows distant. "Not the sea of clouds, but the *real* ocean. It's as mesmerizing as your stars." She glances up at the blue sky, then back to her son. That comment perked him up. "However, that does not mean one does not have to suffer beneath the next. Power is but a game, Jarnes. It ebbs and flows. Like energy, societal power is neither created nor destroyed, but merely shifts from one to another. And that's what this is all about." Her face is stern with determination.

A youngkin sitting at another table over Jarnes' right shoulder, props herself on the back of her chair, facing Lady Fae, and offers a subtle wave. Lady Fae returns the greeting with a large and beautiful smile. Dutiful, but genuine, too. The youngkin continues to stare at her, but Lady Fae returns her attention back to her son.

"We'll never find a suitable match for you, will we?"

"Mother!"

"It's true. You're in your prime—young, handsome, well-educated—yet your elderly mother is the one who receives the ogles and gestures from the masses. I—"

"It's because they fear you, mother."

She glares at him. "I'm not to be feared. Look at this café, for instance. I give back to the citizens and I join them in their daily activities. I acquaint with all. Sure, I make tough decisions as the matriarch, but I am fair."

Her son rolls his eyes. "You are fare, and you are iron-fisted, I would agree." He smirks. "So why can you not place one of these suitable matches across from me in place of yourself."

She gasps, placing a hand on her chest as she recoils. "Jarnes…" Her shock shifts to disapproval rather quickly. "You're tainted. That's why. Had you not soiled your reputation by laying with that De'wi, the fate of our house wouldn't be in question."

Jarnes looks down at his closed book, thumbing the pages, and shaking his head. He could care less if the power they discuss shifts to another house.

"Maybe that half breed she whelped is the answer to our house woes."

"Perhaps."

Her son looks pensive. Lady Fae has never asked him how he feels about being a father to a child he will never see. They put the incident behind them rather quickly. Thankfully, only a handful of the great houses can hang that over their head. He may have to settle for a mate from a lesser house, but that wouldn't be much better. The outlook of House Arilight, the ruling house for millennia, does not look bright.

"Where is Yester?" he asks. "I was hoping she would accompany you, today." A spark ignites in his eyes. A spark that she needs to snuff out.

"Yester is an Arilight handmaiden. She is beneath you."

"Yes. That would be delightful, wouldn't it. But is any elf truly beneath me, mother?" He stops thumbing the pages of his book and opens it up, returning to a world where his mother cannot antagonize him.

"No thanks to the lustful taint that blemishes you to this day. How did I raise such an insolent son?" She shakes her head at him.

The youngkin from the table behind Jarnes pops from her seat and scurries over to Lady Fae with a shyness in her step.

"Hello, there," she says to the youngkin whose hands are behind her back. She wears a weathered, dark grey dress with pockets sewed onto the front. "And what can we do for you?"

"Thank you, Elder Fae, for all that you do." Her voice is tiny, delightful, and practiced. The youngkin stares for a moment, clearly with more to say that she cannot quite figure out how to get out. "I… I…"

'Yes, sweet youngkin, what is it?"

"I made this for you." She pulls her hands from behind her back. In one hand is a chocolate truffle. In the other, a delicately crafted flower. She offers the paper flower to Lady Fae. "It's a rose. I made it from a paper napkin."

"How wonderful, dear. This is remarkable. You've just made a bright spot on my bland morning." She glances up at Jarnes who's face is back to being buried in his book. "How lovely. Thank you." She accepts the paper rose.

"You're welcome." The youngkin turns to hurry back, but stumbles over her own feet and falls into Lady Fae's lap.

Lady Fae nearly leaps from her seat to avoid the child but catches her instead. "Are you alright?" she asks.

"Err… sorry." The youngkin isn't looking at Lady Fae, so much as her white dress.

Lady Fae follows her gaze to see the chocolate truffle flattened and oozing down her white gown. "Ugh…" She shoves the youngkin from her lap. "Get back to your parents. Inconceivable gracelessness…"

"I didn't realize chocolate could be so bitter…" Jarnes doesn't even bother taking his eyes from the page. His mother sneers at him.

5 ESTRANGED EBISU

"What do you suppose they're discussing?" Veras leans into Mira and nudges her shoulder inadvertently, almost falling on her.

"If you'd keep your tongue in your mouth, I might be able to hear," she speaks through her teeth as the points of her ears twitch. She shoves him away. "Quiet."

Veras, with his slim stature, returns to his respectable warrior's stance, like all the other warriors in line with them—shoulders square, hands laced behind their back, fins shoulder-width apart. "Where's Gally?" he adds.

The tension in Mira's body softens. Suddenly, she's willing to talk. "He should be here." She hesitantly leans forward to look beyond the line of warriors. The rest of the clan is in attendance, distracted from the festivities they would otherwise be fully immersed in. All the music, the singing, the merriment. It all washed away the moment the Ebisu plowed through the kelp forest and into their sanctuary. "What could he be doing that is more important than an invasion from the estranged Ebisu?"

"Estranged?" His left eyebrow pops into his forehead. "Is that what you call them? Estranged? It's been thousands of years, well before any of our lifetimes…" He shakes it off. "Gallagher has been swimming close to the ceiling quite often lately." Veras talks with his hands, signaling a flat ceiling then a spear throw. "Hunting most likely, but his proximity to the ceiling has been noticeable. Hopefully he didn't get tangled in the Eye of Solari. It's more violent than usual" Veras points, followed by a whirl of his fingertip. The clouds are looking rather grim beyond the knuckles, with darker greys and swirls of purples and the occasional flash followed by a thunderclap.

"You're right," she agrees. "But not within the knuckles. Those bulwarks have protected us from everything under the clouds including the raging clouds themselves. Except the drifting wraiths, of course. Vile creatures." Her mind wanders to the wraith swarm they were fending off, wondering what ever became of them. "He *has* been swimming close to the ceiling," she adds, "but the idea of him getting swept away seems absurd."

Veras shrugs. "Waterspouts are common, Mira. And dangerous."

"Not within the knuckles, they're not." Haltuk butts into the conversation from the line of warriors behind them. "Does your mind always take you to the worst possible outcomes, Veras?"

He and Tanniv could be brothers with how similar their appearance is. Haltuk is a smidgeon taller with longer ears, and he's longer in the face, but alike in all other aspects. Both are finely tuned warriors in both physique and skill.

"But with that fin of his…" Haltuk points down to his own fins. "If the winds are too strong…" he trails off, looking above the bulwark in the distance.

Mira dismisses the idea with a wave of her hand.

"He's more likely to get abducted by the Indra swimming that close to the ceiling." Tanniv joins the conversation that she tried to avoid to begin with. "If the Ebisu have found us after all these years, you never know."

Her gaze shifts to the top of the knuckles where Veras was pointing. The disquieting storm looming in the distance is thick and daunting with clouds that wouldn't blink an eye before devouring a youngkin. It sneaks closer. Waterspouts will strike before the day's end.

Waterspouts are the least of Mira's worries, though. She fixes her gaze intently at the rallyhouse where the Elders and the ambassador of the Ebisu converse on the large wooden deck wrapping around the building. She can only speculate the nature of the conversation. They didn't arrive with peace offerings, dowries, or anything that would suggest a means to mend the past. Why now? After such a long drought without as much as a sighting of the dark elves, Mira is eager to know.

They were commanded to form ranks and wait while the Elders determined the nature of this surprise engagement. The silence that followed was felt by all who were in attendance. By now, the entire Morshine Clan has gathered by the ocean shore where the Ebisu dismounted their seadragons—all except Gallagher, as far as she can tell.

Several warriors gawk at the creatures with murmurs of envy. Mira would much rather see them freed and dispersed back into the ocean where they belong. The Morshine Clan utilizes carabao for hauling heavy loads, but not against their will. They're rewarded with kelpmallows, a tasty treat for the beasts that they wouldn't otherwise be able to obtain, as they grow high atop the bull kelp. They're free to graze wherever they like, often speckling the seagrass meadows just north of their colony, and they continue to return at their own will. Easy treats as a reward for a small effort.

These Ebisu, though… It's apparent they don't treat life with the same level of preciousness. The domesticated seadragons look withered where they're tethered to the stilts holding up the rallyhouse. The foliage-like fins protruding from their spines are droopy and their heads hang in the sand. Their short legs look as though they can hardly hold the weight of their mass. It leaves Mira in a state of unrest.

Two Ebisu enter the rallyhouse with the Elders while the rest stand guard outside the building. They don't have an ounce of warmth to them. "Why are the Ebisu standing guard where the finest elves of the Warrior's Guild should be?" Mira mutters. "This is wrong."

She knows why. Because the Warrior's Guild doesn't prepare for uninvited guests other than wraiths. The Ebisu stormed in so quickly and knew exactly where to go because the rallyhouse is the clear centerpiece of their colony. The point-elves failed them, and the warriors were unprepared.

"How long is this going to take?" another warrior whines. He receives glares from his peers.

"He's right," Andolas agrees, standing in line a few elves down from Mira. "Why would we stand idle while these Ebisu tread on our territory with hostility? We should cut them down where they stand."

Mira steps out of line to address the warriors. It isn't her place to do so, but if their chief encourages upheaval, she must say something. "We cannot advocate violence while the Elders are in parley with the Ebisu. We don't know why they're here yet. Maybe they're just full of jelly spittle by nature with good intentions."

"Good intentions?" Andolas raises his voice. "Get back in line. Your pretentious attitude is getting old. Just because your father is Elder Rayfin, doesn't place your opinions on top."

"And an uprising against the Elders' command will remove yours completely." Mira glares at him for a moment before stepping back in line. It should be enough to let the rest know his opinion is flawed. They cannot go against the Elders. What kind of warriors would they be if such a decision was made?

Andolas leans his head out of the line and looks at her. "Maybe you should tell your father the truth of how you earned that stone. Your lies go against not only our Elders' word, but our entire culture."

Her head snaps in his direction. "You know nothing about the truth of that day." Her words could shear through a leviathan's belly.

How could he know what happened? Mira was alone when the incident erupted. She and the leviathan. The others had gone ahead as they were supposed to. He doesn't know the truth of it. He only speculates. *Right?*

"We all know the truth of that day, Mira," Andolas replies. "All of us who were part of the harvest. There's no denying you weren't where you should've been."

"I was chased." That's all they need to know. "It was my first encounter. I did what I knew best—swam fast."

"Then maybe you should've been a harvester," he criticizes.

"Harvester or warrior, I'd fight an elf to have her on *my* team," Tanniv comments when he shouldn't.

"Tanniv Windstalker!" She violently whispers with a nudge of her elbow.

Andolas pokes his head out of the line to glare at Tanniv. A silence follows. Only the sound of waves crashing into the shore can be heard as the looming storm swells the waters.

Andolas is right. A harvester would have been a better fit, but even then, she would have found ways to get lost while scouting for the Blue Tears. She firms her warrior's stance—shoulders square, hands laced behind her back, fins shoulder-width apart—and remains quiet.

It isn't long before the Ebisu exit the rallyhouse. Not a blade is raised, or trident in their case. The dark elves look disappointed as they walk down the steps from the spacious deck at the entrance. With their pure black hair, dark eyes and brows, and charcoal-colored attire, they're more ominous than the impending storm. The elf in the lead is stout with stark streaks of white in his hair. An Elder, perhaps? Or a chief? All are a head taller than any elf of the Morshine Clan. The armor they don, obviously enhanced by the essence of Blue Tears, doesn't make them any less threatening. They appear ready to slaughter an entire clan of youngkins. Thankfully, they flee toward their mounts.

"It's done," she whispers. "They're leaving." She removes herself from the line, disrespecting Andolas, but he deserves it. He's nothing more than an over-inflated noggin with pointy ears.

"Mira!" Veras speaks in a heavy whisper. He remains in line.

She hurries toward the rallyhouse. Not knowing what is happening is worse than the consequences she'll face for breaking command.

She searches the horizon for Gally while she swims. *Where is he?*

The rallyhouse is a simple structure. All their dwellings are mounted on stilts for when the storms brew harder and raise the tides. It's made entirely of driftwood and dried kelp fabric with a wraparound deck. Bull kelp is a staple used for many purposes from clothing to building materials. Mira isn't sure where the driftwood originates as they don't have forests within their borders, but it lines their shores, and they take advantage of it.

The typical guards they'd have at the entrance of the rallyhouse are all in line with their ranks, making it easy to slip in. She pushes the doors open quietly and sneaks into the back of the room, hoping to go unnoticed long enough to eavesdrop on their council.

All three Elders debate on one side of the grand circular table in the middle of the room. Her father, Elder Rayfin sits between the other two, a masculine complement to the femininity that both Elder Zyla Falklan and Seya Melonia wield ruthlessly. His dark hair with streaks of wisdom is pulled back into a tail displaying his hard facial features that have survived nearly half a millennium of turmoil. His dark blue eyes match the depths of the ocean and demand respect.

Mother Seya carries an invincible beauty donning an elegant green cotton gown with brown leather trimmings. Golden tresses frame her high cheek bones and drape below her shoulders. And Elder Falklan, a bit nastier in her counsel, carries a similar beauty, but with brows naturally bent inward, a permanent frown, and judging brown eyes. Her russet-brown hair is a stunning complement to her cream-colored dress with bronze seams.

"Ahem…"

Well, that didn't last long. Assassin is out of the question should she be looking for another role soon.

"My apologies," Mira says. "The severity of the situation overpowered my ability to make good decisions. Now… May I ask, what is happening?"

"Garrik, I see patience is highly valued beneath your roof." Mother Seya, the matriarch of the clan, quips. She's beyond four century marks. She's seen many Solaris and her wisdom is rarely questioned. Although Mira's father technically holds rank above her, her voice carries much weight.

"Indeed, it is, Mother Seya." Her father's soft eyes harden as he looks at Mira.

"Oh, stop it, Garrik. Mother Seya?", she questions his tone. "No need for formalities. Your daughter is well aware who's in charge around here."

"Somehow I don't get the impression it's me." He shifts in his seat with a flat expression.

"Your daughter is," Mother Seya adds with her chin pointing in Mira's direction. "Look at her. Refusing to wait to find out the future of her clan. Challenging the Elders' customs when pinned against the unknown. She makes a fine warrior and will make an even finer Elder when the time is due." She smiles at Mira. "Glad to have you here, dear."

"Please…" Mira presses her palms together and raises them to her mouth, eager to know. "…what is happening?"

"We've requested time to weigh this heavy decision."

"Which is?"

"We're debating whether a peaceful takeover is a wise choice," Mother Seya answers.

"Of course it isn't." Mira's words snap at the matriarch. "I'm sorry. I'm sorry. A takeover? A takeover of what? Our clan? Our youngkins? Our culture? Our Tears? Our freedom? Will it involve bonds like their seadragons? Why is this happening?"

"You see, Garrik. She refuses to lie down. She asks questions needing answers. Do you have answers?"

'Err… Seya… Mira is a fine warrior, and an honorable daughter, but this is hardly the time to be doing this." Many lines form in his brow.

"Peaceful takeover?" Mira throws her hands in the air. "We are warriors."

"Mira, you are not an Elder, regardless of the levity Seya gives you." He sends a pointed look her way. "You are not part of this conversation."

"They are brutes dependent on machina. It's fastened to each of their chests. Didn't you see it? This isn't a culture we would bow to. Ask any of the warriors lining the shore." A swift hand waves in the direction of the beach.

"Mira!" Her father's voice is sharp, his patience receding.

"Why do they attack the colony?" Mira's eyes narrow as she refuses to back down. "There must be more to this if you're considering submission. Why… after so many centuries of peace?" She folds her arms across her body. "And with the borders you insist on having, it forms the accusation that you were anticipating this. What did you do that would have them hunting us for centuries? I know you have the answers, father."

"I did nothing!" he shouts. "I only protect tradition, and *our* ancestry. Get out!" her father yells at her.

Mother Seya remains stoic, unphased by her insolence. Elder Falklan, on the other hand, holds a murderous glare. She would banish elves for less if she were the head Elder.

A loud crack is heard and the floor beneath them rumbles. The table in the center of the room jolts, as do their seats. Mira balances her stance.

"Elder Rayfin?" Elder Falklan leans on his expertise for answers. Her gaze invokes more threats than inquiries.

"The storm?" he replies. "I don't know." His eyes bulge and his fins spread wide to hold his balance as another shift is felt in the floor.

Shouts are heard from outside the rallyhouse. Then another quake rumbles. Sounds of metal clashing against metal, and more shouts.

"The seadragons!" Mira cries. "They were tethered to this building. They're trying to tear down the building!"

"Get out! Get out!" Garrik ushers the others.

The floor beneath them drops out. Quick to react, Mira leaps, but the ceiling proves to be an obstacle. The building collapses with no chance of escape.

Moments later, Mira lies within a mess of driftwood, kelp, and limbs. She cautiously rolls her neck, then flexes her arms. Nothing feels broken or damaged beyond the healing capacity of a ration of spice. She pushes against the driftwood lying across her abdomen, but the weight is too much. She's trapped.

"Help!" she cries.

She can only imagine the damage dealt to the Elders. And what of the Ebisu? It sounded like a battle was taking place. Would they attack the warriors and the rest of the clan with such small numbers? There was only a score of them, and their seadragons hardly make a difference in close combat. They wouldn't stand a chance.

An obvious and intentional attack with all the Elders in one place. How stupid of them. How naïve.

A dark gloom is visible overhead where a piece of rubble is tossed from the pile. Her clanmates already work to free them. A sigh of relief escapes her.

The winds press through the crevices of the wood and kelp, sending a shiver up her spine. The storm isn't just near, it's on top of them. It howls with such vigor it sounds like a monstrous beast raging throughout their bay.

A large piece of driftwood disappears from the top of the pile, creating much more visibility. Nobody is there to have removed it, though. Then a large beam shifts, tumbling down the wreckage. The winds grow stronger, reaching through the debris and punching at her flesh. A terrible feeling swells in her gut.

The wind is here to fight. It throws driftwood at her, pinching limbs and body within the rubble. Sharp pains are felt everywhere, as if a thousand lacerations open up at once. As if her body is being torn apart. Through squinted eyes, she sees a mass with limbs flying overhead.

A body? Only the winds of a waterspout could muster such forces.

Mira claws at the rubble, but her movement is limited, and her strength isn't enough. Screams in the distance cut through the howling winds. She desperately wants to be there to help, but she's stuck. Helpless.

Driftwood flies away in large quantities. She's suddenly free of the wreckage. The storm around her rages, ready to devour everything in its path. Large pillars of clouds, mud, and debris spin out of control, plucking driftwood from the structures, ripping bull kelp from their grove, and stealing elves from their homes. Coral shards fly by, and Mira thinly escapes the fatal blow as the waterspouts make it hard to control her movement.

The seadragons the Ebisu escape upon are slow to swim up and over the rocky knuckles, pushing off ridges with their large, hoof-like fins here and there. It gives them quick boosts in elevation, but not so quick that Mira cannot catch them. If only she could escape the winds of the waterspout.

Mira thrusts toward the retreating Ebisu, and she understands, now, why the seadragons are so slow to escape. Mira makes little progress, not taking her eyes off the rocky knuckles where the dark elves climb higher and higher, seemingly out of reach. They aren't alone, she realizes. Several of her clanmates are draped over the seadragons, across their laps. The dark elves are taking prisoners. An act of aggression. An act of war.

Mira's strength stumbles when another bright red coral shard zips past her. She twirls to evade it, and the chaos of the waterspout consumes her. She spins in circles, a spec of insignificance within its turmoil. Her fins are no match for the winds. It tosses her about freely. She climbs closer and closer to the ceiling of clouds without intention. The pressure is immense. Her limbs feel as though they're being torn from her body. And then…

The air is thin, absent of wind. The world around her shines brightly. Too bright to keep her eyes open. Squinting, she sees the ceiling of clouds beneath her and feels the energy of the sun on her skin. Her breathing cuts short as she gasps for air. Her body becomes heavy. Heavier than she's ever experienced, and that terrifying feeling explodes from her gut into every limb as she finds herself falling.

6 MACHINA AND SPICE

"*Y*ou're saying I *have to* wear this—" Gallagher's words are cutoff by wheezing and shortness of breath. "…wear this…" He hunches over the side of the reclining chair Brunswick has him resting in. "Blasted machina!" He shoves the device in his mouth, and it does nothing. He gasps for air, never able to get enough.

Gallagher closes his eyes to focus on his breathing techniques. It must be intentional, and even then his lungs burn as if the air is laced with sand. Breathing has always been a given, like seeing and feeling, but within the Caelum Realm, he's finding out he must work for it. It's constant, like feeding a stomach of everlasting hunger. He cannot stop feeding his lungs with air, or they cry out in pain.

Brunswick hurries to his side, and situates the machina device properly into his mouth, pulling the other end over his ear with slight tension in the line connecting both ends. A clicking noise is heard, followed by a pinch.

Gallagher winces and easily shoves Brunswick away with one arm. The sky elf stumbles and falls backward onto his rump.

Gallagher takes in a deep breath, all gasping and pain instantly gone, as if a smooth liquid has rinsed away the poisonous grit terrorizing his lungs.

"This *blasted* machina will keep you alive, Gallagher," he says with a delighted voice from a seated position on the terrace pavers. "It'll only be for a short while until you acclimate. Like the shades you wear. You must put your feelings aside, I would suggest."

Gallagher glares at him from beneath the tinted lenses Brunswick has him wearing. They don't have the same machina vibe the breathing apparatus does, so Gallagher was more apt to put them on. The sun's glare is brutal above the clouds.

Brunswick struggles to rise, and Gallagher does nothing to help him. He *is* Indra, after all. Why would he help him? Though, it leaves him feeling guilty to watch his struggles as if it's entertainment.

Once Brunswick finds his legs, he slides a chair a short distance across the terrace. The metallic legs create an uneasy sound scratching over the surface of the stone pavers. He plops into it like a bag of sand filling a void. Parts of his body squish through the openings in the chair where they're snug to fit. A deep sigh escapes him. "There we have it." A smile finds his face. "This is nice, isn't it?"

"It's a bit cold," Gallagher replies honestly.

"Ah, well you should wear more clothing, perhaps. You De'wi don't keep a robust wardrobe, do you?"

"It's not cold in the Terra Realm. Clothing is an afterthought. We wear enough to keep each other from blushing."

"You're breathing, though! How does it feel?"

"I remain a skeptic, but I'm grateful to not feel like I'm breathing grit into my lungs." Gallagher offers him a subtle nod of gratitude. He tugs on the apparatus stretching from the corner of his mouth to his ear. It's locked in tight, but not in an uncomfortable way. He hardly notices it. "Is it...permanent?"

Brunswick smiles. "No, no, no. Wearable machina attaches to your flesh, yes, but a release mechanism is always present. Nothing is permanent."

"No. Nothing is, is it?"

Brunswick eyes him with uncertainty.

"You're right, Brunswick." Gallagher reclines into his chair. It's covered in soft cushions, and he finds himself wanting to stay put for a while longer. He continues to recover from the wraith venom, his body achy and fatigued, but that is not why he intends to stay put. It's the same feeling he gets when he soaks in a hot spring back home. His body is in a state of bliss that he wishes would last forever. He quickly sits upright, not wanting to be deceived by Indran culture.

"Jelly spittle and canker sores..." Brunswick's hands fly into the air. "...that isn't right! I'm never right. Or so all the naysayers say. What are you saying?"

He's an odd fellow. Gallagher suspects amongst his own race as well. They haven't left the estate, so he hasn't seen another Indra besides Brunswick, who he is rapidly finding ways to relate to his own race. The elf is as intriguing as they come, and thus far, he hasn't discovered anything menacing or threatening about him as the Elders would have Gallagher believe. Quite the opposite, rather, he's extremely trepid. Full of worry.

"The noctilucent clouds. They're brilliant." Gallagher presses his back into the chair again, with his legs elevated as he watches the sun go down for the first time ever.

"Remove the shades. The sun won't hurt your eyes any longer."

Gallagher is hesitant, but he submits to his request, placing the shades on his lap. The oranges and blues and everything in between suddenly become more vibrant. The image burns into his mind. How he wishes Mira were sitting in the chair next to him.

No mountains, kelp forests, or anything to obstruct the horizon. They sit at the edge of Brunswick's terrace floating above a plain of supple clouds as far as he can see. The noctilucent clouds high above glow brighter as the twilight takes over the sky.

Gallagher holds onto the armrests of his seat, clenching tight, unsure what to expect next. The motion of the sun—which he is eager to stare directly at, but his eyes refuse it—is slower than a sunstar creeping along the seabed. "A star!" Gallagher shouts with a finger pointed to the sky.

"Haha!" Brunswick bursts with a jovial laughter. The sky elf laughs and bobbles until he's red in the face. "*You* are brilliant, young warrior. It is like watching an infant experience the world for the first time, except better. You have *words* to express yourself accompanied by the uncontrollable delight on your face. *You* are brilliant!"

Gallagher shrugs his shoulders without taking his eyes off the sky. Just as Brunswick said, he is lost in the depths and wonder it provides, all uncertainty vanquished by beauty and delight. How it can change color; how it can reveal hidden gems sparkling in the night; how it can entrance the observer, a little speck beneath its grandeur. "The *sky* is brilliant. I cannot wait to share this with Mira…"

"Oh no, oh no, oh no, no, no." His voice is low. "You cannot share this with anyone. I suspect Mira is a young maiden from the Terra Realm?" Lines crease into his forehead. "She *cannot* come here. *You* are not supposed to be here. Your retrieval was a mere accident. I was fishing, young friend. And not for De'wi *or* wraiths, I might add. The winged guppies…" He closes his eyes and presses his short fingers to his mouth. "…they're a savory delight with the right seasoning." His eyes snap back open, fierce, and back on point. "There's a truce. Our worlds are separated for a reason."

"A lousy catch."

"Maybe at first." Brunswick locks his eyes on Gallagher. "But I'd say it's shaping into something bountiful. Wouldn't you?"

Gallagher finally takes his eyes off the sky. *Bountiful?* He has so many questions. Thus far there have been so many novelties presented to him that the questions have been rapid-fire and limited to the surface. He knows nothing of their culture, why they stay above the clouds, what their history is regarding the De'wi and the Indra's hesitancies to cross paths. Can he even trust this Indra? Are these novelties a distraction to persuade or dissuade him from something he hasn't a clue about? And their fins…

"Why are your fins missing their webs?" The question erupts from Gallagher. "Are you blighted like me? They *look* like my fins, but you have no webs. And your toes are shorter, but I suppose that aligns with your nature. But why no webs? How do you swim?"

Gallagher looks back and forth between the two pairs. Brunswick has finally removed the foot coverings he wore, and both are elevated atop the ottomans at the end of their chairs. He referred to them as *shoes* previously.

Brunswick smiles. "We have so much to learn about each other, don't we. These…" He wiggles his toes, then adjusts the odd single lens covering his left eye. "…are feet. We don't have fins. I suspect before our people separated ages and ages ago, they may have been more alike. Whether we both had fins…" He gestures to Gallagher's. "…or we both had feet…" he gestures to his. "I don't know. But by the Indra, I do know we were once alike. A single race of elves is what we're led to believe."

"Feet?"

"Yes. We don't swim, Gallagher. Look where we live. The air is thin. The same reason you wear the machina respirator is the same reason we do not float in the air at this altitude. We have no need for fins. We walk. And occasionally… and let me emphasize *occasionally*…run." With a smile, he grabs two handfuls of his belly, squishing it between his fingers and jiggling it.

"Oh…" Gallagher contemplates that for a moment. It is exactly as his Elders preach—the Indra have allowed their machina to reduce them into helpless elves. They don't move much, and they have grown lazy and weak. This certainly would be a detriment to the De'wi culture. If they didn't train, they would never overcome the leviathans. And if they didn't overcome the sea demons, their most prized resource that prolongs their lives and fends off most ailments would not be accessible. If they learned from the consequences the Indra present to them, could they not overcome the ineptitudes displayed by this sky elf? He's not very malicious as the Elder's would have him believe. He's just lazy.

"I always suspected the Indra to be an angry and vile race," Gallagher admits. "But I don't sense that from you. Why do we stay away from each other? What do your Elders teach you?"

Brunswick's brow furrows and his eyes grow sad. He pops the lens from his eye and fumbles it between his fingers. "I suspect fear, young warrior. I suspect it is due to a history not wanting to be repeated. As you probably know, there was a great clash of arms many, many generations ago, long before our time. Differences between wanting to live a higher life…" He raises a palm over his head, facing down like a ceiling. "…and wanting to stick to tradition, fearful of undesirable change." He swings a pointed thumb in Gallagher's direction. "There's a balance needed. Some wanted to grow and change faster than others. That is where it began. Since then, I think we have both held onto the tradition that the other is wrong and hateful. A vengeance indoctrinated between our races that has nothing to do with anyone alive now."

Gallagher sits in silence, taking his eyes to the sky again. The noctilucent clouds are shining brighter than before. The sun is hidden beneath the horizon, but its energy can still be seen climbing above it, reluctant to separate from the sky.

Could he be right? The only stories that pass through the De'wi are those of villainous Indra and their malicious machina. That they'd enslave the De'wi if they didn't stand and fight. It's why the De'wi pride warriors and focus on strength and cunning. They must always be ready to defend their culture. It's why they have outposts to watch the skies and waters, because the vile beings living within the other realms are violent and threatening. But Brunswick isn't to be feared. He's a plump elf with oddities and passions just like any De'wi. Not like the dark elves he encountered before waking up in the Caelum Realm.

"The dark elves!" Gallagher blurts. "I've forgotten. All your wonder has distracted me, and I've forgotten. I need to get back to the Terra Realm. They're under attack!" He snaps to his fins without any grace and walks closer to the edge.

"Attack? By whom?"

"Ebisu! I need to go."

Brunswick's face contorts and his excess weight jiggles. "An attack…" He puts a hand to his cascading chin, which is almost not a chin at all, but layers of loose flub that fold into his neck. "So, it's true. The observers have recorded battles amidst some of the other isles recently. I thought maybe it was a flaw in their observations, but an eyewitness is empirical evidence. The Ebisu have reengaged the Machina Wars." A frown presses into the flub beneath his mouth.

"Another race with tainted ancient relations. They have no reason to show aggression. They've been living peacefully for generations."

"How do you know all this?" Gallagher asks, his suspicions of the elf resurface after an evening of pleasantries.

"We live in the sky, Gallagher. With machina. We have the means to look beyond the floor of clouds to see what happens beneath us." He points to a metallic table with a reflective surface at the edge of the terrace. "Mine is limited compared to the observers. Only sees a short distance beneath the clouds with an obscured visual. No different than trying to see through the densest fog imaginable. But it allows me to see where the fish are." A smile curls into his cheeks before quickly fading. "Entire teams of Indra monitor the Terra Realm every day. I suppose the same reason the De'wi have outposts, we have our observers—to watch for signs of the peace dissolving. Albeit this Morshine region offers much interference. I suspect it is due to the large quantities of magnetic ores in these mountains."

Everything Brunswick says raises a plethora of questions, but Gallagher is out of time. "I must go. Can I jump?" He looks over the edge.

"It's too late, Gallagher. If your clan was under attack when I retrieved you from that wraith swarm, whatever battle occurred has already claimed its casualties. That was days ago."

"Days?"

"Yes. The wraiths took a toll on your flesh. I pumped you full of Tears, and you slept for days before waking."

Gallagher looks at his hands. *Blue Tears?* He hadn't noticed. Then his gaze darts to his fin. It remains disfigured.

Brunswick eyes him precariously, noticing the brief hope turned to dismay. "It doesn't heal old scars, unfortunately. It will help the recovery process, but not if you've already recovered."

Gallagher tries to pull the machina respirator from his face. It doesn't break free.

"There's a release mechanism, remember."

Gallagher dismisses Brunswick's advice and tugs at the machina. Pain strikes at his ear and lip where it's fastened to his flesh. Anger and distrust quickly wash over him as he continues to fumble with it.

"Please, allow me to help?" Brunswick insists as he puts a hand on Gallagher's jawline.

Gallagher knocks his arm away and is about to tear it from his face regardless of the damage it will cause, but he feels a pressure release. The machina slides from his face with ease.

"Did you…"

"Like I said, there's a release. It's near the ear. Just a button. Machina is not evil unless an evil elf uses it for evil deeds."

He steadies his breathing to take in the thin air. He cannot stay to debate the maliciousness of machina. "I must go."

"You're right. Should the Elder or any of the vermin within the Greater Houses discover your presence here, who knows what would become of you. There is so much more we need to discover about each other, though. Please, keep the machina. I do expect you to return. We will bring our people together. What do you say?"

"Bring the Indra and the De'wi together? Not just a truce but an alliance? To help defend against the Ebisu?" he asks.

"More than that. To shed the stigmas between our races and make us more clairvoyant of each other. Perhaps the Ebisu need the same offering." Wrinkles form upon his already folded face.

"An alliance between the De'wi and the Indra…" Gallagher hesitates. It would be a blessing for all the realms to not live at odds with one another. His clan will degrade him, make him lesser than a blight if he suggested such an idea, but he has nothing to lose. Short term, it could help with their current predicament with the Ebisu. "Perhaps just a seed." He holds up the machina respirator as a salute to their new friendship. "I will plant the seed, but I'm not much of a gardener. I'm a warrior."

"Understood. And friend…" Brunswick arduously climbs to his feet from his reclined state. He walks closer to Gallagher and peers over the edge. "Our cities tend to drift. A controlled drift if there's such a thing. The Greybeards are always searching the floor beneath us. Always observing. Don't expect to return where I extracted you."

"Thank you." Gallagher nods.

"One more thing." Brunswick's short finger points into the air. "Our machina are intended to help where we fall short. It supports our lives. A little too much as we've become dependent on it." He pinches the flub of his belly again. "Don't let it make you lazy like us."

Gallagher holds up the machina respirator, confused how it would make him lazy.

"Not that. Stay put. I made something for you while you were recovering." With that, Brunswick disappears into his abode. His home is formed with clean, straight lines of metallic columns and beams and leafy foliage climbing all over it. Light washes over the building from machina devices. It's so different from the world he's accustomed to.

Gallagher turns back to the starry night, patiently waiting at the edge of the terrace. The noctilucent clouds have faded along with the sun's energy, but the stars are evermore present. Where Gallagher was reluctant at first, he now finds himself grateful for the connection he has made here. An ally in the clouds could be just what they need to defend themselves against the Ebisu. But what has Brunswick gone to fetch? Nerves boil to the surface of his flesh. The respirator in his hand is hardly machina worth fretting over, but it could be anything. And he may have to leave his new friend in a state of disappointment.

A short while later, Brunswick returns. In his hands is something shaped like a fin. "I noticed your damaged fin when you arrived. I thought this might aid you. Nothing much, but maybe it'll be of some assistance." He hands the device to Gallagher who's cautious while accepting it.

Gallagher holds it up, inspecting the blasphemous machina as if touching it will soil his wellbeing. It's a hollow fin made of the Indra's metallic machina. He's speechless. He's confused.

"It's intended to fit over the one that's gone missing." He points to the fin that earned Gallagher his blighted status. "I hope it helps."

Gallagher is at odds with how he should react. He cannot accept this. It is Indran *machina*. A poison to society. His clan will berate him for it. Yet, if it helps him swim, it will change his entire world for the better. A blessing? His lack of words manifests into Brunswick taking the device back.

"I know it's a lot." He taps on Gallagher's knee, gesturing for him to raise it. Gallagher does so out of confusion. "It should be a good fit." Brunswick quickly slides the machina fin over top of Gallagher's and a click and pinch follows. It bites into his flesh with a subtle pain.

Gallagher leaps back. "What have you done?" His voice rises. "I cannot wear this! My clan… The Elders… I cannot wear this!" His voice turns into a shout. With his backward lurch he stepped too close to the edge. His heels hang over the lip of the terrace and he slips.

"Oh no…" Brunswick steps back, unable to do anything. The look on his face is distraught and full of guilt.

Gallagher kicks the fin about as his gut lurches into his throat. He can hardly tell he's wearing it at all, but it could be the novelty of plummeting into the clouds overcoming his emotional and physical state.

As he falls, he calls to the sky elf. "How do I get it off?"

Brunswick calls back, but Gallagher can hardly hear him with the wind whooshing past his ears in his rapid descent.

"Goodbye, friend," Gallagher mutters to himself. He knows Brunswick had good intentions, but this machina must be disposed of before he returns home.

7 SEVERAL WILD DAYS

Darkness curtails Mira's vision. Night has taken the land and turned her world into a labyrinth within the unknown. Her body is pocked full of scratches and bruises from her fall into a densely packed forest. Had the storm not left her perception unsettled and twisted when it tossed her free, she would have been able to swim to safety, but that wasn't her fortune. She plummeted toward the mountainous terrain like a dishwasher tossing out their wastewater.

She hunkers into the canopy of the trees for the night, hoping the predators aren't nocturnal out here in the wild. As much as she enjoys exploring, she's not so fond of having to spend the night unprepared.

Tomorrow is the Solari Harvest. Their stock of Tears will run dry unless the Elders deem it top priority over recovering from the waterspout. And with the threat of the Ebisu at their doorstep, they may not have the strength necessary to defend themselves if they run out of the spice. Their world is centered around it. It offers strength. It enhances their senses. It provides rapid healing and nourishment, prolonging life. Even if the Ebisu abandon interest in their decimated home, without the spice, their colony will decline. The Blue Tears are the heart of their culture.

Thanks to the guild's vigilance and store of Tears, this evening isn't as dark as it could be. Her eyesight pierces the shadows. Prior to the storm, the entire Warrior's Guild and the Elders were all instructed to prepare themselves for the worst, which meant consuming Blue Tears to enhance their readiness. Civilians had to make do with what they had stocked, and it often isn't sufficient. If she were an Elder, rations would have been given to every clan member. Every one of them could be roaming the wilds like she is.

The downside of the Tears enhancing her senses is that she's also more susceptible to the cold temperatures at this higher altitude. The invisible hairs on her flesh stand tall as she hugs herself to fend off the chill. A sleeveless, leather warrior's corset and high cut sarong overtop leather tassets and greaves isn't the best attire for the cold weather.

She's experienced worse, though, and she sees less risk here. It's time to stop acting like a guppy.

Mira puffs out her chest and exhales, grabs a thin strip of kelp from the leather pouch at her hip to tie her hair back, then beats her fins to break through the top of the forest canopy, unknowing whether she heads in the right direction.

An hour into her dark journey and recognizable landmarks remain absent. No Knuckles of Morshine—the most prominent landmark. No Crisper Coral. No kelp forest. No driftwood beaches. Not even a glimpse of the ocean yet, and they're surrounded by it. It's a large island—it would take weeks to travel as the ray swims—but she had always assumed the ocean was visible from any peak on the island. Discouragement settles in with familiarity gone to the wayside.

If she can find the shore, her way home will be thoughtless from there. Only two choices—follow the beach in one direction or the other. It's only been forest canopies and stone ridges with the occasional grove of kelp. She has no doubt she's within the heart of the Morshine Peaks, the centerpiece to the isle. So long as she swims downhill, she'll find what she's looking for.

When she returns, she'll advocate for exploration scouts to map the unchecked terrain. If they ventured outside of their borders once in a while, she wouldn't be lost.

She continues swimming, skimming the surface of the forest canopy until dawn breathes light into the sky.

Finally, she sees something of interest, an edge to the land. Not a shore like she's accustomed to, but a cliff. She doesn't recall any sheer cliffs near home that could harbor such a landscape element, so the exhilaration radiating from her is warranted only by her freedom to discover out here in the wild. She swims to the edge.

The vastness of the land before her steals her mind. Mountain ranges tower to her left and right, the Morshine Peaks suddenly visible now that the view has opened. It feels like the edge of the world. The mountains disappear into the ceiling of clouds so far away, but seemingly right within her grasp.

Kelp forests aplenty shade more than half the land below her. A different type of forest she's never seen before catches her eye. The brown roots of each tree grab onto the terrain like a giant digging its fingers into the sand. Could they be the mangroves her mother and father have mentioned so many times? She makes note of it for exploration on another day, after she persuades the Elders to develop a scouting team.

The ocean is distant. Dull light from the horizon shimmers across it, meshing with... *It couldn't be.* The cerulean iridescence of the Blue Tears covers the ocean and shines bright where the daylight hasn't quite touched its surface. Blue Tears in abundance wading through the swells of the ocean. Could this be an anomaly on the day of the harvest? Are the Elders aware? The sight unravels her knotted thoughts, allowing them to drift away in disbelief. Its beauty is remarkable.

Beyond the kelp forests and across the ocean, a faint orange glimmer shines with a dark, ominous sky above it. A haziness lingers around it, enhancing the orange glow. What could it be? The diluted sunlight emerges over the horizon to her left, which means she faces south, and the orange light gleams just to her right, which is in the direction of Rhizo Isle. She dismisses it, knowing nothing about the land, and elevates it to another wonder to explore in the future.

A squadron of manta rays cut through the air above a plethora of rivers meandering the hillside. Easily one thousand in total. Her gaze sits on them for some time. Something deep within her wants to make the leap to join them. She wants to abandon duty to explore all of it. The thought of Rivee is the first to deter her. She could never abandon her, nor Gallagher. Her clan is in need right now, but the desire pulls at her, regardless. If this is how far the wild stretches, imagine the other isles, the Ocean Realm, and the Caelum Realm. This is where she belongs, pioneering on the edge of discovery.

Though, she must turn back. She must find the shore, and her colony—whatever remains of it. She closes her eyes and turns her back to the unexplored land. Her colony isn't down there. What good would it do her to discover the truths behind the legends—sea nymphs, armored hydra, feathered falcons, and... grendelins!

A chill sweeps through her at the thought, followed by a warm energy she only feels once a year. Her eyes spring open to see the sunspot allowing a sliver of light to shine through.

Today is the Solari!

Mira inhales a deep breath and closes her eyes to take in its magnificence. She arcs her back and falls backward into a dive, allowing herself to plummet down the cliff's face. Her obligations pull at her as she allows her velocity to pick up, careening downward. Then she curls forward to swim back to the top of the cliff, resisting all temptation.

Following the edge of the ridge to the east, she swims for hours until it meets with the land below. Curiosity sidetracks her on only a handful of occasions and she finds herself smiling at a smidgeon of colorful skittles parading through a grove of kelp. Tiny, playful creatures. Mira could spend hours with them. Duty calls, however. With determination, she moves on, eager to be home.

By the time she plants her fins onto the sandy shore, the cloud cover shows signs of night. The marbling whites and greys shift to darker shades of purple and charcoal on the horizon. The Solari Harvest has come and gone, and she has missed it. Guilt, a burden heavier than the anchors pulling her into the wild, weighs her down. Regardless of whether it was within her ability to avoid it or not, she has let her clan down. She has let her mother and father down.

Feeling warm and salty from the nonstop travel, a dip into the waters before night falls sounds pleasant and might be what she needs to unload her thoughts.

Mira unfastens the leather tasset around her hips, followed by her leather greaves and bracers, and sets them on a large stone boulder protruding from the ocean swells. She unbinds her leather corset, then tugs at her sarong, folding it and placing it atop her armor.

Last, she removes the circlet from her head, tucking away the strands of hair it pulls loose, and places it on top of the pile. She stares at it for a moment and picks it back up, thumbing the stone in the center. She slides it back onto her forehead. Strength emanates from it, whether it's mental or physical, she isn't sure, but she feels more comfortable wearing the circlet out here in the vast wilderness. It has become a part of her. It has more meaning to her than what the other warriors see it as, which is strength. To her, it is a memento of the damage she's caused. She will never forget.

It's uncommon for her to disrobe before a swim, but spending the night in wet attire doesn't sound as pleasant as a refreshing dip.

She steps deeper into the waves wearing only her circlet and undergarments. The shimmer of Blue Tears she witnessed across the ocean surface has either faded with the Solari or it's undetectable at close range. Suddenly, a serenading song fills the air. A pod of whales sings an undulating tune offering both peace and a haunting aura to the twilight.

Her stomach rumbles, disrupting the serenity. She hasn't had anything to eat since... the waterspout? ...no, since before she began her training the morning prior. The Blue Tears in her system staves off the hunger for a long period of time, but she's overdue, and without a daily dose, her body will slow and her eyesight will return to normal, both of which have been assisting her travels. The longer she stays out here, the more danger she puts herself in.

She dives into the ocean waves and finds a rocky base in the shallows where she can scavenge for food. Tossing rocks about and pillaging through the weeds for several minutes, she collects several edible shellfish. Hunting leaves her at unease, but her opinion of fish and shellfish alike is similar to wraiths. They're mindless creatures, so prying into them for a snack doesn't impact her the same as when she's expected to hunt seal or porpoise. None of her clanmates have caught on to the fact that she has never made a kill.

Without a blade, primitive methods are needed to crack them open. Swimming deeper, she locates a collection of larger, jagged rocks that ought to work. She smacks the shells against the rocks one by one and drops the meat down the back of her throat, swallowing with a big gulp to avoid the slime from lingering on her tongue too long.

Mira leans against the rocks anchoring her fin into a small crevice surrounded by seagrass to prevent her buoyancy from carrying her back to the Terra Realm. She sinks backward and fatigue slams into her like a rockslide. Her fins are weak, as is her entire core. It's not something she experiences often. She's never swum such long distances, or for such a long period of time. With the Blue Tears wearing off it's having a stark effect.

She closes her eyes and leans her head back.

Something curls around her thigh and her eyes snap open.

Hesitant to agitate whatever it is, she cautiously peers through the darkness to get a glimpse, but the twilight has submitted to nighttime. It's too dark, and her vision isn't as good as it was just a day ago. Whatever it is, it's not small.

She pushes off and pain strikes as the jagged rocks tear at her fin, and whatever curled around her thigh, tightens its grip. She hammers it with a fist, over and over. Another one finds its way around her calf while the original retreats. Mira kicks, and a third one—maybe the original—curtails her retreat, binding both her legs. Terror strikes, but she's been in worse predicaments.

She feels for the circlet atop her head, and miraculously it's still there, along with her stone. If she can overcome a leviathan of the deep, she can save herself from whatever these small, sticky, creepy creatures are.

Mira grips an overhead ledge, readies her fins, putting a slight crouch into her stance, then pushes off. Her might breaks her free from the creature's grasp, and she doesn't look back to see what it was. The darkness wouldn't allow for it, anyhow.

With a gentle climb through the shallows, she bursts into the air like a playful porpoise, and her low mass lets her continue to swim through the dense air. She's free from the terrors of the dark water.

The sudden struggle takes a toll on her body. Fatigue sets in yet again, and she snags her attire from the rock it was sitting on before finding a dry spot of land to rest. She flops down on the sandy surface, both arms and legs limp and exhausted from the struggle. Her vision is better out of water, so she keeps her eyes open to watch for more predators.

She's heard the stories of octopus and their relentless tentacles, but never has she encountered one. Nor did she know they grew to such sizes. That must have been what she encountered.

Overdue for a substantial, genuine rest—not an unintended doze waking to an attack—she quickly gets dressed and finds a steady crevice within a rock ledge that looks worthy. She thoroughly checks the surroundings for predators and sees none. Protected on most sides except above and in front of her, she hunkers down and hesitantly closes her eyes.

An octopus! The moment was terrifying, but the memory has already become encouraging. Her mind wanders around the moment until her fatigue must be ignored, yet again.

The rock she chose as a haven shifts behind her.

Her eyes spring open, bulging with terror, and she pushes off, swimming away. Behind her is a giant stone mass covered in kelp and seagrass and bigger than any creature she's ever seen. Larger than the leviathans of the deep, and it resides here…in the Terra Realm. It has the general shape of an elf: two arms, two legs, and a head, but its mass is the size of a mountain with only minor exaggeration exuding from her terror. It's a legendary grendelin.

As she swims away to a safe distance, exhilaration finds its way back into her and she smiles. The crooning song of the whales fills the air once more. She looks out over the ocean to see the glow of the Blue Tears shining through the dark ocean currents. It hasn't faded as she suspected. She has only been away from the colony for a little over a day, and the adventure she's experienced is worth a thousand tales. Terrifying to be sure, but only because she's unprepared. With provisions and protection, and a healthy dose of Tears, it would be an adventure to boast about. This is where she belongs.

But first, she must find her way home.

8 HELLO KILLER FIN

With a new fin and the knowledge of his clan being under threat, Gallagher powers through the air with more velocity than he has ever experienced. He would be lying if he said fear of his clanmates' fate was the sole reason he swam so hard. He cares for them, but the truth is, he tests his abilities with his new machina fin and doing it with a smile so bright his clan might think a second Solari is on its way.

Gallagher curls over the Knuckles of Morshine and arrives to where his colony should be, and his smile vanishes. He treads high above, petrified by the sight.

Driftwood and rope lies scattered everywhere. The mill, where most of his days were spent hauling and unloading kelp, is gone. Carabao are nowhere in sight, though they could be grazing in a nearby meadow. The smithy, where Gallagher hoped to be honored with a steel yari someday, is gone. His house is leveled. The destruction is catastrophic.

Not a single building is left standing. A few clanmates pick through the rubble, and they look like forlorn vagrants while doing so, scavenging through garbage heaps, looking for anything of value. Anything recoverable to aid their new homeless lives. They don tattered clothes and are covered in the grime of the rubble they dig through. A deep anger replaces the lofty emotions driving his travels. Why would the Ebisu level their colony? And with as few mounted riders as they had, *how* could they level their colony? His rage forces a guttural torrent from within.

He joins his clanmates' scavenger hunt, heaving driftwood from the larger piles to look for bodies. He only finds rubble and remnants of their livelihood—stone and shale tools, woven kelp linens, food stores, and the like.

"Nice of you to join the fight, Gallywog."

Gallagher's jaw tightens. He pulls his head from a pile of rubble to see Andolas standing before him. "Andolas." It comes out low and stern. "What happened?"

"Where were you? Not that you could have helped the situation, but it's rather spineless for you to disappear like you did." He pauses for a reaction, but Gallagher gives him nothing. "You know what else doesn't have a spine? A wraith. Are you made of jelly spittle, Gallywog?"

To tell Andolas of his whereabouts would be accepting unknown dire consequences. The Indra are the enemy, and for him to have been acquainting with one, *in* the Caelum Realm, he wouldn't receive anything but animosity from his clanmates, or worse. Especially Andolas. "I was busy fending off the wraith swarm. Are there survivors beyond those who I see? Where are the others?" He thinks of Mira and Rivee.

Andolas' eyes are full of hate. He dismisses Gallagher's question, instead focusing on why he was absent. "A shame they didn't consume the Gallywog. We're stronger without you."

Gallagher shoves Andolas' nonsensical and hateful comments to the side, storing his anger for another day. "What happened here? The Ebisu could never have done this to our colony. Not with the limited number of mounts they had."

"And what do you know about the Ebisu?" he demands.

"Get off your high cloud, Andolas!" He gains height on Andolas. "The Warrior's Guild might be privileged to information the rest of us don't have, but…" He lowers himself, considering the notion of aquatic elves. "I suppose, none of us actually believed them to be a threat. Has anyone seen one until now? They're no different than the grendelins or the armored hydras. They're mere legend until you see one with your own eyes. Did the guild know?"

"What…is…that?" Andolas points to Gallagher's machina fin. His wide eyes narrow into a look of irate disgust.

Damn it! Gallagher knew the fin would be problematic, but he forgot he was wearing it with how natural it feels to him. The devastation that has become of his colony consumed him and he forgot to remove it. He bends over and pulls on the metallic devise, his face burning with heat from embarrassment. He cannot remove it.

"I was only…" It won't come off. He didn't anticipate having to convince fellow clanmates why he was wearing it, let alone Andolas of all elves. Gallagher rises back up, looking down at the metallic flipper. "It's not important right now." He sidesteps whatever lame justification he was going to come up with. "Where is everyone? Mira? Rivee? The Elders?"

Andolas must agree. His disgust dissolves and is replaced by unease. He draws a hand and turns to point behind himself. "They're scattered. A waterspout hit. Tore our world apart. Those of us who are able, are searching for survivors. We've gathered near the Crisper Coral." He rounds on Gallagher. "Current events may distract us from that atrocity you're wearing and where you've been to retrieve such taboo, but you'll get your due. Come. Elder Rayfin appoints duties, Warrior Guild or not. He's directing our priorities to overcome this mayhem." He glares at Gallagher before turning his back to swim away.

Gallagher follows loosely behind him. He knows the way to the Crisper, and he'd rather not have the brute try to start up conversation. Plus, he's hesitant to convene with the Elders. What will he say?

His thoughts shift back to the devastation around him. A waterspout! On the same day an estranged race shows up on their doorstep. Waterspouts aren't unheard of, but one large enough to level their entire colony is. And within the Knuckles of Morshine is even more alarming.

The Crisper Coral is unscathed. The coral is bright and full of life. The only difference is the fish have abandoned the immediate area, and makeshift structures assembled from remnants of driftwood line the coral beds. The waterspout must have tapered off soon after destroying their world.

Andolas leads him to a wooden structure that looks like it could collapse with a gentle gust. Their swimming slows as they come upon it.

Inside, around a distressed table, sit the three Elders: Elder Garrik Rayfin, the patriarch, seated in the center, Elder Seya Melonia, better known as Mother Seya, on his left, and Elder Zyla Falklan on his right. All don tattered robes and carry much weight in their gazes as they watch Gallagher enter the chamber.

"Ah, Gallagher," Elder Rayfin addresses him.

"Elder Rayfin." Gallagher offers him a curt bow in due respect. He's rigid with formalities around the elf. "How may I be of service?"

"There is no easy way to present this." His lips flatten as he looks down at his hands crossed before him on the table. He slowly blinks and when he opens his eyes, they're pointed at Gallagher. "Mira is among the missing."

"What!" He doesn't mean to show his desires so blatantly. Not in front of Elder Rayfin, or any of the others, for that matter.

"There are many others. Missing. Injured. The only reason they're hanging on is because of their dose of Tears. However…" He rubs at his jaw. "We've missed the Solari Harvest for the first time in the history of the harvest. We have not prepared for this. We prepare ourselves for the grueling nature of the annual harvest, but we've failed to prepare ourselves for missing a single harvest. The stores of Tears we've recovered from the aftermath of the waterspout will not last. It has been decided to ration it to the injured warriors and harvesters who have earned it per our tradition. It will not last."

"And my parents?" Gallagher, sadly enough, hasn't given them much thought. The guilt settles into his gut. With the wraith swarm, the introduction to the Caelum Realm, and now this, his parents haven't been top-of-mind. Selfish or not, he feels the guilt now.

Elder Rayfin shakes his head in silence. Gallagher glances at the other two Elders. Both remain silent and unknowing.

"Deceased?" Gallagher struggles to say the word.

"No." Elder Rayfin responds. "They have been found but are in critical condition. They're in Bailey's care. There may still be hope for them."

"Without Tears?" Gallagher glares. The resentment rears its ugly face unintentionally. His family has only been given Blue Tears on the most bountiful years. They reserve the miracle spice for the warriors, the healers, the Elders, all those who have earned their share. Kelp pickers, farmers, carpenters, smiths…they will be left to fend for themselves.

A forlorn silence overtakes the room. Gallagher does not know how to respond to the situation. Their entire world has been shuffled and not everyone will survive the forced changes.

"And Mira…could she be alive?" It's a dumb question. She has a larger ration of Blue Tears and she's a fine warrior. The odds are better for her.

"We surely hope so."

"Where have you looked, and where can I go?"

"We have scouts from the Warrior's Guild who are more qualified for this. And harvesters who are faster. You'd do better to stick to your normal duties. We'll need kelp, and lots of it. Food. Shelter. Bandages. Do you have your sickle?"

"I…" He hesitates as his arm opens over his hip. He doesn't want to pick kelp. He wants to search for Mira. "I might know where it is, but—"

"No, Gallagher." Elder Rayfin silences him. "I know you care for my daughter. More so than I approve. It's why I told you of her disappearance. But you're not a warrior, Gallagher, and you never will be. My daughter *is*. Thus, you have no business courting her."

Gallagher tries to speak, but the Elder silences him.

"Do you know why Lady Rayfin so often sits in council with the Elders, Gallagher? Though, not an Elder, she is bound to us as if she were one. Marriage is a bond for life, a unity between two mates that endures all things. It would be irresponsible of you to have her endure a blight." His words thump Gallagher in the gut, causing more pain than when he lost half his fin. "The Warrior's Guild will handle the search. You mustn't force this, Gallagher. You have your duty, now go."

"I..." Gallagher cannot disrespect him. Even if he doesn't approve of the Elder's decision, he is the patriarch *and* Mira's father. Gallagher loses no matter what he chooses. "Yes, Elder." His head slumps between his shoulders.

"Elder Rayfin?" Andolas speaks up.

"Yes."

"There's something you should know."

"And that is..."

"Gallywo... err... Gallagher taints our culture with machina, Elder." He glares at Gallagher, folding his arms across his body in a moment of proud triumph.

In his mind, Gallagher burns across the room and puts a fist between his eyes.

"Is this true, Gallagher? Where?" Elder Rayfin replies.

"This is a punishable offense," Mother Seya speaks. "If this is true, we must evaluate the consequences."

"He should be banished," Elder Falklan asserts. "Machina are forbidden within our borders."

Elder Rayfin raises a hand to silence them. "Where is it?" He looks Gallagher up and down, but he obviously cannot see Gallagher's fins from the table he's sitting at.

Andolas points down. Gallagher refuses to lift his fins and finds himself holding back a smile. Not because of his firm resistance to Andolas' conceit, but because he can now use fin in plural form. He has two complete fins thanks to the machina. Unfortunately, he must remove it as soon as he finds out how to.

Elder Rayfin rises to his feet, as do the other two Elders. "For Ceto's sake, Gallagher! You've really done it. Where did you get that?"

"I..." He stutters a lot around Elder Rayfin. Perhaps the elf's authority makes him nervous, or that he's the most respected warrior in the clan. Or it could be that he's the father of the elf he desires. Too many reasons exist, and he must not disrespect him. But he must not tell him he was in the Caelum Realm either. "I found the machina here in the Crisper Coral. Just…" He pauses to recall how long it's been. "…two days ago, I believe."

"Not the first that's fallen from above. A sloppy race of elves, they are." He looks up at the ceiling as though he can see the Indra. Then his black and white peppered brow puckers as his gaze settles on Gallagher. "The first to fall that is readily usable. Remove it." Elder Rayfin moves closer to Gallagher. "We must destroy it before any others get word of this. We'll have the smiths melt it down and forge steel tools from it like all the other machina we find. We cannot have this blasphemy here within our colony."

What colony, Gallagher wants to say. Their colony is no more. But he remains dutiful and keeps quiet despite the comments tearing down all the euphoria the machina brings him. Gallagher gestures to the seat Elder Rayfin just rose from, requesting to sit down.

"Of course." Elder Rayfin ushers Gallagher in a hurried manner.

Gallagher places his calf overtop his knee and yanks. "It's a bit tight." He cannot get the machina fin to budge. "I… I'm trying." He pulls harder without any movement in the fin whatsoever. It feels as though the entire thing wants to rip off at the ankle.

"See, Gallywog, not much of a warrior, are you?" Andolas receives several contemptuous glares from the Elders. He shies away back into his corner.

"There's a release mechanism. There's always a release mechanism," he repeats Brunswick's words and receives funny looks. "I… I don't know where it is, though."

"Let me try." Elder Rayfin carefully puts a hand on the fin, inspecting it and rolling his fingers across the metal. He inserts his fingertips where the machina stops and the flesh starts. He pulls. Gallagher's winces, but he doesn't spit out the tiniest of cries. "It pulls at your flesh. They've made advancements." He speaks quietly to himself. "It's not like it used to be. It refuses to release itself as though it has a mind of its own. Evil Indran machina." He shakes his head.

"We have only one option." Mother Seya rises.

"I'd suggest an amputation," Andolas interjects. All eyes in the room cut off his tongue. He has an inclination for immaturity when around Gallagher.

Mother Seya continues, not taking her glare away from Andolas. "He must be banished." Her gaze quickly cuts to Gallagher.

"I would agree." Elder Falklan scowls at the machina fin as if it will burn the very air it touches. "We cannot have it within our colony. If Gallagher cannot remove it, we must remove Gallagher. There is no other way."

Gallagher's head darts back and forth as each of the Elders speak. Andolas offers his opinion as well, but Gallagher doesn't hear him. He remains quiet, lost in disbelief as to what they're considering. Banishment?

Elder Rayfin raises both hands and waves them about slowly to calm the room. "A decision of this magnitude will not be determined with such haste. He is not banished." His head snaps to Gallagher, his face full of disgust. "Yet!"

The word bites at Gallagher.

"But we must remove you in the interim. I hereby exile you from the Morshine Clan until further notice. You must refrain from entering our boundaries, or suffer the consequences. You must not interact with any of the clanmates, or suffer the consequences. Should the point-elves find you disobeying these orders—and they have hundreds of years proving they see everything—you will suffer the consequences. I hate to do this to you, Gallagher, but with yet another lousy choice…" He points to the machina fin, referring to how he damaged the fin in the first place. "…you limit our options. Andolas will escort you outside the boundaries where you will remain until further notice. You are on your own, Gallagher." He shakes his head at the young elf.

Andolas smirks in the corner.

"But…" Gallagher is stumped. What is happening? He never caused anyone harm. He only ever wanted to be a prestigious warrior, and in turn, take Mira's hand. "…there's a release mechanism!" He scrambles to discover it. His hands grope the metallic fin, pressing and prying along its many contours and ridges.

A calming hand lays on top of his frantic one. "We have always protected our clan above all else." It is Mother Seya with a soothing tongue. "We will figure this out, Gallagher. Your timing comes during an upheaval we've never experienced. I trust this will be temporary, but Garrik is correct in his decision. You must flee the clan immediately before any other elf lays eyes on this fallacy."

Gallagher refuses to understand. "How will you find me? When this… *interim* ends, how will you let me know the final decision?" There will be no finding him once he leaves. He's sure of it. They may not be feeding him lies, but they have no intention of making this right. They will be focused on rebuilding and forget about him. This *temporary* exile will mold into permanent execution. Gallagher is banished from the Morshine Clan indefinitely.

"We have trained warriors for that." Elder Rayfin shakes his head at Gallagher. Sorrow overcomes him.

"No you don't!" Gallagher shouts. His words force everyone in the room to flinch.

"I understand your anger, Gallagher. I'm sorry this is the way, but it must be the way." The other Elders nod in agreement. "We cannot have that blasphemous machina within our grasp." He says the word machina with utter disgust, spitting the word out as if it were a bitter taste on his tongue.

Gallagher's jaw tightens as he balls his fists. "Why?" He doesn't mean disrespect, but this is his livelihood they're taking away. "I know nothing outside of this colony. Nothing because you don't allow anyone to venture outside the knuckles. And now you'll be so bold as to toss somebody out just because of a lousy piece of finware? Why is machina so blasphemous when it aids me in becoming the elf I aspire to be? It harms no one."

"It will harm your mental capacity!" Elder Rayfin grinds his teeth. "Machina is a blight on any culture. It may start out as a simple aid, but too soon it will promote excuses, and excuses cultivate ineptitude. I will not have it!" His voice elevates enough to rattle the makeshift walls surrounding them.

"This is our culture you question, Gallagher." Mother Seya interjects as Elder Rayfin finds his calm. Her airy voice subdues the rising fury within the room. "These machina threaten our way of life. And now *you* threaten our way of life. The machina are atrocities beyond comparison. They are not natural. Ceto condemns these creations. Why do you think the Indra have fled to the Caelum Realm? To further themselves from Ceto." She points toward the ocean where Ceto dictates the waters. "Without Ceto, and without the Ocean Realm, our lives are nothing. We all exist because of him. Because of the waters flowing through this world. And the machina are a means to separate ourselves from him. That is why you are no longer welcome here. Figure out how to remove it, and we will discuss alternate consequences. But until then..." She looks to Elder Falklan, then to Elder Rayfin. "...we expect to never see you again."

The words slam into Gallagher the same as the waterspout annihilated their colony. He suspected Elder Rayfin would recognize his value as a kelp picker, especially in this time of need. And the side of him who is the father to Mira... What will *she* think of this—wherever she is? All three Elders are in agreement. Winning this argument is not a reality. Not when their decision is built on a thousand years of tradition. Not for an elf who was already considered a blight on the colony. Now he's a blight on the culture, too. A blight on the blighted. His slumps where he stands, a melted version of himself.

Indefinite banishment could be forever. Do the Elders truly expect Gallagher to flee this land, never to come back? Is he no longer welcome in the Morshine Clan? That's what they're saying, but he's struggling to come to terms with it. His entire world is slipping away from him. He will never see Mira again. Or Rivee? And what of his parents? What will they think? He didn't mean to have it this way.

Dejection quickly morphs into anger. Gallagher bottles it and puts a cap on it. Lashing out, disrespecting the Elders will get him nowhere. It will only make matters worse.

"Come, Gallywog. Maybe your death will be quick outside the protection of the Warriors Guild. You can finally be rid of your blighted nature."

Andolas' arrogance is too much for Gallagher. With a machina powered kick, he bursts headfirst toward the weak display of an elf. Fists outstretched, he catches Andolas off guard, and blasts him in the gut, keeling him over into a heap of limbs and fins.

"I'll escort myself, thank you." Gallagher, careless with his final actions in front of the Elders—the elves he's spent his entire life trying to impress— exits the rallyhouse in an uncontrolled rage. Nothing representative of how a warrior should behave.

His burst of anger melts away and is replaced by anguish. His head slumps between his shoulders as he swims above the Crisper Coral, lost for the first time in his life. What is his purpose if it is not to become a warrior? What is his desire if Mira is no longer within arm's reach?

And what of his family? His parents? Rivee? He hovers over the refuge searching for those he cares for. He saw the infirmary tent on his way in. His parents could be there. Maybe Rivee, too.

The camp is mostly empty, likely because everyone is either in the infirmary or out searching for more charges to fill the beds. He pokes his head into the tent and is quickly shooed.

"Go, go!" Bailey, the caretaker, insists. "If you're not injured or dying, you don't belong here. Search the area. Find those in need."

"Rivee Rayfin?" he asks as an overwhelming aroma of incense wafts from the infirmary. Medicinal therapy, she always claims, but the smell is powerful.

"Not in here. Thank goodness. That little sprite has been swimming amuck looking for you and Mira. Go find her. Maybe she'll finally get some rest."

"My parents?" he urges before he's shoved back through the entrance.

Bailey's face sinks. "They're stable." Her voice is weak, lacking confidence.

"Can I see them?"

The caretaker stares at him. Her silence crushes him. "Come." She grabs his hand and ushers him to the back of the tent.

Bailey has a few helpers bandaging wounds, stirring up salves, and mincing and rationing Tears into adequate piles. They're the same youngkins who are always apprenticing under Bailey's expertise, expect Gallagher typically only sees one at a time. Today, four aids scurry about, making the space cramped with the surplus of charges, too.

His parents lie in separate cots side by side. Their bodies are covered in linens, and their eyes are closed. Gallagher sees his mother's fingers poking out the side of the blanket. With a gentle hand, he curls his fingers around them and clenches delicately. Her hand is warm. "Will they survive?"

"I can only offer hope, Gallagher." Bailey's voice is soft.

"Then please give them all the hope you have." He turns to his father and places a hand on his chest. It heaves up and down, too slow. "You're a Lightcloud, father. You're full of excellence. See this through." His eyes squeeze tight, and he clenches his hand into a ball, still resting it on his father's chest. "Goodbye, father. Goodbye, mother." He turns back to Bailey and stares for a long moment.

"Goodbye?" Bailey moves closer to him with a look of disdain. "What are you implying? That your caretaker doesn't have the means to remedy this situation." She huffs and crosses her arms tight across her chest.

"Err…no. It's not that. I just…" Without bringing attention to his fin and his exile, he doesn't know how to reply.

Her eyes soften. "I will do what I can, Gallagher. I promise."

"Thank you, Bailey." Gallagher wastes no more time. If he hurries, it might save a life. With so many elves out in the wild, defenseless, starving, and potentially injured, every moment is urgent. He cranes his neck toward the caretaker. "Bailey…" She looks up at him, already having moved on to take care of her patients. "In case I don't see you again…goodbye to you, too." He doesn't wait for a response. He kicks his fins, shooting into the sky for a better view.

"Gally!" the caretaker calls after him from the tent opening. "What is that on your fin?"

He waves her off and continues skyward.

"It better not be what I think it is!" she shouts after him.

The guilt tears at him, but the velocity he's able to achieve overcomes it. After wearing it for just short of a day, he doesn't understand what is so horrific about machina. It is only making him more capable, just as Brunswick said it would.

The elf he swims toward next isn't likely going to leave him feeling good about himself, but he must speak to her.

"Lady Rayfin…" Gallagher shows his respect with a heavy bow just as he plants his fins to the ground.

"Gallagher."

She remains stoic to his approach. Gallagher has never felt warm around her. Not necessarily uncomfortable, but not jovial either. Her auburn hair is pulled back into a distraught bun, and her forehead matches with lines pressing every which way. Even under duress, she maintains her beauty, just like her daughter. Lady Nessa has lost her prize. She's lost her daughter, and it shows in her amber eyes.

"I'm sorry to hear about Mira." Gallagher offers her a comforting hand. She takes it with both hers and allows him to pull her in for an embrace.

"Thank you, Gallagher. I'm confident she'll return. She's a fine warrior. She can take care of herself. It's only a matter of time." She withdraws from his grasp.

"So, you have no clues to her whereabouts?"

"Of course not. Otherwise, I'd be out there searching right now." Her brow turns inward. "She could be anywhere, Gallagher. The Caelum Realm. Or leagues from here with how turbulent that waterspout was. We've never experienced one so destructive. Or…" Her eyes glaze over as tears pool in the corners. "…she could be in the Ocean Realm with the leviathans. Pray Ceto has mercy on her."

"As you said, she's a fine warrior. We'll find her, Lady Rayfin." He tries to grab her hand again, but she pulls back, looking down.

"What is that?"

"It's… it's…"

"It's machina," she answers for him. "Why do you have that? Why are you wearing that?" Her eyes amputate his leg, then go for his throat. She looks ready to murder. "Do the Elders know of this?"

"I… It's…" Gallagher cannot get any words out.

"It's preposterous! Take it off and destroy it. Before anyone else witnesses it." She reaches down to grab at it.

Gallagher pulls his fin back. "It doesn't come off, Lady Rayfin. I've already tried. Or…I don't know how to remove it, rather."

Her eyes light up as she looks at him from one knee. "Why would you do this?"

"I was…" He was curious. But that would never be a good enough answer in any of the De'wi's minds. He was excited to become whole, but, again, any of his clanmates would shun him and call him weak for submitting to his vices. Except…it's not a vice. It's a means to fit in. It's a way to remove his blight. She'll never understand. None of them will. They've never been deemed unfit. They've never been cast out and told they're not good enough. Gallagher wants to tell her all this, but he bites his lip instead, trying not to let his anger get the best of him like he displayed for her husband. "It was a mistake," he falsely admits.

"This is absurd. Leave. Leave now. I cannot be seen around you. Not with that thing on your fin. My husband will find out about this, you know. And your consequences—"

"He already knows," Gallagher cuts her off. He couldn't bear whatever she was going to say next. She was going to drop him even lower than he already is, as if being blighted isn't low enough. "I've been exiled. I was just saying my goodbyes. Have you seen Rivee?" His voice is low and withered.

Lady Nessa glares at him, but after staring for a moment in silence, her aggression softens. "I'm sorry. I haven't seen her. She is around here some-where, however. Probably doing something she's not supposed to like searching for Mira. Out near one of the outposts, perhaps." She turns her head and waves him away. Not another word.

"Goodbye, Lady Rayfin." He looks upon her for a moment longer, but she won't return the cordiality.

Gallagher swims back to the sky to search the area for Rivee. If he doesn't say goodbye, she may never forgive him. Although, if he *does* say goodbye, she might try to follow him.

Too soon, he sees a group of warriors swimming in his direction. He might be able to outswim them now, but what good would that do. He knows he's no longer welcome here anymore. The Elders, Andolas, Bailey, Lady Nessa, they're all offended by the machina. It's either pursue another life with machina or be a part of the colony, and he already made that choice inadvertently when Brunswick put the fin on him.

"Escort yourself, huh?" Andolas leads the group of warriors. Gallagher wonders why the Elders, Elder Rayfin specifically, ever put this elf in charge. He's a lousy leader. Displays of envy, of hate, pursuing vengeance on Mira due to a manifested story of why Alariya died. Gallagher may have been deemed blighted by the Elders, but so too should Andolas.

"Just saying my goodbyes." Gallagher replies, defeated.

"And your time is up." Andolas grabs his wrist. Gallagher doesn't resist. "Blighted and exiled at such a young age. How old are you again, sixty… sixty-five? You had an entire life ahead of you, Gallywog. It's a shame to see you go. It was a pleasure taunting you."

Tanniv and Veras are with him. No doubt Andolas chose these two warriors specifically to escort him, for they're the two Gallagher gets along with better than any other. Tanniv refuses to make eye contact, obviously ashamed by his current duty. Veras' mouth distorts as he shrugs his shoulders.

"Killer fin." Veras admires it. Gallagher manages a half smile.

"Yes, killer it is," Andolas interjects. "It's a monstrosity, and it's why he must be released into the wild. We cannot have monsters living amongst us. Let's go, Gallywog. It's time."

Andolas leads the way. Tanniv and Veras flank Gallagher on his backside, and all four of them swim beyond the borders of the Crisper Coral and up the western bulwark of the knuckles. They swim much farther than Gallagher would have thought. Well beyond the outposts atop the knuckles. The point-elf stationing it, no doubt watches them from afar with a lens. He didn't know the warriors came out here. The colony's border ends at the far edge of the knuckles, but they escort him into the vast open terrain until the knuckles become a hazy mirage in the distance. The ocean is no longer visible. No kelp forests within sight. Only a few coral bushes here and there and dry, cracked terrain. It's a wasteland.

"This is good." Andolas turns to leave. "Never show your face within the Knuckles of Morshine again. The Elders have deemed you a threat to the colony with permission to engage with lethal force should you return."

"Lethal force?" Gallagher calls him out on his lie.

"Yes," Andolas asserts.

Tanniv and Veras look at each other. Confusion and shock on their faces. They don't say anything, but they do offer Gallagher an apologetic look before all three of them swim away.

Gallagher watches them until they are no longer in sight. He's alone. His desire to become a warrior is gone, but he can still find Mira, and he won't stop searching until he finds her. Maybe if he escorts her back home, there will be second thoughts about his exile. The waterspout couldn't have dumped her too far. He spins in place, scouring the vast terrain he must search. She could be anywhere, in any direction.

"Nice machina!" a little voice is heard.

"Rivee Rayfin!" Gallagher spins to face her. "What are you doing here?"

She shrugs her shoulders with a smile.

Gallagher bursts through the air to embrace her. "Thank Ceto, you're alive."

"No, no, no." She pushes away from him. "Thank me. I take care of myself."

Gallagher smiles. "Thank *Rivee*, you're alive!" he mocks, and embraces her once more.

Rivee pulls away to inspect his fin. She reaches with a cautious hand, hesitant to touch it, but getting close enough for a thorough examination.

"Argh!" Gallagher shouts when her face is close enough to kiss his fins. She peels back, scrambles, and falls on her rear. Gallagher erupts with laughter. A good smile to hold onto, for it may be his last, but it fades rapidly as the reality of his exile slams into him once again.

"You scared me. That wasn't nice," she insists as she climbs back to her one fin and pushes off the dry terrain into the air. Since her incident, she has always been more comfortable treading than standing. Understandable for an elf with only one leg.

"No, but the look on your face is one I can hold onto for eternity. And well worth it because I may never see you again." He smiles at her. "You must go back, Rivee."

She folds her arms and grimaces at him. "C'mon." She turns to swim away and waves an arm for him to follow.

"Wait!" Gallagher reaches a hand into the air, but she's not looking. "That's not the way back to the colony. Where are you going?"

She gives him a sidelong glance over her shoulder. "We have a maiden in distress to rescue."

Gallagher stands still, puzzled. "Rescue?"

"Mira, you fool! Mira!" She waves another arm for him to follow. "Bring your stupid machina and c'mon!"

9 HEART, MIND, OR SOUL

Comforting marbled, grey clouds return to the skies. Mira has not been without Blue Tears for many years, and she has forgotten what it is like to travel in the dark without it. After having experienced some of the dangers, she's thankful for the light.

A tall, rocky berm follows the shoreline, and it couples with the western knuckle in the distance. The Crisper Coral, in all its magnificence of bright hues, is just on the other side. And her colony just beyond that.

Her excitement turns grim the more she thinks about it. The storm's rage wisped her away from what was becoming a place of turmoil and struggle, only to toss her into the beautiful and natural wonders of Solaria. She won't be heading back to a place of warmth and comfort. Not compared to where she's been for the past two days. She's more likely to find death and destruction. She picks up her pace.

The point-elves within the outposts spot her before she can even make out the shapes of the buildings atop the knuckles. Their conches sound off, almost in unison. Three quick bursts to notify the clan it's not an enemy. A job well done. If only the point-elves stationed in the eastern outposts could have reacted so quickly when the Ebisu invaded. But she cannot fault them entirely. Her squad was deceived by the wraiths the same as the point-elves were.

Curling over the top of the knuckles, the oranges, blues, and purples of the Crisper Coral bring a touch of comfort. That is, until she gets about halfway across the bed of life and sees driftwood shacks lining the opposite end. A cascading frown forms. What was once an escape into wonder, an area predicated on being a refuge for life, has become a refuge for her colony.

In the shallows, off to her right, several rinsing rituals are taking place all at once. Only during the worst of the Solari Harvests has she seen more than one warrior experiencing a rinsing. They float on their backs with two or three aids surrounding them, and the aura of the Blue Tears radiates around their bodies. It is only performed for those near death. And only on those worthy of the Tears.

Mira swims past a large kelp tent and glances inside the open flap where Bailey works her wonders. At first look, Mira knows she's exhausted. Her typical kelp-fashioned tunic is tattered. Muddy scuffs and scrapes cover her flesh, and her eyes are set deep into her skull with dark rings about them. Bodies— more than Mira would like to count—line the inside, as Bailey rapidly tends to each of them with much help from all the aids she's mentoring.

She pulls open the tent flap all the way and approaches the caretaker. "What happened, Bailey?"

Bailey's eyes nearly burst when she realizes who is asking the question. "Mira!" She swiftly embraces her and refuses to let go for a long while.

Mira has never had a close relationship with Bailey, but it's nice to know her return is appreciated. Bailey retracts and looks her up and down.

"You're healthy. You're intact. No missing limbs? No lacerations?" She grabs at her hair, undoing her messy bun, and combs her fingers through it. "A bit disheveled, but you're a warrior, right?" She embraces her again. "Your parents will be delighted."

"But…" She never answered her question about what happened.

"Go find your parents. They'll tell you everything." Her words are quick and unsettled. She ushers her outside the tent and points toward a driftwood shack that doesn't look safe to enter. "The Elders have been amassing in there until we can rebuild," she says.

"Disheveled?" Mira is stuck on the word, thinking the same about Bailey. "Have you seen yourself? You need rest, Bailey." Mira looks past her, into the tent.

"Precisely…" Bailey's eyes follow Mira's. "More and more continue to be recovered. It's a blessing. And because of it, there's no time for rest."

"And the Ebisu?" Mira turns her eyes back to the caretaker. "What happened of the Ebisu?"

Bailey replies with a shrug and points to the shack. "I only care for the injured. Find your parents."

"Thank you, Bailey."

Mira swims to the makeshift rallyhouse. Two warriors stand on either side of the door. Baratok, the one on her right, slowly exhales a breath of relief, giving her a solid nod of appreciation. He doesn't say anything, but Mira knows he's grateful she's standing before him. Fandor, on her left, abandons his duty, throws his yari to the ground and embraces her, wrapping his arms around her own so she cannot reciprocate the hug.

"Good to see you, Fandor." She smiles. He's not an elf she would expect a hug from, merely another warrior who spars alongside her from time to time. The trauma from the disaster must be impacting him hard.

"You too, Mira. You, too." He lets go and moves to retrieve his yari. "Between the waterspout, those murderous elves, and the wraith swarm, we were afraid we'd lost you to one of 'em for good. It's been several days."

"Several wild days," she admits. "What of the Solari Harvest? Did it take place?"

"No." His head slumps. "We missed it."

"Dire times are ahead of us, Mira," Baratok speaks up. "Go. Retrieve your duties from the Elders. Your speed and skill will be needed."

Mira gives each of them the warrior's greeting—heart, strength, mind, and soul. Each elf reciprocates it, and Fandor returns to his post as Mira enters the forlorn structure.

The rallyhouse is a place for Elders alone to speak freely, and their guests and counsel are only to speak upon invitation. When Mira enters the shack, all formalities are lost.

"Mira!" is heard from several different elves, two being her mother and father. They welcome her with a group embrace. She's relieved to see all three Elders survived the collapse of the former rallyhouse. A part of her knew they would endure because of the amount of spice they consume. A few other elves are in attendance as she interrupts a council meeting already in session.

Unconcerned with the interruption, she dives into her adventure immediately, explaining her sight above the clouds, the vast world beyond their borders, and the octopus and goliath she encountered. When finished, it's apparent the Elders don't share her same excitement or wonder.

Her father grips both of her shoulders and stares at her for a long moment, until Mira feels awkward about it. "We are so glad you've found your way home, Mira." He looks past her toward somebody at the entrance. "Find Andolas. Let him know of Mira and call off the search."

"The search?" Mira interjects. "But shouldn't you continue searching for all the others?"

Elder Rayfin grins. "Of course, of course."

"Wait, did you have a special search party just for me?" Her brows push inward. "That's absurd, father."

"You're a fine warrior, Mira, and an even finer daughter. Your place within this clan is valuable and well worth more eyes to ensure your survival."

"What of Rivee? What of Gallagher? Have they been found? Veras? Tanniv? Haltuk?" She lists off all the elves closest to her. "Are they here?"

Lady Nessa's eyes narrow. "Do not be concerned with them at the moment, Mira. You have duties. You may have just arrived, but like your father said, you're an asset. Elder Rayfin…" She looks to him to continue. Not for his approval, but rather to avoid showing disrespect by giving orders to one of his warriors in front of everybody. Even if Mira is her daughter, she has been a warrior first and foremost since she joined the guild.

"Duties, of course mother." She offers a half smile, then looks to her father. "Am I allowed to know what happened, first?"

Elder Rayfin tells her of the waterspout's destruction, of the missing De'wi they're aware of, and their need to rebuild.

"And what of the Ebisu? What happened to the Ebisu? I watched as they rode off with prisoners. Has there been a rescue party established for them? They are the ones in danger."

"Aside from destroying our rallyhouse before the waterspout touched down, we don't know. They've returned to wherever they came from, I suppose. And that is where you are needed."

"Yes, Elder." Her jaw tightens with a cold dutiful stare. "I'm ready."

"She'll get a day's rest and a solid meal, no doubt," her mother interjects. "Right, Garrik?" She addresses him informally. Likely to touch his empathetic, fatherly side.

He gives her a sidelong glance but says nothing to her. He turns his focus back to Mira. "We're sending a scout team to track down the Ebisu, and we would like you to lead that team, Mira."

Mira is thrilled, but she holds in all her excitement. She has too many questions. "If I am to hunt them—"

"Not hunt." He cuts her off. "This is only a scouting mission. You're not to be discovered. Stealth and speed are of importance. We only need to know where they are and what they are up to?"

"What about the De'wi they took prisoner?" She huffs. "I cannot knowingly leave them there, wherever *there* is, while I watch and gather information. That would be preposterous."

"If they were going to kill them, they wouldn't have rode off with them alive. We must understand the enemy before we retaliate. You must find out what they are up to, and that is all. That is your role."

Mira openly shows her fluster. "What *are* they up to?" She shoves the question back at him, knowing more information is being withheld from her. "What did they say while you were in parley?" She has no authority to ask such questions to Elder Rayfin. "If you are to send me on a mission to uncover their whereabouts and their doings, I need to know everything about them. Everything you know… Elder." She squares her shoulders, folds her arms behind her back, shifts her stance so her fins are shoulder-width apart. If she is going to get answers out of him, she'll only do so by being a warrior, not his daughter.

"The whole story?"

"Yes, Elder."

He stares at her for a moment, pondering the necessity. He turns his body and gestures to the table behind him. "Have a seat." Looking at the few other elves in the room, "You are dismissed. We'll reconvene at a later time. This is of utmost importance." He points to the exit.

Everyone except the Elders and Lady Nessa exit the shack. Bound by marriage, she is tolerated, and even welcomed amidst the dealings of the Elders. They share all things. Their life is one.

All three Elders, donning tattered robes and looking a bit disheveled themselves, sit down at the table. Lady Nessa stands behind her husband as he sits in between the other two. He looks the part of a formidable leader, the distress of the moment not having any impact on him.

Mother Seya, a most elegant elf by nature, although wearing robes frayed at the hems and possibly dragged through the sand, remains in tiptop shape as if she hasn't experienced the same duress as the others.

Mira's mother, similar to Mother Seya, even if her hair were distraught, her face was caked in mud, and she donned rags, would wield a beauty that would be the first thing to shine through a desolate room. She looks more respectable than that now, but less elegant than her typical.

Her mother circles around the table to sit next to her, across from the Elders. The table is supposed to be round, but more so resembles a crescent moon due to a damaged section, likely torn free from the storm.

Her father's face is sullen with wrinkles in the corners of his eyes and across his forehead. "It is time you understood our history and the other elves we have distanced ourselves from."

"Distanced…" Mira mouths the word, hardly audible outside her own head.

"Our focus is on the Tears and the strength and longevity they provide; our focus is on high praise of becoming a warrior to protect the clan from the dangers of the wild, such as leviathans and…" He pauses to make eye contact with Mira. "…goliaths."

"You *knew* the grendelins were more than legend?" Mira interjects.

He waves a hand to dismiss her question. "We've been around for too many generations, Mira. The Elders know many things, but the grendelins aren't of importance right now. Harmless giants, they are. The Ebisu on the other hand…" He pauses, looking to Mother Seya for her approval to continue. She silently nods. Then he looks to Elder Falklan.

"Yes, Elder," she responds. "With the Ebisu's encroachment, I do think the time capsule has been uncovered, and the chronicles of the De'wi will be revealed regardless of our attempts to contain it. It's best to come from us. Tell her."

He clears his throat. Mira waits patiently with her hands laced together in front of her. All eyes seem to be on her, even though her father is the one speaking.

"We are all part of the same family, Mira. The De'wi, the Ebisu, and the Indra. We are all elves born of the same race and evolved into what you see today: the sky elves of the Caelum Realm, the warrior elves of the Terra Realm, and the aquatic elves of the Ocean Realm. Different enough that you would never suspect we are the same. But many generations ago, we all lived as one race of elves on the Isle of Imperius."

Mira's lips part. She had no idea their history was connected in such a way.

"The Indra," her father continues, "as we are all aware, have taken to the skies with their machina, and they've grown plump and lazy because of it. The Ebisu dove into the ocean where their size evolved to compete with the monsters of the deep and they developed a darker tone to blend with them, too. Our differences have an ancient history, but all our cultures are predicated on the need for one resource Solaria offers us."

"Blue Tears…" Mira whispers.

"Correct. The Ebisu use it to thrive in the ocean's deepest crevices, and the Indra use it to power their machina, which allow them to fly the skies. Of the three races, we, the De'wi, are the only ones to have rationed our consumption of the spice, and thus, we are the only race left who has not outgrown their crop."

"But—" Mira tries to correct what she knows to be untrue. Elder Rayfin raises a commanding hand with a grimace to accompany it.

"We have been in hiding on the Morshine Isle for ages, Mira. We've suspected the Indra knew of our whereabouts, but we've given them no reason to intervene with our doings. We monitor our growth and maintain a smaller clan, and because of this, we thrive. Peace between our races continues."

A glance at Lady Nessa tells Mira there's more he's not divulging regarding the Indra, but she remains silent and patient.

"The Ebisu…" he continues. "They have not known of our whereabouts until now. How they swept past our outposts unnoticed, I don't know, but here we are."

"It was the wraith swarm," she answers casually as she ponders everything he's saying. "It distracted both our outposts *and* our warriors. The largest I've ever seen." Her voice is distant because her thoughts are on the Indra, and Ebisu, and the Blue Tears. None of this makes sense.

"The wraith swarm. Of course." Garrik looks to Mother Seya. "Coincidence?"

"It would be naïve and reckless to simplify your enemy. They have learned to live beneath the waves. I would think they're capable of such deceit, wouldn't you?"

"Yes, yes. But I don't like it."

"You haven't told me anything, yet," Mira interjects. "Why are the Ebisu our enemy?" It's a question that has always been skirted around. "So their culture is different. So they prefer the use of machina, but that doesn't mean we're enemies. Why is there such animosity between us? There must be more to this, father."

"Mira!" Her mother reprimands her with a nasty glare.

Mira's lips flatten. "Sorry." She looks to her father. "Elder."

"Your daughter is persistent, Garrik," Mother Seya says with a grin. "Tell her what you know, or we'll all have to endure a tongue lashing. If you're going to send her on this excursion, she deserves to know who she's dealing with."

Elder Falklan raises an interrupting hand. "Are you sure about this?" She looks to Mother Seya, then to Elder Rayfin. "This will change everything."

Silence fills the room. All eyes are on Elder Rayfin as he stares at his daughter. The look on his face is something between anger and pensiveness with a touch of irritation. Whatever he's considering revealing is not light.

"This information doesn't leave this room." His overbearing gaze starts on Mira before scanning all eyes in the room: Lady Nessa, Elder Falklan, and Mother Seya.

"Yes, yes. Go on with it." Mother Seya shakes her head and waves a dismissive hand at his gravity.

Elder Rayfin rolls his eyes at her. "Mira." He settles deeper into his seat. His baritone voice rumbles through the quiet space. "The De'wi have an unsavory history. One to dig a hole and forget about in an unmarked grave. One that we have buried with our ancestors, only passing along the truth to the chosen Elders. Though we have not been burdened with aggression since the Machina Wars, thousands of years ago, our truce with the Ebisu has come to an end..."

"And what forced the truce?" Mira asks the right question, leaning in, intent to know the truth. "What started the Machina Wars?"

"The numbers were high, those who valued tradition over this new discovery of machina. It was an Arilight..." The Elder puts a hand to his chin. "Mother Seya, what was his blasted name?"

"Vanford Arilight. Your mind is under duress. It's okay." She lays a comforting hand on his shoulder with a mocking smile.

He shrugs her off. "Vanford Arilight. The elf who experimented with Blue Tears and the inventor of machina. It was a simple invention. Not much different than a crane with a pulley system, except no elves were burdened with heaving the load. It was the start of a new era. More inventions were procured from Vanford for various undesirable tasks. Excitement buzzed through the culture. Many harbored the potential it could have for society, others shunned it. They looked beyond the excitement and comfort it would bring our culture and saw it as the blight it was. The blight it *is*."

"If there was excitement, what did the De'wi do to stifle it?" Mira asks.

"The Elders were in the latter consensus, and they carried much weight. They shunned the technology. Tried to banish it. Vanford secretly kept a group of apprentices, not wanting his creation to dissolve as if it had never existed. More and more machina continued to surface, and those who were caught with it were exiled. There wasn't any escape from society on the Isle of Imperius..."

"Isle of Imperius..." Mira repeats in a whisper, her eyes dilated and dreamy. The first time he mentioned it, it sounded as if he were giving her legends of their history, but this time it sounds real.

"Its whereabouts are lost. Don't be enraptured by it." He waves her off and continues. "Those who were exiled had to find a new island to call their own. The isles are distant, though, so all were given a boat to rest, assuming their legs couldn't carry them there in one stint, and enough food rations for a score of days. It was a just consequence."

"Doesn't seem bad enough to hold a thousand-year grudge," Mira interjects.

"That was the *just* consequence. Give the exiled a means to start a new life outside of their borders."

"Precisely. An entire world opened up for those who sought it. In fact, I don't think it was severe enough, father. They could have given them a week's worth of rations and no boat. Make them swim the entire way, air or ocean. Make them hunt for their food."

Garrik's eyes narrow. Mother Seya smiles at her, and her mother nudges her with an elbow. Mira grunts irritably and goes back to silence.

"The worst of it…" Her father's eyes grow distant. "I can say I'm grateful I did not live in that era, Mira. The worst of it…" He struggles to continue. "…the De'wi were an oppressive race. Execution from the Isle of Imperius was the publicly witnessed consequence. The worst of it was the separation of families. If a youngkin was the offender, they were pried from their family and treated with the same banishment. Families were torn apart. And the Elders didn't wait for machina to surface, allowing it to grow and spread where they couldn't see it. No. They hunted for machina users. They used methods of torture when they discovered consumers. They ripped the information out of elves to find the machina's source. They even went as far as torturing youngkins to collect information about their blasphemous parents. It was a dire time. They created everlasting enemies."

A heavy stillness takes the space.

"This is why you treat machina the way you do?" Mira speaks up. "Because you don't want it to creep through society forcing monstrous choices that lead to villainous actions. You don't want to be forced to create enemies." Mira understands why her father is so committed to keeping the machina out, but why is machina so bad. If the people want it…

"Oh, it is too late for that, Mira. I don't need to create enemies because our ancestors already have. This is why the Ebisu challenge us today. Eventually, the De'wi migrated from the Isle of Imperius, venturing throughout the Terra Realm, and they carried their dominance with them. Machina was shunned throughout the Terra Realm, and those who sought it had nowhere to go except above the clouds or beneath the waves. And… well… they developed the machina to make it happen. Those who created it were referred to as wizards henceforth because the technology became so robust, most didn't understand it.

Magic was born… And the Machina Wars began. There was no victor. It depleted all the races. The De'wi were diminished from a grand society, consuming multiple isles to minute and distant clans. Since then, the Morshine Clan has kept our existence a secret to all for the safety of our own."

"So, our ancestors are the reason the races scattered across the realms?" Mira asks for confirmation. This is a lot to take in. "Our culture was the dividing factor that forced the elves into the other realms. If they could not live by our standards, they were forced to escape. And thus, the three realms were populated."

"Precisely. The Indra seem to be content in the skies, but the Ebisu are eager to take back the Terra Realm. We are not hiding from machina, Mira. Although it *is* a good reason," he adds, "the truth, we are hiding from a dominant race that holds a grudge." The discomfort is apparent in her father's posture. "This is a heavy burden to bear for elves who made the choices thousands and thousands of years ago."

"It left an everlasting imprint on the Ebisu, I'm afraid." Mother Seya speaks up. "They said as much when they barged in here."

"This means…" Mira pauses, uncertain if she wants to speak the words out loud. "…if you look at recent years, we are the heroes, protecting our clan from the invading forces. But if you begin the story at the beginning, where you ought to, *we* are the antagonists. *We* are the cause for the Machina Wars."

Another silence takes the room. Lady Nessa places a comforting hand on her daughter's shoulder.

"The Terra Realm is vast," Mira adds. "I've witnessed its magnificence. Why not just take another isle and call it a day? The Ebisu must know that we cannot defend all the Terra Realm."

Elder Rayfin shifts in his seat. "It's more about eradicating a culture than it is about conquering the Terra Realm, unfortunately. According to our point-elves records, we have reason to believe other isles have been invaded."

"How many do we have left?" Mira asks. "…to defend our clan."

"A third," Elder Rayfin responds, looking more comfortable with the swift change of tune. "We find survivors daily. The search will continue. Our stock of Tears will not."

"So the Ebisu have no intent to enslave us," she confirms, "or allow us to live at all? They seek genocide."

"Correct. Which is why we need to send our fastest on a scouting mission. We need to know strengths, weaknesses, anything you can find out about them, and we will stage a plan from there. This threat is real, Mira, and we're putting our trust in you to not only venture out into the unknown world, but to return. We need you to return with every bit of information you can muster to give us a lasting hope of survival."

"Why not pick up the clan and leave? The waterspout already gave us a nudge. We should just go! What's holding us here?"

All three Elders look taken aback. Mira's mother nudges her in the side again with her elbow.

"What? It's the truth. Let us find a new home. If death is on the line and we have a third of our warriors and no means to defend ourselves, we should flee. Where is the cowardice in keeping your clan alive?" Mira clenches her jaw and flattens her lips. How could they not recognize this? They're the Elders. "And where in the jelly spittle is Gallagher?" It just comes out. She sinks into her seat, feeling embarrassed.

"Gallagher." His name comes off her father's tongue with abhorrence. "How about the knuckles, for one. Those stone bulwarks and the cascading mountains they draw from protect us on three sides. Even the grendelins refrain from scaling them. And our crop of Blue Tears. They heal our injured. They help us thrive. We should defend them."

"Tears?" The word almost spits off her tongue. "I don't mean to cause doubt, father—Elder Rayfin—but the Tears are in abundance. I may have intentionally left this part out while briefing you of my escapade, so as not to cause unrest, but I witnessed it in the wild while standing high on a ridge in the Morshine Peaks. The entire ocean in that region was glowing with its radiance. I could see its splendor with leagues separating us. There are no lack of Tears."

The Elders all glance at one another. Mira speaks of things that are not to be known to the clan. If she cannot keep her mouth shut with these secrets, she wouldn't put it past her father to exile his own daughter.

"If we flee our home," her father replies, "what of the survivors who remain in the wild? We'll be abandoning them. We cannot flee, Mira. It would be irresponsible."

Her jaw tightens. She agrees with his reasoning, though she doesn't like it. They cannot flee for the sake of all those still lost. "Understood," Mira replies. "And of the Indra? Have there been any threats?" Her tone is low and calm. A challenge as she struggles to keep her composure.

"We have our suspicions that they're probing our defenses and making plans to invade."

"How so?"

"We've encountered a traitor amongst our ranks."

"Who?" That is absurd. All the De'wi know the Caelum Realm is off limits. Nobody enters it. The closest anyone gets are the youngkins who play in the geysers, but they touch the cloud ceiling, and quickly flutter back. How could anyone make contact with the Indra?

"Gallagher." He responds bluntly, and his tone is sharp. It stabs right through Mira. "He returned home with evidence of his contact with them."

"Gallagher… evidence…" Mira is at a loss for words. Why would Gallagher contact the Indra? His entire existence is centered on the idea that he will someday become a warrior. And becoming undisciplined is not in his nature. He wouldn't do this.

"He returned with machina, Mira." Mother Seya responds.

It was a family conversation when only her and her father were speaking, but this is proof the Elders are in agreement. They believe Gallagher is a traitor. "Wait!" A sudden understanding dispels the emotional tidal wave that was about to wash over the room. *"That…* I was with him when he discovered it. We were venturing through the Crisper Coral. Right here within the boundaries. It was just a piece of junk that fell from the sky. Nothing out of the norm. I thought he was going to bring it to the smithy to melt it down into something useful. Where is he now? And Rivee, too? She was there."

Her father shakes his head. "No, Mira. This was no piece of junk."

"Yes, it was!" She raises her voice. "Where is he, father?" She addresses him personally, not as an Elder.

"It was unanimous, Mira," her mother speaks up and places a hand on her shoulder. The other two Elders at the table nod.

"What was? Where is he? Where is Gallagher?"

"He's been exiled, Mira." Her father's voice is not of condolence or compassion, but rather anger. "We cannot have machina within our colony. We just visited this topic. It is a threat to our way of life. We have seen what it can do to a civilization, and we don't need our people to fear the Indran presence within our borders. The truce is still intact for all they know."

"Truce. So, there never was a truce." Mira shakes her head. "It's all fabricated, so we can remain in hiding. We're not warriors at all." She rises from the table. "We're guppies hiding under a stone boulder, hoping to go unnoticed." Her lips purse. "I am going to excuse myself. A much-needed rest is overdue, and I'm afraid if I don't leave your presence right now, I may behave rather rashly."

"Twilight, tomorrow, Mira," her father says as she turns her back. "If you're not on the shores by then, your commitment to the guild will be reevaluated, and duties realigned with your level of devotion."

Mira, angered beyond clear reasoning, escapes the rallyhouse. She's of the mind to kick out one of the boards and watch the entire shack collapse on them. *How could they?* Her own parents exiled the elf she cares for most. Why? Because he's blighted? She saw the machina he found. He's no traitor. He's Gallagher, the only elf with enough passion and dedication to truly be honored as a warrior.

What does she do now? Torn apart by all the lies that've been revealed, she doesn't know whether to disregard her father's rule and chase after Gallagher, or to follow Elder Rayfin's order and set out on the expedition to uncover all she can about the Ebisu. Or maybe she can dismiss them all and befriend the grendelin she encountered in the wild.

She shoots for the ceiling of clouds. It's a long distance, but her rage remains explosive when she gets there, and it bursts forth, manifesting into a roar of pain, disgust, and fear.

The Eye of Solari has come and passed, venturing away from the Knuckles of Morshine. As long as she can see it, she knows Gallagher is close by, somewhere beneath the same clouds. Her heart longs for him. She had always believed she would do anything for him. But exile had never crossed her mind.

Her mind craves the mysteries of the wild. *A grendelin encounter in one short visit! What else could be out there?* What consequences would unfold if she chose to disobey her gut feeling—her soul—and chase after legends?

Her soul binds her to duty. Duty to her clan, her kin, and her Elders. These are her elves and her livelihood. Duty births virtue and longevity and should never be taken for granted.

She lives in a world built on lies and deception, and now she's faced with a choice to abandon heart, mind, or soul. Adversity pulls her apart and she doesn't know if she has the strength to find alignment.

10 AMBITIONS BEYOND REACH

allagher strikes a fragment of black shale against a smooth rock over and over in a uniform motion. "Like this, Rivee." He sharpens the edge, crafting a blade from the fissile stone.

"And why are we doing this?" She rolls her eyes with lazy strikes of her own.

"Because we don't know anything about Solaria outside our borders."

"We know the leviathans dwell deep within the canyon." She lifts her blighted leg. "They don't live in the deserted regions of the Terra Realm. I can tell you that. I mean, look where we are. There's a bushel of coral over there and that's all the life I can see. Unless you consider those rock crops life. Do you think fiends are just going to come out of the blue?"

"I do." Gallagher pauses his motion to give her a hard stare with a smirk. "And all I have to do is swim faster than the slowest one here." He tosses her the sharpened shale. "A gift. So you have a chance in the wild."

Rivee's ears twitch as she dodges it. She picks up a round stone to throw back at him.

"Hey!"

"You deserve it, Gallywog."

"Now, that's just uncalled for." He smiles at her. He's not so offended when the insult comes from another blighted elf, but as soon as an outsider tosses them around, fisticuffs are at the ready.

She laughs at him, then goes back to sharpening her own stone knife. "Still not sure what good these are going to do, but whatever." She strikes at her stone several more times.

"Rivee…" Gallagher's tone moves to a different, less jovial mood. She looks up at him from her shale. "…what's it like living in the colony without parents?"

The question catches her off guard. She's still smiling from her previous jab, but it dissolves quickly. "I don't think about it much, I guess. Nessa has always been good to me. She treats me like a daughter. And Mira treats me like a sister." Rivee shrugs. "I don't know any different, I suppose. Why?"

"I don't know if I'll ever…" He pauses to look Rivee in the eye. He doesn't need to share any of his burdens with her. "Never mind."

Rivee rolls her eyes at him. "You can't do that. It's frowned upon more than that taboo machina you're wearing, you know. You can't start to speak in a meaningful tone just to say, 'Meh, never mind.'" She shakes her head at him. "It's asinine and downright rude."

Gallagher cannot withhold a chuckle. "I'm sorry," he says between merry quakes of his body.

"Well?" She won't let it go.

"I left my parents in Bailey's care." The mood grows solemn. "I don't know if I'll ever see them again, Rivee. There's an emptiness within me I don't know what to do about."

Rivee's face distorts. "Bailey is a magnificent healer. What do you mean?"

"They're kelp pickers, Rivee. And their son is blighted and banished from the colony. My family is the least of her worries. And with the Solari Harvest come and gone, and no spice to go around, they may not survive their injuries from the storm." All goes quiet for a long moment. "I didn't even get a proper goodbye."

"Sorry, Gally." She stares at him with sympathy but doesn't have anything more to say. She's never had parents to lose. Lady Nessa is *like* a mother, but Nessa has made it clear she is not. She is only there to help nurture and raise her to a worthy adult elf. Nessa distanced herself more when Rivee stopped growing.

Silence overtakes the wild for a long period of time. Only the wind howling through the cracks in the dry land can be heard. The two blighted elves are pensive, staring at everything and nothing at the same time, both lost in thought.

"Hey, Gally?" Rivee breaks the silence.

Gallagher flinches with the suddenness. "Yeah?"

"Do you think I could try your fin on sometime?"

Gallagher's face darkens. "If I could, I would, Rivee." He tugs on the machina to show her how well it's attached to his fin. "There's a release mechanism somewhere. I'm sure of it. But it seems to have permanently fixed itself onto my fin. I can't remove it."

"Wicked." She grins and reaches out to touch it. "Can you feel it?"

"Nah." Gallagher taps on it. The fin is rigid where the toes extend out with a flexible material for the webbing between. "It's much better than the kelp fins I used to make. They'd tear after a few beats."

Rivee rubs her fingers along the webbing. "Do you think they have any that would fit me?"

Gallagher looks at her leg. She lost it in an accident with a leviathan that burst out of the canyon depths. Luckily Mira was there to kill it, but not before it took Rivee's fin and lower leg. That was about fifteen years ago, and she wasn't on the list to receive any Blue Tears being a youngkin and all. They probably could've saved it had they recovered the limb and she had been given a dose of the glowing spice. But the Elders are strict about rationing it. The Elders probably have a large enough stock to last themselves to the next harvest, but Gallaghers assumptions are merely sparked from envy. He doesn't know.

"The Indra who gave me this one said he made it just for me. So, yes, Rivee, I do think they have one that will fit you." His smile is sad. He doesn't believe they'll ever make it up to the Caelum Realm. That was a mistake to begin with. Even Brunswick admitted he shouldn't have been there. To go back would be too risky. But the kind-hearted Indra would know how to remove the machina fin. Gallagher's eyes grow wide.

"What?" Rivee gives him a disgruntled look lined with curiosity.

He recalls his first incident when he was captured and hoisted into the Caelum Realm. It involved spice bait at the head of a waterfall pouring from the clouds. Brunswick was also fishing when he was reeled above the clouds. With all that has been going on, he completely forgot about it. He would only need to look for the spice in the sky to find his way back. It could be the answer to his problem.

"What is it?" Rivee folds her arms into her body. "And you never told me you met an Indra." Her lips purse.

"Oh…" Gallagher pauses for a moment. His face scrunches into something odd. "Don't tell anybody?" His request comes out more like a question.

She smiles at him and sticks her amputated leg into the air. "Us blighted have to stick together. Right?"

"Right!" He makes a fist and bumps her stub. "Alright, you think these are sharp enough?"

She glares at him with flattened lips and shakes her head.

"Right, you don't care. They're useless. But just you wait and see. When we run into those elf-eating hydra that are ten times our size, then you'll be thanking me."

"No. I'll be using my sharp rock to hack off that machina fin of yours, so I can swim to safety. I only have to swim faster than you." She grins and twirls into the air. "Come on! Let's go find Mira."

Gallagher picks up the useless blade he tossed at her and follows behind her.

Hours later and the terrain remains the same aside from a few more bushels of coral and more hills. No signs of Mira anywhere. The search is rather taxing and hopeless.

"What are you doing?" Gallagher chirps.

"What!" Rivee cuts a glare in his direction. "I'm looking for Mira. Same as you are."

"No you're not. You're staring at the clouds, daydreaming. Mira isn't in the clouds."

"How do you know?"

"She just isn't. Keep your eyes on the horizon."

"Fine."

A few moments later, Rivee bumps into Gallagher.

"Rivee! Stay focused."

"I am focused."

"Then why'd you run into me? There's an entire world out here, leagues upon leagues of endless terrain, and you try to occupy the same space as me. You're not paying attention."

"Well, it's incredibly boring out here." She puffs her chest, folds her arms across her body, and swims a good distance away from him.

"Warriors don't pout," he scoffs at her as she tries to keep her distance.

"Where are we?" she asks.

"What does it even matter? Mira isn't out here, and it's not like we can go back to the colony." Gallagher pouts in silence for a moment, regretting his words immediately. "Any clues on your side? She would've had a steel yari I imagine. And her circlet. Both easily lost in the winds of a waterspout. The ambient light from her stone would be easy to spot. Anything?"

"Wow... You're really reaching here, aren't you?" Rivee's lips twitch as she stares at Gallagher, dumbfounded by his comments.

"I just want to find her, okay?"

"I do, too, Gally." She swims up beside him. He won't look at her. "She was important to both of us. But remember…she's a warrior. She can handle her own."

"She was tossed by a waterspout." Gallagher's words are grim. Hopeless. "She could be anywhere. What are we doing out here? Why did you come with me, Rivee? I can't help you out here. Your life would have been much better back at the colony. Out here, you're with a blighted elf who'll only get you lost or worse…killed."

"Ha! Killed by what? Desert sand? Maybe some of that quick variety might sneak up from behind and swallow us."

"Shut up, Rivee!" Gallagher yells at her. She freezes. Gallagher has never spoken to her in that manner. "This is serious. You asked where we are. I don't know! I don't know *where* we are, and I might not be able to get you back to the colony. And I don't know what we can eat in such a lifeless region. I don't know, Rivee. And this is no time for smiling and laughing because we might die out here."

A frown forms on her face. She stops swimming and lowers herself to the terrain beneath them where she plops into the sand.

Gallagher drops beside her. "Go home, Rivee Rayfin. It's what's best for you. We can start heading back in the direction we came from and keep our eyes peeled for the knuckles." He glances over his shoulder to double check if they're within sight, but he knows they're not. "Much easier to spot the bulging knuckles jetting out of the shoreline than the missing accessories of a princess warrior."

"Blighted…" She raises her nub, then kicks her good fin to gain height. "They treat me just the same as they treat you. I'm short and defective. I'm worthless in their eyes."

Gallagher casually fist bumps her nub. "We stick together." Gallagher shakes his head, not entirely convinced this is the right choice. He should escort her back home. "Okay." He looks her in the eyes. He enjoys her company, but he doesn't know where to look for Mira. It's hopeless. "But this could get ugly."

"That's a good thing. I fit in with ugly." She drops back to the hard sand.

"Hardly." Gallagher crouches to lower himself to her level. "You're a charming young elf. Look at this unkempt hair…" He combs his fingers through it, and she jerks away from him. "…and those beautiful green eyes…the color of kelp…"

"Or a seadragon, you turd herder." She shoves him away.

"Ah, yes, the alluring seadragon," he agrees as he waves for her to follow him. He continues the search at a mild pace. "Could you imagine having that many fins?"

"Um… I don't think they're all fins, Gally."

He looks at her, confused.

"They're ornamental. They're intended to make it look like sea foliage for camouflage."

"Oh… Well imagine if you *did* have that many fins. You could speed through the air or water with ease. You could be the finest warrior in all Solaria. No leviathan or wraith would stand a chance."

"It's fun to dream. Isn't it?"

"Dream? Err…" Her words slice through his ambition like a sickle through kelp. "Yeah… dreams. I suppose it'll never happen, will it? Me becoming a warrior. I'm blighted whether I have a damaged fin, or one made of machina."

They both swim in silence for a while.

"How'd it happen, Gally? Your damaged fin. Were you born with it?"

"Have I never told you?" He looks at her, shock stricken.

Rivee shrugs her shoulders while continuing her search, not looking at Gallagher but in the opposite direction.

"Hmm… Well, it's probably because it puts me in bad light. It's not a story I share often." He goes quiet.

"Just tell me!" she blurts. "Blighted…remember?"

"Yeah…okay." Rivee wears it like it's a badge of honor. Gallagher doesn't share her same feelings. He'd much rather be whole and be good enough. "I was twenty-eight…" His face distorts as he looks upward like he's searching through his thoughts. "Twenty-nine, maybe? I don't know. It was a long time ago." He throws his hands in the air. "I was foolish. I was invincible. I was the best—"

"But were yoooouuu…" she interrupts. "Were you really the best?"

"Rivee Rayfin!"

"Yes, yes. Go on. Sorry." She apologizes half-heartedly.

Gallagher takes a moment to dig through his memories again. "The waters are as smooth as a sheet of glass. The air was dense and swimmable, as always. The everlasting cloud cover was a tad brighter on that day. It was the day of the Solari Harvest. I was sitting on the reef's edge waiting for the sun to break through the cloud cover and shine into the depths of the Ocean Realm. I wanted to see the glow of the Blue Tears. I had never seen it in the deepest, darkest depths. It had only been described to me. Still to this day, I've only seen it above the ocean's surface. I can only imagine its brilliance is everlasting.

"At twenty-nine years of age, I was still a youngkin. And as a youngkin, I was far from qualified to join the harvest team, but I was ready. My fins were dangling in the ocean waters, and somewhere in the depths was the crop of bio-luminescent spice. Ambitious thoughts ran through my mind. What if I could get my hands on just a small bushel? It would've given me the strength to outper-form all the other elves when I began my training in the Warrior's Guild. As a kelp picker's son, it would've changed our lives. No longer would we be last in line to receive rations of Tears. Even the smiths and carpenters have a higher status. If I were to become a warrior, I could've elevated my entire family. Like Elder Rayfin."

Gallagher goes quiet for a moment, pondering what it is about Elder Ray-fin that he admires so much. It would take centuries to reach the status of an Elder, in which spice rations would be limitless. But he doesn't aspire to be an Elder. And the Blue Tears are only a means to become better. He doesn't chase after the resource itself. It's Elder Rayfin's status as a five-stone warrior that he elevates above all else. Though, with all the recent misgivings, he isn't sure if admiration is the right word anymore. Envy, perhaps.

"I was tired of leaning on the kindness and generosity of those *fit* to lead the clan. I was eager to take the Tears for myself. All I needed was a ration of the spice and I'd be unstoppable. I'd become the warrior I always dreamed of. I could have competed with Mira, the highest prospect at the time, soon to enter the guild, herself."

"Ahh…so it's about a girl?" Rivee interjects. "Always about a girl, isn't it?"

Gallagher gives her a sidelong glance requesting her silence, then he con-tinues.

"One of the older elves swam up behind me. His companions following right behind to join in what I knew would become a mocking session. They were several years older and due to take part in the harvest as greenbloods."

"Who was it? Do I know them?" Rivee interrupts.

"Andolas. You could've guessed. He proceeded to tell me I wasn't safe on the edge of the reef because, despite the leviathans preferring the depths, they travel where the meals are, and they eat little pollywogs like me. I immediately found myself swimming in the ocean as soon as he was done speaking. He shoved me from behind, and I remember hearing laughter on my way in. It muf-fled and faded as I swam deeper, unwilling to surface where I wasn't wanted. I had no interest in being taunted further, so I just kept swimming deeper and deeper until I reached the underwater canyon. It was the deepest I had ever swum."

"You didn't!" Rivee's eyes light up as her head snaps in his direction.

Gallagher nods. "I did." His face scrunches into something impish. "I dove below the border."

"Gally…" Rivee's words are cut short by a gasp. "Why have you never told me this? Does Mira know?"

Gallagher ignores her questions, eager to tell her the full story now. "The deeper I traveled, the darker it got, but I couldn't see the ambience of the Tears anywhere. Desperate as I was, I disregarded movement in the shadows."

Rivee bursts into laughter. "You had zero training. None! I don't think it was the darkness that impeded your vision. You were as blind as a cave shrimp to begin with." She continues laughing.

"All I needed to do was slay a leviathan. You don't think I could've done it as a youngkin?" Gallagher flexes his muscles and bursts forward in a twirling torpedo motion with his new fin. He slows down to allow Rivee to catch up.

"No," she replies bluntly.

"Yeah, well I said they were ambitious thoughts…"

"Okay, okay, we know you made a stupid decision, but how'd you lose the fin?"

"I treaded just below the top of the canyon for a while, dreaming about the days when I could help protect the clan from those malicious water demons. A green light flashed in the depths and swiftly disappeared. My first stone was within reach."

Another gasp from Rivee. "Fool…"

"The silhouettes of the warrior elves were high above. They were preparing for the harvest at the surface. I knew I had to act quickly if I wanted to take advantage of the opportunity. Strength and prosperity were awaiting my family.

"The pressure of the depths was felt immediately, but I swam deeper. The diffused light traveling through the clouds and into the ocean depths faded out completely. And still, I swam deeper. The darkness tore at my courage, but I refused to let it flounder me. Brave warriors endure the challenges presented to them.

"Something moved in my peripheral. Jerking my head and kicking backwards stirred the water around me as I gawked at the darkness. Imagine having no eyes. That is what it was like. I was blind. There was nothing to be seen. Just another game in my head. I propelled deeper.

"The pressure grew more and more hindering, but if the greenbloods could do it, then so could I. And then the green aura of a stone revealed itself. It floated there, in the depths, shimmering like a lone star in the night sky—"

"A what?" Rivee interrupts again.

"That's another tale, for another time, Rivee." Gallagher winks at her and keeps on swimming. "Careless about any evil lurking in the depths, I was mystified by the brilliance of the stone. Arms outstretched and fingers spread wide to snatch it as quickly as possible, I reached for it. The tips of my fingers brushed the stone's surface, and it shot out of reach, as if my touch had the force of a thousand tidal waves. What replaced it were large, terrifying teeth snapping at me. They were as long as I was tall." Gallagher holds a hand over his head, simulating a measurement of his height. "One brushed against my leg, and it was all the motivation I needed to burst out of there—as if seeing the fangs wasn't enough. I'm a bit dense at times."

"I can agree to that." She smirks at him.

"I twirled to point in the direction of the surface and kicked my legs with the force of a waterspout. One beat. Two beats. And pain struck at my right fin. I was swept away into the depths. I don't know how far, for I couldn't see anything. And I don't know whether it was the pressure of the depths or the pain thundering through my body, but the darkness faded to nothing."

"What? Then what happened? How'd you escape?"

"Other than the warriors pulling me from the depths, I don't know. They weren't too far behind me, remember. They found me, harvested the Tears, and one of them was rewarded with a stone. The same stone my fingers brushed against. I was this close, Rivee." He holds up a hand with his forefinger and thumb a fingers-width apart. "This close."

"Yeah, that close to being fish fodder, you idiot. I cannot believe you considered such a brash achievement." Rivee shakes her head at him. "But I'm glad you were rescued. Sorry about your fin."

"Yeah, one horrible choice and it's haunted me my entire life. Had we been more than a kelp picking family, the Tears could've helped in my recovery, but I wasn't awarded any rations. Not only because it was a mild harvest and our status didn't permit it, but because of the added risk I put on the harvest team. As a punishment for my idiocy, I was forced to live with my mistake, damaged beyond natural repair. Blighted for life. I haven't been able to swim properly since then. Until now." He kicks his machina fin outward to put it on display.

"After all that, you still want to be a warrior?"

"Yes. Yes, a thousand times over. It's all I've ever wanted."

"Not true. What about the girl?"

Gallagher's face flushes. "Yeah, that too."

"Speaking of Mira, where to next? We've been heading deeper and deeper into this wasteland for hours. Shall we look for a change in scenery?"

"That's what Mira would do." He looks to Rivee and smiles. "Yes. Ocean's in that direction, right?" Gallagher points to his left. "Shall we?"

"We shall."

11 REDEFINING BLIGHTED

Mira's eyes flutter open. Forgetting where she's at, her limbs jerk outward, and her kelp hammock dumps her to the ground. She's in the makeshift barracks of the Warrior's Guild trying to accomplish an overdue rest, but her thoughts tear her apart.

An odor wafts through the air as she's crumpled on her hands and knees on the sandy floor of the crude structure. Her nose cringes, wondering if it's her. It *has* been a few long days.

Climbing to her feet, she wraps her sarong around her body, covering chest to thighs, and makes for the spring to wash. She's expected to set out on her scouting mission to locate the Ebisu today. Should she refuse, she will be chasing after Gallagher. Either way, she anticipates a long departure from the colony, and a wash is overdue just the same as that rest.

The spring is a quick swim away, just past the tiered rice crops and waterwheels, nestled into a large rocky crag with a small waterfall on one end. Bushels of coral line the spring and offer privacy.

Mira removes her sarong and undergarments and dives in. She curls through the water and surfaces near the waterfall. The fresh water pours over her head as she runs her fingers through her dark tangles. Although they spend much time in the ocean currents, the fresh water is pure and is much appreciated. She spends an hour or so trying to relax in the springs and clear her mind, attempting to understand the Elder's reasoning for banishing Gallagher. Her mind spins in circles.

One elf with machina will initiate exception as the new standard. More and more elves will discover fallen machina and attempt to reengineer it into something useful. History will repeat itself. She understands this logic, but it also presents a potential for change within their culture. Change isn't always bad, nor is it always good, but it allows a culture to grow. Growth is important. Besides all this, it was just a hunk of junk. The Elders had no excuse to banish him.

Gallagher wasn't responsible for bringing the machina to the colony. He only found it. To be banished for such an act, any elf could suffer the same fate. Others bring fallen machina to the smithy regularly. It's where all their steel comes from. It doesn't make any sense to her. Maybe Gallagher had already modified it into something else or was in the process of doing so. That could provoke the Elders' extreme punishment.

Mira would know more if she hadn't stormed out of the rallyhouse. She must talk to Gallagher. She needs to find out which way they escorted him. One of the other warriors would know. Maybe Rivee would like to join in the search. It would be a good expedition for her, assuming it wouldn't take them too deep into the wild. Oh, how the Elders would have a fit if they found out she went to look for him. Her anger is enough right now, she would do it just to spite them.

Except Mira is bound to the Warrior's Guild and expected to chase after the Ebisu and her fellow clansmen. Not Gallagher. Maybe if she hurries, she can do both.

She climbs out of the spring and covers up. As quickly as she can, she returns to the barracks where she prepares herself for a journey, slipping on a warrior's corset and tying her sarong around her hips, securing it with her leather tassets. She braids her hair and ties it behind her head with a kelp band, slips on her garter with a dagger fashioned into it, pulls her circlet over her head, then grabs her steel yari, and exits the barracks to find Veras. Outside of Mira and Rivee, he's Gallagher's closest friend. He'd know where Gallagher was taken to.

It doesn't take long to find him stationed outside the rallyhouse. Mira doesn't bother entering. She's not ready to discuss anything with her parents, *or* the Elders. Not until she speaks to Gallagher. "Veras, good day."

"Is it?" He tilts his head to her. "Maybe it is now that you're here. Good to see you alive, Mira." He nudges his head backward toward the rallyhouse entrance. "I watched you storm out yesterday. Thought you might be going to do something brash."

Mira narrows her gaze, followed by a devious grin. "It's not too late for that. Do you know which way they escorted Gallagher?" she asks, getting right to the point. She spent too much time waking up in the spring. How can she converse with her good friend *and* accomplish everything she needs to?

His mouth morphs into a frown. "I shouldn't say." He looks suspiciously to the west.

Mira smiles. "Thank you, Veras. You're an elf of the most wonderful kind." She moves to disappear in that direction but remembers something. "Oh! And Rivee Rayfin?" She looks back at him, hoping he'll know where she is, too. "Have you seen her?"

"Nah. Haven't seen her."

Mira purses her lips. "Okay. You're still a wonderful elf, Veras." She winks at him and swims away.

She finds Bailey next. Rivee often spends time at the infirmary helping the caretaker with anything she needs. She enjoys helping the injured warriors after a long day of training because of the stories they tell. She gets even more excited after a Solari Harvest. It's dreadful they missed it this year. The first time since it became tradition. The Elders must be distraught about it. Maybe that's why they were so harsh on Gallagher.

"Excuse me, Bailey," she says as she sneaks into the infirmary tent. The incense claim her senses briefly. A large ration of Blue Tears sits on a platter. A mesmerizing ambient glow of blues and greens radiates from the spice. It's like watching flames dance through the air. Mira stares at it for a moment while Bailey divides the heap into bowls and ushers them to each bedside with care. Some of the charges are awake and don't hesitate to indulge. Others look as though they wouldn't be able to feed themselves even if they were awake. And too many of the charges are left without the Blue Tears, ogling the others, envying the quick recovery they'll have.

It's a shame.

She sees Gallagher's parents amongst them, asleep in the back of the tent, but there isn't anything she can do for them that Bailey isn't already doing.

"Oh! Mira!" Bailey sees her standing in the entrance.

"I see you still have your hands full." She looks over the crowd of patients. Her staff of youngkin aids remain hard at work, too. "Have you seen Rivee by any chance? I have a task for her?"

Bailey's lips purse as she shakes her head. "I haven't. Last I saw her, she was fixated on Gallagher being escorted beyond the boundaries." Her face contorts. "Did you hear?"

Mira focuses her attention on the nearest warrior lying in a cot to deflect any signs of frustration she might show. "I did," she replies and leaves it at that. She doesn't want to talk about it because she'll only spit out anger like the rogue fireballs of a mythical dragon. It is not proper for her to be publicly angry about banishing an elf for something as taboo as bringing machina to their land. Especially as the Elder's daughter. "Did you happen to see if she followed them?"

"I watched her follow them away from the colony, up toward the western outposts, but I didn't pay any attention after a while. I have too much going on to keep up with that little sprite's shenanigans." She gestures to her charges.

"She wouldn't have followed them beyond the knuckles, would she?" Mira's concern grows for the youngkin.

"Doubtful. She's fiery, that youngkin, but I don't think she'd venture that far."

"Very well. Thank you." Mira disappears through the tent flap without saying goodbye. She needs to hurry. Her father will put together his own scouting team and send them off without her if she's not at the shore by twilight. Veras admitted he thought she was going to react to the news of Gallagher. Word has obviously spread about her feelings toward the situation. They could easily write her off as a hopeless cause, unfit to lead the mission. Blighted just like the elves she's seeking. The consequences are more than she'd like to endure.

She swims high enough to see over the driftwood structures, the small groves of kelp, and the plethora of coral. It appears most of the life calling the Crisper Coral home have disappeared since their encroachment into the area. The fish have evacuated. No seadragons, otters, or sun devils, all of which would roam this area. She also cannot see Rivee anywhere. Granted, a few days without a dose of Blue Tears will hinder her eyesight, but she should be able to spot the youngkin from a higher altitude if she were out and about, as she most often is.

Her urgency to chase down Gallagher quickly turns into a concern for Rivee's whereabouts. She doesn't want to believe it, but she knows it to be true—Rivee followed him.

She swims through the refuge asking every elf she passes whether they've seen Rivee, and not a single elf has seen her in more than a day.

Mira's anger turns into a boiling fury. The Elders are to blame for all of this. Gallagher was exiled for a less-than-worthy cause and, more than likely, Rivee has gone with him.

Veras remains standing guard outside the rallyhouse. "May I enter, Veras?"

"Depends on your state of mind and purpose," he responds dutifully.

"I mean to castrate the Elder, and I plan on doing so with a smile on my face." She says it without any hint of facetiousness.

"Oh…" He stands quiet for a moment. "…well, if you're in a happy state of mind, I don't think I should—"

"What's that?" Mira points to his right and slips past him when his line of sight follows her finger. She shakes her head at the simplicity of the trick that works nine out of ten times. It could be the most intelligent elf in all Solaria, and they would be duped if there were trust and surprise involved.

Mira enters the room with a calmness blanketed over her fury.

"Mira…" Her father addresses her. The three Elders appear to be in a hot debate sitting around the table. This new rallyhouse is small. Too small for the large decisions being made during these trying times. "We're not expecting your expedition to set out for a few more hours. Twilight. Please dismiss yourself. We have matters to discuss."

"And I have matters to discuss with the lot of you." She remains calm, taking to her training as a warrior, owning her emotions.

Mira looks over her shoulder as Veras enters the tent and stands just behind her with a sheepish look. He remains quiet. Her father grimaces, and the other two Elders glare at her with disapproving looks, but they don't intervene between father and daughter.

"Is this a house matter? Or a clan matter?" her father asks.

"Both."

"Speak." His tone is irate.

Mira approaches the table they sit around. "Rivee has gone missing. I don't have evidence just yet, but I have good reason to believe she followed Gallagher into the wild. We need a search party to set out immediately."

Vocal groans are heard from around the table, and all roll their eyes, including her father. "No evidence? Just a hunch?" he says. "I'd take this seriously if Rivee didn't spend most of her hours testing the confines of our borders. She's always dallying about somewhere, unawares to the rest of us. This is hardly a clan matter. Please remove yourself."

"This *is* a clan matter!" Mira's voice gets louder. "Rivee has disappeared, and I suspect she has followed Gallagher into the wild. Would you have your clan divided? The blighted and the fit?"

Elder Rayfin sighs heavily. He shoos Veras outside of the tent with a wave of his hand, who unquestioningly abides. "Sit down," he says to Mira.

"I'll stand, thank you. It's helping me contain my anger." She glares at her father.

"This was your mother's decision just as much as it was mine—sending Gallagher away." Her father uncharacteristically sheds blame for a decision he's capable of making on his own. Weakness. Maybe because he doesn't fully agree with the decision. Maybe because he knows how much pain it causes his daughter. "Argh… blasted machina. Tell her Seya." He waves an arm in her direction without taking his angered gaze off Mira.

The matriarch holds Elder Rayfin in her sight for a moment before clearing her throat and straightening her posture. Her golden hair has a few tight braids, but otherwise cascades around her shoulders. "Wherever Rivee has gone… If she is outside the protection of the knuckles, we did not send her there. You know we would never do such a thing."

"Do I? You exiled one of your finest, at a time when every elf makes a difference albeit, because of some ancient tradition you've adhered to that hardly has any meaning in today's world. I don't know any of you as I thought I did." She regrets her words immediately after saying them, but her anger is nearly boiling over. Depending how they respond, they might get to see her explode.

"You entitled little imp!" Elder Falklan rises and spits on the floor while glaring at her. The reaction causes Mira to cringe. She presses her hands into the table, leaning in, and glares at Mira from behind her dark brow.

"Mira, you are a fine warrior, but you are about to lose your privilege if you continue to show disrespect within these walls." Her father rises.

Mother Seya remains seated and observant.

"I am not a fine warrior. That would be the issue at hand." Mira pulls her circlet off her head and rubs at the green stone in the center. "You have deemed Gallagher blighted for making one childish and damaging mistake, when he has more heart than any elf within the Warrior's Guild. Including you!" Her finger jabs at her father.

"Mira—" he starts.

Her voice rises above his. "We are a clan at risk of slaughter by an age-old enemy, and you have exiled a healthy and capable elf. Why? Because he tries to better himself to protect his clan? To protect his culture? To protect *you*? I find the Elder's judgement lacking—"

"That is it! Mira! Get out! I will deal with you later." Her father is rigid with a jaw clamped so tight he might shatter his teeth.

"Elder Rayfin!" she hollers back, matching his volume. "Do you know why Rivee has been deemed blighted? Why she lost her leg the day I earned this stone?" She holds up her circlet. "Too much has been left unspoken. It is time for you to know the truth of who your daughter is."

The Elders take to silence. Mira has their attention.

"It was my first harvest." Mira's voice calms with a subtle shake as her anger tempers. Her eyes narrow on her father. "As the daughter of the greatest five-stone warrior…the Tears flowed through my blood, giving me an undeserving confidence. My eyesight was keener. My senses, more alert. My speed, swifter than any greenblood in competition. I have always pushed myself to prove I am reliable, but I was born into this. I had an advantage above the other greenbloods, and it made me careless.

"I was confident in my abilities, but my mind wandered from the moment I swam over the canyon's rim. I had no interest in the Tears because I've been consuming them my entire life. The ocean is vast and unexplored. My eagerness to discover new horizons possessed me.

"It was always said that swimming beyond the spice crop was too risky, but if you can outswim a leviathan, where's the risk? Stay away from its nasty teeth and the risk is averted. I know I was alone in this opinion—*am* alone in this opinion. Those thoughts are what drove me to earn this that day." She fumbles the circlet in her hands. "Not very warrior-like." She fingers the stone within the circlet, shaking her head in shame.

"Mira…" her father speaks, "having thoughts of veering from your duty is hardly—"

"It wasn't just thoughts." She looks at him from beneath a tight brow. "In the dark of the canyon, I could see little. Even with the aid of the Tears. Outlines of the canyon walls revealed themselves and the occasional deep lurker swam by. I knew nothing of whether they were deadly or harmless, and it enthralled me. My gut told me to follow the harvesters. My head told me to explore the depths.

"The harvesters knew exactly where the spice grew and wasted no time swimming there. The warriors flanked them on all sides, and the greenbloods trailed. Typical scheme we've always trained for. Except, I swam where my head told me to go.

"I allowed myself to fall behind. I was only an awkward appendage to the harvest team, anyways. And, with my speed, I could recover the distance lost if it was only a minor detour. The opportunity to explore couldn't be neglected.

"Another deep lurker shifted through the high-pressured waters in my peripheral. It disappeared into the darkness, along with the harvest team, leaving me alone.

"I brushed my fingers across the algae-covered rocks, feeling my way around, flipping the occasional stone even though I could hardly see anything. I came across a cluster of sea anemone shedding a gentle ambiance into the canyon depths. A bioluminescent anemone! Can you believe it? It was my first experience, and it was a delight. A spectacle in the depths. I couldn't resist a poke.

The sticky touch offers an odd satisfaction." Mira's lips curl upward in gentle fashion.

"Further down the canyon, back into the darkness, my speed did nothing to help me find the harvest team. My exploration was intentional, sure, but it was only intended to be a detour. The harvest team was nowhere to be seen, and a fork in the canyon emerged…"

"Fork!" Her father interjects. "There is no fork."

Mira stares at the green stone within her silver circlet. "I beg to differ. Maybe we ought to explore our surroundings with more vigor." Her eyes quickly cut to her father, compassionless.

"Hmph…" Her father crosses his arms and stiffens his posture.

"I went right," she continues. "That's when I saw the iridescent glow of the Blue Tears. The splendor left me motionless for a short while. My heart beat heavier when the harvest team never came into view. It wasn't possible for them to have completed their harvest and return without us crossing paths, but what other explanation was there? Had I taken the wrong path? Another impossibility because there was only one crop within our reach. Or so we've always been told." She observes the reactions of all three Elders. They offer only irritated expressions.

"I only realized just recently the truth of what happened on that day, when I witnessed the abundance of Tears blanketing the ocean west of here. The crop we have been harvesting all these years is hardly the only one available to us. What I found that day was a second crop. A crop my harvest team was oblivious to.

"Regardless of my foolish actions, I'd have been a bigger fool to pass up the opportunity to harvest the Tears. With the scrutiny of what I had done, the least I could do was return with my own share of the spice. But this crop was different than what had always been portrayed. Scattered throughout it were camouflaged polyps the size of my fist. Oddly shaped versions of the light traps the leviathans carry. And within the polyps…embryos. I had stumbled upon a nest." Mira shakes her head, looking down at the table. "The terror that filled my soul in that moment…" She looks up at the Elders, rubbing her finger over the stone in her circlet. All are intently focused on her.

"Why have you never spoken of this before now?" Mother Seya asks. The air in the room is heavy. The driftwood groans and creaks as a calm wind flows through the leaky walls.

Mira raises a finger, suggesting she'll return to that thought. "A dark and vague mass shifted above me. Undeniably a giant of the deep. If I was brave enough, I could have tickled the belly of the beast. It was that close. If I was hardened enough, I could have run my yari through it and spilled its insides. I could have claimed my first stone right then. But I was neither. I was enamored."

"Mira…" Her father's voice is filled with sympathy. She raises her hand to quiet him. The other two Elders remain patient.

"That leviathan was protecting its offspring. Nothing more. I couldn't slay it. I chose to let it live. It hovered above me for the longest time, unmoving. I could only wait so long before having an itching to flee the scene. Instead of grabbing a proper harvest, I snatched a few bushels and bolted into the depths. It was a poor decision. The leviathan curled into my escape route. The swiftness of the giant was no less than a skittle zipping through the reef. Its snapping jaw nearly took off my legs, but I was able to dodge the attack and push off its bulging snout to give myself a needed burst of speed.

"I kicked with all the power of Ceto's tidal forces and refused to look back. The rapid change in pressure impacted my eyesight and senses, making the ocean fuzzy. I only needed to make it above the canyon's edge, and I knew I'd be okay. I would be safe because the leviathans never leave the canyon.

"The shimmering radiance of the surface was overhead, along with the silhouette of the canyon's rim. I finally glanced down where my fins stirred the waters. Gargantuan teeth as long as an orca's fin, and as gnarly as a riptide's curl, were too close for comfort. The leviathan had kept up with me, and it wasn't slowing as we came closer to the shallows.

"Without losing a beat, I curled over the top of the underwater cliff and allowed myself to tumble across the seabed. Lying on my back, stabilizing my lungs, I was staring at the silhouettes of several clanmates swimming along the surface above. I exhaled as I tucked away my yari and reflected on what had just happened. But too soon, the dark shadow burst from the depths. A massive leviathan. A hungry predator. I led the beast to our clan. There was nothing I could do to save the swimmers above.

"The rest, you're aware of. The bellowing conch… …the chaotic scramble of the elves at the surface… …the leviathan exploding from the waves… …Rivee's life-altering injury… …Alariya's…death." Mira's head sinks between her arms as she finds a seat at the table, squeezing the circlet within her grasp. "And the inevitable strike of my yari to slay the leviathan." Her words fade into a mumble as she speaks into her arm, choking away tears and emotion.

"Mira…" Her father's voice is low and comforting.

She lifts her head, lost in the terror of her memories. "The crimson haze that clouded the waters…"

"It's okay, Mira." Mother Seya comforts her. "Death is not easy for anyone."

"Too many bodies floating in the water…"

"Nearly all of them healed with only minor scars as a memento," her father says.

"The terrifying screech from within the cage of fangs…"

"Rivee survived, Mira." Mother Seya consoles her. "Alariya helped her escape."

"Alariya…" Mira's eyes meet Mother Seya's. For the first time, it's as if the Elder sees her for who she truly is. "…she died." Mira tucks a few loose tresses behind her ear, then places her forehead in hear hand, lowering it to the table.

"She's no warrior, Garrik," Elder Falklan proclaims. Mira doesn't bother looking at her or try to deny it in any way. She agrees.

"I fell to the shore as the weight of a thousand leviathans slammed into my gut," Mira continues her ramblings. "I wandered outside of my duties. I provoked the leviathan. I led it back to the clan to unleash its malice.

"Andolas knew. With a hateful glare he dropped the light trap into my palm. 'Sometimes there are casualties…' he said as he gripped my hand so tight, I could not break free from his grasp. '…but never have I seen murder.'

"He punctured the light trap with a dagger and set the blade straight into my palm. Chaos consumed the shore, and I refused to share my shame with anyone. He pulled the blade free, pried the stone from within the light trap, and shoved it into my bloodied palm. 'Regardless of my suspicions, you've earned this,' he said.

"I received it, numb to everything around me. *Earned* this? I *earned* this?" Mira's tone angers. She looks at the scar on her palm, then wrenches down on the circlet, snapping it in two. "Trust in your stones, they say. How can I? I didn't earn this stone, father. This stone crushed me, and I've been trapped beneath its weight since the day Alariya died. Since the day Rivee became blighted."

Mira tosses the pieces of circlet on the table. The stone pops free and spins in front of her father.

"Elder Falklan is right. I'm no warrior, Elder Rayfin. I am as blighted as Gallagher and Rivee. You just can't see it."

Mira flees the rallyhouse and disappears into the skies.

12 Caelum Invictus

R ain has taken to the skies. It falls thick as if all the Indra above are dump-
ing buckets of water from their piers. It's been several days of searching
for Mira without any signs. Gallagher, his dark hair slicked back, and
Rivee, with hair matted to her face, tread through the air, hopeful for a turn of
events, desperate for any clue of her whereabouts. The Terra Realm is vast. It's
like searching for a ray of sun beneath the ceiling of clouds.

"Hey! A geyser field!" Rivee darts forward. "C'mon!"

It's the only excitement they've seen in at least a day. There was a squad
of rays undulating through the air. They kept their distance because the starkly
colored animals are known to pierce that which they find threatening with the
arm-length spines protruding from their tails.

Gallagher hurries after her, and with a missing leg, she isn't hard to keep
up with. He pities her fortune. He so often feels sorry for himself with his damaged fin, but Rivee is missing a fin entirely, and beyond that, she's shorter than
an Indra. He relates to her for these reasons and will always hold her close to his
heart, *and* because she's a spunk on a rainy day. She brings a jovial attitude to
any situation.

A burst of screams and laughter erupt along with the geyser. Rivee flies
into the air hundreds of fins high.

Gallagher finds himself grateful this particular geyser isn't too powerful.
Some can carry an elf into the clouds, and the last thing Gallagher needs is for
Rivee to shoot into the Caelum Realm.

Several geysers erupt. Gallagher, without hesitation, hops into one in pursuit of her. The blast from below is powerful, but a beat of the fins makes it

bearable. What's most uncomfortable about them is the temperature of the water. It's nearly scalding. Gallagher shoots past the geyser's pinnacle and into the air where he finds Rivee carelessly swimming about with twirls and smiles.

"Hey!" She offers him a mischievous grin. "You said you met an Indra. Let's go!" She somersaults in the air, then bursts upward toward the Caelum Realm.

Gallagher watches her for a moment, shaking his head at her youngkin maturity. She disappears into the clouds, and his jaw drops. *She's serious!*

"Rivee Rayfin!" He chases after her. The cloud cover is too thick. Gallagher can only see a dozen strokes away. Rivee is nowhere to be seen.

She'd never swim above the clouds. She must be playing games with him. The threat of the Indra is a mere risk, but the light air is a direct hazard. Without practiced breathing or one of the Indran breathing devices, she wouldn't last long.

He swims through the clouds searching for her.

The damp air is heavy on his lungs. He wonders how Rivee holds up with her underdeveloped body. Would her lungs have issues swimming through the clouds too, or the ocean depths? He's never seen her leave the Terra Realm aside from playing in the shallows of the ocean. She doesn't seem to have issues swimming at these heights. For Gallagher, his mass combined with the rain and altitude bring a noticeable struggle to his swimming.

His concern grows. He cannot find her anywhere in the clouds. His jaw tightens with frustration. "Wraith fodder and jelly spittle," he mutters to himself before calling her name. "Rivee! Rivee, your games are trying. Where are you?"

His head pops through the cloud cover and he immediately shields his eyes from the bright radiance beaming down on him. He scans the surface of the clouds, but they're too fluffy and billowy, like the cushions Brunswick had on his furniture. Even though his visibility is clear, the lumpy surface of the clouds prevents him from seeing anything useful. He needs to get higher, but the light air doesn't allow it. Swimming within the Caelum Realm is an impossibility. The density of the air is so much different, and colder. A shiver runs over his wet flesh.

Gallagher drops back into the clouds until he's beneath the ceiling. There's no sign of her. His frustration is beyond its limits, and his fear... His fear takes him to places that he needn't go.

With the power of his machina fin, he propels himself upward, increasing his speed with every kick. The moisture of the clouds puffs at his flesh like a spray of ocean mist in the heart of a storm. He bursts through the topmost part of the ceiling of clouds into the Caelum Realm. His velocity projects him into the air like a whale breaching the surface of the ocean. It gives him enough altitude to view the horizon.

Rivee's head pokes through the clouds a short distance away. A moment of elation hits him, but his breathing stops when he sees an Indran landship flying in the distance.

The fall steals his stomach away momentarily. Once his body plunges into the density of the clouds, he jets straight toward Rivee's location, but he still cannot find her. The clouds are too thick with limited visibility. With a burst of speed, he erupts from the clouds once again to get a better visual, and she's another fifty strokes away and moving. Her course aligns with the landship. Gallagher yells but penetrates the clouds again where she disappears from view.

He breaks the surface of the clouds like a dolphin playfully hurdling the breaking waves of the tide, except Gallagher isn't having any fun. His heart beats heavier, reality pulling him into the exact fears his mind was drifting toward moments ago. She continues to disappear into the clouds and surfaces in new locations, closer and closer to the landship.

"Riv—" He drops into the clouds, then resurfaces. "Rivee!" And he drops back into the clouds.

A great shadow blocks out the sunlight. The landship is above them. Gallagher finally catches up and grabs her by the arm to prevent her from disappearing again. They tread the air within the cloud cover, invisible to the landship above.

"What were you thinking, Rivee Rayfin?" A mixture of anger and love consume his voice like a disciplining father.

"Did you see it?" she responds, brushing off his dismay.

"Of course, I saw it. It's right overhead. And they're not friendly, Rivee. They're dangerous, just as the Elders have suggested."

"What?" A look of confusion creeps onto her face. "But you said…"

"I said I met an Indra. I didn't say they were all our friends."

"But how'd you get the—"

"There was *one* Indra. *One*! Look at Andolas, for example. If he was the only De'wi you ever met, you'd think we were all arrogant assholes full of jelly spittle. But we're not."

Rivee gasps.

Gallagher's tense muscles soften. "Sorry. They are to be feared, Rivee. And my own fear is lashing out at you. I'm sorry." He pulls her in closer and embraces her. "Their machina is powerful."

Projectiles pierce through the clouds all around them. Gallagher curses under his breath, his head darting back and forth, and before he can do anything, the two of them are netted and pulled into the Caelum Realm. Rivee screams, but Gallagher hardly hears her as his thoughts frantically search for a way out of this.

An apparatus, only familiar to him because of his first mistake dallying too close to the cloud ceiling, hoists them into the Caelum Realm.

"Rivee, slow your breathing, okay. The air is thin up here. Slow inhales..." Gallagher puffs out his chest with air. "Slow exhales..." Gallagher slowly releases. "And hold the air in your lungs longer than you'd typically do. You must be methodic about it. Okay?"

"What? What? We cannot breathe up here?" She squirms and tugs at the netting. "You never said anything about poisonous air." She hysterically pulls at the netting and screams.

Gallagher questions his earlier thoughts about her bringing a jovial attitude to every scenario. She's clearly not ready for life-threatening situations. "Hey *warrior*, you have to calm down or you're going to faint."

She halts her panic with a hard stare at Gallagher, creases forming in her brow and a flat frown on her face. The comment helps her relax. "What do we do, Gally?" she says in a calmer tone.

She picks up the breathing technique quickly. Gallagher was hyperventilating when he first encountered the air, but Rivee is managing it well. Maybe she *does* have some warrior in her after all.

"They're civilized from what I could tell. Brunswick was polite and much of a conversationalist. So...we wait." He shrugs his shoulders. "I don't believe they'll be hasty with any actions, whether murderous or benign."

"Murderous..." Her eyes grow wide as she whispers the word.

Gallagher cringes, wishing he'd check his language around her a little more. It's an anxiety-driven moment, but that's no excuse when he has a young-kin in his presence. He needs to be resolved and dignified.

"Brunswick?" she questions.

"The Indra I met. The one who gave me this." He attempts to raise his machina fin but is quickly curtailed by their tangle of limbs within the netting.

They're hoisted overtop the rim of the landship. A clicking noise is heard and the two of them fall to a platform below. Rivee starts a scream, but cuts it into a chirp, whether from the exhilaration of falling for the first time or trying to hold to his comment about being a warrior.

They hit the ground in a heap. Gallagher untangles himself from Rivee and gets to his fins quickly before helping her up.

A crowd of Indra gape at them. All are similar in stature: small frames, plump around the midsection, and skin folding into their necks where a chin ought to be. They all look young and dumbfounded, too. Maybe they didn't intend to retrieve a couple of De'wi. Maybe they're anglers, fishing just as Brunswick had been doing.

They're at the edge of a pier with machina lining one side. At the source of the pier, tall structures climb high above the base of their landship. The scene is covered in green foliage. Trees and vines climb the structures—as he first witnessed during his last escapade above the clouds. Some are in the form of tall boxes; some are high arcs cascading across the ship; and others appear to be made of the same material as their machina with no foliage at all. Against the blue skies, it's a mesmerizing sight. A new world. And yet again, he cannot wait to share this with Mira. Will he ever find her?

"Out of the way! Out of the way!" a squealing voice is heard. The crowd shuffles away as a slightly taller, slightly plumper Indra works his way through the crowd. A brief hope that it could be Brunswick comes and goes from Gallagher's thoughts when the sky elf comes into better view. "What in Ceto's name?" He turns to one of the shorter Indra and mumbles something into his pointy ear. The little squirt runs off. "How did you get here?" he questions.

Gallagher is the one left dumbfounded now. *How did you get here?* Why wouldn't he know? It was their machina that hoisted them into the Caelum Realm and onto their landship. Rivee, however, doesn't hold back.

"What a manatee's rump of a question." She points to the machina. "You brought us here. Why did you bring us here?" She folds her arms across her body and taps her fin impatiently.

The Indra looks up. The machina has a loose-hanging net attached to it. He mumbles something to the nearby Indra, keeping a close eye on the two of them all the while. "Yes, yes. Of course, we did." He glares with a pouty face while he tucks his hand into a pocket of his overcoat and retrieves a shiny mechanism. Miniature machina. He flips it open, gazes at it briefly, then snaps it shut and puts it back where he found it. "Why were you swimming so close to the boundary? You know the Caelum Realm is off limits to your kind."

"We were minding—"

"Rivee Rayfin!" Gallagher places an aggressive hand on her shoulder as he cuts her off. "My apologies. We were enjoying ourselves in a geyser and caught one with a little too much gush."

The Indra flinches. It's subtle, but Gallagher notices it. He isn't sure what about his comment disgusts the Indra, but the sky elf is clearly appalled by something.

"That explains the sloppy, wet attire."

Gallagher looks down at his tunic and malo, then to the Indra. There's a stark difference between the two. Where the Indra has clean garb with neat folds and buttons, Gallagher's looks like a used washcloth in comparison.

"Why would you swim in this region of the Morshine Isle?" he asks.

"This region? The Morshine Isle?" Gallagher cocks his head. "That implies—"

"Ray!" The Indra shouts and puts a hand over his mouth as if he's trying to stop his words from coming out. "We were angling for the mantas, not this." He waves an ugly arm at them. "We've never encountered De'wi swimming around this section of the misty seas." One of the other Indra mumbles something into his ear. He crouches slightly to listen.

"This section? How do you know where the De'wi swim?" Rivee asks with enough suspicion looming in her tone that she might as well call the elf a liar.

The sky elf grunts. "We've moved beyond primitive technologies. We know…" He pauses and crosses his arms to match her posture. "No, no, no… I see what you're doing. I'll ask the questions. Were you snooping? What reason do you have to poke so closely to our realm?"

They continue asking questions of each other, with hardly a response. Stubbornness at its finest. Nothing but idle threats, and never does the tension escalate between the two.

More Indra move into the scene—Indra who have more of an authority to their presence. They're still short and plump, but with a little more puff to their chests, along with a uniform fully covering their torsos and legs. Each carries an odd looking staff with a conch shell mounted at the top.

"Welcome to Caelum Invictus," one of the Indra greets them as the authority surrounds them. With one subtle dab of the staff, Rivee drops to the ground, unconscious. Gallagher instinctively leaps into the air and falls right back down to the pier. He can't swim above the clouds. He knows this but has never trained for battle in such an environment and knows not what else to do. The conch taps him on his forehead, and all goes dark.

Gallagher's eyes snap open. He wakes in a sterile room with white walls, three small windows located high on the wall, and a bed across the room from his own. Someone is laying in it. "Rivee!"

Gallagher kicks his linens off and stumbles out of bed, getting tangled in the blankets as he hurries across the room. The bed is empty. Linens jumbled together is all. He's lost her. He's lost Rivee. This is what he'd feared when she joined him in Mira's search. He never thought it would be Indra capturing them. Maybe a wraith attack or some other unknown beast threatening their lives, but never the Indra. And now he's lost her and is trapped in an Indran cell secured by machina magic.

Or *is* he trapped? He hasn't even checked the door.

Gallagher makes for the door with haste and notices his damaged fin feels off. Looking down, his heart sinks when the machina isn't there. His head snaps back and forth frantically, looking for the machina fin, and something tickles his cheek. With a frenzied hand, he swats at it, and his fingers tangle in a wire strung taught from ear to lip, followed by a sting like a skittle bite. A metallic taste fills his mouth. Carefully, he pulls at the wire, but it's fastened rather well, and laced through his lip.

He drops to the floor, quickly moving his focus past the machina on his face, to look beneath the beds and under the single table in the room. His fin is gone. He's lost his only means of becoming a warrior. *And* he's lost Rivee.

An overwhelming weight falls on him, anchoring him to the floor. The smooth, sterile floor. He'd be fine lying there until the Indra drag him away to do whatever it is they intend. He's failed.

Gallagher lies in his misery for a moment longer before his thoughts drift to Mira. Wherever she is, she's okay. He knows she is. She's not lying on the floor of an Indran cell. What would she think of him if she saw him now? She certainly wouldn't desire an elf who's given up, and for that reason he refuses to give up.

He has yet to check the door. Maybe he can escape, find Rivee, and retrieve his machina fin. Then flee this wretched flying landship. Yes. He's a warrior, and warriors overcome their doubts and fears. Warriors achieve their goals. And right now, Gallagher must escape his cell and locate Rivee. He presses off the ground and jumps to his fins.

As he reaches for the mechanism to open the door, it casually opens before him, and in walks an Indra: proud, confident, and short.

Gallagher stumbles backward. He's not sure why. The Indra are hardly intimidating by nature. He watches as the sky elf wanders over to the plain table and sits down, a scepter firmly in his grip.

The sky elf stares at him for a moment, looking him up and down, then focuses on his damaged fin. He gestures to the seat across from him. "Sit. Let's discuss the future of the De'wi, and the role expected of you."

His role? Are the Indra puppet masters seeking to control the De'wi from above? What does that mean? The comment doesn't settle well. "Where is Rivee?" he asks. The Indra offers him a blank look. "You know, the short one…" he says, holding out a hand parallel to the floor. "…she came with me."

"Who?" His tone is almost mocking.

Gallagher isn't sure if he's serious or not, and it intensifies his anger. "Why have you locked me in a cell? We have done nothing. Let us flee your realm and get back to our own. I don't believe either of our races intended for us to be here."

"Intended…" The Indra shakes his head. It looks odd with how his skin folds into itself and hides any form of a chin, like a wadded linen twisting back and forth. "But grateful, yes." His wadded linen stretches up and down with a knowing grin above it.

"Where. Is. Rivee Rayfin?" Gallagher's voice rises.

"Don't escalate the situation, young elf." He taps the butt of his staff on the hard floor. The sound bounces off the walls of the hollow chamber.

"I only want to know where you've taken my companion. Where is she?"

"She is in good care. Trust me."

"Trust you?" Gallagher mocks. "How could I? You've sewed wires to my face and locked me in a cell." Or *is* he locked in? He has yet to check the door, and he watched the Indra walk right in and sit down. There were no latches or clicks to be heard.

Gallagher rushes to the door, nearly slamming into it, and tries the handle. The door doesn't move the slightest as if it isn't a door at all, but a wall. Gallagher rams his shoulder into it. Nothing. He continues ramming with no effect.

"That will do you no good," the Indra states calmly. "You're looking less and less like our champion, and more like a crude Ebisu come to terrorize our landship. Come. Sit down and we'll discuss this further."

Gallagher's head snaps toward the Indra.

"Ah, so I have your attention." He straightens the collar of his jacket with an arrogant smile.

"Ebisu?" Gallagher doesn't know what to ask. Too much unfolds around him. Too many questions arrive and flee from his mind just as quickly. Are the Indra and Ebisu at odds? Why would the Indra require a champion with all their machina magic? What does Gallagher have to do with any of this? And where is Rivee, for Ceto's sake?

Gallagher crosses his arms and plants his fins shoulder width apart. Chest puffed and chin up, he says, "Until I see my companion, I will not discuss anything with you."

"Oh, I'm sorry, my elven friend, you will not be making any demands." The arrogant grin doesn't leave his face.

Gallagher has no interest in discussing the matter further. "Then I will find her myself."

With a deadly glare, he charges the sky elf, who sits calmly, shaking his head and wadded linen of a chin. The Indra's staff rises. A quick tap on Gallagher's shoulder as he charges, and he falls to the ground, sliding to the feet of the short, pompous, sky elf.

13 RECONNAISSANCE TO RESCUE

Twilight has arrived. Just as Mira's father requested of her, she has prepared to set out on an expedition to uncover the secrets of the Ebisu who threaten them. Duty to her clan is engrained in her, and she cannot shed it away like a light outer garment on a humid day. Chasing after Gallagher would be selfish. And she already has her mother's word that the point-elves are on watch for Rivee's whereabouts. If she's with Gallagher, she's safe.

Warriors line the shore, each in an attentive stance with arms folded behind their backs. Mira stands before the three of them. She's not a typical leader within the Warrior's Guild, but today she will act as the chief of this squad. Their guild lacks ever since the waterspout hit, with many warriors gone missing and others in recovery—which she assumes is why she was chosen to lead this mission—lack of reliable leadership. Now, she's one of the more experienced and proven with the single stone she's *earned*. Though, she doesn't wear it today, and she'll likely never wear it again.

"The lot of you have been selected personally by me, not because you are the best warriors in the guild, but because I thought you would perform better together than any group of individual warriors." Mira swims down the line. The purples and oranges of the twilit evening cloud cover glimmers off the ocean's surface creating a mild silhouette of the elves she speaks to. "You're here because you're respectful—"

"Hmph… Hardly," Tanniv interrupts, followed by a wink.

"Tanniv! C'mon…" Veras speaks out of turn. "She might be a youngkin in your seventy-plus-year-old eyes, but she's proven. She wears a stone. We address her as chief."

"Where is it?" Haltuk asks. "Where's your circlet?"

She knew she'd have to address this eventually, but so soon. She runs a hand through her hair, brushing her fingers past where her circlet should be. "I know it is not customary, but I wanted us to all be equals as we set out on a journey unlike any other." It's the truth, what she's saying, but she ignores the fact that she discarded the stone in anger. "We need to be a team. We need to have unity. And although I will be leading this expedition, we are all equals."

"Jelly spittle, Mira. What did you do with it?" Tanniv asks.

Her eyes narrow. They don't need to know. Not only is she embarrassed by her unchecked emotions, but she willingly tossed away an undeserved stone and self-proclaimed she was blighted. Now she takes a group of warriors on a mission to spy the Ebisu. Something that has never been done before. It would only display weakness if they knew.

"That doesn't matter." She takes a hard stance, shoulders square, hands laced behind her back, and fins shoulder-width apart. A stern voice comes forth. "What matters is that we are set to go on a journey beyond our borders. Beyond the outposts to places we've never seen." She remains solid, but inside, a flutter of excitement wants to erupt. "Perils exist out there equal to, if not worse than the leviathan's that earn us stones. What I'm saying is that the stones are irrelevant out there because their measure of a warrior are nothing compared to what we'll encounter."

Veras' eyes grow wide, Tanniv smirks, and Haltuk narrows his gaze. "How do you know this if we're going beyond explored terrain?" the skeptic asks.

"Haltuk…" Mira pauses for a moment. He is a strong warrior. Firm in his decisions and quick to react. He's solid. But he's wary of what he does not know. It is another reason she chose him. He will question her decisions where the other two will not. He will hold her accountable. "…I know this because a waterspout tossed me into the wild." Her eyes narrow and she leans into him. Her voice lowers into something dark and menacing. "And in that brief absence, I encountered creatures far worse than any sea demon in the canyon. Creatures that use guile to strangle the life out of you. Creatures that can create waves in the ocean more powerful than any waterspout." She pulls back and calms her intensity. "Plus, we're on a mission to track down the Ebisu. Everything about this journey is beyond our teaching."

All three of them stare in silence. Their minds pondering the adventures they could endure. Tanniv has a mellow aura about him, but the other two look petrified.

"You'll keep me alive, chief?" Haltuk rubs a hand through his hair. The expression on his face is anything but excited.

"I promise, Haltuk Coradrin." Mira can only hope the tone of her voice doesn't betray her emotions. She fears for each one of their lives. "I will keep you all alive," she continues. "Although we have fellow clansmen that were abducted by those Ebisu scum, we are not going into battle. It's just reconnaissance." Her eyes settle back on Haltuk who looks the most concerned with venturing into the unknown.

"Why not a rescue if there are De'wi to be rescued?" Haltuk questions.

"Elder's orders. If they wanted them dead, they wouldn't have carried them away. We must understand our enemy."

"Of course you'll keep the other two alive, chief," Tanniv responds. "Me, on the other hand. I'll decide my own fate but thank you for your consideration."

Mira rolls her eyes at him. "Yaris, daggers, and any other trusted armaments equipped?"

"Check." The warriors say in unison.

"Spice rations stowed away?"

"Check."

"Armor fit and effective?" She gently stabs the leather breastplate of each warrior as she walks down the line. All respond as she does.

"Are you ready?" she asks with a burst of adrenaline.

"Hold!" a voice is heard from behind her, cutting off her attempt to build her team's enthusiasm.

It's her father. She was hoping to escape before having to talk to him again. She waves a hand at her team gesturing for them to stand idle while she deals with the Elder. Technically, they are *his* to command, so she cuts off her father before he gets too close. She also doesn't want the others to overhear their conversation.

"Elder Rayfin," she addresses him formally.

"So, you remain a part of the Warrior's Guild, I see. You haven't thrown that away, yet. Unless you're stealing away our clan members to start a rebellion." He scorns her.

Part of her wants to entertain his snide comment. "Is there something you need, Elder? If not, we have a long journey ahead of us."

"I had a different party in mind." His frown deepens. "What is it about these stoneless warriors that have your attention?"

"You've already pinpointed it, Elder." Mira stands tall and confident, unwavering with her decision of warriors.

"Stoneless," he repeats. He ponders her words, staring the warriors up and down.

"They have everything to prove, and they're a balanced team."

"How so?" Elder Rayfin turns his attention back to her.

"Tanniv Windstalker is fearless. Not in a reckless sort of way, but he's not of the mind to think too far ahead. It allows for impulse and instinct to own his strategies—if they can be called such. Veras Elreid tends to think too far ahead. It can petrify his decision making, but his mind works out scenarios the rest of us wouldn't fathom. And Haltuk Coradrin is a skeptic by nature. He will challenge all our decisions. Together, they are the finest of warriors and would outperform even a five-stone commander." Mira holds eye contact, unblinking.

Elder Rayfin returns the challenge. They stare for an awkward moment before her father speaks up. "You don't have to do this, Mira."

"Let me be clear, Elder Rayfin. I do this for Veras, and Tanniv, and for Haltuk. I do this for the guild and for Alariya. I do this for the clan and our clanmates that were taken. Because I owe it to all of them. I'm not setting out on this life-endangering mission because my Elder requested it of me. And I will not stand down now. Not even if my father begged it of me. It would be very… *blighted* of me to do such a thing. It is my fate to seek new horizons, father. You have always known this. You only refuse to acknowledge it."

Her father grunts at her insolence. "So be it."

"Am I free to depart, Elder?"

Another grunt from her father with a begrudging nod. "Watch out for storms, Mira. Especially those that reach from the heavens to beneath the waves."

She hardly acknowledges the warning, taking it as an insult because of her recent encounter with a waterspout. She turns her back to him to return to her party.

"And Mira!" Her father calls to her. She halts and stands idle with a slight tilt of her head, but she doesn't look at him. "Don't get lost."

"Explorers don't get lost, Elder. They're cartographers. They start their journeys lost." They could be the last words she speaks to her father. Cold. Distant. If there were any onlookers who didn't know their relationship, they'd think they were commander and warrior.

She walks away, back to her party, thoughts tossing around in her head like a maelstrom. Why did he ask her to handle this quest? Will she return? Will she ever see Gally again? Or Rivee? She wants to stay. She wants to search for her missing clanmates, and for Gally, but she owes her life to the guild. She will never be able to atone for Alariya's death or for Rivee's injury. And because of her mistakes, she owes full determination and self-sacrifice to the Warrior's Guild. She won't accept anything less.

Mira stands attentively before her party, and they all straighten their posture. "Every elf is prepared?" she asks. "You've said your goodbyes to your loved ones?"

Each of them nods as she looks at each one individually.

"And you?" Haltuk narrows his gaze on her, then looks over her shoulder where her father stands deliberately at a distance.

Mira grunts something ineloquent. "Do try to keep up. Let's go." She leaps into the air without hesitation.

The four elves swim high past the dreadful ruins of their leveled colony, then above the kelp forest to the east, away from the waning and diluted sunlight. Some of the kelp pickers are back to work despite the chaos of the aftermath, heedlessly laboring to get back to something normal, even at these late hours. Gallagher, obviously, is not one of them, but she cannot take her eyes off the forest, regardless.

A small border of coral and rock crops covers the landscape just before it abruptly climbs toward the knuckles. The cloud cover is lower today, hiding more of the Morshine Peaks than usual. One of the easternly outposts comes into view high atop the bulwark. It wasn't destroyed in the storm like the rest of the colony. Mira swings an arm forward, pointing toward the structure as she shifts her direction straight for it.

The outpost stands tall on six legs crafted from the largest and longest driftwood available. Each of the legs is easily ten times her height, and she finds her thoughts wandering to the land they come from. The Elders say the forests surrounding the knuckles produce the driftwood. Although Mira's experience with trees is lacking, she has never seen any as tall as these. The forest canopies she encountered in the Morshine Peaks weren't as large, and the mangroves she witnessed from a distance, too far to make clear of anything, didn't look like the source. She'd rather believe they're the skeletal remains of the goliath she encountered. Wouldn't that be a discovery.

Atop the tall legs sits a simple round structure with a pointed roof crafted from lighter driftwood, mud, and canvases. It houses two sleeping quarters and a common space within, accompanied by a wraparound observation deck. The point-elf manning the outpost greets them upon arrival and shatters Mira's wandering thoughts.

"Not often we get company outside of shift changes," she says. She's a hardened elf of a few hundred years. She was a warrior once but stepped away honorably after enduring one too many battle scars from the leviathans. She's a retired two-stone warrior who felt her experiences would create hesitations, and in turn be a danger to the guild. She's a proud point-elf and takes her role seriously to continue her protection of the clan in a different way. Two dark braids drape to one side of her face, and the rest is pulled into a tight tail. Her conch shell is secured by steel links wrapped around her neck. Mira has no doubt she doesn't let it leave her side, even when off duty.

"Saheela." Mira greets her with a warrior's grasp and a pat on the back. Despite the many years out of the trench, her grip remains firm. Mira admires the elf. Not because of her stones, but because of her ability to step away from the guild and still find a way to be of service to her clan. "Can you point us in the direction of the Ebisu? Did you see them come or go?"

"Aye, I wasn't stationed here when they arrived, but I hear the wraith swarm caught Cranton with his pants down. The young warrior is being too hard on himself if you ask me. The Ebisu haven't been seen in generations. And I hear they swept right into the kelp forest unnoticed. My bet, they swam around the knuckles and right up onto shore. No one was looking for 'em. Never again, though. The lazy eye will be banished. Our eyes will see everything."

"Did you see them go?"

Her lips flatten and she shakes her head. "No. I'm sorry. If you're willing to trust the point-elves' senses still, I've been getting an ominous feeling from that region yonder." She pats a flat palm to her chest then points to the horizon.

Dark skies loom in that direction, but it's also because the light has fled the east to allow for night.

"What's out there?" Mira asks.

"Too far to see. I couldn't tell you, but an everlasting gloom hangs over it. In all my years as a point-elf, I don't recall a ray of light shining down in that area. The storm is everlasting and unmoving. Odd."

"Just a hunch, then?"

"The ocean canyon meanders in that direction and the Ebisu came from that direction, so my instincts tell me if you follow the canyon, you'll find more Ebisu than you desire."

"A renowned elf once told me that disturbance in your gut is what will drive you to make good decisions. 'Follow that instinct,' he said." Mira places an arm on her shoulder. "Saheela, your instincts are good enough clue as any. I trust they'll guide us in the right direction. Thank you."

"My pleasure, young warrior." Saheela cocks her head with a disgruntled look. "Wait!" She eyes her discerningly. "You mean to go there. What in Ceto's name would drive you to do such a thing?"

"Elder Rayfin's orders," Mira replies. "We cannot sit idle any longer. And *we* are the lucky bunch."

Saheela frowns. "A stoneless bunch, perhaps. No offense, but between the four of you there is only one stone." Saheela looks Mira up and down, searching for it. "Where is it?"

Mira turns away as she rolls her eyes, so the respected elf doesn't see it. She pretends to search the horizon. "This mission doesn't require the ranks of stones, Saheela. This mission requires trust. Determination. Stealth. The leviathans and the honor we take from their demise is not a test of what we will endure out there, I'm afraid."

"And the Elder chose you four?"

Mira turns to face her with a sour look. "Thank you for your guidance, Saheela. It was helpful. But it's clear we'll have to endure without your vote of confidence. We shall be on our way."

Saheela grabs onto Mira's shoulder. "My apologies, Mira. This journey is beyond my reasoning. I only fear for your safety. Be careful. And do return home."

Mira musters a smile on one side of her mouth. "It is my duty to the clan. I—*we* will return."

The young warrior elf turns to face her party. "You heard her. We're headed to the Ocean Realm into an area that doesn't see the light of day. Everyone as excited as I am?" She smiles, half facetiously because she understands no sane elf would be excited, and half genuine because she truly is eager to go. "I don't know how far or long we will be away. Does every elf have a hefty ration of Tears to last the journey?"

Tanniv feigns a sob without real tears. "Yes, chief." He whimpers and sniffles and wipes his cheeks with his knuckles.

Mira rolls her eyes at him. "You're an idiot."

The other two don't give a confident response. If only they had access to that massive crop she saw west of the colony. It would take a week's journey, maybe more to make the swim. It was clear out in the ocean on the way to Rhizo Isle. She has already taken a day to rest. Time will not allow it. With the looming threat of the Ebisu, there is no telling when they will return. Her mission is of utmost importance.

"Wait here!" Saheela says from behind her. "I have a small ration. It will be of better use beyond our borders than to watch them." She swiftly disappears into the outpost and returns a quick moment later. She hands a small kelp-woven pouch to Mira.

"You've given us too much, Saheela. Again, thank you." Mira accepts the Blue Tears. "Err…but I have one more request."

"Of course, young warrior. Name it."

"Do you happen to have any weather-proof parchment?"

Saheela cocks her head.

"I cannot let this excursion go to waste. I expect to return with more than just information regarding the Ebisu."

"Very well. I happen to keep my daily logs, and a personal journal of sorts. I can spare a few pages."

She disappears into her quarters and returns promptly for the second time, handing Mira a bound roll of parchment. Mira hands it to Veras.

"This is yours," she says to him with authority. "I trust you have ink."

"Yes, Mira. Almost always." He pats the pack hanging over his shoulder, then tucks the roll of parchment away.

"Good." She turns back to Saheela. "Thank you, again."

"No, I must thank you." Saheela embraces Mira with a pat on the back. "And I will keep a pointed eye out for your return."

"Warriors! Our journey into the unknown begins." She turns to stand at the edge of the outpost looking upon the wild. She takes a deep inhale and slow exhale, not to calm fearful nerves, but to suppress her excitement.

Her three companions stand by her side, all marveling at the dark horizon where they have never been and are about to go. Vast terrain separates them and their destination. Wild terrain. All are equipped with yaris stretching across their backs and enough dried meats and flatbread to last. Should they fall short of food, they are all capable of scavenging or fishing, and they have a decent ration of Blue Tears to power through their shortcomings. They will be fine.

Mira takes the lead and leaps from the observation deck swimming in the direction Saheela pointed. It's a long way off and may take days, maybe weeks to find the Ebisu, but whatever it takes, they will endure.

She dives low, cutting through the jagged protrusions of the rocky bulwark to drop down to the land below. There will be less visibility, but they too are less visible. The warriors follow her closely.

The land is filled with groves of kelp, seagrass meadows, and ganderberry bushes. The coral, so common around their colony, soon becomes a rare sight.

A field of garden eels can be seen in the distance, only their vertical wormlike shape visible in the dim light. They follow the shoreline, waiting to dive into the Ocean Realm until they absolutely must.

"Chief, wait," Veras calls from behind her.

She stops swimming and plants her fins on the sandy shore. The outpost they just left behind is hardly visible, only seen because she knows it's planted atop the knuckles that can be seen for leagues. "What is it, Veras?" The others find ground and huddle around.

"I... Well... This is the farthest any of us have ever journeyed away from the colony, Mira. Right there." He points to a robust bushel of coral. "It's the last coral we may see for leagues. We're headed into the unknown, and... well... I wanted to take a moment." He breathes a heavy sigh.

"He's right," Haltuk agrees. "This is new territory. We're now explorers more than we are warriors."

Mira cannot resist a smile. She has excelled so well at hiding her desires, but to hear Haltuk say it out loud, her smile explodes onto her face. "And we will be the best explorers the Morshine Isle has ever known."

"Aye, you're damn right we will," Tanniv boasts.

Haltuk pats Veras on the back, who doesn't look as excited.

"Veras," Mira starts, not really knowing what to say to ease her friend's fearful mind. "If there is one thing I can assure you, we will claim new experiences, we will discover new life, and we will encounter new dangers. It will all be worth it. We *will* survive the unknown because we have each other. We will share the knowledge we gain, but the experiences you claim... they will be yours. They will be mine. That is what you need to hold onto. Right here." She pats her chest.

"How can you be so confident we'll return?" Haltuk questions her.

Mira's gaze shifts to her fins as she digs her toes into the sand. Mira knows only one way to reply to that question. She pulls her eyes from the ground to look at Haltuk. "Make your decisions with this." She points to her temple. "Follow this." She rubs her gut. "And let this drive you." She pats the left side of her chest. "Do that, especially in the face of danger, and this will take care of the rest." With a heavy fist, she pounds the right side of her chest. "You will return home. I can assure you."

It's just another iteration of their common greeting: heart, strength, mind, and soul, but it leaves her companions pondering her words.

Tanniv digs into his food stores and retrieves a slice of flatbread. Mira gives him a funny look. "What?" He bites down on it. "It'll get soggy as soon as we cross borders." Dry crumbs spew from his mouth as he speaks. "The ocean'll ruin it." He holds up the thin cracker.

Mira shakes her head at him, then her eyes spring open. "Speaking of the ocean destroying things, Veras." She turns to him. "That parchment should be good for sky, land, or sea. They only give the best to the point-elves. The Elder's don't want any excuses for them not jotting down their daily logs."

He pats the satchel at his hip. "Yes, chief." The other two look at each other with confusion.

"Okay, all set?" she says. She receives nods from each of them. "Then, let us explore." A smile reaches from ear to ear. She turns and steps across the threshold into unexplored territory.

They carry on swimming for days, stopping for rest occasionally, starting up fires during the daylight hours only to cook what they've hunted, and taking turns keeping watch at night as the others sleep. None of them sleep well, though. Not out here in the wild where not one of them has experience. They don't discuss it, but they all feel it—the weight of the unknown.

Tanniv flexes often and pretends as if he's the protector of the green-bloods. And Mira finds smiles beneath every overturned rock. But they don't sleep well at night.

Mira stands watch on this night, and a new day is almost upon them. The clouds overhead show signs of light as her companions begin to stir. Their camp sits between several large boulders on the shoreline. Enough privacy to evade predators, but not enough to evade something with intelligence.

"Shall we?" she asks to anyone listening.

"A morning bite would suffice before we head out, I do think." Tanniv starts digging into his pack.

Mira allows her team to feed themselves. All three consume a fish roasted over the simmering coals from the evening prior. Mira requests a small portion of flatbread from Tanniv, who's hesitant to share. Once they fill their bellies, tidy up their gear, and straighten their attire, they set out for another day of exploration.

The terrain is much of the same out here in the wild, but Mira cannot keep her sight straight ahead. Although she swims in a direct line, her eyes meander across the open air, the terrain, and down into the depths of the ocean. Thus far, their exploration has been downright uneventful and boring. Mira holds onto the excitement of the possibilities, though it is but a hope.

"At what point should we tread the waters?" Haltuk asks.

Mira doesn't know. It's one thing to see the vast terrain from high above in an outpost, and another to travel it. She doesn't remember seeing any land-marks that would indicate when they should dive toward the canyon. "We could travel the rim of the canyon the remainder of the way, I suppose. But we'd lose our vocals."

"And our flatbread would go bad," Tanniv interjects with a frown.

"There are better meals in the sea," Haltuk replies, dismissing the bland snack.

Mira's lips flatten at the comment, her bitterness toward hunting revealed. She eats meat, as she understands the nutrition it provides, but taking lives is where she stumbles. It's not something she speaks openly about. It's not warrior-like.

"Don't worry, chief. We won't let you eat soggy flatbread. Haltuk will land you some meals." Veras must have noticed her distasteful expression. He understands her. "You know your unwillingness to kill helpless prey will benefit you one day," he adds.

"No need to kill what isn't a resource." She denies his accusations. She can't have them thinking their chief is soft-handed.

"Just saying… Good fortune comes to those who spare a life. Those who are rightfully merciful and have the best of intentions. That's all."

She sighs. "Thank you for the good fortunes, Veras. I'll keep that in mind."

Haltuk shakes his head. "Mira can spear her own fish. That's what the back of her yari is for." He holds up his own yari and rubs his thumb along the side of the spearhead. "They don't make these things double-ended for nothing." He thrusts it back and forth with focus.

"You're full of jelly spittle, Hal." Tanniv punches him in the shoulder.

Mira looks to the waves, getting her mind back on task. "We ought to check to make sure the canyon is still within reach. I'm not sure if it goes on forever or how far…" Her words peter off as her thoughts wander into the vast-ness of Solaria. *Could it go on forever? How far would that be?*

"Chief!" Veras' voice shatters her wandering mind. "I'll dive in to check." His hand swoops in a diving motion. "No harm in sending a scout. In fact, it'll benefit us. And aside from you, I'm the quickest." He makes a swooshing sound as his hand darts forward.

Mira's convinced, yet disappointed *she* didn't think of it. But that's why she recruited Veras. He's always looking ahead. "Yes. Yes. Please. We will continue at the same pace. I trust our stoneless bunch will be easy to spot roaming the shoreline." She waves a hand for him to proceed.

Veras dives toward the ocean currents and disappears into the shallows with hardly a splash. The other three continue a steady swim toward the unknown, following the shoreline.

It doesn't take long for the thoughtful elf to return. Water drips from his long, brown hair and sprays them all when he whips it behind his head. "Err...sorry." His face reddens as he pulls it into a tightly bound tail and squeezes to desaturate it.

"So?" Mira stands tall with her hands on her hips and a tapping fin. "How'd your parchment hold up?"

Tanniv and Haltuk both look at each other with perplexity, again. "What's this about parchment?" Tanniv asks. "What's so important about the parchment?" The two await some answers, arms folded across their bodies.

"We've decided to document our journey. Because the Elders offer so little knowledge in this area, we are taking it upon ourselves to cartograph the land." She looks to Veras. "Oh! And be sure to take notes of anything interesting we encounter. You know, like a grendelin."

All three offer her strange looks at that comment.

"Never mind. Just you wait..." She knows nobody will believe the legend is true until they see it with their own eyes. Nobody except the Elders seem to know the truth of it.

"And what of the parchment?" Haltuk gets back to the question. "You intend to map out *everything* we see? What if we swim for weeks, leagues upon leagues? Do you have enough parchment?"

"Do you have enough flatbread for that?" Veras jests, then turns his attention to the beach. He locates a large, flat rock, and pulls out a reed of a rush plant and a small jar of ink from his satchel. "I'll have to make small scribblings, I suppose, if we intend to adventure for weeks."

Mira cannot resist a smile as the cork pops from his ink jar.

He puts reed to parchment and starts marking out his sightings. "Here's the outpost and knuckles for reference." He points to a small circle and jagged scribblings drawn on the left side. "The Morshine Peaks to the north." His head pops up from the map-in-progress to ensure they're still there before marking them on the parchment. "The canyon meanders through here." His reed squiggles to the east. "I counted the distance in strokes from canyon to shoreline, so it's a rough estimate, but distance aside, I witnessed no end to it. An aerial view might do us better. With the canyon's edge in the shallows, I assume it can be seen from the sky. My best guess: it curls around to the eastern side of the island, and that's where we'll find our Ebisu." He stops his markings with only what he has witnessed, not allowing guesswork to make it to his documentation.

"Any signs of Ebisu?" Mira asks from above his left shoulder.

"No signs of any Ebisu where I mustered the courage to look over the edge. The waters are dark. The only thing I saw were fish and sea plants aplenty."

Mira's brow hikes. "Anything unusual?"

"An octopus, I think." He shrugs. "Looked like tentacles, but it was hard to see."

"Interesting."

He cranes his neck from the map to look at her. "I don't see why this is important *or* interesting."

"I was attacked by an octopus only days ago," she says. "I didn't get a good look. It was a terrifying experience. We should inspect the waters to confirm if the same creature lurks within these shallows. We must know what dangers we're up against." She would love to see one while the diffused light shines above. "How about now?" she says with a sweeping arm falling on the ocean's surface. The others give her a confused look, expecting an explanation. "A dive into the shallows," she clarifies.

The others aren't convinced.

"Veras already said he saw no signs of the Ebisu," she adds. "In the daylight, when we can see, it does us no harm to swim the rim of the canyon as opposed to the shoreline."

The other three warriors remain silent. The sound of the wind brushing across the sand and through the rush is all that can be heard.

"Come. Let's go," she orders and leads the way.

"But my flatbread..." Tanniv whines behind her.

A slight shimmer moves across the surface, but otherwise, the ocean is clear as the air they breathe. That will change as they dive deeper into it, however. She pulls out her pouch of Blue Tears and places a small pinch on her tongue. Some elves will tuck it in their cheek or even beneath their tongue, but Mira prefers the tip of her tongue where she can savor the sweet flavor of the bioluminescent spice. She closes her eyes and imagines the energy of the simple plant flowing through her. It works much more subtly than that, and she won't notice the effects until her vision is clear in the depths of the ocean and her breathing is light. Without the Blue Tears, they would be prey for the smallest guppies, let alone the sea demons lurking in the depths.

Mira waits for all the others to consume a ration of Blue Tears and ready themselves. Tanniv proceeds with stuffing his mouth full of more flatbread.

"Don't be wasteful," he says with crumbs spewing out.

Mira and Veras roll their eyes and shake their heads. Haltuk pulls out his own loaf of bread.

"What's that?" Tanniv spills more crumbs out of his mouth.

Haltuk's lips curl into his cheeks. "A departing gift from Crumbaker."

"Is that..." Tanniv lurches forward to get a better look as Haltuk unwraps the small fist-sized loaf of bread. "How'd you... Why *you*? A loaf of Crumbaker's crumble cake!"

"I told her about the journey. She managed to salvage some from the wreckage of her bakery and figured it would suit us just as well as the harvest team, since their journey stopped before it began. It was the only loaf she had, however."

Tanniv ogles it, then waves it off like he doesn't care. "Meh...A loaf for an oaf."

"Not much, but a sweet delight before a taste of night will do us well, I'd say." Haltuk crumbles the small loaf into four sections. "Here you are, chief." He hands the first portion to Mira.

She waves a hand to it. "Tanniv is drooling over it. He can have my share."

"Seriously!" he replies.

She laughs with a reassuring nod. "Be quick. We don't know how long or far we must journey."

"Yes, chief," they all reply, and all devour the sweet crumble cake laced with Blue Tears.

The team of four make for the ocean waters with a leap into the air and a dive into the shallows. The pressure differential from air to water is subtle, but what is noticed most when diving into the deep blue is the temperature change. It's cooler than the air and gets colder the deeper they dive. The taste is also drastic, from nothing to salty, but Mira rarely opens her mouth within the ocean.

Mira remains close to the surface until she sees the canyon, inspecting the terrain all the while. She comes to a halt, wading beneath the ocean's surface. Something isn't right.

The others stop beside her, all four wading in the shallows. Mira points to her eyes with two fingers, then points to the canyon, signaling a gander. A familiar glow emanates from the canyon. It's the same glow the Blue Tears emit— a bluish-green radiance. It's familiar in this sense only. Everything else about it is unusual. Its location, for instance, and its intensity is much more brilliant. The entire rim of the canyon glows.

Wary of what they'll find, all four warrior elves slowly approach, and plant their fins onto the grainy ocean floor before they peek over the edge.

Veras looks to each of them with a shrug of the shoulders. If they could speak underwater, Mira knows he would have a barrage of questions before allowing them to proceed. The four of them stand idle, shoulder to shoulder, staring at the glowing canyon, but not so close they can see into the depths. Mira is in thrall to the novelty of the moment, but she fears she presents too much unnecessary risk for her squad. Finally, Tanniv steps forward.

"Pst…" Mira tries to speak but blows bubbles instead. She grabs his attention before he gets too close. She presses her palm in a downward motion for him to get low and she kneels to the ground herself. He drops to his knees and creeps toward the canyon's edge. Mira follows, and the other two get in line right behind her.

On knees and elbows, the four of them peek over the ocean shelf. Even if they could speak, not one of them would in this moment.

Leviathans swim in a line against the gentle current flowing through the canyon. They travel east, the same direction Mira and her squad are headed. Ushering them are a group of dark elves, hardly visible within the depths aside from the reflection of the leviathan's light traps and their own augmentations. The Ebisu are ornamented with glowing breastplates and two-prong tridents. The blades glow the same as their chests, both obviously augmented with the essence of Blue Tears.

Their own clan infuses the spice into steel like these elves have done, and it adds a particular element that enhances the durability and sharpness of the blade. Though, within the De'wi clan, only three-stone elves are awarded this type of weapon, whereas it would seem standard issue amongst the Ebisu.

Mira pushes away from the ledge and stays low, crouching on her fins. The others follow her lead. She points up to the surface where they can have a clear conversation.

Just as Mira is about to press off the ocean floor, several glowing tridents emerge from the canyon. The Ebisu rapidly circle around them. Hoping the others will follow suit, she leaps upward with a swift beat. She's halfway to the surface before she looks back. Three of the Ebisu are on her tail, and the remainder surround her companions.

"Sht..!" Bubbles spill from her mouth as she attempts to curse at the blasted situation. She cannot leave her companions behind.

A swift somersault in the water, and she's rapidly torpedoing toward her three pursuers. A moment of confusion sends them scrambling out of the way, and she darts right between them to join her companions on the ocean floor.

With a few hand signals she gets them all to form a tight circle with their backs to each other. A half dozen Ebisu surround them. Mira and her companions wait for the Ebisu to make a move, slowly circling, yaris in hand, and keeping their fins on the move, always at the ready.

Every dark elf stands a head taller than the De'wi warriors. The males are even taller. Tanniv, who is the tallest of her companions, comes to the shoulders of the shortest female. Their breastplates are comprised of a thick metal with an iridescent glow emanating from a central insignia of three teardrops. Much sturdier than the leathers the De'wi adorn. Their features are dark and menacing. Long, dark hair, pulled tight into a tail. Flesh darker than the De'wi's and bulging with muscles. The females are a tad softer without as many striking contours, but intimidating, nonetheless. These dark elven warriors are too much for her team to overcome. If they stand and fight, they will lose.

A blue trident jabs at them, and chaos erupts. Haltuk deflects the attack. Mira, gripping the chain attached to the butt of her yari, sends hers harpooning toward the nearest assailant. It's knocked down with ease, and she retracts it just as fast. More tridents jab at their tight pack, all deflected. Tanniv, Haltuk, and Veras all strike, whirling their blades this way and that without much effect.

Mira nudges Tanniv and signals for him to lead the others to the surface. Mira is quick. She can keep them all entertained while her companions flee, then escape once they're above the surface.

Her three companions push off the ocean floor, straight to the glimmering surface above. As soon as their fins are above her shoulders, which happens in the blink of an eye, her yari extends and swings into a whirlwind of fury. The Ebisu all leap back to avoid being struck. One of them pushes off to chase her companions, but Mira quickly redirects her yari, striking that Ebisu in the thigh. Crimson stains the waters around him and halts his pursuit.

Multiple Ebisu lunge toward her and she moves to break free of their encompassing attack, shooting upward in the same fashion her companions did. A hand grabs onto her ankle and ratchets her back down. Her yari flies in the direction of the Ebisu holding onto her and she breaks free, but multiple tridents point at her throat, close enough to draw blood should she struggle any further. Mira is trapped.

A yari that is not her own knocks away several of the tridents from above. Haltuk has returned to save her, and he's done enough for her to break free. She pushes off the ocean bed once again and jets to the surface.

Mira kicks and kicks in a rhythmic motion, breaking away from the dark elves. She doesn't see which way Haltuk went, but she cannot stop to find out with several Ebisu on her heels. Her speed sends her through the ocean surface and into the air without a skip in her motion.

Can she trust that Haltuk escaped to safety? She needs to find a place to hide. She can outswim the Ebisu, and even lead them away from her companions, but for how long? She doesn't know where they fled to.

A rock crop and a thick grove of kelp lie ahead. She swims toward it.

Her maneuvers are swift, but it's like swimming through the bristles of a hairbrush. There's only so much speed available. Curling her body this way and that, she cannot see anything aside from more kelp. The Ebisu and their glowing tridents are gone, but so is her squad.

A few moments pass before her courage allows her to flee the cover of the kelp. When she does, she witnesses the six Ebisu wading at the shoreline. Two restrain Haltuk as he squirms to break free. A thwack from a trident on the back of his skull and his body goes limp. Mira cringes where she remains mostly hidden from sight.

The four not dealing with Haltuk weakly scan their surroundings. It doesn't take long for them to turn and dive into the shallows. The two carrying Haltuk pull him beneath the waves and disappear back into the Ocean Realm.

Mira hunkers into a crevice between two large boulders, unsure if they will return for her. Her breathing is heavy, eyes wide, and muscles tense.

After a long moment, Mira breathes easier, but her gut is tied into a knot. She's safe for now. Her companions, however…

She cringes and squeezes her eyes shut. How could she let this happen? She led them right into the Ebisu's grasp when they were supposed to remain unseen. Eyes beneath the water, that is all, and she allowed Haltuk to be captured.

She remains hidden within the rock crop pondering her next move. The Elder gave direct orders that she is not to attempt a rescue, but that order was given under a different pretense. The circumstances have too quickly shifted from reconnaissance to rescue. She only knows how to swim fast. She knows nothing about rescue missions, but this is where she's at. She must locate her other companions and find a way to save them.

Mira balls her fists as tight as she can to refrain from yelling.

14 A DEFEATING VICTORY

The white walls taunt him. Pure. Clean. Perfection. Nothing like his captors. Gallagher stares at them day and night, drifting off to sleep occasionally, but not for long periods. He only sleeps out of necessity. He would be planning an escape and Rivee's rescue if he knew more about the facility outside his white cell. They bind his hands behind his back and bag his head when they take him to the latrine. Apparently, they don't want him tainting their white room. The thought *has* crossed his mind. Childish it may be, he'd like to punish them, but he'd also be punishing himself. He's the one confined here, and he'd prefer to hold onto dignity as long as he can.

He lies on the floor in the middle of the white room. The three squares high on the wall are blue right now. When darkness falls, they'll morph into a deep purple, then black. They're no longer windows. All that can be seen are the colors of the sky, but even that has lost meaning. How many times have they changed color? Aside from morning or evening, time is lost.

Regular meals are delivered. Meager, but sufficient. They don't torture, aside from confining him to this mentally draining cell. They only want his cooperation, and it seems they'll leave him here for eternity until they get it.

The door to his cell clicks.

Gallagher lies on the ground without a care. He tried to ambush them once as they entered, but the door is charged with an energy that sent him flying. The pain from the energy-burst he can withstand, but he's not fond of that falling sensation—moving through the air without control. It feels like his insides are twisting and morphing, then it vanquishes as soon as he hits the ground.

In walks one of his captors. He's a portly Indra. Though, most of them are. He has a conical shaped head, pointed ears sticking out like shoulder canopies, and flabs of skin in lieu of a neck folding into a round, bulging body, all plopped atop skinny peg legs. Gallagher is surprised he can walk. Looking at the Indra upside down from his place on the floor, Gallagher is of the mind to poke him to see if his top-heavy figure will topple over.

Their machina has kept him from being violent, and it has kept him breathing. The wire on his face is a more advanced version of the breathing apparatus Brunswick had given him. Without the use of their machina, he may not be able to survive within this realm.

Any escape attempt he has mustered has led to their scepters rendering him unconscious. The magic lies within the conches atop their meticulous and intricately designed metal staffs. The first sign of aggression, and a touch from that conch knocks him out. Gallagher is out of his element. Never, in all his days of training solo, would he have thought he'd be confined to an Indran cell, unable to swim, and so easily put to bed with a stick. The least they could do is tuck him in, but he's always left in a lump on the floor. It is the worst of conditions for a De'wi warrior. Not that he is one.

The Indra stands over him. His feet, covered with shoes as Brunswick labeled them, stomp down beside his head, and the bottom of his staff thuds as he slams it against the white floor.

"Get up!" He pounds the staff against the floor a second time. "We're going to see your companion."

"Rivee Rayfin!" A burst of energy and sanity flood back into him. He rolls over and climbs to his fins.

The sky elf is rather casual standing before a warrior elf—a *blighted* warrior—who's nearly twice his size. They have too much trust in their machina.

With a swift kick of his fin, he knocks the Indra's staff loose, and takes it for himself. He pokes the sky elf with the conch end, but nothing happens. He pokes him again and the Indra stands poised, smirking at him.

Gallagher wants to swing the staff at him as any warrior would do. They don't poke their enemies like these Indra do. With the staff gripped in both hands, his arms tense, he's ready to strike.

But the Indra said they were going to see Rivee.

He can be an impulsive warrior, who is no warrior at all, or he can be a patient warrior. He hands the staff over to his captor.

"They only work with the elf they've been imprinted on. Come." He turns his back to Gallagher and walks to the door.

"No bag?"

"No bag." He taps the door with his conch, and it clicks and pops ajar for him to open the rest of the way with his hand.

"No bindings?"

The sky elf turns and looks at him from the open door. "No bindings." His face is stoic.

Gallagher is hesitant to follow. Why the sudden change in stature from prisoner to guest? And it's the first time they've mentioned seeing Rivee.

Two more Indra, both armed with scepters, step in behind him once he exits his cell. He looks at them with disdain and follows in behind the leading Indra. The corridors aren't as white as the cell he's held in. Metallic portals frame the hall with bright white machina torches lining the ceiling. It's unnatural, but a welcomed change to what he's been experiencing.

A few stretches of sterile corridor later and the two guards halt on either side of a door. The leading Indra opens it, and they step into another white room. One of the walls is made entirely of glass, black if you peer past the reflection of the white walls, and the room itself is tenfold the size of his cell. Height and width. On the other side of the glass, a substantial, looming figure waits in a dark cell.

"Is that—"

"You call them leviathans, yes," his captor cuts him off.

"You keep them alive?" Lines press across his forehead as he steps further into the room, both curious and rattled. "And above the clouds?"

"The Greybeards study them. Angler fish." He looks at Gallagher pensively. "It's where we've come up with the idea to bait you—not *you* in particular, but the De'wi. You all seem fascinated with their bioluminescent adornment."

"Bait…" Gallagher recalls his first incident with them. He wasn't aware they were targeting the De'wi. He thought they were merely fishing within the sea of clouds. There are other, more favorable catches they could land. Why De'wi?

"Yes, bait. Unfortunately, we only ever had one bite, but the elf got away."

The looming figure shifts, and Gallagher sees it now—the green glow of its light trap. They house a leviathan in a cell. "But wait… We were pulled in by a net. No bait. And the crowd who reeled us in was befuddled. They were as thoroughly confused by our presence as we were by theirs. I don't understand," he admits.

The Indra subtly shakes his head, but the flab of his chin amplifies it. "Yes. It would seem the anglers down at the piers are much better equipped and capable than those of us who were baiting the De'wi. They witnessed an unusual fish leaping from the sea of clouds, and you and your companion are what they reeled in. A mere happenstance that turned into the catch of a lifetime." A devious grin appears. "As we've been trying to tell you, we need your help." His face turns sour. "Although, I'm extremely reluctant with how much resistance you've shown thus far. You may not be our emissary."

"Why would I ever?" he almost shouts. "Emissary for the Indra? I would never betray the De'wi like that! What kind of warrior do you think I am?"

"A *blighted* warrior, to be sure." The sky elf glares at him, then down at his damaged fin. "Yes, we know much about your culture despite your attempts to remain hidden."

Gallagher has the urge to remove him of his staff and pummel him with it. It's one thing to be mocked by warriors from the guild—those who've earned their ranks—but to be looked down upon by a short, plump, and clearly lazy Indra flares his anger.

"How could you possibly expect me—" Gallagher starts but is quickly subdued with a tap of the conch.

An unknown amount of time passes, and his eyes flutter open, staring at a white ceiling. He's back within his white cell, his anger smoothed away. If only he would try to listen. Maybe it would get him somewhere other than these white walls of agony. They have Rivee, and they have his machina fin. If he is ever to get either of them back, he needs to do something different.

"Feeling better?" a voice asks.

Gallagher hops to his fins and find himself in the same room with the same Indra who rendered him unconscious. He's not in his typical white cell. "How long?"

"It's only been a few minutes."

A few *minutes*? His body feels reenergized. His mood is calm. "How?"

"Are you ready to listen?" the Indra asks with his arms folded across his body, staff still in hand.

Gallagher is slow to nod. He's not ready to cooperate but listening won't do any harm. He will listen to what the squatty elf has to say.

The sky elf walks across the room, moving closer to the glass wall and the leviathan behind it. Gallagher follows, hesitantly.

"I know your race of elves are fearful of the machina. We don't blame you for it or think lesser of you for it. It is embedded into your culture from eons of tradition."

"I'm not fearful of it," Gallagher interjects.

The Indra looks him up and down, then fixates on his damaged fin. "Clearly." He turns to face Gallagher. "Where did you get that machina fin you arrived with?"

Gallagher gives him a sidelong glance then turns his focus back on the leviathan. "I can't say." His mouth flattens.

"Understood. Loyalty." The Indra turns back to the glass wall. "An admirable trait, which you display with annoying tenacity, but I am not here to ask you to be disloyal. I am here to ask you to be an ally. The entire De'wi race, not just you. This unspoken truce we have needs to grow into something more. It needs to be nourished in order to thrive. I am here to wipe away any anger, mistrust, or hate the De'wi have for us, and I'm starting with you."

Gallagher lowers his brow. "Why me?"

"Well…" He gestures toward his fin with an open palm. "You're a fan of our machina? It was the connection we needed. Had you not arrived with it, we may have tossed you back beneath the clouds. Like I said, a catch of a lifetime."

"Brunswick…" Gallagher mutters under his breath. Was he in on this from the beginning? Did he offer Gallagher that machina knowing it would soften him to their culture. Gallagher thought he was a friend. A true ally between the races.

"A name. Very good." The Indra smirks.

Gallagher slipped. He doesn't know if Brunswick was being deceitful, and by the look on this Indra's face, Gallagher may have just put his life at risk. What has he done?

"Why do you need me? Why are you trying to build an alliance?" Gallagher asks. "What is it you want?"

"Blunt. Another good trait…if you're trying to hold others at a distance, acquaintances and kin alike. It doesn't make others feel welcome, you know."

"White cells don't make others feel welcome, either." He returns a glare.

"Enough. Solaria has encountered a shortage of Tears, as you may already know." The sky elf looks at him, silently studying Gallagher.

A shortage of Blue Tears? Gallagher would never know. It's not part of his daily life. His clan is limited to the crop within the canyon, but maybe that's why the Elders ration it the way they do. Maybe the rationing isn't because of how challenging it is to get, but because of how valuable it is.

"You don't know…" the Indra trails off and studies him a bit more. "Shortage might be…err…the wrong word. It is all a matter of perspective, I suppose. Another way to look at it is that our societies are outgrowing the supply. There is not enough to go around. And the leviathans you challenge to claim your share, they are not the only thing protecting the Tears, Brunswick. There are—"

"Gallagher," he interrupts, realizing he never gave his captors his own name. This Indra must have thought he was offering his own name when he said Brunswick's name.

The Indra looks at him skeptically and confused.

"My name is Gallagher."

"Ah…" A moment of understanding crosses him. "Helyer Elgary." He offers a hand to Gallagher.

Gallagher looks at it for a moment, unsure. Does this mean he's being cooperative, or is this just a customary greeting? He doesn't want to send the wrong message. He slowly reaches his hand toward the Indra, who shakes it aggressively. Gallagher shifts his posture to a readied warrior's stance, and the Indra lets go, staring at him with more confusion. How different they are, not just physically but culturally, too.

Helyer looks back toward the leviathan. "As I was saying, they're not the only thing lurking in the depths, Gallagher. I'll try not to be patronizing, but if you don't know of the shortage of Blue Tears, of which all races rely on, then you may not be aware of other things us Indra think of as common knowledge. Have you ever heard of the Ebisu?" He looks at Gallagher.

"I know of them." Gallagher clenches his jaw to overcome the emotions he feels toward them. "I've only recently encountered them."

"Consider it a blessing." He shakes his head and turns his attention back to the glass and the dark figure on the other side. "The Ebisu have slowly but consistently been picking off the De'wi clans. They recently obliterated the Rhizo Clan, and all for their large crop of Tears. If anyone is a threat to your existence… it is not the leviathans. It is the Ebisu."

"They recently invaded our home," Gallagher states.

Helyer studies him again, then turns away. "Interesting. It couldn't have been for the tiny crop of Tears. Has she already made her move?" he murmurs to himself and remains quietly pensive as he stares at his feet. "Could she have formed a bond with the Ebisu? Why else would they attack? Unless…the Ebisu are not after the Tears at all." The squatty elf looks up to see Gallagher staring at him intently. He waves a hand to brush away the comments. "Never mind.

Indran quarrels. Nothing that pertains to you," he announces in a louder voice. "We can only see so much, you see—looking through the Terra Realm and into the Ocean Realm. Our machina has its limitations, but we know the Ebisu have setup an aggressive front somewhere in the region due to other incidents. The Morshine Peaks cause much disturbance for our observers and the tools they use."

"And that's why you need me?" Gallagher questions, suspicions rising, if it's possible they could rise anymore. "To be your eyes in the ocean."

"Precisely. The Ebisu are on a mission to take sole control of the Tears. They threaten the crops of all the De'wi and the Indra alike."

"With your machina, why do you need my help?" Gallagher asks. This all sounds fabricated. "If the Ebisu threaten your way of life, why not use your magical machina to lay claim to what you need. And what were you mumbling only a moment ago? You said their invasion couldn't have been for the Tears. If you're trying to build trust, it isn't working."

Helyer smiles. "You might hold our race in high regard because of our machina, but we are not warriors, Gallagher. If we were on a scale of fit and unfit, we would be worthless." He grabs at the flabby flesh around his chin and jiggles it.

Gallagher is disgusted by the elf. He's self-aware of his weakness yet does nothing about it. Lazy.

"Your scepter. It puts me to sleep." Gallagher points to his staff.

Helyer looks up at the conch, which is gripped by several finger-like appendages protruding from the top of the metallic scepter. "Yes. Effective on one warrior, and only until it is…" He looks to Gallagher. "…never mind that. We don't have the means to take on the Ebisu alone. It will help to have fins in the water." He kicks off a shoe and wiggles his toes. His webs are missing, and his toes are much shorter. "These don't work well in the currents, I'm afraid. Nor do these." He waves his short arms. "We tend to be buoyant and slow."

They both turn their attention back to the green ambiance of the leviathan. Helyer slips his shoe back on, then silence consumes them for a moment.

"Will you help us?" Helyer asks.

"No." Gallagher is blunt. He will not betray the De'wi.

"Very well." He turns away from the glass. "Come. I have something more to show you."

They exit the large white cell, stroll down the corridor, not too far, and enter another large white cell. Again, with glass consuming one entire wall. It appears to be the other side of the leviathan's ocean cell.

Somebody waits within an antechamber attached to the large glass aquarium. Suddenly, water rushes into the antechamber, the floor consumed immediately. The person within leaps into the air, obviously startled by the situation. Intuition tells Gallagher who's held captive in there, but he doesn't want to believe it. He rushes to the window to see for himself. "Rivee Rayfin!" he calls to her as he smashes a fist on the glass. She turns to see him, fear embedded in every feature of her face. She speaks, but Gallagher cannot hear anything she's saying.

Helyer casually walks closer to the antechamber at his own comfortable pace.

Gallagher turns to him. "Why? Let her out!"

"I cannot do that," he says upon his approach.

"Let me guess, you fill the antechamber with water, then open the gate, removing the barrier between her and the leviathan."

Helyer nods. "Precisely."

"Why? Why do this?"

"A means to persuade you," Helyer suggests.

"A means to threaten me. An ultimatum. Save my kin or betray my clan. That is what you present me with."

"Yes." He nods enthusiastically. "Precisely. So…"

"Never! I won't betray my clan."

"Even for the life of your friend, here." He gestures to the antechamber. "Even though your clan has already betrayed you by giving you the blighted label." He points to Gallagher's fin.

Gallagher's line of vision follows his finger. His clan *has* betrayed him. In a way, they have. They've turned their backs on his abilities as a warrior. They turned their backs on him completely when he returned home, prepared, and capable of their warrior ranks. No matter his effort, they turn their backs on him.

He presses his hands to the glass and stares at Rivee. She stares back. The two both unknowing of what to do, both stricken with fear. The water is up to her waist.

It is not the warrior's way to betray his clan. She must do this on her own. She must battle that leviathan and save herself. He cannot betray the De'wi to help the Indra.

"You'd let her challenge that angler fish?" Helyer asks. His presence is calm. "She is just a child of what, fifteen years, twenty years?"

Gallagher turns and faces him. "She is a warrior braver than most!" His voice is stern and abrupt. "She may not have the physical attributes, but she is as courageous as they come. I will not betray my clan!" His last sentence comes out in a roar.

Gallagher turns back to the glass and pounds on it recklessly. It's unyielding, sturdier than any of the structures they build back in the Terra Realm. His knuckles turn red and bloodied, but he continues to pound on the glass. He doesn't know what else to do.

"It'll never break under your power alone," Helyer says.

Gallagher stops pounding and looks at the sky elf. Plump, round, squatty. His only power is in the staff he wields. That staff is imbued with the magical qualities of Blue Tears. It must behave the same as the cerulean steel they wield back home. Will it be able to shatter the glass?

With a quick jab, Gallagher slams his fist right between Helyer's eyes. The blow stuns the sky elf. Gallagher snatches the staff from him with ease and whacks him in the back of the head with the bottom end before turning around to slam the conch into the glass.

First blow ricochets off with a blunt thud. Second blow the same. The vibration works its way into Gallagher's hands.

"I've told you." Helyer grunts with a hand covering the back of his head. "It has no power within your grasp."

Gallagher turns to face him. He grabs the squatty elf by the collar to pull him closer and puts the staff in his grasp, holding onto his hands with a ferocity that could tear them off. Controlling him like a puppet, he swings the staff at the glass antechamber and several lightning bolts climb through its surface rendering the wall full of cracks.

Rivee swims in the center of the antechamber, the water now over her head.

Gallagher shoves Helyer away but maintains grip on the staff. The sky elf stumbles and falls to the ground. Gallagher turns his attention back to the glass to relentlessly pound on it with the metallic weapon.

"What have you done!" Helyer shouts at him.

Gallagher knows exactly what he's done. He's found a way to save Rivee.

Helyer scrambles on his hands and knees toward the exit, but he's too late. The glass shatters and explodes into the white cell. Rivee rushes past Gallagher on a wave and tumbles into the back wall. The water floods the chamber with haste, and now the white cell and the leviathan's tank are directly connected with a small opening growing larger. Soon it will open enough for the leviathan to share the same space as them.

Water rushes past Gallagher through the antechamber and carries shards of glass with it. Gallagher casually evades the threat of getting cut with his primary focus on the dark figure looming on the other side. Its green light trap is the only illumination within the tank, but it is enough to see shimmers of its enormous fangs waiting patiently for a meal. The dark figure stirs as the water rushes into their chamber.

Helyer tries to get the exit open, but he's powerless without his scepter. The water is above their heads now. Rivee remains near the exit with Helyer, who is floating on the surface of the water. As the water climbs, so does he, whereas Rivee and Gallagher remain in the depths where they're more comfortable.

The leviathan stirs. The door is nearly wide enough for it to squeeze through.

Gallagher pries the conch from the end of the scepter to turn it into a multi-pronged spear. The conch is powerless in his hands, so he lets it drift through the water to the floor. He readies himself for a battle. He will not let Rivee die, and he will not betray his clan.

Their white cell is now full of water with a dangerously wide opening into the leviathan's tank. Glass shards drift through the water. The larger pieces having already sunk to the bottom, but the smaller pieces drift more carefree as the raging waters calm and the turmoil settles. The green ambience and the dark figure looming behind it swim toward them.

Rivee remains near the locked door on the other side of the chamber. Helyer struggles at the surface of the water, making a ruckus of splashes. He might be trying to swim. Gallagher isn't quite sure because it doesn't look like swimming, but he can't fathom the sky elf intentionally drawing attention to himself.

Gallagher readies himself for a fight. A chance to redeem what he lost so many years ago.

The leviathan leisurely swims through the opening into the light of the white chamber. Its pure black eyes are as large as Gallagher and stare into oblivion. They are hollow, wretched black holes that devour all light, enflaming the fear of its prey. Its teeth are twice as long as Gallagher is tall. All three of the elves could be one small meal for this beast. Its fins are more like appendages. Arms with elbows and massive fins in place of hands. In the rear, two tails with even larger fins calmly paddle it forward.

A current of water pushes Gallagher away as the leviathan's large mass swims past him toward the splashing imbecile. It creates an eddy that sucks him back in toward the beast's rear fins. When it does, Gallagher pierces a fin with the spear and holds on tight. The tails whip violently as the giant fish picks up velocity. Gallagher struggles to hold on but refuses to let go. He whips back and forth in the water as the leviathan gets closer and closer to Helyer. If the sky elf gets eaten, then any chance of them escaping this room is lost. He needs to slay the leviathan before it gets to Helyer.

Gallagher tries to issue resistance, but it does no good. Maybe with his machina fin, but that's wishful thinking. Right now, he might as well be an algae eater suctioned onto its underbelly for all the attention he's getting from it.

It breaks the surface of the water and slams into the wall where Helyer is, its fangs snapping at anything in its path. The self-inflicted blow stuns the fish and Gallagher takes advantage of the opportunity. He withdraws the spear from its fin and bursts forward, closer to its snapping jaws, but a raging tremor explodes through the fish and knocks Gallagher away, too far to do any damage with the spear. The giant fish circles the tank.

Helyer continues to splash around on the surface. He hasn't been eaten yet, and the leviathan's attention is pulled toward the Indra once again with his inability to swim. If only he'd bob in place like his body wants to, and stop that ruckus, Gallagher would be able to draw the leviathan away from him.

Gallagher might be able to cut the fish off, but it would mean swimming directly into its snapping jaws. He kicks his fins and bursts forward.

With his spear stretched outward, he swims at an angle of pursuit to cut the fish off from its attack. Helyer splashes like an imbecile, continuing to draw its attention. Gallagher is almost there, and the leviathan turns in his direction at the last second, jaws open wide. He points the spear perpendicular to the fish and jabs it into its mouth, propping it open, and gaining him just enough time to slip in between its fangs and into its mouth. He yanks on the spear and its mouth slams shut.

Just as Gallagher planned.

The space is cramped, and a strong sucking force pulls him into its belly. He cannot see anything, but he doesn't need to. The fish surrounds him on all sides. Gallagher allows his body to flow freely as he jabs his spear into the fish all the way into its gut. He retracts it and stabs again. He does this over and over, relentlessly attacking the fish from the inside. The water around him grows warmer. The taste becomes wretched, and he finds himself struggling to breathe. He needs to get out.

Even with the breathing apparatus strapped to his face, it's like inhaling poisonous fumes. His lungs become tight, and a coughing fit attacks him. He drops the spear and digs his fingers into the fish's throat to pull himself toward its mouth. He climbs and climbs, coughing the entire time. Its jaws remain clamped shut. He's trapped.

He pushes his fins into the leviathan's tongue and presses his back into the roof, attempting to push its mouth open, but he's not strong enough.

The blood is thinner in the mouth, but it seems to be thickening the longer he remains trapped. His lungs burn.

The taste of blood antagonizes him. He holds his breath and pushes. The machina strapped to his face isn't filtering the juices flowing around him. His legs weaken. This isn't working. He grabs onto one of the fangs and pulls with all his might. They're anchored too deep into its jaw. Will this be his final resting place? He hadn't thought about how to get out.

As fatigue settles into his muscles and desperation to breathe tears at his lungs, he feels a current swoosh past his skin. The water and blood drain from the leviathan's mouth, and Gallagher sucks in a lungful of air. It provokes a coughing fit, but he quickly focuses and contains his breathing.

A white light shines from between the leviathan's fangs, and it grows brighter. Someone or something is prying the mouth of the fish open. Before long it is wide enough for him to slip through, but he remembers all too well how Alariya lost her life, and how Rivee lost her leg. It was a moment just like this.

Gallagher kicks and kicks at the leviathan's fangs but they won't break loose. He must squeeze between them.

With closed eyes and a scrunched face, he grips two adjacent fangs, then pulls with all his might. His body splashes free of the liquids pooling in the fish's mouth and slides right between the leviathan's fangs where he falls to the once immaculate floor, now tainted with fish guts and blood. The room has been drained of all the water.

"Come on, Gally. You're safe now. It's dead."

"Rivee Rayfin!" He sees her silhouette against the bright lights. She's sitting on the floor. He would've thought she was another Indra if she hadn't spoken to him.

"Yeah, it's me. You killed it, Gally. I'd help you, but this light air doesn't bode well for me."

Gallagher flops onto the ground of the white cell once he climbs free. His muscles feel like they've been shredded. He can hardly move. Rivee crawls to his side and grabs hold of his hand.

"Where's Helyer?"

"Hel-who?"

"The imbecile splashing around on the surface."

She points to his limp body sitting by the exit.

"Is he dead?"

Her mouth distorts. "No, unfortunately."

"Are you okay?" Gallagher asks, struggling to form words as he's still trying to collect himself.

"Sure, but *you stink*. Are you? What's on your face?"

"Do me a favor," he pleas.

"Sure."

"Help me up, so I can fetch that stone." He points to the leviathan's green light trap attached to the appendage protruding from its head.

"How?" She looks down at her missing leg. "You want me to slither over there and bite it off?" She sasses him.

"If you must." Gallagher is straight-faced.

"Seriously?"

He opens his mouth to fire back, then closes it and keenly looks at her when he realizes what she meant about the light air. Rivee cannot swim nor walk within the Caelum Realm. She can hobble or crawl, and that's it. This isn't the place for someone with one leg.

Several Indra swarm into the chamber before Rivee can do anything. Two check on Helyer, and the rest circle around Gallagher and Rivee, all armed with their scepters.

"You've slayed a leviathan, but do you truly think you can save your friend from our machina?" One of the Indra taps her on the head with his conch and Rivee falls limp into Gallagher's arms.

"Fine," he mutters under his breath. He just defeated his first leviathan, and he feels nothing like a warrior. He only feels defeated.

"Fine?" the same Indra repeats.

"I'll do what you need, if you allow her to return home." He drops his head. "Safe and unharmed," he quickly adds.

"Agreed."

Rivee is carried away by a few of the Indra, while Gallagher is escorted back to his white cell, still a prisoner of the Indra, nothing gained from conquering the leviathan.

15 THE GRENDELIN

Killing wasn't to be part of this mission. Mira is not a trained killer of elven races. They train to defeat the leviathans, battle the wraiths, and any of the other vicious sea creatures creeping in the wild. This is all her fault. Had she not led her team into the Ocean Realm, this wouldn't have happened. Her curiosity drove her decisions, and now she finds herself alone. Her heart is heavy.

Mira wanders through viscous thoughts as her body curls in and out of the rock crops, brushing her fingers through the seagrass, not swimming more than a body's length above the ground. The glow of the midday clouds makes visibility far and wide. She does what she can to stay hidden behind the collage of obstacles while scanning the terrain.

Sharp glances over her shoulder plague her solo travels. Nothing is there. And nothing has been there the last dozen times she looked. She checks too often, but she will never let another Ebisu sneak up on her again.

Where are you, Tanniv Windstalker? Where are you, Veras Elreid? The thoughts run through her mind constantly as she searches.

Mira hangs close to the shoreline, not wanting to stray too far, and not wanting to get too close to the ocean waves. The longer she holds out searching for Haltuk, the farther away he and his captors will get, but she cannot abandon Tanniv and Veras. She balls her fists, wanting to scream at the conundrum tearing her apart.

A throng of skittles catch her eye, dancing within the seagrass up ahead. Wary to get too close for fear of scattering them, she observes their behavior from a distance. The colorful little creatures, with tails of a fish and torsos of an elf, calm her anxiety. There's a playfulness to their movements. Some bob in place, feeding on algae, while others chase one another through the knee-high blades of green grass. None are larger than her hand, and without an ounce of predatory malevolence they are a delight to watch.

Suddenly, a firm hand wraps around her bicep. She thinks to put up a struggle, but this elf's hand is too strong. It would be like a youngkin trying to escape her mother's expectations. It's not going to happen. She reaches for her yari.

"Mira!"

Hearing Tanniv's voice brings much needed relief. She spins and Veras is by his side, too.

"Allowing your subordinates to sneak up on you, eh?" Tanniv says.

Mira drops her yari and lunges forward, wrapping Tanniv in her arms.

"Good to see you're alive, chief," Veras says.

Mira pulls away from Tanniv and moves to embrace Veras. He lurches backward, but not enough to escape her. "Thank Ceto, you're alive." Her head snaps back and forth between the two as she lets go. "I wasn't sure. I saw you escape the Ocean Realm, but then…"

"Haltuk?" Veras jumps right to the problem at hand.

"I watched him get carried away."

"Aye, as did we," Tanniv replies. "So, what are we waiting for? You hunting skittles?" he asks with his yari jabbing in their direction.

"You see them as a snack?"

Tanniv shrugs. "Yeah?"

Mira grimaces at him. "C'mon. Let's follow the shoreline. Their intention wasn't to kill. They carried him away like a prisoner, so they're surely taking him to wherever they reside. At this point, we presume the canyon will lead us directly to it. Right Veras?" She looks to him for confirmation, but she hardly needs it. A burst of renewed determination permeates her with the arrival of these two.

"Yes. That's what Saheela led us to believe," Veras replies as he pulls out his parchment to review what he's documented. "Nothing has changed my opinion of the matter."

"Then, let's go. But we'll stay out of the shallows for now, only probing to ensure we're on the right path. Agreed?"

"I can be your scout." Veras raises his parchment into the air.

"And I can be your bodyguard. Protect you from those vicious skittles." He jabs his yari at them and hollers. They disperse, fleeing beneath the grass.

Mira isn't delighted to have them leave, but his comments leave her snickering. "Very well, bodyguard. May your courage scare off all the beautiful villains, so they don't have to suffer the rumblings of your ever-hungry tummy."

Their journey continues along the shoreline. Despite their missing friend, their hopes are high that they will be successful in his recovery.

The landscape doesn't vary too much from the corner of the island where their colony is tucked away. Less coral and smaller groves of kelp, but otherwise it's similar. Larger boulders in the rock crops, perhaps. The Morshine Peaks remain on the left, towering into the ceiling of clouds, as they will for the entirety of their journey as they circle around the island.

What happens if they *do* circle the entire isle? Do they go home defeated? How long would that take? The thought of it both excites *and* pacifies Mira. They will find Haltuk and all the other De'wi who were taken. They must.

"Is it time to check on the canyon?" Mira asks her companions, specifically looking at Veras.

Veras shifts uncomfortably while swimming beside her. "Mira..." He looks to the diluted position of the sun, then his fingers pop into the air as if he's counting them. "It's hardly been an hour. I can't imagine the canyon has disappeared."

"But better to be sure than to imagine," she insists. "Trust in your stones," she says to instill confidence, but it's mostly to instill confidence in her own decision making. It doesn't sit well after breaking her circlet and denouncing her stone's significance.

"Very well." His tone lacks excitement. "I suppose it'll be better for my cartography the more precise it is." Veras swims off toward the shallows and disappears beneath the surface with hardly a splash.

Tanniv and Mira continue following the shoreline. The terrain becomes hillier with larger boulders, and seemingly taller groves of kelp. Rock crops provide a lot of cover to duck behind should they need it. So much that they cannot clearly see down the shoreline anymore.

"What will you miss most?" Tanniv initiates conversation.

"Huh?" Mira looks his way. He swims sideways, facing her.

"C'mon. We don't know how long this journey will last. What will you miss most while we're out here? I already miss Crumbaker's baking." A frown forms, but quickly slips away. "Mira?"

"I...err..." Gallagher and Rivee are foremost on her mind. Her mother's morning lectures. Her father's resolute guidance. "The Crisper Coral..." She settles.

Tanniv's face contorts. "You miss the skittles!" he mocks.

Mira turns sharply and darts in his direction to give him a thump, but Tanniv easily curls out of the way.

"C'mon, Mira. There must be something you'll miss. Or do you despise us so much, to escape into the wild is a release of all the pain and suffering we cause?" His smile is half-hearted attempting to conceal a frown.

"I'm sorry," she says. "I just... My father... The Elders... Their inexplicable decisions..." Her fists tighten into a ball.

"Gallagher?" he questions.

Mira makes eye contact with him briefly, then looks away. "Yes. I just don't understand why they exiled him. And Rivee followed after him."

"Rivee *what?*"

"She's gone, Tanniv. Bailey saw her following Gallagher as he was escorted beyond the border. I couldn't locate her anywhere."

"Rivee is out in the wild!"

Mira nods.

"And you didn't go searching for her? You didn't strike up a rescue mission?"

Mira's brow furrows. "What was I supposed to do? The threat of the Ebisu..."

"Abandon us. Chase after Rivee. She needs you."

Mira's lips flatten. "That'd get me banished just as quick as Gallagher."

"Maybe..." Tanniv comes to a halt and plants his fins on the sandy shore.

Mira stops beside him. "I'm worried, Tanniv. Everything is falling apart. The Ebisu… the waterspout… Gallagher's banishment… missing the Solari Harvest. Only days ago, all our clanmates were jovial with the eve of the Solari Harvest spiking their spirits, while the warriors on the harvest team melted away with anxiety coating their brave journey ahead. It was all as it should be. Now…" She sighs. "Look at us. What does this all mean?" An awkward silence fills the space between them. "Never mind. What good does it do to burden myself with things of the past. Haltuk is our only concern now."

"Err…" Veras rapidly comes to a halt where they stand, treading in the air with water dripping from his saturated clothing. It's why the De'wi warriors minimize their attire. "We have more concerns than just Haltuk at the moment." A flat hand raises high in the air and holds as if he's referring to something near the ceiling of clouds. "Come. Hurry." He speeds ahead. Tanniv and Mira follow close behind.

Around a curve in the shore, where the terrain turns even rockier with limited visibility, Veras' worries come into view. Emerging from behind what looks like an unnatural levee, larger than any elf could make without machina, is a stone giant.

"Is that…" Tanniv's jaw hangs, leaving his sentence unfinished.

"A grendelin." Both Mira and Veras quietly flutter the words out of their mouths as if speaking it too loudly will provoke the creature. They look at one another, bewilderment consuming each of them. Mira's lips slowly curl upward, and she looks back toward the astonishing sight.

"They're real?" Tanniv shouts.

Both of his companions shoosh him. "Quiet," Mira adds with a frown. "There is much we'll discover now that we're in the wild." Her inward brow, directed at Tanniv for lacking caution, softens. "So much…" A beaming smile finds her face. "So much to uncover. Can you imagine what else we'll find? The hydra, sea nymphs, maybe blustering cities of races unknown…" Both of her companions are now staring at *her* in bewilderment. "Blue dragons! Or the Isle of Imperius!" Her eyes light up.

"Don't be foolish, Mira." Veras stops her dreams from bleeding out of her mouth. "That island isn't real."

"Nor are grendelins." Mira points to the stone giant.

All their attention redirects toward the fascinating image of a stone mountain rising into the sky. It's arched back straightens upright. Green aquatic foliage shimmers in the diluted light from the everlasting overcast. Its shoulders and head begin to differentiate from a mountainous shape into something more elf-like. A thundering roar erupts across the land. A fearful roar. A strained roar. Its arms flail through the air as it lunges forward, swatting at something. It tilts its head back and screams at the clouds. The vibration of its monstrous cry rumbles through the terrain causing the land to quake.

A colorful steel chain flies through the air and curls around the giant's forearm. Not just any color, but the color of Blue Tears. Its vibrant glow is a striking contrast to the dark, chiseled stone coloring of the grendelin. It cries out again. Its head whips in the direction of the three companions, sadness exuding from its stone-grey eyes.

"It's suffering!" Mira cries out. "We need to do something!"

Both her companions stare at her, speechless, mouths agape.

"Come." She swims closer to the levee, keeping low until she summits the rock wall. A gasp escapes her. "Are you seeing what I am?" She looks around, but neither of her companions are near her. Craning her neck over her shoulder she sees them rooted firmly at the bottom of the levee refusing to come any closer. She waves them off and focuses on the incomprehensible scene.

The rock wall she scaled is part of a great ring of boulders, like a nest or bedding ground. It's just as the song expresses. The tune starts playing in her mind, *Kings, kings, kings of the isle, giants of old, bringing a smile, stepping over mountains, bedding in stone rings...*

Within the circle, a small battalion of Ebisu elves assault the stone giant. Masculine and bulging with stone muscles, it would seem impossible to challenge and expect a victory. The augmented chain hooked around the creature's arm is anchored to a heavy ballista manned by two Ebisu. Another chain bombardes the grendelin. It launches from another ballista, twirling through the air until it closes around the giant's other arm, forming a tight bind. A curdling scream shakes the land as the grendelin rears back its head and roars to the heavens, its stone muscles flexing and foliage-like hair tremoring in the light. Mira's heart sinks.

She turns and slumps into the rocks in one smooth motion. Her clanmates have finally decided to join her by her side. They stay out of sight of the awful scene developing on the other side of the wall.

"You didn't get eaten, so..." Tanniv spills a hand over her shoulder. "...that's good. Have you had enough? Can we go?"

"Enough..." Troubled lines press into her forehead.

"Is Haltuk over there?" Veras swings a pointed finger up and down as it artfully hurdles the wall.

"Not that I saw. Dozens of Ebisu and a clamoring grendelin. That's all."

"Oh. That's all, she says." Tanniv rolls his eyes. "I suggest we give the giants a wide berth. Yes, they are *all* giants, Ebisu and grendelin alike."

"Are you not the courageous one?" Mira spouts. "No beast too large? No challenge too overbearing?"

"I'm not suicidal. You want to save the giant…" He pauses. "I can't believe those words just came out of my mouth." A deep sigh follows, and he lowers himself onto the rocks to sit beside Mira. "We're discussing whether or not to save a legendary grendelin from a race of aquatic elves of which neither have been part of our world until a week prior."

"It's surreal. Absurd even," Veras adds where he stands before the two on a lower rock meeting them face to face.

"What can we do to help this giant, Mira? Machina. Ebisu. This is out of our realm." He tilts his head and shrugs his shoulders. "Well… within our realm, but with races from outside of our realm." He looks to the sky, pondering whether he said that correctly.

"Maybe my father was right?" Mira's voice is soft.

"Huh?" Tanniv prods for an explanation.

"About the machina. Look what it is capable of in the wrong hands. They use a standard ballista and augment it with Ceto's power." Another startling roar shakes the land. "That sound tears at my heart."

"Really?" Tanniv shifts where he's seated. His hands cup his ears. "Hurts my ears and soils my trousers."

Mira gives him a pointed glare.

"What? You must be tone-deaf if you can say that sound isn't painful."

Veras is visibly withholding a laugh.

"I'm serious," Mira asserts. "Look at how they use the power of machina? They target other powerful beings, either to destroy or…" She taps a finger on her temple. "Or to control it." Her gaze is distant, staring at the rocks surrounding them. "My father was right. Machina cannot be trusted in the hands of elves. Gallagher!" She gasps and looks up at her companions, brushing fallen tresses from her face. "Did either of you see the machina he allegedly brought into the colony?"

"Not allegedly, Mira," Veras replies.

"It was…" Tanniv's lips curl on one end and his head tilts back and forth as if weighing the situation. "…it was slick. Looked good on him."

"What was it?" Mira's voice is soft, but urgent.

"A fin. After the storm struck, he returned with a machina fin. Everything was in turmoil with the Ebisu, the aftermath of the waterspout, and then Gally bringing the forbidden machina home, I don't think anyone even bothered to ask where he got it. He was exiled immediately. In and out. The Elders were quick about it."

"A machina fin…" Mira's head hangs low where she braces it with hands on her forehead.

"Yeah, to improve his odds of becoming a warrior, no doubt." Tanniv runs a hand through his hair. "That damn fin of his. If only it were whole without the need for machina. He'd probably be leading this charge. No offense." Tanniv balks at his insulting comment.

"What has he done…" That isn't the Gallagher she knows. He is loyal to his clan. He is a warrior deep in his heart where it matters most. For him to knowingly bring the forbidden machina back home, what was he thinking? She doesn't know what to feel. Anger? Disgust? Sympathy? "Where could he have gotten such a thing?"

Both of her companions shrug their shoulders.

"What now?" Veras asks. "It's not within our means to help that grendelin, chief. I would suggest we continue back to the shoreline to our previous purview. Finding Haltuk."

"But are we not out here to gain knowledge of the Ebisu?" Mira questions him. Something Haltuk would have beat her to if he was here.

"Good point," he replies.

"We hold for a few minutes. Enough to gain intelligence of this brutal race and nothing more. We can't be seen." Another screeching roar cuts her off and Tanniv grabs at his ears.

The companions lay low and peak over the top of the rocks to witness the chaos unfold. The grendelin has a broken chain whipping around in a frenzy. Ebisu leap to grab it without success and Mira questions what good that would even do. A ground layer of judgement forms regarding their decision-making abilities. But maybe the Ebisu are much stronger than they appear. Not strong enough to withstand the power of a grendelin, though. Right?

The chain flails with enough velocity to bludgeon any one of them. Eventually, one snags the end of the chain and is carried off his fins and tossed into the air only to find a crushing blow against the rocks on the opposite side of the ring. A limp body hangs within the rocks just above a group of seadragons huddled together.

"C'mon, chief." Veras' tone is shaky. "Let's get out of here before we're outed. This giant can handle its own. The Ebisu are no match for it."

She breathes heavily. "Okay." The reluctance in her voice is thick.

The rock levee grows taller behind them as they swim lower, shying away from the atrocious scene on the other side. Another deathly scream sounds off followed by a thud and a crack.

"Watch out!" Veras calls to them.

All three dart in different directions. Boulders the size of small huts tumble down the wall, too heavy to bounce, and find resting places in the hardened, sandy terrain near the base of the wall. A stone hand covered in green kelp and seagrass, larger than the boulders, grips the top of the wall. But it doesn't pick up a boulder as Mira presumes. A weapon as simple as a stone could make a difference in a goliath's hand. Instead, another hand and forearm curl over the wall, then the grendelin's head. It pulls itself up, trying to escape the ring. Its stone eyes beg for mercy.

It clambers free of the ring, pulling itself up and over. Then it tumbles down the rough slope and smashes into the sandy terrain, spraying mud, just as the boulders did.

Moments later, Ebisu emerge on top of the wall, filling the skyline with their glowing silhouettes. More and more peak the levee, one after the other, until dozens are in view.

"What have we here?" one of them says in a voice that could carry across the ocean. Mira doesn't know which, as all she sees are dark shapes with glowing breastplates contrasted against the dull, grey sky.

"Let's go, Mira!" Veras shouts at her.

"This creature needs us!" she shouts back. "We must help it."

"Mira, no!"

"Enough squabbling," the presumed squad leader says. "You three can come back with us. Detain them!" A dark arm waves through the sky and several Ebisu descend the wall. They don't leap into the air or swim, however. With strained muscles, they physically climb down the rocks, one leg after the other, one arm after the other. Occasionally, one risks a drop to a larger boulder below, but not without caution.

"Is this a joke?" Tanniv asks.

Mira turns to Veras, not intentionally ignoring Tanniv, she just has too many thoughts stampeding through her head at the moment. "Do you think the spice has any impact on it? The grendelin, I mean."

Veras swims closer with his palms turned upward. "If it does, it will take an ocean of Tears to make a difference on a monster this size."

"Monster?" Mira glares at him.

The grendelin moves slowly, attempting to get up.

"What can we do, Mira? Tell me." Veras folds his arms across his body as he loses patience. "Those Ebisu will not hesitate to attack if we don't flee right now."

Tanniv joins the huddle. "They look rather slow to me. Ceto's shits, they can't even swim."

"Tanniv Windstalker!" Mira degrades him for using Ceto's name in vain. "Wait…" She examines the Ebisu slowly making their way down the levee. "But they reside in the Ocean Realm…" The look on her face morphs into something awkward. "How could they not swim? That doesn't make any sense."

"Look with your own eyes, Mira," Tanniv asserts with a jabbing finger in their direction. "They can't swim. Not up here within the Terra Realm, anyways."

"Hmm…so all we need to do is figure out how to get this giant back upright. If they can't swim, all it must do is climb the mountainside to escape. The effort wouldn't be worth the chase for the Ebisu. C'mon! Help me! Before they get to the bottom."

"Help you with what?" Tanniv throws his arms in the air. Veras shakes his head with wide eyes. They seem to react to their chief in that manner too often.

"You really think we can help a stone giant to its feet, Mira?" Veras makes no move to help her.

"Yes! Yes, I do, Veras." Mira doesn't wait for them. The grendelin is already on its hands and knees. She swims beside it, whispers words of encouragement to the creature, knowing it likely doesn't understand, then proceeds to push upward along its boulder-like shoulder. She won't give up. Not when an innocent life is on the line.

Veras and Tanniv look to the Ebisu, halfway down the wall, and hurry toward Mira. They hunker beneath the goliath's chest and heave upward.

"Is it working?" Tanniv asks. Nobody answers. Mira and Veras are too engrossed in helping the grendelin. There doesn't seem to be any change, however. The grendelin is immovable. With its dense might, how could the Ebisu ever overcome such power. It's no different than moving a mountain.

Mira stops kicking and swims to the side of the goliath where she can get a view of the encroaching Ebisu. Tanniv and Veras join her.

"What next? Is it time to flee?" Veras asks with much urgency.

"Machina…" A burning anger grows within her. "It's an evil thing, isn't it? They use it to dominate the innocent, and they'll continue until they find resistance."

"Let me guess…" Veras tilts his head in her direction. "…we're that resistance?"

Tanniv balls a fist, then reaches for the yari on his back. "Very well, chief. I hope you know this is suicide."

"We don't fight." Mira throws up a hand for him to put away his yari. "We distract. If they cannot swim, we will taunt and distract until the grendelin can climb to safety. Veras, can you help guide it while Tanniv and I take care of the Ebisu?"

"How do you suggest I do that?" he asks with flailing arms.

Mira looks at him with a disappointed stare. "Veras…" This whiny, scared version of Veras isn't going to help them. "I need the thoughtful, problem solving Veras, right now. Not whoever this is." She waves a circling arm around him. "We are in a new world, but you must collect yourself if we're to be successful."

A flying chain splits the air between them, breaking up their conversation. Veras, with renewed determination set into his posture, swims with vigor toward the head of the goliath. Mira and Tanniv swim toward the advancing Ebisu.

"What is your intention?" Mira calls to them as she treads air above the Ebisu who have descended the wall. "Why do this?"

One of them responds. "You expect us to answer that?" He is the tallest and thickest of the bunch. His dark hair, pulled back into a braid, is streaked with greys and whites. His face looks like a weathered piece of leather beaten by the waves for hundreds of years, but his arrogant smile and toned physique tell Mira this elf is capable. "Bold. Blunt. But this is war, darling. I have no *intention* of telling you anything."

"War…" Mira responds. Tanniv treads air by her side, waiting for direction.

"Yes, war." His voice carries weight. "It would seem all you De'wi believe the Machina Wars ended over a millennia ago, but it was only a calm. We have not forgotten. The war will never end. Not until every last De'wi is enslaved or dead." His eyes narrow into something malicious. "I prefer the latter."

"General Merces…" One of his subordinates looks to him, then to the grendelin, which is on its feet and moving away from the shore.

"Damn it!" The dark general glares at Mira. Without taking his eyes off her, he commands his soldier. "Take half the squad and head it off. Retrieve your seadragons if you must. If we don't return with that goliath there will be consequences."

"Yes, sir." The soldier gives Mira a sharp look before he heads back up the levee with several of the Ebisu in tow. She scowls in return, unsure what she did to deserve such hate.

"As for these De'wi…" He addresses Mira, now. "We are always in need of expendable soldiers. What do you say?" His eyes follow her curves, up and down. "Hmm…yes… Or servants of other talents." A disgusting smile finds his face. "Would you like to be reformed?"

"Reformed?" Mira doesn't know what he's talking about.

The General erupts with a boisterous laugh. "Detain these two. Try not to kill them, but if you must, you must. They're expendable." He turns to follow the others.

A chain shoots from a handheld machina that one of the Ebisu soldiers wields. It's not as heavy as the chain used on the grendelin, but worthy of a fatal blow if they aren't careful. Mira and Tanniv easily dodge the first shot and move out of reach.

"Tanniv," she calls to him with an aggressive whisper. "The seadragons…"

"What about them?" he replies as he regroups with her.

"It's what they rode in on when they invaded our colony. Without them, they've lost their speed."

"And…"

"Come. We'll set them free." Mira disregards the Ebisu below them, who have no means of attacking other than their flying chains, which are easy enough to dodge. She speeds off toward the levee, high above the Ebisu climbing through the boulders, and at least three times faster.

"This isn't one of your ideologies to protect all life, is it?" He calls as he moves to chase after her.

The seadragons are huddled on the far side of the grendelin's ring. Mira's mind wanders through the lifestyle of such a large creature. Is this ring its home? Its bedding ground? It is an obvious obtrusion to the natural terrain if its intention is disguise. Perhaps it hides from something other than the rodent-sized lifeforms they would appear to be from its perspective. Maybe the boulders offer a sense of comfort? How have they remained out of sight for all these years? Is their colony so isolated, so hidden, that not even a giant would cross the knuckles to find them. It's not like the grendelins are incapable of climbing over a mountain. Or do the Elders have a means to deter such creatures? Have the Elders witnessed a grendelin before? They must have. Why do they keep their clan isolated from such wonder? Too many questions invade Mira's thoughts. Enough to overwhelm her.

"Mira!" Tanniv waves a hand in front of her face. "Mira! Where are you?"

She shakes away her wandering mind. They've arrived at the seadragons. "Sorry. I'm here." She looks down at the wonderous creatures. "My mind...it runs amuck... I'm sorry."

The seadragons are full of vibrant greens and blues, similar to the colors of the Blue Tears but without the iridescent glow. Leaf-like extremities run down their spines giving them the appearance of foliage if seen from a distance. Their long snouts and body shape are more akin to seahorses. Their legs are short, but sturdy, meant for galloping through the water with fin-like hooves. Witnessing them up close sends a flutter of excitement through her veins.

"What now?" Tanniv asks.

"Shoo! Go!" Mira waves her arms. The seadragons flinch and scurry backward but remain huddled together. Their reaction makes Mira recoil.

"C'mon, chief, you've battled a leviathan and resurfaced. No need to be afraid of a handful of delicate dragons." He smirks at her.

"Eh...why won't they flee. They can swim over the levee I presume. How else would they've gotten in here." She looks beyond the wall toward the Morshine Peaks hoping to see Veras and the grendelin, but the wall is too tall for her to see anything more than the ceiling of clouds.

"Are you sure we need to do this, Mira? Maybe they don't want freedom. Look, they're saddled and bridled." He gives the reins a gentle tug. "They augment everything, don't they?" Mira looks closer to see a subtle glimmer of the spice. The bridle and reins are infused with Blue Tears. "They must have a surplus to last generations if they use it to reinforce something like this. You think they feed 'em the spice, too?"

"We must do something!" she urges. "If the Ebisu get back on these seadragons, they'll catch up to that grendelin and we'd have made no difference at all."

"How can you be so sure?"

"I saw them ride into our colony." She places a gentle hand on the lower neck of one of the seadragons. Its large eyes stare at her with a soothing calmness. An undeserving trust. Or perhaps an oppressed acceptance that it must endure whatever is handed to it. "These seadragons have been broken," she mutters. "But they are fast. Faster than you or I. If we don't release them, that grendelin is bound to suffer a similar fate. *I* may want to *just* save a life..." Mira makes eye contact with Tanniv. "...but think of what the Ebisu can do with a stone giant within their control. You heard him talk about war. They mean to destroy us. We must set these creatures free. We must." She looks to Tanniv for his endorsement.

His gaze veers toward the approaching Ebisu. His jaw clenches. "Errgh…fine. We can't be having them sending grendelins to attack our clan." He places a fin on the left finhold attached to the saddle and throws an ungainly leg over the nearest seadragon. "Could you imagine anything worse?" He situates himself in the saddle as he pleads for Mira to join. "C'mon. We'll herd 'em."

Mira stands still with her arms folded, undecided and pondering the idea of sitting atop a dragon. What would Rivee think of this?

"You want to save them, don't you?" He waves an urgent hand for her to get on.

"Yes." She clenches her fists together and looks toward the opposite side of the ring. The Ebisu, already down the wall, sprint in their direction with long strides. Mira hops onto a seadragon and hollers as she squeezes her calves into the side of the creature. It squirms, then bursts straight toward the incoming Ebisu.

"Wrong way, Mira! Up and over. Up and over."

Mira tugs on the reins and instinctively squeezes tighter with her calves. It steadies the creature but does nothing to change direction. She stands up with a solid yank of the reins and a slight lean, and she breathes easier. The seadragon changes course.

She cracks the reins to pick up speed. The herd ahead of her stir with anticipation. Not allowing for an arms width of separation, she whizzes past the seadragons, exciting them, and provoking them to follow.

"Atta girl, Mira!" Tanniv calls to her. "I'll pick up the rear."

The levee wall is tall and steep. She redirects the seadragon to head straight for it, not allowing an ounce of velocity to go to waste. The herd follows behind her, and Tanniv in the rear just as he said. Not knowing what will happen next, she readies herself to be tossed from a seadragon unwilling to intentionally smash into a boulder. Her eyes squeeze halfway shut as they approach the wall. She firmly grips the reins and raises her arms as if pulling up will make the seadragon swim higher. When they are within a few strides, the seadragon thrusts upward, sending Mira flying backward from the saddle.

With haste, she turns her ejection into a swift and elegant curl through the air. Within seconds she's swimming alongside the head seadragon, still guiding the herd up the steep, uneven, grendelin-made terrain.

"Yeah, Mira!" Tanniv calls enthusiastically from the rear.

The speed of the seadragons exceeds her own. Leaving her behind, they curl up and over the top of the levee wall. Tanniv remains in the saddle for a while as Mira pursues the stampeding herd.

Looking ahead, Mira sees the grendelin duck behind the crest of a mountain, already a long distance away within the Morshine Peaks where the giant will find camouflage. A large smirk fills Mira's face ear to ear, and a burst of laughter escapes her as they swim for the mountains.

Tanniv ejects himself from the speeding seadragons and curls into a swim just as Mira did. They follow the herd until they lose sight of them in a valley of rolling hills leading to the mountainous terrain.

"Come!" Mira redirects their course. "Veras went this way," she hollers at him with wind pressing into her cheeks. It's the feeling of freedom. For the first time in her life, her heart, mind, and soul are in the same place. Peace fills her to the brim.

"And what about Haltuk?" Tanniv calls to her from a short distance away.

His words reel her back. The gravity of the situation instantly crushes her. She slows to allow Tanniv to catch up. "This was only a casual interaction with the Ebisu," she says. "If their machina can be used to overcome a grendelin, imagine what else it's capable of. The General spoke of war, Tanniv!" She turns her head to look at him.

"I'd rather not imagine any of that," he admits.

"Blasphemed machina! It's as horrendous as the Elders have always made it out to be. How are we going to defend ourselves if they return to eradicate us? You heard the General, he prefers death." Mira runs a hand through her hair as they continue swimming. "And to think they enslave people…"

"One step at a time, chief."

She stares at him for a moment, pondering the next steps. "Yes, Tanniv. One step at a time. First, we rendezvous with Veras. Then we rescue Haltuk." The horizon ahead of them is filled with steep valleys, sharp ridges, and forests. "And all the while, we embrace the adventure." She turns her body to face him, still swimming ahead. "What do you say, Tanniv? Despite the challenges we face, let's enjoy this while we can."

He looks at her with a grin. "That I can do. But first, do you have any more flatbread, by chance?" He grabs at his stomach.

"Look!" Mira points toward the distant sky. "Another waterspout is forming." Although, this one doesn't appear like any other waterspout she's seen. Small bursts of lighting climb through the funneling clouds as it reaches into the Terra Realm. Then an object spits out of it as if it magically appeared from a distant world. The waterspout dissipates and the lightning vanishes as if it was never there. "What is that?"

"Your guess is as good as mine. Maybe our friend, Gallagher, coming back from another escapade within the Caelum Realm." He shrugs.

Her brows curl inward. "It's too big to be an elf. Nor is it a ray. It looks like a carriage." She looks at Tanniv. "Indra?"

Tanniv grunts. "Wouldn't that be a fun adventure. A full-scale war against both the Ebisu *and* the Indra." He shakes it off with a smile.

"Yeah, you're right. Out here in the wild, it could be anything. Let's go find Veras."

16 A Thirst for De'wi

*e*lder Fae stands idle in the lift as it climbs to her quarters. Her personal guard line the perimeter, blocking the windows that overlook the beautiful cityscape of Caelum Invictus. Lady Fae stands in the middle of all of them as if she were a prisoner of her own guard. At least her long, draping gown, that fans outward on the floor, keeps them at a distance as they carefully avoid stepping on it.

"Next time, I travel the lift alone," she says, standing still and looking forward, anticipating the doors to open. Her guard don't say a word in response. As they shouldn't. Some days she just needs more space. This box is too overcrowded. *Caelum Invictus* is too overcrowded.

The lift comes to a halt and the doors slide open in silence. She steps off the lift into the antechamber of her quarters where her guard disperse and systematically line the open chamber. Lance is the only one courteous enough to open the door for her. After a curt nod of appreciation, Lady Fae continues into her quarters.

"Yester…" she calls out to her handmaiden, anticipating her to be there. "…what do you think about us developing a new landship. Caelum Invictus is getting rather overcrowded, don't you think?" She strolls deeper into her quarters, looking around for her handmaiden. "It might be time to deport a portion of the working class and a few of the lesser houses. It'll be a new opportunity for all of them. A means to start a new, and it will give me some space to breathe." She cranes her neck around a few partitions within the chamber to look for her handmaiden. "Yester?"

No response.

"Hmm…"

A silhouette shifts out on the balcony. Perhaps she's tidying up outside.

"Yester, dear…" she starts as she steps outside onto the metal deck. The wind picks up her hair and tugs gently at the circlet about her forehead. Her brow turns inward when she sees Yester giggling. "Yester." It comes off her tongue sharper this time.

"Oh… Lady Fae…" She rises to her feet from the plush cushions of the patio furniture. "My apologies, I was just—"

"Jarnes…" She cuts off her handmaiden to address her son. "Are you swooning my handmaiden?"

"I *was* having a delightful conversation with Yester." He refuses to rise, lounging comfortably on the sofa. "That seems to have come to an abrupt halt, however. Thank you, mother."

"This is objectionable within our realm. Jarnes, you know this is unacceptable. And Yester…" Lady Fae's glare is red hot. "…you lead him on with your smiles and giggles. You know your beauty is undeniable. I ought to sew that mouth shut and make you wear a mask in my quarters if my son is going to be so discourteous and just barge in here at his own discretion. How would you like that?" Her burning stare snaps from one to the other, back and forth. Both remain quiet for a long, awkward moment. Her son rolls his eyes at her from the comfort of *her* furniture.

"It was my fault, Elder." Yester puts her head down. "It won't happen again."

Jarnes finally rises to his feet. "Ridiculous. *I* am the one who came looking for Yester. I basically chained her to the furniture as I begged for her company. Yester is free of misconduct. I take full responsibility. But, honestly, I had other reasons to be here, mother. Reasons you must sit down to hear. I only took the opportunity to chain Yester with my words when I noticed you were nowhere to be seen." A sinful smile crosses his face with a subtle glance at her handmaiden.

"Yester, please." Lady Fae waves her arm back toward the entrance of the balcony. "You're dismissed. Let the two of us speak. And do start wearing gowns a bit less form-fitting."

"Elder Fae." She curtsies. "Master Arilight." She offers a second curtsy accompanied by a smile. Then she disappears off the balcony.

The two of them watch her go, then Jarnes gestures to the sofa across from him. He sits and leans back to get comfortable, then crosses a leg over his knee while his mother finds her seat.

"So…" she says. "What rumors are so important my legs cannot bear the weight." She sits like a proper lady, legs crossed, acute posture, and her hands folded into one another atop her lap. Her darling gown of light blues and golds drapes to her ankles with a transparent gold shawl covering the revealing thin straps at the top. Her hair, aside from the gentle gusts of wind, is flawless. Royalty.

Jarnes, on the other hand, dons a simple dark grey suit with white pin-stripes. His vest and overcoat are out of alignment. His trousers hike higher into his calves than they ought to while he crosses his legs, and his shoes are scuffed. His blond hair, the only aspect of him that is in proper order, is combed to the side with a part of perfection down the other side.

"The Godmadinas are working at something big," he says.

"Big? How so?"

"Are you aware of the two De'wi elves being held captive within your city?"

Lady Fae's mouth opens, but she's speechless.

"Mother…"

"De'wi?" she questions, looking for confirmation that she heard him correctly.

"Yes."

"And you're certain? This isn't just some childish game being played at court?"

"I witnessed it. I happened to be traveling from the Sky Plaza taking a shortcut through the detention facilities to meet with an acquaintance, and it was as if they had no intention of hiding him. He was a giant amongst the Indra. Every elf around him looked like a child. And his attire… So lacking… and brutish. An uncivilized race to be certain."

"A De'wi within Caelum Invictus." Lady Fae speaks, trying to convince herself to believe this ghastly development. Her gaze cuts to her son rather sharply. "Do you know what the Godmadina's intentions are?"

"At the sight of him, I couldn't *not* poke around to get more information. I figured the Godmadinas wouldn't be straight forward, so I made haste to a parlor I frequent."

Lady Fae's face turns sour.

"I don't condone in that sort of behavior, mother. A lounge to mingle and remedy a parched throat."

"And which parlor would that be?" she asks, a frown lingering on her face.

"As if I would tell you. You'll have to trudge through your sources if you're that interested. I need my space, too, mother. But I will admit, I have a handful of contacts you wouldn't be proud of—gentle elves to be sure, but not of the lofty status you'd approve of." His mother's lips flatten, showing her disapproval. He continues, careless of what she thinks. "Anglers at the piers have been using more than just nets for their daily catches. They've been baiting the De'wi with Tears."

"So, you've been mingling with anglers, have you?"

"Irrelevant, mother. My company, although full of good tidbits of the goings and comings of our fruitful city, can spread rumors at best. They don't have any facts as to why the Godmadinas are baiting them. But I did find out they have another in the detention facility. They hauled up *two* De'wi when they brought them aboard the piers."

"Warriors? Both of them?" she asks.

"One, yes. The other…" Concern is rampant in his eyes. "We're drifting above the Morshine region, no?"

"We are."

"The other was no taller than you or I. A female youngkin. But a youngkin nearing adulthood. She should be grown to full height."

"What are you getting at?"

"We were drifting above the Morshine region twenty years ago, mother. Our last interaction with the De'wi. Do you not recall?"

Her eyes grow wide. "Could it be?"

Jarnes sits forward, matching his mother's posture. "I think it is." It looks as though he's trying to restrain a smile.

"Riveria Arilight…" The name comes off her tongue in a whisper. Too many thoughts and memories whirl through her head for her to land on any one emotion.

On one hand, this De'wi could be the answer to her house woes. It would take quite a bit of convincing of the greater houses, but it could be done with some coercion and influence. What that would look like for future generations is a toss of a spear into the sea of clouds. Not even the best observers could predict where it would land. But it is certainly a path laid before House Arilight. A path they could start walking down if these speculations are accurate.

On the other hand, this De'wi is the one who damned their house to begin with. And now Jarnes is tainted through the lens of the greater houses. If only Fae had birthed more than one son.

Both her daughters have joined other houses through marriage. Jothra, her second born, married into House Ohmsmire. Chrigan is a good companion for her, and it has been a fruitful marriage with two sons, Smika and Paka, who both have matches in the works. A well-respected house and a good addition to the Arilight name as a whole. And Haley, her second daughter, married into House Jonesook. Dunbell Jonesook is a good elf and a good mate. Lazier than some, but he has good wits about him. They, too, have had a fruitful marriage with Vinbell, their first daughter, Horbell, their first son, and Mabell, a second daughter, all of which have good names amidst the court.

Jarnes, however, is plagued. Jarnes was her only means of carrying on the house name. How did it end up just the two of them? So many ifs... If only her husband were still alive. If only she had more than one son. If only her son would have kept his trousers on twenty years past.

Lady Fae's expression turns sour and focuses on her son. "Our past comes back to haunt us." She settles on anger. "These De'wi must be removed immediately."

Jarnes, with an obvious bias, raises a finger in objection. "Or... Or we could lay claim to her. The Arilight name is fading and *that* is our biggest adversary, more so than even the Ebisu who threaten the three realms with their brutality. Think of the possibilities..."

"Think of the distasteful glares. They will toss us from the landship. Their very own Elder. They will make us swim with the De'wi."

"And what is so bad about that?"

She glares at him. "It is not the De'wi specifically, just their primitive culture."

"The elves of our realm thirst, mother. They are parched, and the water we import to the sky realm will not wet their throats. What they thirst for is interaction with the De'wi. They thirst for more than these limiting landships where they fly throughout the heavens. They want to get back to their roots. Why do you think the Godmadinas have brought the De'wi aboard and flaunt them about like treasures."

"Am I so out of touch?" she asks as her lips flatten, and she stares out beyond the terrace to the city she rules over.

"It is nothing that is spoken, mother. It's a thirst that you can only see in their eyes... in their behavior. They want more."

"We all want more. Always. Growth is what makes us feel alive."

"This is different. The Godmadinas are already referring to one of them as a champion."

"A champion to what?" Lady Fae blurts out.

"A champion to the Indran race. A means to fight the Ebisu and keep them from thrusting their dominance at the sky. It is only speculation, but I suspect they are using him as a means to reacquaint with the De'wi and stop the Ebisu from stealing our crops of Tears, mother. The Godmadinas are doing this. They undermine their Elder to feed the elves. But it's not too late for you to own this. All we must do is swoop in and lay claim to it as the Elder House. The elves want it. Their mouths are salivating to get a taste of these De'wi."

"So we lay claim to a new heir to bring our races together, and we get a bonus champion in doing so." Her hand goes to her mouth as she ponders the downside. If it's what the people desire, she sees none. "If they lust for the De'wi, we will show them we are twenty years ahead of them. Where is this youngkin? My granddaughter?" She smiles at her son.

17 HEIR OF THE SKY

I ntrinsic to Gallagher's being is the ability to survive. Damaged or not, he has the will to press forward. It has always been there. But today, he isn't so sure. He has agreed to bend his will and break his principles for another to survive. What does this mean? Is he blighted just as the Elders have always labeled him? His head hangs between his shoulders as he sulks in the corner of his white cell, pondering this conundrum.

"I would like to know, who is the elf who has labeled you blighted?"

Gallagher looks up from beneath his brow. In walks an Indra, followed by another, and another. Then three more females. Aside from a few youngkins when he and Rivee were first captured, he hasn't seen a female Indra. They're curvier than the males with defined chins, but still plump around the midsection and even shorter than their counterparts. Each wears a long flowing gown as opposed to the collared vests and trousers the males wear.

The first Indra through the door, the one who asked the question of Gallagher, approaches him. "You've slayed a leviathan, young elf. How do you feel? Come, come." He reaches a hand out to Gallagher to pull him to his fins.

Gallagher ignores his hand and lifts himself up. "I feel…"

"Never mind. Never mind." He waves his arms about. "How you feel is irrelevant. *You* are *our* elf. We are certain of this. A fine display of courage and strength. You nearly killed Helyer in the process…" The Indra looks over his shoulder to where Helyer stands. Gallagher hadn't even recognized him in his ominous mood. "…but all is well."

"Why am I here?" Gallagher is blunt. He has no interest in joining this Indra in his excitement. What is there to be excited about? He lost his clan

permanently with this betrayal. He has certainly lost Rivee's respect and friendship. And what of Mira? They are worlds apart if she still lives.

"Rather than tell you, I would like to show you," the short elf replies
smugly. "I have seen enough to understand where your values lie, and I would
like to open some doors for you. But first…" The sky elf turns and gestures
toward the three females. "…we would like to get you cleaned up." He looks
back toward Gallagher and he cocks his head. "And get you some proper attire.
You will have many eyes on you, so we cannot have you wearing those rags."

Gallagher looks down at himself. He dons his typical malo, a kelp-fashioned loincloth, and a leather belt. No tunic, as it isn't customary for the De'wi
males to wear anything more than a malo.

"Ladies, please." He waves an open arm, gesturing for them to do something. "And remove that apparatus from his face. He can do without by now."

Gallagher presses a hand to his face, fingering the wire attached between
his ear and lip. The male Indra make their way toward the exit as the females
pull out string to measure his torso, limbs, and every part of his body. They pull
his arm taught to get the first measurement.

"Wait!" Gallagher calls. "Who are you?"

"Ah, yes." The Indra turns to face him. "My apologies. I am Aricent Godmadina, righthand and second born, heir to our house matriarch, Vicenya Godmadina, of whom you will meet soon enough. Please…" He waves a hand for
the ladies to continue, then he exits the white cell.

The three maidens stand Gallagher before a pane of reflecting glass. He stares
in wonder for quite a while before saying anything. "What is this magic? Is that
what I look like?"

The ladies giggle.

Gallagher has never seen his image so clearly before. They have looking
glass within their culture, but it reflects a faint image. Nothing he's paid much
attention to. This glass shows his reflection without flaw.

He stares for a while longer, not only looking at himself but the reflection
of everything within the room. He bends at the knees to see the ceiling. He stands
on the balls of his fins and wobbles left and right to glimpse the entire room. He

would not be able to differentiate between reflection and reality if it weren't wrapped in a metallic frame.

They have him wearing grey trousers, a matching jacket with small tassels at the cuffs, and a white, collared vest beneath the jacket. It's so foreign, Gallagher has never even dreamt of such attire. It's wild, exotic, and restricting. He raises his arms to feel the fabric slide across his skin and inhibit movement. His hair isn't so exotic as it is perfect. It's combed to one side and clipped finely on the opposite side. Every strand of hair in a precise location in line with one another. They've made him look like an Indra in this attire, but not in size or shape. What is he doing? This is disloyal to his clan.

"You are a handsome elf." One of the ladies says. She stands next to him in the looking glass with a proud smile on her face. "I wasn't quite sure what to do with those." She gestures to his fins. "Tailoring an outfit is much faster than a shoe. I'm afraid you'll have to go barefoot."

"Fin," Gallagher corrects her as he wiggles his toes.

"Excuse me?"

"They're fins. Not feet. Barefin."

"Oh…" She chuckles and Gallagher's gaze lands on her smile. "You're ready. Come." She ushers him away from his reflection toward the exit.

They enter a long hallway, stretching far in both directions. The floor has a steady movement in the center of the hallway. Standing still atop the moving floor are dozens of Indra traveling up and down the corridor without moving their legs.

"How is this so?"

His escort giggles but says nothing.

"It's a conveyor," a new voice speaks.

Gallagher looks around to see an elegant maiden elf approaching them. No more elegant than the three who transformed him into an Indra, but she carries a lofty air about her. She walks toward them with confidence as if every other elf will trip over themselves to get out of her way. The white gown she dons is tight around her thick midsection and flows freely to her ankles. The sleeves are embedded with tiny sparkling stones and her hair matches with majority of it bound atop her head and sprinkled with similar stones, leaving only a few tresses intentionally framing her face.

She receives many eyes from passersby on the conveyor. Gallagher's three escorts step behind him as this beautiful elf approaches. Several Indra with scepters line the corridor. All appear to be disguised as common elves going about their day, but it's obvious they're with this maiden elf when they all have reason to stop as she does.

"It's no different than a conveyor in an assembly line. An asset to all industry."

Gallagher remains silent. He is clueless about what she says.

"My apologies. It's an Indran means of efficiency." She looks to Gallagher's escorts. "You are dismissed. I will take it from here."

The three female Indra break away from them and disappear onto the crowded conveyor without another word. She is certainly an elf with authority.

"Vicenya?" he asks.

"Excuse me?" her brow presses inward.

Gallagher shakes his head. "Nothing." She must not be the same elf Aricent mentioned earlier.

"Now you have me curious." She tilts her head and looks at him up and down. "If you believe a pretentious elf like Vicenya would lay a foot near this place, House Godmadina are instilling false expectations. I'll have to evaluate and rearrange whatever they've told you about the Indran culture."

"They haven't told me anything." Gallagher glares at her, giving her no more respect than any of the others. Whatever authority she wields, it means nothing to him. "They have only offered ultimatums."

"Hmm…good." She swiftly turns away before he can react and steps onto the moving walkway. Gallagher reluctantly follows.

Several elves already on the conveyor shuffle to get out of their way. A plump Indra falls behind them, tripping over himself. Gallagher turns around and offers an aiding hand.

"Thank you, young champion." The elderly elf stares at him with admiration.

Gallagher cocks his head at the elf's gratitude. Helyer made mention of a champion as well. He dismisses the oddity as Indran culture he doesn't understand.

The halls are filled with other Indra, all who stare without guilt as they pass by. It's as if they've never seen a De'wi before. Unless they're staring at the elven maiden who escorts him. But their eyes seem fixated on him.

The corridors are long and many, with too many extremities branching out to count. The moving floors eventually carry them to a grand chamber where multiple corridors congregate. The chamber is busy with green-leafed trees and other foliage. Some with thick blade-like leaves, similar to seagrass but grown to epic proportions. Several bushes hold bright colored blossoms. Large leaves and small leaves of countless shapes. Navigating around all this foliage are pristine, white trails with miniature creeks that would offer a peaceful acoustic if it weren't for the bustle of the crowd. Gallagher pokes at one of the leaves to see if it's alive.

"The atrium," his escort announces, pulling his attention away from the beautiful foliage and toward the Indra going about their business. Most glance or stare at Gallagher. A small one runs up to him.

"I knew it was true." His words come out in a child's voice. "You're the De'wi who'll champion our people!" The child Indra clutches Gallagher's hand. "Thank you." Then, he runs off.

"What was that?" Gallagher asks the maiden escorting him. "Champion?"

She says nothing. She presses a hand on his lower back to usher him forward. As they move to the exit and she opens the door, Gallagher takes note of the normal door with a lever. Not all are operated by their machina magic.

They step outside and the buzz of the scene petrifies Gallagher. The plaza before them stretches across the landship like a vast meadow set in the middle of a forest with towering structures on all sides. An odd melody fills the air, or multiple melodies, perhaps. Chatter overtakes it as elves of many sizes, shapes, and colors skitter around on miniature carriages pulled by nothing. They scream with a high-pitched whine that forces Gallagher's hands to his ears for protection. Standing high on the steps of the atrium they just exited, he witnesses a sea of heads bobbing and zipping without much room in between. So many Indra...

He closes his eyes and takes a deep breath. Refocusing, he looks to the skyline. The surrounding towers are all built with metallic, rigid elements and lots of glass. Green foliage climbs every one, transforming them into green pinnacles of land cascading into the air. Some have waterfalls and others are adjoined at the top, creating an arch of foliage. Between each tower is where Gallagher finds the most joy. The deep blue color fills every crevice of the sky where a towering green structure is absent. He's in the heart of the sky city.

The smells of their realm, of their culture, fill his nose. It's fresh, almost scentless. The salty aroma he's accustomed to doesn't exist above the clouds. Aricent was right about him not needing the breathing apparatus anymore. He's acclimating to their world.

He shouldn't be acclimating, though. He clenches his jaw. What is he thinking? He should be planning his escape. What is stopping him from escaping right now? He could run and break free of their grasp. All he must do is find the edge of their landship and make the leap. Except... Rivee. He doesn't know where Rivee is. He doesn't know if she's been freed yet.

"Come." The maiden's soft but persuasive voice ushers him to continue walking. Her smile is flawless.

Gallagher follows her. As do her entourage of not-so-stealthy guards.

Too many Indra fill the plaza for them to travel in straight lines. There must be tens of thousands, and they all have somewhere to be, walking with a heavy pace or riding in the odd individual-sized machina carriages. They do a lot of resting while venturing to their destinations. A small guardrail encapsulates the two-wheeled machina, all made from similar material to the machina fin he owned for such a brief time.

"We refer to them as ferries," the maiden states when she sees him ogling them. "An efficient means of travel. Caelum Invictus isn't as small as the colonies you're accustomed to. The Sky Plaza alone warrants the use of them."

Gallagher looks down at his bare fins. He held a small sample of what it felt like to power through the air like a normal warrior, not so different from how these Indra power through their thoroughfares, and it was taken from him. His desire to get the machina fin back is almost as much as his desire to take Mira's hand. Maybe more because it's a means to be worthy of her hand.

He only finds admiration for their machina, and maybe a hint of envy. Yet, he has always been told how evil it is. How harmful it is. He doesn't witness any of that within the city. The machina only seems to help them with tedious tasks, like walking long stretches through a city in which they don't have the ease of swimming. He can only imagine how long it takes those without the ferries to get to their destinations. Gallagher looks up and down the plaza to gather the full distance from one end to the other. Their short legs could fall off by the time they walked that far, but it seems as though some make the jaunt. And those who are walking, also don attire which has seen better days. Some are even barefoot like Gallagher. And those who travel by ferry present themselves in pristine whites and light grey wardrobes with shiny or sparkling accents. Not a spot of filth to be seen on them.

The maiden escorts him to a larger white carriage with doors trimmed in silver, fully encapsulated, unlike the others that look like buckets on wheels. This one is a full-sized carriage with four wheels.

"How do they…err…go?" he asks.

His escort smiles at him, believing it a jest at first, until she finds the earnest expression on his face. "The essence of Blue Tears, of course. The Greybeards are wizards when it comes to machina."

It is all so mystifying to him. He climbs into the carriage. Inside are seats covered in plush, crimson fabric, softer than the silkiest sands within his bay. So elegant and luxurious. Is this the life all Indra live? Except maybe the few wandering barefoot out there.

"Where are we headed?" he asks after he's done admiring their machina.

The maiden takes a seat across from him. "The hydration station."

"Hydration station…" Gallagher is bemused.

"Aricent will explain it to you when we arrive."

"Aricent?"

"The elf you met earlier today," she says with much derision. "Have you already forgotten?"

"Sorry. There's a lot…" Gallagher watches pedestrians zip by through the window. The carriage travels at a fast pace. Faster even than Mira can swim. "There's a lot to take in," he finishes his sentence without looking at her, his gaze instead transfixed on the passing objects outside the window.

"Indeed. I cannot fathom what you must be experiencing." She stares at him, whether with admiration or intrigue, Gallagher isn't sure. "You're the first De'wi most of us have seen in person, you know."

Gallagher isn't sure how to respond to that. He's experienced so many firsts in the past week, and he cannot wait to tell Mira. A frown finds its way onto his face.

"What is it?" she asks.

"What is your name?" Gallagher asks in return.

"Fae."

"Fae. A beautiful name."

"Thank you."

"I'm Gallagher."

They sit in silence for a moment while Gallagher ponders her last question. He may never see Mira again. Or any of his clanmates. For all he knows, he will be a resident to the Caelum Realm for the remainder of his life. His frown deepens.

"You're sad. I don't know what House Godmadina has done to you, but I will assure you, we do not all behave in whatever way they are treating you. Most are tender. Accepting. Forgiving. Hate, nor violence, are becoming of the Indran race. House Godmadina on the other hand have allowed envy to creep into their hearts, and they display more and more of these negative traits by the day. Please do not judge us all by what you are experiencing."

"House Godmadina? That was Aricent." Gallagher looks for confirmation.

"Yes." Her voice is sharp with much disdain.

"And what if I were experiencing perfection and euphoria?"

"I would call you a liar, then repeat myself. Do not judge us all by what you are experiencing." She smiles at him. Tender, indeed.

"Mira would love to meet you someday."

"Mira?"

"Never mind. It will never happen." Gallagher turns his attention out the window.

"A loved one?"

"Something of that nature."

"Ah, a courtship undone."

Gallagher cringes. "More like a courtship never begun."

"I hope this was not our doing."

Gallagher shakes his head, never pulling away from his blank gaze focused out the window. "Blame will never solve a problem. I refrain from doing so." The Indra may have taken the final blow to his courtship of Mira, but Gallagher is the only one to blame. He refused to court her before becoming a warrior. His hesitancy is the only thing he can blame, and she may be lost forever.

The carriage slows to a stop, nearly indetectable aside from the scenery outside the window coming to a halt. The door opens and Gallagher steps out of the carriage into another large plaza. This one is beautiful in a vastly different way than the last. The towering structures around him are all metallic without the green foliage. Bridges connect the buildings in several locations, creating a labyrinth of passageways in the sky. A cold aura fills the space, and a smell of something sweet and acidic. The acidic odor can almost be tasted, like bile finding its way up your throat. The sweetness is familiar, but depicting it is beyond Gallagher at the moment. The same blue sky frames every building, filling him with an energy he doesn't get beneath the clouds.

"The hydration station." Fae gestures to the large structure before them, which is in the form of a massive sphere with towering silos surrounding it.

Not nearly as many Indra roam this plaza, and their attire differs from the majority in the other plaza. The colors are less brilliant with more noticeable frays in the hems. Gallagher is ushered toward the entrance of the building before he can take in anymore of the scenery.

"There he is!" A jovial voice bellows. It's Aricent, accompanied by Helyer and a few other Indra. "Where is your escort? The ladies I left you with should have accompanied you here."

Gallagher looks around to find Fae no longer with him. The carriage is gone.

"Never mind. Never mind. Come in."

Gallagher is reluctant to take part in whatever they have in store for him, but his options are limited. Why would Fae have left him at the entrance without a word of departure? He allows for the group of elves to welcome him into the building. "What is this place?"

"You're about to find out," Aricent proclaims. "Follow me."

The entire building appears to be one giant machina. Everything within is metallic and cold. The walls, the doors, the floor, and ceiling. They're all varying colors of grey with a shimmer to them. Similar to the exterior of the structure, bridgeways fill the space above him, interweaving in an intricate maze.

"We're thoroughly excited to have you on board," Aricent says to him. Helyer grunts at his comment. "Well… most of us." He shrugs. "Helyer has his reasons to not be as enthusiastic as the rest of us. I think you understand."

"Because he almost died?" Gallagher is blunt. "This should be a proud day for him. He survived a leviathan. Even amongst the De'wi, not many can say the same." Gallagher makes direct eye contact. "You should be proud."

Helyer shrinks away, unconvinced. He looks a bit disgusted by the comment. Gallagher shrugs it off, unconcerned about the weak elf.

They walk through a set of double doors, which Aricent opens with the touch of his scepter. This must be a more secure area like the white cells. Once through the doors, all the Indra step onto one of their personal ferries, of which all are parked along the side of the corridor in an organized fashion. Gallagher chooses to walk. They follow this long, wide corridor for quite a while. With minimal effort, his longer legs keep the same pace as their ferries.

The group passes through another set of double doors at the end of the passageway and the sweet scent Gallagher was smelling outside slams into him like a kelpmallow pie plastering his face. The strong aroma nearly knocks him back.

When he gathers his senses, he's shocked yet again by the bluish-green glow emanating from a large vat centrally located in the room. Gallagher follows the skywalk bordering the vat, hanging onto the metallic guardrail as he does.

"Careful. Don't lean over the edge," Helyer instructs. The Indra stare at Gallagher with concern. They must not be used to having such a tall body walk their skywalks. The guardrail comes up to his waist, whereas it rises all the way to their chests. Gallagher doesn't feel unsafe around it, though. He grips it with both hands and shakes it a bit. All the Indran bodies tense.

Gallagher laughs internally. "The rail is secure," he says confidently.

"Of course it is," another Indra imposes his opinion, clearly offended.

"Calm down, Golistian. We now know the engineering is above standard regulation. You can give yourself a pat on the back."

If his stubby arms could reach it, Gallagher humors himself, but refrains from saying it out loud. "What is this place?"

"The hydration station," Aricent replies and moves toward him along the skywalk. "This is the heart of our livelihood. The legacy of the Greybeards."

Gallagher cocks his head at the small sky elf. "You've brought the enemy to the 'heart' of your livelihood?" He asks the question mockingly.

"I suppose we have different opinions of one another. You are our champion, Gallagher, not the enemy."

"And have I agreed to this?"

"You have, when you defeated the leviathan to prove your value and said you would help."

"I don't even know what it is you need help with." Gallagher's brow tightens.

"Precisely why we are here, Gallagher. Please, let me explain."

The other Indra move closer, all circling around the central vat along the guardrail. All their little arms reaching for the rail.

Gallagher could handle them all in a fight if he had a weapon. And the ability to swim. And if they didn't wield their machina scepters. "Ergh…please do."

Aricent starts into his explanation. "What you see before you is the essence of Blue Tears. The Greybeards have engineered a means to process the spice, breaking it down into its finest form where we can extract its oils and waters. The essence is then used to power everything you see before you." He waves an arm, arching it from the vat to over his head. "And the byproduct we can infuse into our food, offering a most nutritious and balanced diet. The Tears are the source of life for all elves, not just the De'wi. However, unlike the De'wi, the Tears are not only consumed by the Indran race. The Tears power our way of life. An energy source for mind and machine alike."

Gallagher doesn't have the mind to correct him. The De'wi use the essence of Blue Tears within their blades to enhance longevity and sharpness. They are not ignorant of the concept. Their culture simply chooses not to indulge, especially in machina. But it raises the question: where is the line drawn between an augmented tool and machina?

Aricent points to several tubes leading from the vat to the towering column overhead. The chamber they're in is a massive hollow structure climbing as far as he can see. Skywalks cross the hollow in too many places to count.

"Typically, you would see every one of those ventilation tubes emanating the same blue-green glow as the vat. This entire column should be glowing with life." He raises his hand high gesturing to everything above them. "Our supply of Tears is running in short supply, Gallagher. This is why we need you."

Gallagher isn't comprehending what he's saying. If they've always had such a lavish supply, why would they need a single De'wi to gather more?

"Why don't you have your machina help you. That's what it's for, is it not? To do everything you don't want to. Why call upon a De'wi to gather your Tears?"

Aricent chuckles. Gallagher looks around to see several of the elves smiling at his comment.

"No, no. We have our own methods for that. Solaria, I'm afraid, has lost its surplus of the energized spice. The small crop within your clan's boundaries is one of the last the Ebisu have not overtaken. We've—"

"Wait!" Gallagher interrupts. "You had me fight that leviathan! What was it for if not to test my ability to retrieve my clan's supply of Tears?" Gallagher tightens his jaw and firmly grips the rail. "You *do* want me to gather Blue Tears for you? Though, we De'wi are warriors, not gatherers." Gallagher cringes inside, knowing his role as a kelp *picker* could just as easily be labeled a kelp *gatherer*.

"Please, Gallagher. Listen." Aricent turns to face him. "First off, the De'wi are not all warriors. So many more clans reside outside the Morshine Isle, as you're probably aware, and not all wield a stick for battle."

Gallagher grimaces. "It's called a yari."

"Your tiny crop would hardly make a difference. This problem goes far beyond your leviathans and your Blue Tears. That was a test of courage, resolve, and of your loyalties. You see, we are not asking you to betray your clan. We are not enemies of the De'wi. We have our differences, but I think we are all mature enough to know there is room for both of our cultures amidst Solaria. We have our Caelum Realm, and you have your Terra Realm. We do not wish for you to turn on the De'wi. We hope for you to be our emissary. We hope for the Indra and the De'wi to make an alliance. And we need this to happen soon." He gestures to the nearly empty vat containing the essence of Blue Tears.

"Why are the Tears so important? I've only consumed a small sample in all my life. Clearly, we can survive without it." Gallagher flexes a bicep, but it's not seen beneath his uncustomary jacket.

"The essence of the Blue Tears energizes our machina, Gallagher, as I stated earlier. Including the landship you're walking on."

Gallagher looks down at his fins.

"Nice touch, by the way. Your fins. I see they didn't have any shoes to accommodate your large size."

Gallagher ignores the comment. "So…" He pauses, gripping the railing tight as he thinks about the dilemma the Indra are in. "…if you run out of Tears, your entire landship falls from the sky. Are there more landships? Are they all in the same situation? Why not just abandon this one and move onto the next?"

Aricent grips the rail next to Gallagher and looks down at the essence of Blue Tears. "This is only a minor issue—our landships falling from the sky. This is a problem for all Solaria. The Tears are a resource all elves consume, and when a resource engrained into our societies is depleted, it will bring chaos and war to the world.

"Oceanus Salus is also dependent on the Tears, you see. It is the only way the Ebisu can function as they do within the Ocean Realm. I've never witnessed it firsthand, but I hear their civilization has outgrown itself. There is only so much space for them to breathe and walk freely down there without getting wet. But it's all dependent on the essence of the Blue Tears, just as our culture is.

"The primitive De'wi—no offense intended, just a reality—are the only civilization without a threat to their culture. Without the Tears, we will all be forced back into the Terra Realm. And this…" He turns to look at Gallagher, a look of sincerity and desperation on his face. "This will lead to war if we all try to exist amongst one another."

The subtle din of machina parts shifting and breathing like an overexerted elf, is the only sound that follows his dire proclamation.

The Indra are all focused on Gallagher. He's not quite sure what they expect of him, but he knows it's not going to be a light task. Two of Solaria's cultures have extinction looming within eyesight, and somehow Gallagher is to make it all better.

"Why not address this with the Elders?" Gallagher asks. "Why me?" He turns to face Aricent, desperate for a good answer. With lives on the line, he knows he will never be able to turn this down. Whatever needs to be done, he will do it. But why choose Gallagher? "Why a blighted warrior?"

The door to the chamber swooshes open, and in walks another group of Indra. The sky elves turn to give them their full attention, bowing their heads as they do. They each carry a hidden expression holding a mixture of disdain and guilt.

"Thought you could keep this honored guest out of my purview, did you?" The beauty entering the cold, hollow chamber dons a white, flowing gown laced in crimsons and silvers. Her hair is made into fanciful curls and spills in ways Gallagher has never seen. Atop her head sits a crown emanating a subtle blue glow. Her glare, directed at the other Indra, overpowers all the brilliance of her aura.

Beside her is a male donning a suit of equal elegance, and a youngkin, also dressed in a beautiful, eye-catching gown draped to the floor. A tiara is propped atop her head. These individuals are Indra royalty.

They walk with silent feet on the metallic skywalk. Their grace and elegance are a stark contrast to the industrial vat and cold metal enveloping the chamber. The other Indra all shuffle to the rail as the royalty walk past them, and the beauties stop before Gallagher.

His mouth hangs open, for he knows both the lady elves. But he doesn't know them as royalty. "Fae?" It's the same maiden who intercepted him at the white cell and escorted him here. But when did she have time to make an outfit change?

She pinches her gown with both hands and offers a curtsy.

Gallagher takes a second glance at the youngkin standing next to her. Then a third. She stands tall with *two* shoe tips exposed from beneath the beautiful gown that nearly touches the deck. He stares in amazement, befuddled at who he's looking at. "Rivee…" He can hardly say her name amidst his shock. For the first time, Gallagher realizes Rivee is an adult. Short she may be, but as she stands next to Lady Fae their height doesn't show much difference. Rivee is hardly taller than the Indra. And her elegance and beauty have diminished all her child-like qualities.

A nasty glare and a nudge from Fae drives Rivee to offer Gallagher a curtsy as well.

"Stop that." He pulls Rivee up. "What are you doing? What is this? Why's she dressed like this?"

"She's royalty amongst the Indra," Fae responds. A look of shock is apparent on all the other sky elves' faces.

"An heir!" Aricent blurts out. "Blasphemy! Who has sired this youngkin?"

Lady Fae glares at him. The open disrespect doesn't seem to be anything new between these two. Then, Gallagher remembers Fae saying something about House Godmadina and the envious ways they've taken to. Is Gallagher witnessing a longstanding rivalry between two elite houses?

"Jarnes, you imbecile. It was outside the traditions of wedlock, but she's an heir all the same. And more importantly a daughter and a granddaughter."

"How so? Where's the mother?" Aricent rebuttals.

"Are you suggesting this child was born without a mother?" she says mockingly. A few of the other elves grin at the idea of such absurdity.

"No. Of course not. You won't get away with this so easily, Elder Fae." Aricent says her name with contempt. "You will have to show evidence."

"The same evidence that has resulted in my son being blacklisted amongst all the eligible maidens. Do you mean that evidence?"

Gallagher cannot believe what he's witnessing. Aricent appeared to be a decent elf, and nearly had him convinced to help save their race. But in the presence of Elder Fae—Gallagher's attention turns to her—Aricent's personality turned into that of a sibling throwing a tantrum. Is this the envy she warned him of? Is Aricent manipulating Gallagher to do his own personal biddings without the consent of their Elder?

Elder Fae dismisses the elves of House Godmadina—shooing them, rather—and she doesn't continue until the last one flees the chamber.

"Young hero, we have much to discuss, but we will have time for that this evening when you join us at the celebration to welcome our Riveria home."

"Riveria…" Gallagher stares at Fae, then at Rivee, his mind whirring like a raging storm. All of these house squabbles and talk of royalty and war are over his head, literally where they belong, yet he finds himself pulled directly in the eye of the storm, unknowing how to escape it all.

18 INTO THE HEARTLESS VOID

"Dragons, Mira…" Tanniv cranes his neck to see her. "We rode dragons! Can you believe it? Maybe a half century ago, when I was a young tot, I would have believed this…but now? Never. I cannot believe we sped through a *forest* of all places—with real trees of wonder—on the hides of dragons." His smile reaches ear to ear.

Mira cannot resist joining him in his moment of elation. This is everything Mira dreamed about. Except…she always had Gallagher and Rivee by her side when imagining a world like this. And never was she in pursuit of lost or imprisoned companions. "Seadragons, Tanniv. Seadragons."

"What's next? Do we ride the waves gripping the shell of a sea turtle." His eyes light up. "Or perhaps we bounce through the clouds on the backs of manta rays. This is unbelievable!"

"The blue dragon," Mira mutters just loud enough for Tanniv to hear above the wind whirling past their ears.

He looks over at her as he backstrokes through the air, bemusement swathed over him. "Not to shade your dreams, Mira, but the blue dragons are untouchable. After experiencing that grendelin, I can say I'm more prone to believe they exist, but—"

"But could you imagine?" Mira's tone grows louder with more excitement. Her arms spread wide as if she's gliding. "Wings covered in feather-like scales, spreading wide. They soar through the currents of the ocean like a ray on the clouds. Their long tails propel them with elegant yet powerful beats. I wonder if they breathe fire?"

"Fire! Now you're being preposterous. Dragons don't breathe fire. Especially not under water. Regardless, you'd have to swim deeper than any elf has ever swum to find one. You know the legends. We're talking head-implosion deep. Is an imploding head worth the thrill of riding on the back of a blue dragon?" His head follows her as his body twirls through the air, giving her a hard stare as if he actually expects her to answer that question.

"*Please*, keep your imploding head focused ahead of you. Last thing we need is for you to smash it into a tree or a low-hanging branch."

"Good point, chief." He raises his hand with a pointed finger. "Don't run into trees." He looks back at her again with a playful grin. "This is all so new to me—swimming through a forest and all—I would have never thought of that, but I'll remember that one. Don't run into to trees." He checks off an imaginary box.

"Smartass." She shakes her head at him. "The blue dragons are…err…never mind." She pauses, unwilling to say what she wants to. Revealing her dreams to anyone other than Gallagher or Rivee feels awkward, and even this she has never spoken to them.

"Are?" He continues ahead, not looking back at her. "Are what?" He comes to a halt when she doesn't respond. "C'mon, Mira. What is it? You want me to go head first into a tree trying to figure out what you're saying? Am I really that bad?"

She shakes her head and swims past him. "No, it's not that."

"Then what?" He speeds up to swim by her side, pressing her further.

"I can't."

"Can't what? I'm never going to let this go now. You have me intrigued."

'Ugh…fine." She stops kicking her fins and treads in place. "The blue dragons, they're…"

Tanniv rolls his eyes at her. "Get it out already."

"I…err…" She stops treading and plants her fins on the soft soil of the forest floor. "Sorry, this is hard to admit."

"Go on." Tanniv lowers himself to the ground beside her, his full attention ready to hear what she has to say.

"I often sit at the edge of the shallows. And stare."

"At what?" Tanniv asks.

"The darkness."

"Seems interesting."

"There's a serenity to it. The glimmer of light breaking through the surface only to be devoured by what? Nothing? Where does it go? Does the light just disappear? Is darkness so powerful that it consumes all? I have stared into the depths for hours at a time wondering what could down there. What could steal the light away. Is it the Ebisu? Perhaps, but I don't believe that to be true. I know it's not true."

"You're scaring me, chief. But I'll ask the question. How so? How do you know?"

"I've seen one, Tanniv. A blue dragon."

Tanniv holds back a burst of laughter.

"I think they absorb the light. It was only a glimmer in the depth, similar to the light breaking through the surface. But the source of light was coming from the depths, and it moved, unlike the Blue Tears. It moved, Tanniv. I think they absorb the light and create the darkness. They are both the magnificence and the terror of the depths. They are…"

"Not real." Tanniv playfully jabs her in the gut and laughs at her. "You're right. You shouldn't have told me. C'mon. Let's continue ahead." With that playful jab, he leaps into the air and swims back toward the canopy of the forest.

"I should've never said anything," she mumbles to herself. To ride a blue dragon would be brilliant, but he's right. She needs to keep her focus. She needs to keep her wandering mind grounded if they are to get through this. "Keep swimming," she yells up to him to regain a sense of control. "We'll have a rest when we peak that ridge just ahead." The Ebisu should be more than a valley or two away by now. They can afford to rest.

Tanniv raises a hand of acknowledgement and narrows his body to speed ahead. Mira casually takes up the rear. When they reach the peak, Tanniv strolls to the top of a steadfast rock protruding from the mountainside, offering a good point of view above the tree line. Mira joins him.

"Can you believe we're in the Morshine Peaks?" She looks up. "If you stand on your toes, you can almost touch the clouds." She reaches her hand skyward.

"It's all too surreal to comprehend. I don't have the wandering heart you do, Mira, but even I can admit, experiencing what we have in such a short time in the wild, is beyond thrilling. I would do this again." His bare chest heaves up and down as he releases a big sigh.

"It's colder up here," Mira suggests, folding her arms across her torso.

"Any signs of the grendelin?" Tanniv's gaze narrows, scouring the rugged terrain. "Hard to believe such a large creature could go missing."

"Agreed. But it *does* look like a mountain itself, so…" She shrugs.

They can see all of Solaria from this altitude. The mountain ridges reach away from them toward the shoreline like fingers gripping the land. The ocean glistens in the evening light. Oranges and golds paint the clouds as the hidden sun merges with the horizon.

"The Eye of Solari is so distant…" Her gaze sits where the cloud cover is brightest in the west with a dark ring encircling it. She can hardly see it. But she *can* see it. Gallagher is out there somewhere. Hopefully with Rivee right by his side.

"I can't believe we missed the Solari Harvest," Tanniv adds, reflecting on the hectic days that have come and passed.

"Look at that treacherous storm out *there*." Mira points east, away from the golden horizon.

"Ominous for sure. Wouldn't surprise me if the Indra had something to do with the storms. Oh! And look over there. A storm within the ocean!" His finger jets toward what appears to be a massive waterspout fostering a whirlpool in the ocean.

The clouds above could be an illustration drawn with coal, they are so dark. The whirlpool's turbulence is certainly an area to avoid. A blight on the world.

"The Ebisu's ocean lair?" he asks. "It would explain why they're so malicious. Dealing with constant warring currents like that."

Mira smirks. "Yeah. They're good for holding a grudge, it would seem." Her smile fades as she focuses on it. "I've never witnessed anything like it. My father mentioned something of storms reaching into the ocean…" She looks at Tanniv but withholds further comment, unsure what it means.

"It's like the one that leveled our colony," he says, pointing to a different and distant storm. "Lightning and all."

"What?"

"You didn't get to witness it. You were in the rallyhouse." He pulls his gaze away from the storm to look at Mira. His eyes are wide with excitement. "It was wild. Three turbulent waterspouts circled around the bright eye in the sky. It's unheard of, right? Especially for them to touch down in our little chunk of shoreline. The winds don't push storms beyond the knuckles, Mira. It's not supposed to happen. Chaos erupted instantly. Chaos everywhere."

"You think…" Mira starts, but she's not sure what she's about to ask. Is it coincidental the Ebisu arrived just when a storm of a millennium arrived? Is there a correlation between the dark storm and the dark elves? "…err…never mind. How about a small fire?" She rubs her hands together to warm them.

"What about the Ebisu on our tail?"

"What tail? We don't have tails, Tanniv." She says it with an honest tone.

"Wha… That's… I didn't mean we had tails…"

She smiles and he grimaces in return. "It would take them weeks to climb this terrain," she insists. "Without their seadragons, they're no different than carabao ranging a hillside."

"Did you see where the seadragons dispersed? If they locate even a few, they could find their way up here before dawn."

"They broke away deep into the hills. It would take them days at minimum to find the ones they lost."

"Yeah, okay," he agrees with reluctance hanging in his voice. "It might help draw Veras out, too." He scours the terrain one more time. As does Mira. A stone giant shouldn't go missing. But then again, if they've been dwelling on the same island together for millennia, they're probably good at blending in.

The two of them gather underbrush and spark a flame with dagger and stone. Mira has never been so appreciative of a campfire. They sit beside it and Tanniv pulls out dried meat from a pouch at his hip to warm it by the fire.

"It's already been cured, Tanniv." Mira questions his behavior.

"Aye, but a warm meal is better than a cold one, isn't it?"

"I would say you have a refined approach toward what goes in your mouth."

"As we *all* should, Mira. As we *all* should."

Her lips delicately curl into her cheeks. Though, for as many smiles as she discovers on this journey, there is a frown to accompany each one. How can she be happy when they started with four and are down to two.

"Do you think we'll find Haltuk?"

Tanniv's mouth flattens as he clenches his jaw. "I don't know, Mira. I try not to think that far ahead. It draws hope. It manifests gloom. It creates internal turmoil. All of which are delusions out of my control. I'd prefer to stay right here with my thoughts. Right now." He rotates the meat he placed next to the flame.

"Yeah, I suppose it sparks unnecessary feelings, but it can help us derive a plan if we consider what lies ahead."

"And that is for you, our chief, to dwell on. Not I." He looks up from the flame, his face glowing in the dancing light. "Tell me where to go, Mira, and I will do as you think is right. As a warrior of the Morshine Clan, I don't fear what lies ahead because I don't think about it. Instead, I embrace the moment. You have my blade. I trust your decisions."

"Thanks for the beacon," a new voice calls from beyond the light of the campfire.

"Veras!" Mira hops to her fins and quickly embraces him without giving him a chance to walk into the light.

"So soon?" Tanniv doesn't bother getting up.

"What a loving reunion, Tanniv," Veras mocks him as he and Mira find a seat around the flames. Veras pulls out his parchment and immediately begins scribbling on it.

"Aye, it's only been a few hours. I never doubted your livelihood. Take it as a compliment, young warrior." He raises his meat to him, then takes a large bite out of it.

"Hmm…well at least one of us never doubted my livelihood." He looks to Mira. "How'd you fare?" He cracks his knuckles. "You're alive. But I fear your beacon will reunite more than we'd like."

"We removed their means of swift travel. The seadragons are roaming the mountains somewhere." She gestures to the rugged terrain before them. "Hopefully they made their way back to the ocean where they belong."

"Seadragons, huh? Did you ride them?"

"Eh-yeah…" Tanniv responds with a large smile. "You have to try it."

"The Ebisu, they're incapable of swimming through the air like we can," Mira says. "Too heavy, I suppose."

"Yeah, too heavy until they realize they can remove that ridiculous armor they wear." Veras acts out peeling away a breastplate.

"I wonder…" Mira's gaze grows distant and concerned.

"What about you, Veras?" Tanniv asks with a mouthful of meat. "How'd you get that giant to follow you?"

"With bouquets of compliments." He unfurls his hands as if he's presenting a gift and offers a slight bow to go with it.

His eyes light up, and he pulls out his parchment to jot down more notes as he glimpses the terrain in between writings. "There too much to observe out here in the wild. So many findings to record."

"Serious, you fool, I must know. I mean…it was a legendary grendelin, and *you* persuaded it. Where is it now, anyways?" His head twists over each shoulder.

"It was easy, mostly. But I'm all out of Tears." Veras pats at the side pouches strapped to his belt, then continues scribbling on his parchment.

"You gave that thing your Tears?" Mira spits out. "What if it had an adverse effect? What if it went berserk and dominated all of us?"

"Well…it would have saved its life, just as you wanted." He shrugs his shoulders with his hands raised. Mira's brow furrows. "Getting it to understand I had the sweet treats was the tricky part. I basically had to shove my hand up its nose, and once it smelled the sweet scent, its fear melted away. I tossed half of it into its mouth, and swam toward the mountains, hopeful it would follow."

"Where is it now? We searched for hours and saw no signs of it. How'd you make it disappear." Tanniv's eyes narrow, appearing both malicious and mischievous in the dancing orange light. "You didn't use some of the Indra's machina magic, did you? Veras…"

A small puff of laughter escapes Veras. "No. I gave the last of my spice to it, and it followed a bit longer, but eventually turned away when it realized I wasn't offering any more. But…" A scheming look suddenly appears on Veras' face. "I did manage to snatch this away from one of the Ebisu before we separated." He pulls out a small device from his pouch, hardly bigger than the palm of his hand.

"Veras!" Mira's voice is motherly and full of ridicule.

"I haven't used it. I just thought we'd fare better if they had one less of…whatever it is." He turns it over in his hand, inspecting its nature.

"You know Gallagher was banned for having machina?" Her motherly tone presses deeper into him.

"We're not within the boundaries of the colony, are we?" Veras looks at her from beneath his brow, orange light reflecting off his face and the device he holds.

Mira purses her lips. "I suppose not."

"I think it would be wise to figure out what it is. It will help us understand what we're up against."

"A warming welcome…" a fourth voice enters their semi-circle from beyond the light.

All three De'wi warriors snap to their fins, their yaris at the ready.

A tall elf arrogantly strolls closer to the campfire. The orange light dances a little darker on his flesh. His chest and thighs are freed from their armor. The evening sky behind him has all but lost its golds and yellows. The small glimmer of light refusing the darkness to take hold of the night sky is washed away with his grim nature.

"It is nothing more than a zephyr. Allows for a dry moment beneath the waves. A means to take a breather, not unlike you have here."

"Where are the others?" Mira asks the General.

"Oh, they're surrounding you. I felt it would be a bit forceful if we all revealed ourselves at once. I didn't want you relieving yourself in your garments."

"Veras! Tanniv! Go!"

They hesitate. Mira narrows her gaze on Tanniv, who moments ago said he would do as Mira requested. With that glare, Tanniv shoots into the sky. Veras, still hesitant, pursues him after a quick mental debate of the situation.

"You can have me."

"But I want all three of you." General Merces waves a hand, and Mira can hear twigs crack and rocks tumble around her. She presumes several elves leaped into the air to chase after her companions.

Mira kicks the burning coals at the General and leaps into the air to join her companions. These dark elves are large, so all three of them should be able to outswim the Ebisu.

A firm, strong hand grabs Mira's ankle as she's lifting into the air, and it pulls her right back down to the campsite. Her body smashes into the rocky terrain, and all goes black when her head ricochets off the boulders.

Mira awakes with a startling submersion into the Ocean Realm. Water and bubbles attack her flesh. Her vision is blurry, taking a moment to wake. The darkness around her doesn't help, but she can make out several bodies swimming on all sides of her. She naturally tries to stroke her arms and kick her legs, but they are bound together. She is being dragged through the water like a recent kill, its hunters waiting until they return home to fillet the meat. She tries to scream away her frustrations, but only bubbles spill into the dark water.

Each of the Ebisu surrounding her have reequipped themselves with their glowing breastplates and ancillary pieces of armor. It provides the only light aiding in her ability to see where they are headed. They dive deep, and fast.

A sliver of darkness emerges before them, darker than what was already completely void of light. Mira recognizes it as the underwater canyon. The same canyon they intended to follow in hopes of discovering where the Ebisu dwell. They plunge into the depths.

Hours pass by per Mira's best gauge. With the darkness, the scenery hardly changes, and the time might as well have stopped altogether. And she struggles to keep track of how far they've traveled. Her stomach hasn't begun rumbling yet, which offers some semblance of time.

Eventually, a dim light permeates the canyon ahead of them. Her emergence from the black nothing into something visible fills her senses but drains her courage. Something unnatural lies beyond her vision, and an empty void consumes her heart, leaving her desires back in the darkness.

The light grows brighter as they continue ahead. The canyon walls smooth into flat panels with intricate carvings. Shapes of sea creatures, mountains, clouds, and one deity binding them all together. Sharp contours fill the voids between the etched pictures. Beyond the wall art, stone columns and a beam form a portal into a monstrous deep-sea cavern. Turbulent waters flow past them like an underwater river pushing them forward as they break into the open space, but it quickly subsides as they swim deeper into the cavern. The source of the light obliterates all Mira's fears and desires, leaving her lost in wonder.

Tiny sparkles of light line the ceiling and walls creating depth to the space. In the center is a giant glowing sphere with a diameter extending from the top of the cavern to the bottom. Within it, a platform stretches the distance of the sphere and holds an entire city—countless buildings, waterfalls, inhabitants traveling the thoroughfares, which appear as moving specs from a distance, and many, many bright white lights.

Her captors drag her through a rigid, rectangular entrance. At the end of a long corridor, stairs carry them from the ocean water into a subterranean city, where her body stops floating and smashes into the sharp contours of the steps. Pain seizes her ribs and stops her short of breath.

Loud banging drums echo through the underwater city, pulverizing her ears as she comes from the silence of the depths. The aroma is not so different from back home—salty air with the subtle tang of seaweed. Except breathing is a challenge. Her lungs aren't getting enough air.

The Ebisu seamlessly transition from a swim to a stroll, insensitive to the groans billowing from her as she pounds against each step. The level platform, when they're done climbing the steps, is no less painful. It tears at her flesh like violent waves pounding her against a sandy shore. Finally, her captors drop the chains and leave her lying in an outstretched, bruised and bloody mess.

"Another neophyte," General Merces says. "To the reform block. She'll require a solid interrogation with a heavy hand before being converted. See to it."

Mira glares at the General as he directs his subordinates what to do with her. Lying in agony, bound at the wrists and ankles, she's helpless to do anything more.

The General and his battalion walk away as if this is just another day in their life. Is it their regular duty to capture the vulnerable and return them to this godless city? The General said *converted*. She would die first. They have no idea who they've captured.

Two dark elves pick up her chains and proceed with dragging her. She tries to remove her mind from the gritty platform tearing at her flesh, but the burn is unavoidable. Through squinted, tortured eyes, her perception of the world she's entered is biased. Nonetheless, she tries to take it in. To learn more about the Ebisu.

Steel buildings with corrugated walls stand tall and many. White lights sterilize everything shining from high above near the sphere's surface. If this is where the Ebisu live, it's no wonder they are heartless. Warmth is missing from this place.

A rumble different than the beating drums fills her ears and throbs her body beyond the grinding already flaying it. A flat carriage wheels past them, down what seems to be a thoroughfare. Several machina sit atop it, all similar in appearance to what they used against the grendelin. Ballista used to mutilate the giants of Solaria.

Nothing within this city resembles culture the way Mira knows it. Elves do not walk the streets. No youngkins. No smiles. Nothing is adorned beyond armor. Soldiers form in large groups, line after line, thrusting tridents and grunting, and others walk in uniform lines down the thoroughfares, no detours allowed as they focus on their destination.

Either she has been brought to a military encampment, or the Ebisu are the ones who need reformation. A splash of sunlight, and perhaps some of Crumbaker's crumble cake to sweeten their day. Life within this place is glum.

"What's with the staff, Salus?" One of the guards says to the other as they drag Mira through the encampment.

"It was detained from the envoy that showed up the other day. Each of the guards carried one. We removed their weapons, but not without one of the Ebisu falling flat on his face. Something about these scepters packs a punch, and I'm determined to find out what that is."

A chuckle follows. "I doubt it'll be missed. Seems like a weapon that'll get you reformed yourself."

A loud smack of metal-on-metal rings through Mira's ears from the staff hitting the deck. "Just you wait and see. Weak as they seem, I know they would carry more than just sticks to guard the envoy. There must be something more to it."

His sinister tone crawls through her skin. This Ebisu is one to steer clear of.

A door squeaks on its hinges, much more painful to the ears than the wood hinges she's accustomed to. Mira finds a short breather from the grinding pain as one of the soldiers stops to close the door behind them. She hears it click shut, and the pounding of the drums quiet, only to be replaced with more pulling and yanking of her limbs. Several corridors later, they stop. A substantial, metal door opens beside them.

"Ugh, this place reeks," one of the Ebisu soldiers puts a forearm to his nose as they drag her into the chamber.

More white lights are centered in the ceiling of this room, dimmer than the corridor and only giving the dark space just enough light to see across the chamber. All are without a flame. How they work is a wonder for another time.

"You'd think they were rolling around in their feces and smearing it on the walls," the other soldier replies. "Filthy reforms. I don't know why they're needed. A taint on our society if you ask me."

Steel cages line the perimeter hanging in the shadows with bars reinforced from floor to ceiling. All have the subtle glow of the spice. Metal everywhere. Cold and uninviting.

"It's so less Ebisu must die, you imbecile. If they're reformed into fighting for our cause, then that's one less Ebisu on the front lines when we take down the next De'wi clan. You know…eventually this battle will take to the skies."

Another clicking is heard and a cage door opens. The Ebisu's hands grip Mira's underarms, their hands large and firm. Their strength is noticeable. She is gracelessly tossed into the cell and falls into a heap in the center. The door clicks shut behind her.

"Never. Above the clouds? You think that's true, Salus?"

"Lord Tenebrous is determined, maybe a little insane. You truly believe he'd stop with the De'wi?"

"But the envoy? The skies…" Their voices fade as the chamber door shuts behind them.

"Mira…" a defeated voice, barely audible, calls to her from somewhere within the chamber.

Her eyes pop open, alert. "Haltuk?" Still bound at the ankles and wrists, she struggles to lift herself upright. She falls against the bars to her cell, searching for him. Too many cells line the chamber. Too many steel bars interfering with her sight.

"Mira…" he repeats. This time with more vigor.

Another De'wi is curled into a ball across from her. It's not Haltuk. The elf appears to be sleeping. She steers her mind away from whoever it is. In the next cage, two squatty elves look morose and defeated. They're plumper than any De'wi from her clan. Indra, perhaps? Would the Ebisu hold Indra captive? In the far corner, she sees him.

"Haltuk?"

He presses into the bars. "Mira…" His voice is low and sullen. "No, Mira. Not you, too." He slumps against his cage.

"Haltuk? Are you okay?" No response. "Haltuk?" He remains quiet, slumped against the steel.

"It's the food," a quiet, feminine voice says from the cage adjoining hers. "They don't offer much until they need us for the trials. Keeps us lethargic."

She's hunkered into the far corner of her cage, draped in a dark cloak. Mira cannot see her. "Where are we?" Mira asks.

"Best to rest. You'll need it if you're to resist their treatment."

"Treatment?" Mira presses tighter into the bars trying to glimpse her neighbor. "The reformation?"

"They warned you. Better treatment than most. It's not a pleasurable experience. You're better off knowing nothing."

"Have you begun the reformation? How do you know?"

"Once they pull you, you'll never return. Not in your current state."

"How do you know so much?" Mira asks.

The elf rises into the light and peels back the linen draped over her head. She's tall and dark, with a mess of pure black hair. She easily stands a head taller than Mira, maybe more. She walks to the shared bars between their cages.

"I'm one of them," she admits.

Mira moves to take a step back and stumbles because of her bound ankles. She falls flat on her back and smashes her head on the hard floor. Pain cascades throughout her body, and she allows it to overcome her. She lies in her cell broken and defeated. Only for the moment, though. She needs time to recover. That is all. The soldiers were right. This place reeks. She closes her eyes and drifts away.

19 A STORMY INTRO

Harrowed by Fae's proclamation of Rivee's lineage, Gallagher broods the entire way to the celebration. How could they have been harboring an Indra within their clan and not known about it. Rivee looks nothing like an Indra. She's short, but her frame is petite unlike the Indra, who are all plump and robust. Although, Gallagher never did see her wearing a breathing apparatus like he had to wear. Could she be Indra like they say or is this all a hoax to set the anchor for an alliance between the two races?

He stares out the window watching the city lights zip by. A maiden sits in the carriage with him now, but he hasn't paid her any mind. He's too lost in thought and is vexed by the entire situation. Should he help the Indra, or should he rescue Rivee and escape this strange and wonderous world?

The lights outside the window slow and soon come to a complete stop as the carriage parks in front of yet another massive structure within the sky city. The carriage door opens and Gallagher steps out. He doesn't know the maiden's name, nor has he interacted with her more than just a few glances, but that doesn't stop him from reaching a hand out to her as she moves toward the carriage exit. She hesitates momentarily and studies Gallagher. After a quick deliberation, she takes his hand, and he helps her down from the carriage.

"A gentle elf," she says quietly as she stares at her feet.

"A warrior," Gallagher corrects her.

This draws a quick glance from her, and a smile.

He lifts his elbow for her to take hold. Again, a hesitation, but she acquiesces, allowing Gallagher to escort her into the celebration.

"Your culture is so…lavish," he says as he stares at all the sparkling lights. The building is stippled with them, and other fixtures shoot beams of light toward the sky. They must all be powered by their machina magic for they shine much brighter than the flame torches Gallagher is accustomed to.

"Lavish? We celebrate the return of an heir. You haven't seen anything yet. These are simple beacons to mark the entrance of the festivities."

"Beacons?" What he really wants to ask her is how Rivee is the heir to their realm. How could this be?

"Do you not have them within the Terra Realm?" she asks with a sidelong glance.

"We have none of this." Gallagher shakes his head in wonder. "Lights. Massive structures. Carriages." He turns his head to look over his shoulder. "This is all so…" He trails off.

"Brilliant. I would be delighted to be your escort this evening." Her words are quick and certain. Gallagher hadn't even asked a question. "I can teach you about our culture, and I'm certain I have much to learn about yours." She squeezes his arm gently.

"Yes…" he agrees, but his attention is drawn toward the entrance. A massive archway stands before them, an open portal to the festivities. Beyond it, Gallagher witnesses the sun sinking low on the horizon. Though this will be the second sunset he's witnessed, he cannot take his eyes away from it. His escort watches him intently as they pass through the archway.

Through the portal, the chamber is filled with mingling guests. But it is no chamber at all as Gallagher had assumed. The archway was a mere façade replicating a towering building. What lies before him is an open courtyard with a cloudless, twilit sky above him. The first stars sparkle amidst the deep blue and purple hues. Walls house them in on three sides, whereas the fourth is absent. What borders the courtyard in place of a wall is a small pond and a waterfall pouring over the edge of their landship looking out to the horizon and the setting sun.

An escape.

"It's beautiful, isn't it?" she asks.

Gallagher turns his head to look at her as they walk deeper into the party. "I'm sorry, I don't even have the pleasure of your name."

"Yester." She smiles "Handmaiden to the one hosting this lavish party, Elder Fae." She pulls her arm away from Gallagher's clutches to pinch her fine, light blue gown, and bow to him. A custom not seen amongst the De'wi. Elf-maidens stand tall amongst all the other elves as equals. A nod of the head or a firm grip of the forearm is how they make their introductions. None of this bending at the knees and lowering oneself before the other.

Fae had Rivee do this to him at the hydration station as well. It seems to be limited to the elf-maidens and not the males.

"Nice to meet you," he says, brushing past his unrefined thoughts.

"We ought to start introducing you to the eager eyes," she suggests.

Gallagher gazes at the crowd of elves. Numerous small circles of mingling elves, and too many glancing eyes. It's obvious all conversations are about him. The thought of his name slipping off so many tongues this evening makes him cringe inside, but what can he do? He's technically a prisoner, if not by manacles, by coercion. His escape route is within reach, but he cannot leave without Rivee. Would she even want to leave now that she's discovered a life of royalty? Or is this all fallacy? A game the Indra play to persuade him.

"Come, come," Yester says. She leads him away from the ogling eyes and toward a little knoll that extends beyond the edge like an extremity to the landship.

"It's extraordinary," he says as he looks upon the waterfall pouring over the side. Could these be the same waterfalls that pour from the clouds into the Terra Realm? The same waterfalls all the youngkins play in, and that feed the flying fish. An odd connection between two realms.

"Yes, it is, but that's not why I ushered you over here." She waves a hand over the party. "Look, see. You have a view of all the guests."

Gallagher nods, unsure what the reasoning is.

"There are many houses to cover, you see. I don't expect you to remember all of them but do your best." She pauses and looks at him for a moment. "Are you a visual learner or hands on?"

"Uh…"

"Never mind that. We'll brief you on the important ones, regardless. And it's always nice to have a visual log, so we'll start over there…" She points to the left side of the party. "You see the elf in the off-white jacket and blue, bulging belly hanging out of it. He carries a scepter without a conch."

Gallagher scans the growing crowd of hundreds of elves. A distinguished group catches his eye. They don dark robes reaching to the floor with loose fitting sleeves. Each has a full grey beard—the only elves he has ever witnessed with such facial hair. He shakes his head at the anomaly and continues scanning the space until he sees the elf she's pointing out.

"That is Melly Medirt, the patriarch of House Medirt. They're a struggling house, and the only reason I mention them is because they will insert themselves where they don't belong. You'll often hear whispers calling him Melly Meddler, to be frank. It's not kind, but annoying elves draw out unkindness from the best of us." She points just to his right. "The elf-maiden he speaks to, she's Sariah Haslit. A beauty, she is. Look at the long, dark hair flowing down to her back-side. She maintains those curves so well. She's the matriarch of House Haslit, an underhouse of House Godmadina. She's the second daughter, so heir to noth-ing, and her marriage to Jareth Haslit was merely to strengthen the Godmadina house. They've been busy growing their family with Ludonia, Hoglet, Didymust, and Tobylias, all of which have started families of their own. A re-spectable house, but clearly pumping out the runts to gain power by numbers.

"And over there…" Yester points a little further toward the center of the crowd. "…you have Gariel Elgary dressed in the flowing crimson gown with gold lace. She's married to Jarstian Elgary, and is also daughter of Arisean and Vicenya Godmadina, and sister to Sariah Haslit. In turn, House Elgary is also an underhouse of Godmadina. You see, Godmadina—over there—" She points to-ward the archway where they entered. An elegant couple stroll through the por-tal. The elf-maiden wears an iridescent, white gown resembling the color of a pearl. The elf escorting her dons a sky-blue five-piece suit trimmed in the same pearl color. He carries a scepter with a remarkable conch emitting the glow of the Blue Tears. "…is a competing house to the Elder House, House Arilight. That is Arisean and Vicenya Godmadina, patriarch and matriarch of the house. And House Arilight is the Elder House—"

"Fae?" Gallagher interrupts.

"Precisely."

"And where are they?"

"They have not arrived yet. This is Riveria's induction into the culture, you see. This celebration is for her, and they can present nothing short of a grand entrance."

'I see. Any other houses I should be aware of? Any that are a bit more offended by a De'wi's presence within their realm?"

Yester smiles at him. "Of course. That would be all of them. The De'wi are primitive nitwits in the eyes of the Indra."

"Then why am I here?"

"You see, Gallagher, they're offended because you're different. We Indra are immature in that way. You're only the primitive nitwit if you allow yourself to be such a thing. Tonight is not only for Riveria's introduction, but for you to demonstrate what it means to be De'wi." She places a gentle arm upon his shoul-der.

Gallagher suddenly feels the pressure of the realms on his shoulders. The weight is heavier than a pile of leviathans stacked upon him. He scans the crowd, slowly growing larger and larger, and he's supposed to be the representative for all De'wi? Why him? An uncomfortable warmth settles into him.

"So, am I to remember all these names you give me?"

"Gallagher, dear, you'll do fine. In time, you'll remember them. Their pride won't have it any other way." She faces him and places a hand on his chest accompanied by a smile. "You'll do fine," she repeats.

Gallagher smiles back. Yester, even though he's just met her, offers a comfort in this strange realm.

"Come. It's time." She takes a step off the knoll and turns back with an outstretched arm. Gallagher accepts it, and she curls her arm around his.

"Thank you, Yester."

"It is my duty," she says without taking her eyes off the crowd.

Eyes follow them as they move through the crowd. Gallagher, struggling to accept the attention, looks up to find more stars have arrived in the night sky.

"Is this our champion?" a voice calls to them and denies Gallagher his escape into his own thoughts.

She is a beautiful elf-maiden. Though, they all present themselves that way. Based on what he's seen thus far, he doubts he'll come across anything less.

"Time will tell," Yester responds. "Gallagher, this would be Vinbell Jonesook, daughter of Dunbell and Haley Jonesook, and granddaughter of Elder Fae."

"Er… Nice to make your acquaintance." He moves to clutch her forearm into a warrior's embrace as he would greet any elf informally. She flinches and retracts a half step. "Uh…sorry. Still learning Indra customs." He looks to Yester for guidance.

She offers Vinbell a short bow with open arms. Gallagher emulates the action but with much less grace.

Vinbell looks amused. Not threatened or disgusted as Gallagher would have assumed. "Show me," she says with a smile. "Your customary introduction."

"Vinbell…" Yester asserts in a whisper.

"Oh, stop. It's fine. Show me, young champion." Her eyes tear through his attire, looking him up and down.

"Err…" Gallagher doesn't know what to do. He would typically grab a warrior's forearm and pull them in close with a gentle double-tap on their shoulder, but this is a female Indra, *and* a formal gathering. Does he dare present them with a traditional De'wi greeting?

With a balled fist he pounds his heart. "Heart." Then he pounds the right side of his chest with the other fist. "Strength." He reaches for his head with a graceful pulling motion like he carries his mind down to his soul, central to his core. "Mind and soul." Then he reaches open hands out toward Vinbell with a gentle bow of his head. The last part he just made up. Gallagher's mind circles around Mira as he does this. The last time he made the motions of a traditional greeting, she curled into him insisting heart, strength, mind, and soul were equally valuable. "We don't often lower ourselves before others. Not even to our Elders."

"Not even the Elders…" she repeats. "Such unrest. How do you show your respect to those above you?"

"Ah, but Gallagher here is our champion. Who could be above him?" Yester interjects.

Gallagher isn't sure how to respond, so he offers a fake smile. All elves are above him within his clan. He's blighted, but is this common knowledge among Indra?

"My apologies, Lady Jonesook, but many others wait to get an introduction."

"Understood." Vinbell offers Gallagher a curtsy. "Nice to make your acquaintance, Gallagher." She winks at him.

Gallagher, unsure what the custom is within this realm, also curtsies. Both elf-maidens offer him a snicker in return, while Yester pulls him up straight.

"Never a curtsy. It is a feminine act," she whispers to him as they move onto the next introduction. "A bow is fine, but never a curtsy." She looks up to the next couple. "A good evening, Aricent. Ariskye…" She looks to one, then the other, and offers them both a curtsy.

"Good evening." Gallagher offers them a short bow.

Yester smiles at him. "Gallagher, you've already met this fine gentleman…" She gives him a flat smile. "But how about a proper introduction?" She holds an open palm out, gesturing to the sky elf. "This would be Aricent Godmadina, first son and second born to Arisean and Vicenya Godmadina—the elegance you witnessed enter the party from the knoll. And his youngest sister, Ariskye."

Gallagher smiles at the two of them. Though, he wouldn't mind dueling this short, pompous elf for creating so much complexity in his world. He was anchored in his decision to save Rivee and escape, but this elf had to enlighten him about the woes of an entire race. Gallagher blames Aricent for meddling with his simple world.

"With Gariel, their oldest sister, having joined House Elgary, Aricent is the heir to the house. And some day, Lady Ariskye will find a suitor of her own, no?" Yester says it with wide eyes and a surplus of anticipation.

"Lady Yester... Please."

"Oh, but we all have witnessed how your eyes wander toward Smika..." Yester snickers.

"Lady Yester. Unfathomable." Aricent adds. "It would never be. An Ohmsmire and a Godmadina? It would turn the backs of every house. They'd make us walk the edge." He gestures to the horizon.

"Only a jest, Sir Aricent."

"Or..." Lady Ariskye narrows her gaze at Gallagher. In a mischievous voice, "What about a De'wi?" She grips his hand with both hers as she moves in closer.

"Ariskye!" Her brother condemns her. "Stop that." He glares at Gallagher, who has done nothing but watch this conversation unfold.

"But look how handsome our champion is, brother." Her playful smile fades as she stares at him with an obstinate glare. "It could be the future. The bond needed to bring our races together. I do find his muscles rather..." She looks up at Gallagher, still holding close to him. "...intoxicating."

Gallagher stiffens.

"Okay, okay, Lady Ariskye." Yester interjects. "Enough of your fantasies. I am tasked with the introductions, so we must be moving on."

"Oh, of course, Lady Yester." Ariskye's lips flatten as she allows Yester to pull Gallagher from her grasp.

"Nice to make your acquaintance," Gallagher says as he's pulled away.

"Sorry about that," Yester whispers to him. "Nobility, unfortunately, doesn't remove desperation."

"I found her...entertaining."

"Yes. I suppose you could say that." She moves through the crowded courtyard, escorting Gallagher along. Countless eyes follow him as he walks by. He stands much taller than any Indra in the room by at least a head, so all they must do is look across the courtyard to make eye contact. He avoids this at all costs, either looking at his fins or out at something in the distance.

Across the bed of clouds beneath the gentle light remaining on the horizon, he sees the clouds whirring. Yet another wonderous sight, to be above the clouds and see what could be the birth of a storm.

"Gallagher, allow me to introduce you to Chrigan Ohmsmire."

Yester's words pull his attention back to the party.

This elf he recognizes. He was at the hydration station when Elder Fae arrived. This elf is of more importance than the others. If he didn't know by his attire alone—a light blue suit with intricate silver trimmings, hair fashioned in a crisp and meticulous way, shoes made from the tusks of a narwhal and a scepter to match with an obscure glowing conch sitting atop it—he would know based on where this elf makes a presence. Not presuming Gallagher, himself, is of importance, but Elder Fae, rather.

Another introduction. Gallagher sets into the same De'wi tradition he used with Vinbell, so as not to look like a stumbling idiot. Consistency leaves others feeling confident and comfortable. A balled fist thumps his heart. Then another finds his chest and moves to his forehead pulling his mind into his soul. Then he offers it to Chrigan with a single open hand.

The elf stares at him, unmoving at first, then raises a hand to the flab of skin that Gallagher believes is his chin. "Interesting." His tone is vile. "Is there a reason for this? Does a warrior always offer themselves to others in this manner?"

Gallagher looks to Yester, uncertain, then back to Chrigan. "It's… err… a formal greeting… Sir."

"Odd. It must mean something, otherwise it just looks like a primitive beating of your chest. Unsophisticated at best."

Gallagher's brow curls inward at his insult. He goes through the motions again. "Heart." He beats the left and the right side of his chest. "Strength." He reaches for his head. "Mind." Then to his core. "Soul." He refuses to offer it to Chrigan a second time. "The prime attributes of any warrior. Fuel these. Make them your own. Understand what they mean, and failure is not possible. Failure is irrelevant. This is what it means to be a warrior."

"And what do they mean?" he says with a mocking grin.

"*That*… you will have to find out for yourself. A warrior cannot know these things. A warrior must discover them." Gallagher sees Yester smiling in his peripheral after she squeezes his forearm. He looks to her with a subtle comfort growing inside him. She says nothing. She just looks at him.

"Absurdity…" He scoffs at Gallagher. "Sounds like hope and—"

A loud boom sounds, cutting off the arrogant elf. Gasps tremble through the crowd like a rolling wave. A flash of light, followed by another boom. Gallagher looks out to the horizon where the turmoil is originating. Likely that storm getting too close to the landship. A sprite reaches for the upper atmosphere and lights up the night sky, followed by a crackling noise as if the sky itself were splitting in two. More sprites. More booms and crackles. The clouds whir in a spiral motion, gaining velocity. A waterspout pushes downward leaving a funnel where flashes of light are visible within the clouds. Then, suddenly, the water-spout reverses, climbing into the sky.

"Get back!" Gallagher shouts. "Get back!" He raises an arm to Yester sig-naling for her to stay put, then he rushes to the edge of the landship, trying to get elves to evacuate the area. But they remain put and look rather peeved that he's trying to usher them to safety. "It's a waterspout! It isn't safe. Get back!" he continues to yell. "It'll toss you about like an empty shell in an undertow. You'll end up in the Ocean Realm if you aren't careful. Get back!"

Many of the elves stare at him in disbelief. Others look offended. None listen to his words of caution, and their attention quickly turns from him to the storm behind him.

Gallagher follows their eyes and sees a small landship elevating within the reversed waterspout. Two elves stand atop it in the center. The waterspout carries their platform closer to the party, sprites flashing all around them as it gracefully approaches. It butts up to the landship and becomes stationary. The storm dissipates and the night sky goes back to normal. The clouds calm. The stars twinkle. And all flashing and booming subsides with a single spotlight shin-ing onto the platform from somewhere high above.

An elf on the platform speaks. "Ladies and gentle elves…" a loud voice addresses the crowd. "…your Elder, Lady Fae." The elf bows to the crowd and gestures toward the royalty standing behind him.

She wears a white gown accentuating the curves of her upper body with an elegant, free-flowing skirt draped to her feet and covering much of the floor. Extending into the air behind her are colorful tufts of hair on sticks. They present a pattern of circles and waves, exotic in every way.

"She's beautiful, no?" Yester whispers to him as she finds his arm to re-acquaint with him. She curls her arm around his as if she won't allow him to leave her side again for the rest of the evening.

He glances around the crowd, and everyone seems to have quickly put his rash behavior in the past. A warmth overcomes him, both from embarrassment and from the elf clinging to his side. Her gentle touch, and desire to remain close by his side is comforting. He gazes upon her briefly as she stares ahead at Elder Fae. "What are they?" he asks.

"Excuse me?"

"The colorful plume behind her. What is it? I've never seen anything like it."

A single eyebrow hikes into her forehead. "Feathers..." Gallagher stares at her with a blank face. "Have you never seen a feather?"

Gallagher's face distorts with a shake of his head. He's as oblivious as a youngkin learning how to walk. Swimming comes easy, but walking is unnatural to the De'wi.

"A bird?" she questions.

Gallagher's face squishes into something awkward. "Just stories. The Elders have spoken of them. Do they exist?"

Yester giggles and places a gentle hand on his chest. She allows it to linger. "Of course, Gallagher."

"Gally." He smiles back at her. "My friends call me Gally."

Her lips flatten and she stares into his eyes for a moment, pondering his words. "Gally," she repeats. "Okay, then." Her lips curl just enough for Gallagher to recognize it as a smile.

"I would like to see one, someday."

"I believe we can arrange that," she replies. "Oh, shh...shh... She's about to address us." Yester nuzzles into Gallagher. He looks down at her, feeling a natural sensation to pull away as Mira flashes into his mind. But Yester is doing no harm. He lets it be.

"Great houses, lesser houses, and all those in between..." Lady Fae pauses to ensure the entire crowd quiets its murmurings from the grand entrance. "Tonight, we have so much to celebrate. As you all know, we have rough times ahead of us if we refuse to take action. Our culture...our freedom...are in dire shape if we cannot regain control of our supply of Blue Tears. And tonight... Tonight, we have made progress in fortifying our future with not only a champion to guide us to victory, but a bond to strengthen our alliance with the De'wi. With our two races...our two realms joining together, we can take back the crops of Blue Tears the Ebisu have stolen from us."

Applause breaks out accompanied by murmurings throughout the crowd. It fades rapidly as they are eager for more from their Elder.

"Some of you have already made acquaintance with our champion, Gallagher Lightcloud." The Elder gestures to Gallagher standing in the front row with Yester. He refuses to look around to see all the eyes on him. "But there is another who accompanies us tonight. Not another warrior. A mere youngkin to the De'wi, and royalty amongst the Indra."

The crowd stirs with quiet murmurings. No applause.

"I present to you, my granddaughter, Riveria Arilight, daughter to Jarnes Arilight, and one day heir to the Caelum Realm."

Rivee, in a stunning gown of marbled whites and deep blues, steps out from behind Elder Fae's plume of feathers and offers the crowd an eloquent bow.

A mixture of applause, gasps, and crude mutterings take place. Gallagher wonders why such a fallacy would be claimed if it has the potential to divide their realm.

"The Godmadinas won't be happy about this," she whispers to Gallagher as if she were reading his thoughts. "With Jarnes not marrying and having off-spring of his own, House Godmadina had a chance at taking Eldership within the next few hundred years. But with an heir presented before the realm, their ability to lay claim to the realm has just been postponed."

Gallagher stares into the distance, not hearing anything else Elder Fae has to say. Rivee isn't Indra. How could she be? If she was, how did she end up within the Terra Realm? She's short, sure, but she looks nothing like the Indra. She's slender and built like a warrior. She's a De'wi.

The reality hits him like a stone. Rivee's parents came from another island. Drifters looking for a better life, except…they didn't survive the journey. Only Rivee did. She's been raised by the clan, primarily by Nessa Rayfin. They all look out for her. Gallagher has never thought much of it other than having sym-pathy for her from time to time. They don't have great and lesser houses within the De'wi ranks, and all members of the clan are treated like kin, so her upbring-ing didn't differ much from others. Was the island her parents drifted from Cae-lum Invictus? Could Rivee be an Indra?

What does this mean? Should he steal her away as he hoped to? Will this bring the two realms together as Elder Fae suggests? These are not questions a warrior is trained to answer, but he's in this position and the only way out is to answer them. He can continue to entertain the Indran game and let this all play out or he can grab her right now and take the dive.

Gallagher stares at Rivee for a long while as Elder Fae continues address-ing the crowd. Rivee stares back at him. Both silent and confused. She looks uncomfortable, but life in royalty could be better than life as a blighted De'wi. This adds more complexity to his decision of whether he should help the Indra or not.

He takes his eyes off Rivee to look at Yester. She's kind, and Gallagher has quickly grown fond of her. His thoughts shift rapidly to Mira, who will al-ways hold his heart…his strength…his mind and soul. But she may not even be alive anymore. And Gallagher is also blighted within the ranks of the De'wi. Here, he's labeled a champion. Here, he was given the opportunity to slay a leviathan and succeeded. They have been treating him like royalty as well.

Yester looks up at him and smiles. It's a beautiful smile.

Maybe he can stay for a while longer and feel it out. Maybe the Indra are honest elves, and the De'wi have had it wrong all this time. A few more nights. Another week. He can entertain Elder Fae's requests to learn more. What harm could come of it?

Another sprite attacks the upper atmosphere, startling him out of his thoughts. More shoot off in multiple directions, more violent than the last. A loud crackle and boom follow, and Elder Fae rushes off the platform, ushering Rivee alongside her. This time the crowd backs away from the sudden storm.

The clouds fill with lightning bursts and a waterspout emerges as it did before, carrying yet another vessel. It looks more like a transport vessel for individuals as opposed to the royal barge Elder Fae and Rivee arrived on.

Large metallic anchors shoot into the air and land in the courtyard, anchoring the small vessel to the larger landship. Several sky elves disembark, shouting and swinging maces with glowing balls of iron attached to the end of them. Gallagher finds himself in need of a yari, or at least his sickle. He carefully pushes Yester behind him and readies himself for battle. Buttons fly as he tears off his restrictive jacket and vest.

It does him no good. A net flies through the air and covers him. Before he can begin to struggle his way out, it pulls tight and yanks him from the landship and through the air where he's left dangling from the transportation vessel.

The assailants return to their ship, anchors are cut free, and it quickly disappears into the clouds with him dangling from its side.

20 PRISONER OF WAR

Mira's eyes flutter open as she regains consciousness. Her head screams in agony. She rolls onto her side and her body does the same. It hurts to move. Her flesh is marred from being dragged through the encampment. Her ribs feel as if they were squeezed by a grendelin. The bindings on her wrists and ankles make movement even more challenging. She lies still.

The chamber door creaks open. She's eager to hop to her fins and demand answers, but her aching body, combined with the bindings, prevents her from doing so. She climbs to her hands and knees, despite the pain.

A tin bowl slides aggressively through a small opening at the bottom of the cell door, nearly spilling its contents, followed by a smaller mug. Two guards deliver meals one by one down the line. The thick contents slam into the tin and he bends over and shoves it under the next door. Mira takes a quick tally on the quantity of cells, struggling to count them with the amount of bars lining the chamber. Her best estimate is eight cells in total. This will only give her a few moments to elicit information from these guards.

Ignoring the food at her fins, she grabs the mug of water and presses into the bars. "What do you intend to do with us?" she asks first, then proceeds to take a large gulp of water. They act as if they cannot hear her. "Why have you taken us as prisoners?" If what she heard previously is accurate, they intend to enslave them. But how do they enforce obedience? She may not want to know the answer.

They ignore her inquiries and stop at the cell with the Indra across the way after delivering food to them. It's the same guard who brought her here. Salus is the name she recalls hearing. The one who was excited about his staff, which he doesn't carry with him now.

Mira cannot hear their whisperings, but it sounds as though tensions are rising between the Indra and the Ebisu guard. The tall, dark elf smashes his fist against the cell bars and moves on to the next cell.

"What's the reformation?" Mira yells across the way as they slide a meal beneath Haltuk's door, still not paying her any mind. Nagging prisoners must be a norm in their lives. "And when can I expect to have it done? I'd like to get this over with." One of them finally looks up at her, but only offers a glance. Mira rattles off more questions. "Can I speak to an elf of authority? I'd like answers as to why I'm here. How long can I expect to be in here? Is a maiden allowed a trip to the privy?" She chugs the rest of her water. Her mug was less than half full. It baffles her why they would skimp on water when they live within the ocean. Yet another question needing answers.

"One visit per day," the guard finally responds. He points to the end of the chamber. With the obstruction of her cell bars, she can hardly see it, but a door-less privy sits in a small alcove. "It's not time."

"Hardly a privy." She grimaces. "Where's the privacy? And if I need to go now? Can it be the time?"

The tall elf walks closer. He's not tall in comparison to his own race, but he stands much taller than Mira. Up close, in a low-tension moment, the elf almost looks soft and compassionate. He points to the corner of her cell where the hard, gritty floor is stained. "Looks like your predecessors have already marked a spot for you." He bursts into laughter.

Spittle accumulates on the tip of her tongue. She purses her lips. What elf would speak to a maiden in such a way? She swallows it, putting herself above this elf, regardless of which side of the bars she's on. She knows better.

The chamber door creaks open and a third soldier walks in. He draws the attention of the other two and speaks quietly with a look of urgency. Mira abruptly cuts off whatever crude response was about to escape her, so she can eavesdrop.

He speaks quietly. Mira pins the side of her head against the bars to hear better. "Shine your armaments. Shine your barracks. And for Ceto's sake, clean out the shit pots. There's no reason to make them live like this. You only make life worse for everyone who enters this place." He puts the back of his hand to his nose.

"Now?" The guard replies so the entire chamber can hear.

"Yes, now!" The third soldier moves his fists on his hips and furrows his brow. "Lord Tenebrous will be arriving shortly. He's already enroute from Oceanus Salus. You know he'll stop by to see the candidates for reformation. He always does."

"But he hasn't been here in…"

"Get it done, soldier. Or you'll end up in one of those cells, too."

Mira glances toward the girl adjacent to her, wondering what her story is. She's hidden beneath her linen in the shadows of her cell. Mira looks back toward the conversation and their superior is already exiting the chamber. The door shuts behind him.

The guard smacks his metal truncheon against the cell bars and drags it down the line creating an intolerable rhythmic alarm. "You heard him." He cocks his head as he walks down the line creating the awful noise. "Or maybe you didn't. And if you didn't…the Elder will be here shortly to ensure you're all in good working order. Prime candidates to reinforce his front lines. So, get your act together. Eat your savory meal. Spit-shine your cells. And let's put our best fin forward." The other guard in the room remains standing near the entrance. His face says he's in disagreement with everything his comrade is saying.

"We're behind bars—" Mira starts but is cutoff when the Ebisu in the cell next to her grabs onto her bicep, reaching between the cell bars. "What?" How did she pop to her fins and pounce on Mira so quickly?

"Not worth it…" she whispers. "That one is an imbecile and he'll push the matter beyond where it needs to go just to spite you."

"What was that?" The guard struts toward them.

"I… I…" It irks Mira to behave submissively but she's intelligent enough to take heed to her prison mate's advice, Ebisu or not. In order to be successful, sometimes you must lower your game to the level of your opponent. "I thought maybe now would be a good time to use the privy." She looks back to the stained corner of her cell, then back to the guard who's standing before her, now. "Before we spit shine our cells."

His gaze attempts to undress her schemes. But she has none. She only needs to use the latrine. It'll be painful to squat before the entire chamber but better than doing it in the corner of her cell.

"Very well," the guard says. He moves to unlock the door.

The maiden elf discretely slips her linen through the bars. With a subtle shift of her body, acting as though she's retreating into the cell to allow room for the door to open, she grabs the linen and wads it into a ball. Her hands and legs are still bound, so she has no place to hide the linen.

Afraid the guard will take her privy curtain away, she acts irrationally.

The iron door creaks open into the cell. The guard steps in to usher her out. A few swift and unexpected movements, and she has the linen around the guard's neck with his shoulders pressed tight against the cell door. She lurches forward to slam it shut, keeping a barrier between her and the guards. The Ebisu claws at the linen, kicking his legs. Not a sound escapes his open mouth as he struggles for air.

Mira lets go of the linen when the imbecile's dead weight drops him to the floor. He falls into the cell, pushing the door open again. He's only been rendered unconscious. Not dead.

"Thanks for that," the other guard stands idle, still at the entrance. "I can hardly listen to him talk sometimes, but it's beyond me to do anything about it. Don't want to end up like that one." He gestures to the maiden Ebisu. "Now, get to it, so we can get you locked back up in a timely manner." He gestures toward the privy.

Mira struggles to get over the guard slumped at the entrance to her cell.

"Oh, here, let me get that." The guard lowers himself to her ankles and taps an odd handheld device to her manacles. A click sounds and they pop open. Despite her reservation for machina, she does find the technology fascinating. He does the same for her wrists. "Tough to do your business with restraints, eh?" He looks down at the guard on the floor. "Though, somehow I think you would've managed."

She eyes him with caution and confusion. She takes a step for the privy and the guard stops her.

"Hold up." He reaches down toward the unconscious imbecile. "Don't want to leave your curtain behind, eh?" He hands the linen to her. She accepts it but says nothing as curiosity overtakes her.

She makes toward the privy. "That's not what I had in mind," the Ebisu behind bars says as she passes by. Mira shrugs.

Haltuk follows her behind his bars as she strolls toward the back of the chamber where the privy is.

"You good?" she asks.

He responds with a nod. They both know that now is not the time to start up a conversation. Not with a guard lying unconscious on the floor and another ushering her to do her business.

Mira squats and holds the linen out in front of her blocking out the view of the chamber. The remaining guard starts up a conversation with the other prisoners, which she's grateful for. Nothing more embarrassing than relieving yourself while a crowd waits in silence.

"For the newcomers…" the guard starts, "…a few things you should know about the living situation beneath the waves… First, air is less dense than what you're accustomed to—not for the Indra in the room. You may experience struggled breathing from time to time, but you're not dying or being reformed by toxic air pumped into the chamber. Acclimation will be quick. Second, water is limited. Our filtration systems have a heavy load. Constantly malfunctioning, and even when they're working at full capacity, we don't have enough, so preserve your energy. Don't sweat. Limit your trips to the privy…"

"How could water be a scarcity beneath the waves?" one of the prisoners asks.

The guard ignores the question. "If you would be so kind as to finish your meals in rapid fashion, you might just find an extra serving come next time."

"This food is no better than what's in that latrine," another prisoner replies. It's a pompous response. It wasn't Haltuk. Nor was it the Ebisu caged next to her.

"Oh, no. It's all the leavings from the mess hall. This is good stuff. All the flavors of a meal in one bite, eh. Savory. Now, get to it. Finish up." A few grumblings are heard before he continues addressing them. "Come now, come now. We're going to pair up, so we can wipe the filth from these cells." A metallic ding is heard, followed by a click, and the creak of a cell door. "Let's all shuffle to one side, eh. You don't want to be in firing range when we rinse 'em clean, I imagine. Although…" The room goes silent for a moment. "…some of you could use a rinse yourselves. What do you think? Shall we clean up our guests before Lord Tenebrous arrives?"

Mira lowers the linen to her lap and pulls up her undergarments one-handedly. She proceeds to fastening her leather belt and tassets, then adjusts the sarong around her waist. The Ebisu have not removed the leathers she was wearing while captured. She would think they would strip her bare to ensure she isn't hiding any armaments, but then again, with the machina they wield, maybe primitive armaments hold no threat to them.

The guard already has all the prisoners moved to the cells on one side of the chamber. He waits at an open door closest to the privy. "We really ought to put a door on that thing. Nobody wants to see that. Come on. Come on." He ushers her into the cell and locks the door behind her. "You best pray you get reformed before that one recovers. I'll be back with buckets and mops," he says to her before he walks away.

He drags the guard from the chamber and leaves the prisoners to themselves.

"Mira!"

She turns around to see she's in the same cell as Haltuk. She grimaces at his bloody image, and it reminds her of her own pains. "How'd you fare?" She moves closer to embrace him. "You look horrible."

"I think you lucked out with that one," he replies. "Most of these Ebisu are dreadful, jelly spittle sucking—"

"Hey!"

Mira and Haltuk both swing their heads toward the Ebisu. Mira hadn't noticed her hiding in the shadows of the same cell. She holds the linen out with trepidation. After all, she *did* just use it while sitting on the privy.

The Ebisu snatches it from her grasp. "I could suffer your same fate for that, you know." She wraps it around her shoulders and over her head. "You use *my* shawl. *My* shawl. Now he's going to think I had a hand in planning your shenanigans." She shuffles back to the shadows. "It was only a courtesy. Not a means to escape. You'll never escape."

"But... I... I didn't want him to take it. My hands were bound... I had..." Why is she explaining her actions to this Ebisu. Yes, she was courteous with her use of the shawl, but her fellow dark elves have imprisoned them. "Why are you in here? That guard mentioned sharing your same fate over something miniscule. Is this Lord Zen... Hen..." Her brow tightens.

"Lord Tenebrous," Haltuk aids her.

"Yes." She nods her appreciation to Haltuk, then moves closer to the Ebisu. "Is this Lord Tenebrous a brutal ruler? He's your Elder, no?"

The Ebisu chooses silence.

"Look. All we want is to escape and prevent our clan from being overtaken by your own—if you consider them as such." Mira casually gestures toward the bars surrounding them. "Anyways, if we have an inkling of how to get out of this place, it will go a long way. You must know something. We only try to survive."

The Ebisu remains silent.

Mira sits down beside her. Not too close as to invade her space, but close enough to have a meaningful conversation. "Thank you for the shawl. My wits weren't about me with my hands bound. Fear took over and I acted. I'm sorry if your fate turns for the worse." Mira begins to rise.

"Rela."

"Excuse me?" Mira sits back down.

"My name is Rela."

Mira softens. "Mira." She offers a hand, but Rela dismisses it with her eyes.

"He deserved it and more."

"The guard?"

"Yes." Silence fills the space for a moment. "There are others like me. Not all Ebisu are dreadful." Her gaze shifts to Haltuk with piercing eyes.

"And what exactly are you?" Mira's question comes off her tongue with hesitancy.

"A blade that goes against the grain." Her voice lowers to a whisper. "So many have already been reformed, but there's a coalition out there. Not all of us prefer a life of war. Not all of us have a vengeance to fulfill. Not one of us were alive when the Machina Wars began, so why hold onto that aggression. Why bring history into the present?"

"Lord Tenebrous…he means to slaughter our clan, doesn't he?"

"That or enslave you."

"What good would that do? Enslaving us? Does he use slaves for entertainment? For labor? For…pleasure?" She struggles to admit the last could be a possibility.

"De'wi and Indra do not exist within our society. That would taint it." She pauses. Mira sees the two Indra pressed against the bars in the cell adjacent to them. "The Elder only uses his slaves for war. The front line." Rela's face twitches. "Maybe the occasional escape into euphoria for some of the less disciplined commanders." Her gaze becomes distant and filled with pain.

"How is that possible? And why? Why bring back the Machina Wars? If I ever meet this elf, I… I…" Mira's shoulders slump. "I suppose I'll ask him why he lusts for blood."

"Recompense for a life stolen."

"Stolen!" Mira nearly shouts the word, and she rises to her fins. "We have been hiding from the Ebisu and the Indra…" She glances at the two hanging on the bars. "…for millennia. If anyone's life was stolen, it is the De'wi."

"You know nothing of our history." Rela looks up at her from beneath her brow. "The De'wi oppressed us all. That's how the war began. The Ebisu fled to the ocean to get away from the De'wi's reach. Our ancestors literally sank beneath their enemy, and this is what we've become," her gaze tightens on Mira, "De'wi." Her last word is as sharp as her gaze.

"It's true." A voice is heard from the cell next to them. "The Indra fled above the clouds, where the De'wi could not swim. Driven away by fear.

Although, vengeance isn't the culmination of our society like the Ebisu. We have let bygones be bygones."

Mira stares at him for a moment taking in the sight of him. He is short and plump, as is the elf next to him. Their attire…fully clothed from neck down including fin coverings. Her stare lingers into an awkward moment, then she replies as she looks down at her own fins. "We have been in hiding for millennia. Sealed away from the threats of the outside world."

"I cannot attest to the history your Elders preach," the Indra says, "but it is widely known amongst the Indra that we were driven from the Isle of Imperius to the skies out of necessity. Our ancestors rebelled against an oppressive force. And it would seem the Ebisu have the same story. Odds are your Elders, scholars, or whoever keeps the records, are mishandling the information."

Mira folds her arms across her body, suddenly feeling the chill of the dingy cell. "No, you're right. Our Elders have been withholding this information from us."

Haltuk stands idle, leaning against an outer wall not comprised of bars. "What are you saying, Mira?"

"The De'wi were the cause of the Machina Wars." Saying the truth out loud stings her. If the Elders hadn't given her this information before their expedition, she would have called these Indra liars. But their story aligns with the Elders. "It's true."

"Impossible. How do you know this?" Haltuk shakes his head and raises a flat palm to her, waving her off. He doesn't want to hear any more.

"A conversation about the archives, if it wasn't destroyed in the storm, might be worth a conversation with the Elders." She glances at Haltuk, who gaze is now distant and angry. "Still." She continues, focusing on the Ebisu. "The history of the realms is no reason for genocide. I must do what I can to prevent it. What does this alliance reform look like? Is there any way to avoid it? Any way to fake it?"

"There's no escape, De'wi," Rela answers.

"There's always a way out." She turns her attention to the Indra. "Do you know? How do they reform us? How could they possibly get us to stand on the front lines and fight our own?" Anger brews in her words.

"Machina!" The Ebisu responds. Mira cuts a glare in her direction. "They use machina. Just as this war began, they will use machina to end it."

"What?" Mira's mouth is agape. "You mean they use their machina to torture us? To force submission?" Mira doesn't want to think about all the blasphemous ways they could use machina. After witnessing their attempt to subdue that grendelin, she knows they're capable of extraordinary measures. And they lean toward diabolical.

"There's no torture involved. A fight, perhaps. It's an implant."

The door to the chamber opens and several Ebisu soldiers line the walls before an elf with obvious authority enters. Behind him, the elf she recognizes as General Merces enters the room, plus a few more soldiers. The space between the cells is packed full of Ebisu. The smell of their musk almost overpowers the rotten smell of the chamber.

"Does anyone ever clean this place?" the authority speaks, looking around the room, slapping disgrace on every elf he makes eye contact with. Like General Merces, he's tall with hair darker than the shadows, highlighted with greys and whites. His face has weathered more than a few centuries beneath the waves. But despite his obvious ancientness, his build is sturdy. He's not an elf to cross paths with.

Mira and her cellmates stay quiet, as does every other prisoner. Most have drifted back into the shadows of their cells. Only Mira stands out in the open.

"Lord Tenebrous," the General speaks, "these are your captives worthy of alliance reform."

"Worthy of reformation?" His arm jets out to the cell holding the two Indra. "What kind of outpost are you running? They're hardly battle worthy. Slow. Short reach. They move like seasnails amongst barracuda."

"Yes, however…put a trident in the hand of an expendable life and it's an Ebisu you will spare. Decoys, perhaps. Besides, these two won't make it past the trials."

"Perhaps…" Lord Tenebrous scans the remainder of the cells.

"Here. This one over here is a higher quality specimen." He points to Mira who stands in plain sight. "Most, unfortunately, are feeble, weak elves. This one, however…" His eyes grope her and leave her feeling like a victim. She cringes and berates herself internally for having thoughts of weakness.

"Slender. She looks fast, but where's the muscle? She looks like a worn princess."

Mira flinches at the audacious comment.

"Possibly the fastest elf I've ever encountered. Where her lack of muscle falls short, her speed more than supplements it. I hate to admit this, but she nearly killed one of our soldiers with a sheet only moments ago."

Lord Tenebrous looks her up and down. "And this is the best you can produce?" They speak as if she isn't standing right before them.

"Yes. Unfortunately, most prisoners are cowards who refused to fight when we engaged or were severely injured."

"Ah, no matter. The Terra Realm is all but ours. Only a few more De'wi clans to squelch before all resistance is abolished." He pulls his gaze away from Mira.

Her disgust for the elf overcomes her. She spits and it sprays the side of his face. "You'll never take the Terra Realm. Not while I still have a breath in my body, you won't."

Lord Tenebrous makes a small motion with his hand and General Merces repeats it. A guard quickly shuffles to the cell door and fumbles with a similar handheld device that unlocked her manacles. The cell door clicks and in steps Lord Tenebrous, fearless of the inmates. He approaches Mira with calm. She refuses to break eye contact, not backing down from his intimidation. He stops before her, looking down from where he stands more than a head taller than her. A swift hand grabs a wad of hair at the base of her skull and her cheek smashes against the cell bars, squishing her face into a wretched ball of pain.

Mira can hear Haltuk screaming at the elf, but nothing happens to break her free. She cannot see much with her bloodied face squished into the glowing bars. A warm trickle runs down her forehead and into her eye.

"Not so fast, are you?" His strength is undeniable. Despite all of Mira's squirming attempts to free herself from his grasp, her head remains pinned to the metal bars. "You De'wi are all alike. A pretentious race, and most of you aren't even aware of it. It's the reason we discovered the latest clan—I presume *your* clan. One of your fellow warriors ventured above the clouds as if the borders don't apply to him." He lets go.

Mira slumps into a squatting position, holding her head to keep the blood from spilling down her face and to put pressure where the pain resides. *Gallagher!*

"It triggered your location. When word was delivered, we acted immediately, offering a means to convert peacefully, of course. Then, I heard a blasted waterspout attacked our battalion." A subtle glance toward the Indra follows. "Set things back, and now it would appear you De'wi are on assault, still pretending as though you're the superior race. Just like every other clan we were forced to slaughter."

She doesn't want to believe it. Gallagher is the only one she knows who ventured into the Caelum Realm. Was it he who set all of this into motion? Are the Indra and Ebisu working together to eradicate the De'wi? Did the machina he brought home have anything to do with this? Inadvertent or not, it has led to so many deaths, and potentially the death of the entire clan if she cannot escape this place.

"You're ambitious. Courageous." He lifts his chin as if pondering a grand scheme. "I'm curious to see how those qualities translate into a reformed soldier." He remains stoic as he looks down at the jaded mess that Mira is. "A fine asset you could make. As the General said, most of the pathetic worms we collect qualify for a first strike at best. Expendable lives to protect our own. But your tenacity alone won't be enough. We need to see your skills in action to see what kind of weapon we can make out of you." He looks to his guards. "This one is first. Prepare her for the trials. Let's see how she manages the Pit of Reform. And give her a worthy opponent. Her blade could be the one to assassinate their Elder."

"What! No!" Mira cries as she finds the strength to rise up.

"You cannot do this?" Haltuk shouts. But it's a feeble cry, and everyone in the room knows it. Lord Tenebrous' mere presence makes all others submissive, and Haltuk's cry is but a whine in the wind.

21 House Orillian

"Reel him in! Reel him in!" a desperate voice shouts as Gallagher is hoisted up the side of the ship, slamming against the metallic hull, still confined by the net. The vessel speeds through the dense ceiling of clouds. Visibility is nonexistent. Where they are going, or who has captured him this time, he doesn't know, but he finds himself wondering why him? Why has a blighted De'wi become so relevant in his typical world of irrelevance?

The net is pulled in a smooth motion over the edge of the vessel and Gallagher thumps onto the cold, metal deck in a heap of disarray. These nets they use are indelible. Whenever he gets through this mayhem, he must find a way to train himself for these situations. They make him too vulnerable.

"We have you, young friend. We have you."

Gallagher knows the voice. He looks up from beneath the heavy netting to see Brunswick, in all his formal and elegant attire, standing over him.

"Err… Thank you."

"Get this net off him." Brunswick waves his scepter around as if it will magically help his elves move faster. Several elves rush in to untangle Gallagher.

"What is this? Who are these elves?" Gallagher asks as he struggles to climb to his fins, pulling strands of the net free from his limbs.

"Yes, yes. Many questions. Many answers. Time will tell. And time will heal. We'll get through this, young warrior. You'll see."

"Let's start by answering what is going on?" Gallagher insists.

"Okay, okay. But let's get you some food and drink. You must be ravished after having to deal with all the tongue-tantalizing and idolizing going on amongst those magnificent houses." Brunswick throws his arms in the air. "Great houses, lesser houses, and all those in between," he mocks.

"And what kind of house are *you*?" Gallagher asks, needling through all his jests to get some answers. Anger from everything that has happened boils to the surface. The machina he fastened to his fin; the banishment it caused; their induction into Caelum Invictus; and now this abduction. None of it would have happened if it weren't for Brunswick. "The machina you left me with, it destroyed my life."

"Of course." His smile flattens, and the monocle nearly pops from his face when his brow squeezes into it. He adjusts it with a finger on either side. "You have my sincerest apologies. I did not intend for any destruction. I would have removed it had you not bowed out so swiftly." He raises open palms into the air. "As for the house, I am a rebel house. We lie not in between, but on the outskirts. Orillian is the name. And we refuse to take part in their house games."

"Instead, you create your own games…" Gallagher looks around the vessel. "…and rules."

"We do," he replies. "Go! Go!" he shouts to his subordinates, and they rush off into a cabin sitting atop the deck. "Come, let's reacquaint and fill you in." Brunswick wanders toward the cabin himself.

Gallagher follows behind, uncertain and wary. His previous engagement with Brunswick was authentic, he has no doubt about that, but he knew nothing of his rebellious side. It shrouds their growing friendship in a cloudy veil. He steps through the door into the cabin, and the door clicks shut behind him.

He walks into a large chamber full of windows with a single staircase leading beneath the deck. He follows Brunswick down the stairs.

Many corridors lead to closed doors. Gallagher has an urge to crouch even though the ceiling is tall enough for him to stand upright. Looking at Brunswick ahead of him, the Indra is nowhere near hitting his head on the ceiling. Gallagher is out of place in this world. He should have charged for Rivee and taken his chance to escape when he had it. Now what is he to do? His fate is in Brunswick's hands, whether he likes it or not.

The sky elf opens a door at the end of the corridor to a concave chamber lined with windows on three sides. It must be the front of the vessel, for the clouds outside in the night sky stream past in great quantity and velocity. They're hardly visible, but it's obvious they're moving faster than he could ever swim. The thought brings him to stare at his damaged fin. A fin the Indra, with all their machina magic, couldn't even find a shoe to fit. He looks at the rest of his attire, realizing he'll need to find something new to wear whether he returns to the Terra Realm or the Caelum Realm. He dons only a pair of trousers because he ripped off his restrictive suit to battle the rebels who claim to have rescued him.

Brunswick finds a seat at a table adjacent to the windows. "Sit. Sit."

Gallagher sits.

"House Orillian is who we are. Not joined together by wedlock, birth, or anything of the like. Our house is comprised of loose ends untethered to the culture of the Indra. Bastards. Disappointments. Brave souls. And..." He narrows his gaze on Gallagher and leans in. "The blighted." He leans back and relaxes in his chair. "If you'll have us, of course."

If *he'll* have *them*? What choice is there to have? He's stuck within the confines of Brunswick's vessel while Rivee is pampered by Indran royalty on the sky elves' landship. There is no choice. Gallagher must follow Brunswick to get back on that landship and to save Rivee.

"Why are you doing this? What are you rebelling against? This seems preposterous to acquire a blighted warrior. I'm not even a warrior. I only dream of becoming a renowned savior of my clan. Why are you rebelling?"

"Not a warrior, eh? You have me, and all the other Indra fooled."

"Why are you rebelling?" Gallagher repeats.

"Yes, yes. You should know, I would agree. Why would you—*a warrior*—join the fight without knowing who or what we fight? Their vanity and unnatural ability to idolize self-worth is a start. They are kind elves on the surface, no doubt about that, but their culture is at risk of crumbling away. We are not talking about house feuds tearing down society, we are talking about their machina failing and turning their world into ruin."

"I know this. Elder Fae explained it all to me. Your sky cities require an abundance of Tears to power them, and the Ebisu threaten your survival. It's why they brought me aboard the ship, to become an emissary between the two realms. To create an alliance to abolish the Ebisu." Gallagher sits back in his seat, suddenly overwhelmed by the magnitude of the situation. He hasn't stopped to think what this means—for him, for Rivee, for all De'wi.

"True, true. But there is so much more. The Indra are no different from any other race—any species of life trying to thrive on Solaria for that matter. They will do what they must if their survival is threatened. Where you see the Ebisu attacking other clans and crossing realms to gain control over the Tears, the Indra are no different." Brunswick leans in. "Elder Fae and all of House Arilight will honor the alliance they promise, but what happens when the battle is won. Elder Fae won't let go of power so easily once she has it. She will force the De'wi to convert or find a way to control your people, all the while having complete reign over all sources of Blue Tears."

"And why should I believe that?" Gallagher is in over his head. Elder Fae said quite the opposite. She claimed House Godmadina were the envious and power-hungry elves of their culture. Gallagher doesn't know what to believe, and he'd rather not have to deal with any of it. He likes Brunswick, but this all seems too conspiratorial. He is only a kelp picker, and a blighted one at that. He doesn't belong in the meddlings of opposing races.

"You can believe what you want, but it won't stop the truth from revealing itself. House Arilight has been suffocating their competition for eons."

"That explains the grumblings when Rivee was announced as heir to the throne?"

Brunswick's brow curls inward. "Rivee?"

"Riveria Arilight as Elder Fae announced her. She's a De'wi. A youngkin that I've known since she was an infant." Gallagher rubs a hand through his hair. "None of this makes sense."

"A new heir. But what of Jarnes Arilight? How can she bypass the true heir? Unless…" Brunswick's eyes grow wide.

"She's Jarnes' child. A bastard, hidden from your society. I don't know the truth of it, or how an Indra could have been born within our clan." Gallagher scratches his head. "Or was she adopted by the Elders?" He trails off and stares out the window unsure what he's talking about.

"Hmm… The Godmadina's aren't going to be happy about that. I'd speculate she's not going to last long amongst the Indra. The plotting has already begun, no doubt."

Gallagher cuts a nasty glare at Brunswick. "What do you mean, 'not going to last long'? Is she in danger?"

Brunswick removes his monocle and rubs at his eyes. "She's important to you?"

"Every De'wi life is important to me." Gallagher is relentless with his hard stare.

"A fighting spirit. What would you do to save her?"

Gallagher leans in. "I would fight every last Indra until I was the last elf standing." He refuses to break eye contact.

"Ha! A warrior's spirit, indeed. So, you'll join us then? Can we name you an Orillian?"

"Will you help me rescue Rivee?" Gallagher replies.

"Of course, young warrior. Of course."

Gallagher reaches a hand across the table. Brunswick grabs it with a firm grip with a large smile on his face. Gallagher, however, isn't so quick to be excited about the makings of this alliance. Not until Rivee is safe and back within the Terra Realm where she belongs.

The Orillian vessel surfaces above the clouds, revealing the starry night sky, and ambling to a halt to dock at the same residence where Gallagher first met Brunswick. He recognizes the terrace, which he spent a good amount of time at while recovering from the wraith attack. At the time, it was only Brunswick staying within the estate, but today it houses a large group of rebels.

"You invite the rebel force into your home?" Gallagher stands next to Brunswick staring beyond the bow as they arrive.

"Indeed. They've abandoned their own houses for our cause. I would never refuse them a place to call home."

"Is it safe?"

Brunswick responds with an emotionless expression. "It has been up to this point. I'm careful with my dealings among the greater houses. None should suspect anything."

"So, you remain part of the elitists, then? You interact with the greater houses even though you work to tear them down?"

"Of course. Of course. It's how I maneuver around Caelum Invictus and manifest what I need in order to do our biddings."

"Caelum Invictus covers the entirety of this landship?"

Brunswick cocks his head to look at Gallagher. "Sorry, young warrior, I must remember you know nothing of our realm. Caelum Invictus is what we call *this* landship. It is the capital of our realm. The dominating city in the sky."

"There are others?"

A chortle escapes Brunswick. "Oh, yes. Many, many more."

"All as large as this one." Gallagher's eyes could challenge the brightness of the full moon. He suddenly feels threatened by their dominance of the sky, and miniscule as well.

"No, no. Caelum Invictus is the largest of them. Twice as large as the next."

"And where are all these other landships?"

"Why, they circle Solaria. Wherever there is sky, they can go. The only limit is up." Brunswick points and turns his pupils into his eyelids. "And down, of course. It's rare we venture beneath the clouds anymore."

This information leaves Gallagher unsettled more than it gives him relief. The Caelum Realm is far more robust than Gallagher ever realized, and Brunswick is a rebel at heart with a socially elite façade. Why would he risk his status to challenge the entire system of corruption?

One of the Orillians, a taller Indra with fewer unsavory bulges, approaches the two of them. "Shall we depart, sir?" he addresses Brunswick formally like a subordinate would address a chief in the warrior's guild.

"Yes, yes. Please, escort our champion to his quarters."

"Yes, sir."

Gallagher allows him to lead the way. "What now?" Gallagher asks the elf as they walk through the terrace toward the abode. A shiver runs through him as a gentle breeze gusts past his modified wardrobe. He's never experienced temperatures this low in the Terra Realm, so it didn't even cross his mind that removing his shirt and jacket would be an issue. He was only thinking about having enough flexibility to go into battle. Little did he know he was being stolen away by allies. So it would seem for now.

"We wait."

They enter Brunswick's home through the large doors off the terrace and pass through a few familiar corridors until he stops in front of a closed door. Gallagher, with his larger strides nearly steps on his feet before coming to a halt.

"Err...sorry..." Gallagher isn't sure how to address him. "Name?" he asks.

"Fandor." He turns to leave.

"Why are we here, Fandor? What's the Orillian's purpose?" Gallagher needs more answers. Thus far, their hearts seem to be in the right place, but then again, so did Elder Fae's. Gallagher doesn't much appreciate getting caught up between the squabbles of the sky elves, he just needs to find Rivee.

"Peace," he puts it simply. "Avoidance of death." And the elf escapes Gallagher's interrogation by swiftly disappearing down the hall.

Avoidance of death? Who's dying?

Gallagher walks beyond the antechamber into his quarters where he finds the room fitted for his size. The bed is large enough for him to stretch his legs, and he's grateful their culture appreciates a good bed mat just as the De'wi do. Large windows overlook the veranda and the horizon beyond, where infinite stars speckle the black sky. He moves to the wardrobe, which is made of the same metallic materials that everything within the Caelum Realm seems to be made of.

He flinches upon opening it, as he finds suitable clothes for him. Stepping back, he looks around like this is some sort of gimmick. The only explanation is that Brunswick has been anticipating his return. The Orillians must have had his capture on their agenda for some time. He looks to the bed with suspicion, wondering if it was also sized adequately just for him. Focusing back on the wardrobe, he shuffles through the clothes to find something more appropriate for settling in for the night.

After donning a light tunic and a more comfortable, less restrictive pair of trousers, Gallagher sprawls out on the bed, stretching out his legs, his toes, and his arms. The clothes aren't nearly as comfortable as the malo he's accustomed to, but they're flexible enough that he hardly knows he's wearing them at all. Good enough to rest in. A knock on the door is heard just as he closes his eyes. He's hesitant to get up. It's been an extremely long day thinking back on it, and his body would much prefer to rest.

With reluctance, he rises to answer the call.

"Brunswick?" Gallagher guesses, and opens the door to let him in.

The elf steps into his chambers, but not so far as to impose. "Before we get too far into this, I wanted to give you this." He reaches into his long surcoat and pulls out a steel blade about the length of Gallagher's arm. "I know these mean a lot within your culture, and I wanted to offer it as both a token of respect and evidence that we value your culture and your strength." He offers the blade, pommel first, to Gallagher.

Gallagher is confused at first. Swords are not idolized in the slightest fashion. A handful of warriors have had them crafted, but the yari is their primary weapon. For Gallagher, a sickle would be his preferred weapon as he's so familiar with cutting down the kelp with one. It is what he has trained with his entire life.

He inspects the blade in detail. On the textured, metallic handle are five concave circles, one filled with an embedded stone. A gentle green glow radiates from it. He grips the blade and holds it out to measure its weight and balance. "From the leviathan?" Gallagher can hardly refrain from smiling, but he manages to maintain a stiff face and posture.

Brunswick nods. "The blade is infused with Tears, but it's my understanding these stones are a tribute to your strength and class as a warrior. You've earned it, Gallagher."

"Cerulean steel…" he mumbles, hardly audible. He's left speechless. He is undeserving of such a blade. Only the three-stone warriors have the renown to carry the weight of such a weapon. After the debacle with the machina fin, Gallagher has hesitations to accept the gift, but it's not machina, right? It's no different than the cerulean steel honored to the best of warriors. He'll have to do more to earn it, sure, but the blade is not taboo amongst his clan. He allows a smile to break through. "Gally," he replies without taking his eyes off the short sword. "My friends call me Gally."

"Gally, then." He pats Gallagher on the back. "I'll leave you be for the remainder of the night. Get some rest and we'll discuss matters more thoroughly in the morning."

"Yes." Gallagher stares at the blade, more specifically the stone embedded within the hilt. "And…" He breaks his entranced state to look Brunswick in the eyes. "Thank you, Brunswick. You have gifted me a new beginning." His emotions nearly pour from his eyes, but he takes a sharp breath to cut them off.

"My pleasure, Gally. It's good to have you aboard." He steps through the open doorway. "Oh… And Gally… That is a machina blade. It might take some getting used to." The sky elf exits his chambers before he can ask what that means.

Suddenly full of mixed emotions, Gallagher sinks back into the bed mat and closes his eyes where he dwells on how a blade can be considered machina and what this stone means for his future. He earned the stone. He slayed that leviathan. But would the Morshine Clan recognize it? They didn't witness his achievement, but that doesn't change the fact that he has his own stone. Gallagher's world is changing, and for the better. Now he just needs to find Rivee and get her back to the Terra Realm where she belongs. He ponders this for some time. Sleep takes him eventually.

A loud boom wakes Gallagher. How long he's been asleep, he isn't certain. He pops from the bed and rushes to the window. The sun remains hidden beneath the horizon, leaving him unable to see much, but he *can* see dark shadows scurrying around on the veranda. The glass shatters and he swiftly ducks out of the way.

His mind goes straight to his short sword, and he shuffles toward the bedside where he left it.

Assailants spill through the broken window, shattering more glass and making the opening wider as they invade the chamber. Dressed in black attire and black hooded cloaks, three assailants stand ready to fight. Each wields a scepter with a glowing conch on the end. And all are short and plump like most Indra Gallagher has encountered. They look a lot like the Greybeards he witnessed at Rivee's ceremony, except their faces are concealed by black fabric.

Gallagher holds his short sword at the ready unsure how he's going to defend against those magical conches wielding the power of dormancy.

The first Indra moves in casually with the scepter outstretched. Gallagher bats it away with an arm to get closer to the assailant and swings his blade. It bounces off the intruder, not even slicing through the soft fabric of his cloak.

Gallagher leaps back and quickly inspects the sword. He looks to the cloak the assailant is wearing. Could it be some form of machina embedded within the cloak like the Ebisu's breastplates? Their cloaks aren't glowing, though.

He smacks the side of the blade to see if it will activate whatever machina lurks inside it. Nothing happens. Then, furious that Brunswick gave him a dull blade, he pounds the pommel into his palm, and a swift whoosh is heard followed by a tense strain in his hand. He sees nothing, but the sound was as clear as the brilliant stars in the night sky.

Two more attack simultaneously. One swings their scepter high, while the other swings it low, and the first foe jabs directly at his gut. Gallagher leaps into the air toward the assailants, turning his body sideways to dodge both attacks.

Accustomed to denser air, he cannot twist his body correctly to plant his fins back on the ground and he ends up tumbling toward their feet.

A scepter swings down at his face and Gallagher deflects it with the short sword. The other scepter knocks him in the head. Aside from a headache and a future bruise, it does nothing. The assailant's eyes grow wide beneath the shadow of his cloak.

"Immunity!" he screams.

The assailant carelessly swings his scepter. Gallagher knocks it away with ease and scrambles to his feet. He doesn't know why the scepter didn't knock him out this time, but this opens the door to victory.

Gallagher, with far more speed than the assailants, swings his short sword and cuts one down without much resistance. The blade cuts right through his cloak and into his flesh with ease. Not looking for answers at the moment, he accepts the newly found edge and moves onto the next foe. The two of them are stricken with fear and move to flee, but Gallagher won't have it. He cuts one down, then the other without any fight.

Three bodies lie dead within his chambers. He looks out the window to see others fighting on the veranda, both Orillians and these cloaked Indra. He leaps through the window to help.

A dozen or so cloaked figures are scattered across the terrace. Gallagher sprints to the closest in combat. Scepters whiz through the air deflecting the maces the Orillians wield. Bodies fall. Gallagher swings at the nearest cloaked figure and drops the elf to the ground. He cares not for tending to the injured, only stopping the assailants from doing more harm. He moves onto the next.

Their scepters seem to be useless against him. Aside from delivering a blunt pain upon impact and the occasional scratch, they are worthless against his short sword. One by one, Gallagher moves through the battlefield slicing through every one of them until no more assailants stand on their feet.

With heavy lungs and a heaving chest, Gallagher looks around at the aftermath. Bodies, both cloaked and uncloaked, are sprawled across the veranda. Several of the Orillians remain standing. Some stare upon him with fear. Others in wonder.

"Who are you?" one of them asks. Gallagher recognizes the elf from the vessel, but he doesn't know who he is.

Brunswick finds his way onto the veranda, casually strolling out toward Gallagher. None of the others seem to notice as they all make Gallagher the centerpiece of their attention.

"House Orillian," Brunswick addresses his members as he approaches Gallagher. He stands by Gallagher's side and places a hand upon his shoulder. "This is the newest member to our house, Gallagher Lightcloud. An elite De'wi warrior ready to fight for our cause."

One of the elves hoots. Other murmurings are heard as they all approach to congratulate him on the victory. He doesn't listen to what they're saying, however. He can only think on Brunswick's words, 'elite De'wi warrior.' He's no longer a blighted warrior. He's no longer an irrelevant kelp picker. Within the Caelum Realm only his damaged fin has become irrelevant. Amongst the Indra, Gallagher is an elite warrior.

22 PIT OF REFORM

B ack in manacles, Mira stands on one side of a wide open ring. Not so different than the ring of boulders the grendelin created, except this one has metal walls, cold and dark with iridescent oils gleaming the surface. In the center of the ring lies an unnatural pond shaped in a perfect circle. They wouldn't be so foolish as to offer an easy escape route into the ocean. It must be a tank of some fashion. But for what? Training underwater?

A dull drumbeat fills the arena. It seems to be coming from somewhere else within the encampment, and not intended to add seasoning to her trial. The rhythmic tune has been constant since she was dragged in through the ocean walls. She cringes. Both at the thought of ocean walls and the everlasting beat. Neither should be a thing in existence.

Far on the other side—maybe ten large strides, one momentum-filled bound over the pond, and another ten strides—stands another manacled De'wi. These trials of reform, do they mean to pit the prisoners against each other? Mira's heart weighs heavy.

Several guards enter the pit from a side entrance. Above the walls, terraces with steep seating border the entire circumference of the pit. Several Ebisu are in attendance, but not so many as to fill the stands. She locates Lord Tenebrous and General Merces among them, surrounded by a team of soldiers who are not there for the entertainment. How she would like to go up there and settle this right now.

She leaps into the air and falls right back to her fins. A hopeless attempt. With how light the air feels passing through her lungs, she figured they had done something to prevent swimming within their outpost. The machina used to create this world is no doubt the cause for her limitations. Another reason to detest machina that can be tossed onto the growing heap of reasons.

The guards stroll closer. Three to each side of the combat pit. Everything about them and their culture thus far is foreign. They walk as half-giants compared to Mira. They don machina wardrobes augmented with the spice and arm themselves with two-pronged tridents. They war with their surroundings only to gain, not to defend or survive. They are a dominating race. Mira's heart drops out of her chest. How is she going to survive this? Even if she defeats this De'wi it will crush her soul to do so. Either way she loses.

With the possibility of death at her fingertips, Mira ponders the value of the De'wi's primitive traditions. They hold onto a world without machina while the realms around them grow and thrive. Are their traditions worth fighting for? Why *does* she fight to survive? Why does she fight to defend her clan? Why not accept a dominating culture as her own? She understands, now, why the Elders considered defeat before any battles played out. If this is how the Ebisu war— pitting the De'wi against one another, forcing us to battle our own on the front lines—it begs a worthy debate. It wouldn't be a simple battle of hate and pride. If De'wi line their ranks through means of machina magic, then they would be shedding their own blood. The De'wi can survive if they choose to accept machina in their lives. Or would Lord Tenebrous allow their survival if there was no more warring to be had?

"This will be a fight to the death," one of the approaching guards says. "Are you ready." He halts before her and the butt of his trident pounds into the gritty arena floor, puffing up a tiny plume of dust.

Mira grinds her teeth. "I am." She stands tall and confident before the guards. Inside she's a rambling mess of thoughts and indecisiveness.

The guard on her right kneels to unbind her ankles while the guard on her left unbinds her wrists. They step back, and the guard in the center offers his trident. Suspicion washes over her.

"It would be a waste of time if you weren't armed. Take it."

Mira grabs the shaft of the trident. It's lighter than the yaris she's accustomed to. This one isn't glowing with the iridescence of the spice like the tridents the Ebisu wield.

"May Ceto claim the defeated and wash them anew. Good fortune to you, warrior."

Mira's jaw tightens. *Good fortune!* They force her to battle to the death, then wish her good fortune? How brazen. She is not fond of these elves in the slightest.

They withdraw from the battle pit, as do the guards across the pond. The two De'wi stare each other down. Uncertainty fills the metallic arena.

From this distance, the other De'wi is just a dummy to thrash upon, but she knows when she gets within striking distance, her opponent will become an elf. A living, breathing elf, for which she will be forced to take his life. She must figure out why she fights, or she will falter. A loss here is the death of her entire clan.

Who else will warn her clan of the raid to come?

When she departed, the Elders were uncertain when or *if* the Ebisu would ever return. That storm did exactly what the Ebisu intended, all except for make sure none of the De'wi continued to breathe. Someone must warn them. And she doesn't see that someone being anybody else.

The Ebisu won't stop warring until all the De'wi are eradicated or enslaved. Her clan rebuilds in the same location, naïve of the Ebisu's true intentions. However, she questions whether the Elders are naïve or just arrogant. What they need to do is find allies in the remaining De'wi clans. They must build a worthy army to defend themselves. And for Ceto's sake, they need to relocate. Stubborn Elders and their inflexible tradition.

The drumbeat enters a new tune intended for the crowd's entertainment. Her eyes narrow as her hands grip the staff so tight they feel like they are going to snap the trident in two.

The two combatants guardedly approach the center of the ring where the pond mirrors their surroundings like a sheet of glass. Mira halts at the rim, as does her opponent. He's frail. Shirtless with striations of ribs pressing through his chest. His flesh is pale and bruised. He looks like he's been here for months. Though, Mira cannot feel empathy for the elf in this moment. Right now, he is not a fellow De'wi. He is her enemy. He must be her enemy.

A ripple in the pond pulls their attention away from one another. Gentle rings undulate the surface, off center and rhythmic. A sharp, purple claw delicately pierces the water. It's attached to a tubular arm of a moderately different shade. Another claw breaks the surface. Three more arms emerge, and that's when Mira recognizes it for what it is.

"Get back!" She yells across the pond to her opponent. "It's an octopus. They're vicious. Get back!" He takes heed to her warning and warily steps backward. A tentacle spews forth from the water, seemingly never ending and curls around its first victim. The frail elf is helpless. The tentacle, the length of half the battle pit, pulls the elf into the water without any struggle. A swift splash and her opponent is gone.

The silent audience stares upon the combat arena as if an elf didn't just get murdered. Lord Tenebrous and General Merces stare at a machina device unfamiliar to her, not giving the scene any attention. Although, she could say that about any machina device: unfamiliar.

"Is it not over?" she yells up to them. "Am I not the victor?" Not one elf in the crowd acknowledges her. That would be too easy. It was no trial at all to watch her opponent get whisked away by a plethora of tentacles. Which means…the elf was never her opponent. The octopus is the trial, and she's its next victim.

If her judgement of its tentacle length is accurate, that octopus can reach every inch of the floor without leaving the pond. Safeguards are miniscule around the pit. She's not safe anywhere. Where does she gain an advantage? Running around the surface with a pointy stick prodding at the beast's arms *or* joining it in the water where she can pierce the beast's heart?

She sprints for the pond and bounds into a dive with the tip of the trident taking the lead.

Visibility within the water is beyond good. Much better than the depths of the canyon where she's accustomed to battling aquatic beasts. Even though they're an unknown distance beneath the waves, it is like swimming in the shallows at the Crisper Coral. White lights shine from the ceiling above creating a large shadow that shrinks as she swims deeper.

The octopus, with a mass several times her size, not counting its tentacles, is wound into a tight ball on the edge of the cylindrical tank. The walls are glass, and on the other side, more spectators. They slap the glass with excitement where the octopus devours its first meal. Crimson stains the water around it, providing the beast concealment.

What would cause the creature to attack on cue like it did? Maybe they only feed it elves. Maybe Mira and the poor, frail elf are the only meal it has been offered in weeks. Regardless, if this is her challenge… If the Ebisu are so brutal that they must see lives lost to find worth… Then Mira won't let it be her life that gets suffocated. Not until she sees an end to this warring forced on the De'wi. She swims closer.

The floor of the massive glass tank is lined with a metal grating open to the ocean. Could this be an escape route?

Swimming closer, not interfering with the octopus feeding along the rim, she tries to stick an arm through the caged floor. It's large enough for a school of fish to pass through, but nothing as large as an elf. She tries pushing through anyways, shoving an arm and a head into one of many holes. It doesn't work. She lodges herself in a tight spot like a fool.

It was a hopeless attempt at best, and she knew it before even trying. She grimaces as she pushes against the grated floor with her left arm, which also refuses to let go of the trident. She's stuck.

Mid squirm, and she suddenly finds herself petrified. Beneath her, a terrifying sight swims into focus. It starts as a large shadow in the black waters. As it approaches the glow of the aquatic cage she's trapped herself in, she sees not one gnarly head reveal itself, but three heads swim by, followed by three long, scaly necks, and one bulging mass beyond measure that might be as large as the entire Ebisu outpost. It's a sea demon. A demigod of the worst kind. A protector of Ceto himself.

Mira rapidly tries to free herself, and if it were not for the powerful stroke of the demigod's tails sending an underwater current her way, she may not have been able to break free. She pops loose of the grated floor in a panic. Staring past the floor, she watches it disappear back into the black void.

She would not find this a worthy escape route even if she could fit through the bars.

Thankfully, the octopus sharing the cage with her remains distracted by its first meal.

Mira pushes away from the floor and trains her focus back on the antagonist at hand. Its many tentacles leave her wary of playing games on the outskirts of its reach. It would exhaust her and leave her vulnerable before she made any difference in the outcome of the battle. She goes straight for the kill while it's distracted.

Swift and powerful, her trident attacks the beast's head, plunging deep into its flesh. Chaos unfurls all around her. Tentacles squirm this way and that, sliding up and down her flesh. They smack the glass, frantically swinging throughout the well-lit tank and tangle within the grated floor, shoving its mass every which way.

Mira struggles to hang on, and only extracts her trident when a moment of calm breathes between chaos. She stabs again, holding on tight as the octopus pushes away from the glass. An elven body is left behind as the two of them speed through the water toward the center of the pit.

The octopus has no means of escape, either. The wide-open tank provides nothing for camouflage or shelter. It heads for the pond's surface above the tank. They break through the water and back into the light air of the battle arena. Its thick tentacles flail, reaching for survival, spraying water across the metallic surfaces as a curdling noise escapes it.

The razor tips at the end of each arm fly overhead, like spears flashing through the sky. None make contact like the octopus' dark watchful eyes. They're sad and helpless. Between them, a small metallic object shimmers with the iridescence of the spice. Another moment of calm gives her the opportunity to extract her trident.

Now on her fins standing firmly on the arena floor, she pierces the unnatural machina, jabbing the spear in and out to ensure its destruction. Chaos resumes for another long, dreadful moment, until the tentacles lose their zest and fall to the ground. The octopus is dead. Its mass is sprawled across half the pit like the veins of a blight spreading its toxin.

Mira leaves the trident protruding from its skull and squats between its limp arms. She falls to her rump and leans back to lie down, suddenly realizing her body is consumed with pain. She raises an arm before her face, then the other. Both are covered in blood. Her entire body stings with lacerations. She hadn't noticed the swift and painless attacks, but the octopus did a number on her body. If she hadn't killed it when she did…

A deep sigh of relief escapes her.

These Ebisu are brutal. Forcing death through entertainment. Choosing to conquer all life around them. Do they hold any values outside of domination? Do any of them attempt to live a peaceful and prosperous life or are they all war mongers?

Excitement fills the meager crowd above her, but she pays it no mind. Mira closes her eyes, fatigue from the quick trial taking a toll on her body. A few moments pass before she is heaved to her fins by two Ebisu guards. They escort her away from the monstrous heap as two different guards dive into the pond in a hurry. Eager to clean the tank for the next bloodbath, perhaps?

The doors slide open and Lord Tenebrous and General Merces enter the battle pit among a dozen or so guards flanking them on both sides.

"Your name?" Lord Tenebrous demands.

Mira refuses, and General Merces reveals it for him. "Her name is Mira, Lord. I extracted it from the guards who overheard their conversations in the cells."

"A quick victory, Mira." Lord Tenebrous says. "Impressive."

"Too quick," General Merces adds. "It left no suspense."

"If you want suspense, fight one yourself." Mira denigrates the General. Although tall, muscular, and threatening by appearance, she recognizes only cowardice in this elf.

The two of them chuckle at her response. "I'm at least one hundred years past my prime," the Elder says to his general. "What about you, General?"

"I stopped after a thousand or so kills. Lost interest." He smirks, and his eyes never seem to fail in molesting her anytime he looks at her.

"What was the shiny device between its eyes?" Mira asks, skirting past their arrogance. "Do you control all your subjects with machina?" Her voice is raspy and struggled as the pain consumes her more and more.

"You noticed," Lord Tenebrous responds. "You'll get one soon enough. But first, we need to understand your competencies. What are you capable of?" His hand moves to her chin. She tries to raise her own hand to swipe it away, but the guards have her restrained. "Is there any sweetness in this fierce warrior? Is there any empathy we need to obliterate?" His hand moves to his own leathered chin. "Looking into those eyes, I suspect we might have an assassin on our hands. Swift. Quick to kill. Guile might be the next trial. And if you find success, we may just put the Elder's life in your hands."

"Which Elder?" Mira flinches. They wouldn't put her up against her own father. They could never force her to kill any member of her own clan.

"So, you have a connection, do you? Your body language… it screams a relationship beyond Elder and subject. And given your youth…" Another hand graces her chin. She jerks away. "…daughter?" He smiles at her. It's a smile devised from malicious thoughts. "But which Elder?" He pulls back from her and paces between her and his guard.

"There is only one true Elder of the De'wi, you know." He looks at Mira from his peripheral without halting his pacing. "When all the De'wi dispersed into hiding thousands of years ago, after accepting their cruel nature for what it was, they formed their own small allegiances. They had to. One large society was an easy target for the machina forces we were generating. The De'wi knew they didn't stand a chance, and a hundred smaller clans would make genocide more difficult. Cowards." He sends a sharp glance in Mira's direction.

"And although each clan named their own Elders, there remains only one true Elder of the De'wi. A descendant of the Elders of old. The true heir to the Isle of Imperius." He stops his pacing and faces her. "Thanks to the clumsiness of one of your clanmates revealing your location, we recently discovered that Elder is isolated in the bay you De'wi have labeled the Knuckles of Morshine. And I intend to murder that heir and all other De'wi in existence."

Mira holds steady. Lord Tenebrous is looking for giveaways in her reaction, but she won't have it. Her brow furls as she stabs through him with her glaring eyes.

"Only a handful remain," he continues. "The Rhizo Clan, admittedly, were a tall order. It was a battle we'll remember for eternity. They set us back. We continue to recover from our losses, but in the end, we set their world ablaze. Water, land, and all."

"You!" Mira gasps. "You did that?" He's referring to the orange glow she witnessed on the horizon while lost in the wild. The orange glow she found mesmerizing at the time was the Rhizo's world burning down.

"It's not like we take honor in murder…in war. Genocide is a means to eliminate the hateful, oppressive nature that dwells within all De'wi." His face turns into something menacing. The hate behind his eyes is real and full of pain.

"This is vengeance, Mira. We will wipe Solaria clean of your kind and reclaim the Terra Realm for our own. We already have a settlement in development. Although, Ceto has blessed us as a superior race while dwelling so close to his origin, we don't belong beneath the waves, Mira. No elf does. The De'wi forced us into this life. Soon, Oceanus Salus, the metropolis that it has become, will be nothing more than an abandoned ruin. A lost city beneath the waves. We will take back the Terra Realm before the next Solari, and your kind will be eradicated."

Mira spits in his face, and a swift fist comes down across her left eye. Her body falls limp, still in the grasp of the guards and unfortunately, she remains conscious. To be free of pain is all she can hope for right now.

"You all are murderers," she mutters.

"It's not murder. It's retribution," the Elder responds in a passive manner.

"You not only claim the lives of the De'wi, but you also claim every life you encounter." She winces from the pain in her eye. "You say the De'wi were oppressive. That the De'wi forced you into the ocean. Do you not see what your doing is no different? Worse, even. You're enslaving lives. You're murdering innocent elves who had nothing to do with this Machina War you're holding onto. And the machina… You abuse its power just as the De'wi suggested during the Machina Wars. This is why they shunned the technology. You're fulfilling every foresight the Elders had back then."

"It goes full circle, doesn't it." A subtle grin forms. "Yes, I do think we'll use you to finish off the Elders. And the best part is, when your reform is finalized, you are aware of your surroundings… your actions… but you have no control over them. An absolute puppet. It hasn't failed us yet. And once I get my hands on Ceto's Equation, even the Indra will bow to our rule." He pauses and studies Mira for a moment.

Mira glares without a response.

"I trust you witnessed the demigod within the depths. It was an offering from Ceto. It's the evidence of our superiority. Why else would Ceto deliver a demigod to our doorstep other than to embrace the three realms and make us whole again. The demigod is our first step on a path to finding Ceto's Equation."

"Ceto's equation?" she murmurs.

"Ah, yes. Ceto's Equation: the understanding of everything you see, feel, hear… everything your senses absorb. Once we understand the world as a deity does, nothing will hold us back. With Ceto's Equation even the Tears will be irrelevant. It is life's great pursuit." He breathes a deep sigh. "You see, the mundane settle for pursuing smiles. As many as they can find. But the more ambitious… we choose wisdom. The euphoria of a smile lasts moments. The euphoria of success lasts a lifetime."

"Wisdom only comes with time," she lashes at him with a snide remark. "Every elf knows this."

A smirk smears across his face. "Yes, of course. Once we claim the Terra Realm with the help of our demigod, next on the agenda is the Caelum Realm. Once we have the Greybeards at our disposal then we'll have that wisdom to seek whatever we desire. The stars in the heavens?" He looks up at the dark dome above them speckled with thousands of small white lights. "The deepest, darkest depths of the ocean." He waves a hand gesturing beneath the deck they stand on. "Or Ceto's Equation. The three realms will only be the beginning. If we have Ceto's intellect at our fingertips, we could create worlds of our own. Worlds without dark, callous oceans." What was an excited and ambitious tone quickly lowers into something malicious.

Silence overtakes the small group standing in the middle of the pit. The Elder's comments bounce around in Mira's head, breaking down barriers she didn't even know were there. And based on the blank stares of the others, the same applies to them. The thought of new worlds… New horizons… The vastness of everything possible should they understand what Ceto understands. She quickly shakes it away.

"It's a fool's ambition to chase what isn't obtainable. Ceto is a god. We are mere vessels."

"So you believe. Unfortunately, you won't be around when my ambitions become reality. Your clan—whichever one you belong to—should expect the demigod to pay a visit." He turns to exit the scene.

"I belong to the Morshine Clan," she shouts at his back. The guards tighten their grip on her. "You know why your efforts will be fruitless, Lord Tenebrous? You know why the De'wi of the Knuckles of Morshine will not find defeat in this war you're dragging out for millennia?" The Elder halts and looks over his shoulder with curiosity. "We fight for our principles. The values we hold closest to our hearts. Tradition. We fight for what we believe in."

A restrained burst of laughter escapes him. "Tradition is for those who choose comfort."

"You're wrong. Tradition isn't for the sake of comfort, but for embracing the strength of your roots and holding onto principles that have helped you grow into the life you have. Tradition is honoring your heritage and the opportunities it delivers. Tradition is the foundation of culture, and without culture what is life but a plethora of meaningless moments in time."

"And you think tradition is going to save you with your primitive roots?"

"Roots alone are not enough." She shakes her head as her eyes veer toward her feet. "There must be growth. There must be branches to explore the skies while the roots anchor into the depths. Culture is a living beast that doesn't want to be tamed, you see. It won't be baited down one path or tethered to another. Culture is a hybrid of the fearless and bold who push forward, offering fruit for the picking; the skeptics who criticize and resist, anchoring reality and tradition; and the futurists…the intellectuals. They hold the key to analyzing and weighing the fruit. Is it bountiful? Is it rotten? Will it nourish the roots and promote growth? It must all harmonize for culture to thrive. The De'wi are strong in this. And what you nourish… The culture you've developed beneath the waves…it has no roots, and its branches are pruned. They fight out of the hate and fear you've instilled in them. They don't fight for you or any of their own. And for this, you will fail."

23 WHERE GREAT WARRIORS RISE

odies remain scattered about the veranda of the Orillian safehouse. Disposing of them is unnecessary because all the elves are gathering their important belongings to flee the estate. The location is compromised and no longer a viable option for Brunswick and his rebellious house to lay low.

"Only take what is necessary," Brunswick calls through the halls as he hurries to his quarters. "Armaments, treasured belongings, only what you can carry with you." His instructions aren't reaching everyone because they're all scrambling through the halls doing what they already know is necessary, but Brunswick calls to them regardless. "We must dissipate. Hit the streets. Dissolve into the crowd. You don't exist for several months, and we can reacquaint when the time is right. I will find you." His voice echoes through the corridors. "I will find you. Go now. Go fast."

Gallagher hurries to his quarters where he doesn't have anything to collect. He already has his short sword in hand. What else does he need?

After scanning the room, his gaze lands on the wardrobe. Proper attire for setting out into the city would better suit him than the sleeping attire he's currently wearing. He attempts to set down the blade, but he cannot let go. It's as though his hand and the hilt are one. He tries to pry his fingers away with his other hand to no avail. His hand is stuck to the hilt.

He doesn't have time for this absurdity. He grabs what he can with one useful hand and hurries to the exit, where he waits for Brunswick.

It doesn't take long for the head of house to arrive. Gallagher thanks his instincts for waiting in the correct location. Brunswick could have left the building from any of the side doors, or even the veranda where his sky vessel is moored.

"Are you planning on battling the working class with that blade? Put it away." Brunswick hurries past him to a carriage waiting in the front courtyard.

"I don't know how! And I have no scabbard if I did. I have nowhere to put it." Gallagher follows behind and hops into the carriage after him.

"I suppose you don't have anywhere to go, either?" Brunswick adds.

Gallagher shrugs his shoulders.

"Here." Brunswick reaches for the blade.

Gallagher cringes at the act. Never would he intentionally reach toward an unsheathed blade. Not unless the armed elf was handing him the blade, hilt first. But Gallagher allows Brunswick to reach toward him, careful to point it away from his friend.

"I had the Greybeards craft it especially for you," he says, "knowing a sheath would only hinder your efficiency as a warrior. Pound the pommel, like so." He grabs Gallagher's hand and smacks the pommel against his open palm. A release in tension followed by a whooshing noise, and his hand is free. In conjunction with the release of the blade, a heavy fatigue also sets into his body. Like the weight of a thousand battles hanging over him.

Brunswick runs his stubby finger along the edge and pulls it away, holding it up for Gallagher to see. No blood.

Gallagher's eyes dart back and forth from his finger to the sword. The blade doesn't look any different. Maybe a slightly different sheen, but Gallagher wasn't watching close enough to notice.

"Tuck it into your surcoat. You should have several loops and pockets for such."

"But how did…"

"Like you said, Gally. Magic. The Greybeards are full of it." Brunswick pats the tip of the blade with his palm. "See, there's a thin, nearly invisible sheath crafted from the machina. The effect of the blade is nullified until you pound on that pommel." He hands the sheathed blade back to Gallagher. "How do Tears allow your bodies to heal faster, or make you stronger? That's what the De'wi use it for, no? It's the same way it allows our steel to be manipulated. It's a matter of harnessing the energy the spices are chalk full of. You'll need a wizard to explain it to you. I don't have the wits about me to understand such things."

"Wizard?"

"Yeah, the Greybeards. I suppose if you're only consuming the stuff, you probably don't have wizards within your culture, do you? They're the ones who've molded our realm into this." He gestures out the window to all the grand structures covered in green foliage and bright lights. "They've figured out how to harness the energy and use it to create what you see. There's a mysterious circle of privilege going on there, which only the most special Indra are privy to. Superior beings, they are. Our battle isn't against them."

"And who is our battle against, exactly." Gallagher tries to find a spot to nestle his blade into his coat. "You haven't given me much information, yet. No information, really. I'm only here to rescue Rivee at this point. Anything else is beyond me. I don't know your cause."

Brunswick stares out the window, allowing a moment of silence before he responds. "Our war is against all nobility. All the great houses, all the lesser houses. We work to tear it down." He looks at Gallagher, waiting for a response.

There's a long pause before Gallagher responds. "So you're a youngkin revolting against authority, testing your boundaries, is that it? Rivee does it all the time, it's how we ended up here. She felt that a casual poke into the Caelum Realm was a good idea." He shakes his head at their conundrum. "Seems like a futile war, don't you think? Is your culture not predicated on the nobility? Would another house not rise wherever you squashed one?"

"Brawn *and* wisdom. It's a shame our house was raided before I could properly introduce you to everyone. Someday. Someday, Gally, you'll get to meet the heroes who believe in a better world for the Caelum Realm." Brunswick turns to look out the window again. He's contemplative. Lost in a painful memory if Gallagher is reading his expression properly.

The carriage speeds down the thoroughfare, a combination of metal and green foliage zipping by and very few elven citizens. It's early enough that the city is half asleep.

"Where are we headed?" Gallagher asks.

"Another safe house."

"Is it…safe?"

Brunswick pulls away from the window with a half-smile. "They're all safe until they're not." His smile fades. "It's a long excursion to the other side of the city and the view won't change much." He frames his face between his hands. "Get some rest while you can. Now that you're an Orillian, you never know when you'll get another wink." He goes back to looking out the window.

Gallagher leans his head against the inside of the carriage and closes his eyes. He cannot sleep, however. What has he gotten himself into? Only weeks ago, he was an unfit kelp picker among the De'wi. Now, he's an elite warrior within a gang of Indran rebels. And he still doesn't know how he's going to save

Rivee. He could flee the carriage and head straight to whatever royal chamber they're holding her in, but he doesn't know where that is. It would be reckless. Brunswick is his lifeline within the Caelum Realm, so he's at the mercy of his decisions.

Eventually, Gallagher fades into slumber and doesn't wake until the carriage slows to a halt.

Brunswick steps out of the carriage, and Gallagher follows, looking around the pavilion and stretching his muscles by reaching high into the air. The sun beams down on them, having climbed high enough into the sky to creep between the tall structures. Gallagher has been here before. It's not the safehouse Brunswick had mentioned before he dozed off. They're at the hydration station.

"Brunswick." He nudges the sky elf. "I shouldn't be here. *We* shouldn't be here."

"Don't fret, young elf." He whips around with his scepter in hand. "The elitists only show their faces around here when it benefits them to do so. And the working class are no stranger to my cause. Especially the ones tending to our source of life." He turns back on his heels and heads toward the entrance to the massive structure. "Come. I want to show you something."

The giant dome and silos tower above them. They enter through the same entrance as when Helyer first introduced him to this place. Gallagher cannot remember the specific corridors they walked before, but it looks the same. After a long walk through the facility, Brunswick places his scepter on a familiar door. A subtle flash of green light appears from the scepter, invisible unless you're staring directly at it when it happens, and the door quietly opens. It's the same chamber Helyer had him visit with the large vats of Blue Tears, the infinitely tall ceiling, and skywalks aplenty, spanning across the hollow chamber as high as he can see.

"I've been here, Brunswick. Helyer—I'm sorry, I don't recall which house he belongs—brought me here to convince me of their needs. He said your culture will collapse without more Tears." He waves a hand to the half-empty vat of Blue Tears.

"Elgary. That would be Helyer of House Elgary." Brunswick leans into the rail as if he's attempting to look down into the vat. "Yes, it's nearly empty isn't it. We should probably refill the distribution vat." Brunswick waves an arm to another elf standing on a skywalk above them. The elf nods and disappears into another chamber. It's not long before the vat begins filling with swirls of blues and greens.

"What's happening?"

"This is the main distribution vat. This is what feeds the city. All the surrounding tanks fuel the different sectors of the city. You see, we can cutoff any one of these as needed. It's not all or nothing. If this were truly a crisis, there are control measures we could implement."

The iridescent liquid rises within the vat. It is mostly blue with gentle green swirls depending where the overhead lights reflect off it. Gallagher gets the feeling it is a natural substance despite the toxic appearance it holds. The main vat fills to the top and stops, then the essence pumps into surrounding, smaller vats.

"You see, these buckets of energy are not all we have remaining. Even if they were, they've powered everything you have witnessed up to this point. Has it drained any less than when you saw it prior? The carriage we were escorted here in, the lights, the doors, all the novelties you've come across. It powers them all. But the most important thing they power is the distribution of our water. Come." He raises his scepter and points it further down the skywalk.

"Where are we going?"

"You need a *proper* tour."

Gallagher follows Brunswick down the skywalk to a door on the opposite side of the chamber. The waft of a pressure release sounds off when Brunswick taps it with his scepter, then the door swings into the next chamber.

"Requires a different level of security with what goes on behind this door. They'll know we were here, so we don't have much time."

"Then why'd you bring me here?" Gallagher was suspicious when they arrived, but the fact that Brunswick knows they're putting themselves at risk leaves him unsettled. What choice does he have? Where can he run to?

"It's fine. You've seen how quick the nobility move." He waves off Gallagher's worries.

The chamber they step into is as tall as the previous with skywalks lining the perimeter as opposed to spanning across it. It's a vast, hollow cylinder.

"Don't look down," Brunswick says with a smirk.

Of course Gallagher looks down. The hollow cylinder extends down a short way, then opens to the clouds beneath the landship. They swirl in a circular motion around the cylinder, similar to what would be seen at the start of a funnel cloud. Had Gallagher never experienced falling, he wouldn't think anything of it, but now knowing that feeling, his legs become uneasy. He steps away from the guardrail, which to him, is more of a tripping hazard.

"What is it?" Gallagher asks.

"This is how we extract water from the Ocean Realm. It sucks through this chamber, then feeds through a system of machina where it eventually distributes throughout our city, similar to how the energy is distributed. We have the different sectors segregated. Between this powerful bit of machina and the machina keeping our city aloft, that is where majority of the energy is used."

"What does this mean? What are you telling me?"

"Don't you think Elder Fae and the great houses would do more than recruit a single De'wi champion if their entire city were at risk of falling into the Terra Realm? Don't you think they would secure other means if their primary water source were at risk of malfunctioning? This isn't about gaining access to more Tears. Especially not the small crop your clan have claimed. This is about control, Gally. The Ebisu are a threat to their existence, and they mean to utilize the De'wi as a weapon."

"This isn't news. They plan to use me as an emissary to create an alliance between our two realms. They've dubbed me their champion."

"And why do you think they would lie to you about the depletion of the Tears. Sure, an unlimited supply is absurd, and they need to properly maintain and secure the crops they have, but it is not at risk of being depleted. It's at risk of being stolen. The Ebisu are their enemy, not the De'wi. Elder Fae... the great houses... they care nothing for your race. The De'wi have become irrelevant just as they intended. Please, take heed to this warning. They are only using you to fight the Ebisu."

"Who leads this charge? House Godmadina or House Arilight?" Gallagher is stunned this question came out of his mouth. The Indran nobility are no concern of his, yet it sounds as though he's being sucked right into the heart of their quarrels.

"Both. It doesn't matter. They both wish to squish the Ebisu when and where they can to maintain their supply of the resource. This is one thing they have in common and will work together to see through. Arilight is the leading house, however."

"Why would we not join you? The De'wi, I mean. The Ebisu are evidently our enemy, too. Why would you want to stop us? Your life is at risk if the Ebisu take control of your crops. Why are you doing this, Brunswick?"

"Come. We should go." Brunswick shuffles past Gallagher on the sky-walk.

"No." Gallagher grabs his shoulder.

Brunswick turns with malice in his eyes, but Gallagher refuses to let him walk away. He needs answers. Thus far, all these sky elves have done is feed him little sweet bits to keep him interested in their cause, but it's time he was given some meat. He needs real substance to continue.

When Gallagher refuses to back down, Brunswick's anger melts away. "Fine." He sounds defeated. "But let us have this conversation back within the safety of the carriage."

Gallagher nods and releases him. The two elves walk through the facility in silence. Gallagher analyzes all the machina and what Brunswick has told him about the hydration station, connecting the dots between the Indran-created waterspouts and the waterspout that demolished his colony. Was it intentional? Do they know the damage they've caused within the Terra Realm? The Indra could be the cause for Mira's disappearance. They could be the reason he may never see her again. He's ready to retrieve Rivee and get back to her. He's had enough of these Indran games.

His roaming thoughts slip away when they reach the carriage.

"Your story?" Gallagher asks as they get settled, sitting across from one another.

"Yes, yes." Brunswick rolls his eyes.

"Let's take this back to where it all began." His eyes grow distant as he strolls through his memories. "For eons the sky elves have drifted above the clouds, peaceful and fruitful. But we must travel to a time before then. A time when we were all joined as one race and were merely labeled as elves. The Ebisu, the De'wi, the Indra... we all lived in as good of harmony as any species could. It wasn't until Vanford Arilight puffed that first breath of life into cold steel that the cracks started forming. As we all know, the cracks formed into rifts that could not be bridged, and thus led to the Machina Wars.

"This is when the elves scattered. Since then, the Ebisu have dominated the Ocean Realm, the De'wi have spread thin across the Terra Realm, and the Indra took claim of the Caelum Realm. The De'wi are the only race not dependent on machina or Tears. Your culture allows you to live with or without it."

Gallagher shuffles in his seat. He is all too aware of this, as he has lived his entire life without it, and has been striving to acquire a regular ration since he was a youngkin.

"As you now know, we Indra rely on it to stay afloat in the skies, and the Ebisu depend on it to maintain their colonies beneath the sea. I don't know enough about the Ebisu, but up here above the clouds the sun is always shining, and the stars are always twinkling, which means we don't get much precipitation. It's why we utilize the machina to create waterspouts. The reason I'm reiterating all of this is to point out that water is a valuable resource up here within the Caelum Realm.

"The Tears have become a permanence in our lives. It will always be, and nothing will change that. To relate, for you, it's like having land beneath your feet. It will always be there. Now, I know that's not a reality, but the point is, our society doesn't think much of the Tears. It's baked into every portion of our food, it powers our entire life, and we shuffle along not giving it much thought until the Elders and greater houses say we must be concerned about it, that is. If our society lost the spice, it would be detrimental. Don't think I'm downplaying its importance, but it's nothing we think much of on a regular day. Water, on the other hand... it is a daily consumable, and it's used to leverage the lesser houses. The Orillians were one of those lesser houses."

Gallagher notices he said, 'were,' and he has an idea where his story is headed.

"We were a rising house, doing everything we could to live the way the nobility expected us to, and when one house is inserted into what is a tight circle of distrust, then it must force another out. What you sow with this social structure are lovely but extremely delicate flowers that come and go, and the only thing that survives long-term are the roots and stem—House Arilight and their converging houses.

"House Godmadina has been the only exception, rooting themselves within the circle of nobility. A weed in the eyes of House Arilight, who are the founders of our civilization thanks to Vanford Arilight." He pauses to take a solitary moment within his thoughts.

"Back to House Orillian. You see, I was heir to the house at the time, and had much influence throughout the city. This allowed my inquisitive side to explore where I now know I shouldn't have. I had no lust for control or power within the ranks of the nobles, I only wanted to learn their names and understand who they were. The other nobles didn't quite comprehend this mindset—I see in hindsight—because the only way for an elf to live is the noble way—to strive for the top of the hierarchal food chain at all costs. This is how Elder Fae views the world. She's sweet, dignified, and full of beauty, her flowerings in full bloom for all to admire, but if you pluck those away and get too close, you'll suffocate from the grip of the ruthless, thorny vines beneath."

Brunswick inhales and exhales slowly, shaking his head and looking out the window. His forehead has lines pressing across it and his frown grows deeper.

"I had the opportunity to meet her one day."

"Elder Fae?" Gallagher asks.

Brunswick looks at him in earnest. "Yes, yes." He looks back to the window. "I was cruising through the pavilion we were just at. I was on a ferry outside the hydration station when I saw her. She's a rose in a field of weeds, you see. It was an opportunity I couldn't pass up."

"A rose?" Gallagher questions.

Brunswick gives Gallagher a peculiar look, and then he realizes why Gallagher is confused. "I forget your Terra Realm is a different world, young warrior. Excuse me. A rose is the most beautiful of flowers. The sight of one would catch your eye from across a garden, and its perfume would stop you in your tracks. Lady Fae is not a sight to be dismissed." He pauses with a deep sigh and a distant stare. "Maybe it's just me." He waves an arm in the air to dismiss his thoughts. "There was a meeting of the great houses that day. So many were in attendance, I was able to slip into the lot of them unnoticed. You can say I was intrigued. You can say I was entranced. I just wanted to know more about her. I cared nothing for the games of nobility.

"I followed them into the hydration station where a council took place. This is the first time I had been inside the hydration station, and that too, motivated my impudence. Half of me expected an informative tour, but there was none. This place wasn't new to all the others like it was for me. I stocked up the questions: How does it work? What happens if an irrigation line breaks? How does the water get into the hydration station? Are there more stations than just this one? I am a curious soul, you see. I only wanted to know.

"The council took session in the central chamber. The one housing the essence of Blue Tears. Elder Fae addressed her guests and went on to discuss a distribution plan for the greater houses should a limited allocation of water become necessary. They were all in agreement that the working class was too valuable to remove from the equation. Although our machina is self-administered for the most part, the small population of working class wouldn't have a dramatic impact on the overall design of their plan. Never would they go back to working with their hands, you see. That is what the working class are for. The lesser houses, however…" Brunswick trails off, clenching his jaw.

"I suddenly felt uncomfortable, wondering if I had inserted myself into a council I oughtn't have. I remained quiet and tucked behind the others trying to be a weed amongst weeds.

"She went on to discuss the twelve major pipelines feeding smaller stations throughout the city—that answered one of my questions—and gave control of these smaller stations to each of the houses, stating that it was a group effort to maintain the balance. She insisted shutting off irrigation lines was only to take place if urgency demanded it. But she was talking about shutting off the water source to the lesser houses, you see." Brunswick cuts a glare into Gallagher, not intending it for him, just out of pure anger. "The water is a primary means for survival, Gally. Without it, we would die. She was talking about eliminating the lesser houses one by one with precision and intention.

"It was then, after I had become mortified of the discussion taking place, that I decided to clear my throat and raise a hand to call attention to myself.

"'Excuse me,' I said." Brunswick raises his hand as if he's there, in that moment. "'Lady Fae?' The group split, all looking over their shoulders to see who spoke. I was now in direct line of sight to Elder Fae who held her chin high and looked down at me over her nose. 'I don't believe I know you,' she said. I brushed past her comment, not wanting to reveal my identity. Normally, I would devour a good introduction, you see. I love making acquaintance. But not then. Not when self-destruction stood before me. So, I went on asking her for clarification on the situation, and if she meant to cutoff the lesser houses from the resources. The entire council remained quiet. I had spoken what was intended to be left unspoken. 'What house are you from?' she inquired. I refused to answer, and instead went on to make a recommendation. 'Just one,' I clarified, pointing a finger in the air. 'I presume our energy source is depleting,' I said as I swung an arm to the half-full vats of Tears. 'And if this is the ultimate challenge we're dealing with, we can all make sacrifices to reduce our energy consumption. We can shutoff irrigation lines in a strategic manner and take turns limiting our resource intake. It doesn't need to be all or nothing, am I right?' I looked around the crowd, seeing if there were any nodding heads. There were none. Again, I spoke what was intended to be left unspoken. 'I mean, we're talking about eliminating houses before eliminating luxuries. Maybe we should make a list of what we can do without. Lists always help. A good brainstorming, you see. As you said, house elimination should be a last resort, and quite honestly it shouldn't even be discussed at this point, if you ask me.' I went quiet and looked around for affirmation of my claims. 'Nobody asked you anything, except who you are.' Elder Fae's aggravation was growing."

"What did you do?" Gallagher interrupts. "Did you run?"

Brunswick raises a hand to quiet Gallagher. "I continued the debate. They needed to hear their absurd plans out loud. 'Are we at least trying to find new sources of energy?' I asked. 'Or perhaps looking into ways to expand the crops of Blue Tears?' That was only met with silence. Those fools didn't want to hear any alternatives. 'Somebody remove this elf,' Elder Fae insisted with a raised voice. 'And find out who he is.' That's when I ran." Brunswick simulates a running motion while seated in the carriage. "Not easy for an Indra, you see." He cocks his head at Gallagher with a touch of pride.

"You clearly escaped. But how?" Gallagher asks.

He smiles. "The nobles were all too lazy and self-righteous to follow. And there were intentionally no working class within the vicinity due to the subject of conversation, so I just ran. Nobody followed." His smile falls away as if it just walked off the edge of the landship.

"Years passed, and all had seemed forgotten without consequence. I never mentioned it to anyone. I knew what the penalty would be should I raise a hand. Cowardly, I know, but it seemed like empty preparations by the nobility. It was a means to tell themselves how much better they are than the rest, and that was all. Part of me had faith in Elder Fae and the great houses to find a solution before it came to cutting off water supplies. Despite the moment seeming to be forgotten, I began to develop safety nets within the city and amongst other houses. I built relationships. I spread out my investments. I developed a strong respect amongst the working class. I did all of this to have fallbacks should the great houses try to eliminate me.

"One day, coming home after a day in the city, I found my water supply cutoff. No other houses, just House Orillian. It wasn't immediate death, of course, but inevitable death to be sure. Indra are stingy, you see, and to offer water to another house would be beneath the greater houses, absurd to the lesser houses, and not a possibility for the working class. The machina was designed to distribute the water, and always had, so the process and inconvenience alone dissuaded most. Could you imagine having to walk to a well only to retrieve a bucket of water at a time. Where would you store it? How would you get fresh water if the machina failed you?"

Gallagher raises his hand to speak, but Brunswick waves him off.

"Stop, stop. You don't live within Caelum Invictus. You would understand how challenging this is if water was at the twist of a faucet your entire life. Back to the point, House Orillian eventually shifted into the working class, having to scrounge for resources as opposed to being handed them. We struggled to survive. Our health became worse. The house was dismantled and became irrelevant to all. House Orillian was destroyed all because of my inquisitive nature to learn more about Elder Fae and the hydration station."

"That is absurd!" Gallagher interjects.

"It is." Brunswick looks out the window, pondering his thoughts. "I had the means to fall back on," he adds. "House Orillian was but a phantom of what it once was, and I, Brunswick Orillian, would make sure it remained that way, forever determined to dismantle the nobility and institute a better hierarchal system for all."

"And what would you put in its place?" Gallagher asks the right question.

"I know I will never eliminate power, but there must be a means to allow for equal opportunity during power shifts. Change in power should never involve hateful crimes against others. It won't be my system to replace this monstrosity, it will be a discussion."

"I'm glad I'm a De'wi," Gallagher says to him as he pulls the short sword from his surcoat. He thumbs the green stone and stares at it with admiration. "We are measured by our actions, and that is all."

"The De'wi don't need the Tears to exist like the sky elves or the aquatic elves do. We live complicated lives. We'll do what we must to gain control of this limited resource because it gives us our water, and it gives the Ebisu pockets of air beneath the waves. It is a war between the Indra and the Ebisu, and we're trying to drag your clan into the middle of it, Gally."

"Is there any way to avoid it?"

"We go into hiding."

"Who? My entire clan? If I don't deal with this now, your nobles will find another De'wi to drag into this. We don't have time for that. Rivee is in danger. You said it yourself. The Ebisu have already struck my clan. Hiding isn't an option. I'm going to save Rivee and return home to deliver this information, whether they'll have me or not. Where is she?"

A smile slowly curls onto Brunswick's face. "I like your style, Gally. You have heart." He hits his chest. "Let me show you."

Their carriage slows to a stop soon after. Gallagher eyes his Indran friend with suspicion as he opens the door to climb out.

"What?" Brunswick shrugs his shoulders with a devious grin. "I knew we had little time. It was already on the agenda to scout her estate, so we could devise a plan."

"Sly." Gallagher climbs out of the carriage behind him. "If all Indra are like you, I can't trust a single one of them."

Brunswick has brought them to a plaza more magnificent than any of the others. Iridescent white pillars line the plaza, rows upon rows of them, shooting high into the sky like the kelp forests back home. Behind them, on a knoll in the distance, is a large building of similar color with too many spires to count within the skyline. The ground they walk on is also made from the shining white stone. It's brilliant and pure, as if nothing in Solaria could taint its perfection.

"The Arilight Plaza," Brunswick announces with a wave of his hand. "We must be discreet. Not many visitors venture this way, and only those who are invited."

"You carry us straight to her front door?" Gallagher questions.

"No, no, young warrior. Where we parked is well within public domain. Her front door would be down there." He points to the white structure filling the skyline. "The Arilight Palace. And that's where you'll find Riveria, second in line to House Arilight."

"So, Rivee Rayfin is in there, and you believe she's in danger within those shiny, white walls?" Rivee would dream of living in a place like this. A droning feeling digs at Gallagher that constantly undermines whether he's doing the right thing by attempting a rescue. She could be so happy here. She might even love the drama involved with these elves. But if her life is in danger...

"Indeed." Brunswick moves forward and waves a hand for Gallagher to follow. "Come. Let us get closer."

They stroll through the plaza with the towering pillars slowly passing by, which are more of a marvel up close. The size of each is tremendous. Gallagher is uncertain how they would get each to stand upright, let alone how they are crafted.

"You will see as we get closer, House Arilight has many guards. The pillars lining the pathway to their palace each have machina built into them, not only to defend against an attack, but to alarm those within the walls." Several moments pass in silence as Brunswick casually strolls with his scepter in hand, clanking against the white, stone pavers with each step while Gallagher ogles all the brilliant white structures.

"If your eyes are keen enough, you'll see the drones hovering about their palace as well." He points his scepter to the skyline where small dots circle the spires.

If he were back home within the Crisper Coral, he'd think they were no more than a flock of hunting manta ray.

"What's a drone?"

"A type of machina with the sole purpose of prolonging the life of the Elder. Similar to the pillars, they will alarm the guards within the palace of approaching guests, *or foes*, but these machina aren't built to defend, so much as they are to attack. They are armed with the same magic as our scepters..." Brunswick taps the rod of his scepter. "...and they will detain any elf deemed a threat to Elder Fae's survival."

"So, how do we get around them? There must be a back entrance."

"Stop." Brunswick holds out his scepter to block Gallagher. Then he points it at the top of one of the pillars. "See. It glows with the spice's aura when activated. It knows we're here."

Gallagher readies himself, for what, he isn't sure.

"Calm down. For all it knows, we are a flock of birds flying by. They recognize movement, and that is all. Should we continue forward, it will activate the next one. And then the next. If they see a pattern, they send the guard. If the pattern persists, they send the drones and more guards. And should anyone make it beyond that, I don't know."

"You've done this before?" Gallagher asks.

Brunswick turns on his heels to face the warrior elf. "Of course. We must know our enemy."

"*We...* Who are the others within House Orillian? If I am to do this with your team, I must know who they are."

Brunswick's lips flatten as he folds his arms. "They're all like me. Houses destroyed by the culture we live in. Some are from the working class, and merely seek a better life. But they won't be involved in this one. This is your mission, Gally. And yours alone. I can't have them risking their lives to save an heir to the Arilight throne. The only way they'd go for it is if it were an abduction—a means to damage the culture."

"Call it what you will... Abduction, rescue... It doesn't matter, we're stealing away an heir to House Arilight."

"Yes, but they would expect to have control over her once they captured her. Setting her free within the Terra Realm would have no benefit, you see."

"How am I to gain access and save her by myself." Gallagher's voice rises.

"You're a warrior. Unsheathe your short sword."

Gallagher stands there in disarray, unsure what his intent is.

"Your short sword!" Brunswick insists. "Unsheathe it." He swings his scepter at Gallagher.

Instinct, and maybe decades of training interlaced into his daily kelp picking, sets in. Gallagher quickly pulls out his blade to deflect the scepter. A gentle green flash comes and goes. Brunswick stands down. Gallagher remains in a defensive stance, uncertain of Brunswick's motives.

"I saw it when you were defending the estate. Their scepters had no impact on you, you see. You have a defense against our machina magic. And I believe the green stone embedded within your sword has something to do with it. I cannot think of another explanation."

"What proof do you have? You didn't even touch me with your scepter. I'm not traipsing in there with false hopes."

"Then allow me to do so." Brunswick shrugs and waves his scepter in the air.

Gallagher stands idle for a moment, contemplating the ramifications. "Okay."

"On your knees," Brunswick suggests.

Gallagher cocks a suspicious head at him.

"In case I'm wrong and you collapse."

Gallagher acquiesces. Once on his knees, and with the short sword still in his grasp, Brunswick taps Gallagher's forehead with the scepter. The stone glows, and nothing happens to Gallagher. He remains upright.

"Ha!" Brunswick chortles. "Again, again. This time without the blade in your grasp."

Again, Gallagher cocks his head with suspicion, but decides it's best to understand the limitations. He sheathes the blade and drops the sword in front of him while leaning on his knees. Brunswick taps his forehead and Gallagher collapses into a limp pile of limbs and body.

Gallagher comes to after another tap of the scepter.

"What happened?"

"The Greybeards are brilliant elves!" he shouts. "The blade. It must be within direct contact…or the stone, perhaps…" His brow crinkles. "I'm not sure. It sits within the hilt, so either way, it should work as long as it's within your grasp." Another large smile curls into his cheeks. "Splendid!"

Gallagher retrieves his sword and climbs to his feet. "Okay, so I have a defense against your magic. What about the numbers? One blighted warrior against an army of Indran guards?" Gallagher inspects the curious blade, running his fingers along the hilt.

"*Blighted?*" Brunswick violently shakes his head. "We've already established this, Gally. You've rightfully earned that stone. You are a champion. An elite warrior of House Orillian. You are not a blight."

"Blighted or not, the odds aren't in my favor."

"Nor will they ever be. This is how great warriors rise above the rest."

An annoying thrum churns overhead. Gallagher looks up to see several machina flying above them. Each has a gentle bluish-green glow at their center.

"Run!" Brunswick yells. He heads back toward the carriage, but Gallagher has a different plan in mind.

Gallagher charges down the brilliant path toward House Arilight.

24 Enduring the Trials

T he cell block is a defeated mess of inmates. Her captors have returned her to her original cell. Nothing has been cleaned as the guards intended. The stains continue to taint the cold floor. The smell, however, has either been diluted with fresh air or, perhaps, the Ebisu *did* clean the latrine. A privacy curtain is strewn across the front of it now. Mira nods her head to the speck of decency shown by whichever Ebisu installed it, but it doesn't change her overall disgust for the race.

Too many days have passed. Mira isn't sure how many, but they have been locked away for quite some time. Days are unknown beneath the waves, a distant legend like the grendelins, holding a false existence until you go hunting for them. She wonders how all these Ebisu don't go mad without the natural clock of the sunrise and sunset. The day and night offer a peace of mind that Solaria and Ceto continue to press on. Down here, she isn't so sure about that.

The guards bring two small meals each day, she presumes, which helps her keep track of the time. Mira is skeptical of the meals, but she must eat something. Not skeptical of poison. The Ebisu have no reason to poison their prisoners if they intend to convert them into soldiers for their own cause. And that is why she's skeptical. They've been delivering porridge blended with spice. Why feed their prisoners Blue Tears? Is this how they reform their prisoners? Is every bite not only refueling her body with the strength she needs, but also altering her mind? Could their machina magic do such things?

The Ebisu prisoner, Rela, is in the cell adjacent to hers, hunkered deep into her preferred shadowy corner. Haltuk is in the farthest cell, opposite her own. One Indra remains, but all other prisoners are gone. The cells are half empty with only four remaining.

"Haltuk!" She tries to keep her voice low, but the distance between them doesn't allow for it. "Haltuk Coradrin, you alive?"

"Quiet, De'wi! My head hurts," Rela comments from her dark corner.

Mira ignores her. "Did you endure the pit, Haltuk? Did they offer you spice?"

"Yes." His voice is hoarse. "The pits, the spice, the defeat…"

"Defeat? But you're here!" she replies.

"Ah, but we're all defeated, young maiden," the Indra pipes in.

An exasperated sigh escapes Mira and she slouches deeper into her cell. "Yes. We are, aren't we." She sits on the cold floor. "And what of you Indra? How'd you survive the pit?"

"It is nothing I wish to relive. My companion and I… the sea demon… the guard and his relentless torture… we are not warriors. Fighting is not the Indran way."

She doesn't feel much sympathy for him. Based on his few words, her own experience wasn't much different. Except the torture part. She doesn't know if he is exaggerating or being literal, but she doesn't have the energy to muster that conversation. She *is* perplexed by how these elves with such a short reach could possibly overcome an octopus like she did. "Name?" she asks.

"Paka Ohmsmire, second son to Chrigan Ohmsmire, part of a two-elf envoy come to retrieve the Elder for negotiations. General Merces had the nerve to imprison us." Mira sees the shadows around his face curl into something angry. "Horbell Jonesook was my companion… He was an admirable elf…" His voice fades as his head bows.

With all the light shining down on the passage between the cells, leaving the cells themselves dim and shadowy, she cannot see if the elf is weeping, but his whimpers suggest as much. "An envoy. We witnessed a carriage-like vessel traveling the skies before we were imprisoned." Her gaze tightens on the Indra. "Paka, what kind of negotiations?"

Between sniffles, he responds. "I'm not privy to such information. Grandma Fae…err…Elder Fae sent us to escort the Elder. That is all. She requests his presence to discuss matters beyond me. Elder to Elder."

"Are the Indra threatened by the Ebisu in any way?"

Paka's eyes turn in her direction without a single movement of his body. They shoot toward Rela in the cell next to her, then back on Mira. "It's widely known that tension rises for the control of the spice. If there is a threat, that would be it. Why?"

"No matter. My mind only wanders. The possibilities with the Indra and the Ebisu joining together in conversation are concerning, to say the least."

"And what that could lead to for the De'wi, you mean?"

"Yes." She eyes him cautiously.

"You must know, the De'wi are no enemy of the Indra. A tainted past, sure. A foul taste in our mouths, sure. But not an enemy. There isn't enough aggression within our race to ignite any means of war upon the De'wi. We don't give much effort to fighting."

"Then what do you think these negotiations are about?"

"Control of the spice. If I must speculate." He slumps away from the bars of his cell back into the shadows.

Mira sinks back into her cell, as well. Aside from lack of food and a rumble in her stomach, the fatigue she should have, isn't there. After enduring all the lacerations from the octopus and the battering she suffered from Lord Tenebrous, she should be down in her spirits, but she's quite the opposite. Each dose of spice they offer her has helped liven her back to her original state. It concerns her why they require lively prisoners. Why else would they give them the spice. To heal, perhaps? Whatever they have in store for them, it can't be good.

Mira turns to the dark shape huddled in the cell next to her. "What else do you know about this reform? How do the machina implants work?"

Rela grunts in return and shuffles her linen tighter around her head as she sits hunched against the bars on the far side of her cell.

"Your trial must have been hard-earned, I take it." Mira finds the most comfortable position she can, lying on her side with an arm supporting her head. "I could use a wash," she admits after noticing the stink of several days. It's an odd comment when they currently reside beneath the waves, but swimming through the salty waters doesn't allow for much of a bath. It leaves the skin sticky and wrinkly if not washed away with fresh water. It's no wonder the Ebisu use machina to stay dry. It's no wonder they want to get back to the Terra Realm. But how do they get fresh water to drink? Come to think of it, Mira has only been offered small rations of water since she's been here. Thirst strikes her. The thought of the springs back home leaves her mind wandering. She needs to find a way to get back there. She needs to find a way to make her clan safe. But how? How can she escape the depths of hell, down here beneath the waves.

"My trial comprised of a thrashing. Nothing more."

Mira's neck arches backward as she looks toward Rela, still lying down. "I'm sorry," she replies. "In our clan, we don't have any rebels, but we do have those we consider a blight on the colony. Unintentional...but they're hamstrung emotionally. Told they're not worthy."

"Worthy for what?" Rela asks.

"For anything, really. They are allowed simple tasks. Fulfilling if you lack ambition, but unfortunately the blighted are full of ambition when they're told they cannot do something." Mira pauses a moment. "I'm not sure how that compares to a physical beating. Sorry, I shouldn't have brought it up."

"It's natural to seek power and control, isn't it? Even with my rebellious nature, all I do is fight to gain some sense of control of my life. Some sense of power. That's all we ever do. Shift the power from one to another. Shift the suffering from one to another."

"Hope," Mira replies. "As long as we have something to strive for, it doesn't matter where the power is."

"Unless you're beaten senseless by the power..."

Mira ponders the violent nature of the Ebisu. Rela is right. If those in charge are evil to the core, as Lord Tenebrous presents himself, the power shift is important.

"What can I do to help?" she asks.

"Get us out of here. We don't stand a chance while caged within the reform block. Once we're implanted, there's no turning it off. They'll turn us into fools without our will, controlled by the battalion commander."

"No will..." Mira looks at an empty dish in her cell. "How does it work?"

"You'll see soon enough. No need to rush toward death. Get some rest. The trials are not over."

"Yeah, rest..." How could Mira possibly rest?

What does this all mean? The Ebisu are at odds with the De'wi, but is Lord Tenebrous picking a fight with the Indra, too. And that monstrous demigod beneath the outpost... could it truly be within their control? That octopus had a small implant and seemed to attack when they needed it to. They *do* utilize seadragons for travel. General Merces and his soldiers were after that goliath, too. Is it possible their machina gives them so much control over their environment? The devastation it could bring. Mira can only hope Lord Tenebrous was bluffing about the demigod. The De'wi are no match for such a creature. Leviathans, goliaths, and seadragons...

Mira wakes with a start, not realizing she had dozed off. Sweat dampens her hairline. Her dreams ran amuck through the disasters that became of the Isle of Imperius where the Machina Wars began. It was far more fantastical than the stories tell it. Ravaging machina, seemingly alive in the form of beasts, tore through the rocky, forested hillsides. She stood on a sandy shoreline watching the chaos around her. Trees, greener and thicker than what is possible, lined the beaches. Blue and green lights darted through the underbrush. Screams from the elves who created the beasts sliced through the air, overpowering the sound of the wind and the waves that make a beach intoxicating. This was anything but that. Horrifying would be the purest description of this beach.

An omen.

Two bowls slide into her cell. One with a half serving of the mess hall's leavings, and the other gets filled with a mouthful of water.

"Eat up," the guard says as he walks by with a ladle and a bucket.

Another guard carries the bowls and a jug of water, serving the prisoners as they're filled with slop, and pouring the water into the bowl once they're on the floor of the cell. Neither guard is the same as when she was first tossed in here. There has been a different guard each day.

Mira gives a sigh of relief. She's dreading the day she encounters the guard she assaulted, and each day he doesn't show face is a relief. She's sure to pay the consequences for it eventually.

With only four prisoners in the block, they quickly make the rounds and exit.

"I never see you eat." Mira quietly speaks to Rela.

"I get enough. The water is more important." Rela crawls to the water bowl and positions herself against the cell bars. She takes a sip off the bowl. "Sleep is important, too. Didn't sound like yours was restful."

"Eh…" Mira wipes the back of her hand across her forehead before picking up the bowl of slop and attempting to pour it down her throat.

"Bad dreams?"

"A bit distasteful, yes. Worse than the meals." She holds her bowl up.

"They lace it with the spice, you know. They want strong soldiers for their trials."

"Yeah, I noticed." Mira inspects the contents closely to see what else might be in there. The shimmer of the spice's iridescent veins reach through the bland white contents. Not so much that she can taste its sweet flavor, though. "The Ebisu are generous with the Tears, aren't they?"

"The ocean is vast. Ceto blesses us with bountiful crops. Enough to thrive. Enough that some believe Ceto has chosen us as the superior race deserving of such glory."

Mira halts mid-sip and looks toward Rela. She pulls the bowl away from her face. "And you believe that? The superior race?" She scoffs.

"Does that leave a sour taste in your mouth? Is it so unfeasible that you cannot swallow it.?"

"Why would the creator choose one life over another?"

"Centuries of disappointment…" she suggests.

"Perhaps." Mira rolls her eyes, knowing Rela likely cannot see her. "If the Ebisu have an abundance of the Tears, then Lord Tenebrous' intention is purely vengeance. What else would drive his war mongering? Only hate for the De'wi."

"Yes. And it's why so many of us are resistant."

"So many?"

"I'm not the first Ebisu in the reform block." She taps on her ear. "Look for the sign of a machina implant. You'll see it fastened around their ears. Each Ebisu who wields one was once part of the resistance. Well…some were just fools. And the General found a way to fix stupidity."

"The implant is inserted into the ear?"

"Partially."

"Seems like an easy fix to get off the Elder's reform list. Why not just pluck it out?"

"Not so easy when your mind isn't your own. What do you hate the most in life?"

"Am I being interrogated, now?" Mira glares then turns her shoulder to the prisoner.

"What do you hate?" Rela insists.

"Eh… hate… I don't know." *That Gally was banished… That the Ebisu invaded our colony.* "Wraiths are rather despicable. Vile, mindless creatures."

"Imagine if all the things you cared about, your companions—she gestures to the cell across the way—your clanmates, your kin… Imagine if all you saw when looking at them were mindless wraiths. That is what the reform process will do to you. It changes your perception of reality. It changes who you are. You won't know any better. You won't have thoughts of your own that aren't tainted by the Ebisu ideology. You will want to fight for Lord Tenebrous. You will be willing to die for Lord Tenebrous."

"Mira…" Haltuk calls from across the block. "…what are we to do?" Haltuk sounds broken. She doesn't have an answer for him. His chief, who is responsible for his capture, doesn't have any solutions to save him.

Knowing the meals are laced with Blue Tears, and feeling a rejuvenation in her body, she grabs onto the bars and pulls. It's hopeless. They're also augmented with the spice, shimmering with blues and greens. Her fists tighten around the bars until the blood stops flowing into them. "We fight, Haltuk," she finally responds. "We are going to fight our way out."

The door to the cell block creaks open. In walks the dreaded guard she challenged a few days back. Mira wonders why she ever made such a rash decision. The guard is easily a head taller with a physique that could snap her arms in half. His eyes hold onto her with a knowing smirk on his face, and he walks right past her down the line.

A sigh escapes her. Maybe she can use that dark braid of his to choke him out next time. Or perhaps steal his trident and take on an army of Ebisu with two prongs of fury. Her ideas are frivolous and fruitless. She has no idea how they're going to escape the Ebisu.

A total of eight guards enter the chamber. She recognizes one other. The one who praised her for quieting the haughty guard. Maybe one or two others had passed through to serve a meal, but their faces aren't memorable. Until you get to know them, they all look alike with spice-augmented metallic plates covering their chests, shoulders, thighs, and forearms; defined physiques built for war, bulging out of their armor; and dark braids with a few loose tresses framing their battle-hardened faces. Two guards stop before each cell door. One taps a machina device on the locking mechanism. Four clicks are heard throughout the chamber, followed by the grinding of metal on metal as the hinged doors open inward. The guards step into each cell, one holding manacles, the other ready and maybe even eager for a fight.

None of the prisoners show any signs of resistance. They are all manacled, foot and wrist, and bound together into a parade of misery. Rela stands in front with the Indra behind her, Haltuk behind him, and Mira in the back. They exit the cell block with guards on all sides, and march through the thoroughfares of the outpost.

The sky above is as dark as midnight with bright, white lights illuminating the dome. How do they tell the difference between night and day? It's weird to know the ocean is on the other side—above her, and all around her.

Metallic buildings erected in rows create thoroughfares throughout the outpost. She assumes they're barracks and more cell blocks. The quantity indicates they could house hundreds of thousands of soldiers. The thought of one hundred-thousand armed Ebisu soldiers arriving at her shoreline comes into view. A quick shudder slips through her and she shakes it away. Some must serve other purposes, such as crafting those ravaging machina beasts she dreamt about. A preposterous idea, but there could be machina research taking place here. She needs more information. She needs a miracle.

As immense as this facility is, and knowing it is only a military encampment, she wonders what Oceanus Salus is like, the city they've developed beneath the tides. She imagines a similar dome four times as large filled with towers of metal and white lights. They must have music other than terrorizing war drums. What is their food like? Do they hunt ray and whale and gather kelp like the De'wi or is their diet synonymous with their behavior. Maybe they only consume the leviathans and octopi of the ocean. Anything with fangs that could tear them in two or vegetation that could paralyze them, like dragon's tongue.

And what of the youngkin, and mothers and fathers. No society can exist without them. Would their innocence rebel against Lord Tenebrous' methods or does their culture dismantle their innocence from the moment they're born, teaching them they are something they're not.

Mira's wandering mind is shattered when the rhythmic sound of metal chains dragging across a metal deck come to a halt. They've arrived at the Pit of Reform where they will find out what trials await them.

"What do you think they'll have us fight this time?" The Indra whispers amongst the prisoners, but he's not so quiet the guards cannot hear.

"How did you even survive the first trial?" Haltuk questions. "No offense intended, but if you battled an eight-legged sea demon like I did, I find it hard to believe you survived the beast." A few chuckles come from the guard, who are otherwise ignoring their conversation.

The Indra glances over his shoulder before he addresses the pride-crushing comment. "It would seem the eight-legged beast choked on my cohort upon devouring him." His head slumps between his shoulders. "My guess is the trident made a lethal blow upon consumption. My companion saved me."

"I'm sorry to hear that." Mira speaks before anyone else can mock him. "Your companion was heroic. Ebisu trials or not, to die defending your own is always an honorable death. May Ceto bless him in the afterlife."

"Honorable, indeed," Haltuk agrees.

Rela remains silent. Focused on the trials ahead, perhaps, as they all should be. The discussion of the Indra's death causes them all to follow her lead. They enter the Pit of Reform with only the sound of metal chains scraping along the deck. The weight of the pit falls heavy on all of them.

They line up just in front of the pond in the center of the pit. Mira looks to the crowd, which is fuller today, and more boisterous too. Wooden strongholds have been erected within the pit. Four of them equally spaced, defending against the central pond.

General Merces enters the arena with his personal guard flanking him. Lord Tenebrous is nowhere to be seen.

"Prisoners. Today's trial will have only one victor. You will fight to the end."

"And what does the victor earn?" Mira brashly asks.

"Another day in their wretched existence." General Merces glares at her momentarily and a tantalizing smirk follows. "But for you, perhaps we can reward you with the bed of a champion." Mira is left speechless, having never been spoken to in such a manner. His gaze lingers, making her feel disgusting, before he cuts toward the elves who escorted the prisoners. "Soldiers. Adorn them with a fighting chance." On that comment, he turns on his heels and exits the pit with his guard in tow.

A rack of armor is wheeled into the pit upon his leaving and each prisoner, one by one, is dressed in a machina breastplate. The armor presses overtop her form-fitting warrior's corset, cold metal striking her flesh where the corset leaves it revealed. Mira feels a quick pinch near her collarbone, followed by a sudden surge of power running through her veins. They've adorned each of the prisoners with the same breastplates the Ebisu soldiers wear. Shoulder guards, bracers, and greaves included, and it is all made of heavy metals. It's no wonder why they cannot swim within the Terra Realm. How is she going to engage in any kind of a successful battle plan wearing anchors? Maybe the strength the Blue Tears offer will neutralize the weight of the armor.

The prisoners are fitted, their manacles are removed, and tridents are placed in their hands. Arming the prisoners would seem foolish in most cases, but these Ebisu are powerful elves, and they outnumber them two to one, not considering the hundreds, or thousands, or tens of thousands filling the encampment. It would be rather foolish of the prisoners to attempt anything.

Prior to evacuating the pit, the guards escort one prisoner to each stronghold. An eerie silence overcomes the crowd as they anticipate the battle ahead. The black sky and well-lit arena add to the surreal aura of the moment. The pond in the center is flawless. The trial participants await whatever nasty creature is about to break the tension.

Mira's forehead is damp. Her armor is heavy and awkward despite the strength it offers her. The silent anticipation is as painful as being chased through the abyss by sharp teeth and an empty stomach.

She peers over her miniature stronghold, which is comprised of horizontally braced wood slabs about as high as her breasts. If it's another octopus, this stronghold will do nothing. Haltuk waits directly across from her. The Indra is to her left and Rela is to her right.

A single ripple grows across the surface of the pond.

"It's here!" the Indra shouts. She cannot see him directly, but the tip of his trident bounces behind his stronghold like a nervous guppy. The other three combatants, including Mira, watch carefully, only their eyes visible from beyond the wooden barriers.

A steel spearpoint emerges first, elegantly slicing through the water, followed by a long shaft. The head of something elven-like comes next. Water casually slips off grey, serpent-like braids, pointed ears, a slender nose, and full lips of a purple tone. Her body lifts out of the water as if she's being elevated by a platform. Water trickles down her pale flesh, which sparkles with the radiance of Blue Tears amidst the overhead lights. Full nudity on display, which Mira is certain gives the creature an advantage over the male warriors, for every curve of her body is feminine and exploits the natural beauty of an elf maiden. The only thing terrifying about her are her uniform, stone grey eyes without pupils or irises.

"For all the wonders in the world... Are we staring upon Ceto?" The Indra pokes his head out from behind his stronghold.

"Far more terrifying," Rela yells across the pond. "Stay behind your wall!" she adds.

"What could be more terrifying than Ceto?" Haltuk asks. His eyes are locked on the beautiful creature.

"I believe you're ogling a sea nymph, Haltuk." She snorts with distaste. "She's blind. Look at her eyes."

"A creature of the deep," Rela adds. "She doesn't need eyes where she belongs. But if all of you continue running your yaps, she'll know precisely where you are. Keep quiet!"

The platform the sea nymph stands on closes off the pond entirely. Mira is grateful this fight will be on land, out of its element.

"What's the plan?" Haltuk shouts.

The sea nymph's head cuts in his direction. She leaps through the air, covering the entire distance. Her spear impales the wooden stronghold and nearly Haltuk's heart if it weren't for a quick flinch and the steel armor he dons.

"Fight the sea wench!" Mira yells. "That's the plan." She flees her stronghold and sprints toward Haltuk and the sea nymph.

The creature spins on her heal extracting her spear in the same motion and stabs toward Mira. She drops to a slide to evade the speedy attack and follows through with a roll to get behind Haltuk's stronghold with him.

An ear-piercing screech antagonizes the arena. All the combatants and spectators alike cover their ears. The sea nymph circles around the barrier and stabs down at the two of them. They dodge the attack and split ways. Mira runs toward the direction of the Indra and Haltuk toward Rela.

The sea nymph screeches again and bounds toward Mira, cutting her off.

"If it's blind, how does it know where I'm headed?"

"Echo location," Rela shouts from behind her stronghold. Her voice is muffled and strained.

The sea nymph's cold glare penetrates through Mira. She blocks the way to the Indra, who continues to squirm behind his stronghold. Its spear stabs and Mira easily knocks it out of the way with a twirl and strike of her own. Her trident nicks the sea nymph in the side causing another traumatizing screech. Mira ducks out of the way of its spear and rolls toward the worthless Indra.

"No, no. Stay away!" the Indra yells at her.

"If we all die, what do you think is going to happen, you fool?" Mira glares at him. "Are you going to kill her on your own? If you can't fight, the least you can do is be a distraction."

Just as she finishes lecturing him a spear slips past her throat. The Indra acting as a distraction for Mira and not the sea nymph as she intended. A thin, red line forms on her neck and the Indra yells, horrified by the situation.

Another strike and the Indra is silenced for good. The spear severs his vocal chords.

Mira's two-pronged trident stabs the sea nymph in the back while it focuses on the Indra. A curdling screech blasts the air, forcing her to cover her ears, but then it fizzles out. Mira must have punctured whatever creates the horrific noise. The sea nymph turns on her, not dead from what would have been a fatal strike to any De'wi, and the trident slips from her grasp. Without hesitation, Mira sprints away from the sea nymph toward her companions.

The creature closes the gap with one bound, knocking Mira to the ground. The spear tip anchors her in place, having punctured her shoulder and quite possibly the metal deck, too. She cannot move without pain tearing through her shoulder. A foot smashes into her back, cold and dreadful, amplifying the agony. The spear slides from her shoulder and Mira knows she must act quick. Pushing through the pain, she rolls to her side, slipping free of the sea nymph just as the spear tip slams into the deck. Mira's leg swoops behind the creature, dropping it to one knee, and just then, another trident flies through the air and pierces the sea nymph's naked chest. It slumps forward leaning into the shaft. Its stone grey eyes remain gazing ahead, hard to decipher whether they're lifeless or not. Its serpent-like braids fall over its face like a curtain in a closing act.

Mira breathes a heavy sigh, lying on her back, and the pain in her shoulder forces a cringe that in turn causes more pain.

Rela retrieves the trident from the sea nymph and stands overtop Mira. "Only one victor," she says.

The trident comes down at her chest, but Mira is able to move quick enough that it graces the steel breastplate and sticks in the metal deck. Mira hops to her fins, pushing through her pain, and creates distance between herself and Rela, who struggles to remove the trident from the deck.

"Only one victor…" Mira repeats, confusion plastered on her face. She glances toward Rela's stronghold and sees two fins lying on the ground, motionless. "What have you done?" The anger in Mira's voice sends tremors throughout the entire pit.

Mira swoops in, kicks the trident loose, grabs it, and knocks Rela to the ground all in one swift and precise attack. She stands overtop of Rela, staring down at her with enough hate to murder. "Concede!"

Rela moves to grab the trident and Mira slams it down on her neck. "Concede!" she yells. The two-pronged trident is anchored into the metal deck. Rela flails her legs and pulls at the trident to no avail. She is pinned and losing air quickly. Her gasps are empty and struggled.

"Concede!" Mira repeats. Never having yelled so angrily at anyone, it startles her. Is she capable of the same violence these Ebisu wield?

Rela's arms stop squirming, and her legs stop kicking. She goes limp. Mira puts a fin on her breastplate and presses down as she pulls the trident free. She thought she was gaining an ally in this Ebisu rebel. She was wrong. They are all full of the same brutality.

War drums fill the arena, declaring Mira's victory. She pays them no mind as she rushes to Haltuk's side. Blood pools on the deck from a large gash in his abdomen just beneath his breastplate.

Mira leans into him. "I'm sorry, Haltuk. I tried, and I failed." She has no tears to shed with the chaos of the moment still overwhelming her. "Another De'wi warrior dead because of me." She slumps into him, embracing his lifeless body.

Finsteps can be heard all around her, and she lets the Ebisu guard carry her away, not giving any effort to walk alongside them. More Ebisu guards tend to the fallen as she is escorted out of the Pit of Reform, the only survivor. But it makes no difference. She will get the machina implant and be converted into an Ebisu soldier, all the same. Her prize is to live another day with the pain of having failed her companion. The guilt and misery of her victory swathes over her in a dark shroud.

25 A LIFE OF RELEVANCE

Pillars zip by as Gallagher races down the long path to Arilight Palace. The machina crafts hovering overhead move as fast as Gallagher's legs, no faster, no slower, but they make no move to attack. They only follow.

It's a long while before Gallagher sees anything other than white pillars, green hills, and the drones above. As the palace gets closer, and the sun climbs into the sky, he is welcomed by a line of Indran guards standing atop pearly white steps. More than a dozen, all armed with scepters, and ready for battle.

Gallagher slows down and comes to a halt at the base of the steps. He handled a similar number of guards back at House Orillian. Can he do it again?

He places one foot onto the first step, and the guards split, allowing for Indra nobility to pass through.

"Champion..." An unfamiliar sky elf stands before him at the top of the stairs. "It's nice of you to return to us. We weren't sure if that deviant from House Orillian had manipulated you with his fallacies. But I must ask..." He looks down at the blade Gallagher wields. "Because you come armed, are you here to join our cause, to become our emissary and create an alliance with the De'wi?" He folds his arms across his body. "Or are you here to fight House Arilight?"

Gallagher looks down at the weapon in his hand. They don't know that he was running in to take back what doesn't belong to them. They may have witnessed him arrive with Brunswick, but they don't know why. For all they know, Gallagher was running to escape House Orillian. Gallagher taps the pommel of the sword, and a sheath consumes the blade. He tucks it away beneath his surcoat. "Who are you?"

"Forgive me." The mallow-shaped elf bows from the top of the stairs. "Smika Ohmsmire. Son to Chrigan and Jothra Ohmsmire, Grandson to Elder Fae of House Arilight, heir to House Ohmsmire. I bid you good welcome."

Gallagher understands little of what he said other than he's related to Elder Fae. "I would like to see Rivee Rayfin."

Smika looks down at him with a perplexed expression. "Who?"

How could this sky elf not know who he's referring to? He arrived with the youngkin and rescued her from the leviathan. "Oh...err... Riveria Arilight," Gallagher says, struggling to recall her Indran name. "I would like to see her before I commit to anything."

The sky elf holds his chin high. At least that's how Gallagher translates his body language. It's difficult to see his chin with all the folds of skin beneath it, but it feels rather pompous, especially with the quick and audible exhale to follow, as if Gallagher is ludicrous for making any requests at all.

"Follow me," he says.

Gallagher climbs the steps two at a time. Smika loads into a ferry and Gallagher follows on foot.

They enter the palace through grand, double doors just as white as the pillars and stone pathway he charged in on. Trimmings of gold and silver accent it in an unusual way. They look like artistic scratches curling across the walls, but white is the predominant color of everything Gallagher sees.

They stroll through a grand foyer and down several corridors, Indran guard in tow, and all armed with scepters. Gallagher isn't sure if they're here for him or if this is typical for this son-of-a-thousand-pompous-elves nobility stuff. He wouldn't put it past the elf to have more than a dozen personal guard.

Smika ushers Gallagher to wait when they reach the base of a grand staircase with none other than white balustrades, white stone steps, and silver and gold trimmings. It's all illuminated from bright white lights hanging from the tall ceiling above.

Smika's ferry, unexpectedly to Gallagher, climbs the stairs. The elf hasn't walked a step, and Gallagher realizes why the race, in general, tend to be plumper with many more chins than they were born with. They allow their machina to put forth much of the effort just as Gallagher's Elders have always presented. It makes them physically weak.

Gallagher looks down at his damaged fin. Would the machina he wore have made him weak, too? He felt so powerful within the Terra Realm while wearing it. His speed doubled, and he could have competed with the best of warriors to earn his stones. Maybe the question is whether it would have stopped there. If one small piece of machina invoked such powerful emotions, would he have wanted more? And what of the rest of the De'wi? If he proceeds with joining House Arilight instead of stealing Rivee away to take her home, he has no doubt the machina will be introduced to their culture. It would benefit the rebuilding of their colony after the waterspout ripped through it, and it would benefit his clan if they go to war with the Ebisu. Perhaps, knowing the vice the machina can have on its wielders, they could prevent it from making them weak. Perhaps, they could implement certain measures to prevent the abuse of machina. It could help them. He could get his fin back.

"Our champion returns, does he?" Elder Fae arrives at the top of the stairs. "Please, join me." She turns and disappears without waiting for a response, leaving Smika in her wake.

The plump elf stares at him from the top of the stone staircase. Gallagher looks around at the guards who block all the exits. He looks back to Smika and starts up the stairs.

They pass through a grand foyer, a few corridors, and up several ramps before entering a chamber where she waits seated at a table with beverages ready for consumption. The palace is built for their ferries to travel throughout. Smika never once stepped foot off the wheeled machina.

After being requested to do so, Gallagher sits across from the Elder. The table, surprisingly, isn't white, but rather an illuminated, metallic frame with a frosty glass surface. They add their machina magic in places where it benefits nobody. Gallagher's eyes shift to the contents of the glass, after silently scrutinizing the table.

"There is nothing to be suspicious about. I have no reason to pacify our champion, do I? But I won't be offended if you allow it to go to waste."

Gallagher puts the glass to his lips and takes a drink. It's bitter and dry, and somewhat sweet. How a liquid of any kind could make him want to consume more liquids is beyond his understanding, but this one does. He sets the glass down, uncertain if he should consume anymore.

"My apologies for the way in which you were forced to depart our celebration." A short silence follows when Gallagher doesn't respond. "So, you've met the rebellious side of our culture. How was it? What did you think?"

Small talk? Is this an attempt to deceive Gallagher and extract information from him? They still don't know where his head is at, and they know he's being persuaded by multiple agendas. How did he become such an important pawn in another race's noble antics?

Gallagher isn't sure where his head is, either. On one hand, he could bring two races together and introduce machina to his culture in an attempt at prosperity for all three realms. On the other, he could be introducing corruption accompanied by machina and the inherent weaknesses it spreads throughout a culture. This could be the seed of demise for the De'wi, and Gallagher the one who sows it. No better than the irrelevant kelp picker he is.

He decides to keep his responses short, and to listen intently at what she has to say.

"The rebels are nice," he says.

"Nice?" She looks at him with indifference and maybe a hint of disgust, as if the words *rebels* and *nice* don't belong in the same sentence, but she's trying to be polite and swallow it regardless.

Gallagher nods.

"Smika informed me you expect to see Riveria before you make any final commitments, is that so?" She takes a sip of her beverage. Her motions are eloquent and practiced.

"It is true. I would like to consult her on this matter."

"But she is only a youngkin. You mean, you would like to make sure she is safe."

"Youngkin or not, I value her opinion. Is she not safe?" Gallagher's eyes narrow.

"She is more than safe. Nobody would dare intrude upon my doorstep. Plus, you've seen the defenses we carry. There isn't an Indra who could enter the grounds of my palace undetected."

"Is there reason for someone to invade your palace?" Gallagher treads lightly but persists with his audacious questions to see if he can draw out her true colors. Brunswick hasn't done anything to be distrusted but this culture is still new to Gallagher, and Brunswick's motives are personal. He has no reason to help the De'wi, only reason to take down House Arilight. If Elder Fae would speak to her true motives, it would help Gallagher know what to do.

"You tell me. How is Brunswick doing? I noticed he didn't craft you another fin to wear."

She knows of their first acquaintance. Gallagher shifts in his seat, wiggling his toes at the mention of his damaged fin. He has yet to put on a pair of shoes as the rest of this culture does.

"Will you force your machina on us?" he asks bluntly.

"Of course not. But the De'wi are welcome to it." She smiles, knowing its novelty and effectiveness are undeniable.

"Can I see her?"

"You can." The Elder raises her hand to a guard standing at the exit. He steps out of the room.

A few moments pass with more small talk and no significant information passing from one to the other. Then, the chamber door opens.

"Rivee Rayfin!" Gallagher rises from the table to greet her.

"Gally!"

The two embrace each other. It isn't until Gallagher pulls back that he realizes something strange about her.

"Rivee, you're beautiful." He bounces a tousle of her curls in his hand, admiring the drastic change. Her hair was always straight, and distraught. "Your gown is lovely." It's long, flowing, and blue, the color of a cloudless sky. "And you're standing on two legs?" The last comment comes out as more of a question. He hasn't had an opportunity to talk to her about these new developments.

Rivee pulls up her gown just enough for Gallagher to see the machina leg she has equipped. It has the same metallic appearance as the fin he wore, but with imitation muscle and sinew weaving around the metallic bars. It dons a shoe coordinating with her gown and, of course, her other shoe.

Gallagher ponders this for a moment. Either Elder Fae's tailors are more prolific than whoever sized him up, or Rivee's fins are more compatible with shoes.

"I'm no longer blighted, Gally. They've given me my leg back. Isn't it wonderful?"

Gallagher embraces her once more, and smiles. Although, it quickly fades. He's happy for her, but he wonders if it will last. Gallagher's didn't. He was offered a taste of what life could be with two whole fins, then it was torn away. Fortunately for Gallagher, he's been roaming about the Caelum Realm since it was removed, so it hasn't been noticed. But once he returns to the Terra Realm, where they predominantly swim, it will never go unnoticed. He'll constantly be reminded of his blight.

Rivee, on the other hand, requires the machina she wears to get around in the Caelum Realm, and it obviously makes her happy. This tears Gallagher in two.

Gallagher whispers in her ear while they're still embracing. "Do you want to go home?" A simple question, but he's not confident he'll get a simple answer.

She remains silent. He pulls back to look her in the eyes, and they're full of uncertainty.

Gallagher turns to Elder Fae. "It's obvious you've allured her with your lofty customs." His words are abrupt and coated with aggression. "She's happy." Gallagher cannot pull her from this place. She'll despise him for eternity and always strive to return. The only way Gallagher can remove her without severe consequences is to show her the dark side of machina. But how? Gallagher doesn't even know what that is. Beyond that, the sky elves claim she's Indra. Maybe she belongs here.

Gallagher pulls a chair out for Rivee and nudges it in when she sits—a smile on her face all the while. Gallagher joins them at the table.

His hand runs through his hair as he stares at the table. "Can you please elaborate on how an Indra youngkin ended up within the Terra Realm? How does this happen? And how is it possible we were never aware?"

"You De'wi are not incapable of deceit, you know. Mighty warriors, sure, but immune to greed, envy, and self-fulfillment, no." Elder Fae looks to Rivee with genuine care. "I think that story isn't mine to tell, however. It would be best if it came from her mother, Nessa Rayfin."

"Excuse me!" Gallagher cannot fathom this. "Lady Nessa?" He needs confirmation. Did he hear her correctly?

"It seems I've already given too much. In time. Riveria must hear this from her mother. Not her grandmother."

"Grandmother?" Gallagher stares in bewilderment, unable to think straight.

"And my father?" Rivee speaks no louder than a mouse.

Elder Fae looks to her. "I've been holding off the introductions for the right time. Riveria, would you like to meet my son, Jarnes Arilight, first born, heir to House Arilight, and… your father?"

Rivee's head snaps to Gallagher, both with excitement and a request for permission, as if Gallagher can grant that. "You've always been like an older sibling to me, Gally. You and Mira. How I wish she were here." Rivee and Gallagher both. Rivee's head turns down to the table as she fiddles with her fingers.

"She's okay, Rivee. She's out there somewhere. She's the mightiest of them all." Gallagher attempts to lift her spirits, but he knows it's hollow. Gallagher's words are carried only by hope, and they both know it.

"And with my new leg, I could be just like her." Rivee's head pops back up, her eyes lit with a newfound fire. "You're right, Gally. She's out there somewhere, and one day I'll be able to show her who I've become." She scoots her chair back, swings her legs to the side, and pulls up her gown to admire her machina leg. "Gally…" She looks at him. "Would you like to meet him, too?"

Gallagher reaches out to grab her hand. "Yes, Rivee Rayfin. It would be an honor to meet your father."

Elder Fae raises a hand to the guard at the door. One of them slips through the exit. "It won't be long," she says.

Gallagher stares at Rivee for a long moment. Her beaming smile is contagious. She's no longer irrelevant and blighted like Gallagher. She's royalty. If he brought her back home with that machina leg, he'd only be dragging her down with him.

Gallagher's smile fades as he looks to Elder Fae. "She's safe within your home?"

Rivee's brow quirks, but Gallagher pays it no mind. He's looking for confirmation from Elder Fae.

"Yes. You have my word," she responds with her eyes fixed on Gallagher.

Gallagher inhales a heavy breath. "Okay." He doesn't bother to hide the hesitancy in his voice. He doesn't like it, but Gallagher cannot remove Rivee from this new position. "What do you need from me?"

26 BOON OF TEARS

Seadragons casually swim past Mira, led by Ebisu soldiers. They are the only thing swimming within the bubble. Limp and floppy fins suggest they aren't thrilled to be part of the Ebisu army. Perhaps they aren't controlled by machina like the other creatures.

"Let's go," the soldier escorting her says. He yanks on the chains attached to her manacles and she stumbles, bringing her wandering mind back to the moment, and back to the excruciating pain from the gaping hole in her shoulder.

Haltuk's death hasn't fully sunk in. It all happened so fast. Death. Defeat. Triumph. Chains. And here she is taking a victory lap through the streets of the outpost, back to her cellblock. What will happen next?

The cellblock door creaks open. The chamber is colder than she remembers. Dark steel plates cover the floor, the walls, and the ceiling. The cell bars have a tint of the spice exuding from them. The stench remains the same, billowing into the nostrils upon entry, and worthy of dropping the weakest to their knees. This is what victory has brought her. Defeat may have been the preferred choice.

The guard escorts her into her cell. "What happens next?" she asks. Her head is sunk between her shoulders staring at her fins. Void of any fight, she trudges into her cell.

"They reform you, then they assign you." He pauses a moment, staring at her from his peripheral. "Did you think there would be some kind of reward for winning?" he asks with a smirk on his face. "It's called the Pit of Reform because it reforms you. Nothing else."

Mira slumps into the cold bars in the corner of her cell.

"I'll tell you what. For your hard-earned victory, I'll have the mess hall serve up an extra dish for you tonight."

Mira grunts in return. Not a discourteous grunt. A defeated grunt.

The guard exits the chamber and leaves Mira to her miserable brooding. Days go by, or so she thinks. Her only means of telling time is the amount of meals brought to her. The guard stood by his word, and she received two bowls of gruel the night of her victory. A prize to cherish for eternity—a dead companion, the death of a rising ally, chains, and two bowls of gruel. Sums up her feelings toward the Ebisu and everything they value.

Mira lies on the cold, metal floor with her eyes closed. Not sleeping. She closes her eyes to snuff out the light, to allow darkness to take her. What else does she have?

The door to the cell block suddenly creaks open. "Can we get this reformation over with already?" she says without opening her eyes.

No response.

She anticipates her door to open and a dish to slide in. Instead, the cell door next to hers opens. This prompts her to open her eyes.

A body stumbles and drops to the floor. Limp. Seemingly lifeless if she hadn't seen it stumble. Another prisoner of reform. Another expendable piece for the Ebisu army. They don't require such forces to take on the scattered De'wi colonies. The army they build could be for only one thing. To lay claim to all three realms: sky, land, and sea. Lord Tenebrous intends to go to war with the Indra.

Why does she bother fretting over it? She will be part of it soon enough.

"You're still here?" a weary voice says from the cell next to her. The voice matches the condition of the body.

Mira rises to a sitting position, leaning on one arm, and peers into the dim-lit cell next to hers. It's an Ebisu. Another rebel Ebisu? The prisoner pushes upward to lift themselves. Not until Mira sees a face, does she recognize her for who she is. "Rela!"

A boiling anger rises inside her. An anger she didn't realize was there. Only defeat remains. She has no room for anger. But here it is, climbing to the surface from the depths of the darkness that has consumed her.

Rela was dead. If not dead, reformed. "How did you survive? Why'd they send you back here?"

"I suppose I deserve that." She crawls to the corner of her cell where, surprisingly, her linen remains. She drapes it over her head and presses her back into the cell bars on the far side, away from Mira. "There was to be…" A cough interrupts her. "Excuse me. One victor. I had to."

"Nobody forced your hand." Mira's words are sharp.

"I did!" Rela snaps back. "I forced my own hand. I had to."

A growl escapes Mira as she attempts to shake the bars. She only shakes herself, however. The bars are rigid. She's of the mind that she could bend metal right now, but spice-enhanced steel proves to be too much. She lets go and drops back to the floor, anger and defeat battling to take hold of her mind.

"You lost a good friend, and… and… well, maybe I've become numb to it." A coughing fit erupts from her.

Mira stares at her for a moment, undecided if she should pry further. Does she care why Rela killed her companion? "Numb to death?" she asks. "Because you don't seem very good at it."

"Or you're bad at executing it," she spits back, clearly taking Mira's comment as an insult.

"Are you a spy? Do they use you for some sort of mental anguish. To break me and open me up?"

Rela shifts where she sits and more coughing echoes throughout the mostly empty cell block. "They would *physically* torture you for information. The Elder isn't so sophisticated with his tactics as to play mind games." Rela's words are choppy and slow. She's taken a severe beating of her own. Whatever happened to her, it's not from the Pit of Reform.

"Why are you back here?" As little as Mira wants to talk to the nasty elf who killed Haltuk, questions continue to spill out of her. "One victor. You should be dead or reformed. Why haven't they reformed you?"

"My best guess…" She clears her throat with a gnarly gurgled sound and spits on the floor. "…they want to see me spit up as much blood as they can before implanting that shit into my head. I'm a traitor, Mira. They want to see me suffer." A long pause fills the air as both prisoners contemplate her words. "I know General Merces does," she adds.

"General Merces?"

"Genocide isn't beneath him." Rela pulls the linen tighter around herself. "Genocide… torture… slavery… He treats all life as his tools to mold the world around him."

"What happened? I mean…why have you chosen rebellion? I presume you could have lived a life within Oceanus Salus and away from all this vile behavior. Or do the Ebisu have any normal livelihoods? There must be if you're capable of building such monstrosities. Not everyone can be a soldier of war.

There must be smiths, harvesters, and the like. Maybe a few youngkins survive your brutal nature." Mira's words are full of spite.

"General Merces happened. When it was decided to lay siege to the Terra Realm, recruitment began. They ushered all the strong and capable into their military outposts. Caravans filled with Ebisu both willing and unwilling traveled the depths of the ocean to these outposts to begin their training. It has been going on for hundreds of years, and more recruitment is always needed. General Merces sees to it that all efforts go toward improving our warring technology or our warring battalions. As soon as the youngkins are of size and strength, they are pulled in."

"You had family that were enlisted?" Mira regrets the question as soon as she asks it. Anger still boils at the surface. Knowing Rela's past will only temper it. She'd rather hold onto that anger. Use it to get revenge, or perhaps to fight her way out of this hell hold.

"If they were merely enlisted, I wouldn't be here right now. I would be on the lines alongside them." Rela struggles to continue. Mira doesn't bother intercepting the conversation. Despite all her anger toward this Ebisu elf, she can sense the anguish she's battling. Mira remains silent, waiting for her to finish. "General Merces personally murdered my husband..." She chokes on her words. "...and my son."

Damn it! This changes Mira's outlook, just as she suspected. She prefers the anger. Now, she must deal with sympathizing with this murderous, brutal elf. This elf that killed Haltuk. She has strong motivations to conquer her enemies, just as Mira does. She would stop at nothing to avenge the death of her kin. Would Mira?

"And that is why you murdered Haltuk?" Mira presses into the bars between their cells, holding an ironclad gaze on Rela.

The whites of Rela's eyes shift and become visible in the shadows as she stares back at Mira. It's the only acknowledgment she responds with—a brutally cold stare that brings a chill to the prison chamber.

"Because you must do everything within your power to remain alive. So you can fulfill that vengeance?" Mira adds, her tone flat and devoid of empathy.

Rela holds her chilling glare, saying nothing in return.

Debate fills Mira's mind. She left her clan in anger. Her mother was Gallagher's chopping block and her father the executioner. They made sure he was dealt with harshly and swiftly, so nobody could debate the punishment before it was executed. Mira has good reason to be upset with them. Furious even. And come to find out Gallagher *was* involved with the taboo machina. Now, she has mixed fillings about his loyalties and whether she needs to atone for her actions. If her kin were slaughtered, which they very well could be if she doesn't escape to warn them, would she do *anything* to protect them? Would she take an innocent life? She doesn't know.

"How do we escape?" She considers them both unintentionally, but she means it. Rela has not earned her forgiveness or her trust after what she has done. But she has earned her respect. Maybe if they work together, they can flee this place. "I will help you take down General Merces, but first we must get out of here. How do we do that?"

"A miracle." Her words are growing more distant.

"Rela?"

No response.

"Rela, where is the way out? Assuming we escape this cell block, how do we flee the outpost? There must be weaknesses in the patrols... In the perimeter."

"..."

"Shit!" Sympathy for Rela recedes like a glacier as anger coils deep within her, ready to spring out at the world around her. She lies down and closes her eyes, ignorant of what else she can do.

Unknowing how much time has passed, Mira wakes to the sound of the cell block door screeching open.

"It's time." It's the same Ebisu guard who allowed her privacy on the privy several days ago. "Let's go." He leans his standard-issue trident against the wall and opens the door to her cell. Then, he moves onto Rela's cell. No other guards join him. This must be common practice for their reform. Wither away their prisoners until they have no fight left in them, then introduce their mind-controlling machina.

"That's how it works..." Mira speaks to the guard as she slowly rises to her fins. "That's what the Pit of Reform is for..." The guard doesn't pay her much attention as he inspects Rela's condition. "You use us for entertainment as you break us. You break our heart and soul and cheer us on while you do it, making us think there could be some kind of benefit of survival. You laced our meals with just enough Tears to give us fight, but it's all for destroying our will to survive. You need us in a withered state to control us, and you use entertainment to take us there. Disgusting!" She spits on her cell floor. "You all deserve to die!"

Mira pulls her door open all the way, ignoring the pain in her arm, and quickly rips into Rela's cell. He's bent over Rela's body. His head jerks over his shoulder, and Mira's knee breaks through his jaw. Mira pounces on him.

His body is limp. "Thank Ceto…" she whispers to herself. She doesn't have much fight in her. It was a quick spark of ambition, nothing more. Guilt pings her as she stands overtop his body. He was nice to her.

She quickly moves to aid Rela. Life remains within her, but she's broken. Bruises cover her dark flesh. Cheeks, shoulders, forearms… Dried blood too, where her flesh couldn't withstand the flogging.

Mira scans the room for anything that can be used as a litter. More guilt washes over her as she decides it's best to abandon her. "You are a true warrior, Rela. I don't fully understand why, but it pains me to leave you here. And if I find a way out, I will do everything I can… I will do *anything* to stop General Merces and avenge your fallen kin."

"Wait…" The guard rises to a sitting position, rubbing at his jaw.

Mira rises with much anguish and retreats from the cell to snag his trident. "You don't understand…"

"What is there to understand?" She blocks the doorway, armed and ready to kill. "You intend to take everything from us De'wi. I won't have it."

"I *intend* to give you a fighting chance."

"Why should I trust you?"

He shrugs. "Because I let you have your privacy while you were… you know."

"Hardly a means to earn trust." She pauses, and the tension within her stance subsides. "I do thank you for that, but I don't trust you."

"What if I told you your companion isn't dead. That I can help you free him."

"Haltuk?"

"I'm sorry, I don't know names. The De'wi you seemed most concerned about. In fact, none of the prisoners who shared this cell block are dead. If you didn't notice, healers rushed in after each trial. They are injected with a heavy dose of spice to aid in their recovery before they are implanted with the transmitter."

"Transmitter?"

"It's what creates the neophytes."

"Neophytes?" He speaks words Mira doesn't understand. "The General called me that when I was first introduced to this hell. What is it?"

"New converts. Those who've been reformed."

"Why wasn't Rela given the same treatment? Why wasn't *I* given the same treatment? I can't trust you."

"Rela is a special case. The General has taken a likening to her suffering. She attempted an assassination on him. It's how she ended up here. It's how she ended up like this." He curls over her, inspecting her wounds. He presses a hand on her bare inner thigh examining her groin. "Bruises. As I suspected. The General is a sick individual. A taint on all elven races. He deserves to be labeled a monster." He looks up at Mira. "And you... You're the victor. Obviously stronger than the rest. If not stronger, smarter. Your wits and endurance require more trials. Had there been more prisoners captured, you would have been forced to endure more trials to break you further. You're in luck, however. They plan to finalize the reform today."

"Why not pin me against one of your fabled creatures?"

"We've seen what you're capable of. Unfortunately, the General values those creatures more than the De'wi. The risk is too heavy for him. He'd rather pin you against neophytes, but they too hold a value above the prisoners going through the trials."

"Hmph... Your *General* must have been tossed about in too many waterspouts. His priorities are disorderly at best."

"I would agree," the guard admits. "What if I gave you some of this?" He digs into a pouch at his hip. Mira's grip on the trident tightens. "A solid ration of spice." He holds the bioluminescent algae in his open palm. It's enough to give her strength for a week if she rationed it properly. Enough to fully heal her nearly useless shoulder.

"You offer me Blue Tears?"

"I do."

"But it's not diluted in the gruel. You offer me a fighting chance." She looks at him, forming a conjecture of deceit and games within her thoughts. "And what of Rela?" Mira gestures to her with the tip of the trident. "Please."

The guard gently opens her jaw and tucks a small wad beneath her tongue. "It won't act quickly without chewing, but her saliva will break it down slowly, and she'll come to eventually." He looks up to Mira again. "She is a close companion of mine. Her husband, the one she lost—I'm not sure if she made you aware—was my best mate." A sadness overcomes him that cannot be falsely manifested. "I have my own reasons for stopping this insanity."

"I suppose I don't know any other way out of here. If I trust you... If you bring me to Haltuk and help us escape... Help *all* of us escape..." She gestures to Rela with the trident again. "How will you get us out of here?"

"I have a means to tamper with the implants." He rises to his fins. "You must follow through with the reform. Your companion, along with all the other neophytes, are contained within the halfway house. Whether you like it or not, you will have to trust me. And you will have to behave as if your will is not your own, which will be the hard part."

"Act a slave…" She lowers the trident to her side and steps closer to the Ebisu guard. "I can do that." She holds out her hand. "Name?"

"Tiolas." He reaches for her hand, and she quickly slaps it away.

With a shake of her head, she says, "The spice."

"Of course." He hands her the wad of Blue Tears.

"Nice to meet you, Tiolas." She shakes his hand. "Mira."

27 QUARRELS AMIDST THE STARS

Y et another grand plaza full of splendor and desire. The Caelum Realm
doesn't fall short of pleasing the eye. The sun has just fallen over the
horizon and the first celestial bodies shine their light upon Solaria, also
inviting a coolness to the realm Gallagher isn't accustomed to. He pulls the collar
of his surcoat taught to keep the chill off his neck.

Jarnes Arilight, in an attempt to get to know his daughter, has invited them
to view the stars—one of many passions he explores. His guard, also acting as
servants, unpack an instrument in the shape of a long cylinder on legs.

"What is it?" Rivee asks. The cold doesn't seem to bother her. Although,
Elder Fae insists she presents herself as a lady and has her wearing a full gown

covering her legs plus an overcoat. It could be that Elder Fae is also embarrassed by the machina she uses to walk.

"Oh, Riveria, if only I could answer that in simple form. What you have asked is a broad question." He stands proud next to his instrument donning a dark blue surcoat draped to his calves with a matching vest beneath it. His long blond hair is pulled back into a tail without a single strand of hair misaligned. His face is young and soft, contradicting his firm and resolute demeanor.

He taps the instrument with the conch at the end of his scepter. "This is a view into the past. This is a means to explore beyond Solaria. This…is the beginning of the future." He taps the instrument again. "Take a peek."

Rivee's face squishes into something abnormal.

"You put your eye to the lens, just here." He offers her a sincere smile.

Gallagher scouts the plaza with his eyes as her father tries to get to know her. Jarnes' guards all stand at a lazy attention around the two, giving them their space while creating a perimeter. It's nothing like how the De'wi warriors would act in this situation. These elves poke at each other, laugh, and have no eyes on their surroundings. He looks back at Rivee, who seems content with laughs and smiles of her own. Leaning on the dangers Brunswick implanted in his head, Gallagher doesn't like this one bit. Rivee out in the open of an unknown garden plaza he isn't familiar with. He doesn't feel like he can protect her out here. He convinces himself that checking the perimeter is necessary.

"I'll be back shortly," he says to one of the guards. "Checking the perimeter," he repeats his thoughts out loud.

The guard's lips flatten in a perturbed manner. What they both know, that wasn't said, is that Gallagher is doing their job for them. He cannot let go of what Brunswick told him about Rivee's safety. He's already had to battle House Arilight's elite guard once, some of whom may have been these guards' companions. And that was only for running away from what felt like imprisonment. If House Arilight and House Godmadina are involved in a permanent war with one another, what would prevent House Godmadina from coming after both heirs to House Arilight? Tonight would present the perfect opportunity.

The plaza is a vast green field covered in trimmed grass. Nothing like the seagrass within the Terra Realm, but grass none the less. A small knoll sits in the middle with a pergola placed on top and white stone-paved trails curling throughout. Around the pergola are brilliant-colored flowers, visible even in the starlight. Bordering the plaza are the tall, foliage-covered structures in which the sky elves dwell in. They're tall buildings, and their abodes are stacked on top of one another. Perhaps, all the elves prefer the miraculous view of the edge when they rise in the morning, and when they bed down at night. It's a beautiful sight, and one to envy, but they build their homes as if they're confined to them and incapable of walking out here to edge. The only effort, an evening stroll. Another societal statement fully displaying the indolence engrained within their culture.

Gallagher strolls toward the pergola where he'll have a better view of the entire plaza. Not exactly the perimeter, but he should have a good view of it. At least, that's the excuse he tells himself. Curiosity draws him in, wondering if those flowers are the roses Brunswick spoke of when discussing Elder Fae.

Several sky elves stroll through the plaza, most in hand with another elf. An extremely small minority of willing couples enjoying the nice evening, perhaps. There aren't so many that Gallagher cannot keep an eye on all of them.

He stops to examine the flowers. Folds of petals upon petals curl around one another. Whites, reds, indigos, and violets, just to name a few of the colors. He puts his nose to one and quickly jerks back, the aroma much stronger than he anticipated. He tries again and breathes in the intoxicating smell. Suddenly, Gallagher has a new understanding of how Brunswick felt about Lady Fae. There was a deep passion there, and she treated him as a weed in her garden. He feels sympathetic for the elf.

In the distance, a flash of the blue-green iridescence catches his eye. It's the glow of the scepters these Indra arm themselves with. Across the plaza at the far edge. Then, a few more. Gallagher wouldn't think much of this, except he's only witnessed the conches glowing when being used to attack someone, and that someone has been him in every instance.

His muscles tighten as he stares from afar. Could this be an attack on House Arilight? Should he head them off and disrupt the incursion before it begins? Or is he being overzealous.

A warrior would not wait for an attack. The least he can do is get closer to investigate. However… He looks back in the direction of Rivee and her father. The guard continue to be unobservant and hardly worth the scepters they wield. If Gallagher investigates the glowing conches, he'll put Rivee at risk by creating too much distance between them. He won't be able to protect her from such a distance. His eyes patrol the rest of the plaza. Nothing is amiss, and it's enough to convince him to investigate the activity on the far side.

Gallagher strolls down the curling pathways with his hands intertwined behind his back. He wishes to run, but he doesn't want to look out of place.

He dons the same uncomfortable attire Jarnes is wearing. It's not fit for a warrior, but Jarnes insisted. It's a symbol of class and prosperity, and the prideful elf wanted him to fit the role while spending the evening together. In short, he didn't want to be acquainted with a working-class elf, or any elf of lower status.

An heir to House Arilight has minimum expectations, which makes sense if you're a warrior. If you cannot trust the others in your squad, you may as well toss them into a wraith swarm and be done with them. And when the best isn't actually the best, and only dressed to emulate such, nothing good will come of it when put to the challenge. To avoid suspicion, Gallagher leaves his long surcoat on despite wanting to toss it to the ground to ready himself for an attack.

As he gets closer, his tension dismantles. The group of elves are merely youngkins enjoying themselves, and the green glow is painted rocks, not glowing from the essence of Blue Tears, but rather the moonlight from above. They're playing some form of a game.

"What is it, he asks?" The youngkins freeze. "The game you play, what is it?"

Wide eyes and mouths agape, they stare. "Are you..." one of the youngkins stammers.

"He's a giant!" another blurts.

Gallagher flinches, and the youngkins startle, picking up their rocks and scurrying off into the night. He hadn't thought much about the way he might appear to Indra youngkins. He's average height within his clan, but to an Indra who has never seen an elf taller than a rice paddy, he must look like a giant.

Gallagher shrugs off the interaction and follows the pathway as it curls back around, closer to the edge of the landship and back in the direction of Rivee and Jarnes. All is calm. All is well.

He wonders if he wanders too close to the edge as he peers through the darkness at the moonlit clouds beneath him. Too close to the edge, figuratively, as he tends to never let his guard down, always leaning into the gravity of every situation. All is peaceful and enjoyable in the plaza this evening, yet Gallagher finds threat and danger everywhere he looks. Rivee is happy. Jarnes, thus far, seems genuinely interested in being a father. She will live a good life in the Caelum Realm. Maybe Gallagher can visit her from time to time? Or maybe the Morshine Clan will welcome visitations despite her machina leg?

Gallagher yearns to go home. He longs for Mira's presence. Though the Indra want him to be an emissary between the two races, he doesn't see the need. Rivee is already that connection. Gallagher's duty, both to Rivee and to the protection of the De'wi race, is complete. He no longer wears his machina fin, so maybe they'll welcome him back home. All he needs to do is take the leap. He stops and turns to the edge. It's unsettling—the sensation of falling—but he knows once he penetrates the ocean of clouds, he'll be able to swim the rest of the way home.

Gallagher doesn't dare do it, however. He must say goodbye to Rivee, first.

A scream pierces the calm evening. Gallagher dismisses his forlorn thoughts and looks for the source. Fear tears at his flesh as his utter failure reveals itself. Rivee and Jarnes are under attack.

Gallagher rushes the scene, disregarding the curling stone pathway, making a straight course to Rivee. Glowing conches dance about in the darkness. Some belong to Jarnes' guard, but far more than that close around them. They are outnumbered by at least double.

The guard put their backs to Rivee and Jarnes as they fend off the assailants, but Rivee and Jarnes are backed up to the edge of the landship. Gallagher flinches in his sprint as Rivee trips over Jarnes' instrument, kicking it over the edge, and tumbling toward the edge herself. Jarnes manages to grab a wad of her gown and pulls her upright. They're trapped between the assailants and a leap into the Terra Realm.

Gallagher engages in battle, withdrawing his short sword and unsheathing it at the same time with a tap of the pommel. An energy surges into his body as if the machina unleashes tendrils crawling throughout his veins. He feels invincible. Knowing that is a dangerous place to be in the head, he subdues the thought.

His blade clashes with a scepter and he easily cuts down the first attacker. Another enemy approaches with a swinging scepter. It smacks him on the head but has no pacifying qualities thanks to the machina blade he wields. The pain stuns him, however. He's smacked again and again, until he retaliates with a piercing blade. Their scepters do no more than offer bruises and headaches and that's when Gallagher realizes these morons brought sticks to a swordfight.

Their blunt weapons are no match for his size, strength, or weaponry. He moves through the crowd, cutting down foe after foe, dropping the robed figures until those left standing realize their grave situation. They retreat, back into the darkness of the plaza. A few of Jarnes' guard pursue them, but with little effort.

All others stare at Gallagher, some with their jaws hanging open, others with a burning glare. He isn't sure what he's done to deserve such attention, but he disregards it and rushes to Rivee's side.

He sheaths his sword and a wave of pain floods over him as if every impact of their scepters smack down all at once. A brief dizziness consumes him before he shakes it off.

"What are you?" one of the guards asks.

Gallagher doesn't pay him any attention. "Are you okay, Rivee Rayfin?" He barely gets the words out. His lungs are on fire from the heavy breathing in this thin air. She lies on the ground near the edge of the landship.

She doesn't respond to his question as she lies injured on the ground.

"You moved faster than any warrior I've ever seen, Gallagher," Jarnes says.

"Hardly," he responds as he inspects her body for injuries. He sees none.

"And that sword. All I could see were flashes of blue and green like a light show in the black of night."

Gallagher rises with Rivee cradled in his arms, ignoring Jarnes' comments. He turns to stare him down. "I trust you understand my decision."

"You mustn't," he cries. "Not while she's in that state. There are no remedies within the Terra Realm."

Gallagher gives his words no heed.

Rivee may or may not forgive him for this, but he knows what must be done. She is not safe within the Caelum Realm. Not until the Indra can dismiss their quarrels and behave like mature elves.

With his back facing the horizon, Gallagher allows himself to fall with a gentle push to clear the edge.

Rivee's father, with an aggressive reach to stop them, steps too close to the edge himself. His shoe slips, and his arms flail as he careens toward the Terra Realm in their wake.

28 Becoming an Ebisu

rayed along the edges, bruised, and bloodied, Mira plays the role of a
defeated prisoner as Tiolas trots her through the open thoroughfares of
the outpost. Having just consumed a pinch of Blue Tears, she already
feels the energy surging through her abdomen and into her limbs. With the hasty
fashion the guards take to mend their future assets and Tiolas' extra dose, the
damage done to her shoulder will be on pace to be fully healed by the end of the
day.

Another guard tows Rela in a litter where she truly is defeated. They managed to get more spice into her, so she ought to be feeling livelier just in time
for the reformation.

Haltuk was likely carried to the reform chamber in the same manner, and
all the others, too—a sliver away from death. She can only hope and trust that
Tiolas is offering sincerity with his information about Haltuk. And it is enough
for her to continue the fight.

"How are you doing, Rela?" she calls back to her, making sure her own
voice is tired, so as not to alarm the guard towing her. A few moans are all she
gets in return. Nothing delineable.

The trek to the reform chamber is mostly quiet. A few squads look them
up and down only to have disgraced eyes fall on Rela in her litter. Nobody likes
a traitor. Even with the machina implant to realign her loyalties, Mira doesn't
think she'll get good treatment by any of her fellow Ebisu. If the Ebisu reforms
don't die in battle, she's most certain their comrades would be more than willing
to take on the task.

Come to think of it, Mira has not seen any reformed soldiers around the outpost. She assumes the machina implants would be noticeable. Especially with the subtle or vibrant glow of the Tears that all seem to have.

The chamber they approach is nothing special. Just another metallic building without windows, just like her cell block. They step over the threshold and an odor wafts over her. Much more pleasant than the cell block she's been restricted to. It smells like a blend of blood and spice. Something metal in nature combined with the sweet aroma of the Blue Tears. It must be the general smell of machina amplified with the abundance of it stored in this chamber.

The smell makes her weak in the knees. It draws out a fear she wasn't aware she had. Not a fear of machina itself, but a fear of being controlled beyond her will. The sole purpose of this chamber is to extract the soul and replace it with another. A fake soul. A machina soul. She places a hand over her abdomen.

"How do they do it?" she whispers, more to herself than to Tiolas.

"They gore you, like so." The thumb of another soldier presses into her gut and slides upward between her breasts. "They rip out your insides." The elf is face to face with her. She hadn't even realized anyone else was in the chamber as she was distracted by the different variants of machina. "All of 'em. Can't leave any of you in there." His breath is hot. "And we stuff you full of that!" His finger jabs toward a wall of glowing metal parts.

Beneath the wall of machina sits a large bucket on a stained table. Within it, a mess of elven parts. Mira's stomach turns in agony. She quickly pulls her eyes away from the scene.

When the elf takes a step back, she realizes who it is. The same elf she put to sleep when she first arrived here. The same elf who likely holds a grudge from the embarrassment she induced.

"Salus! Enough of that." Tiolas jumps in to separate the grudge-wielding elf from Mira. "Mira, this way."

Salus narrows his eyes on Tiolas. "Mira?" he questions. "Going by given names with the neophytes are we?" He lunges forward. "Maybe we should snip your ears, too." He playfully attacks Tiolas, but in an awkward fashion as nobody else in the chamber is looking for smiles. Tiolas nudges him away with an arm and a peeved glare, and knocks over the bucket of elven parts, spilling them all over the floor.

"Damn it, Salus!"

"They're..." Mira's brow twists into lines of worry and disgust. "They're..."

"Ear tips. Now, sit down," Tiolas demands with more authority than request this time.

Mira finds a seat in the cool, metal chair. Why does everything have to be so cold within their culture? Cold and brutal. She stares at the ears on the ground. Small triangles of flesh. Some large, some small. Some decaying, others fresh as if they'd just been clipped.

"Is that going to happen to me?" Her words escape in a gasp, suddenly realizing what she's in for. She pops from the chair, maybe a bit too lively, as she's supposed to be a defeated elf. Not an elf full of vigor and fight.

Both Tiolas and Salus grab her arms and force her back in the chair with a thud. Mira fights, but their strength is beyond her own. They fasten her arms to the chair with leather straps, then her ankles. One or two attempts to free herself and the straps prove to be secure. She loses her fight, holding onto the feeble trust she has in Tiolas.

Salus leans into her, close enough to put his lips to hers. With a quick jerk, he snaps at her ear with his teeth. "We can bite 'em off if you'd like?" He holds up a pair of curved shears. "It's quick. Don't you worry."

Mira's eyes get as big as the bright white lights shining down on them. They're going to cut off the tips of her ears. Leave her with a blight full of mockery. What will her clanmates say to this? Will they sympathize with her? Will they shun her? A frown etches into her face. Or will she ever see her clanmates again to be concerned with such vanity? Or—her breathing stops—is this reform taking her mutilation beyond vanity? She's having machina implanted into her head, for Ceto's sake! Will the Elders exile her the same as Gallagher?

Panic strikes at her. She hopelessly struggles. The most she can wish for at this point is for the machina to take her mind entirely, so she doesn't remember any of this. She trusted Tiolas. She believed he had good intent.

Tiolas fumbles with a small device. Mostly dark grey and metallic like everything else in their world, with fine white trimmings. It's curved like the rim of a mug on one end and pointed like a typical elven ear on the other. Mira's eyes haven't refrained from bulging out of her face since she realized how deep of a mess she's in.

"Calm down, reform. I need you holding still, or it'll get awkward. Trembles and all. Simmer down. You'd hate to have your handmaid nip one of your braids while getting a trim. Well…" Salus points the shears at her. "…this'll be a tad more permanent." A smirk smears across his face, followed by a conniving laugh. He jabs the shears just behind her ear with a quick snip, and one of her braids slumps to her shoulder and falls to the floor. Mira flinches with a toxic anger waiting to unleash on this vile elf.

Tiolas shakes his head at Salus. "Just one," he assures her with a hard stare. "It's standard procedure."

"You couldn't form the machina properly for an elf's ear?" Mira's question is full of putrid loathing.

"It's the mark of the slave, you winch." He grabs a wad of her hair and pulls it over the back of the chair. Her neck stiffens as her head slams tight to it. "Not that we couldn't tell whether a De'wi was inferior, but like Tiolas said, it's standard procedure."

A searing pain consumes her right ear as she sees flesh fall to the floor in her peripheral. She clenches her eyes shut. She desperately wants to reach for it. To coddle it. But she cannot. It burns like a wraith sting. A warm sensation trickles down her ear and along her neck, followed by a burning to replace the sting at the tip of her ear. She cringes.

"It needs to be cauterized," Tiolas insists with a hand gently placed on her shoulder.

Is that supposed to comfort her?

Her eyes open into a piercing glare directed at the Ebisu who she so gullibly trusted. These elves are evil to the core.

Tiolas walks behind her with the machina in his hand. He reappears on her right side and swiftly slides the machina over top of her snipped ear. A clicking noise is heard, followed by a shot of pain behind her earlobe. The pain shoots deep into her spine.

Tiolas bends over to examine the device. "And now is the time to play the slave, soldier," he whispers into her ear. He rises. "All looks good. Next." He gestures to Rela, whom Mira didn't even realize had been towed into the room with her, she was so caught up in the reformation process.

Is that it? Has she been reformed? Is she now an Ebisu soldier in mind? She feels the same, aside from the burning pain in her ear and the awkward, dull sensation originating in her neck. And with the Blue Tears she consumed before coming here, the pain quickly subsides. Her mind remains her own.

Suddenly terrified of how she is supposed to behave, she stares blankly, straight ahead. Tiolas didn't dupe her after all. She is to play the role of a slave. A neophyte as they call them. Her brow furrows. He could have briefed her on the mutilation part, but she may have not gone through with it if she had known. How do slaves behave?

Salus snaps his fingers in front of her left eye. She blinks and remains stationary. She doesn't have much choice with her arms bound, otherwise she may have swatted his hand away. He snaps again, in front of her right eye. She blinks with a subtle flinch.

Tiolas and Salus unfasten the straps binding her to the chair. She remains seated, unsure if she's allowed to act of her own will, or if she only responds to commands. Should she respond to anybody's command, or just specific soldiers? Tiolas could have done a much better job in briefing her about what to expect.

"Get up, get up, you worthless front-liner." Salus tugs on her arm and pulls her from the chair. She walks toward the edge of the room and waits. Salus keeps a close eye on her, inspecting her every move.

"Get her in the chair," Tiolas commands.

Salus gives him a disapproving look before helping the third guard who towed Rela into the chamber. "Our infamous traitor. You know, General Merces is going to have fun with you after what you did to him." He grabs her underarm and the two guards hoist her to her feet. "How could any soldier have the nerve to assault him? He leads us to a better world. A world where Ebisu are not forced to live beneath the waves. A world filled with daylight and weather. We can get away from this permanent darkness where only the blind dwell. Maybe one day, we'll aim for the skies." He looks down at Rela and spits in her face.

They plant her in the chair of reform and bind her legs and wrist the same as they did to Mira. Rela isn't all there. Despite the spice they stuffed into her mouth, she has a long recovery ahead of her. The General, or whoever is responsible for her condition, took her life to the edge. She can hardly hold her head up on her own. And with Tiolas' reaction to the brief examination he gave her, it's quite possible she was defiled in the most horrific way, too.

Mira's jaw tightens as she holds down the rage within her.

The shears come out. Tiolas braces Rela's head with a hand under her chin and another holding a wad of her unkempt hair. The sound of metal on metal terrorizes the room as the blades of the shears slide past one another. A chunk of flesh falls to the floor. Rela flinches and Tiolas secures his grip on her. A hot iron, in the form of a simple metal rod with one red hot end, carefully rolls across the top of her ear and is placed back in the furnace from whence it came. For how ugly Salus is on the outside, he takes a lot of care in what he does.

Tiolas finishes her off by clamping the petite machina around her ear and impaling her neck just behind the jaw underneath her lobe. Mira's hand lifts and slides across her own implant. She drops it suddenly, unsure if she should be moving without command. None of the Ebisu seem to notice.

Rela's eyes spring open at the final pinch and she stares straight ahead, seemingly visionless while being fully alert.

Mira wants to address her, call to her, but it would give away her false reform. She remains still in body, but not in mind.

They pull Rela to her fins and usher her to stand beside Mira. She's pleased to have an example of how to behave now. She can follow Rela's lead.

"Something isn't right," Salus suggests. "Something is off. You saw the De'wi flinch, right?"

"This reform process has never failed us yet," Tiolas replies. "It's as effective as it can be. You know this. And it often takes the machina a moment to train the body. To align the will of the General with the nervous system of the neophyte. Or maybe she's just a weak De'wi. Have you ever reformed one before?"

Mira flares internally, but remains in an attentive, soldier-like state—arms behind her back, fins shoulder-width apart, and a steadfast posture.

"Only recently. The one who shared the cell block with her. He didn't flinch."

"So you have a sample of two." Tiolas looks at him with a wrinkled brow.

"None of the Ebisu flinch, either." Salus stands before Mira, looking her up and down.

"De'wi are weak," Tiolas repeats. "Look at 'em. She's petite. How could she possibly have the same resilience as an Ebisu. Plus, that other De'wi was nearly lifeless. You're looking at the victor of the Pit of Reform. You should be eyeing her with admiration."

"Admiration?" Salus takes his attention off Mira and swings it to Tiolas. "Never! A De'wi? You've lost your mind."

Tiolas smirks at him. The tension is momentarily gone. "Go inform the General. He'll want to inspect these two himself. Maybe put them back into the Pit of Reform to test their skill and endurance against each other. These two reforms are a caliber above the rest."

Salus' brow curls inward. "The General?"

"Yes. Lord Tenebrous made a comment about this one." Tiolas points to Mira. "I suspect, given the General's history with Rela and the Elder's special interest in this one, he'll be interested to inspect the two of them."

Salus rubs the back of his neck, uncertainty strewn across his face. "The General also doesn't like to be disrupted. This isn't normal procedure."

"And these aren't normal reforms."

What is Tiolas doing? Why is he trying to bring the Elder and his ruthless general here?

A fist slams into her gut unexpectedly. She hunches over.

"I may not get another opportunity to do that." Salus smiles from ear to ear. "Damn, that felt good. For your insolence back in the cell block." He stands before her, waiting. *Waiting for what?* "Why isn't she getting back up?" Salus jabs a finger at her. "You see, something's wrong. What's going on?"

Mira grabs his pointing finger and bends it backward. A snap is heard, followed by a cry of pain.

"You little piece of…"

Mira's fist slams into his face. With the Blue Tears intoxicating her system, her strength and already commendable speed are enhanced. She whips around his backside while he's off guard, knocks him to the floor. She curls her legs around him to hold him down, locks his arms behind his head, and puts him in yet another choke hold.

The third guard in the room is slow to react. Tiolas lunges at him, unsheathing a dagger at the same time, and the elf drops to the floor with one quick and unexpected strike.

Salus struggles for a short time. His legs kicking and moving them across the hard floor. Mira's back slams into a table and ear tips tumble over top of them, followed by the clanging of a bucket. Mira refuses to let go. Salus, unable to speak or make a sound beyond a choked gargle, eventually drifts away.

"Well…that didn't go as planned." Tiolas shrugs as he stands above her and Salus.

"There was a plan?" She glares at him and his lack of communication.

"We should get out of here," he replies.

"Where's Haltuk? I need to retrieve Haltuk."

"The other De'wi? There's no hope for him. He's with all the other reforms in the halfway house, learning to cope with his new identity."

"Then that's where I'm headed. Where's the halfway house?"

"He won't know who you are, Mira. It's hopeless. He'll most likely treat you as an enemy as that is how he's been reprogrammed."

"Reprogrammed?"

"Yes. The machina…" He points to hers. "It channels some kind of energy into the brain. It blocks your memories. It draws out anger and hatred. And somehow it aligns the mind with the Ebisu. It reforms ally and foe with an injection into the brainstem." He points to the implant at the base of her ear. "He will attack you, and so will all the other neophytes."

"That doesn't make sense. Why would the other neophytes not attack him? If they're all programmed to attack De'wi…" She throws her hands up. "Why are we talking about them as if they're machina. These are elven lives."

"That's all I know, Mira. I'm not a Greybeard. Only the wizards understand these things."

"Greybeard?"

"They engineer the machina. They're the masters of the technology. Vanford Arilight was the first of them. A name you might recognize."

Mira grunts. "Where machina originated… Yes, I know the name." They don't have time to pry into the details. "I don't care. I must rescue Haltuk. With or without you."

"With you," a third voice says.

"Rela!" Mira's gaze snaps in her direction, as does Tiolas'. "I wasn't sure…" She pauses. "You're with us! How do you feel?"

"I'm good. No time for frivolous talk. Let us get to the halfway house," she insists.

Rela leads the way. Tiolas grabs a trident from a rack on the wall. Mira moves to grab one as well, and he puts a hand on her wrist. "You're still a prisoner. Reformed or not, you're not allowed to roam freely with a weapon." The two hurry out of the reform chamber to catch up to Rela.

"You cannot just walk in there," Tiolas says to Rela.

"Precisely why you're going to be our escort. Mira, get in line. Follow my lead. Tiolas, take charge. Maybe show some Ebisu decency and be nasty to us, so it's more believable."

He looks over his shoulder at them after stepping in front to lead. "But I'm never nasty to the neophytes."

Mira cannot see while looking at their backs, but based on Rela's grumble she presumes it was accompanied by an eye roll.

"This halfway house…what can I expect?" Mira asks.

"Shh…" Rela straightens her posture and turns her stroll into a march. Mira follows her lead. A squad of Ebisu soldiers come into view as they walk past the corner of the building.

Mira holds back a gasp when she witnesses more than just a squadron of Ebisu. The thoroughfare turns into a vast plaza larger than her entire colony back home. It must be a place for the entire outpost to congregate, for it is that large, and it appears the majority of the Ebisu are already here. Squadron after squadron of Ebisu arrange in combat formations, sparring with one another. So many, Mira nearly stops in her tracks to gape. Ten thousand would be her minimum guess.

The soldiers' formations create a straight path through the plaza, which Tiolas marches down. He doesn't stop to inspect the threat as Mira wished he would.

The march lasts an eternity. Rhythmic grunts and clashing tridents fill the air along with awful drums. It's all choreographed, similar to De'wi training, except these Ebisu do it flat on their fins, not in the air. It's ironic that they live in the ocean, yet they don't swim anywhere within the world they've constructed. Mira has never marched so much in her entire life.

They find their way past the plaza of determined soldiers with their grunts and clangs fading into the distance and enter another thoroughfare with large metallic buildings on either side. It looks the same as every other street. Mira could easily get lost in this place. Thankfully, she can easily look up and see where the edge of the dome lies.

The trio march further into the maze of buildings and eventually approach one unique in size, shape, and overall appearance. "It's a fortress…" Mira mutters.

"Shh!" Both Rela and Tiolas respond to her without looking back.

Stout towers stand guard at each corner of the building with ornamental spires reaching for the dome above with multiple twisted iron workings. It reminds Mira of Rivee's short, unkempt hair: chaotic and out of control. The corner of her lip curls upward.

This is the only eccentric thing she's witnessed within the outpost. The first sign of a culture beyond rigid control of everything surrounding them.

Between the many towers stand walls just as firm as the guard towers. Windowless with large sheets of metal slabs riveted together in an attractive pattern. The building is tiered, stepping higher than the spires surrounding it with windows decorating all the higher levels. Ebisu guards patrol the top of the wall at every layer and at the regal entry gates.

Mira finds her neck craned upward to stare at the various components of the structure, and quickly corrects it. She is but a drone, and a drone wouldn't admire the architecture.

She wonders why they require something so overdone for the halfway house. The security makes sense. The over-the-top details in the architecture of the building don't. She cannot ask Tiolas or Rela as silence is the current expectation. Her assumptions run wild just like the spires.

"More neophytes" Tiolas addresses the four guards standing at the gate. Two on either side.

A nervousness strikes Mira. She isn't sure why. She remains a prisoner as she has been since first introduced to this place. The only difference is that she isn't in manacles. And, perhaps, that she needs to keep her emotions and overall behavior in check. She is clueless as to what kind of flexibility she has. She already knows flinching is suspect. Is she allowed to scratch at an itchy nose? Is she allowed to blink? What if she needs to use the privy again? Are bodily functions expected of these controlled slaves?

A roaring sound of the gates opening pull her out of her whirlpooling thoughts that were bound to take her into a fear trodden state.

They walk through the gates and into the bailey of this grand palace. The open courtyard is easily one hundred paces wide and deep. It's empty of Ebisu and slaves. Moderately sized pools of water decorate the space. Small fish, urchins, anemone, and seagrass are illuminated within the glass tanks. Vibrant coral lines the walkways following the many paths to the other side, all maintained at a uniform size. It's almost as if this place is intended to be tranquil. A peace offering before they enter the doom of the halfway house. They trod down one of the pathways to the other side where matching gates stand tall. The end of tranquility and the beginning of turmoil.

Before the gates open all the way, a thunderous boom shakes the entire outpost, nearly knocking Mira off her fins.

"What in Ceto's name?" Tiolas braces himself, arms and fins wide, with his head snapping back and forth searching for the cause.

Rela turns to face the outer gate, looking past Mira. Her mouth is agape and her eyes distant. Mira cranes her neck to see what the fuss is.

On the far side of the outpost, back where her cell block was located, water pours into the dome in mass as large pockets of air fight to escape. The protective barrier has been shattered. Towering above all the buildings stands not just one, but two stone giants.

Mira must hurry. This chaos is her opportunity to collect Haltuk and be free of this place.

29 The Blighted Warrior

G allagher holds Rivee tight within his grasp as they plummet at an incredible speed through the ceiling of clouds. The air thickens when they burst through, and his lungs thank him for it. The falling sensation dissipates when he points his toes and arcs his back to slow their velocity.

The Indra accidentally pursuing them doesn't have the same instinct to slow down. His heavy mass plummets past them, a curdling scream escalating, then dissolving as he does.

"Jarnes!" Gallagher yells after him. "Kick your fins!" He yells before remembering the Indra don't have fins. Their toes aren't long and webbed like the De'wi. Besides that, he's wearing shoes.

In a rush, Gallagher dives after him. With Rivee in one arm combined with the velocity at which they travel, it's a struggle to grab hold of him. Gallagher manages to grip the tail of his surcoat, and with all his might slows him down to a reasonable pace.

"Have you never swum before?"

Jarnes looks at him with wide eyes, his jacket flapping in the wind and his hair enjoying a bit of freedom from its typical combed perfection. A smile curls across his face. "Only in a pool. Never beneath the sea of clouds."

"Ceiling of clouds." Gallagher smiles and points upward. "Now, it's the ceiling of clouds."

"Of course, of course."

Gallagher's smile fades. "We're not going back up there, Jarnes."

"I don't expect you to." Jarnes looks down at the terrain and waves his arms in an arduous attempt at swimming.

They swim through the air, still with an urgent pace in case any more Indra decide to pursue them.

"Rivee, we've escaped the Indra. No longer will you be a pawn in the games of nobility. You're safe now, Rivee Rayfin."

No response.

"Rivee?" Gallagher brings his swimming to a halt and treads in the sky. With one hand beneath her underarm to prevent her from drifting away, he tries to wake her with a nudge of her chin, then a gentle shake of her body. "Rivee Rayfin? Are you okay?"

No response.

"She needs to return to the Caelum Realm. There's nothing you can do for her," Jarnes suggests as he flaps his arms raucously. He looks back toward his home above the clouds. "We can—"

"Never!" Gallagher shuts him down. "We're not going back there. Bailey can get her the spice. Bailey can fix her."

"I presume this Bailey is a caregiver?"

"The best."

With much effort, Jarnes swims closer. "I didn't see what happened to her, but her injuries don't appear serious enough to warrant this level of fatigue. Which means…there is only one explanation for her unconsciousness.""

"A blow of an Indra scepter? They don't…err…dissolve an elf from the inside out, do they?" Gallagher knows the idea is absurd, but he doesn't know the limitations of their machina. One thing he does know is House Godmadina would like to see her dead, and it's possible they were successful.

Jarnes looks into his brow with a hand over his mouth. "I'm not sure. I suppose the Greybeards could make such a scepter if they found value in it." He looks toward Gallagher who's petrified by his response. "But not that I'm aware of," he quickly adds. "She's likely just unconscious. Not…err…dissolving. If it was from a Godmadina scepter and not an accidental brush against an Arilight—"

"We need to get her to Bailey. C'mon." Gallagher doesn't want to hear any reason for them to head back to the Caelum Realm. Bailey can fix this. He wastes no time in cradling her back into his arms. Not knowing what ails her, speed is of the essence. How that machina fin would come in handy right now.

The Knuckles of Morshine come into view. The bulging rock formations sprouting from the shoreline are unmistakable. A bellow from a conch sounds off. A point-elf has spotted them from one of the outposts. He drops low to swim between the contours of the natural bulwark, not letting up on his aggressive swimming. Two more blows of the conch are heard. They must not think of him as an enemy.

Jarnes is a good distance behind, but he's coming along. Gallagher doesn't wait for him.

The kelp forest he harvests from passes by in a blur and opens up to the ruins of their colony. Knowing what he does now about Caelum Invictus and the waterspouts it creates, this could all be the result of the Indran landship. If it *was* the Indra, they have utterly disrupted everything the De'wi know including passing over the Solari Harvest. Their stores of Blue Tears are low because of it, and Rivee may have to suffer for it.

The makeshift structures of the refuge within the Crisper Coral grow in quantity, and it appears new, more permanent structures are being erected. Gallagher swims toward what he believes to be the infirmary but is quickly intercepted by three elves of the Warrior's Guild.

"You've been banished, Gallywog," Baratok asserts. This elf is often influenced by Andolas and his arrogant demeanor. Gallagher brushes his slight away, unoffended by those who have yet to earn his respect. "You're not welcome here. And what are the two of you wearing?" He looks him up and down, scoping the full suit and jacket he dons, along with Rivee's gown, and evidently notices he no longer wears the sky elves' machina. His eyes come to a halt on Rivee's machina leg, however.

"I need to get her to Bailey!" Gallagher insists. "I don't know what is wrong with her."

"She's probably poisoned by that machina, you imbecile! What did you do to her?" He shoves Gallagher's shoulder and rips Rivee from his arms. She hovers in the air before him, limp and unconscious. The machina leg weighs her down and she slowly drops to the ground.

"Hey! Don't put your hands on her!" Jarnes yells from behind the trio of warriors.

Gallagher methodically closes his eyes and cringes. He's brought an Indra into their home. First machina, now this. He might as well dive into the canyon with the leviathans. With the rush to get Rivee help, and the amount of time he's spent getting to know the Indra, he let that concern slip past his purview.

"Move aside, Baratok. I need to get her to the caretaker," Gallagher tries to distract him from the slowly approaching Indra. "I won't let you stand in my way." He withdraws his short sword and unsheathes it. All fatigue he acquired from the journey vanishes.

All three warriors freeze.

"He has a stone," Baratok says to the others. "Where'd you get that? Are you a thief now, too?" His words are sharp and full of hate.

"Never mind the stone. He has an Indra!" One of the other warriors points at Jarnes, who has no finesse in the sky. It would be comical if not for the magnitude of the situation.

"It doesn't matter," Gallagher insists. "There's no time. Can you not see she's injured? Please, just swim aside and let us take her to Bailey."

"No!" Baratok firms his posture and puffs his chest. "You bring blaspheme within our borders. I cannot let you pass without a decree from one of the Elders." He gestures to Gallagher's blade. "And it's clear you're a threat to our colony. Seize him!" He points to Jarnes.

"Don't do this. I only want to save Rivee."

The warrior readies his yari and moves to attack Gallagher. To avoid confrontation with an elf he wishes to fight alongside one day, he flips in the air and dives down toward Rivee. The yari swings past where he was, just missing Gallagher's fins as he snags Rivee and swims lower, leaving Jarnes to be captured.

They won't torture the Indra or send him to battle leviathans. The De'wi are not so extreme. He'll be fine.

Gallagher doesn't look back to see if they're in pursuit, but he knows at least one or two are. He kicks his legs with extraordinary force beyond measure—even more so than when he had the machina fin—and heads straight to the infirmary, hoping it remains in the same location.

He looks over his shoulder to see how close the warriors are, and it's clear they didn't attempt the chase, for they are nowhere near him. He shakes his head with disapproval. That sort of lazy behavior isn't common for any warrior. Perhaps the Indra was the perfect distraction. Perhaps the Indra was the perfect *excuse* to allow Gallagher to get Rivee the care she needs. Baratok, although overly confident at times, is no stranger to compassion.

Gallagher plants his fins on the ground, sheathes his sword and tucks it away in his surcoat. He doesn't want Bailey to consider him a threat, too.

He casually opens the door so as not to give her a scare, but hard enough to warrant urgency. He finds the caretaker still addressing injuries of the unlucky who are not awarded a speedy recovery with Blue Tears. The sight makes him realize this is Rivee's fate unless he can convince Bailey otherwise. She takes her eyes off her task to look at Gallagher.

"Bailey, please. She's in dire need." He forces his way into her space and lays Rivee on an unused cot.

"Gallagher." Her voice is poison. "You oughtn't be here."

"No, but *she* should. She needs your help, Bailey. Please. Her wounds require any spare Tears you have on hand."

"I'll be the decider of that," she argues. She looks Gallagher up and down as she moves closer to him. "Where have you been? What are you wearing?" Then she looks at Rivee and a restricted gasp escapes her. "Rivee!" Her head snaps back to Gallagher. "What have you done, Gallagher?"

Gallagher shuffles backward. "She... err... she followed me. We were... err... captured. I did all I could to rescue her." His stammering voice shifts to a whisper. "But it wasn't enough." All Gallaghers feelings of irrelevance suddenly wash over him. He tried to be a warrior, and he failed.

"There are no injuries that I can see." She says it with an air of delight, then lays her head on her chest. "Her heart beats, her lungs pump, but her head is not right?" She straightens upright with a furrowed brow directed at Gallagher. Then she looks down at Rivee's leg. "It's this blasphemed machina on her leg. Take it off!"

How could she be so accusing? Just like the warriors and every other ignorant De'wi. She's the caretaker. She's supposed to diagnose what the ailment is, not blame it on the misunderstood.

"It's not the machina!" Gallagher asserts. "She was knocked in the head with an Indran scepter." Gallagher's voice lowers and his head sinks between his shoulders. "Or so I think. I didn't get there in time."

"An Indran scepter?" the caretaker questions.

"A Godmadina scepter to be precise. One of the great houses." He waves off his comment when Bailey looks at him with utter confusion. "We were captured by the sky elves. They use their machina magic to subdue their enemies."

"Machina magic?" She rubs a thumb across Rivee's forehead and brushes her hair out of her face.

"They use the Tears, Bailey. Wizards imbue their machina with it. It's how they've become so powerful."

"Powerful?" she spits. "Hardly. They are cursed."

Gallagher shrugs. "In a way, yes. But not all of them."

"You befriended them?"

"Some, yes." He's uncertain if he should mention Jarnes. She'll find out soon enough. "The Indra are no different than us—elves born into an ethos created before their time. The nobility are corrupt and damaging to their culture, but that is all beside the point. What can we do to save Rivee? She needs the Tears."

"And the Tears she shall not have. You know our traditions, Gallagher. Corrupt or not—which I do not believe they are—she's blighted, Gallagher. Her rank amongst the Morshine Clan isn't high enough to receive even a pinch of the spice. Fatal injury or not, we make no exceptions. You know this."

"But with her new leg, she's no longer a blight on our clan. Look at her. She's a whole youngkin, now."

"And will likely be banished just like you if I cannot get this thing off her. I shouldn't even be speaking to you. Get out. Get out." She waves her hands, shooing Gallagher toward the exit. "I'll do everything I can, Gallagher," she says as she pushes him out the door. "You know I will."

"No. You won't. If you refuse her Tears…" He glares at her. For the first time ever in all his years, he's upset with Bailey. He feels guilty for it. "…you are refusing Rivee the one thing that ought to heal her." A long silence parts them as they stare each other down, unmoving in their viewpoints. "If you won't offer her what she needs, and the Elders won't allow it, then I will retrieve it myself. You cannot stop me from healing her with what is rightfully mine."

"Gally, no!" She cries from the doorway. "That's suicide."

"Rivee deserves it. This is my fault."

Gallagher moves to leave when Bailey grabs his hand. "Gally, wait! Your parents…"

He looks over his shoulder at her.

"I'm sorry, Gally…" She shakes her head and continues holding his hand, grabbing onto it with both of hers, pleading for his forgiveness.

His parents are dead. Dead for the same reason Rivee will die if he doesn't take action right now. Why didn't he do this for his parents? Is he to blame? He knew their traditions. He knew they wouldn't receive any Tears. Should he have charged into the depths for them as he plans to do for Rivee? It's in the past. What can he do about it now?

He stares at Bailey for a long moment. He doesn't say anything. What is there to say. He pulls his hand away from hers and turns his back, not another word is spoken between the two of them.

Gallagher swims toward the ocean currents, armed with only his short sword and the ridiculous five-piece, Indran suit. As much as he'd like to grieve for the loss of his parents, he must do this before the Elders get wind of it, and before the Warrior's Guild attempts to prevent it. He must go now.

Gallagher slips his surcoat off, allowing it to drop to the sandy shore, and withdraws his short sword in the same motion as he makes way for the ocean.

He does the same with the vest, disrobing down to only the trousers, knowing the clothes will dampen his abilities within the depths of the ocean.

"Gallagher, halt! You are unfit—a blight in the name of the warriors of the Morshine Isle. You are incapable of such a feat."

He slows and plants his fins on the ground. The ocean is only a dive away. Gentle swells roll through the water. He's at the same beach where he first dove into the depths when he was a youngkin. He was taunted from behind when he made the decision to leap in. It was a choice that changed his life for the worse. He won't make the same mistake twice.

"Who are *you* to judge who's a blight on our society?" Gallagher turns to face Lady Nessa. Never in his life would he ever speak to Mira's mother in this manner, but the situation is dire. He has an opportunity to help Rivee if he can only recover the Tears from the deep.

"It is not my judgement. You know that." She folds her arms across her body.

Several warriors swim up behind her and stand at the ready. Elder Rayfin is just behind them.

"And this is not my choice. I must fulfill my duty to Rivee by any warrior's standard. I have an opportunity to save her, and I will, regardless of what you think of her. Or me. Or any elf deemed blighted. The reason she is in her current state is because I allowed it to happen. It is my doing. I have no choice but to save her. Your rules and traditions cannot prevent this."

More warriors arrive at the scene including a bound and gagged Jarnes. Then, the two remaining Elders, a few kelp pickers who picked alongside Gallagher, carpenters, smiths, and even some youngkins all slowly accumulate around them. A crowd has formed.

"Even with the machina she wears?" Elder Rayfin speaks as he steps in front of his wife.

"What does that have to do with any of this?" Gallagher's entire body tenses. Now he must disobey not only Mira's mother, but her father, too. He cringes internally.

"She will be exiled, just as you are. And you risk your life for her. I see you have had your own machina removed, Gallagher." He gestures to his fins. "We can reassess your exile, and possibly lessen the consequences. You don't need to do this."

"You don't get it!" Gallagher yells. "This isn't about me." A short pause as he gathers his words. "I just found out I lost two parents, Elder. Two. They were alive when I last saw them. Now they're not. You know what could have prevented that. A warrior willing to dive into those depths and recover the Tears they needed to continue living." Another dramatic pause. The growing crowd is silent.

"This isn't about the clan. This is about doing what is right. This is about standing for what we believe in. This is about principle, and I am not about to throw aside my principles to elevate my own wellbeing. This…" He raises his short sword to show the stone to the crowd. "…is about being a true warrior."

Ogling eyes shine through the crowd, but not from Elder Rayfin, Lady Nessa, or any of the other Elders.

"Where did you get that?" Lady Nessa is the first to speak.

He doesn't want to be distasteful, but they are earning such behavior. "I will tell you, if you tell Elder Rayfin the truth about Rivee." His eyes cut to where Jarnes is restrained by two warriors.

Lady Nessa takes a step back, pressing a hand to her chest as if she's lost her words, stunned and silent from his audaciousness. Her gaze cuts to the Indra, and a moment of shock and disbelief flashes across her face.

Elder Rayfin's brow creases as a frown forms. "You will not speak to her in such a manner," he says. He shows no interest in what Gallagher just said. "Warriors, detain him!"

Four elves of the Warrior's Guild step forward.

"Now *this* is something we don't have to do," Gallagher says. He readies his short sword. He doesn't believe running will better the situation as he did when he was younger. He must prove to them he is capable. Though, how he's going to defend himself against four trained warriors armed with yaris, he doesn't know.

They surround him in a half-circle with his back to the ocean. His only options are to fight or flee, in which they will most definitely catch up to him with his damaged fin.

"We don't have to do this," he insists.

The warrior on his right is the first to attack. Gallagher swings his blade with finesse to deflect the incoming yari and drops low with a swinging leg to uplift the warrior. He easily evades it with a leap into a swimming position.

The next attack comes from his left—a jabbing yari. Gallagher dodges it and grabs onto the staff with his free hand, pulling her in closer. His eyes narrow as he glares at her. They attack with the means to kill, not subdue.

"Stand down before this gets ugly," he commands.

Two of the warriors smirk at him. The warrior whose weapon has been seized, on the other hand, burns with a red heat. She's ready to murder.

She yanks the yari away from Gallagher and nearly takes off a few fingers in doing so. Gallagher loses interest in trying to calm the situation. Their arrogance and disinterest in discussing the matter are apparent. Gallagher attacks.

He moves faster than the other warriors, as if they only train but once a year. His short sword cuts right through the two yaris with shale blades but doesn't make them any less effective. He knocks a yari away from his face with an open palm, punches a warrior in the gut, slaps his fin across someone's face, and pounds the pommel of his sword into the temple of another, sheathing his blade, and dropping the warrior to the ground in a limp pile of limbs.

His blade is no longer bound to his hand, and a yari slaps it away, knocking it into the shallows. Gallagher thinks to recover it, but in his brief moment of debate, he's attacked again. This warrior is suddenly faster. More powerful. The yari slices into his shoulder leaving a deep gash and Gallagher stumbles backward into the water. Another attack, and Gallagher barely evades it. Two more yaris strike. One cuts through his trousers, the other lacerates his bicep.

How did they gain so much speed and strength? His eyes glance at the short sword in the shallows. It's not them who gained power, it's Gallagher who lost it. To fend off warriors of the guild, he needs his blade.

Only three remain. Gallagher back peddles and steps on his short sword in the water. Hesitant to bend over and retrieve it, he leaps into the air instead with his legs flying out in front of him and his body curling into a backflip. He splashes flat into the water to retrieve his short sword. One of the warrior's fins steps on top of it, and the tip of three yaris can be felt near his neck. He wasn't quick enough.

Gallagher is better than this. He trains more than any other warrior. He refuses to accept defeat.

Gallagher inhales a deep breath with his face submerged in the shallows. The yari tips dig deeper into his shoulders, just below his neckline, and he accepts the pain without worry. A strong exhale and he grabs onto his blade, rolls with a violent splash, and pushes off the ocean floor into the air where he hovers above the three warriors, ready for a second attempt at victory.

Blood drips down his chest. He strikes the pommel of his sword on his hip, and it binds to his hand, making him one with the blade. A surge of power rushes through him. He can feel the machina traveling through his veins.

He strikes, knocking all three of the warriors' weapons to the side and tackling one in the process. His speed has recovered. His power is suddenly uncontested. He knocks the warrior out with a strike of his elbow, rises to his feet and pummels the next right through the jaw with the heel of his fin. Both are rendered unconscious. He finds himself standing face to face with the last warrior.

"You will not detain me. You cannot detain me. I am not bound by the limitations of the guild. I've already been banished from this clan, and I will do what is necessary to save Rivee. And you will do nothing to stop me. Stand down or be defeated by a blighted warrior." Gallagher flexes his muscles unintentionally with a shift in his stance, and the warrior flinches.

Gallagher takes advantage of him with a remarkable blow right between his eyes. The warrior drops to his knees and splashes in the shallows.

Gallagher fixates on the crowd. All remain silent. He shakes his head at all of them, primarily focusing on the Elders who could have avoided this.

"Gallagher please…" A soft whisper is heard from Lady Nessa. She steps forward. The remaining warriors begin to follow, but Elder Rayfin holds up a fist to stop them. Mira's mother approaches Gallagher in the shallows, a gentle swell washing over her bare ankles.

"The Ebisu have taken our stores of Tears. Even if our ways permitted us to offer Rivee a ration, we wouldn't be able to." She speaks only for Gallagher to hear. "There is a reason we only harvest on the Solari, Gally. What you do is dangerous. The light of the Solari dispels the leviathans. They don't hunt where light removes the effect of their light trap, Gally. And you travel into the deepest, darkest corners of Solari." She forces eye contact. "Do you know the way?"

"I do," he replies with confidence, though it isn't true. He's never been down there.

"Do you know what must be done?"

Gallagher's brow curls inward. "Is Rivee your daughter?" he blurts in a hushed whisper. The din of the ocean waves crashing against the bulwark should be enough to keep their conversation private.

Nessa's lips flatten while she ponders her next words. "It's… It's a long story, Gally." Lines crease across her forehead. "Not one we have time for at the moment. Garrik is aware. You will get answers, I promise. Now that you've brought her father here, everyone will. It is unavoidable." Her expression is sorrowful.

"He cares for her, you know." Gallagher's eyes skirt away from Nessa, toward Jarnes. "He's not villainous as our Elders would have us believe."

"I know. I carried his child, Gally." A momentary silence casts over them. "It's time for you to go. Remember, more predators besides the leviathan dwell down there."

"Yes, of course."

"The wolf eels can be the vilest, but if you swim too deep, watch out for that dragon's tongue. It is by far the deadliest. If you've discovered it, you've gone too far. Refrain from touching anything other than the spice."

"Understood," Gallagher responds quietly.

"And of course, the leviathans. Don't let them fool you. If you see one light trap, another is not far off."

"Yes, Lady Rayfin."

Nessa squares him up, placing a hand on both of his shoulders. She looks up at him, dread consuming her. "You do the impossible." Her lips purse as she shakes her head at him. "Yet you stare down your task with resolve. Save her, Gally. Save Rivee for me." She has the face of a mother denying the death of her daughter. Tears pool within her eyes and she turns away.

Lady Nessa returns to her husband's side. The crowd, which looks to have grown into the entire colony, stares at him in anticipation.

Gallagher thumps the left side of his chest. "Heart," he says with a loud, assertive tone. Then the right side. "Strength." He taps his forehead and his gut. "Mind and soul." And he offers it to the crowd with a giving, open-palmed gesture of his hands. "I offer all that I am in the service of my clan, whether you accept me or renounce me. This is what it means to be a warrior." Without another word, Gallagher dives into the ocean, blade in hand and nothing more.

30 UPHEAVAL AT THE OUTPOST

Pearlescent barriers lower from the top of the dome like curtains calling an end to the act. It's a transparent film, nearly invisible aside from an array of pink and purple shimmers. It spans the entirety of the dome. A shrill slurping noise resonates through the air, loud enough to have come from the two stone giants. When the thundering sound of the flooding waters is muffled to a dull hum, Mira knows she and her newfound companions have been sealed off from the breach.

"A safeguard?" Mira questions.

"Yes," Tiolas responds in a hushed voice, still overwhelmed about the distant scene. "We live beneath the waves. We have many."

"But never has there been a breach so vast," Rela adds. "Never have we witnessed half the dome fill with chaos and destruction."

Both their eyes are wide and mouths agape.

"Is this the uprising?" Tiolas asks.

"From whom? The Ebisu rebels?" Rela stops ogling over the destruction and looks at Tiolas with a dumbfounded stare.

"Yes. Why not?" he says.

"Do you know how to tame a grendelin?"

"Err…" Tiolas scratches his head.

"That's something only specialized Ebisu soldiers know how to do," she says. "If it wasn't intentional, it's an incredibly stupid and disruptive wrangling accident."

Mira narrows her gaze on the two grendelins. Giant hands dip into the fast-flooding waters plucking what appears to be soldiers and tossing them into the air. Stone arms blow against the rigid metal buildings, leveling them with one swipe. The grendelins are attacking the outpost. But why?

The grendelin Mira encountered back in the Terra Realm didn't seem to have an ounce of malevolence. It only wanted to escape with its life intact. Yet these two attack the elven outpost with vigor. They'll draw the attention of the entire army, General Merces and Lord Tenebrous included.

"Let's go!" Mira shouts, startling the other two from their stupor. "Back to infiltrating the halfway house. This is our opportunity to rescue Haltuk and the other reforms."

The gates into the halfway house burst open. Tiolas quickly shuffles his two reforms back into line as Ebisu soldiers come pouring out of the building. They sprint past the trio, nearly knocking them off the path and into one of the aquariums decorating the courtyard. No cropped ears or machina implants are visible. Only their standard issue machina breastplates and two-pronged tridents. These are true Ebisu soldiers. And right out the other side of the bailey they go, no doubt headed for the breach.

Not one of the soldiers stops to address them. A few undeserved glares and sidelong glances, but they all spill into the courtyard and exit just as fast. Until the end of the line where General Merces holds up the rear. Mira's entire body tenses.

"Soldier." He stands tall and firm, looking directly at Tiolas. The permanent wrinkles around his eyes deepen. "Dump them into the holding tank until we have time proper to assimilate them."

"Yes, General." Tiolas turns to follow orders, and Rela starts following immediately as if tied to him with an invisible chain. Mira, with a slight delay in her step, follows suit, looking at Rela's back, and nothing more. She steps past the General and lets out a small sigh of relief.

"Hold, soldier."

Tiolas halts, as does Rela, and Mira too, but with a stutter in her step.

"This De'wi would be our victor, no?"

Mira continues to look forward. She clenches her jaw.

Tiolas pivots to face the General. "Yes, General. It would be."

"Too fresh?"

"Still on the chilling block. These neophytes are as dumb as they get. They haven't had an ounce of training."

The General puffs out a grunt. "No matter. I'd like to see what she's capable of. She comes with me."

Mira's eyes light up as bright as the overhead lights. She slaps herself internally for the body language, but with her back facing the General he cannot see. Her lack of discipline is without consequence for the moment.

"Yes, General, of course." Tiolas walks up to Mira and turns her around with a nudge of her shoulder, then points to the General.

What is she supposed to do? She doesn't know how these neophytes behave. Does she act on voice commands? Does she have a will of her own, and only her alliances are reformed? She knows nothing.

Mira attacks.

A swift fist to the ribs where no armor covers him, followed by a spinning kick to the back of his kneecap. It drops him to one knee where Mira puts him in a chokehold. Her mistake is leaving one of his arms free. He reaches behind his head and grabs a braid. She flies over his head before she can do anything to counter.

The General stands above her, his face stern before a grin slowly forms. "Feisty." He rubs his ribcage. "Stupid. We'll have to teach her friend from foe, but she has spirit." A large firm hand wraps around her upper arm and easily pulls her to her fins. He acts as though she struggles—but she doesn't—and he presses her tight to his body with one arm wrapped around her upper torso, hand pressed eagerly on her chest. The other gripping her hip, fingers suspiciously close to her groin. "C'mon, reform," he says into her ear, his breath warm and toxic. "We have some grendelins to detain."

The General drags her in the direction of the chaos. She catches one wide-eyed glance from the two friendly Ebisu before being pulled out of sight.

"C'mon, reform. Use your own legs."

Mira's heart screams. She obeys and scurries forward so he's not pulling her along. His strong grip remains firm. *What now?* Without the advantage of swimming, the General is too powerful for her to fight one on one. Plus, he's armed with a short blade at his hip, which she's grateful he didn't use a moment ago. She has no other option but to follow him into battle. But then what? Does she turn on the Ebisu? The thousands of Ebisu who battle the grendelins. Or will she be set free to act as she desires, in which case, she can go back to searching for Haltuk. The possibilities overwhelm her. She tries not to think about what she's stepping into. What she has no control over.

The Ebisu soldiers who exited the halfway house with the General head down the main thoroughfare toward the scene. The General has a different plan, however. The two of them split off down a tighter path between many buildings. *A shortcut?* Her instincts scream out loud to do anything within her power not to follow this elf, but her legs continue to shuffle to keep up with his long strides. What other choice does she have?

They reach the transparent barrier. It radiates with pinks and purples in a pearlescent fashion and splits right between the two buildings on either side of them, blocking their path. On the other side are the flooding waters rising deeper than the buildings.

The General puts a hand to his ear where he wears a similar transmitter to the ones the neophytes wear. An odd high pitch noise beeps in her right ear causing her to look in his direction. "*Soldiers. Ready the ballista. By whatever means necessary, nullify those grendelins.*"

Mira sees the General speaking and hears his words, but somehow they're magnified within her ear.

The General turns to look at her, his eyes doing their typical ogling, up and down her body. He shoves her against the wall of the building.

"We're not jumping into action, just yet." His hands press firmly on both her shoulders, pinning her back to the wall. "At least not the fighting action. Feel free to be aggressive, neophyte."

Mira doesn't know what to do. Is this some form of training to get her to react properly? Does he expect her to resist him? Fight back like she did only moments ago?

With one hand still pinning a shoulder to the wall, the other gropes her body. The General's eyes are lost in lust. That's when Mira realizes the severity of the situation. This isn't training, or some portion of the reformation process. He means to force himself on her.

Mira cannot hide her repulse. She flinches when a hand touches the underside of her chin and slides down her flesh toward her breasts. Her chest rapidly heaves up and down. She flinches when fingers slip between the laces of her leather corset. He pulls at the seam, loosening it. Mira's muscles tense throughout her body, from her jaw clenching tight all the way down to her toes curling inward. What is she supposed to do?

He leaves her corset partially undone and moves his hand down to her leather belt. He leans in to put his lips on her forehead as his hand struggles with the buckle. She cringes as she feels his tongue touch the side of her face.

Mira cannot allow this. She must break the act. She risks everything. She will lose the one advantage she has, the belief that she is under his complete control. Which is a huge advantage. But she cannot allow this. Every muscle in her body screams as she remains stiff, unmoving, while the General's hands familiarize themselves with her body.

He breaks her buckle loose and immediately slips a hand beneath her sarong. Mira cannot resist the fight any longer.

Her teeth dig into his cheek where it lingers too close for comfort, followed by a knee slamming into his gut.

The General cries out in pain with an unsavory curse to follow, but he refuses to let go. His strength overpowers her. He grabs her with both hands, spins her around, and slams her face-first into the wall. A dull pain stuns her as her skull smashes into the cold metal. The taste of iron fills her mouth. A hand continues to grope her body as he presses her tight against the wall, relentless with his lust.

She is the daughter a five-stone warrior. His teachings have made her better than this. *She* is better than this.

She forces an elbow into his ribs and manages to curl a leg around his own, contorting it enough for him to release his grasp on her. With one more final blow to the back of his head, she stuns him, and doesn't stick around to challenge him further.

She instinctively dives toward the pearlescent barrier with the assumptions that it is an escape route. Reflexes throw her arms out before her, but instead of hitting a solid wall, her hands go right through it and into the flood waters on the other side. Her terror transcends into a swift and powerful swim.

The salt in the water bites at her mutilated ear, and the sudden change from dry, thin air to water shocks her lungs. A few quick gasps overtake her before she calms her breathing. This is a much starker transition than going from the dense air of the Terra Realm into the ocean. Something about the air within the dome isn't natural. However, getting back into the ocean waters rejuvenates her senses as if she had just consumed another dose of Tears.

"Foolish neophyte." The voice comes from her right ear where she has the machina transmitter implanted. "I thought you might be something special. Maybe there's still time to prove yourself."

Did she not give away her fallacy? The General still thinks she's under his control. Maybe the neophytes are expected to resist the machina. Maybe what she just did is a normal part of the reformation. She puts the thoughts aside, no longer concerned, as she swims away to safety, not looking back to see if he follows.

Her hand rubs across the machina implant, feeling its pointy nature emulating an elven ear. She attempts to speak herself, wondering how it works, but only a gurgle and bubbles spew from her mouth. Somehow the General speaks to her through the machina implant. This must be how he gives direction to all the other slaves.

A faint glimmer pierces into the depths from the overhead lights. Just enough to be able to dodge the bulging structures surrounding her as her pace dips and darts in rapid succession. The maze of buildings provides cover but also acts as a deterrent to get back to the halfway house. When she feels confident the General is not on her tail, she swims toward the surface.

The higher she swims the more current she battles from the inflow of flooding, but it seems to be relatively calm compared to when the breach first occurred.

Water presses into her face and through her hair offering a cleansing she wasn't fully aware was needed. She runs her fingers across her scalp, down her arms, and past her underarms scrubbing away the filth she's accumulated while being locked away in the stank-trodden cell block. It doesn't cleanse the repugnance she acquired from the General's assault, however. Only time will erode that filth.

She abruptly stops scrubbing when the grendelins come into view. Gargantuan stone legs tromp around on the flooded metal deck of the outpost, leveling buildings with a single step. Mountain-sized fists pound through the water like a rockslide, the water having no impact on the force of their blows. Deep, guttural cries find their way beneath the surface of the water adding to the chaos of the moment.

The grendelins tower over everything, standing nearly as tall as the dome itself. The water has risen as high as it will, leaving a small pocket of air at the top of the dome. The white lights sparkle along the surface creating a light show throughout the battle scene.

Ebisu soldiers work together to subdue the two giants. Several risk their lives swimming within an arm's reach, acting as obvious targets while others circle around their legs with glowing chains. Mira wants no part of this...until they wheel forth the ballista loaded with spice-enhanced bolts large enough to pierce a mountain.

A sigh in the form of bubbles escapes her. Why do they have weapons capable of such destruction?

With her current vantage point she can see from wall to wall of the entire dome with only a smidgeon of haziness through the pearlescent barrier. She pinpoints the halfway house. Its twisted spires, easily spotted, are on the opposite side of where she's wandered to in her escape from the General.

Her mind pulls her toward the halfway house, knowing that is where Haltuk resides, but her heart sinks for these two grendelin. Haltuk has Rela and Tiolas working to secure his escape, right? Her gaze cuts back to the dramatic scene of stone versus metal. A glowing bolt pierces the forearm of one of the grendelins and a painful groan bellows from the giant like a wounded animal crying for help. Mira cringes. It's enough to anchor her decision. She cannot knowingly allow these gentle giants to be enslaved by the Ebisu. She swims toward the scene.

She's careful not to get too close to the battling Ebisu, staying on the perimeter and offering wide berths when needed, contemplating her plan. But then she remembers... *She* is one of them. Her hand grazes across the implant, and it gives her a meager confidence to swim closer to the battle. They might treat her with disdain, but as long as she holds up the appearance she's helping work toward their common goal, she should be safe.

The closer she gets, the faster her heart beats. Ebisu soldiers, armed with tridents and harpoons swim all around her. Not one of them blink an eye at her presence, but then again, she's not the one with fisticuffs made of stone. Regardless of where their attention lies, the mark of the slave, which she will forever carry with her, is working. She swims with the enemy. Now, is there any way she can join sides with the giants without getting detected? Is there any way to shift the balance in favor of the grendelins? As a neophyte, whatever she does, it must look like an accident to maintain her cover.

Then, his voice speaks in her ear. Instinctively, she looks around, but nobody is immediately around her. And she's under water.

"Soldiers. A neophyte fool marches amidst your ranks. I suspect fallacy. Be on alert. Detain her if you see her."

The transmission goes quiet.

Mira's eyes dart around, searching the waters for approaching soldiers. The space between her and the next elf is vast. The soldiers are split far and wide, so as not to give the grendelins an easy target. It seems to be helping her situation. Their focus remains on the larger, more immediate threat. Her nerves calm, and she breathes.

With the speed of a seadragon she dives toward one of many elves stationed at a heavy ballista, careful not to be seen. The ballista are spread farther and wider than soldiers distracting the grendelins, so finding an isolated ballista is hardly a challenge.

With the elf's full attention on the grendelin, he doesn't see her coming. The swiftest of motions follow as she snags a blade from his belt and finds his throat within the same beat. Crimson waters billow out around him and Mira yanks the lifeless body from the seat of the ballista. He drifts away to the metal deck.

Her heart races. Guilt piles on top of her like a grendelin's pile of feces. The weight of killing an unknown in the silence of dark waters is unimaginable. It had to be done, though. All the ballista need to be destroyed, and the vile Ebisu who aim to enslave the giants as well. They're a disgusting, war-mongering race, but somehow Mira still holds onto a ping of guilt for murdering this elf unawares.

At least another half dozen more ballista surround the grendelins, periodically firing between reloading. Glowing bolts fly through the dim waters, all tethered by chains of which are anchored to the monstrous weapons. The few that aren't firing already have a chain secured through a giant's arm or leg. The grendelins are as rigid as stone, maybe even made of stone, but it looks tremendously painful, regardless.

Suddenly, a hand grips her shoulder and she freezes, berating herself internally. How could she let this happen? The emptiness lingering in her gut from her silent murder is quickly washed away by fear. It manifests into a hasty spin and a reckless attack.

Her blade comes to a halt at the throat of a companion she thought she may never see again.

"Tanniv!" she blurts out, but only bubbles and gurgles spill forth. Veras swims up beside him as well.

Veras' eyes light up as he points to her ear. Mira outstretches her pointer finger and thumb into the form of a check mark and thrusts it away from her body, attempting crude sign language that she never studied well enough. Veras' brow tightens. It takes a moment, but he replies with a nod when he realizes she's trying to tell him they'll discuss it later.

She points to the four fasteners, gesturing that she needs to pry them free. Tanniv looks dumbfounded. Veras waves off her idea and proceeds with pulling an unfamiliar device out of his side pouch. It's a little larger than the size of his palm, dome shaped, and metallic with bluish-green lights shimmering within it. Mira nearly slaps it out of his hand when she realizes Veras is holding a machina device.

He places it on the floor of the outpost and taps on it. The colors react, growing brighter just before the water around them whirls like an underwater eddy. The currents grow stronger, reaching upward, and within moments a pocket of air forms around them. A much smaller, personal version of the large dome that makes up the outpost.

All three of them fill their lungs with a deep inhale. Shifting from breathing water to air is a bit awkward when unexpected.

"Where did you get that?" Mira yells at him promptly. "Put it away! Don't you realize it'll draw attention? I have a cover to maintain. The Ebisu!" She waves her arms about gesturing to the army all around them. She moves toward the device, but Veras steps in front of her.

"It's okay, Mira. This is Ebisu machina."

"I know!" She throws her hands in the air. "Exactly why you need to turn it off. It's forbidden!"

"We witnessed them being used all over the dome before I decided to use it. We believe the soldiers use them to talk to one another within the depths. To take a breather from the ocean. I can't believe they live down here."

Mira inhales the light air. It's the same air that fills the dome. Not like the air within the Terra Realm. She exhales and the tension in her muscles loosens. She leans in and gives Veras a big hug. While embracing him, she eyes Tanniv standing behind him and reaches out for him to join in. He grabs her hand in a welcoming manner, avoiding the group hug. Smiles beam on all of them.

Mira pulls back. "This better not draw attention," she says, accompanied by a nasty look.

"We saw others." Veras waves his arms about as if several examples are within view. "It shouldn't."

"How'd you get here?" she asks.

Tanniv points to the stone giants warring in the water.

"You brought them here!" Her tone isn't that of an impressed chief, nor a jubilant one. "Do you realize you've sacrificed their lives for one of your own."

"Two of our own," Tanniv interjects. Mira replies with a spiteful glare.

"Where's Haltuk?" Veras asks.

Mira shakes her head and paces back and forth within the pocket of air. "Still locked away. A slave." She reaches for the machina on her ear. The sting of the mutilation has subsided, likely due to the saltwater closing the wound.

"Your ear? Are you ready to explain, now?" Tanniv asks. "It's rather stylish." He reaches to touch the device and Mira slaps his hand away.

"I didn't know it would be a lasting mark," she says with a frown. "This is how they build their army. They create slaves utilizing their machina magic." She shakes her head, thinking about how many neophytes there must be.

"What does it do?" Veras leans in, curiosity consuming him. He tries to touch it as well and Mira flinches, stepping away from his prodding fingers.

"It's supposed to steal away my will or something like that, but it also functions as a communication device." Her brow turns inward as she runs a hand through her hair and rings the water from it. "Mine is a fake."

"Doesn't look fake to me" Tanniv suggests. "What will the Elders think of it? And your ear! They clipped your ear, Mira!"

"I know, Tanniv. I was there." She rolls her eyes at him. "We need to focus on the problem at hand. Haltuk remains imprisoned and his implant is real. There's a good chance he won't recognize us for who we are. He may even try to kill us."

"Haltuk would never…" Tanniv starts but trails off.

"If their machina implants do what they say, his will won't be his own. The General was certainly trusting of their machina. He allowed me to swim freely, believing I would obey his command without question. It ended with a little scuffle…" A shiver trembles through her body. "That's how I got here."

"Does it come off?" Veras asks.

"Not without much pain and effort, I don't think. The forbidden thing is jabbing into the base of my skull."

"Really?" Veras' tone is more excited than concerned. Mira glares at him again. "I mean…that sounds dreadful."

"Look!" Tanniv points outside of their personal bubble. The look on his face is grim.

Mira follows his line and sees the water glowing with the color of the spice. The glow originates in one specific area and spreads outward into the dark waters like the tendrils of a leaf. "What is it?" she asks.

"Stick your head outside the bubble," Tanniv replies. "You'll see better without that reflective glare."

"I'm not sticking my head through that thing!" Mira almost shouts back at him.

"I wouldn't recommend it either," Veras pipes in. "We don't know what it's made of, or what it'll do. It could pop the bubble, or quite possibly sever a limb."

Tanniv ignores all concern and shoves his head through the outer rim of the bubble. Similar to how Mira leapt through the pearlescent barrier keeping half the outpost dry, Tanniv is able to penetrate the odd substance without impacting their pocket of air, nor does it look like he's lost his head.

He pulls back in. "We gotta go! Now!"

"What is it?" Mira asks.

"The rest of the army. They're loading into the pool by the hundreds, then dispersing throughout the tank." His arm points and follows one of the visible tendrils. "That glow you're witnessing is their breastplates and tridents."

"And judging by the intensity, it's a force we cannot evade if we don't leave now," Mira says.

"Precisely."

"I was of the mind to rescue the grendelins with this ballista, but there's been a change of plan. We need to get back to the halfway house where the neophytes are held. Our objective…free them all." Mira waves an arm for them to follow as she dives through the bubble.

The encroaching army is rather easy to avoid as they swim at a shallower depth to engage the grendelins. Mira is the first to spear through the iridescent barrier. She arcs her back just enough to land on stumbling fins as she catches her balance. Next comes Tanniv. His transition through the barrier is much less graceful, and Mira's wouldn't have been considered graceful by any elf's imagination. Tanniv flops onto the metal deck in a dripping heap. A moment later, a toe, followed by an entire fin, slowly emerges from the wall of water. Then Veras' hand pokes through. Mira grabs it and yanks him all the way.

"Your caution isn't needed here," she says. "If you can give us guile and strength, that would be ideal."

"I've got your strength!" Tanniv shouts from the floor. "But it's sopping wet." He pulls out the remnants of Crumbaker's crumble cake. Mira rolls her eyes.

"What *is* it?" Veras turns around to examine the barrier, poking more fingers at it.

"Machina magic. What else?"

"Phenomenal."

"C'mon. This way." Without attempting to dry off, Mira plows forward in the direction she recalls the halfway house to be. Tanniv scrambles to his fins, and Veras throws up a hand of caution, but Mira ignores it. The two elves hurry after her.

"Mira, did you not just caution toward using guile?" Veras speaks in a loud whisper.

"Ahh, right. But as you can see, this place is mostly deserted. All the military enforcement has been sent to the breach. As long as we stay off the main thoroughfare, we should have free rein until we get to the halfway house."

"Halfway house? How do you know? How do you know any of this?"

Veras isn't usually the one to question her, but without Haltuk around, he must feel the need to speak up. "I don't know anything," she admits. "But we need to take advantage of this opportunity. I know the way to the halfway house, which is where Haltuk will be. And I know we have some allies there already."

"Allies!" Both Veras and Tanniv sound shocked.

"Turns out, not every Ebisu is malicious and out to murder us." She throws her hands in the air, looking over her shoulder at them as she continues to run.

Several buildings and a few thoroughfares later, they arrive at the gates to the grand halfway house.

"Ergh...thank goodness." Tanniv hunches over with heavy breaths pumping from his lungs. "How do they tolerate this madness? Do they truly walk or run wherever they go? What good are fins in a place like this?"

"This is marvelous!" Veras spurts while ogling the massive, twisted spires overhead. In rapid fashion, he withdraws his parchment and reed and starts scribbling away. "I would have never imagined the Ebisu could accomplish such feats. The Elders never made any mention of any of this."

"I've come to realize the Elders withhold a lot of information from us, Veras. But I have faith that it's all for good reason. You've witnessed the destruction their machina is capable of, have you not. It's just as vile as a wraith swarm invading a sleeping colony. Catches them unawares and lays havoc on the land before anyone realizes the devastation they've caused. Come." She waves a hand for them to follow. "Haltuk is within these gates."

"The Elders should at least allow us to create grand structures like this one," Veras whines as he follows Mira to the gate. He scribbles on his parchment as he walks, looking up at the building between scrawls.

"I'm good with a hammock and Crumbaker's bakery. I don't need anything more." Tanniv says.

"Your yari might be of some use, too." Mira gives him a narrowed sidelong glance.

"Yeah, but..." Tanniv refutes. "We were discussing architecture... And privileges..."

Mira holds the gate open for them. "Get your heads in order. We're in an enemy encampment. Should we fail, we will all be turned into war slaves. And should that happen, that yari of yours is likely to impale a fellow clanmate. How would you feel if it were your blade that pierces the heart of my father."

The two warriors nod. 'Yes, chief," they reply in a low droll. They lower their heads as they walk past her into the courtyard filled with aquariums of fish and sea life.

"They live beneath the waves." Tanniv jeers. "Is this real? They keep fish as slaves, too."

"I think they're decoration," Mira replies. "There's a tranquility to them. Could be a manipulative tactic to subdue the slaves."

"Is this where you've been held this whole time?" Veras asks.

"No. I didn't have such pleasantries." Mira's gaze searches far, almost as if she's looking through the gate on the other side of the courtyard. Her mind circles back to the stench of her cell block, the open latrine, those who didn't survive the trials. They could all be behind those gates. "Rela and Tiolas should be somewhere in there." She points to the gate with the dagger she's still holding. She had forgotten she even had it.

"Who?" Veras asks.

"The Ebisu rebellion. More reside behind those gates, so I'm told. Maybe enough to secure our escape."

"Ok, then. Let's get to it." Tanniv marches toward the gates.

"*Unleash the demigod!*" Mira hears the words through her earpiece. They're choppy and distorted, but she knows what she heard and shudders at the command.

"What's the matter?" Veras asks.

"The demigod…" she whispers. "It's a monstrosity. A leviathan ten times the size of what we encounter back in the Knuckles of Morshine."

"Here?" Veras is perplexed.

Tanniv halts his charge and turns around. "There's more?" Now Tanniv sounds like the whiney one.

"I can hear the General's commands." She taps on her implant. "I wonder if it's for the grendelins?"

"So… Does that change what we're doing here?" Veras' arm bobs up and down with a finger pointing at the floor.

"We need to get those grendelins out of here. The Ebisu have an advantage over them in the ocean waters. They're sure to enslave them. And with that demigod added to the mix, they don't stand a chance. Or… Or we could figure out how to drain the water. Patch up that hole you created and turn this place back into an underwater refuge."

"Military outpost, chief," Veras corrects her. "It was never a refuge."

"Slave camp, really," she agrees.

"What about Haltuk?" Tanniv asks.

"Haltuk is my responsibility. You two go. Figure out how to get our stone companions to safety. I will continue ahead to retrieve Haltuk, then circle back to find you."

"No, Mira!" Veras blurts. "Chief," he corrects himself. "Then we are back to where we started. Tanniv and Veras playing with the grendelins and Mira and Haltuk imprisoned within the Ebisu outpost. No offense, but your command is absurd."

Mira's lips flatten. She goes quiet, pondering his words. He's right. That would put them right back at square one. "But we need to secure an exit," she argues. "Unless you know of one?"

Veras shakes his head. "No, I don't."

"Let's go get Haltuk!" Tanniv says, as if it's already decided.

"I don't know what's on the other side of the gate." Mira whips around to look at it.

"Since when has the unknown kept you at bay?" Tanniv smirks at her.

"It's my team I fear for."

"We're soldiers of the Morshine Clan, chief. We conquer leviathans for a living. Whatever is on the other side of that gate is no match for three of Solaria's finest warriors." Tanniv puffs his bare chest and puts his fists on his hips, staring into the distance as if he could see a horizon.

"You're a fool, Tanniv Windstalker." Mira smiles at him. "I'm glad to have you on my side." She looks at Veras. "You too, Veras Elreid. There's a reason I chose the two of you to be on my team. Together, we are capable of much more than the finest warriors of Solaria."

"Indeed," Tanniv agrees.

Veras looks at her with a skeptical eye.

"Wait!" Tanniv's gaze cuts to Mira. "We *are* the finest warriors. That's what I just... Are you saying..."

Mira smiles at him. "Got any more of Crumbaker's crumble cake? We might need it."

Tanniv smiles. "Of course." He reaches into his side pouch. "Just a nibble, though." He tears off small bites and hands it out.

"Okay. Let's do this."

The three De'wi soldiers charge toward the gates of the halfway house, ready to take on whatever lies on the other side.

31 THREE STONES A GLUTTON

Quick and steady, Gallagher slides through the dark currents of the canyon. He has trained for this his entire life. His breathing, although strenuous, is under control. His fin, although damaged, adequately propels him through the water. His eyesight, although adjusted to the absence of light, can see nothing beyond his reach. He's swimming blind with his short sword acting as an obstruction detector, and his free hand pushing off the canyon wall when he gets too close. His only saving grace, the subtle green glow from the stone embedded into his short sword. Fear is prevalent.

Why he ever thought to do this as a youngkin is beyond him. What a bold, stupid child he was. This place is a living nightmare without eyesight. Any predatory creature could devour him in the blink of an eye, and he'd never see it coming. At least the leviathans have a telling sign.

Gallagher heeds Lady Nessa's warning, doing his best to stay within the center of the canyon. Should he linger too long near the walls, the eels or something with a lethal toxin will find him. He pushes off when necessary, which becomes more common the deeper he swims. For the moment, all is clear. Although, that could change with each stroke he makes.

A gentle light creeps into view. Not a glowing light trap, but a shimmering blue-green iridescence. A mark. The Blue Tears are within sight. It offers relief to his fearful mind. Though, doubt remains strong. It should have been harder to find. And deeper, too.

No eels or leviathans, and he isn't deep enough to have reached the toxic sea life. All is good. All is eerily peaceful.

The weight on his chest grows with each beat of his fins as he dives deeper and deeper. The crop is nearly within reach when he realizes the mistake he's made. Blue Tears are not the only bioluminescent lifeform within the canyon. Something that should have been on the forefront of his mind. Perhaps his eagerness to harvest the Tears and get back to Rivee are overshadowing his wits. A patch of glowing sea anemones shimmers before him. The hunt continues.

Except... Gallagher finds himself face to face with the canyon wall and a wolf eel staring back at him from within the same crevice the anemones grow.

It remains still. Cautiously watching him. Waiting. Its lips are parted, revealing tiny razors within. Dark eyes blend with its splotchy grey and black skin, making it nearly invisible within the crevice if it weren't for the surrounding anemone reflecting off its slimy flesh.

Gallagher looks around where the faint light allows him to. More eels are tucked within the nearby crevices. Their heads sway ever so slightly in the gentle currents within the canyon. Some with fierce teeth baring. He can only guess as to how many are *not* visible. He slowly retreats away from the wall.

Caution precedes. No aggressive maneuvers. Once he's beyond arm's reach he pounds the pommel of his short sword to unsheathe the blade. It latches onto his hand and the stone glows more vibrantly as an energy surges through his core and into each limb. The intensity of it would be painful if it didn't also enhance his strength.

He retreats to the center of the canyon with noticeably better vision cutting further into the depths of the canyon. Not great. Not even adequate, but better.

The eels remain within their burrows, and Gallagher swims deeper, eager to flee the nasty creatures. The threat is real. Anxiety quickens his pace. His breathing grows more and more arduous, but not as bad as he would have thought without the spice in his system. His legs feel stronger than ever. He feels alive.

Again, Gallagher sees a faint glow within the depths. Wary from the first encounter with the anemone and eels, he refuses to get excited. As he gazes at the bioluminescence, still a good distance beneath him, he wonders how such a luminous plant can grow within these depths. Darkness all around him which even the rays of the sun struggle to penetrate on the day of Solari. Only Ceto should be able to navigate these depths, yet life finds a way.

His mind shifts to Mira. Would she find the dark corners of the world as wonderous as the Terra Realm? He imagines her swimming before him, accompanying him with this burdensome task. Her dark hair flows freely, nearly invisible in the darkness. The green aura dancing in the water reflects off her beauty. She smiles, filling him with the energy to finish this task alone.

Gallagher blinks to wash the alluring image from his mind, but the green reflection bouncing off her eyes doesn't fade. Lurking just above him is not one green light trap, but two. Everything else is black.

He swiftly taps the pommel of his sword. The blade releases his hand, a shimmer casts over it, and the stone dims. A faint glow never leaves it, but it oughtn't draw attention. Suddenly the weight of the water feels heavier both on his legs and his chest. His breathing is almost unbearable. His legs feel as though he swims through weeds, and the harder he kicks, the heavier his breathing gets.

He flips at an angle where he can keep his eye on the light traps above, yet continue his dive. He presses onward with the same tactics, his short sword a detector of obstacles and his legs and freehand a force to propel him deeper.

His training works in his favor, primarily his breathing technique. If he couldn't remain steady and calm, he would have been discovered long ago. Undoubtedly, living amongst the sky elves for a short while must have strengthened his lungs, too.

He swims up to the patch of bioluminescent spice without a single encounter, and without a doubt in his mind, these are the Blue Tears he seeks.

His fingers brush across the feather-like substance. It's soft to the touch, and wherever his fingers graze it, the spice temporarily loses its luster. It reacts to his touch. It's so wonderous Gallagher cannot pry his eyes away. The plant in harvested form is a limp weed with a fraction of the glow. To see it within its natural habitat is brilliant.

As he beholds the glory of its existence and the energy it offers, his fingers brush past several polyps within the small crop. They resemble a leviathan's light trap, only a smidgeon smaller and more transparent. Hundreds of them. He leans closer to get a better visual. Within the spherical bodies are tiny lifeforms. He glances over his shoulder, knowing only one fish could lay eggs of this scale.

The thought crosses his mind to smash every one of them. He would put a halt to an entire cohort of leviathans. But if he did, he could never call himself a warrior. Not by his own standards. It would be no different than the Ebisu or the Indra finding a De'wi nursery and murdering all their youngkin. The battle is not with the unborn. The battle is with the clashing cultures. He looks over his shoulder toward the lurking leviathans. All is black. They've disappeared.

Urgency settles in. Gallagher has little to carry the Tears. He stripped off his surcoat with all its hidden pouches, and he has no satchel like the harvesters would carry for such an excursion. He can use his trousers, but he has many trepidations with arriving back home in the nude. A pantleg will suffice.

Just when he's about to grab onto what looks like a chunk of coral to anchor himself, he freezes. It's not an urchin or an anemone, but could it be the dragon's tongue Lady Nessa spoke of? He's never seen it himself. It appears to be a smaller form of coral with a few plant-like features. As he churns the water around it, it resembles a flame within the depths of the ocean. Gallagher carefully backstrokes, unwilling to find out.

Hesitant to touch anything except the Blue Tears, he proceeds with slicing a pantleg from his trousers while floating a safe distance from the plant life. He ties the fabric into a makeshift sack and hurries to pluck the Tears, cautious of anything without the bluish-green iridescence.

Gallagher packs it in, and even stuffs a few leaves in the waistline of his trousers. Plenty for Rivee and a surplus for the next excursion, which he'll gladly share with the clan. He turns his focus back toward the surface.

Danger has hardly brushed by his side, and it makes him anxious of what's to come. He's evaded the eels, snuck past the leviathans, and avoided the toxic sea life, but he still has that return trip. Looking up, the leviathans are nowhere in sight. It's more terrifying than seeing the two light traps bobble above. At least then he knows where the danger is.

His chest feels like he's squished between two boulders, but he has the Blue Tears, and his journey back home has commenced—if he can still call it home.

The black ocean remains black in every direction. The glow of the Tears in his waistline and the stone within his blade are too dim to see the canyon walls unless he's right next to them. He could easily bump into an eel or dragon's tongue and not know until it's too late. He tries to keep a straight line toward the surface, careful not to climb too steep of an angle to avoid his lungs bursting from the pressure differential.

Gallagher's line of good luck comes to a halt when the green glow of the leviathan appears from behind a bend in the canyon. Laying low until it swims past would be his best option. The alternative would be to engage, which part of him desires another stone to claim for himself. His culture is to blame for these idolized lusts. Rivee is more important in this moment, however. Engaging would put her life at more risk than it already is. He waits.

The leviathan lurks overhead, swimming closer, several body lengths above him. Its casual movements are the only thing keeping him calm. The flesh of its belly shimmers in the faint glow of the Tears, nearly close enough to reach out and touch. Gallagher looks down at his waistline, careful not shift his head too fast. He's turned himself into a beacon of light and might as well have put a prey sign on his back to light up. He cringes at his idiocy.

The angler fish comes to a halt a short distance away.

Gallagher refuses to take his eyes off the aquatic beast wondering if it stares back. An elf can lose itself in those empty, black, spheres that are its eyes. A vague outline of the creature and numerous fangs the size of a small elf are illuminated by its light trap. Its size is enormous. Bigger than the leviathan he battled in Caelum Invictus. That one was a child compared to what floats before him.

With sword in hand, he swims higher, hoping this aquatic beast will let him pass. Its eyes are larger than Gallagher's head and dark as the midnight sea. Watching. Waiting. The glow of its light trap is blinding. Like staring at a flame in the late evening, everything around it becomes imperceptible. Gallagher casually swims higher.

Its jaw opens slowly, then chatters closed as if it has an itching to attack. Gallagher continues to stare, unsure how to react.

Suddenly, its long twin tail pounds against the water. It jets forward. Gallagher cuts in a different direction, evading its lunge. Its jaw snaps shut. The act is silent to his ears, but in his mind, he hears a clap of lightning jolting fear throughout his body.

Out in the open water, he's a helpless guppy, especially with his damaged fin. He got lucky this time, but he doesn't have the power to evade such an attack every time. Gallagher swims closer to the wall. The bite of an eel would be less fatal than the bite of a leviathan, after all.

The leviathan attacks.

A firm handhold on the wall is his savior, as he's able to pull himself out of the way, just dodging its gangly teeth. He continues climbing to grow the distance between them, but he knows he cannot do this all the way to the surface. And he knows he cannot outswim the sea demon. Mira is perhaps the only elf worthy of such a task.

So why does he swim away?

Gallagher pushes off the wall and turns to face the leviathan. He pounds the pommel of his sword on his thigh. The blade interlocks with his hand, the stone glows brighter, and a noticeable shimmer flutters through the blade as its protective coating retracts. A power surges through Gallagher. His breathing calms. His anxiety subdues. His confidence heightens. He looks at the stone within the blade, accepting the magnitude of what his friend has gifted him.

The leviathan lunges at him again. Feeling nimble and powerful, Gallagher dodges the strike, and with a swing of his blade slices through the leviathan's upper lip. He circles over top of the beast and stabs down through its skull. The leviathan rages. Fins and tails flail through the canyon. Its dual tail curls and whips at Gallagher, almost piercing his body with the spines protruding from it. His impact with the canyon wall is likely just as painful, but not fatal.

It takes him a moment to recover, and the leviathan is on him again. Its jaws snap and slice through Gallagher's thigh. His muscles tighten and lock, but he doesn't allow the pain to overcome him. He counterattacks. Pushing off the wall with a swing of his blade, he spins in a cyclonic twirl and impales the leviathan, shattering its glasslike eyeball. Fits of rage overcome the beast. Even if he could let go of his sword while it's unsheathed, Gallagher refuses. He grips it with both hands, tossing through the water with the leviathan, and only when the beast calms, does he remove his sword and stab again. And again. And again. One more quick fit erupts from the sea demon before its life fades.

Gallagher has slayed the leviathan.

Lack of time squashes any chance for a victory boast, however. At least one more lurks nearby.

Gallagher moves to retrieve his stone, but he hesitates. Rivee is more important. He needs to get back. Although, she would berate him from her death bed if he didn't collect it. It'll be quick. He severs the thin line it's attached to and cuts into the light trap where the stone shines brightly on the inside. The intensity fades as he holds it in his open palm.

While fumbling with where to put his badge of honor, two more leviathans arrive. Gallagher cringes at how his fortune has turned.

Just like the first, they appear from around a bend in the canyon. Gallagher instinctively freezes, but he refuses to be prey that falls limp, willing to accept death. With the added power of his machina sword, he bursts upward at an unrivaled speed.

The leviathans engage in the chase.

Gallagher, with all his might, swims as fast as he can possibly swim. It's not fast enough.

One of the leviathans surges above him. The other chases from behind. He tries to climb, but the higher he goes, the closer he swims to the terrifying creature. They're working together, cutting off his angle of escape. He's forced to curl through the canyon away from his colony or dive deeper, neither of which will bring him to safety.

Gallagher abruptly comes to a halt. The leviathan pursuing him opens its jaws wide, and the warrior elf is swallowed whole. Its jaws snap closed, but not without a sword piercing through its skull. The leviathan dies immediately, and Gallagher is left trapped within its jaws. It makes for an easy kill, but the challenge of the escape almost isn't worth it.

He scrutinizes himself for making this stupid mistake for the second time. He should have learned after intentionally getting swallowed the first time.

Squirming through its insides, Gallagher makes way for the belly, where he knows it will be easier to escape through the thin, boneless flesh. Time is against him. The mixture of blood, ocean water, and whatever juices digest its prey prevent him from breathing. He acts quickly. In the open space of its belly, he hacks at the inner lining and spills free from the beast.

Gasping for breath, he hurries to retrieve his third badge of honor. He leaves the light trap intact and tethered to its line, severing high so he can tie it around his waist.

The second leviathan attacks while he's distracted with his treasures.

Jaws opened wide, teeth ready to impale, and it charges. Gallagher bursts backward toward the canyon wall and slams into it. The leviathan's teeth slide right past his face, the hard enamel pressing against his cheekbone. Gallagher manages to squeeze into a tiny crevice where the leviathan cannot fit. Its jaw opens and chatters closed, trying to snag any part of Gallagher and yank him out into the open.

Gallagher shimmies deeper into the crevice. Safe for the moment, he sheathes his blade and thumbs the stone embedded within it. Brunswick knew the importance the stones hold within his culture, and he allowed for growth, but was he aware of the power imbued within them? Four more concave slots wait to be filled. Gallagher only assumes the stones are relevant, and if more can enhance his strength, it's worth a try.

Gallagher pops the smooth stone into the slot intended for it. Slightly larger than the size of his thumb, it's the perfect fit.

With much anticipation, Gallagher smacks the pommel of his sword against the rocks. The blade shimmers. Both stones glow with a light more brilliant than when he had a single stone, and a power surges through him more intense than ever, tugging at every muscle within his body. When the transition finalizes, he inhales a deep breath to calm his nerves. He can see across the canyon. His breathing is light. His energy is rejuvenated. He is ready to take on one more goliath of the deep.

Gallagher watches as the jaws of the leviathan continue to snap before him. They chatter every time they close. Timing it just right, he waits for the jaws to close. But before he can attack, the leviathan disappears in a flash of teeth and scales more monstrous than the leviathan.

Scales swim past him at a slow rate, the only thing visible for a long while. After a moment of shock, petrified within the crevice he's chosen as a haven, the twin tails of a leviathan swim past. The tip of each tail is as large as one of the leviathans he just defeated. His jaw hangs low as he remains frozen in place.

Just when Gallagher finds his courage to swim for the shallows, he feels a small pinch on his calf. A wolf eel has latched onto his leg. He pushes away from the wall with haste to find dozens more waiting within the depths. He quickly removes heads and tails, and tries to swim away, unconcerned about the eels latched onto him.

They're too fast. The fry of eels surround him, nipping at his flesh, tearing away small bites with each attack. Gallagher swings, but too many join the frenzy. His stones give him no advantage here.

The blade slashes through the water. His legs kick. His free arm slaps at them, but nothing is effective. The eels are too slithery, and too many. Fatigue grows on him like a rotten cancer spreading through his flesh. He can hardly move his arms. After defeating two leviathans, his gluttony for pride, for honor, for relevance may be the end for Gallagher.

He swings his blade for the last time, and the eels disperse. Before losing consciousness, something grabs him by the arms and pulls him toward the surface. He allows the darkness to settle in, and he closes his eyes.

32 HALFWAY HOUSE

A surge of energy pumps through her veins. It won't last long with the small ration of soggy crumble cake she consumed. Tanniv pulls open one door, Veras the other, allowing Mira the first steps through the gates of the halfway house. Treatment for regality if they weren't charging toward unknown dangers. The *ladies first* courtesy falls flat in this moment.

The metallic doors appear antiquated with bits of rust growth around the hinges and along the seams of the stiles, but they open freely without a squeak.

Mira steps into a grand foyer three stories tall. Shimmering iridescent and metallic panels line the walls with sporadic lamps illuminating them with white light. The room is wider than it is tall with stairways climbing away from it in various directions. Some lead to an upper hall and others to the third story. Some lead directly to closed doors. Some disappear behind walls.

The space is empty and quiet.

"Well, this doesn't seem too efficient," Tanniv breaks the silence. His voice carries throughout the foyer. Both he and Veras step into the room behind Mira. Veras pulls out his parchment and unfurls it.

"What are you doing?" She questions his timing to document.

"Mapping out their halfway house." He looks up at her with many lines spreading throughout his forehead as if it's obvious.

"Oh… err… good idea."

"I don't think we'll ever come back to this drowned hell once we get out," Tanniv says.

A loud clank startles them all when the door slams shut behind them. Mira shoots Tanniv a disappointed glare.

"A façade, perhaps?" Veras questions.

"Or a labyrinth to steal their wits," Mira suggests.

"Which way, chief?" He points his yari at a few of the staircases.

"I haven't been this deep. I… This isn't what I anticipated." She steps further into the large room.

"Could they have been dispersed into battle?" Veras steps up beside her.

"Perhaps. Do we each take a separate stairway?"

"Ludicrous!" Tanniv blurts out. "So we can lose our way *and* lose each other."

"He has a valid point," Veras chimes in.

"This is ridiculous. If only we had the ability to swim through this maze." Mira clenches her jaw, furious at the absurdity. "No need to dwell on what we cannot control. Come." She sprints to the right with her dagger in hand.

"Mira!"

She recognizes the voice as Rela's. Mira whips around to see where it came from. A moment of scanning all the stairways high and low, and she sees Rela's hand casually gesturing for her to follow. She's on the other side of the foyer on their level.

Tanniv and Veras are on guard, yaris in hand, each with a keen, determined glare.

"Stand down. This is the ally I spoke of. Come on." Mira rushes toward Rela. Tanniv and Veras are skeptical, but they follow.

"How'd you fare?" Rela asks. "I was hoping you'd find a way back here. I've been checking the entrance regularly. Didn't want you venturing into the hands of Lord Tenebrous." She points upward.

"Lord Tenebrous?"

"Come. We talk as we move." She hurries toward a stairway leading down. "Aye, he resides on the top floor when he's here."

"Wait! He's gone?" Mira chirps.

"Tiolas said he departed just before your final trial. I don't know anything more." She pauses. "His place looks like a palace, right? His utmost, highest, most refined elegance must have the best."

"So… He resides in the halfway house with the prisoners?"

"Above them. Yes."

"What if there's an insurrection?"

"Like right now?" Rela looks over her shoulder with a grin.

Mira has never seen her with this level of enthusiasm. She didn't believe she was capable of more than a frown. "There are many securities in place. As much as we would prefer to go to the heart of the evil and destroy it, not only is he rarely here, but we are ill prepared." They hit a landing and turn to go down more steps. "The elf is armored beyond our understanding. We must rescue the neophytes and escape. Recoup and reassess."

"How many reformed?" Mira asks with a mild pant in her voice.

"Thousand?" Rela's hands gesture that she doesn't know. "Tiolas is down there now, working up a plan—"

"A thousand reforms!" Veras interrupts. "How are we going to rescue a *thousand* reforms? We came here for two! Also… what's a reform?"

"Veras!" Mira ridicules him. "I know you're not one for surprise, but you're a warrior. We take each challenge as it is presented to us. Think of all the lives you'll be saving. Think of all the soldiers you'll be removing from the force that intends to obliterate your clan. If there are one thousand reforms, there are one thousand lives we must try to rescue."

"So the reforms are the war slaves…" he deduces.

"Neophytes," Rela corrects him. "That's what we call them."

"This is a stairway to hell." Tanniv pipes in. "We keep going down. I think we've ventured deeper than Ceto himself."

Mira rolls her eyes. "You were saying, Rela?"

"Err…Tiolas. He's on the lowest level—"

"Hell," Tanniv corrects her. Mira is ready to push him down the stairs.

"He's in *hell*," Rela continues, "working out how to open the cells and avoid being attacked while removing the implants."

"These *thousand* prisoners are going to attack us?" Veras questions her. "Mira…"

"Yes, Veras. They have been reformed into Ebisu soldiers. They will appear as enemies, but they are not." She shakes her head at him. "You've acquired a rather whiny persona since we've reacquainted. What happened?" They come to the final step with a single door leading into a vast chamber. Rela bursts through. Mira halts and puts a hand up to stop her two warriors. "Veras, you okay?"

"Sorry, Mira. Anxiety, I suppose. I never anticipated we would find ourselves in—"

"Hell!" Tanniv blurts and receives glares from both Mira and Veras. He shrugs.

"The Ebisu were but a story mere weeks ago. They weren't a *real* adversary. Grendelins, too." A deep sigh escapes him.

"Haltuk is somewhere down here. Some of our other clanmates, too. Keep your mind on them. Think of your fellow warriors and the lives they deserve. Those lives have been taken from them by the Ebisu scum. They need you, Veras. They need us."

"Of course, chief." Veras straightens his stance into that of a warrior. Back straight and tall. Shoulders firm. Hands locked behind his back. Fins shoulder-width apart. "I'm ready, chief. Let's go save Haltuk and the others."

Mira grins at him before turning to lead the way through the door and into the open chamber. She nearly trips over a downed guard lying in a pool of blood. Scanning the room, she sees a few more Ebisu soldiers removed from action, limp on the floor. However, the dead bodies are a lost memory when she focuses on the expanse of the chamber they've walked into.

"Hell…" she mumbles as she stops in her tracks.

"See!" Tanniv steps up beside her. Veras stops, too.

Metal bars with their subtle glow line the walls as far as she can see. The chamber must span the entire width of the outpost. The cells are stacked four high on both sides of them with skywalks at each level. A wide space separates the two sides, large enough for an entire army to assemble. White lights wash the front of the cells in uniform order as far as is visible.

"And we're supposed to release all of these prisoners?" Veras stands still, no hand motions or facial expressions.

Tanniv pops out a short laugh. "Yeah, let's get to it, warrior." He slaps him on the back, knocking him a step forward.

"Tiolas is down this way," Rela calls from a long distance away. Her voice echoes throughout the hollow chamber.

The three companions follow her lead. "Keep a lookout for Haltuk," Mira breathes a heavy sigh. "This could take days."

"Weeks," Veras adds.

"Are these prisoners all from the other De'wi clans?" Mira asks Rela as they get closer. They walk down the center of the chamber.

"Some. A good portion are Ebisu resistance. Less are Indran emissaries. I've only ever seen the two that were locked away with us."

"Do all the neophytes go through the trials?" Mira asks.

"Most, but not all."

"So, most of these prisoners have experienced death at some point."

"Near death. They're quick to get the spice in them. Plus, the victors come here, too. There's nothing special about a trial champion. Sorry." She glances over her shoulder at Mira. "They mostly have those trials for their entertainment.

Aside from that, it lets the General determine where each elf's skillset is at. Are you capable of being a blockade, a dead body to slow the enemy, or are you capable of killing? You either slow the enemy or you remove the enemy. Allows the General to understand whether you belong on a driving flank or a dying front line."

"Where do they get all the ore for these cells? For *all* the underwater structures for that matter?" Veras asks with a wave of his hand, gesturing to everything around them. He pulls out his parchment and starts counting down each line, making scratches as he does.

"There's a big mining operation back in Oceanus Salus. Tunnels carve into the underwater mountains where plenty of ore is discovered and there aren't enough miners to excavate it. It's a prestigious role to own. Machina does all the major excavation. Gives them new mineshafts and corridors to venture into, but the Ebisu take pride in it. My husband was a miner."

"Your husband…" Veras starts, but Mira puts up a hand to silence him.

"I see," Mira interjects. She has many more questions, as she suspects Veras does too, but she allows a brief silence to respect Rela's fallen husband. "And I suspect you have many harvesters for the Tears?" she asks after a long silence. "I cannot imagine what it takes to power all this machina. You must strip the seabed clean."

"Harvesters? Err…pickers. I think what you mean to say are pickers. I suppose we have quite a few…"

She stops listening to Rela. The term *picker* sends Mira's mind wandering toward Gallagher. He's out in the wild somewhere, abandoned by his clan like the Ebisu enslaved in this prison. Except he's forced to live his days in solitude. Which life would be worse?

Perhaps he has Rivee by his side. Maybe they found each other. She can only hope.

Although, now that she has experience with the destructive qualities of machina, she understands *why* he was exiled. Look at all the machina in this facility. She suspects some have good intentions, like perhaps the dome offering them air to build a civilization. But what about the machina implants used to imprison slaves? What about the machina ballista used to entrap their enemies, and the enhanced tridents used to defeat their enemies? What about the machina cages used to contain their slaves? The slaves they use in an effort to dominate all of Solaria. In the hands of elves, machina offers too much opportunity for destruction. If her clan were to be contaminated by machina, they would use it to tear into the leviathans. Every warrior would be a five-stone warrior. But not truly. Not in the same manner her father can boast about it. Perhaps the Elders made a good decision to exile Gallagher. A single tainted seed could take over the entire culture.

Although… With his strong heart, Gallagher might be the exception. His soul is blessed with goodness. He has the mind to stray away from the ugliness in the world. Maybe it's not the machina, but the vicious heart of the elf who controls the machina. An everlasting conundrum. They will never truly know if the machina is the evil that persists or if the ugliness is seeded within the elf. Perhaps the machina wars should be rebranded as the eternal war, for it will never be decided. There will never be a resolution.

Mira lets go of these brooding thoughts that could drown her in misery, and she refocuses on the task at hand. "Is there any way to find out where our companion is? We don't have time to search every cell."

Tiolas finally comes into view. He stands before a machina station.

"That's what Tiolas is trying to determine. Come." Rela sprints ahead.

A gentle blue glow reflects off Tiolas' dark skin as he stares at a machina device mounted to the wall. "I don't know what these glyphs mean," he says as they approach. He turns away from the machina to see Rela has brought more company. "Oh, good to see you survived the General, Mira."

"He puts a lot of trust in these machina implants, doesn't he?" Mira fumbles with the device attached to her ear. "He had no notion I wasn't under his control." She doesn't mention the assault lingering over her. It's like being trapped under a dead seal. The disgust and stank she feels is beyond reason. She's not ready to discuss it. Her anger would only flare in a moment which requires utmost focus.

"The machina hasn't failed him since the early days. Back when we only tested it on the creatures of the deep. He has no reason to believe your machina is false."

"And what of the communication? First, why did you not tell me I would be hearing voices through this thing? Second, why do I only hear the General on occasion?"

"An oversight. My apologies. It's controlled solely on his end. It's a one-way communication channel for him to command his army. The Ebisu armor also has it built in for communicating out in the dark blue. Theirs have two-way communication, so they can talk back and forth. Both have limited range, which is probably why you're not hearing him down here."

"Can he hear me? Us?" she asks.

"Not that I'm aware of." Tiolas looks to the two elves he doesn't know. An awkward silence follows as they stare back.

"Oh, forgive my poor etiquette. Rela. Tiolas. This would be Tanniv Windstalker and Veras Elreid." She gestures to each of them respectively. "These are two of three companions I traveled here with."

"And the third is behind these bars somewhere." Tiolas looks up at the towering wall of cells. "Any thoughts on how to read this thing?"

"It's a layout of the chamber." Veras squirms between the others to get to the machina device. "You see here, every one of these lights aligns with one of the cells. Four high… And be my guest to count how many wide." He waves a hand at the numerous lights. "Down here, there's another four rows of equal length. That would be the wall of cells behind us." He looks over his shoulder and points with his thumb. "The glyphs are typical elven script." His nose scrunches into his brow as he looks at Tiolas.

"Reading isn't a high priority within our culture." He shrugs.

"Very few Ebisu would be able to read this," Rela adds. "We live beneath the waves. Parchment, writing, it's an extravagance down here. Often frowned at by others. No different than strutting around Oceanus Salus with your chin up wearing the finest furs from the Terra Realm. Others would treat you as a first-class nitwit who puts themselves above the rest. Those of us who know how to read keep it to ourselves."

"Interesting." Veras shrugs. "Okay then, back to the pretty lights and malicious machina. I suspect with the way the little life bubble machina worked, this will be of similar function." Veras presses one of the lights.

"Life bubble?" Now Tiolas is the one scrunching his face at Veras.

The sound of a pressure release is heard in the distance, somewhere to their left.

"Did it…" Mira's question trails off as she starts moving in that direction.

"Well, get to it. Start opening them up," Tanniv suggests. "We don't want to spend the rest of our lives in hell, do we?"

Both Veras and Tiolas turn around to face him. Both peeved at the comment. "And how do you suppose we remove the machina implants on a thousand soldiers who are trained to kill us?"

Tanniv quails. "One at a time?"

"That will take too long." Mira's tone is assertive. "There are five of us. We do ten at a time, minimum." She turns back to face the group. "We start with one or two, but as we remove more implants, we can increase the rate. Is there a quick means to remove the implants?"

"Have you tried to remove your own?" Tiolas asks, not anticipating an answer. "It is extremely painful. The implant—well, not yours, because yours is fake—extends deep into the neck toward the spinal column. It's no easy feat. First you must unclamp it from the ear to prevent tearing off the rest of it, then, with caution, you must slide the implant free. If you're to jamb it in further or carelessly yank it free, you can do permanent damage on their aptitude."

"You mean we'll create a bunch of idiots if we aren't careful about the extraction?" Tanniv asks.

"Precisely," Tiolas replies.

"If we come across any fellas you're holding a grudge against, be sure to speak up." Tanniv pounds a fist into his palm with a conniving grin on his face. "One more idiot to live with, but one less asshole." He gets many glares in return. "What?"

"With the precision involved in this task, might I request we start with just a couple?" Veras raises two fingers. "Two muscles to restrain them, and one eloquent hand to remove the machina."

"Good plan. Let's do it." Mira agrees.

"And you've been voted our eloquent elegance." Tanniv wraps an arm around Veras' shoulder and smiles at him.

Veras' brow furls. "Is that…a compliment?"

Mira reaches toward the machina panel and presses another light. Another pressure release sounds off. Mira and Rela both hurry down the chamber in the direction of the sound. The others follow in pursuit.

"They're on the ground floor," Mira states as they approach the two adjacent cells that are open. She comes to a halt in front of the first one. "What's wrong with them?" she asks.

"This might be easier than we thought." Rela stops beside her, then peers into the adjacent cell.

"And look at that." Mira points. "They each have their own privy within each cell. Guess they don't require special linens to do their business." Rela smiles at her.

The reformed soldiers remain content within their cells. One lies in a cot, the other seated on their cot. Neither has the ambition to vacate their cell. Neither are Haltuk.

"Let's be quick," Mira says as the rest of their companions catch up. "Tanniv. Left cell, with me. Rela, Tiolas. You got the cell on the right. Veras, move in when the soldier is subdued. Everyone got it?"

"Yes, chief," both Veras and Tanniv respond verbally. Tiolas and Rela nod their affirmations.

The process is quick. The soldiers put up nothing of a noteworthy fight. They are a bit disgruntled and squirmy, but they submit rather easily. Veras removes both implants carefully and quickly.

"You are part of the rebellion now," Rela says to both of the neophytes after they're escorted from their cells into the open chamber. "How do you feel?"

"Foggy," one answers.

"There is an incredible pain in my neck," the other responds.

"Here." Rela hands each of them a small dose of Blue Tears. "Should help with the recovery. Sit down, let it settle in. We're going to need your assistance shortly. There are many more to rescue." She points down the line, then proceeds with tearing into the linens of the bed.

"What are you doing?" Veras asks.

Rela cuts several thin strips and hands them to the neophyte. "Wrap this around your neck. It's bleeding profusely." He reacts without question, just as he's been trained to do. Then she hands several strips of linen to her companions.

"How long have I—"

"Not a clue," Rela answers before he can finish his sentence. "General Merces has been developing this army for more than a hundred years. Just sit, let your mind wander freely."

The team liberates four more neophytes as the first two recover. Eventually, they start getting aid from the prisoners they're rescuing. Veras ends up managing the machina station to open the cells while a crew stay put on each skywalk to avoid having to hurry up and down the stairs. Emptying the cells doesn't go quite as fast as they intended, but the more they free, the quicker they extract the prisoners.

"There he is!" Mira's heart skips a beat when she locates Haltuk. Third floor up, and about one hundred freed slaves into their operation.

Mira and Tanniv rush into the cell. Haltuk lies on a cot, careless that the two of them are there, but he appears to be in good condition.

"You're alive!" Mira gasps. "Hurry Tanniv, let's release him from this evil."

Tanniv looks at the toilet. "Err…can I have a moment?"

"No! Get over here." Mira isn't sure if he is toying with her or not, but she shuts Tanniv down, regardless of his reasons. "Now is not the time for jests, nor answering nature's call."

"Yes, chief. Hey, we need an extractor in here!" Tanniv shouts as he rushes to Haltuk's side.

They pin him down on the cot. He struggles to break free of their grasp, but not as if his life depends on it. An awkward metal clang rattles the bars behind them.

Mira cranes her neck to see why, and a boiling anger shears through any excitement she had for finding her companion. Salus stands in the open door armed not with the Ebisu's typical trident, but a scepter with a glowing conch in place of what should be a blade or spear tip.

"Rela, help!" Mira shouts. "Tiolas! We've been discovered."

"I've unlocked it's power…" His voice trails. Mira doesn't understand. "I killed everyone on this level," Salus admits with pride. "Your screams will struggle to reach the others amidst the commotion." He takes one step closer. "It tore at me to be a good soldier and put your mockery behind me, but I did. Then you decided to make a fool of me for a second time at the reform chamber." He scowls at her. "Do you know what this is?" He casually holds the scepter away from his body.

Mira and Tanniv remain silent.

"This is Indran machina at its best. This is the Greybeards' masterpiece. Instant control of the mind and body." A terrifying smirk spreads across his face. "The Indra who brought it so graciously helped me unlock its power. It took a few threats… some torture…" He cringes, obviously not comfortable with what he's done. "…and… perhaps a death, but I got what I needed. And with this power, we are unstoppable. *I* am unstoppable."

"You know what, Salus? I don't like your name." Mira scoffs at him.

The comment leaves him speechless.

Tanniv restrains a chuckle.

"It's not fitting of a villainous mastermind, so how about I take that scepter from you, and we move on. You can help us free the other neophytes. Join our cause."

"Your allies will never get to you before revenge strikes." He looks up and down at his scepter with admiration.

"Those who allow revenge to consume their hearts are the weakest links in a society. The Ebisu will fare well without you." Mira stands upright, ready for whatever he brings.

Tanniv doesn't hesitate. He rushes the Ebisu. Salus welcomes the attack by swinging his scepter at the shorter De'wi warrior. Tanniv easily deflects it with his forearm, but he collapses upon impact, falling to Salus' fins.

"What kind of evil magic is that?" Tanniv grumbles from the floor.

Salus casually knocks him on the head with the conch and Tanniv falls limp.

"I don't know exactly, but I like it," he says.

"What did you do?" Mira screams and kneels by his side. "Is he…" *dead.* She doesn't say it out loud.

The malicious smile on Salus' face is fit for a world-dominating tyrant who lusts for power. "The Indran emissaries arrived with them. Naturally, we removed all their possessions when we threw them into the reform block, and I was the lucky one to discover its potential." His smile morphs into ire. "Are you ready to die?"

"Hardly." Mira pulls out the Ebisu dagger she's been holding onto and rises to her fins. She sidesteps as far as the small cell allows and reaches the opposite wall from where Haltuk is now sitting upright. He carries a stoic expression as if his mind is absent.

Salus swings the scepter. Mira avoids the attack with a roll toward Haltuk. Salus presses into a small device protruding from his breast plate, which looks like a similar design to the neophyte's implants. He speaks into it. "*Soldier. This elf maiden is a threat. Kill her.*"

"What?"

Haltuk seizes her from behind before she can comprehend who Salus was talking to. His upper body strength overpowers her, pinning her arms to her body. She kicks her fins to no avail and drops her dagger in her struggles.

Salus lowers his guard and approaches Mira, who squirms relentlessly in Haltuk's grasp. "You *are* a champion, I'll admit. You fight with vigor like tomorrow'll never come unless today is your finest."

"How?" Mira asks, easing up on her fight to get free. "How do you control them?"

His brow creases. "The implants." He shakes his head with a mixture of confusion and curiosity. "I don't understand it myself. Only the Greybeards do. The implants talk to one another when in proximity. I suppose you wouldn't know this, would you? Not with a fake implant." Salus' face turns sour.

"I hear the voices," she admits but says nothing more.

He looks over his shoulder through the metal bars caging them in. "I always suspected Tiolas as a traitor. Now I know for sure. I suspect he's out there somewhere with the growing crowd, extracting the transmitters from the neophytes. It's going to take weeks to get to them all, you know." He turns back to face Mira. "More than a thousand cells need to be opened. Thousands of disgusting reforms that each need to be catered to. And how do you expect to get out of here? Swim through the front door?"

"Yes, thanks to the grendelins. That's exactly what we intend to do."

"It's a bit late for that. The grendelins are submissive creatures. After their initial rage—which is yet to be determined what provoked the attack—they calmed when we stopped trying to defend the outpost. Now they're bound and working on converting the dumb creatures. I have a suspicion you and your rag-tag group were involved somehow, but no matter. The decoy has been subdued. The giants are under control while we reprioritize our forces. The General is already assembling a battalion to engage the halfway house. There's no way out of here except up those stairs that brought you down here."

Salus' smirk is infuriating. Mira's lack of planning doesn't help her anger, either. She needed Haltuk. Veras is smart and all, but Haltuk would have stopped her in her tracks if he felt she was making a ridiculous decision. Look where she's put them. The three of them are behind bars, and Tanniv could be... She refuses to finish the thought. If the stairs truly are their only way out, they're going to have to fight an entire Ebisu battalion. Can it be done?

"Then I certainly don't have any time to make acquaintances with you." She leaps backward, buckling Haltuk's knees and sending him to the floor where she lands on top of him. He gasps for air, stunned, and his grip loosens. She squirms free and charges Salus with haste, careless about his machina magic. She rolls beneath a swinging scepter toward his legs and lands a fin on his knee-cap. The Ebisu soldier screams in agony and falls to the ground. Mira grabs the scepter while it's still in his grip and lands an awkward blow to his skull. The incompetent soldier goes limp.

Mira holds the scepter away from her body as if it will poison her, inspecting it with her eyes. Such power. She wants to discard it, but fears whose hands it will end up in. The mere thought of another Salus getting their hands on it forces her to grip it tight.

Haltuk gets to his fins and looks at Mira with determination. "Need a little help here!" Mira screams out into the vast chamber, hoping someone will hear her.

She has sparred with her companion countless times, but never has she had to defend her life against a fellow De'wi. Not knowing if the scepter in her grasp instantly takes lives or not, she's hesitant to swing it at Haltuk. "Help, please!" She can hear the crowd stirring below her and finsteps on the skywalks above, but nobody responds.

Haltuk attacks with a left jab. Mira knocks it away with the staff, spins, and finds herself behind him. She quickly wraps the staff around his neck and locks it in place by hooking her arms around it. Haltuk reacts with a forward heave. She flies over top of him, landing on Salus, and somehow kicking the door in the process. It slides shut and clicks, locking the two into the cell together.

She's lost the scepter.

The dagger!

It lies next to Salus' limp body. She snags it, and with a hasty pop gets back on her fins with her back to the cell bars.

"Mira!" a voice calls from behind her. It's Tiolas. "Hold on."

"Hold onto what?" she snaps, regretting it immediately. Tiolas hasn't earned her scorn.

"I'll send word to Veras to get the door open." He backs away from the bars and starts counting cells before he disappears down the skywalk.

"Hurry!" she calls after him.

Haltuk engages, relentless without a mind of his own. Mira needs to remove that forsaken implant, then she'll be free of this nightmare. Never did she anticipate having to fight the elf she came here to rescue. This world beneath the waves is all upside down.

A fist flies at her head, but she's quick to dodge it. Then another catches her in the jaw. A black flash consumes her vision, and she finds herself back on the floor toppled over Salus yet again. This time, her recovery isn't quick enough. Haltuk is on top of her with both hands locked around her neck.

Mira pulls and claws at his arms to no avail. She strikes at his face, but his strength is unyielding. She tries to scream for help but comes up short. Haltuk, her fellow warrior, her friend, is going to murder her. She scrambles without respite, though her muscles aren't in agreement with her mind. Her strength is failing her.

The dagger remains in her grasp, but she is hesitant to use it on her companion. Must she decide between her own life and his? Shutting her eyes tight, not wanting to witness what she is about to do, she thrusts the dagger at him.

He anticipates her actions and knocks it away, but not without the blade slicing her palm as she scrambles to hang onto it. The pain is hardly noticeable with the burning at her throat and in her lungs.

The sound of metal grinding on metal fills her ears. The cell door opens. The hands tearing into her throat break free and her body shuts down. Her arms fall to her side, and she closes her eyes as she gasps for breath. The air burns as it comes and goes from her lungs, but she's elated, for the air *does* find her lungs.

"Pin him!" someone yells.

"He's strong for a little De'wi."

"Hold still! We're trying to help you."

The tussle continues for a short period. Tiolas returns to help Mira sit upright.

She jabs an elbow at Salus. "He'll need to be tied up. A solid blow to the head, but I don't know if he's dead or not." Her head snaps toward Tanniv who remains on the floor of the cell. He has not woken yet. Mira scrambles on her hands and knees to get to his side. "Tanniv!"

"Here, try this." Tiolas holds out a ration of Tears.

Mira snatches the blue algae and shoves it into his mouth, working it beneath his tongue, careful not to drip blood all over his face from her own wounds. "Please, Tanniv. I didn't come here to replace you with Haltuk. Please, Tanniv…" She buries her head into his chest. The room is quiet aside from the sound of Salus being dragged out of the cell. Mira can feel Tiolas' eyes staring at her.

"Wait!" She pops up from her lying position to hurry toward the scepter.

The two former slaves stop in their tracks, thinking she's talking to them, and they prop Salus into a sitting position outside the cell. Mira ignores them and forces a grip on the shaft with her bloodied hands, recoiling slightly as the pain from her lacerations flare. Her blood spills down the shaft, following the engraved patterns. It seems to absorb the blood, but she pays it no mind until the conch on the end of the scepter emits a bluish-green glow.

She hesitates, holding the scepter above her companion. Not knowing whether it will do more harm, she has qualms about the outcome.

She taps Tanniv with the conch at the end of the scepter. Nothing happens. She taps again, a little harder, making sure to contact flesh, unknowing if it makes a difference. Nothing happens.

Mira's shoulders slump. She drops the scepter with a clang on the metal deck, and waves off the former neophytes to continue dragging Salus away. She cannot have him in her sight, right now. She kneels beside her companion. "I'm sorry, Tanniv. I didn't mean for this." She closes her eyes and withholds tears with a slow exhale.

"Didn't mean for what?"

Mira's eyes snap open.

"You have any food?" he says as he rises to a sitting position.

Mira bursts forward with a smile and embraces him.

"Hey Mira…" The voice isn't Tanniv's.

"Haltuk!" She lets go of Tanniv and turns to see Haltuk standing near the door. She hops to her fins.

"How could you, Mira?" Tanniv jests from the floor. "You're leaving me for *him*?" He falls back to the floor in theatrical fashion.

Mira hesitates out of confusion, not understanding the joke. She waves Tanniv off and hurries to embrace Haltuk. "You're alive," she whispers to him.

"Of course." He pulls back.

"I saw your lifeless body. You died, Haltuk. I didn't know if it was only the Ebisu's machina magic keeping you alive, or if you would truly wake up from this nightmare." She leans in to hug him once more.

"Okay, okay." He pushes her away. "You're alive, too. Now, how do we stay that way?" He looks around the cell with a wave of his hand, gesturing to the conundrum he's awoken to.

Mira looks to Tiolas for answers. "Salus notified the General. A battalion is headed this way. Is there another exit other than the stairs we came in from?"

Tiolas looks around the cell, pondering the options. "I…" He steps out onto the skywalk, overlooking the growing crowd below.

Mira helps Tanniv to his fins and they follow him out to the skywalk.

"I don't believe there is." Tiolas' voice is quiet and full of worry. "This place was designed to secure the neophytes. In case of an insurrection, they needed to limit the exits." He leans against the metal rail, his hands gripping it tightly.

"What about down? Is there anything beneath us aside from ocean waters?"

Tiolas turns to face her, his face distorted. "You're proposing we make our own exit? And swim to safety?"

"Yes." Her answer is confident as if they have already made the decision. "Unless you would rather play with the Ebisu army with our waking, ill-prepared rebels?"

"We would lose half to the blade and the other half would be re-enslaved." His lips flatten as he turns back to the rail looking over them. "How do you propose we make an exit?"

"The Ebisu are the elves with the machina magic." She inspects the scepter she forgot she was holding. "I'm sure you can figure something out."

"A hole in the shell would flood the outpost," he says.

"Not if the air continues to pump into it. What does it matter, anyhow?"

"There are other rebels, Mira." His face turns sour. "And soldiers with families who fight not for the General or Lord Tenebrous, but for those they hold dear. They don't all deserve to die."

"Then what do you intend to do once you've freed all these slaves? Hide? I thought you were building an army of your own. A rebellion?"

"We need to cut off the head of the beast. If we can do that, the remaining threats will reveal themselves. It won't be many. We don't need to kill them all."

"This conversation is beyond us," she says. "Let's focus on getting out of here. Assuming we *do* get out, we can take refuge within the Knuckles of Morshine. Lord Tenebrous knows we're there now, but access is limited, just like this halfway house. It will be secure."

"And what of the demigod?" Tiolas asks. "You heard the message?"

"We'll have to take our chances."

33 THE FATE OF THE REALM

Lady Fae floats into the Ohmsmire's grand hall. Not literally, but the combination of her elegance and her flowing gown make it as such. Yester accompanies her, tailing close behind, as they are ushered by servants of House Ohmsmire to a large table filled with beautiful arrangements of flowers and a savory meal. House Arilight and its underhouses will dine this evening with many conversations to be had regarding the Godmadinas and their willingness to undermine the Elder House. A stratagem must be put into action, or their place in this realm will fade away into the sea of clouds.

Chrigan Ohmsmire and Dunbell Jonesook, the patriarchs of their houses, rise as the two maiden elves approach the table. As does Smika Ohmsmire, first born son of Chrigan and Jothra. All the lady elves in attendance remain seated but offer kind, welcoming expressions.

The servants push in their chairs as they sit, and the gentle elves wait to seat themselves until Lady Fae and Yester are comfortably situated.

Chrigan sits opposite Lady Fae at the head of the table and his wife, Jothra, to his right. Smika Ohmsmire, their son, sits to his left. Immediately to Lady Fae's left is her daughter, Haley Jonesook and her husband, Dunbell Jonesook. Across from them to Lady Fae's right sits Yester, Vinbell Jonesook, and Mabell Jonesook, both granddaughters of Lady Fae's. It is a family event.

The house servants begin dishing out the first course.

"Thank you for the invitation, Chrigan. I trust you are comfortable with me bringing Yester along to this house invite. She has been with House Arilight too long for me to not consider her family."

"Of course, Elder Fae," Chrigan replies earnestly. He makes eye contact with Yester. "Lady Yester is always expected." He smiles at her as she mouths a thank you, then turns his attention back to Lady Fae. "So…it's true, then? Jarnes and Riveria have abandoned us?"

"Abandoned? Goodness, no. Riveria was subdued by a Godmadina scepter, then they were taken from us by that beastly De'wi."

Yester noticeably shifts in her seat at the comment. She shed a few tears when she realized she may never see Jarnes again, but she holds her composure now.

"Stolen! By our champion?" Vinbell speaks with astonishment. "He was so kind… and modest… and… handsome." Vinbell's gaze finds her plate of food, her cheeks turning red after her admission.

"Yes, he was all those things *and* deceptive," Lady Fae adds. "A good reminder of why we keep to the sky and let them have the Terra Realm. Our worlds don't belong together."

"Yet we send two of our best beyond the Terra Realm, and into the ocean," Chrigan says. "I know I agreed to the envoy, but my gut doesn't. It has left me uneasy since our sons departed."

"Paka and Horbell will do fine. They have a small guard, and all were armed with their scepters. If the Ebisu threaten them in any way, they can easily display the dominance of our machina."

"Aye, but it is not your son who was sent away into another realm, now was it, mother?" Jothra, an elegant elf maiden with dark features, carries all the beauty of her mother and all her brazenness, too.

Haley, who also shares her mother's beauty with slightly darker features, joins the conversation. "Yes, mother, I would have to agree with Jothra. It is easy to dismiss the gravity of the situation when it is not your own sons sticking their necks out."

"They are my grandsons!" Anger takes hold of Lady Fae's tone. She inhales a deep breath, calming herself. "To say I would willingly toss them to the leviathans is an insult. I understand the graveness of what we are trying to accomplish. The future of our realm is threatened by the Ebisu, and your sons have taken on a brave role in trying to negotiate the boundaries of what is rightfully ours. I do not take this situation lightly, but I *am* confident that they will be successful. If any harm *does* come to them, we have the means to enforce the consequences."

"You mean revenge?" Smika questions.

Jothra scoffs at her mother from across the table. "So, you wait for harm to come to our children before you will show our dominance."

"That is not what I said." Lady Fae doesn't withhold a glare of her own. "These matters are delicate. War is an intricate weave of hearts, pride, and ambition. The slightest misstep will provoke the rage that dwells within all elves. Look at the lengths the Godmadinas are willing to go to in order to secure their future. The heir to House Arilight is lying unconscious somewhere, only remedied by using the same scepter she was attacked with. They. Attacked an heir. Of House Arilight! And if we don't act quickly, Riveria may remain in that unconscious state for eternity. We don't know the long-term effects of that machina power. And that's the least of it. They stepped on our pride, knowingly undermining our authority to build an army of their own. An army of De'wi, the weakest of the races."

"Weakest?" Dunbell speaks up for the first time. "I heard our champion slayed a leviathan."

Lady Fae sends a sharp glare his way. "And we secured that leviathan for him to slay, now didn't we?" Her words are feisty. "The De'wi would be slaughtered if they challenged our machina. They are inferior. But that is beside the point. Look how easily a house within our own realm provokes us. The Ebisu will not be as civilized with their reprisal. We must tread this matter lightly."

The table goes quiet, all the elves pondering what a battle would look like between the races.

"A spark has reignited the Machina War, hasn't it?" Chrigan asks.

Lady Fae responds. "A spark in the form of a dark elf with too much grudge coating his heart. Yes, unless we can finesse our way through these negotiations, I do think the Machina War has a new breath of air." Her lips part to say more, but she pauses, hesitant to speak what she has on her mind. "I would like to propose a different tone for these negotiations for when Paka and Horbell's envoy returns."

"And what is our current tactic?" Chrigan asks. "If these Ebisu only want to exact revenge for an ancient grudge, what do we have to offer them in return?"

"They also want our Tears. Don't forget that."

"Are you suggesting we give them our valuable resources *and* let them start a war with the De'wi?" He glowers at her.

"I am suggesting we work with the Ebisu to retrieve our imprisoned family members. Then we deal with the Godmadinas."

"One of which you have only known for weeks." Jothra adds.

"And one of which is your brother!" Lady Fae's tone is aroused. "These are your kin. You would have the De'wi steal them away and not do whatever is within your power to get them back home safely? The Ebisu can do that for us. And I am prepared to offer a crop of Tears for such a trade."

"They have already taken that crop, Elder Fae," Dunbell reminds everyone. "So, do we offer yet another crop of Tears? What would that do to our society? The lesser houses would revolt. We already have that small rebellion to deal with in House Orillian. By doing this you would make more enemies within our own city, and even across our realm amongst the other landships." Dunbell shakes his head, his long nose like the beak of a squawking lorikeet. "I don't much agree with that tactic."

"Dunbell is right," Chrigan says with a soft tone. "If the Ebisu's rage already stirs and thirsts for revenge, we have nothing to offer them. Offering them Tears will only harm our own society. We shall not work with them. They are an evil that needs to be dealt with in a different way. We must suppress their rage and tame the beast before we mount it and ride into battle."

"And how do you suggest we tame it?" Elder Fae scowls, her disapproval finding everyone at the table, regardless of whether they challenge her word.

"We wait for the envoy to arrive," Chrigan answers, "and we ask their Elder what it is he wants. Then we decide from there. We make too many assumptions about what drives these elves. Let us confirm before we make any decisions on this matter."

The room goes quiet. Not one elf has consumed the meal sitting before them. A few of the younger elves poke around at their plates, not wanting to challenge their elders' authority.

A soft voice breaks the silence. "If my opinion holds any weight...I would like to rescue Jarnes." Yester's voice sounds like a mouse in an abandoned dwelling, quiet, yet loud enough for all to hear at the same time.

"As would I," Lady Fae agrees with her, but not without a disapproving glare. Her son and Yester cannot be trusted in the same room together. Perhaps, she could be bartered. No. What would the De'wi want with an Indran handmaid. "Riveria, too," she adds.

"Then I would suggest you find other means to rescue them," Chrigan says. "Sacrificing resources that belong to our entire realm is not the way to go about it. I know they are kin, and Jarnes deserves all our efforts to get him home safely, but your plan would create too many enemies close to home. You would damage our society for the sake of your own house."

"I would." Lady Fae picks up her fork and takes a bite of her meal, parking the conversation for further discussion when the envoy arrives.

34 RISE OF THE REBELLION

*D*e'wi, Ebisu, and Indra all have something in common on this day. They have all been imprisoned by Lord Tenebrous and his war-mongering ideology. The newly released prisoners recover on the floor of the vast chamber while others join in to help release the remaining war slaves. A common goal is shared amongst the three races for the first time in centuries: to escape the machina enslavement of Lord Tenebrous.

The din of the chatting survivors is overrun by a soft roll of war drums echoing through the chamber. It comes from the stairwell—their only known exit. Time is limited. Mira and her companions, all four back together again, have abandoned the task of releasing the prisoners, and instead focus on a means to escape. Tiolas and Rela included.

"Tanniv!" Mira calls to her companion, who's trotting down the line of cells looking for an exit.

He halts and looks around, unsure where she called from. Mira waves an arm to get his attention, and to wave him closer. She stands near the middle of the chamber amidst the neophytes recovering from their time spent without a will of their own. From the bit of small talk she's had with a few of them, they don't recall anything from their time as a slave. They don't know how long they've been imprisoned without a mind of their own, but their memories from a past life seem to be emerging from the fogginess they're currently experiencing.

"We need to bar the entrance," she says as Tanniv approaches.

"Lock ourselves in like a guppy in one of those aquariums upstairs?"

"Yes, like a guppy in a sea tank." She shakes her head, not truly understanding what she just agreed to. "The cots in the cells." She nods to him.

"Consider it done." He beats his chest and turns to charge toward the stairwell.

"And Tanniv!" she calls after him. "Let's build a wall, too. Just on the other side of the control panel, so we can continue to release the neophytes."

"Yes, chief!" He sprints off.

Mira turns back to analyze the chamber from a distance. Four levels of skywalks. Walls lined with bars. Only one way in and out that they're aware of. No weapons aside from the few Tanniv and Veras brought, Tiolas' trident, and the scepter Mira stole from Salus. How are they going to escape from this alive or with their minds intact?

"I think I've found a way!" Veras shouts from a long distance away, near the edge of the vast chamber. "These floor panels. There's a maintenance shaft of some kind beneath them. It looks promising."

The others rush to see what he's discovered, including Tanniv. Her brow tightens at the sight of him, but her loose authority permits it when she also sees some of the neophytes building a wall with cots. They stack them on their sides, two tall and reinforce them with a third and fourth, making elf-sized cubes of sorts. It's flimsy at best but will at least act as a deterrent. If only they had bows or harpoons, they could line the skywalks and attack from high ground. Wishful thinking.

Veras lifts a panel from the floor and tosses it to the side with a loud, tinny clank.

"Indeed, maintenance tunnels just as you said," Tiolas confirms.

"Where do they lead?" Mira asks.

"Everywhere. I've only accessed them on the other side, near the barracks, but my understanding is that they span the distance of the outpost in all directions."

"Escape the halfway house and find an exit on the other side," Mira says. "Then make a quick dash through the gaping hole the grendelins made in the dome. Worth a shot?" She looks around at the group standing above the hole in the floor, waiting for some form of confirmation.

"It's tiny and dark," Rela says with concern. "A single line of prisoners is all we could fit."

"And we'll have more than a thousand by the time they're all released." Veras waves his arms to the various cells surrounding them on all sides of the chamber.

"That could take hours," Haltuk adds. "Is there not a quicker way?"

"Tanniv, you have any more grendelins in your back pocket?" Mira asks him. "We could smash another hole in the wall."

Tanniv pats the leather pouches at his hips. His lips flatten. "Nope. All out. Sorry. I've got this, though." He makes a fist and flexes his bicep with a grunt.

Mira smiles at him. He's a good companion to have around in dire moments.

The soft thrumming of drums beat louder, thundering through the chamber. The growing crowd in the halfway house, once boisterous and filled with the excitement of pending freedom, silences. Faint war chants harmonize with the pulsing drums as the prisoners all freeze and wait for their impending doom. Freedom, now looking bleak.

"They're on their way, just as Salus said they would be. We're out of time." She swings her arm at Veras and Tanniv. "Get the neophytes moving!" She looks up at the dark rebellious Ebisu. "Tiolas, you lead the way, since you seem to be most familiar with these tunnels."

"Will do." He hops into the underfloor channel without any hesitation and looks up at her. "I'll scout ahead to remove any obstructions. Get the neophytes coming, and I'll be back in time to guide them." He disappears beneath the floor.

Rela, Veras, and Tanniv hurry toward the crowd to usher the prisoners. Haltuk stands back with Mira, awaiting orders.

"How are you feeling?" she asks him.

"Like I've awoken from a dreamless, century-long sleep. Just as you could imagine." He stretches his arms outward, then over his head, followed by an arching back. The bandage around his neck is soaked in blood. They don't have enough Tears to help them all heal, but they have plenty of linens to wrap them up.

"You tried to kill me, you know." She narrows her gaze on him.

"Err…sorry. I didn't mean it."

"Don't worry. I'll hold it over you for as long as I can." She smirks. "C'mon. Let's get these elves into line."

The companions usher the freed prisoners to the tunnel beneath the floor. Tall and dark Ebisu, short and plump Indra, and too many De'wi get in line. Rela and Veras help to drop each elf into the hole, one at a time. Haltuk, Tanniv, and Mira guide them into a single file line until the mass of the crowd understands what's happening. Then, they begin directing themselves.

The three companions stand at the rear of the crowd, staring back at the entrance to the stairwell. All three in a warrior's stance—shoulders square, hands laced behind their back, fins shoulder-width apart. Disciplined, dutiful, determined. Rela and Veras join them, only Rela refuses to stand at attention.

A wall of cots divides the chamber. Tanniv must have recruited half the neophytes to get it built so quickly. It will act as an annoyance more than a barrier, but anything to offer them more time to escape is beneficial. More cots and mattresses continue to fly from the upper skywalks, crashing and thudding as they land. Neophytes continue to rush in and retrofit them into the wall.

By Mira's best judgement, at least three quarters of the neophytes have been released from their cells. Several dozen freed prisoners scramble along the skywalks working to save the remainder. If only it were as simple as opening the doors, but each prisoner requires three or four elves to restrain the Neophyte and remove the implants. They're making good headway. If only they can fend off the incoming battalion long enough to free them all.

"Horbell!" Paka, her Indran cellmate, rushes to the other Indra who they believed was lost to the trials. He's alive, just like Haltuk. Their moment of elation puts a tired smile on Mira's face. And more Indra join in their reunion. They must be the rest of the envoy Paka mentioned.

"Did we find any of our own clanmates down here?" she asks Tanniv as he walks up beside her. He's not the tall, handsome elf he was back in the Terra Realm. His dark hair is distraught. He has sweat and scuffs covering his forehead and muscled jawline. And overall, he looks warn. "You look like you've been to hell and back, by the way." She smiles at him.

"Haven't quite made it back, yet." Tanniv smirks. "Casseya, Nicolas, and Mischielly to name a few. Not knowing all who were abducted makes it a challenge to locate them all, so we have to take what we can get."

Mira's face hardens. What else can she expect. "Very good, Tanniv. Thank you."

"Hey! Don't be thanking me. I'm not the one who got us into this mess. You should be thanking yourself." He swings a wide arm to pat her on the shoulder, but she ducks with another smile.

The drums grow louder. A blue and green glow bounces off the walls at the base of the stairwell and grows brighter with every moment that passes. The thunder of the drums rolls beneath their fins, sending shivers of vibrations into their bones. It draws fear, yet the warriors stand ready. Ready to defend the livelihood of these enslaved natives and elves of all races. Ready to defeat General Merces and his maliciously aligned virtues.

The Ebisu soldiers spill into the vast chamber two at a time, for that is all the entrance will allow. They form lines. Like properly trained soldiers, none think for themselves. Not while they're on duty. A trained soldier is not so different from an enslaved one. They are controlled by one mind. It just happens to be a distasteful mind. One that will murder the innocent because of a thousand-year-old grudge.

"We defend, understood?" Mira says to them, speaking mostly to the three companions from her clan. "This has become bigger than our mission to unveil the Ebisu's weaknesses and motives. This is an opportunity to make an impact in this war we didn't know we were fighting. These prisoners need our help. An honorable warrior defends the weak. A determined warrior will see it through. We defend until every one of these elves drops into that tunnel. Heart, strength, mind, and soul." She pounds the left side of her chest, then the right. She grips her mind and pulls it into her gut. "Let's show them what a De'wi warrior is capable of!"

Tanniv grips his yari and hollers. Veras hesitantly follows suit, obviously calculating the odds of five warriors against the unknown number of soldiers filling the chamber. Rela and Haltuk join Tanniv in his war cry but have nothing other than their fists and their strength. At least Haltuk is armored with the Ebisu's standard issue, Tear-augmented breastplate. He's smaller than the Ebisu, but it will offer enough strength to give him a fighting chance. Mira continues to wield the metallic scepter she stole from Salus. It holds an incredible amount of power, but what good is one metal stick against an army.

"When the General arrives, he is our target," Mira commands without taking her eyes off the growing mass of soldiers on the other side of their makeshift wall. "If an opportunity arises, do not hesitate to take his life."

Prisoners fill in behind the five companions, creating a wall of bodies between the assailing soldiers and the prisoners attempting to get away. A large distance separates the good and the bad, with each group anticipating the other from across the massive chamber. Soldiers versus a rebellious band of warriors.

"What's going to stop the General from putting another battalion on the tunnel's exit?" Veras asks. He has a good point, and Mira doesn't have an answer.

"There are multiple exits to those tunnels," Rela answers for her. "They'll have to divide and conquer."

"If Tiolas is quick enough getting them through the tunnels, they should be able to put up a defense wherever they exit. Are there any armories they could raid?" Mira looks to Rela for more answers.

She shrugs. "Depends on where they surface. Let's hope Tiolas has the mind to pick the exit with armaments nearby."

The war drums are heavier than ever. The chanting is loud and clear. Then, abrupt silence. A silence more impactful than the thrum of their drums. A silence that causes their nerves to scream in agony over the unknown fate of the day.

The soldiers shout war cries and charge ahead. They sprint at full speed with trident tips leading the assault. The prisoners and Ebisu rebels stand firm behind their feeble wall of metal bed frames, unarmed and ready to die for the lives they can save. Ready to die to avoid going back to being war slaves.

"Here they come!" Mira shouts, hoping those dropping into the tunnel will find more urgency.

Hardly a ruckus is made when they collide with the wall. The muffled sound of metal clanging against metal and minor shrieks of metal scraping across the floor is accompanied by war cries diluting into grunts. It's as if the battalion came here to rearrange the furniture. No blades clashing, nor screams of agony from frontliners falling victim to war. Only soft slices and hacks as the innards of the bed mats fly.

A trident impales the bed mat directly in front of Mira and rips it away from the metal frame. The cots come tumbling down, one by one, and Ebisu soldiers trip over the mess of furniture. Mira uses the opportunity to thwack as many soldiers as she can with her stick. The screams of agony begin, and soldiers start dropping instantly.

Tanniv and Veras join her in attacking the guards that find their way through the rubble. Bodies pile before them. Arms and legs entangle with the mess of cots and the unarmed prisoners steal away their tridents, increasing their odds. But their defense doesn't last long.

The more thoughtful soldiers don't attack the wall. They push it out of the way and create openings. Ebisu and De'wi reforms bombard them as they do, pushing back against the wall, but it turns bloody too quick as tridents pierce the cots and drop the defending elves.

The wall becomes useless as more Ebisu soldiers learn from their comrades and mimic their actions. The wall is breached.

"Fall back!" Mira shouts. "There's nothing you can do against their tridents."

Chaos ensues at the halfway house. Elves climb the stairs to the skywalks. Some leap from the rails into the crowd of assailants while others charge down the long path to escape behind them. Prisoners scream, ushering each other with more urgency until it becomes pushing and trampling to get to the escape route.

More prisoners climb the stairs to escape, and the Ebisu soldiers do the same, blocking pathways where they can. A few prisoners find cells and wait out their inevitable imprisonment with the dire situation erupting.

Mira refuses to break. She cannot let the Ebisu and their malicious machina win this battle. She must make a dent in their warring ethos, enough to send a message to Lord Tenebrous that the De'wi will not go silently.

A trident gashes her right arm, sending her stumbling backward. She pushes past the pain as blood drenches her forearm and drains onto the staff, making a slick grip.

A roar of frustration bellows from deep within her and she unleashes a flogging on all the soldiers in her vicinity. Her scepter wheels in a circle over her head, fully extended to maximize her reach, knocking heads and slapping breastplates. Elves fall limp all around her.

She halts her actions when she sees the end of her scepter glowing with the iridescence of the Blue Tears. It doesn't always glow. Only when she wields it with intention. A mass of bodies encircles her as more Ebisu soldiers gather around, hesitant to get within range of her attacks.

"Warriors of the Knuckles of Morshine, fall behind me!" She hollers at the crowd of bodies, unsure where her companions are. "Tanniv Windstalker! Haltuk Coradrin!" She swings the scepter at the encroaching Ebisu. "Fall behind me!" She back peddles, working her way closer to the tunnel entrance. "Veras Elreid!"

"I've got you, Mira!" Haltuk flanks her on the right.

"As do I." Tanniv joins her on the left.

"The remaining prisoners are on their own," she says. "They've made choices to abandon the plan. We can no longer protect them."

Three quarters have escaped into the tunnel system, while more wait to drop in, and Mira defends the last of them. But others circle around the chaos high on the skywalks and attempt to escape through the stairwell. They are forced to suffer the consequences of their own actions. Ebisu soldiers scatter throughout the chamber, a frenzy of pursuit and wrestling with those unwilling to go back to slavery.

"Where's Veras?" she asks, her voice heavy and determined.

"Behind you, Mira," he replies.

She whips around with her glowing scepter firmly in her grip. The conch on the end is swift with her movements and swings right past Veras, who stands rather close to her. "Damn, Veras! Be careful. This thing is beyond my control. Don't want you—" She lunges forward after being knocked in the back by her companions who continue to fend off the Ebisu threat. The conch slams into Veras' forehead and he drops to the ground instantly.

"Jelly spittle, Mira! What'd you do to him?" Tanniv yells over his shoulder while swinging his yari out in front of him.

"I... I... It was an accident." She gives the scepter an evil glance, but she cannot let go of it. Not in a crowd like this where anyone could pick it up and wield it's power. Why would the Indra make such a weapon?

"Mira, we need to get out of here, now!" Haltuk shouts. He has nothing to defend himself save for a metal rod from a cot. It's hardly effective.

"Here!" She tosses Veras' yari to Haltuk and he immediately transforms into an effective warrior.

"Where's Rela?" she shouts, as she rises swinging her scepter to fend off the Ebisu.

A loud roar fills the chamber, its source unknown. A bed mat flies from the upper skywalks. It crashes into the mass of soldiers before them. Atop it, an angry and violent Ebisu rebel, ready to murder anyone who challenges her. She rises to her fins wielding two tridents. "I'm here, Mira. Let's get out of here."

The four companions defend Veras and the last of the prisoners dropping into the hole until it is their turn.

"Can you carry him?" Mira asks of Tanniv.

"Of course?" Veras and Tanniv disappear into the tunnels. Then Haltuk.

"Too many Ebisu remain standing," Mira says to Rela. "Someone must stay and fight. Get out of here!" She knocks one of the soldiers across the chin and he falls limp.

"Don't be absurd!"

Mira is yanked off her fins and finds herself falling, followed by a painful crash into the tunnel below. Rela drops in right behind her.

"We'll do better defending the rear from in here where our pursuers can only fit two abreast," she says. "Get up!"

Mira climbs to her fins with a sneer on her face. She doesn't much appreciate being tossed around, but part of her is grateful. And Rela's fighting spirit is contagious.

The two follow the group of escapees, back peddling to keep their eyes on the chase. Mira doesn't have any issues standing upright, but Rela, with an extra head in height, must crouch. The tight space combined with somewhere around a thousand prisoners ahead of them keeps the pace slow. They will defend as long as they must.

Ebisu soldiers drop into the tunnel soon after. They keep their distance, unwilling to get too close to Mira's scepter after witnessing the power it wields. They follow at close range with knees bent and necks lowered, anticipating an opportunity.

Neither side speaks to the other. They snarl. They smirk. They behave as if they are rival gangs of the same clan competing for superiority—dominance the goal, not death. The outcome of this is much more dire than that, unfortunately, but the tunnel limits their actions.

The escape is slow and awkward. Mira jabs her scepter occasionally to maintain their separation. When they get to the end of the tunnel, she'll have to fight them. What other choice will she have? It's inevitable. By waiting, she can ensure the rest of the escapees get out.

"How long *is* this tunnel?" Mira whispers to Rela, not taking her eyes off the Ebisu threat.

"Too long. Shall we engage?"

Mira is silent for a moment. Waiting can ensure the prisoners get out, but fighting has the potential to end the chase altogether. "If we act quickly, we can create a blockade of bodies. Pile them high." She shrugs her shoulders.

"I'm in." Rela lunges forward. "C'mon!" She leaves Mira stunned in her wake, but she hastily joins the charge. The decision is made for her.

The Ebisu put up arms, but lack of room prevents an authentic defense. One of Rela's tridents sneaks right in and ricochets off armor. She's quick to retract it, and Mira follows right behind her with a jab of her glowing scepter. It, too, has no impact on the armor.

"Careful!" one of the soldiers calls to the rest. "Don't let the De'wi scum throttle you with her machina."

"Machina…" she mutters under her breath as she retreats to a defensive position. She hadn't thought of it as such. Machina is powered with the Blue Tears, but its intent advances society and tears down tradition. Weapons are not machina… Are they? Her mind drifts to the cerulean steel her father wields. The thought challenges everything she thought she knew about the De'wi and the Ebisu. If machina is defined by Blue Tears, then her father, the Elder of her clan, has been denying their traditions for hundreds of years. Denying traditions he has fought to defend his entire life.

She lets the thought simmer as they continue to back pedal into an open space with the walkway splitting and circling around a large opening into the ocean waters. "What is this?" Mira asks.

"Jelly spittle! It's the access bay used to transport larger sea life in and out of the outpost. We must hold our ground here or risk being overcome."

"Larger sea life like the…"

"The demigod the General released. Yes. This is where he housed it… fed it…" Rela jabs at Ebisu to keep them back. The soldiers keep their distance.

"Enslaved it," Mira adds with a grunt while she swings her scepter. She steps back and feels the edge of the platform with the heel of her fin. One more step and she'll plunge into the water with that sea demon. "It's not in there, though, right? He released it to battle the grendelins, right?"

Rela's eyes dart in her direction, uncertainty and skepticism embedded in them. "He only releases the demigod to attack the De'wi colonies, Mira."

Mira swings her scepter mindlessly, focused on the words Rela just said. If the demigod was released… What other clan is in the vicinity? That demigod is headed toward the Knuckles of Morshine. "We must get out of here, Rela. We must get out of here, now!"

A surge of anger flows through Mira and into the swing of her scepter. She lands a blow on an Ebisu soldier, smacking him in the jaw and dropping him cold.

"Mira, c'mon!" a voice shouts from behind her, somewhere on the other side of the access bay. It sounded like Tanniv, but she's hesitant to take her eyes off the Ebisu to confirm.

Rela's trident deflects off the breastplate of an Ebisu and rips through her arm. The soldier screams in pain, and another steps into the front line of the tunnel to replace her. "It's too late, Mira. The demigod was released hours ago. It could already be there."

"Hardly!" Mira's tone is full of wrath. She takes it out on another Ebisu soldier, slamming him in the gut, then striking upward across his jaw. He flies backward into the soldiers behind him. "It took us weeks to get here. Impossible that it could already be there."

"Think of how large it is. You saw it, right? That creature isn't natural, Mira. It's a weapon handed to the Ebisu from Ceto himself. It can traverse the depths of the ocean with ease. We need to focus on what's in front of us. On what's within our control."

An enemy trident stabs toward Mira. She deflects it and undercuts the dark elf's legs. The blow makes his legs useless, and he crumples to the ground on top of another body. Rela follows up with a strike of a trident, gashing another's abdomen. It's the start of a slew of attacks. Mira and Rela unleash on the Ebisu soldiers, dominating the limited space within the tunnel opening, thanks to the power of the Indran scepter and Rela's fierce duo of tridents.

Mira lets down her guard when it looks as if no more soldiers have entered the tunnel in pursuit of them.

Rela breathes a heavy sigh. "Fools should know better than to fight me."

Mira wants to ask her what she means, but she's focused on getting out. "Why go back to the surface when we can escape right here?"

"Too dangerous," Rela responds while she fastens her tridents to the harness on her back. "We pump air into this outpost, which presents the challenge of pumping air out. Otherwise…pop!" She gestures an explosion with her hands. "You see that gentle current on the surface." Rela points toward the edge of the pool.

"I do."

"Toxic air is pumped into the water and is released outside the barrier of the outpost. It's gentle here at the surface, but as you get deeper it grows stronger. At the bottom of that pool where it exits into the vast depths of the big blue, that current will suck you out and spit you into a darkness you'd never escape from. Knowing which way is up or down, left or right is impossible. It's a maze without borders. It's not an option."

"Hmm…" Mira isn't convinced, but to throttle all the prisoners into another place they don't want to go might prove impossible.

"Mira, watch out!" Tanniv yells from the tunnel on the other side of the pool.

Mira and Rela both spin around, and Mira is the unlucky one who finds herself knocked off her fins by a lone, persistent Ebisu soldier. She spills into the pool and the current immediately pulls at her body.

35 Danger in the Shallows

"How is he not dead? His wounds are fatal. Chunks of flesh have been torn from his legs and arms. An ear is half gone. Missing digits on his hand. Too much blood has been spilt. The salty waters helped to slow the bleeding, but death is inevitable. Tears will *not* help him."

Gallagher wakes. The fog of a heavy sleep keeps his eyes closed as his mind and senses try to fend it off. The conversation continues.

"We must try." A maiden elf fights for his survival. "Look at the sacrifice he has given his clan."

"And why does he continue to wield a blade within your infirmary, Bailey?"

"I haven't figured out how to release his grip of it. I've tried many tactics. Wedges. Grease. Pincers. Fire."

"Fire?"

"His body is already mutilated. I didn't think it would make a difference. When it didn't, I used the flame to cauterize the nastier wounds."

Gallagher doesn't feel the pain of the wounds they discuss.

He raises the blade and pounds the pommel on the cot he lies on. It's too soft. The blade remains armed, stuck within his grip.

"Gallagher!" Her voice is kind and soft.

His eyes flutter open shaking off the last remnants of sleep. His body is tense. Stiff. He pounds the pommel into his palm with just enough vigor. The blade falls from his grasp, and suddenly he is overwhelmed with excruciating pain. A loud moan blasts through the infirmary and to the world outside. Gallagher isn't sure, but he suspects the noise came from him.

"Elder Rayfin! You can clearly see the stones with your own eyes. By all traditions and merit, he has rightfully earned this."

"Alright, alright. Give him the Tears."

The pain is too much. He closes his eyes and the world around him fades.

"Hello, Gallywog."

Gallagher opens his eyes and instantly narrows his gaze as Andolas pulls back the curtain of his secluded corner in the infirmary. His pain and suffering don't allow him any escape from this elf, unfortunately. He's confined to his cot and must listen to whatever mud flings from Andolas' mouth.

"What are you doing here?"

"I'm here to tighten your manacles."

Gallagher balls his fists as he looks down at his ankles, but he doesn't get the full satisfaction of a tightened fist because his muscles don't allow it. He's not wearing any manacles. He had to take a second look to be sure, though. There hasn't been any discussion regarding his banishment, so it's not far-fetched.

Andolas finds a subtle grin. "Jesting, of course." He struts closer to Gallagher with solid eye contact. "I want to...err...I want to..." He pulls his gaze away and looks at the cot while crossing his hands in front of his waist. "I'm sorry, Gallywog."

Gallagher's face distorts and his jaw tightens. "Sorry?" Another jest. Gallagher is in no mood to tolerate his cruelty. "You can leave now."

"Don't make this harder than it is." His distant gaze turns into a hard stare. "I'm fully responsible for everything that has become of you, Gallywo...err...Gallagher. I know I can do nothing to change what is done, but I want you to know there isn't a Solari Harvest or a day of sparring that goes by when I don't think of the warrior you could've become. The Warrior's Guild would have been a better place with you to elevate us all to a higher stone."

Andolas' mere presence brings Gallagher much tension, and his words aren't making it any better. "Why are you saying this? What's your angle, Andolas? We both know I made the choice to dive into the canyon to retrieve the spice. You had nothing to do with any of this?"

"I pushed you into the water when you were a youngkin. It was that action that started this all."

It's the first time Andolas has ever admitted to pushing him. "I know. Or at least...I suspected as much."

"Had I not pushed you, you would have never become a blight on the colony. Had I not pushed you, you would have become the renowned warrior you were meant to be. Had I not pushed you... you would never have been banished and forced to rescue Rivee. And now——"

"Rivee Rayfin!" Gallagher interrupts him. "Did she get the Tears I recovered for her. Did she get them?" The moment of excitement draws pain, and he sinks back into his cot.

"I don't know. They have her in the shallows doing a rinsing ritual."

"The shallows!" Gallagher suddenly recalls the leviathan he witnessed in the canyon and the Ebisu accompanying it. "The Ebisu are here! They need to get out of the water. The guild. Prepare the guild!"

"Gallagher, what are you saying? Have you lost your mind along with all that meat?"

Gallagher quiets, recalling the massive scales swimming past him. "I saw... It was the largest leviathan I have ever seen. A creature from the depths of hell."

"A leviathan? I thought you just said Ebisu?"

"Both." Gallagher cuts his gaze to Andolas. "They were swimming in the direction of our colony. Whoever pulled me from the depths would have crossed paths with them."

Andolas twitches. "I saw nothing. Whatever you think you saw, you must be mistaken. Maybe those eels stole a chunk of your noggin." He taps on his head.

"Wait... You?"

Andolas rolls his eyes. "Yes, but I didn't see these Ebisu or this leviathan you speak of."

"I'm telling you I saw them."

"Even if I did believe you, do you think Elder Rayfin would? Or any of the Elders? You'd have to charge into the ocean on your own again."

"Then that's what I'll do. Can you fetch my blade for me?"

"What?" Andolas' lips flatten. "That's absurd. Look at you. You're a mess. The guppies would devour you in seconds, let alone a leviathan bigger than any that has ever existed. You're fish fodder, Gallywog. You can't go back into the waters."

"Andolas! If you want to repay me for the damage you've done... If you want to relieve yourself for the hardship you've forced upon me, please...go find my blade."

A heavy sigh blows out of him. "Okay." He turns away from Gallagher and combs loose strands of hair from his face. "I'll find your blade. But if you find your way back into the ocean, it wasn't me who pushed you this time." He struts toward the exit.

"Oh, and Andolas..."

"Yes?" He looks over his shoulder.

"Any sign of Mira? Has she returned?"

Andolas shakes his head in silence, then removes himself from the infirmary.

Gallagher waits patiently, but only because he has no other choice. His body won't allow him to rise from his cot. Treading through the air is a possibility, but the initial push to get himself off the ground is impossible.

He fiddles with his fingers tapping on the stubs of the missing digits. He scratches at the linens. He pokes at the open sores covering his body, flinching with each jab. Most have sealed with Bailey's help, but to regrow the sinew he's lost would be impossible.

He waits.

"It's been too long," he mutters to himself.

Andolas isn't coming back. Gallagher digs his elbows into the cot to shift his weight and tries to sit up. He manages to push himself right out of the cot with a hard crash on the wood planks below. The pain reverberates throughout his body.

"Gallagher!" a maiden's voice calls. It's not Bailey.

Lying face down, he sees two fins rush toward him. Then another pair of fins not too far behind.

"Gallagher, what are you trying to do?" It's Lady Nessa. "Can you help me get him back to his bed, Garrik?" Her request is more of a demand.

The two elves, with much struggle, heave him back into his cot. Lady Nessa leans over with two hands planted firmly into the mat. Garrik looks tired with heavy breathing, but he stands proud.

"I suppose we're not the youngkins we used to be," Nessa starts. "What were you trying to do?"

"I cannot wait around here any longer." Gallagher jumps right into it. "The Ebisu. I'm not sure why they haven't attacked yet, but they are here. And they bring destruction. Get everyone out of the water—"

"Gallagher, slow down," Garrik enforces his authority. "There have been no sightings of Ebisu."

"So you'll wait for the attack instead of being preemptive about it? Is Rivee still in the shallows or was Andolas not helpful in any way?"

"Rivee's rinsing is under way. Tradition, Gallagher. We cannot extract her on the whim of a possible Ebisu attack without any evidence. You were at the edge of your life. How could anything you witnessed be trustworthy?"

"Because I know what I saw."

She continues. "Several elves frolic about the waters while Bailey and the Elders tend to Rivee. We would be there as well, except Andolas refused to have it. He said your summoning was as urgent a matter as there could ever be and insisted we came, despite our attempts to shed him from the ritual."

"Will you stop the ritual if the result is opposite of what you intend? She could die. We need to get her out of the water. We need to get them all out." Gallagher tries to lift himself again. "Argh!" A boisterous scream escapes him. "I hate being blighted! I need my blade!" His voice is frantic and angry.

Garrik pulls the blade from a scabbard at his hip. "And what will you do with it, Gallagher? You're in no condition to battle anything. I doubt you can even swing this blade." The Elder admires it as he holds the sharp steel before him. "This steel is familiar. Certainly not made from a De'wi hand."

"Put it in my hand, please." Gallagher's voice calms. "Put it in my hand and you'll see."

"I had the smith insert your third stone. The one hanging about your neck. I hope you don't mind. I was going to wait to present this to you, but..." Garrik, careful not to touch the edge, delivers the blade to him, pommel first.

"It's not sharp. At least, not yet."

Lines press into the Elder's forehead. His confusion leaves him speechless.

Gallagher lets the pommel drop onto the bed mat with no effect. He was hoping to unsheathe the blade with ease, but he should have known better. He can hardly grip the sword let alone lift it, but with an arduous reach and a struggled fist, he pounds the end of the pommel.

The stones within the hilt glow between Gallagher's fingers. The sword locks onto his hand as if it has invisible tentacles curling up his arm. The revitalizing energy held within the stones pours into his body. His eyes open all the way. He straightens out his body, arcing his back and stretching while lying on the cot. He lifts his hands in the air and flops out of bed onto his fins with the finesse of a gliding ray. He stretches once more, pointing what toes and fingers he has left, and elevates his arms above his head. His attire isn't ideal for a battle as he only wears a malo and nothing more. No armor. But it will have to suffice.

"What kind of magic is this?" Lady Nessa whispers as her mouth hangs open.

"You're glowing!" Elder Rayfin crows and goes speechless after his outburst.

"I'm what?" Gallagher looks down at himself to see the aura of the Blue Tears faintly shimmering anywhere he has an open wound or a chunk of sinew missing. It's mild enough that it would be unnoticeable from a distance, but it's definitely glowing.

"It's machina magic!" Garrik's voice suddenly grows hoarse and violent. "Why do you continue to shame our traditions. Do you have no decency?" His fists ball as he folds his arms across his chest.

"I don't do this to disrespect any tradition or anyone. I do this because it's what must be done to save Rivee. That is all." He offers the Elder and Lady Nessa a curt bow. "Now, if you don't mind, I must be on my way. Thank you for bringing me my blade. I am in your debt." He doesn't wait for a response.

Gallagher leaves the infirmary in a hurry, zipping past other patients on his way out. He finds the shoreline with haste, and just as Mira's parents told him, the shallows are littered with romping elves, splashing and playing as if there isn't a danger in the world.

"Rivee Rayfin!" He spots her a short distance away from the crowd. The Elders swim by her side as she floats on her back. A small ration of Blue Tears surrounds her, making the water glow with a beautiful blue aura. Bailey is by her side as well.

Gallagher torpedoes through the air faster than a seadragon.

"Gallagher!" Bailey is the first to see him. He treads above the plain of the water looking down on them. "What are you doing out of bed?" She back-strokes to create distance between herself and Rivee. "How are you doing this? And your aura? Is this some kind of overdose? An allergic reaction, perhaps?"

The Elders turn to face him. Elder Falklan has a sour look on her face. Nothing out of the norm.

"We need to get her out of the water. The Ebisu are here!" Gallagher nudges forward, but Bailey puts herself in his way.

"I don't think so, Gallagher. What is going on? In all my years caring for the clan, I've never seen the Tears react this way in anyone. It was only a regular dose." Bailey rubs at her jawline in a pensive manner.

"You shouldn't be here, Gallagher. This is Rivee's rinsing. Not yours." Elder Falklan jabs a finger in his direction, then points to the horizon. "I don't care what kind of overdose you have. Get him out of here."

"Andolas mentioned something of an Ebisu attack when he summoned the Elder and Lady Nessa," Bailey cuts in. "He fled to the guild to recruit scouts upon Elder Rayfin's orders. There has been no word that we're under attack. The conches would have bellowed by now."

"There is a leviathan within those waters…" He points out to sea with his blade. "…capable of destroying our entire colony. And it's headed this way." His posture slouches. "Or at least it was before I became your charge."

"The scouts will address the matter, Gallagher." Mother Seya looks up at him and speaks with her soft, kind voice. "Nobody challenges your claims. In fact, quite the opposite. They search the perimeter. We will wait for word from the guild. Until then, Rivee's ritual will continue."

Gallagher looks out to sea, holding his gaze on the horizon. The diluted light from the eternal overcast reflects off the gentle swells rolling into the shoreline. Water as far as he can see. But if the Ebisu weren't headed to the Knuckles of Morshine to finish off his clan, then where were they headed?

His eagerness to jump into battle deflates and he lowers himself into the shallows to get to Bailey's level. "How is she doing? Is there anything more I can do?"

Bailey smiles at him, as does Mother Seya. Elder Falklan continues snarling. Bailey speaks. "You have done plenty, Gallagher. Without your heroic—"

"—and idiotic—" Elder Falklan spits out.

"Without your heroic efforts," she continues, "we wouldn't be able to perform the rinsing. And there was plenty to distribute to the guild, as well. You've done enough. It's good to see your spirit and energy are alive, but you should go. Get some rest. I will come check on you when we're done here."

"Any improvement?"

Bailey shakes her head. "No. But she has not gotten any worse, either. Her condition remains the same. Alive, but in a permanent state of unconsciousness. This is a first for me, Gallagher. I'm not quite sure how to heal her."

Gallagher's attention quickly shifts from Bailey to the ocean swells. A disturbance along the surface, but he doesn't see it clearly. Every conch from every outpost blows loud for the entire colony to hear. He stops breathing, anticipating the worst. Anticipating the terror that is about to unfold, almost as if conch shells themselves are responsible for calling the destruction upon the land.

"What is it?" Bailey and the Elders turn to follow his line of sight.

The haze of a wraith swarm emerges from behind the knuckles where they reach into the ocean. The stony bulwark becomes a blur as the gelatinous creatures pour over the rocks like Samara's dough coming to life, rising in the heat of her oven, and spilling over the edge to escape containment.

Gallagher breathes a deep sigh, relieved that it is only a wraith swarm and not the terror he anticipated. Though, part of him fears for more to come. And the other part of him cringes for his zealous attempt to warn the Elders.

The Warrior's Guild reacts promptly. Several squads rise into the air, armored in their leathers from chest to shins, hair tied in braids, and yaris at the ready.

Gallagher watches as the warriors approach the swarm, but they come to an abrupt halt. Every one of them uncharacteristically stops midair, treading in place, frozen in fear. His eyes shift back and forth from the warriors to the wraiths, curiosity and anticipation binding him just as tight as the warriors he watches.

Just then, a curved spine penetrates the water's surface in his peripheral. Distant. Nearly invisible had he not been so focused in that direction. More spines emerge and retreat with hardly a splash like one of the waterwheels in the creek. The trail of spines is never ending. The warriors of the guild must have a better visual of the monstrosity from above. It's not the wraiths who have them petrified. It's the sea demon Gallagher witnessed in the depths.

"There it is," he whispers.

"There what is?" Elder Falklan scowls at him.

Gallagher points. Gasps follow as the spines continue to penetrate the surface of the ocean just beyond the bulwark.

"Gallagher…" Mother Seya's lilting voice calms him like the serenading song of the great whales. "…this is not your fight. Don't do it" She knows his intentions before he has even made the decision. "The Morshine Clan has abandoned you. You mustn't do whatever it is you're thinking of doing. You have no responsibility here."

He turns to look at her. He stares into her sad eyes. Her knowing eyes. She understands the destruction that is about to claim their colony. She may not understand the monstrosity beneath those waves, but she understands the terror and chaos looming behind those warning conches.

"My clan may have exiled me… My clan may have refused my kin simple aid that could have saved their lives… But are those not selfish thoughts. Me…my kin… I will grieve in time, and I will let my anger surface when I do, but what about the warriors who were able to receive Tears in lieu of my parents?" He points to the sky where they ready themselves for a final battle. "What about the allies I have made within the Caelum Realm? Neither of those would have come to pass without my exile. I should not dwell on what has been… I must focus on what is now. And right now an entire colony of De'wi is at risk of being slaughtered if what I know to lurk just beneath the swell is true. It doesn't matter if my clan has abandoned me. I am a warrior at heart. I have not abandoned any of you, and you cannot change that with your judgement."

Another alarm from the conch sounds off, leaving the elves perplexed. One blow signifies a threat. Three, which is rare, is an incoming visitor. The conch sounds off a third time. And a fourth. And a fifth. The point-elves continue bellowing their horns in rapid succession. The only thing it could signify is absolute chaos because that is what it sounds like.

With his blade leading the charge, he leaps out of the water. Wind thumps against his cheeks and tosses his hair about. The strength the stones lend him is undeniable.

Before Gallagher reaches his pinnacle to dive into the ocean, the beast reveals its true nature. Water rushes off blue and purple scales glistening in the dull light. A head emerges at the entrance to their bay. A head armored with hard plates and spines. Its mouth armed with teeth that could impale a mountain. A forked tongue whips from between its fangs and disappears just as quick.

This is not a leviathan.

Two more heads emerge as it approaches the shoreline. Both as fierce as the first, and each atop a long sturdy neck connected to the same stout, scaly frame. It stands atop four legs with twin tails ripping through the swales of the ocean like a gust of wind peeling away layers of a sandy dune.

What stands in the shallows before him is a demigod. The mythical three-headed hydra. This creature does not exist, yet here it is, ready to devour his clan.

Gallagher weighs his options, frozen in midair, the same as all the other warriors. He could start with the wraiths, only slowing the inevitable, or he could take the quick route to a hero's grave by facing the hydra head on.

The conches bellow relentlessly, no longer an alarm, but rather war horns intended to invigorate the heart of a warrior. They feed his soul, adding to his strength.

36 BORDERLESS MAZE

Water swooshes past Mira, carrying her out into the ocean. Mira strokes desperately with the scepter in one hand, and kicks her fins, but her strength isn't enough to fight the current. Just as Rela said, the deeper she gets, the stronger the current gets. Fighting it is futile. She lets her body relax. It whirls frantically with the motion and velocity of the water until it spits her out into utter darkness.

Submerging into the ocean waters is a breath of fresh air after all she's been through. The salt bite increases the pain of the few wounds she's endured, but she's thrilled to wash away the sticky crust of blood and sweat coating her flesh.

What she isn't thrilled about is the black, borderless maze she just entered. Life has taken her into a depth so deep, she may never recover from this. Her instincts give her a sense of up and down, but it's questionable. She looks in the direction she perceives as up. The same direction she came from, she believes, and the Ebisu outpost is gone.

There certainly is no Eye of Solari down here to guide her and give her comfort. Her companions… Gallagher… Rivee… her parents… Even if they were swimming right next to her, they would be worlds apart in these black depths. She is lost in darkness.

And what of the unknown threats that consider this nothingness home. Threats like the demigod or any other variety of devil fish, like the octopuses. Mira knows she shouldn't fret over what she cannot see, but the tension of the unknown lingers heavily, regardless.

Mira picks a direction and swims. She thrusts herself further into the black nothing.

Time loses meaning. Without her senses to help facilitate anything relative, she knows not whether a few hours pass or a day. Her hunger and fatigue are her only gauges. Both rise to a level of discomfort.

A faint blue dot emerges from the darkness. Miniscule and unnoteworthy if it weren't the only visible spec in the vast, black, aquatic maze. It could be the stupidest decision of her life, but Mira swims toward it.

As she gets closer, the one hazy dot morphs into multiple, larger figures. She halts immediately, backstroking to cut through the velocity of her swimming. It's too late. They're all around her. It's as if they appear out of nowhere, the way one becomes a few, and a few become hundreds in a matter of two blinks.

The one hazy dot was a distant wraith swarm. The gelatinous blob of bobbing wraiths is deceptive as per their usual. And now they're blindly drifting past her. All around her.

She holds still, intentionally, but she might not be able to move if she tried, as the fear grows within her.

They're larger than the wraiths within the Terra Realm, and these vile creatures have a luminescence streaking through their transparent flesh. If it weren't for their subtle glow of blues and purples, they would have devoured her in this blinding darkness.

Staying still would be no different than intentionally falling on her own blade. She cannot let her fear overcome her. She won't survive them. Swinging the scepter will do nothing for her but get her tangled in a mess of stinging tentacles that will make her death quicker. Her only option is to be in the moment and one stroke ahead at the same time.

She inhales a breath of water and exhales. *Never below.* It's utterly impossible, but as long as she focuses on their hoods, she might make it through this.

She shoots ahead brushing past the first hood, then another. She keeps her angles as tight to the wraith's hoods as she can. If it weren't for their sporadic movements, this would be a breeze. Then, a wall of wraiths cuts off her next move. A quick backstroke follows and one of her fins tangles in the tentacles of several wraiths. The bite crawls through her leg as fast as a lightning strike, but thankfully it stops within her leg. She breaks free but is no closer to escaping this fiasco. The wraiths are on all sides of her.

The wraiths grow in number to the point that the black of the ocean is no longer visible. She only sees the blues and purples of the glowing wraiths—a beautiful radiance all around her. At least her death will be a sight to remember in the afterlife.

Another tentacle slaps her shoulder and petrifies her momentarily as the alarming pain shimmers through her. More tentacles invade her space. Her body is enveloped in a pain. Her flesh tries to escape her sinew, and her sinew fights to escape her bones. It all wants to tear apart and break free from one another but is bound together by a wicked fate. Pain consumes all hope.

But never will it consume her faith. Ceto is miraculous in this sense. Like the knowledge one gains, faith cannot be taken from her. She holds onto this thought and allows him to protect her heart until the end.

Suddenly, blackness penetrates the wall of wraiths. The black hole grows larger. It could be the edge of the wraith swarm. Or it could be death casually swimming up to her. She is numb either way.

Within the center of the growing blackness, another hazy blue dot awaits. Just what she needs in this dire moment, another wraith swarm to take the leavings of the first.

A shape takes form. It dances in the darkness with an elegance befitting of celestial divinity. It swims closer and the wraiths vanquish into the black maze surrounding her as if the mindless creatures are terrified.

The blue figure squashes its playtime enjoyment and freezes before her. Mira freezes, too. She stares, oblivious to what it is. She cannot define their separation. She doesn't know how small or large it is because she doesn't know how far away it is. But it's aware of her presence.

Mira's chest heaves into the restricting leather of her warrior's corset. This much time beneath the waves and it starts chaffing, adding to the pain of the wraith venom.

Enthusiastic about the wonder, she would advance but her body doesn't allow it. She'd like to blame her moment of petrification on the pain, but that's not why she remains frozen. Terror crawls throughout her and dilutes her curiosity.

The only defense she has is the machina scepter she has refused to surrender since her confrontation with Salus. It's been a reliable weapon, but she also fears letting it get back into the hands of the Ebisu. She thinks to let go of it right now. She can rid the three realms of the power of this machina magic. But what would stop the Indra from creating more weapons like it. Perhaps, every Indran soldier already wields one of these scepters. She cannot lose it just yet.

It swims closer.

The blue creature, with a mesmerizing green iridescence, flows through the black depths like kelp weed swaying in the tide. Effortless and beautiful. Mira should be swimming for her life, but the proximity to the creature washes away all her fears. Vanquished just as quick as that wraith swarm. It means her no harm. It approaches with curiosity, a mirror of her conviction.

Mira's mouth slowly parts, agape with disbelief. She has already uncovered too many wonders of Solaria during this adventure. The mighty grendelin and a demigod were beyond her expectations. Is she staring at the spectacle of a blue dragon?

It soars through the darkness like a manta ray on the clouds. Though, opposite in contrast, this creature is a light in the darkness. Shimmering scales cover its body. A frill decorates its many wings, short and wide. Threatening claws protrude from its webbed feet.

The dragon swims past Mira, brushing against her, sending shivers throughout her body, and liberating her of all pain. The instant relief leaves her short of breath.

Its long, slender tail curls around her as it swims past, casually spinning her in place. She's petrified with desire.

Desire for what? To touch it? To swim with it? To ogle it? She cannot peel her eyes away from the creature. It's so beautiful to look at. Pure desire.

The dragon circles around her a few times, never taking its crystalline eyes off her. It stops briefly and stares before rapidly twirling her in the water with a forceful nudge and latching on with its graceful claws to whisk her away.

She doesn't fight it.

The blue dragon speeds through the darkness faster than Mira ever could. Faster than the seadragons. Faster than the skittles dissolve beneath the coral when danger lurks. Faster than the gyrations of a waterspout.

Mira ought to be trembling, but the blue dragon exudes only serenity. Being around it lifts all the weight she has ever carried. In this moment, she is free of the burden of rescuing the neophytes from the Ebisu outpost. She is free of the danger of the demigod lurking somewhere within this black maze. She is free of General Merces maliciousness, and of her father's expectations. The blue dragon carries all that weight for her as they power through the black waters.

The white lights of the outpost come into view too soon. Mira isn't ready to go back. She'd much rather live her days shrouded in whatever false securities this mysterious dragon holds over her, but she knows how unrealistic such a desire is. And she doesn't understand why she's having such thoughts. It's almost as if this blue dragon wields the same power over her as the General wields over his slaves with his machina magic. The blue dragon is made of the same energy, except it only has the intention of life.

She can hear the dragon speaking to her, not with words, but intention. It requires her to get more comfortable, and allows for her to climb atop its back, all while continuing their ascent through the black, borderless maze.

Once atop the dragon, mounted securely between its powerful wings, Mira emancipates herself from all thoughts and immerses herself in the calm this dragon offers. She understands it won't last long and takes advantage of the present.

And it doesn't last long.

37 MIRA AND THE BLUE DRAGON

The sphere is such an unnatural cancer amidst the midnight blues of the surrounding ocean. Tiny blue and green dots are stationed outside— Ebisu soldiers. The damage the grendelins caused appears to have been mended. Water no longer cascades into the outpost, and Mira finds herself wondering how they are going to get back inside to help her companions. Or better yet, how does this dragon communicate through intentions?

She can sense a connection with the creature as if it can peer directly into her soul. The only explanation is that this blue dragon is a herald of Ceto himself. The champion of a deity.

Just as a deity can manipulate the world it harnesses, the blue dragon swims right past the Ebisu guards undetected and straight into the sphere. Mira is momentarily stunned by the swift change from wet to dry. It happens so fast. From the guards' perspective, Mira and the dragon might look like a mere flash of blue light.

Suddenly, her stomach finds her throat as they descend at an uncomfortable velocity. They plummet toward the deck. Mira doesn't enjoy the feeling, but an unearned trust exudes from this creature. Something she cannot explain other than she knows she will be safe. Regardless, she finds herself wanting to flap her arms as they plummet toward the metal deck submerged in water.

Her mind eases when the blue dragon unfolds massive wings and dances upon invisible threads of weightlessness. She hadn't even realized it had hidden wings tucked away, but she expected no less from such a stunning creature. The blue dragon no longer swims. It flies through the light air of the outpost on wings spanning twenty paces wide. Her stomach settles and that gross feeling is replaced with glee.

The battle scene comes into view as Mira and the blue dragon circle overhead. Both stone giants are half tethered to the metal deck, anchored by ballista, chains, and stone-piercing harpoons. One of them is on its knees, hunched into a defeated position. Ebisu soldiers splash around in knee-deep water covering the deck as they struggle to keep the other grendelin under control. More soldiers encircle a group of unarmed Ebisu—the neophyte slaves and Mira's companions.

Pointing fingers follow them through the upper atmosphere of the dome. And soon after, pointing bows and ballista.

The thrum of a massive bowstring sounds off, and a harpoon attached to one of their augmented chains soars through the sky. A feeble attempt to take down an elusive blue dragon.

Arrows fly through the dome, both small and large. The dragon circles overhead, waiting for something. An opportunity, perhaps. It takes a few passes around the dome before Mira understands. It's awaiting clear intentions.

Her mind is muddled with the chaos of the moment and all the projectiles targeted at them. And a creature she is unfamiliar with and has no means to communicate with somehow expects her to speak through intention. Yet, somehow her intuition to communicate is undeniable. It's an inexplicable bond. This dragon can sense everything about her, and she can sense everything about it. They are one.

An overwhelming elation floods her.

She ducks as one of the harpoons flies overhead. It wasn't close to hitting them in the least, but instincts take over in a moment like this. They soar beneath the chain its attached to and continue circling the dome.

With the serenity the dragon offers, Mira is able to focus. She's here to rescue her companions and all the neophytes. But in order to secure a safe escape, they must eliminate the threat. Her intentions are formed. The dragon reacts.

Another ballista fires. The blue dragon catches the harpoon with its front claws and tears the ballista it's anchored to from the deck. Several soldiers are caught in its destructive path before its claws release the destructive machina.

They swoop low, within a scepter's reach of the waterline. Mira secures a tight grip on the rod *and* the dragon. She leans outward with a full extension beneath the winged creature and the glowing conch slams into the first soldier. His body sinks into the water as if the scepter melted his legs. The flying duo attack soldier after soldier in a similar fashion, and they all disappear beneath the water's surface.

Effortlessly, Mira and the blue dragon take out squadron after squadron. Arrows fly. Screams echo through the vast dome. Roars from the grendelins send tremors through the water. Mira and the blue dragon fly like a destructive whirl-wind, unscathed and full of power. A one elf cavalry.

With the dragon's speed and Mira's scepter, the Ebisu army doesn't stand a chance. They destroy the ballista anchoring the grendelins and the guards assigned to them.

A roar of approval resonates from the group of prisoners who were surrounded and outnumbered only moments ago.

With a heavy thrust of its wings, the blue dragon forces a wave of energy outward, creating ripples in the shallow water before landing with an elegance befitting royalty. A bow and a full wing extension offer Mira an easy dismount.

Where the floods are knee-deep to the Ebisu, they are waist-deep for the De'wi, and chest-deep for the few Indra in the crowd. The plain of the water strikes the contrast of their height differential. It's incredible that they all share a common ancestry.

"Can we take it home?" a voice bellows from the crowd. Tanniv comes trudging through the water as fast as he can to embrace her with Veras strung over his shoulder.

"And then you show up with this…" Haltuk approaches, shaking his head at her. "A mount worthy to only the most virtuous of warriors. Only those true of heart and intent. Ceto has blessed you, Mira. We thought you were lost."

None of the elves are willing to get close to the dragon. They all keep their distance and ogle at its magnificence.

"This is brilliant, Mira." Tanniv gives her another embrace, struck with glee. "How—"

"It's not over yet." She cuts him off. "Where's the General?"

Her companions shrug their shoulders.

"Mira!" Tiolas emerges from the crowd. He pushes through the water to get closer. Rela steps into view behind him.

"The dome has been mended and the water drains…" Mira looks around. "…a little too efficiently. Will it be as simple as walking out of here? There are sure to be reserves. This was hardly the threat I know exists within these walls." She gestures to all the fallen Ebisu soldiers.

Tiolas' chest heaves in and out. "Come." He starts toward the edge of the crowd encircling them. All their companions follow, listening in. "Skywalks line the perimeter of the dome," Tiolas replies. "We have several unmarked exits there. They aren't easy to recognize on the dome itself, but the skywalks are marked. The outer wall isn't any different from the safeguard barrier currently splitting the dome. The outer wall is rigid in many places, hence the grendelins destructive blow, but it's soft in many areas, too. Just as you flew in, we can exit without issue."

"And after we escape the outpost, then what?" Haltuk asks. "We swim for our lives?"

"We swim for Crumbaker's crumble cake." Tanniv steps forward and pats Mira on the shoulder, letting it linger there. "Right? Hey, looks like that giant they took down is coming back to its wits." He points with a brutish posture. His lack of soberness pokes at Mira.

"Tanniv!" She shrugs his hand off her shoulder. "Haltuk makes a good point."

"Sorry, chief." He smiles at her, then winks.

"I'm serious, Tanniv." She shakes her head. "How did you end up in the Warrior's Guild, let alone my team?" She turns her gaze to the stone giants.

"Because of warriors like you, chief. I stand on the shoulders of giants. Don't you ever forget how Veras and I snuck into this place."

Mira grins, but it fades quickly. The grendelins stretch tall and wide and grumble incoherent noises. Glowing chains dangle from their giant stone masses. They're not dead, but they might be better off that way. The Ebisu will turn them into their war slaves. *Grendelin neophytes…* The thought of it leaves an empty pit in the bottom of her stomach.

"And how do we get them out?" Mira asks.

"I was hoping you wouldn't ask that." Tiolas admits.

"We cannot leave them here. I don't know how Veras and Tanniv per-suaded them, but we all know they didn't come on their own will. Those lives are our responsibility."

Tanniv's chin is up. Guilt doesn't come easy to him. He's too optimistic for guilt. "Mira." Tanniv grabs her attention. "How'd you tame the blue dragon? Maybe that sea-whisperer inside you can do the same to the grendelins."

She shakes her head. "How'd you tame the grendelins?" she spits back.

"Tears," he says. "We lured them here with Tears. So happens it's a snack they fancy." He pats at his side pouch with his free hand. "All out, unfortu-nately."

"Or an addiction they're being lured into," Rela adds with a scowl directed at Tanniv. "Some can't deviate away once they get a taste, you know. You shouldn't feed it to the animals."

Tanniv stutters nonsense, caught off guard by Rela's response.

"If it'll get them away from General Merces, it's worth it. Anyone else have any?" Mira looks around the crowd. It's unlikely any of the neophytes would have any, so she's really asking Tiolas and Rela.

"Sorry, Mira," Rela responds, shaking her head.

Mira folds an arm across her body and puts her other hand to her chin. "Tiolas, Rela…" She gestures to them. "Lead the prisoners to the exits. Let's get out now, while the opportunity is present. Tanniv, Haltuk, you're on the rear. Make sure everyone escapes safely."

"What about Veras?" Tanniv asks.

Mira goes quiet, then remembers how she revived Tanniv. Perhaps she can do the same with Veras.

"Mira?" Tanniv presses her for a response.

Before she can respond, a voice clearly speaks in her ear.

"Taking a coward's stance, I see. Cannot stay and fight?"

Mira looks around and sees nobody. It will take some time to get used to that. "Did you hear it, too?" She asks of Tiolas and Rela. Rela still wears her fake implant, and Tiolas has the communication device built into his armor.

"It was the General," Tiolas responds. "I think that means we need to act quicker than quickly."

Mira stands idle for a moment.

"I don't like the look on your face, Mira," Haltuk says to her.

"I have an idea," she says. "I cannot leave those grendelins in the hands of the General. Not while he's capable of enslaving anything he desires."

"And how are you going to do that?" Haltuk insists.

"Don't worry about it." She grips the metal scepter and points toward the blue dragon. "I'm equipped to challenge Ceto at the moment. These elves need to be taken down a notch."

Haltuk nods his approval.

As does Tanniv, but with more enthusiasm. "Attachief. My kinda elf maiden. Gripping your foes by the…" He pauses to clear his throat and makes a crude gesture. "…and stomping on 'em. I like it."

Her face distorts with disgust, but she smiles internally. She takes it as a compliment, but questions why he would enjoy anyone's elfhood being stomped on.

"Get moving," she says to Tiolas and Rela.

"Don't take his life, Mira," Rela steps closer with an intense look on her face.

"His life?"

"The General's. He stole my family, remember? I need to close that door." Rela holds her close with her gaze, determined to get Mira's word.

"Understood," she replies. Though, she doesn't know how she can promise that.

"Good luck, Mira. And…err…thank you. For everything." Rela embraces her. Mira awkwardly pats her on the back, not expecting such gratitude.

"You're welcome?" Her acknowledgement is spoken as a question.

Tiolas gives her a warrior's nod of respect then turns on his heels and starts ushering the prisoners. "Come! Come! It's time to escape Ceto's hell."

"Nah, nah, we already did that," Tanniv pipes in. "That was the basement, remember. This here…" He swings his arm around. "…this is more like the foyer to Ceto's hell."

He only receives glares from his unnecessary and ill-timed comment.

Rela joins Tiolas, and Mira's companions circle tighter around her.

"Mira, thank you for inviting me on this adventure," Tanniv says with more gravity. He pats her on the shoulder and lets his hand linger. He stares at her as if he has more to say, but he remains silent.

"Tanniv Windstalker… You speak as if you're saying goodbye. I'm only taking up the rear and cleaning up your mess." She smiles at him. "As any chief would expect to do for you."

"Hey…"

"I do it with gratitude. Consider it a gesture of my appreciation. I'll be right behind my best elves."

"This doesn't sit well with me, Mira." Haltuk gives her a stern look of disapproval.

"I don't know how to explain it, Haltuk, but that blue dragon—"

"That *divine* dragon," Tanniv interrupts. "With that beast, you're capable of Ceto's will."

Mira looks at the dragon. It offers undeniable security. "As long as I have it on my side, I know I'll be okay."

"And if you lose it?" Haltuk asks.

"We cannot fear what we don't know, Haltuk." She squares him up and places both hands on his shoulders. "We take risks, small and large, and this one is somewhere in between. That is all. There is no fear to be had. Not while I'm mounted on that... *divine* dragon." She winks at Tanniv.

"What are you going to do?" Haltuk persists.

"I'm going to give you time to escape safely. Then, I'll lead the grendelins out of here in the opposite direction, back to the Morshine Peaks."

Haltuk frowns. "Fine then. But as swift as that dragon is, I expect you to be right behind us. If not, you're going to have another rescue party headed your way."

"No. Unnecessary. I don't need anyone coming after me. And if my father asks, tell him I've found new horizons." She smiles and turns her head away thinking of all the potential with a blue dragon beneath her. No, not beneath her like a vile wraith. Elevating her...above the horizons as a gift from Ceto. This dragon is more than she or any elf will ever be. "I will return. I promise."

"And what about Veras?" Tanniv gestures to the large sack of limbs hanging over his shoulder. "We'll address his condition when you catch up?"

She looks at the scepter, holding it away from her body. With how quickly she was able to bring Tanniv back, she ought to be able to do the same with Veras. "Turn around, so I can see his face," she says.

"That's some powerful machina you're wielding." The shout comes from behind her. Haltuk's eyes peer over her shoulder and grow wide.

Mira flips around to see General Merces at the head of an Ebisu battalion. They linger on the opposite end of the open battlegrounds, looming there like a nightmare that she cannot awake from. Her mouth hangs open, briefly speechless, while the shock of the number of soldiers ready for battle strikes at her.

"Go." She says with a heavy whisper. "Get him out of here. We'll wake him later. Get out, now! Go!"

"But Mira!" Haltuk disagrees.

"I am your chief, Haltuk. This is my mission, and right now I need you to flee. I need you to get back home to warn the Elders of what's to come. Now, go!"

"I'd tell you to trust in your stones, Mira, but you don't need them." Haltuk says to her back. She refuses to take her eyes off the battalion. "You're fearless like Tanniv."

"Fearless, or perhaps stupid. They're often indistinguishable, following parallel paths." She sends a quick sidelong glance and a smirk over her shoulder to Tanniv. She's not worthy of the boast. The only reason they've made it this far is the machina she's chosen to arm herself with and the blue dragon. It's a power beyond her own.

"In that case, stupidity might be a good trait to have on occasion." He pounds a fist into Tanniv's shoulder. "Take care, Mira. And thank you for keeping me alive." She hears him splash into the water, swimming to catch up with the fleeing prisoners.

"I'll have a loaf of Crumbaker's crumble cake waiting for you." Tanniv says. Then she hears him follow behind Haltuk, saving her from having to comb through more emotions. She'd rather fight a battalion of soldiers.

"See you soon, Tanniv," she whispers to herself. "See you soon, Haltuk."

She listens as Tanniv immediately hands out directions to the prisoners as he scrambles to catch up to them. Mira's confident the two of them will get the freed prisoners safely to the Knuckles of Morshine. And with Veras' parchment, they'll know the quickest route, too.

She needs to get back to the blue dragon and the security it provides. She didn't stay behind to prove her might. She stayed to claim victory, and it lies within the blue dragon.

As she gets closer to the enthralling creature, its wings spread far and beat with the power of a waterfall, dispersing a mist into the air from the shallow waters at its feet.

"No!" Mira cries. Its mass lifts into the air as she watches in disbelief. It circles overhead a few times, out of reach, then perches on the shoulder of one of the grendelins. "Why?" Why would the blue dragon have revealed itself to Mira if not to help her? Their intentions were in alignment. She could sense it like a moment of relief when realizing success is within reach. What changed?

The General and his battalion trudge through the water to approach her. They get into formation as obedient soldiers ought to. The General stands no more than ten paces away from her.

"You've caused a lot of ruckus." He nods, smitten with admiration. There's a gruesome wound in his cheek from where Mira bit him. "A fine warrior you've proven to be. Besting us at the grendelin ring—although you had favorable odds, I might add. And taking victory in the reform trials only to evade the final transition." His brow curls inward. "Though, you couldn't have done it without the rebellion, I presume. I see you endured the clipping…" He cocks his head, gaining a better view of her ear. "…and you have the implant, which only means it's a fallacy." He pauses for a moment, looking her up and down.

After his attempt to defile her, it draws out a disgust in Mira she didn't know she was capable of. This elf is leagues beneath the vile wraiths she abhors. It reinforces her decision to stay behind and kill him. She *must* kill him regardless of the promise she just made to Rela. She must.

"Petite things you De'wi are. But it doesn't slow you, does it? You managed to release all the neophytes, dispelling nearly a quarter of my army." He pauses, holding a hard stare.

Mira is ready to gouge out his eyes.

"Why do you do it?" he asks. "Why do you fight the inevitable. The De'wi are a dying race. Ceto has chosen the Ebisu as his superior beings. Just look at what we've accomplished with his might at our fingertips." The General raises his arms above his head and methodically spins in place, gesturing to the spectacle of everything they've built. It hardly measures up to the grandeur he suggests with half of it toppled over by the grendelins.

"And look at how our deity has abandoned you when you need him most." He points to the blue dragon perched on a grendelin. "I must admit, that was quite the entrance, taking out half a battalion. But no more." His facial features turn dark.

"Ceto…" His name comes off her tongue in a whisper so quietly only the deity himself can hear it. She stares down at her fins, pondering the emotions she felt while riding atop the blue dragon. This arrogant, dark elf claims to have direct support of Ceto. "That's it…" she says.

The General holds a confused gaze.

That's what it was that she felt atop the dragon. Her intentions were in alignment with the creature, sure, but what she felt was so much more. Her intentions were in alignment with Ceto, too. The power she felt within her was Ceto, not the dragon. It's so clear and apparent, now that she has articulated her experience. Ceto is bound to her. Within her. All around her.

"What's that?" the General eyes her with a patronizing glare. "Was that a whimper I heard?"

Her gaze fixes on the General, pointed and confident. "Some of us are soldiers, bred to follow orders without question…"

A stifled chortle pops out of the General.

"Some of us," she continues, "are warriors with the heart, strength, mind, and soul to carry out the will of honor and integrity. Some of us are artists, breathing out inspiration in infinite forms. Some of us are miners, raised with strong backs and the undeniable ability to persevere through tough times. We are all fated for something. And I see it now. I sense it." She pats her breast. "Right here. Deep within me. Ceto has taken hold. I am a disciple of his word. It is a feeling you will never know until you find it. I don't need to preach. I don't need to fear. I only need to interpret the will he has imprinted on my soul. And I don't think he much cares for enslaving the life he has created…" Her gaze softens. She relaxes, knowing whatever comes of this moment, she is in the hands of her creator. She is safe.

His gaze turns into something hard and cruel. "I think it's time to enslave you properly, since my soldiers are apparently incompetent to do so." He pulls a heavy mace from behind his back. The spiked ball at the end of the chain glows with the aura of the Tears. "Let's see how you fight on your own. No aids favoring your odds."

He stands more than a head taller than her with biceps larger than her neck.

Mira tightens her grip around the scepter. "Come at me, then."

A quick snap of his mace, and Mira ducks, followed by an upward blow into the General's bracer. It doesn't faze him, and another swing of the mace falls toward her shoulder. She drops, evading the attack, and submerges herself in the knee-deep water. She darts forward.

Mira splashes out of the water with another upward attack, striking his hip, but it does nothing aside from causing a wince.

The General notices the confusion on her face. "Trust me, your Indran scepter isn't going to fare well against this." He offers a curt bow. "I saw the damage you dealt back at the halfway house, and now this..." He gestures to his fallen soldiers. "I've come prepared, armored head to fin."

It's not a strong armor he dons. Only a thin fabric. A small knife would cut right through it, but perhaps the scepter has no effect on fabric. Whatever the reason, she's limited to a blow to the face as it is the only part of him unprotected.

His mace catches her off guard as her confusion momentarily stifles her wits. She dodges it, but stumbles backward, making a large splash in the water.

Mira curls around his backside, staying within the shallow water where her agility is at its best. Circling around him several times, she watches as his fins step this way and that, trying to anticipate her movements. She leaps into the air with an explosive spray of water and sends the glowing conch right into the General's face. He splashes face down. Blood ripples away from his body, slowly dissipating into the saltwater.

Mira stands idle. She looks at the conch on the end of the scepter. Its cerulean glow shines through a coating of blood. She can practically taste the iron aroma exuding from it.

Is that it? Is General Merces finished with one blow to the face?

She inspects the scepter. Aside from the conch on the end, it is merely a pewter stick. Yet it wields so much power. So much potential for destruction. For anarchy.

Her grip loosens and she allows the scepter to splash into the water. Her knees are weak. Her arms tremble.

This is what her father is afraid of. This is why he hides within the Knuckles of Morshine. Power like this draws out envy and lust. Those who find excitement in conquest would stop at nothing to feed their ambitions.

The Ebisu don't seem to be aware of the power it holds. Salus discovered it. But did he tell anyone? Did the General know what kind of power she wielded before engaging? He saw the destruction she was capable of, but did he understand how easy it was?

She recovers the scepter from the water and examines it.

"Aargh!" Mira spears the scepter straight down into the shallows and smashes it into the metal deck. Conch shards flutter away. Its glow gradually dissipates, clearly visible through the knee-deep water. What remains of her scepter is a metallic staff with spear-like prongs. Not quite as sharp as it should be for an effective weapon. And no longer does it glow with the machina power.

Foolish. What was she thinking? She stands before an entire army who have been raised to believe the De'wi are a disgusting, cowardly race, in which genocide is a merciful end for them. She is nothing but an insect beneath their fins, and now she is essentially unarmed. And what about Veras? Will he be able to recover without the scepter?

The soldiers, so accustomed to following orders, stand dormant. It's as if they don't know what to do. Their leader has fallen. Will another rise to take his place without Lord Tenebrous' support? Have they been so fear-stricken by the General and Lord Tenebrous that not one elf will take ownership of the leaderless army?

Mira doesn't wait around to find out.

She rushes toward the skyways where she knows the exits to be. She has yet to solve the problem of how to get the grendelins out of this giant bubble. Although, she may not have to.

The blue dragon leads the stone giants toward the edge of the outpost. Could it be communicating with the grendelins in the same manner as it did with her? Or is it fulfilling her true intentions—to save the grendelins? Does this mean another flood is coming?

Mira looks over her shoulder to see the Ebisu army still standing at attention. Fools cannot think for themselves. However, a small band huddles together to deliberate, and more Indran scepters are dispersed amongst them. When Lord Tenebrous returns, there will be a new general elevated. This isn't over.

She climbs the stairs to the skywalk and pounds on the iridescent barrier housing the outpost. It has a soft, yet rigid texture to it in most places. Then her fist sinks into it and breaks through to the other side. No matter where her arm pokes through, the barrier creates a tight seal around her arm. Wet on one side, dry on the other. If only elven souls were pure, this is what machina magic could do for Solaria. It truly is brilliant technology.

A thunderous roar rolls through the outpost right before a loud crash, like the sound of glass shattering. The grendelins smash through the upper barrier yet again, leaving with a violent and abrupt exit, just as they came.

Mira watches as a waterfall cascades into the dome. She doesn't stick around to get washed away by it. She dives through the barrier into the darkness of the deep blue ocean. She ascends to where the marvel of the blue dragon illuminates the depths, and it allows her to climb aboard, once again. A warrior, her blue dragon, and two stone giants make their way out of the depths of the Ocean Realm, and eventually they'll rendezvous with her companions before returning to the Knuckles of Morshine.

38 GALLAGHER AND THE HYDRA

Silence entrenches the Knuckles of Morshine as the hydra stands tall and mighty, ready to devour their colony. The stone bulwarks towering above them on all sides is miniscule comparatively. The wraiths pour over the rocks and settle into their bay like a low-lying fog blanketing the ocean. The only sounds to be heard are the soft waves rolling into the sandy shoreline, and the low, rhythmic breaths of the demigod as it stares down upon them. The beast blocks the entrance to their bay.

One foot of the beast could stomp out an entire building. One bite could tear through an entire squad of warriors. This demon is invincible to an elven species. Only Ceto could lay waste to a beast of this magnitude.

"Gallagher…" Mother Seya's kind voice pulls his attention away from the demigod, holding an authority more powerful than the gigantic beast. Elder Falklan and Bailey remain by Rivee's side where she floats on the surface of the water surrounded by the glow of the Blue Tears that Gallagher recovered for her. Her rinsing doesn't appear to be effective.

Mother Seya continues. "All good warriors have a cunning mind and a powerful soul to guide their decisions." She points to her head, then pats her stomach beneath the waves as she looks up at him. Her eyes are soft and caring. "*Great* warriors have the strength to power through the turmoil life garnishes." She presses a fist atop her right breast. "*Divine* warriors have the heart to defend their principle, and all they hold dear, regardless of the foes posing a threat to their existence. Even if those foes are the ones they love."

She swims higher to join him at his level, water dripping from her long gown, and she places a hand over Gallagher's heart. Her wet hand is cool on his bare flesh.

"Young, blighted warrior..." Her voice quiets, and she closes her eyes. "If you succeed, I cannot promise our traditions will not be one of those foes." She looks down at his glowing sword and all the dreadful scars tarnishing his body.

Gallagher holds her in his gaze. "You have my respect, Mother Seya," he responds. "See to it that Rivee and her father get better treatment than I have. Heart. Strength. Mind and soul." He goes through the motions.

"Heart, strength, mind, and soul," Mother Seya repeats.

Gallagher turns his back on Rivee's rinsing, and bursts higher into the air to gain elevation equal to the hydra. The demigod studies him as its three heads sway mildly back and forth. Air surges from its nostrils and Gallagher flinches. He treads through the air contemplating the beast, giving the wraith swarm no attention. The Warrior's Guild can handle it.

The hydra strikes without warning. One head lunges forward while the others continue their gentle sways. Gallagher jets to the left and evades the attack. It moves so slow he could strike the beast ten times before receiving a counterattack.

"Gallagher!" A voice is heard from below. Andolas treads air ahead of what appears to be the entire Warrior's Guild. They remain out of striking distance. "We would be honored to fight by your side," he shouts up to him.

Gallagher is not so proud that he won't accept the help of the guild who shunned him. "Don't be foolish. You know it would be *my* honor to join the lot of *you*. But I think the guild is needed down *there*." He gestures for the guild to direct their assault on the wraiths. "And you cannot leave your colony unprotected." He points to the shallows beneath them where the cerulean glow of Ebisu trident tips can be seen emerging from the shallows.

A second head strikes. Gallagher manages an aerial maneuver above it, and counterattacks. His cerulean steel cuts into the armor plate just above the beast's eye. A bellowing roar echoes off the stone bulwarks.

"Looks like you found its weakness." Andolas calls up to him.

"Hardly. It will take a hundred thousand blades of cerulean steel to slay this menace. We don't have enough, let alone the fists to wield them."

Andolas quickly directs the guild, splitting them between the shoreline and the shallows where the wraiths grow closer. Then, he joins Gallagher by his side.

"They're outnumbered," Gallagher chastises his leadership. "What are you doing?"

"And one more will make a difference? I'd say you're outnumbered three to one. And the quicker we can take down this beast, the quicker we can assist the rest of the guild. So, let's get to it. What do you have in mind?"

Gallagher holds an unknowing silence, uncertain what to tell him. Not only does Gallagher not have an answer, but he's not accustomed to Andolas looking to him for guidance.

The demigod rears its head back and narrows its gaze on the two of them with a twitch in its eye. The spines on all three necks stiffen. The hydra steps further into the bay and strikes. Not at Gallagher or Andolas. And not with the head focused on the two of them.

The guild defending against the wraiths disperse, but not all are lucky enough to get out of the way. Two elven warriors and a mouthful of wraiths disappear into the maw of the beast.

Gallagher is not prepared for the loud snap of the jaw followed by a sheared scream, a squelch, and crunching bones.

Listening to the death of his clanmates leaves an empty pit in Gallagher's stomach. He didn't see who was swallowed whole, but no doubt they were dear to someone close to him. The gross feeling rapidly grows into a fury directed at the hydra.

Gallagher doesn't hesitate. A swift twirl follows, giving his blade momentum, and he swings down upon the demigod. His blade sinks into the scaled armor just above its eyes with a speed the beast cannot defend against. Even with three heads, it cannot anticipate Gallagher's moves. The blighted warrior strikes, and strikes again, seemingly never ending like a thousand blades all striking at once. But it's not enough. He needs a hundred thousand blades to take down this monster.

Gallagher breaks away, creating distance and finding a breath as he acknowledges the gap in power between a lowly, blighted warrior and a demigod. Elves were not meant to defend against such creatures. And such creatures were not meant to attack elven colonies. This beast should be in the depths of the ocean protecting Ceto where the stories have it.

The wraith swarm beneath him presses closer to the beach. And the De'wi defending the shoreline are no match against the armored Ebisu. Gallagher suddenly realizes this is a massacre. The Ebisu are here to eradicate his colony from existence, and he can do nothing to stop it. Not while they have a demigod within their clutches.

"How do you move with such ferocity?" Andolas eyes the blade Gallagher wields. "Although…you only managed to distract it. It doesn't appear to have even lost a breath. The beast must have a weakness somewhere."

A compliment and a slight in the same breath. Gallagher turns his gaze away from Andolas, brushing it off. "Yeah, but where?" Gallagher pants, still recovering.

"Keep distracting it. I'll check its underbelly." Andolas doesn't wait for a response. He drops toward the shallows.

The beast's eyes dilate, and its gaze follows Andolas. Teeth bared, its head snaps forward.

"No!" Gallagher screams. It draws Andolas' attention, and instead of swimming for his life, he points his steel yari at the incoming hydra, ready to defend himself.

Gallagher refuses to watch and do nothing. Andolas might be the elf who caused him the lowest life possible within their caste, but community and family far outweigh pride—the deadliest of all flaws. The demigod's attack slows down to the speed of a sea slug. Andolas, too. The air stills. Gallagher kicks his fins, bursting forward and causing ripples of air as if he just dove into a glass lake, followed by a thunderous boom echoing throughout their small bay.

Holding his blade out to his side, he swims past the demigod and slices a deep laceration through its neck. Not deep enough to sever its spine, but deep enough to inflict lasting damage. He then jabs his sword upward through the bottom of the hydra's jaw and presses outward with all his might, opening a hole large enough for a youngkin to swim through. With a final blow, he takes up his sword with both hands and pierces the demigod's throat, jabbing at an angle into the beast's skull until his forearm is buried deep beneath armored scales and flesh. He yanks it free, pulling out a mess of blood, and watches as its head, only one of three, retreats out of harm's way. The glow fades from its blue eyes and the head falls limp.

Everything around Gallagher resumes its normal motion and the beast's head splashes into the shallows, disrupting the battle below.

Another debilitating roar sounds off as the demigod cries out in pain. All battling stops for a long moment as its two remaining heads sway back and forth, considering its foes.

Anticipation floods the bay within the Knuckles of Morshine, all elves, Ebisu and De'wi alike, are uncertain what is to come next. Gallagher, too, doesn't know if he should continue to attack the beast. All things considered, this is the legendary hydra, and he would prefer not to be the warrior to slay it. Doing so could unleash Ceto's fury upon him.

The demigod's eyes focus on Gallagher. What thoughts a creature of its status is capable of, Gallagher can only speculate, but there seems to be an understanding embedded there somewhere. Respect amongst two worthy challengers.

The beast's eyes regain their focus, and the two remaining heads strike at members of the guild, one after the other. The battle between De'wi and Ebisu ensues below, suddenly unconcerned with the distraction caused by the demigod. His clanmates swim above the Ebisu for an advantage, but it appears to be a meager advantage with the demigod snatching De'wi from the air.

In the distance, a group of bodies swim up the steep slope of the surrounding bulwark toward the north. Those clan members who cannot fight are escaping. They head toward the outposts.

A loud crash clashes with the sound of the battle cries below. It's the sound of a mountain crumbling to the ground. Gallagher's head snaps to the east, and the knuckles are doing quite the opposite of crumbling. They rise toward the ceiling of clouds.

Boulders the size of small huts fly through the sky in the direction of the hydra. One smashes into the beast's neck, causing it to stumble, while the other boulder lands with a catastrophic splash, sending a massive wave toward the shoreline. Ebisu, with their heavy armor, are tossed into the sand while all the remaining De'wi are safe from the blast of the wave as they swim above it.

Stunned beyond comprehension, it takes Gallagher some time to realize he is watching not one stone giant climb over the ridge, but two. And buzzing around their shoulders is a faint blue glow, too distant to distinguish exactly what it is.

Assuming the giants are merely clumsy, yet associated with the Ebisu army, his heart sinks. The only answer is to retreat. The Knuckles of Morshine, aside from being their home for generations, is nothing special. There is still time to join his retreating clanmates and flee to safety. Though, how do they flee from a demigod? It's reach is limitless within the Terra Realm. They would need to join the Indra above the clouds.

Wide jaws rush toward Gallagher with teeth bared and the depths of its throat visible. But the beast moves with the speed of a wraith compared to Gallagher. A simple spin and a beat of his fins allows him to dodge the attack and thrust a counterstrike into its neck just behind its jawline. His blade sticks and his body is tugged this way and that as the demigod's head flails.

Gallagher's body jerks backward as its head lunges forward. He's pulled along without a hint of control. Pain screams through his arm, and he's sure it's going to be torn free of his body if he doesn't do something.

He smashes the pommel with his free hand and the blade releases him. The pain grows tenfold and spreads beyond his arm as his body is tossed uncontrollably through the air.

With fatigue the new standard for his disfigured body, he has no strength to overcome the velocity at which he flies toward the knuckles. Not without the power of his machina sword—his crutch. Wraiths scream past him, or rather, he screams past them, feeling a sting here and there until he's free of the swarm and splashes into the shallows at the base of the mountain.

He lies still, eager to do more… to do everything within his power to defend his clan… but he has no power. His crutch is buried in the neck of a demigod. He leans against the bulwark with waves splashing at his face, and the rest of his body submerged beneath the water.

Chaos overtakes the scene before him. Waves knock his head about. Grey mountain-sized feet splash into the shallows. Stone fists grab handfuls of wraiths. The hydra's two remaining heads snap at one another as if their lucidity has been vanquished. Ebisu soldiers, only recognized in Gallagher's dazed and blurred vision by the glow of their armor, fly toward the bulwark just as he did. Loud thuds are evidence that it's unintentional.

Mountains step through their bay toward the hydra with the blue glow still buzzing about their shoulders. Fangs crunch down upon stone forearms. It looks as though the stone giants are defending their colony. Handfuls of wraiths are stuffed into their cave-like mouths with stalagmite teeth tearing into the vile creatures. Ebisu continue to fly through the air, hitting rocks, splashing into the shallows, and some careening over the top of the knuckles.

The wraiths, unable to maintain the structure of their swarm, disperse in all directions, fizzling away into the sky. The glow of the Ebisu army has faded. And the hydra rages, but in a retreating manner, backing out of the bay as the two stone giants bellow murderous roars at the demigod.

More waves splash into Gallagher's face and knock his head into the rocks he leans against. The wear on Gallagher's body seems to have taken hold of his mind. Whatever just unfolded before his eyes, couldn't be possible. He must be hallucinating. Only his heart and soul remain intact. But those too, are soon to fade.

39 BLIGHT OR BANISHMENT

The colony is silent as the daylight fades. Although victory has been found, the clan of warrior elves have many affairs to ponder. Many deaths to mourn. Many decisions to weigh. Some of those decisions are to decide the fate of the blighted.

Their realm is on high alert, for the Ebisu could regroup and attack at any moment, and the Indra could show face for the first time in generations to retrieve their elites. Defenses must be raised on all fronts, both sky and ocean.

Victory has raised the hearts of the clan, but those who look ahead know what is awaiting their fate. Mira, Andolas, Lady Rayfin, and the Elders have been in deliberations since the battle ended.

The revered object that paved the way for victory lies in the center of the table while Mira wraps up the recounting of her tale to the Elders.

"…and now, here we are deciding fates." Mira leans backward into her seat with a slouch and a deep sigh. A burden is lifted from her shoulders after recapping her story.

"Thank Ceto those stone giants didn't make our bay their new grendelin ring," Elder Falklan says. "There have been too many happenings for one day. Shall we rest on this new information and reconvene at first light?"

"What?" Mira's face turns sour as she snaps upright.

Her father quickly raises a hand before Mira starts in on her. "Elder Falklan…" A heavy breath escapes him. "We are all exhausted… but I don't believe our exhaustion should stand in the way of the elves who are awaiting the fate of their lives to be decided. We will have this conversation now." Elder Rayfin looks to Andolas. "Go find him."

Andolas stands idle with a blank expression.

"Gallagher," he nearly shouts. "I'm referring to Gallagher."

Andolas exits the rallyhouse without another word.

All the nerves throughout Mira's body cry with excitement and anticipation. She has not seen Gallagher since the day the Ebisu first arrived on their doorstep. She combs fingers through her hair, needlessly brushes off her leather corset as if she's smoothing wrinkles from a beautiful gown, and she sniffs at her underarm, pulling away with a cringe.

"Err…" Mira raises a hand. "May I be excused?"

Her father glares at her. "What? Why?" His voice is hard.

Her mother rolls her eyes at Mira, then rises from the table to stand by her side. "Our daughter needs a stroke of confidence, dear." She looks at Elder Rayfin from across the table. "That is all."

Lady Rayfin pulls out a small vile of essence from a purse at her hip. She dabs it on her finger then smears two strokes along Mira's neck, just beneath her jawline. "A bit of flavor to sweeten you up." Then, she retrieves a small comb and starts on Mira's loose tresses, yanking on the lighter tangles first. "You've lost a braid."

"It'll grow back."

"And this earwear… I'm not sure if I approve."

Elder Rayfin looks puzzled but waves it off. Mother Seya smiles with elegance, and Elder Falklan scowls with a disapproving shake of her head, as per usual. The three Elders converse amongst each other, and Mira pays them no mind. Her mind races in too many directions.

Lady Rayfin pulls Mira's hair into a tight tail, then kisses her on the head. She leans in with a whisper. "No words express how relieved we are that you returned home, Mira. The vast world awaits curious hearts like yours, and I wasn't sure. A blue dragon could have carried you to any horizon you desired." Mira leans her head back to look at her mother. Lady Rayfin smiles and kisses her on the forehead, then finds her seat beside her husband.

"Don't fret, mother. It fled back to the Ocean Realm after the demigod retreated. Regardless of where my heart takes me, the knuckles will always be my permanent horizon."

Commotion is heard outside the rallyhouse.

"Does it hurt?" One of the warriors guarding the entrance says.

"Which one?"

Mira's heart flutters when she hears Gallagher's voice.

"That one," the guard says.

"Dammit, Claven! Why? Why would you poke at another elf's wounds?"

"You look rough, Gallywog."

"And I feel rough, too," he replies, still standing on the other side of the doorway, out of sight.

"The Elders are waiting," another warrior states. The door opens.

Andolas walks in first and hanging onto him is a worn and defeated warrior with his head hanging low.

Mira's brow turns inward. *Gallagher?*

Andolas hands the warrior his yari and makes sure it's secure in his grip before slowly letting go and allowing him to stand on his own two fins.

Andolas moves to the side and shifts into a warrior's stance—shoulders square, hands crossed behind his back, fins shoulder-width apart. It's almost as if he's mocking this warrior. The stark contrast between the two is enhanced with Andolas standing by his side.

The warrior appears to be incapable of something so simple as a warrior's stance. His back won't form a straight line. He may not even be able to cross his hands behind his back. And his flesh is pockmarked with blight, nothing like Andolas' smooth and firm physique. The elf looks like a withered Elder fated with one thousand years too many.

He rubs at his lumpy flesh and cringes when his hand brushes across the congealed wounds that appear fresh. He rolls his shoulders as if loosening his muscles, but his movements are arduous and irregular. He tightens his grip on the shaft of the yari and forces his back upright, looking as if he's using all the strength he can muster.

"Elders," he says. His eyes widen at the sight of the blade lying in the center of the table. "You recovered it…"

"Gallagher!" Mira's cry catches in her throat. Her mouth hangs open at the sight of her dearest friend.

His grip on the yari loosens and he immediately hunches over, his body unable to hold its own weight. Mira doesn't hesitate, knocking her chair to the ground as she rushes in to catch him. His touch sends vigor spinning throughout her.

"What happened?" she asks.

His body presses into hers as she supports his weight. His aroma is strong with salt water and the sweet scent of Blue Tears.

He smiles and a warmth consumes her.

"You're…" He blinks several times. "You're alive…" He sinks into her in what she believes is a hug, but his arms struggle to fully embrace her.

"So are you." She pulls away just enough to see his smile.

"I don't think my adventure went as smoothly as yours." He stifles a flinch when he gets a closer look at the garment on her ear.

"Oh!" she gasps. "A necessity to escape the Ebisu." Her jaw tightens as her hand finds the white and silver machina. "Mine wasn't so smooth, either. An unfortunate battle scar." She cringes after making the comment, looking at Gallagher with pity.

"Machina looks good on you," he says. The comment stifles her.

"Have they reacquainted long enough?" Elder Rayfin interrupts. He's looking at his wife for confirmation, and she lets out a soft sigh with a nod of her head.

"Oh, don't be so impatient, Garrik." Mother Seya scolds him when his wife doesn't. "They've been through a lifetime of events since they last saw each other. Give them a moment."

Elder Rayfin grunts then lets silence take the room. It becomes awkward rather quickly, as reacquainting isn't as genuine when you have four pairs of eyes staring at you, waiting for it to be over with.

Mira shakes her head at her father with a subtle glare. "Go on, Elder," she says to him. She ushers Gallagher to her seat, struggling to pick it up while also holding Gallagher upright. Andolas swoops in to help her, and they get the battered warrior into the chair. Mira stands behind him, her hands placed on his shoulders to help stabilize him.

"Young warrior." Elder Rayfin addresses him.

Gallagher raises his gaze from the blade to the three Elders. "Heart, strength, mind, and soul." He addresses them respectfully. Although, his arms seem unwilling to cooperate. He sits before them, a half-eaten mess of an elf.

Young warrior! It's the most he's ever gotten out of her father. Perhaps Gallagher is a step closer to earning her father's respect?

"Gallagher…" Elder Rayfin pauses and closes his eyes for a moment with a deep sigh. "You have tainted our culture by intentionally wearing machina. And you have done so on more than one occasion. You have disobeyed your Elders by harvesting Tears out of place and nearly died in doing so. You have crossed our borders and led both Indra *and* Ebisu directly to us. One of these things is disgraceful enough, let alone notching all three catastrophes on your belt. But…" The Elder pauses and tightens his jaw. All eyes are on Gallagher. "…you have also saved lives. Hundreds, I would proclaim. You recovered a youngkin from the clutches of our enemy in the sky. You successfully retrieved Tears for the said youngkin, and even though she was not in line to receive any, your demonstration of warriorship was admirable. You faced a demigod head on, fearless in your approach, and successful in revealing its weakness…" His voice fades and his eyes grow distant and pensive. He regains focus after a moment of thought and looks Gallagher directly in the eyes. "You are the victor, the hero, the reason so many of our warriors swam away from that battle."

"The hydra's weakness, Elder?" Gallagher asks. "Please excuse my interruption, but I don't believe I'm worthy of everything you just spat off. I only did what any warrior would do. I merely had the machina to aid me. With the power at my fingertips, it was my obligation to protect those who could not. As it always is, and always will be for any warrior. Though…I suppose I am not even a warrior." His head hangs low. "I am just a kelp picker. And I am certainly no hero. I apologize for all the chaos that I have left in my wake. None of it was intentional." Gallagher's head slowly rises from the table to meet Elder Rayfin's gaze.

"That hydra was under the control of the Ebisu," The Elder responds. "Similar to Mira's implant…" He pauses to glare at it. "…the hydra had one tucked just behind each of its jawlines. Your last blow pierced the device, deactivating whatever mindlock the Ebisu had on it. From there, the hydra began attacking itself. And then Mira—"

"Not to mention the whirlwind attack he unleashed on it," Andolas interrupts from the corner of the room, "Slaughtering one of its heads singlehandedly. Gallagher was a glowing blur. A waterspout cycling through the air laying out destruction wherever he touched. Flawless." His eyes shift to the sword sitting on the table.

Silence fills the room when Andolas is done. The interruption alone was breathtaking, but then he proceeded to compliment Gallagher. Mira wasn't ready for that, nor does she think anyone else in the room was ready for it.

Elder Rayfin glances toward the other two, Mother Seya and Elder Falklan. Mira assumes a silent confirmation is taking place.

"Taking all things into account," the Elder continues, "your exile has been lifted with permanent banishment no longer a consideration. On one condition." His stare is hard and direct. He looks down at Gallagher's sword, impregnated with three leviathan stones. "You forfeit all machina, including the latest blaspheme you brought to our realm." He jabs a finger at the blade.

Elder Falklan looks at it with apparent disgust. Mother Seya is stoic. Andolas ogles the blade. Gallagher, too, stares at the weapon for a long time, pondering the decision being presented to him. He knew this is a choice he would have to make.

"Gallagher, I will gladly accept you into the ranks of the guild." The Elder adds, while patting the blade before him. "But we will need to find another accessory to adorn your stones with, in which you have also earned the cerulean steel, young warrior. If I had known the truth of this blade, I would have never handed it over." He pulls his eyes away from the machina to focus on Gallagher.

"You may not be able to wield the cerulean steel in battle with your current state, but traditions are traditions. The induction into the guild remains an honor worthy of only the most heartened warriors, and the cerulean steel is a renowned honor beyond what most acquire in their lives. But I'm afraid you'll have to step away from the adventure as soon as you are inducted. We are in need of new outposts with the borders on high alert. A point-elf would be a suitable role, no?"

"May I?" Andolas raises a hand to address the Elders. He receives three spiteful nods in return after his daring interruption a moment ago. He steps forward to stand by Gallagher's side, right next to Mira. "As a warrior of the guild, I admire fortitude—heart, strength, mind, and soul. This is who the De'wi of the Knuckles are." Andolas pauses and looks down at Gallagher. "Look at him. He could hardly walk in here on his own two legs."

Gallagher lifts his head to that snide comment. Truth, so it may be, but Andolas degrades him.

"We all know his heart is more courageous than any we will ever see in a thousand lifetimes. His mind is sharp and diligent. Worthy of leading an entire realm into prosperity. And his soul…" Andolas clenches his own gut. "His soul could mend the three realms. He is already on that path. And what you do… you steal the one remaining piece that will allow him to achieve the greatness we all know he is capable of. You steal his strength."

Elder Falklan raises a hand to cut him off, even though it sounded like he was finished. "Are you saying we should make an exception?"

"Yes. Machina would help him move freely. We've already seen what it's capable of. Look at the Ebisu. They have an entire society constructed of it, and—"

"Look at the Ebisu!" Elder Rayfin raises his voice. "A destructive race. The Indra, too. You know the stories. You all do!" His eyes meet every elf in the chamber with a display of his displeasure. "They found satisfaction in machina in the beginning. It eased their daily hardships, but it was never enough. They made *exceptions*. The desire to have it by their side, assisting them, entertaining them… It grew and grew until it became a necessity. Then that necessity burrowed a hole in their souls telling them it was worth fighting for. Worth killing for. We do not use machina for that reason. And we thrive without it."

"What of the Tears, then?" Andolas' voice is calm in contrast to the Elder's.

Mira and Gallagher both remain silent. Since when has Andolas ever been willing to stand by his side.

"Is it not the same?" Andolas continues when all the Elders fail to respond. "We feel the need to fight for it. To kill for it. It makes our lives easier, and we've become dependent on it. How is that so different from machina?"

"Andolas, please?" Gallagher raises a hand to him. He doesn't need Andolas to fight his battles.

"No, Gallagher. We all deserve an explanation. Of this, and so much more. Like the Indran-mix who's been breaking bread with us since she was born. They've been harboring an enemy for years, and it's time for answers before their silence becomes a plague of its own."

Mira's ears twitch. "What is he talking about?"

Elder Rayfin noticeably cringes. This is obviously something he doesn't want to discuss. Her mother, where she stands behind him, subtly digs her fingers into his shoulders. So this impacts her, too.

"An explanation is due. I agree. You raise many good questions." Her father places a hand on her mother's where it rests on his shoulder. "Every society requires a currency. A means to improve and better themselves. Without a means to improve. Without hope, a soul is smothered out of existence. Blue Tears are that currency. Gallagher here is the perfect example. Look how much effort he exerts to improve. To better himself. He does this not just for the Tears, but for the status it brings him and his family. Blue Tears offer us—"

"A deceased family without the Tears." Gallagher keeps his head down, only muttering the resentful words to himself. It's enough to stop the Elder, speechless.

"…goals," Lady Nessa continues for her husband. "The Blue Tears offer us a chance to improve. Machina…" She twitches. "…does not."

"It could," Andolas argues. "We could use machina as our currency."

"And we would become a lazier clan for it." The Elder nearly shouts back at Andolas. "We overcame the Ebisu, Andolas. We didn't do that with the use of machina. We did that with exceptional training and the strength it awards us."

"Then what do you call that, Elder?" Andolas points to the blade on the table. "Our champion, who had a significant impact on our survival, used that very blade." He throws his arms in the air, then immediately lowers them, trying to recover from any insult he might provoke from his insolence.

Elder Rayfin disregards his comment aside from a quick jab with his eyes. "If you are always looking for ways to make your life easier, then you will surely find it. And you will surely pay the price for it. An easy life produces a soft culture. A soft culture produces a hard life. Endure some hardship and you will find strength. Or endure nothing and you will find hardship. We must always seek a balance. As a unit, our clan will be stronger without it, and we have too many reasons right now requiring our full strength. Machina is forbidden. And that is final."

"Hmph…" He grunts but says nothing further.

"I would agree, Elder, it—"

"Silence, Elder Falklan. I don't need your affirmation on the topic." Elder Rayfin gives her an indignant glare.

"What is your choice, Gallagher?" Mother Seya asks with a soft voice that calms the chamber. "Banishment or Blight?" As the matriarch, she is highly respected amongst the elves. All the Elders are, but Mother Seya carries a certain air about her that never angers, is full of wisdom, and offers guidance. When she presents the question to Gallagher, it's as if the choice is his alone and his mother waits to see whether she will be disappointed or not.

"Mother Seya… I…" Gallagher stumbles his words.

It should be an easy choice, Gallagher. Mira holds her breath.

Gallagher looks at Elder Rayfin. "Will Rivee and her father be treated with decency?"

"Of course," the Elder responds with confidence.

Father? Mira's mouth parts to speak, but she isn't sure if she heard that correctly.

"Both of them?" Gallagher insists confirmation. "Jarnes is not a bad person. If the character he displayed in Caelum Invictus is an example of Rivee's future with him, then you must allow for that relationship to grow. Rivee needs the attention and love he can provide for her. I know you have no flesh in this but think about your wife. She would want the best for her daughter."

A gasping silence stunts further conversation. All eyes are on Elder Rayfin, staring, waiting for the volcano to erupt and send shards of burning rock in all their directions.

"Father, is this true?" Mira is the first to speak.

His eyes meet hers, wide and full of guilt. It is all the admission she needs to understand the truth.

The Elder sighs. "It was…" He knows more deception will only tear them apart. "There was no adultery. Whatever presumptions any of you have made about Nessa, they're utterly incorrect. She is an elf maiden of the most honorable kind and holds all my respect and love until the end of our days."

"What happened?" Andolas asks out of turn. He receives many nasty glares.

"We sought a truce with the eyes in the sky, tired of holding our cover, hiding within the knuckles. As much as we avoid machina and all its maliciousness, we know Solaria offers much more than what we've allowed the clan to experience. But to step out into the world, to see new horizons beyond these stony bulwarks...we required *some* semblance of safety." He pauses a moment, staring down at his fidgeting hands. "We are not in good favor with the other races of elves."

The Elder clenches his jaw, then stares directly at Mira. "Rivee Rayfin is your sister," he admits. "Half-sister if we need to be technical. It is true."

"Of course it's true, but why?" Andolas presses. "Why did Lady Nessa do it? And how could this not be infidelity? This is betrayal of the worst kind. Not only a disgrace to you and your family, but you have betrayed our entire clan. Our Elder, the one we hold in the highest regard is smeared by the one he loves the most, and *without* consequence? There must be an explanation to match the level of betrayal taking place, or I will condemn Elder Rayfin and Lady Nessa as a blight on our colony. A taint to our culture that will dismantle everything we know. Why would she lie with an Indra?"

Andolas stands tall and firm in his conviction, as he should. Mira, although they are her parents he indicts, feels just as much betrayal. How could they hide the truth for so many years?

Mother Seya and Elder Falklan are calm and observant. Were they aware of this scandal? Their faces give away nothing.

Gallagher fidgets in his chair, though it may be from the level of injury his body has sustained.

Mira has never seen this level of insolence from Andolas. He's a haughty elf, but to demand answers from the Elders is unlike him. Does he have the authority to label another elf as blighted? This has always been a mark given by the Elders, and only the Elders, but the three of them seem to be taking the claim seriously.

"As I said..." Elder Rayfin continues. His voice is calm considering the threats made to him. "...we sought a truce. The Indra accepted our peace offering and invited us above the clouds. We couldn't put this burden on anyone else. Not even the bravest amongst the Warrior's Guild. This wasn't a matter of defending our clan, it was a matter of massaging the aftermath of a war nobody ever recovered from. After much consideration, Lady Nessa was deemed our emissary. She was the perfect candidate. She held high status amongst our clan. She couldn't speak for *all* the De'wi colonies out there, but we knew her voice held some weight. Her knowledge of our histories challenges the Elders, and she maintains a lofty beauty, easy on the eyes and unthreatening. An Indran envoy met us in a discreet location away from the knuckles. We had to maintain the secrecy of our clan's location. The Indra escorted her the remainder of the way. From there and above the clouds, it is Lady Nessa's story to tell." He raises a hand to silence her before she says anything.

"It wasn't our intention to create family ties," he continues, "but it happened. If you recall, Lady Nessa was *ill* for a period of time. The deception was necessary while she was away. We implanted the stories of rescuing a youngkin from the wild, and the importance of Lady Nessa's quarantine after recovering that child. She had an unknown ailment, if you recall, and we didn't want to spread it throughout the colony." He frowns as he clenches his jaw. Deep, intense lines press into his forehead.

"It's alarming how easy it is to alter a lie into a truth and have nobody question it. Nobody batted an eye to our story. It was assumed migrants from a distant clan were seeking better lives and only the youngkin survived. Rivee quickly became one of our own.

"Riveria Arilight is the daughter of Jarnes Arilight and Nessa Rayfin." Elder Rayfin's eyes reluctantly meet Mira's, then snap to Andolas. "With my confession, I believe the deception that you call a blight has been eradicated. An announcement will be made for all to know the truth."

Andolas' mouth is agape. It's apparent he wants to say more, but he has no words.

"Why mother? Why did you do it?" Sorrow and shame pour from Mira. "What about father? Why would you do this to him? To the clan? To me?" Mira isn't quite sure if she should yell or cry. The shame they bring to the family is beyond reason.

"Machina…" Lady Nessa replies. "I'm sorry, Mira. I don't want to bring excuses to the table, but that is all I have." Elder Rayfin pulls his wife in tighter to himself, wrapping an arm around her waist. "I wasn't myself while I was away. The Indra… Their Greybeards… They're always working to produce something new. Always trying to develop the latest form of machina. I'm afraid I was part of a trial."

"Excuses…" Mira's voice is quiet, but far from calm. "How could machina force you to…" Her voice trails off. "The same machina magic the

Ebisu use." Her eyes grow wide as she fingers the device on her ear. "You were a slave?"

Lady Nessa pulls her hair back with one hand, and flips her ear forward with the other, revealing a scar just behind her jawline. "The Indra weren't so brutal that they felt the need to mark me a slave. And the device I wore wasn't so stylish, but yes, I was not myself while I was in the Caelum Realm."

The other Elders remain calm as if they knew. Andolas looks confused.

"Mother…" All of Mira's anger is washed away. Having witnessed thousands of slaves she understands perfectly what her mother went through. If Mira wasn't so lucky as to get a fake implant from the rebellion, she might be in the same situation, knowing the ugly intentions the General had.

Mira hurries around the table to give her mother a hug as she loses control of her emotions.

"That explains your hatred of machina, but where's the truce?" Gallagher is far from satisfied based on his tone. "If the bond was made, why was there no truce? And why not be open with your clan about securing that truce? Why lie about your intentions and your undertaking into the Caelum Realm?" Anger engulfs him. "That entire year…we were led to believe isolation was of utmost importance because she and Rivee contracted an unknown malady. Not even Bailey was allowed to see them. And what of the moment Rivee needed the Tears to mend that leg of hers. We could have made her whole. She may be blighted still, but we could have reattached that leg. Yet you refused your own daughter the Tears." He throws knives at Lady Nessa. He has never, in all his years, berated or disrespected Mira's parents. Not so intentionally.

"That was my choice." Her father slams a fist on the table, rattling the blade in the center. "Do not attack Lady Nessa. I am solely responsible for every decision made within the knuckles."

Elder Rayfin clenches his jaw and closes his eyes. A moment passes before he opens them to address Gallagher.

"Fear. Even a five-stone warrior holds fear in his heart, Gallagher." He thumbs the torque around his neck. The stones gleam in the dim candlelight in the room. "We had to do everything possible to maintain our secrecy, including sticking to our traditions with the offerings of Tears. It was all due to fear. Fear of what our clan would think of our decision. Fear of the shame we have brought down on our family. Fear on both sides of the clouds, not just ours.

"Although Lady Nessa remained in their graces for several months, the Indra denied the child was of Indran heritage. Elder Fae shut away Jarnes, and all allegations of the bastard child were denied by the Indra. It's one thing we elves have in common. A child out of wedlock is beyond shameful. Elder Fae would not have her family tarnished by such disgraceful acts. Our negotiations were a failure, regardless of the child born of two realms."

"But how did you escape?" Mira asks, holding her mother's hand, standing by her side.

"They wanted nothing to do with the child. They aren't so brutal as the dark elves beneath the waves. Conniving and valueless in most ways, but they were merely playing with toys. They removed the implant and sent me on my way as soon as I started showing."

"And that's why you had to remain in quarantine?" Mira utters. "Your ailment was pregnancy."

Lady Nessa nods.

Mira looks at Gallagher to see if his qualms with her parents are at rest. To see if their logic and reasoning resonates with his own. Regardless of what is being revealed, she would never have him be at odds with her kin. She stares longingly, awaiting a reaction.

The chamber is silent. Too much information is tossed about the room to process it adequately without a moment of thought.

"Her tune has changed." Gallagher speaks as he squirms in his seat. "I tried to keep clear of the dramatic interweaving nuances of their culture, but I ended up tangled in their mess, regardless. Elder Fae is desperate for an heir to keep the Arilight name in power. Riveria is that heir."

Mother Seya speaks in a soft tone. "It has been a mere two decades, Gallagher. Are you sure about this?"

"Not only do the Arilights wish to recover her, the Godmadinas also chase after her. Except...they want her dead." Gallagher bemoans.

The Elders look at each other with uncertainty.

"The Ebisu," Elder Falklan says. "Could this be why they attacked after so many centuries?"

"Of course," Elder Rayfin agrees. He puts a hand to his chin as he speaks his thoughts out loud. "Gallagher gave away our location when he ventured above the clouds. The Ebisu, angry and malicious as they are, were used as a tool by the Indra. They must have given the Ebisu our coordinates. The grudge-holding elves were aimed at annihilating us, and in return, the Godma... Gomda... Godda—"

"Godmadina," Gallagher helps him.

He nods to Gallagher. "Yes. The Godmadina Indra would crush the heir to House Arilight. It makes sense."

"No," Gallagher raises a hand with a moan, and quickly drops it back to the table. "I don't believe it was the Godmadinas or the Arilights." Gallagher pauses as he attempts to articulate his thoughts. "I... err..."

"Explain yourself." Elder Falklan glares at him. "*Something* gave away our location to the Ebisu. Being that the Indra are the eyes in the sky, it raises suspicion that the Ebisu attacked so soon after your inexcusable venture into the Caelum Realm."

"The Indra... I don't deny giving away our location. It was a mistake I will carry with me forever like so many others I've made." Gallagher lowers his eyes to the table. Nobody disagrees with him. "But the only Indra who knew of our location was Brunswick Orillian." He clenches his fists, but his muscles resist. "He was there when I was first reeled above the clouds. And then again when he saved me from the wraith swarm." Gallagher's words fade as he tries to understand what this means.

"Okay, so it was a different Indra, but an Indra all the same—" Elder Rayfin starts to speak before being interrupted by Claven, the warrior guarding the entrance to the rallyhouse.

"Come! Pardon my interruption, but you must come!" As if in harmony with his words, the voracious bellow of a point-elf's conch sounds alarm. "Another army approaches!"

40 WARRIOR IN THE WILD

With the aid of Andolas and Claven, Gallagher exits the rallyhouse and swims arduously to the heights of the knuckles with all the other on-lookers. Some elves gather into the round deck of the outpost mounted between the two tallest peaks. Others tread air above the rocky bluff. Gallagher finds a crevice formed like a rigid, uncomfortable chair and sits down.

The horizon is vast. The Morshine Peaks climb into the clouds on their left. The big blue and its infinite white caps carries on forever to their right. And in between is the sandy shoreline with rock crops and kelp groves swaying in the wind. Walking toward them on the beach is an enemy battalion, glowing breastplates, tridents, and all.

"What is this?" Andolas cries out from somewhere above him. "Prep your arms! Get the Elders, youngkins, and the blighted to safety. Mira…" Andolas looks for her amongst the crowd.

Mira is already halfway down the other side of the knuckles, swimming straight for the approaching army.

"What is she doing?" Andolas shouts, asking nobody in particular.

A handful of elves in the battalion separate from the rest of the army, leaping into a swim. With Mira's speed, she greets them in a matter of moments. Hugs and smiles ensue where there ought to be pokes and prods of tridents.

"Gallagher…" Andolas lowers himself to stand beside the blighted elf. "Do you have any idea what this is? Why is Mira making friends with the enemy?"

Gallagher shrugs. "When I was above the clouds, life was drastically different, but the personalities were just as diverse as what we see here within the knuckles. My guess…" A grin finds his face. "…Mira discovered the same thing beneath the waves."

"What does that mean?"

"It means you need to get out more, Andolas. You need to experience the world we live in. There is more than one shade of light in Solaria."

Andolas grunts. "You don't know what you're talking about. Claven!" He waves a hand. "Baratok! With me." The two warriors follow him down the mountainside as they chase after Mira.

Gallagher makes his way back inside the knuckles while the thrill of the unknown climaxes and eventually simmers with a heightened energy buzzing about the colony. Where the point-elves blew their conches only once, two more alarms follow, signifying an approaching ally as opposed to a foe. Though, by the time they blew on their shells, word had already widely spread that Mira made some friends outside the knuckles.

Gallagher patiently waits on a rock along the shore for Mira's return. He presses his fins into the sand, burying his toes.

"Gallagher?"

A dull shadow is felt hovering over him.

Tanniv stands above him. "You alright?" he says. "Looks like you were swallowed by a leviathan and spit out."

Gallagher closes his eyes where he sits on his rock and a thin smirk finds his face. If only Tanniv knew the truth of that comment. He shakes his head and looks up to his clanmate. "A tale best saved for an ale and crumble cake, perhaps."

The waters stir where the battalion follows a good distance behind him. They swim around the knuckles instead of over them.

Tanniv gets down to one knee. "My, you really *have* taken a beating." He grabs Gallagher's arm, bending it in uncomfortable positions to inspect it. "You look like you survived a carabao stampede ten times over, then dragged through a field of garden eels and dragon's tongue. Can you get up?"

"Wolf eels, to be precise."

Tanniv flinches at his response. "It was only a jest. Are you serious?"

Gallagher's lips flatten as he nods.

"Come." Tanniv says. "A tale best served with crumble cake. Let's get our hero out of the sand." He gives Gallagher a knowing look.

Now it's Gallagher's turn to flinch at Tanniv's comment. "I'm no hero."

"Word travels fast. From the tip of the knuckles to the shore. It was the first thing out of Claven's mouth when they came to greet us. We've heard about your glowing hide and how you sent a demigod crying back to his home." He grabs Gallagher beneath his arms and hoists him into the air. "Good work, warrior."

"Mira brought giants home…" Gallagher spits out, trying to take the focus off himself.

"Pfft… They're not easy things to wrangle. Did you get to see the blue dragon?"

"What?" Pain shoots through Gallagher's body as he jerks his head to look at Tanniv.

"Yet another tale served best over—"

—ale and crumble cake. Got it." Gallagher smiles.

The simple label of warrior sparks the dying ambition within Gallagher. But it's something he cannot have. Not while residing within the Knuckles of Morshine. It reminds him, he never settled his fate with the Elders. "I need to go see her," he says.

"Mira I suspect? Sure thing," Tanniv says. He helps Gallagher into the air where he manages a casual breaststroke. "You ever going to recover from this?" Tanniv asks as he escorts him.

"Not according to Bailey." Gallagher hurries forward, not wanting to discuss it.

The Elders and Lady Nessa stand outside the rallyhouse at the base of the steps where they greet Mira. An intense discussion immediately develops.

"Why would you bring them here?" It's Elder Falklan who carries the nastiest bite with her words. "This is just as bad, if not worse, than that machina you have on your ear. Why has it not been removed, yet?"

Mira reaches for her ear. "It'll require the tender hands of a caretaker, I'm afraid." She scowls back at Elder Falklan. "It was my ill timing. I do apologize. Instead of defending the clan upon my arrival, I should have made the removal of my implant a priority."

"Mira!" Both her mother and her father glare at her.

"Her comment was hardly fair," Mira pouts.

Mother Seya raises a hand to soothe their nerves, and her voice aids in the undertaking. "It would seem we have become a refuge for all who have lost their way. Can we be respectable hosts and welcome them in? Garrik, it is the right thing to do until we find time to consider the ramifications of this mess."

Elder Rayfin waves a few hands and makes a few orders and several clanmates rush toward the battalion wading in the shallows.

Gallagher pulls his gaze away from Mira as he touches down and instead addresses the Elders. "Excuse me. Elder?" he says, believing it to be a prime time to interrupt the disagreements. "You left the results of my banishment in my hands. A life carried by the strength of my clan, or a life upheld by my strength alone. I believe I have made my decision."

Mother Seya tilts her head with an endearing smile. Elder Falklan frowns with a curled brow.

Elder Rayfin steps forward, escorting his wife with her arm wrapped around his own. "Is that so?"

Gallagher can stay with his clan. He can continue to see Mira and Rivee and live a good life, even though he'll never be able to have her hand. He would continue living the way he has, except... With his current condition he won't be able to offer the clan anything. Even the role of a kelp picker is out of the question. He would drag them down. An unwanted burden. A point-elf would be a good promotion from what he's been doing, but is he capable? Housing away from the colony atop the knuckles, in solitude. Waiting. Watching. More waiting. He looks at Mira with longing eyes. Hope and determination stare back at him.

Despite the strength she offers him, he cannot do this to her. Can he? He will drag her into the depths of the canyon. Into a dark abyss. She deserves so much more. "I..." he says while looking at his heart and soul. Facing her, with more struggle than it should be worth, he pounds a fist over the left side of his chest. "Heart." He pats the right side, which is more of a sweeping motion. "Strength." He touches a hand to his forehead, then to his gut. "Mind and soul." Their common greeting looks so arduous on him.

She returns the gesture silently, mouthing the words as she does so.

He doesn't take his eyes off her. All onlookers, which have grown to more than just the Elders and Lady Nessa, remain silent, awaiting his answer.

Elder Falklan clears her throat.

"I am in more need of the machina than ever before." He scans the Elders and lands his gaze on Elder Rayfin. "But I am stronger with my clan." He glances at Mira. She is his strength. "You place a choice before me that I don't wish upon anyone."

"Agreed," Elder Falklan speaks. "But the choice is yours. Retrieve your machina and be banished for life or accept your blighted status within the clan and be stronger for it."

"I must forsake the machina," he answers quickly, almost cutting her off.

Those who are aware of the choice presented to him offer relieved gasps. Others, who only just joined the conversation look around the crowd with confusion as if they've missed a grand spectacle.

"Samara! Where are you?" Tanniv shouts. "Get your crumble cake ready! We have many tales to tell."

Gallagher's stance is as rigid as his body will allow. Mira stares upon him, inspecting his every move. She knows.

"Very good." Elder Rayfin replies as he places a grateful hand on his wife's arm.

Gallagher's gaze shifts to his fins as a noticeable slump overtakes his body. All his hope of becoming a warrior is gone. Gallagher has made the decision to abandon his personal ambitions to be with his heart and soul. Although he will never truly be with her, he will be able to enjoy her company from time to time. It feels like the right choice. However, the weight of his burden on the clan, Mira most of all, is heavier than he anticipated.

Elder Rayfin sends a warrior into the rallyhouse to retrieve the sword from the table where they carelessly left a tool of such power unattended. The warrior quickly returns and hands the sword to the Elder.

"Then we shall dispose of this taboo machina. The smiths will melt this into something useful. We will find another suitable artifact for your stones, Gallagher, warrior of the guild."

Mira looks at him with bright eyes. "Three stones…" she mutters, her mouth agape with excitement and confusion tangled into the lines pressing across her forehead. "I must have allowed that little detail to slip past me."

Gallagher shrugs away her interest. "Just pretty stones." He looks down at his fins.

"Hardly, Gallagher." She leans into him. "This is an opportunity. This is a means to elevate your family. Everything you ever wanted."

She doesn't know his parents are gone. Now is not the moment to tell her. Not while she has a smile on her face. He looks at her from beneath his brow. "Not everything I ever wanted…"

"But…" She freezes when she realizes how large the crowd around them has grown, and all who are in proximity are staring at her. "Perhaps we can discuss this later." Her face blushes as red as the most brilliant coral.

Mother Seya nudges Elder Rayfin. "Maybe now is the time to make an announcement to the clan." Her voice is as soft as a billowing cloud, serenading only those closest to them.

"Ahh… Yes, we do have some matters to address." The Elder looks down at Mother Seya with utter irritation, but he knows it must be said. He climbs the steps to the rallyhouse, still holding Gallagher's sword, and stops at the top to address all the members of the Morshine Clan. Mother Seya and Elder Falklan remain at the base of the steps, as does Lady Nessa. All the clan members must be in attendance by now for the crowd of elves extends out toward the shallows and past several of the other makeshift quarters that have yet to be rebuilt properly.

"For those of you who have been away…" The Elder's voice booms within the Knuckles of Morshine, "…I regret to inform you that we have had many fallen warriors. Too many over the past few weeks after Ceto's will brought us that storm of a millennium and the Ebisu found their way to our front door. Please, let's offer a moment of prayer to those lost and those who suffer in their wake."

A long silence follows with only the din of the ocean playing as a background tune for the passing of their clanmates. Then, Mother Seya starts up a hymn, and the crowd joins in soon after. The loss is more than any clan should have to bear.

Elder Rayfin continues when the hymn dithers out. "Amidst the fallen… And not to elevate any one clan member above the next, but there is importance behind this one…" He pauses and looks at his daughter. "…our most spirited of youngkins lies dormant in Bailey's care."

"Wait!" Mira blurts out. "Rivee! Rivee is hurt?" She looks to her father first, then to her mother knowing that's where she'll find answers.

"Mira…" Lady Nessa steps forward and reaches for Mira's hands. Her beauty almost hides the sadness she expresses.

"She's not…" Mira chokes on her words. "…dying, is she?"

"No, no, no…" Lady Nessa pulls her daughter in close. "But she remains in a serious condition, unable to wake. Bailey is doing everything she—"

"How?" Mira cries. "How did this happen?"

"Please, Mira." Her father glares at her with ire.

Mira quiets, but the tension in her body language screams louder than the war cries of a battle. Gallagher would join her by her side to comfort her, but to do so would be an event.

"We are doing everything we can to find a remedy," Elder Rayfin continues, "but her condition is due to the very power we abolished a thousand years ago. The reason she lies ill is due to machina magic." Gasps surge through the crowd, but the cause for her condition has already spread amongst most of them.

"I regret to use our beloved youngkin as an illustration for the effects of impunity…" Elder Rayfin's eyes find Gallagher amidst the crowd. Then he looks to the sword in his hand. It looks like a normal sword to anyone unknowing. "…but what has become of her is an irrefutable reminder of what can become of our world when such power finds hands of malice. And because we cannot breed out maliciousness from our hearts, we must eradicate the power. Despite the inevitable clash of cultures that lies ahead…" He points toward the shallows. "…I ask for you to hold true to your beliefs. Machina is the destroyer of civilized societies."

Several cheers and boasts follow that comment. The De'wi have always stood behind the Elder, as renowned as he is, and Gallagher has no doubt he's reinforcing their loyalty now that they're about to be introduced to the two other races of elves.

Mira's lips are parted as if she wants to say something, but her gaze is indifferent, as if she's stumbling through an elaborate riddle in her head. Gallagher watches her intently, mostly because he struggles to take his eyes off her whenever in her presence. To him, it's like staring at waves rolling into the shore, or the flames of a crackling fire. She has a mesmerizing and unwavering beauty that refuses to release him from its grasp. No matter what the moment holds, his eyes always drift back to her.

Mother Seya climbs the stairs to address Elder Rayfin privately. She says something with an adamant look on her face. Elder Rayfin's face contorts, but he nods. Mother Seya steps to the side and remains at the top of the stairs with him.

He calls for his wife to join him by his side. Lady Nessa climbs the steps and stands on the opposite side.

"I will address the manatee in the room in a moment." He gestures to the shoreline where the refugees are being ushered. "There is more you need to know regarding Rivee Rayfin." His powerful vocals can likely be heard at the end of the shallows where the refugees stand by. "Much more…" The second part comes out as more of a whisper, but a loud one at that, for the Elder's voice struggles to find lower volumes. His brow fills with concern as he stares upon Mira.

"What is this?" Tanniv asks in a whisper.

Gallagher lets his question go to the wind.

"The blighted youngkin you know as Rivee Rayfin, the same youngkin debilitated by the machina magic, is also known as Riveria Arilight. She is royalty amongst the Indra." The crowd stirs with mumbling questions. The Elder is patient, but it doesn't take long for them to quiet down as they're eager for an explanation. "The Indra we have been detaining since Gallagher's escapade into the Caelum Realm is Jarnes Arilight." Some gasps fill the crowd, but not as many as there should be, so he clarifies further. "He is Rivee's father. And her mother…" The crowd stirs. "…her mother is Lady Nessa Rayfin."

"She's an Indra?" somebody shouts. And that's when the crowd breaks loose. Sassy, blunt, and audacious comments fly from the crowd. An overlying irate aura blankets the entire colony from knuckle to knuckle. Gallagher would be in the same mindset with this madness if he hadn't discovered it while overwhelmed with the trials Caelum Invictus threw at him. Instead of throwing a tantrum like the rest of his clan members, he watches Mira.

That indifferent gaze she had shifts to something more confused, as if the riddle in her head has stumped her. Then her brows curl inward. Her riddle angers her. Her gaze climbs the stairs to where her mother and father stand above the clan, proud, dominant, and virtuous…until now. She offers her parents a murderous glare, evidently not ready to accept the deceit, then storms away from the crowd in silence. No words. Her mother reaches for her from the top of the stairs—a meager gesture of apology—but allows her daughter to disappear without pursuit.

"Excuse me," a calm voice is faintly heard amidst the crowd. Gallagher wouldn't have picked up on it if the Indra had not squeezed in right next to him. "Excuse me," he says again, but nobody aside from Gallagher hears him.

Gallagher raises a hand to the Indra, requesting assistance to get off his fins so he can gather their attention. The sight of Gallagher swimming above the crowd is enough to deescalate the growing mob mentality. They quiet, whether from the ugliness he bears or his increasing renown as a hero, he doesn't know.

"The Indra has something to say." Gallagher points down to the squatty elf amidst the crowd, but his clan goes back to grumbling their ire and mistrust.

"Excuse me." A booming voice casts through the rumblings of the crowd as if it were accompanied by a wave of silencing goo that locks their jaws shut.

Gallagher looks to Elder Rayfin, thinking it was him, but he looks just as confused. When the Indra pulls his hand away from his face, it's clear machina is the culprit. A small metallic device is implanted into the Indra's throat, sleek and flush with his flesh, yet barely noticeable beneath the flabs of skin hanging over it. Gallagher's brow presses inward. He's uncertain how to feel about their magic.

"Excuse me," he says in a normal tone, now. "I couldn't help but overhear." He points back toward the edge of the bay where the rest of the misfits continue to make their way ashore. "If my assumptions regarding your dormant youngkin are accurate, I may know how you can save the little one."

"And what would you know about the De'wi?" someone from the crowd shouts, and it's followed by agreeing mutterings.

"I admit, I know little of your culture, but that's hardly relevant. If this was the same youngkin who was unveiled at our celebration just recently, then it's likely a forced submission from one of the greater houses." The crowd is silent, waiting for more. "Machina magic," he adds, and the mob enrages once again. He cowers at the reaction.

This time, it takes Elder Rayfin's authority to silence the crowd. Although, it's obvious even *he* has lost their trust with how long it takes to quiet them.

Gallagher remains treading above the crowd. This is where he finds the most relief from his broken body. A few breast strokes from time to time to keep him aloft is all it requires.

Elder Rayfin looks at the Indra. "What can be done… err… My apologies, I don't believe we have your name. What can we call you?"

"Paka Ohmsmire, second son to Chrigan Ohmsmire of House Ohmsmire."

"Hrm… That's a lot of Ohmsmires."

"Yes, we indeed have a healthy house. My brother, first born—"

Elder Rayfin cuts off his babbling before it starts. "What can be done for our youngkin, Paka Ohmsmire?"

"I suspect you require a scepter of the same frequency."

"A scepter?" the Elder asks.

"A tool we use to subdue those who threaten us."

"Machina magic…" he corrects him, "…used to control those who disagree with you." The Elder stares hard from atop his post at the top of the steps with a quick glance at his wife who stands by his side holding onto his arm.

The Indra rolls his eyes. "But not just any scepter," he adds. "Each house has a frequency. You need to figure out which house it was and recover a scepter with the same frequency to undo what is done."

"So…" He points Gallagher's sword at the Indra, not as a threat, but an extension of a simple hand gesture. "What you are saying is that we must introduce machina into our culture in order to save her? Blasphemous!" It takes him a moment to recognize the irony of the sword in his grasp. He lowers it immediately.

"Or—" the Indra starts but is cut off by the mob.

"Why not send her packing above the clouds with her father?" It's unclear who made the suggestion, but more than one elf agrees with him.

"That is even more blasphemous!" Lady Nessa pipes in. "To send one of our own to the sky?"

"It's where she belongs," another elf shouts.

"This is where she belongs!" Lady Nessa is adamant.

"Wait!" Gallagher cries to stop the argument from escalating.

With slow and arduous movements, Gallagher swims toward Elder Rayfin. He makes a silent request for the sword—a gift from Brunswick, whose alliance currently lies in question. Elder Rayfin allows him to take it, but not without apprehension.

Gallagher grips the leather hilt firmly and holds it up, admiring the craftsmanship. The three stones embedded within the hilt glow between his knuckles with a gentle green aura. He taps the pommel on his open palm and a whoosh croons through the air as the blade unsheathes and the power of the stones surge through his body. Gallagher straightens his back and flexes his muscles with a brilliant glow wherever his flesh isn't whole.

"You presented me with only two choices, Elder Rayfin. But I would like to respectfully present you with a third." He lands on the stairway, a few steps beneath the Elder. He stands tall, shoulders rigid, hands crossed behind his back, still with the blade in his hand for it's the only way he can manage, and fins shoulder-width apart.

"If I accept your offer to release my banishment and forsake machina forever, I will forever live a blighted life. An unfulfilled life. I will never be able to have what I desire." His gaze turns to look for Mira. A long silence passes before he sees her sulking, sitting on a rock at the edge of the crowd that is shrouded by a blazing red coral.

"And…" Elder Rayfin's patience is slipping.

"And should I take back my blade…" He holds it out before Elder Rayfin. "…it gives me the strength I need to acquire everything a warrior desires. Though, I don't know how it functions…" A befuddled look appears on his face while he examines the blade.

"Precisely why this magic is forsaken." Elder Falklan blurts out as she stomps up the stairs to join the other Elders.

Gallagher raises a hand to silence her, and immediately regrets the insolence as the Elders glare at him. But he needs to speak.

He has Mira's attention, now, and she looks like she wants to remove his head, but he doesn't know why.

"I understand why you dismiss this technology," Gallagher continues. "It will make our warriors weak. I agree. It will act as a crutch. Unfortunately, I am one who needs a crutch." He pauses to look around at the members of the Morshine Clan. *His* clan. "The third choice I present to you: I will claim my machina. I will accept your banishment. But I will not give up being a warrior for the De'wi race. Riveria Arilight remains unconscious by means of the same magic that flows through this blade. I have witnessed elves come and go from this magic. I, myself, have experienced it. And I cannot stand idle while Rivee suffers this fate."

"And what is it you intend to do?" the Elder asks, his arms folded across his body.

"The banishment is permanent. I understand this. I will remain on the outskirts of your borders. I will not cross beyond the knuckles, as your rules of banishment require, but you cannot stop me from protecting those I cherish most. I will set my sights on the Indra, who have the means to give Rivee her life back. And I will take Jarnes Arilight with me. He is the best hope of discovering and retrieving the remedy." His eyes shift back to Mira in the distance. "Do you accept my decision?"

Mira's head shakes deliberately. A frown sets in as she fixes her gaze on Gallagher. She hurts, but she won't tell him no.

The three Elders look at one another, silently debating within their own minds. Lady Nessa takes a step back as she has no authority here. Each Elder gives the other a nod of approval. What is the downside for them? Gallagher will not taint their culture with the machina, *and* there is hope for Rivee.

"Respectfully agreed, Gallagher Lightcloud, Warrior of the Wild." Elder Rayfin addresses him with utmost admiration. "Your decision is an honorable and noteworthy one. You will be remembered."

Gallagher tries to feign a smile. This is the acceptance he's been waiting for since the day he met Mira. Her father finally gives approval and labels him a warrior with the entire clan in attendance, but it's at a time when they are expected to part worlds and go their separate ways.

"I have one more request, Elder."

"Sure." The Elder nods.

Gallagher's decision doesn't seem to release the tension on the beach. "I would like to gather rations and supplies for my permanent departure. And most of all, say goodbye to my loved ones before I go."

"Of course, Gallagher. But your time is limited. This will be treated as a banishment like any other. As that is what it is." His brow crinkles and lips flatten. "Understood?"

"Understood." Gallagher gives Mira one more long glimpse before turning to depart.

A throat clears behind him. "Gallagher?"

He pauses and cranes his neck, looking up the stairs.

"The machina," Elder Falklan says with contempt. "Please allow us to hold onto it before you go dallying about the colony. Machina is forbidden, remember?" Her scowl is everlasting. "It would be a shame if any youngkins went following down your blasphemous path because we permitted such insolence."

Gallagher thumps the pommel of his sword against his left palm, and it releases him. The energy drains like a receding tide with a heavy undertow. He is left with thighs that hardly hold his weight, hanging arms that pull his shoulders into a slump, and a humped back. As if he did not just stand as a strong and capable warrior, he tumbles down the stairs into the crowd as a defeated and crippled elf.

He can feel the eyes watching him as he digs into the sand, struggling to lift himself.

"Warrior…" A hand presses into his underarm. "You have my support whenever you need it."

Gallagher looks up at the elf. It's Andolas.

Another hand lifts him all the way to his fins. "Hero…" Gallagher looks to his right to see another aiding elf. "I obviously cannot speak for everyone, but I will be so bold as to say you have the support of the Morshine Clan whenever you need it."

"Thank you, good elves." Gallagher knows not what to say. "If you can help me into the air, it is easier on my body."

The crowd begins to dissipate as he swims away. It doesn't take long before Tanniv joins up with him as he retreats.

"Well?" he says. "So that's it? No more crumble cake? You're just going to up and leave?"

"Goodbye, Tanniv." Gallagher looks him in the eye and holds out his arm. Tanniv smacks it away, his face as sour as an overripe ganderberry.

"Banished?" Tanniv continues to follow despite his feelings of betrayal. "Twice in a matter of weeks." He smirks.

"I apologize for having to depart upon your arrival, but it's for the best," Gallagher admits.

Tanniv's eyes narrow. He clearly doesn't understand why being banished would be for the best, but he accepts it. "In the end, it was an honor, Gally."

"Indeed, it was." He offers him a warrior's grasp. "Tanniv…" He sluggishly turns his body in the air to face him. "…where's Veras?"

Tanniv's grin turns sour. "Yeah, about that scepter… You might need to secure two of them. Veras isn't doing so well." He points to the crowd of refugees. Veras is lying on a litter, carried by two warriors. "No fret, though. If anyone is capable, it's you." Tanniv pats him on the shoulder, and it knocks Gallagher out of his swimming rhythm. "Good luck, warrior. I have a feeling this won't be the last time we see each other."

"Gallagher Lightcloud!" a stern voice calls through the crowd. For the first time in his life, Gallagher doesn't want to turn around to look at her.

"Do you want me to fight her?" Tanniv says with a grin.

"Yes?"

A chortle escapes Tanniv. "Sorry, it was an empty offer. I have no problem staring death in the eye, but this is much, much worse. Good luck."

Gallagher turns to face his biggest challenge yet. This moment terrifies him more than going into battle against a demigod.

She stares awkwardly as she takes in the sight of Gallagher. He has the body of an ancient Elder who has seen a thousand years of battles in a realm of constant warring. His muscles are rigid and firm where they're intact but dimpled with imperfections. In some areas, entire chunks are missing, scabbed and still healing.

"What happened to you?" She asks, her tone shifting to a sympathetic whisper.

He smiles to lighten the air. "It was an adventure, Mira! There were so many moments I would love to share with you. I wish you were—"

Mira raises a hand to cut him off, all sympathy fleeing, only to be replaced with disappointment. She spins in the air without a word and swims higher, away from the crowd, obviously expecting Gallagher to follow.

It takes too many grunting strokes to chase after her, but eventually she settles near a crop of deep blue coral. He touches down beside her.

Mira stares into his eyes—not looking up at him but staring straight ahead because of the slump his broken body has awarded him. Her eyes are a mirror of the pain his body feels. Damaged. Distressed. Betrayed. She starts into a stroll through the Crisper Coral.

Gallagher is reluctant to follow. He pushes off the ground with much effort to get into swimming form. "Can we?" he asks.

"Of course." She casually leaps into the air to swim beside him.

"Keep it slow, please. I'm only capable of so much."

She stares at him, not even looking where she's swimming to. "Why?"

Gallagher isn't sure how to respond. He knows it was the right choice for all the right reasons. He won't act as an anchor to those he cares for most, and he will be able to guard them as the warrior he's always dreamed of being. "To save Rivee," he sums up his thoughts.

She stops swimming. The two of them tread above the Crisper Coral where they've engaged in so many adventures with Rivee. Words won't fix the pain she feels. Words won't change the mind of the blighted elf who pines over her. She knows this. He knows this.

"I won't let you off so easily, you know." She looks at him from beneath her brow, a devious glare. "I will find you, Gally. Banished or not, once you have found the remedy you seek, Rivee and I will not allow you to disappear from our lives forever. You know this, right?"

Gallagher smiles. "Your place is here, Mira Rayfin. I know you seek new horizons, but don't you come looking for the banished and broken warrior." He says it with a smile, silently telling her he approves. "You'll never find me."

"Warrior in the wild," she corrects him. "Challenge accepted."

She swims closer to Gallagher with grace and leans in to kiss him. The moment is surreal and everlasting. He would never have been so blunt with his own actions, but now that they are here, interlaced, he will have the moment last to the end of time. His soul flutters. His mind melts away. His heart races. And his strength is fueled by her tenacity and love.

They hold onto each other for some time, hovering above the colorful coral and dynamic fish beneath them. "You'll never guess what I saw?" she whispers to him.

"You'll never guess what I've found." He pulls away. Just enough to beat the left side of his chest with a firm fist. With a warrior's passion, he smiles and kisses her once more.

EPILOGUE

"**e**lder Fae, your grace, your guest has arrived." Her handmaid addresses her with direct eye contact while speaking, then lowers her gaze to the white tile floor.

Fae Arilight stands at one of many windows in her quarters overlooking all the beauty of Caelum Invictus. Her gaze lies past her own estate to the luscious green landscape bordering it. Towers with machina nervous systems line the sky beyond, all covered in the life of Solaria, fresh and voracious. It's a beautiful city. All they had ever dreamed of when her ancestors took to the skies. What more could she ask for?

An heir to House Arilight.

Her son has been tainted by the De'wi, and all who are important within the great houses know this. He'll never find a suitable partner because of it. If only he had kept his charisma in his pocket and his trousers on while attempting a coalition twenty years ago. Perhaps, she should have never permitted the use of that machina to tame the De'wi. Hindsight is a nasty lens to look through.

She turns, her flowing gown dancing on the air as she does, to address her messenger. "Please, have him join me up here in my quarters."

"Yes, your grace." The short elf scurries out of her spacious room.

Fae turns back to the window, admiring everything her ancestors have built over the last few thousand years. She cannot let it slip away without a fight.

"Yester, dear."

"Yes, your grace?" Her handmaiden rises from the plush settee she was sunken into to join her by her side.

"My son's flirtatious exploits of the De'wi were supposed to have brought our two races closer together." She continues staring out the window.

"Indeed." She nods carefully, obviously deciding which way to tread around Lady Fae in this moment. "Although, just because the De'wi wasn't openly accepted doesn't mean we cannot further our efforts. Your son is a handsome elf. He will find another—"

Fae casually shakes her head. "No." She looks at her with a pointed gaze. "No, Yester, you are incorrect. It is beyond that, now. My son has been tainted in the eyes of our culture. No Indra will have him knowing he's laid with a De'wi." Lady Fae pauses to see how Yester will react to the comment. Her handmaiden remains unfazed.

"And how are we supposed to make amends with the De'wi now that my son and granddaughter have been kidnapped by one of their warriors? I hailed that champion. Word has already spread of their kidnapping, thanks to House Godmadina." She rolls her eyes. "If I make amends with the De'wi now, it will cover our white palace in a shadow so dark its grandeur would be smothered, day or night. To befriend the very enemy who slights us—our house would be finished. Another heir is not within our grasp."

Her hand snaps toward the window she stands next to. "Riveria Arilight is our path forward. The De'wi have made their choice to steal away Riveria, who rightfully belongs here. I have no doubt Lady Nessa will do everything within her power to protect that child. So—"

"What are you planning, Elder?"

The back of Lady Fae's hand slaps down across Yester's face. "Do not speak over me, Yester, dear." Lady Fae's voice is calm. She rubs at her knuckles as if Yester is responsible.

"Your grace." The messenger returns to the room, too quickly. The young elf must have escorted Fae's guest to her antechamber prior to notifying her.

She scowls at the messenger before speaking. "Please. Usher him in."

The doors to Fae's quarters are large white onyx slabs trimmed with gold handles as tall as she is. Her messenger is a sixth of its size and looks like an infant next to them. But all of Fae's doors are as large as these ones for she knows who lives within the realms of Solaria. And she wouldn't be much of a host if she couldn't accommodate the largest of the races.

The messenger, with ease, pulls open a door. In steps a tall, dark elf, nearly twice the height of Elder Fae. He's an older elf, weathered by several hundred years of the ocean. His skin is leathery, but only mildly wrinkled with muscles bulging out of his black tunic. He had black hair once, like all the other Ebisu, but time has softened it to a peppered grey. Both his posture and facial features are firm. Much harder than the soft elves of the Caelum Realm.

An entourage of six follow behind him, all as tall or taller than he is. Elder Fae suddenly feels uneasy. Why would the messenger allow an entire entourage into her chambers. This was supposed to be a private meeting. One Elder to another. Then, her own guard shuffle in behind them, twice as many, all armed. Her own guard look like toys next to the Ebisu, but she knows their scepters can render any one of these Ebisu unconscious at a touch of the flesh. Her anxiety washes away, but she remains peeved that so many are in attendance.

"Elder Fae." His baritone voice is accompanied by a subtle bow.

"Lord Zaos Tenebrous. Thank you for making the journey. I trust my emissaries were courteous and made it a pleasurable one."

His eyes narrow. "Indeed." His response is full of uncertainty.

"Please join me on the balcony where we can speak in private." She eyes all the guard crowding her space with contempt. "Yester." She waves for her to attend.

Yester rushes to her side to open the balcony door for her. Her long, flowing gown, gorgeous as it is, is as wide as the opening. She graciously moves to the balcony as if she's floating. With elegance, she smooths the puff and wrinkles from her dress as her body sinks into a couch with over-stuffed cushions.

Lord Tenebrous follows behind her. He pushes down on the cushions with a firm hand before taking a seat, and when he does sit, his discomfort is apparent.

Elder Fae looks at him with confusion. Yester stations herself behind Elder Fae, remaining standing.

Two additional servants serve wine and appetizers—a tray of meats, greens, and other delicacies both novel and familiar to Lord Tenebrous. Elder Fae wanted him to feel welcome, but also have a little taste of adventure.

"Lord Tenebrous, again, thank you for joining us here in the Caelum Realm. Do you like to enjoy pleasantries first, or shall we get to it?"

"What is this?" He shoves a fist into the cushions again. "These pads. They're soft. They make you weak."

Elder Fae flinches at his comment, then forces a smile. "They offer comfort. After overcoming the hardest of challenges in life, we tend to find comfort in luxuries."

"Hmph... Then comfort is a weakness."

"Yes. Maybe it is." She pauses. "So, I trust my emissaries gave you the details of this meeting, otherwise you wouldn't be here."

"Indeed."

"You're an elf of few words, Lord Tenebrous."

"We live beneath the waves. Without significant advancements in our machina..." He looks around the balcony of the white palace, showing clear admiration and envy. "...I have learned to keep my words abrupt."

Elder Fae knows it's only an excuse. Their advancements in machina has allowed for an entire civilization to prosper beneath the waves. "Very well. To the point. Will you help me recover my son and future heir from the De'wi who have imprisoned them?"

Lady Fae sees Yester flinch in her peripheral. House Arilight and its underhouses agreed to have this meeting before making any offers or requests of the Ebisu. Lady Fae, however, must take matters into her own hands. What she faces is vital to the future of House Arilight.

"They have defeated many of my soldiers and caused quite the uproar within one of our outposts. They're not as withered as you might think."

"No, they aren't, are they?" She's annoyed. "Which will make more of a statement when you overtake them." She tries to play to his pride, but she knows an offering is due. He won't accept the challenge otherwise, but what is it he wants in return?

"You do all of this for an heir?" he asks.

"I do. But why do you care for my motivations? There's a history of oppression between our races. They've earned whatever comes their way. Plus, after they embarrassed you with the defeat of your battalion, and a demigod I hear, you want them destroyed, too. No?"

"I would like to make a display of our power, yes, but your motivations reveal your intentions. If it is an heir you seek, and you are willing to go to such lengths to retrieve them, I can plan accordingly."

"You intend to cross me?"

"No." His reply is sharp. "We are not so manipulative as the Indra. If you desire this youngkin as much as you imply, you are less likely to cross *me*."

"I wouldn't!" She gasps.

Lord Tenebrous narrows his gaze. "Lies. However…" He pauses while pondering his next words. "I will retrieve your heir, though not without something in return."

Here it comes. She straightens her posture and acts galled that he would request anything from her even though it is expected of her guest. "Which is?"

"I don't want your plush cushions…" He pounds a fist into the seat. "…but I do want the advancements in your machina. In return for your heir, I ask for your wisest wizard. If you can do this, there shall be a truce between our realms."

Elder Fae remains silent, considering his request. Offering their knowledge—more power if she's honest—to an inferior race could be damning. More damning than just offering a crop of Tears. But with a truce, respite from the consequences is a potential reality. It is more than she anticipated from the primitive race. Is the longevity of House Arilight worth it?

"I thought there already was a truce," she lightly jabs with her words. "That's a hefty price." She pauses to study his reaction. He remains stoic in his expression. "And what of the Blue Tears? A price that steep requires the return of the crops I've already given you. You will stop treading on what is rightfully ours."

Lady Fae sees Yester flinch in the corner of her vision. The elves of Caelum Invictus have been led to believe the crops were taken, but as the Elder of the realm, she's required to stay a few steps ahead. She has seen her house slipping for years, now. The crop was handed to the Ebisu to endow future negotiations. She had to lay a foundation to disrupt whatever the Godmadinas were planning. She failed to anticipate something as bold as befriending the De'wi to build an army of their own. And although she tried to play into it by proclaiming Gallagher as their champion, it did not work out for her. A miscalculation. Now her son and their only heir to House Arilight are trapped in the Terra Realm where the Indra are reluctant to go.

"Crops?" he questions.

"Don't mock my intelligence. When your soldiers arrived and destroyed the machina harvesting our crops, we allowed it to happen. Had I wanted to, I would have reclaimed what your brutes smashed. It was a peace offering. A means to show you there's a potential alliance here. If you cannot see that, then perhaps there is nothing to discuss here. Ten thousand acres of Tears are no longer flowing into our stockpiles. A hefty price. Do you know what kind of damage that does to our society?"

Lord Tenebrous remains quiet, contemplating her words. His confusion seems genuine.

"If it wasn't you, then who was it?" she adds.

"Your own," he says with a sharp tongue, obviously insulted.

"Hmph…" Elder Fae studies him once more. She doesn't know the truth of the matter. They didn't have any observers keeping watch in that region at the time. She only assumed it was the Ebisu. It would be impossible for the De'wi to manage such a task. Could it have been her own? House Orillian, perhaps?

"You will not encroach on any of my crops," she says, "and I will prepare an engagement with our Greybeards to find the most suitable candidate for the Ocean Realm. In return, you will devour the De'wi who kidnapped my heir, and you will return them to me."

"We go as far as the Terra Realm," he asserts. "We meet in the middle for the exchange."

Elder Fae holds her chin up before speaking. "These conditions will be met. You have my word."

Yester clenches her jaw, obviously uncomfortable with the decisions being made, but she remains silent. It isn't her place to debate Lady Fae, the Elder of the Caelum Realm. Plus, it would make their race look weak in front of Lord Tenebrous.

"One more thing." His baritone voice rolls off his tongue like serpent cutting through water.

Elder Fae digs her fingernails into her palm. "Yes," she replies with the utmost civility.

"Territory."

She stares stoically at Lord Tenebrous, not to give away her irritation.

"Oceanus Salus thrives beneath the waves, but elves do not belong in eternal darkness. We will take back what is rightfully ours. The Terra Realm belongs to us. We've already begun eradicating the De'wi."

She remains calm. "There has been discussion about this between our great houses. We saw the ocean aflame. That was you?"

He nods. A single and subtle up and down motion with his chin. No words.

"Your confessions beg the question, why create a coalition with Caelum Invictus if the Indra are not needed?"

"You're correct. The Indra are not needed." His eyes move to the blue sky surrounding them. "It will keep you where you belong. A means to show you there is a potential alliance here."

Elder Fae recoils at his mockery. She has no intention of laying claim to the Terra Realm. The Ebisu grow stronger, but if they remain below the ceiling of clouds, she has no concern. Her son and future heir will be returned, and the Indra will thrive because of it. "The Terra Realm is yours."

"Agreement settled," Lord Tenebrous declares. "Now let's have those pleasantries."

THE END

APPENDIX

RACES & CHARACTERS:

Leading Roles:
- Gallagher Lightcloud: A kelp picker of the lowest rank within the Morshine Clan. He aspires to be a renowned warrior. He has been labeled a blight on the colony due to a damaged fin from an accident in his youth.
- Mira Rayfin: A warrior with a prestigious birthright. Daughter to Garrik and Nessa Rayfin. She is the fastest warrior within their colony with potential to be the finest warrior. Her aspirations are to explore the unknown world.
- Rivee Rayfin (Riveria Arilight): Orphan within the Morshine Clan, like a kid sister to both Gallagher and Mira. Deemed a blight on the colony due to a missing leg from an accident with a leviathan.
- Fae (Elder Fae) Arilight: Elder and matriarch of the Caelum Realm. Mother to Jarnes Arilight and head of House Arilight.

DE'WI:
- Alariya: A warrior elf who died by a leviathan during an incident with Mira.
- Andolas: A two-stone warrior of the Warrior's Guild within the Morshine Clan.
- Brantford Lightcloud: Gallagher's father.
- Daya Lightcloud: Gallagher's mother.
- Garrik Rayfin: Leading Elder of the Morshine Clan. Father to Mira Rayfin, husband to Nessa Rayfin. Renowned five-stone warrior.
- Haltuk Coradrin: Warrior of the Warrior's Guild. Friend to Mira.
- Nessa Rayfin: Mother to Mira Rayfin, wife to Garrik Rayfin.
- Seya (Mother Seya) Melonia: Elder and Matriarch of the Morshine Clan.
- Tanniv Windstalker: Warrior of the Warrior's Guild. Friend to both Mira and Gallagher.

- Veras Elreid: Warrior of the Warrior's Guild. Friend to both Mira and Gallagher.
- Zyla Falklan: Elder of the Morshine Clan.

INDRA:
- Brunswick Orillian: Elite within the Indran social classes. Once part of a lesser house, then turned rebel due to conflicts with the greater houses.
- Fae (Elder Fae) Arilight: Elder and matriarch of the Caelum Realm. Mother to Jarnes Arilight and head of House Arilight.
- Greybeards: Mysterious wizard elves who lay the groundwork for the machina.
- Helyer Elgary: Emissary of House Godmadina who escorts Gallagher around.
- Horbell Jonesook: Prisoner at the Ebisu's military outpost.
- Jarnes Arilight: Son to Fae Arilight and heir to House Arilight.
- Paka Ohmsmire: Prisoner at the Ebisu's military outpost.
- Yester: Handmaiden to Fae Arilight.

EBISU:
- Lord Zaos Tenebrous: Elder of the Ebisu.
- Rela: Ebisu rebel imprisoned within the reform block.
- Salus: Ebisu guard stationed in the reform block.
- Tiolas: Ebisu guard stationed in the reform block.

INDRAN GREATER AND LESSER HOUSES:

House: Arilight (Elder House)
- Fae Arilight, Matriarch, Elder to all Indra
- Jarnes Arilight, First son, First born (Heir)
- Riveria (Rivee) Arilight, Bastard daughter of Jarnes Arilight, Half De'wi, Half Indra.
- Jothra Arilight (Ohmsmire)
- Haley Arilight (Jonesook)

House: Ohmsmire (Underhouse to Arilight)
- Chrigan Ohmsmire, Patriarch to House Ohmsmire
- Jothra Ohmsmire, Matriarch (Daughter to Fae Arilight)
- Smika Ohmsmire, First Son, First Born (Heir)

- Paka Ohmsmire, Second Son, Second Born

House: Jonesook (Underhouse to Arilight)

- Dunbell Jonesook, Patriarch of House Jonesook
- Haley Jonesook, Matriarch (Daughter to Fae Arilight)
- Vinbell Jonesook, First Daughter, First Born (Heir)
- Horbell Jonesook, First Son, Second Born
- Mabell Jonesook, Second Daughter, Third Born

House: Godmadina (Competing House to Arilight)

- Arisean Godmadina, Patriarch to House Godmadina
- Vicenya Godmadina, Matriarch
- Gariel Godmadina (Elgary), First Daughter, First Born
- Aricent Godmadina, First Son, Second Born (Heir)
- Sariah Godmadina (Haslit), Second Daughter, Third Born
- Paneya Godmadina, Third Daughter, Fourth Born
- Aritik Godmadina, Second Son, Fifth Born
- Ariskye Godmadina, Fourth Daughter, Sixth Born

House: Elgary (Underhouse to Godmadina)

- Jarstian Elgary, Patriarch to House Elgary
- Gariel Elgary, Matriarch (Daughter to Arisean and Vicenya Godmadina)
- Golistian Elgary, First Son, First Born (Heir)
- Helyer Elgary, Second Son, Second Born
- Ilariel Elgary, First Daughter, Third Born

House: Haslit (Underhouse to Godmadina)

- Jareth Haslit, Patriarch to House Haslit
- Sariah Haslit, Matriarch (Daughter to Arisean and Vicenya Godmadina)
- Ludonia Haslit, First Daughter, First Born (Heir)
- Hoglet Haslit, First Son, Second Born
- Didymust Haslit, Second Son, Third Born
- Tobylias Haslit, Third Son, Fourth Born

House: Medirt (Struggling House)

- Melly Medirt, Patriarch to House Medirt
- Haley Medirt, Matriarch
- Jolly Medirt, First Daughter, First Born (Heir)
- Gordy Medirt, First Son, Second Born

House: Orillian (Rebel House)

- Brunswick Orillian, Leader of the Rebel House
- Mako Orillian, Adopted by House Orillian

ACKNOWLEDGMENTS

I escaped the dread of cleaning the kitchen on too many occasions to write this book. Always the biggest thank you to my wife and children who allow me the time to write. They are my biggest supporters whether they realize it or not.

Another thank you to those who helped me take a rough draft and turn it into a novel. Mary, you've been a solid anchor to my continuous writing improvement. And Katie, a critical writing friend who has no shame in sniffing out the not-so-pleasant garbage that ends up on the page. It takes more than one person to write a novel, and these two have been essential in this.

ABOUT THE AUTHOR

Jonathan J Michael is a fictitious character who ventures through fantastical worlds, eavesdrops on conniving schemes, and watches epic battles from a safe distance.

In the real world, he's a keyboard warrior who struggles with vocabulary, spelling, art, and everything else involved with publishing a book. But he stares those malicious evils in the eye and dominates them, one by one, with the swift stroke of a key, and a lot of help from his sidekick companions, the thesaurusrex. Will he continue down this epic journey until the end of time? His fate is in the hands of the endearing and wise patron.

THE SOCIALS

Leave a Review:

If you enjoyed this book, the best way to show your appreciation is to leave a review at Amazon, Goodreads, or wherever you desire. Honest reviews equal book success.

Join my Newsletter:

If you'd like to receive book updates and special promotions sign up below. Emails are few and far between.

For more information about Jonathan J Michael visit…

http://jonathanjmichael.com

https://www.facebook.com/jonathan.j.michael.author

Made in the USA
Las Vegas, NV
05 February 2025

17518815R00267